BY HARRY TURTLEDOVE

VIDESSOS CYCLE

VOLUME ONE

VIDESSOS CYCLE

VOLUME ONE

THE MISPLACED LEGION
AN EMPEROR FOR THE LEGION

Harry Turtledove

Ballantine Books

New York

2013 Del Rey Books Trade Paperback Edition

The Misplaced Legion copyright © 1987 by Harry Turtledove

An Emperor for the Legion copyright © 1987 by Harry Turtledove

Published in the United States by Del Rey, an imprint of The Random House Publishing Group, a division of Random House, Inc., New York.

DEL REY is a registered trademark and the Del Rey colophon is a trademark of Random House, Inc.

The Misplaced Legion and *An Emperor for the Legion* were both published in paperback in 1987 by Del Rey, an imprint of the Random House Publishing Group, a division of Random House, Inc.

ISBN: 978-0-345-54258-8
eBook ISBN 978-0-345-54569-5

Printed in the United States of America on acid-free paper

www.delreybooks.com

Maps by Shelly Shapiro

2 4 6 8 9 7 5 3 1

VIDESSOS CYCLE

VOLUME ONE

THE MISPLACED LEGION

In various ways, this book is dedicated to
L. Sprague de Camp, J. R. R. Tolkien,
Speros Vryonis, Jr., and, above all, Laura

I

THE SUN OF NORTHERN GAUL WAS PALE, NOTHING LIKE THE HOT, lusty torch that flamed over Italy. In the dim stillness beneath the trees, its light came wan, green, and shifting, almost as if undersea. The Romans pushing their way down the narrow forest track took their mood from their surroundings. They moved quietly; no trumpets or bawdy marching songs announced their coming. The daunting woods ignored them.

Peering into the forest, Marcus Aemilius Scaurus wished he had more men. Caesar and the main Roman army were a hundred miles to the southwest, moving against the Veneti on the Atlantic coast. Scaurus' three cohorts—"a reconaissance in force," his superior had called them—were more than enough to attract the attention of the Gauls, but might be unable to deal with it, once attracted.

"Only too right," Gaius Philippus answered when the tribune said that aloud. The senior centurion, hair going gray and face tanned and lined by a lifetime on campaign, had long ago lost optimism with the other illusions of his youth. Though Scaurus' birth gave him higher rank, he had the sense to rely on his vastly experienced aide.

Gaius Philippus cast a critical eye on the Roman column. "Close it up, there!" he rasped, startlingly loud in the quiet. His gnarled vine-staff badge of office thwacked against his greave to punctuate the order. He quirked an eyebrow at Scaurus. "You've nothing to worry about anyway, sir. One look and the Gauls will think you're one of theirs on a masquerade."

The military tribune gave a wry nod. His family sprang from Mediolanum in northern Italy. He was tall and blond as any Celt and used to the twitting his countrymen dished out. Seeing he'd failed to hit a nerve,

Gaius Philippus took another tack. "It's not just your looks, you know—that damned sword gives you away, too."

That hit home. Marcus was proud of his blade, a three-foot Gallic longsword he had taken from a slain Druid a year ago. It was fine steel and better suited to his height and reach than the stubby Roman *gladii*. "You know full well I had an armorer give it a decent point," he said. "When I use a sword, I'm not such a fool as to slash with it."

"A good thing, too. It's the point, not the edge, that brings a man down. Hello, what's this about?" Gaius Philippus added as four of the small army's scouts dashed into the woods, weapons in hand. They came out a few moments later, three of them forcibly escorting a short, scrawny Gaul while the fourth carried the spear he had borne.

As they dragged their captive up to Scaurus, their leader, an under-officer named Junius Blaesus, said, "I'd thought someone was keeping an eye on us this past half hour and more, sir. This fellow finally showed himself."

Scaurus looked the Celt over. Apart from the bloody nose and puffed eye the Romans had given him, he could have been any of a thousand Gallic farmers: baggy woolen trousers, checked tunic—torn now—long, fair hair, indifferently shaven face. "Do you speak Latin?" the military tribune asked him.

The only answer he got was a one-eyed glare and a head-shake. He shrugged. "Liscus!" he called, and the unit's interpreter trotted up. He was from the Aedui, a clan of south central Gaul long friendly to Rome, and wore a legionary's crested helm over bright curls cut short in the Roman fashion. The prisoner gave him an even blacker stare than the one he had bestowed on Scaurus. "Ask him what he was doing shadowing us."

"I will that, sir," Liscus said, and put the question into the musical Celtic speech. The captive hesitated, then answered in single short sentence. "Hunting boar, he says he was," Liscus reported.

"By himself? No one would be such a fool," Marcus said.

"And this is no boarspear, either," Gaius Philippus said, grabbing it from a scout. "Where's the crosspiece below the head? Without one, a boar will run right up your shaft and rip your guts out."

Marcus turned to Liscus. "The truth this time, tell him. We'll have it

6

from him, one way or another. The choice is his: he can give it or we can wring it from him." Marcus doubted he could torture a man in cold blood, but there was no reason to let the Celt know that.

But Liscus was only starting to speak when the prisoner, with a lithe twist and a kick, jerked free of the men holding him. His hand flashed to a leaf-shaped dagger cunningly slung below his left shoulder. Before the startled Romans could stop him, he thrust the point between his ribs and into his heart. As he toppled, he said, "To the crows with you," in perfect Latin.

Knowing it would do no good, Scaurus shouted for a physician; the Celt was dead before the man arrived. The doctor, a sharp-tongued Greek named Gorgidas, glanced at the protruding knife hilt and snapped, "You ask too much of me, you know. I'll close his eyes for him if you like."

"Never mind. Even while I called, I knew there was nothing you could do." The tribune turned to Junius Blaesus. "You and your men did well to find the spy and bring him in—not so well in not searching him carefully and keeping a lax hold on him. The Gauls must have something in the wind, though we've lost the chance to find out what. Double your patrols and keep them well out in front—the more warning of trouble we have, the better." Blaesus saluted and hurried off, thankful to get away with no harsher reprimand.

"Full battle readiness, sir?" Gaius Philippus asked.

"Yes." Marcus cocked an eye at the westering sun. "I hope we can find a clearing before dusk for an encampment. I'd feel safer behind earthworks."

"And I. I'd feel safer still with a couple of legions at my back." The centurion went off to make the needful changes in the Romans' marching order, bringing his spear-throwers forward and tightening up the distance between each maniple and its neighbor. An excited hum ran through the ranks. Here a man hastily sharpened his sword, there another cut short a leather sandal strap that might trip him in action, still another took a last swig of sour wine.

Shouts came from up ahead, out of sight beyond a bend in the path. A minute or so later a scout jogged back to the main body of troops. "We spied another skulker in the bushes, sir. I'm afraid this one got away."

Marcus whistled tunelessly between his teeth. He dismissed the scout with a word of thanks, then looked to Gaius Philippus, sure the centurion felt the same certainty of trouble he did himself. Gaius Philippus nodded at his unspoken thought. "Aye, we're for it, right enough."

But when another of the advance guards came back to report the path opening out into a sizable clearing, the military tribune began to breathe more easily. Even the small force he led—not quite a third of a legion—could quickly build field fortifications strong enough to hold off many times its number of barbarians.

The clearing was large, several hundred yards of meadow set in the midst of the deep wood. The evening mist was already beginning to gather above the grass. A stream trickled through the center of the clearing; half a dozen startled teal leaped into the air as the Romans began emerging. "Very good indeed," Scaurus said. "Perfect, in fact."

"Not quite, I'm afraid," Gaius Philippus said. He pointed to the far edge of the clearing, where the Celtic army was coming out.

Marcus wasted a moment cursing; another hour and his men would have been safe. No help for it now. "Trumpets and cornets together!" he ordered the buccinators.

As the call to action rang out, Gaius Philippus' voice rang with it. The senior centurion was in his element, readying his troops. "Deploy as you debouch!" he shouted. "Three lines—you know the drill! Skirmishers up ahead, then you front-rankers with your *pila*, then the heavy infantry, then reserves! Come on, *move*—yes, *you* there, you worthless whoreson!" His vine-stave thudded down on the slow legionary's corseleted back. Junior centurions and underofficers echoed and amplified his commands, yelling and prodding their men into place.

The deployment took only minutes. Beyond posting an extra squad of slingers and some protecting spearmen on the slightly higher ground to his right, Scaurus kept a symmetrical front as he waited to see how many enemies he faced.

"Is there no end to them?" Gaius Philippus muttered by his side. File after file of Gauls moved into the clearing, slowly going into line of battle. Well-armored and powerfully armed nobles shouted and waved as they tried to position their bands of retainers but, as always among the Celts, discipline was tenuous. Most of the men the nobles led had gear far

8

poorer than theirs: a spear or slashing sword, perhaps a large oblong shield of wood painted in bright spirals. Except for the nobles, few wore more armor than a leather jerkin, or at most a helmet. Of the cuirasses to be seen, most were Roman work, the spoil of earlier battles.

"What do you make of them? About three thousand?" Marcus asked when the Celtic flood at last stopped flowing.

"Aye, about two for our one. It could be worse. Of course," Gaius Philippus went on, "it could be a damned sight better, too."

On the far side of the clearing the Gauls' commander, splendid in armor of black and gold and a cape of crimson-dyed skins, harangued his men, whipping them up into a fighting frenzy. He was too far away for the Romans to make out his words, but the fierce yells of his listeners and the deep thudding of spearshafts on shields told of the fury he was rousing.

Heads turned Scaurus' way as he strode out in front of his own troops. He paused for a moment, gathering his thoughts and waiting for the full attention of his men. Though he had never given a pre-combat oration, he was used to public speaking, having twice run for a magistracy in his home town—the second time successfully. The technique, if not the occasion, seemed similar.

"We've all of us heard Caesar," he began, and at the mention of their beloved marshal of legionaries they shouted approval as he had hoped. He went on, "We all know I can't talk that well, and I don't intend to try." He quieted the small laugh from the men with an upraised hand. "No need, anyhow—things are very simple. Caesar is five days' march from here at most. We've beaten the Gauls time and again. One more win here, now, and there's not the chance of a frog at a snake symposium that they'll be able to put anything in our way before we can link up with him again."

The Romans cheered. The Gauls shouted back, shaking their fists, waving their spears, and yelling bloodthirsty threats in their own language.

"I've heard worse," Gaius Philippus said of the speech. From him it was high praise, but Scaurus only half heard him. Most of his attention was on the Celts, who, behind their tall leader, were trotting at the Romans. He would have liked to meet them at the streamlet in mid-clearing, but to do so he would have had to pull his line away from the woods which anchored its flanks.

Only skirmishers contested the crossing. Slingers sent leaden bullets whizzing into the ranks of the Gauls, to bang off shields or slap into flesh. Archers added their fire, drawing back to the breast and emptying quivers as fast as they could. Here and there along the barbarians' line a man stumbled and fell, but the damage was only a pinprick to the on-rushing mass.

The Celts raised a cheer as one of their archers transfixed a Roman slinger as he was letting fly. The bullet he had been about to loose flew harmlessly into the air.

The Celts drew nearer, splashing through the ankle-deep water of the rivulet. The Roman skirmishers fired a last few shots, then scampered for the protection of their line.

The long Gallic sword felt feather light in Marcus' hands. The druids' marks stamped down the length of the blade seemed to glow with a life of their own in the red sunlight of late afternoon. An arrow buried itself in the ground beside the tribune's feet. Almost without thinking, he shuffled a couple of steps to one side.

The barbarians were so near he could see the scowls darkening their mustachioed faces, could tell their leader bore a sword twin to his own, could all but count the spokes of the bronze wheel cresting that leader's high-crowned helm. The beat of the Gauls' feet against the grass was a growing thunder.

"At my command!" Marcus shouted to his first line, raising his blade high over his head. They hefted their *pila* and waited, quiet and grimly capable. Already, with wild whoops, the Celts were starting to fling their spears, most falling short of the Roman line.

The tribune studied the oncoming mass. A moment more ... "Loose!" he cried, sword-arm flailing down. Half a thousand arms flung their deadly burdens against the Gauls as one.

The enemy line staggered. Men screamed as they were pierced. Others, luckier, blocked the Romans' casts with their shields. Yet their luck was mixed, for the soft iron shanks of the *pila* bent as their points bit, making the weapons useless for a return throw and fouling the shields so they, too, had to be discarded.

"Loose!" Scaurus shouted again. Another volley leaped forth. But the Gauls, brave as they were unruly, kept coming. Their spears were flying too, many of them, even if not in tight volleys. Next to Marcus a man pitched backwards, his throat spurting blood around the javelin that had found its way over his shield. The legionaries pulled stabbing-swords from their scabbards and surged forward as the fighting turned hand-to-hand.

A cry of triumph rose from the Gauls as, spearheaded by two huge blond-maned warriors, they hewed their way through the first Roman rank. Even as the buccinators' horns trumpeted a warning, a maniple of the second line was moving into the gap. Their short swords flickered now forward, now back, fast and sure as striking snakes; their tall, semi-cylindrical *scuta* turned the strokes of the foe. The Celtic champions died in moments, each beset by half a dozen men. Surrounded on three sides, most of their followers fell with them. The Romans, in their turn, raised the victory shout.

Marcus sent another maniple to the left flank to deal with a breakthrough. They contained it, but that part of the line still sagged. The Celtic chieftain was there, fighting like a demon. Red light flashed from his sword as he lopped off a legionary's hand, then killed the man as he stood stupidly staring at the spouting stump.

A Gaul charged Scaurus, swinging his sword over his head in great circles as if it were a sling. As the tribune ducked under his wild slash, he caught the reek of ale from the man. He whirled for an answering blow, only to see Gaius Philippus tugging his blade from the Gaul's body.

The centurion spat contemptuously. "They're fools. Fighting is far too serious a business to take on drunk." He looked about. "But there's so damned many of them."

Scaurus could only nod. The Roman center was holding, but both flanks bent now. In close fighting the slingers on the right were more liability than asset, for their covering spearmen had to do double duty to keep the Celts off them. Worse yet, bands of Celts were slipping into the woods. Marcus did not think they were running. He was afraid they were working their way round to attack the Roman rear.

Gorgidas the doctor slipped by him to drag a wounded legionary from the line and bandage his gashed thigh. Catching the tribune's eye, he said, "I'd have been as happy without this chance to ply my trade, you know." In the heat of the moment he spoke his native Greek.

"I know," Marcus answered in the same tongue. Then another Celt was on him—a noble, by his bronze breastplate. He feinted low with his spear, thrust high. Scaurus turned the stab with his shield. The spear-point slid past him off the *scutum*'s rounded surface; he stepped in close. The Gaul backpedaled for his life, eyes wide and fearfully intent on the motion of the tribune's sword.

Marcus lunged at the opening under the arm of his corselet. His aim was not quite true, but the thrust punched through his foe's armor and into his vitals. The barbarian swayed. Bright blood frothed from his nose and mouth as he fell.

"Well struck!" Gaius Philippus shouted.

His sword-arm was red almost to the elbow. Marcus shrugged, not thinking his blow had carried that much force. More likely some smith had jobbed the Gaul, though most Celtic metalworkers took pride in their products.

It was growing dark fast now. Marcus set some men not yet fighting to make torches and pass them forward. His soldiers used them for more than light—a Celt fled shrieking, his long, greasy locks ablaze.

Liscus went down, fighting against the countrymen he had abandoned for Rome. Scaurus felt a stab of remorse. The interpreter had been bright, jolly, and recklessly brave—but then, of how many on both sides might that have been said? Now he was merely dead.

The Gauls pushed forward on either wing, slashing, stabbing, and chopping. Outnumbered, the Romans had to give ground, their line bending away from the covering forest. As he watched them driven back upon themselves, the growing knowledge of defeat pressed its icy weight on Scaurus' shoulders. He fought on, rushing now here, now there, wherever the fighting was fiercest, shouting orders and encouragement to his men all the while.

In his learning days he had studied under scholars of the Stoic school. Their teachings served him well now. He did not give way to fright or despair, but kept on doing his best, though he knew it might not be enough. Failure, in itself, was not blameworthy. Lack of effort surely was.

Gaius Philippus, who had seen more bumbling young officers than he could remember, watched this one with growing admiration. The fight was not going well, but with numbers so badly against the Romans it was hard to see how it could have gone much better.

The buccinators' horns blew in high alarm. The woods were screen no more; leaping, yelling Celts burst forward, storming at the Roman rear. Tasting the cup of doom in earnest, Marcus wheeled his last reserves to face them, shouting, "Form circle! Form circle!"

His makeshift rear defense held somehow, beating back the ragged Celtic charge until the Roman circle could take shape. But the trap was sprung. Surrounded deep within the land of their foes, the legionaries could expect but one fate. The night was alive with the Celts' exultant cries as they flowed round the Roman ring like the sea round a pillar of hard black stone it would soon engulf.

Druids' marks on his blade flashing in the torchlight, the Gallic chieftain leaped like a wolf against the Roman line. He hewed his way through three ranks of men, then spun and fought his way back to his own men and safety.

"There's a warrior I'd sooner not come against," Gaius Philippus said, somberly eyeing the twisted bodies and shattered weapons the Gaul had left behind him.

Marcus gave tribute where it was due. "He is a mighty one."

The battle slowed, men from both sides leaning on spear or shield as they tried to catch their breath. The moans of the wounded floated up into the night. Somewhere close by, a cricket chirped.

Marcus realized how exhausted he was. His breath came in panting sobs, his legs were leaden, and his cuirass a burden heavier than Atlas had borne. He itched everywhere; dried, crusted sweat cracked whenever he moved. He had long since stopped noticing its salt taste in his mouth or its sting in his eyes.

His hand had been clenched round his sword hilt for so long he had to will it open to reach for the canteen at his side. The warm, sour wine stung his throat as he swallowed.

The moon rose, a couple of days past full and red as if reflecting the light of this grim field.

As if that had been a signal, the Celtic chieftain came up once more. The Romans tensed to receive his onslaught, but he stopped out of weapon range. He put down his sword, raised his bare right hand above his head. "It's well you've fought," he called to the Romans in fair Latin. "Will you not yield yourselves to me now and ha' done with this foolish slaughter? Your lives you'll save, you know."

The military tribune gave surrender a few seconds' honest thought. For some reason he was inclined to trust the Gaul's good intentions, but doubted the barbarian would be able to control his followers after they had the Romans in their power. He remembered all too well the Gallic custom of burning thieves and robbers alive in wickerwork images and knew it would be easy for the Romans, once captive, to be judged such.

One legionary's comment to his linemate rang loud in the silence: "Bugger the bastard! If he wants us, let him come winkle us out and pay the bill for it!"

After that, Marcus did not feel the need for any direct reply. The Celt understood. "On your heads it will be, then," he warned.

He turned to his own troops, shouting orders. Men who had chosen to sit for a moment heaved themselves up off their haunches, tightened their grips on spears, swords, clubs. They tramped forward, and the insane smithy's din of combat began again.

The Roman ring shrank, but would not break. The still bodies of the slain and thrashing forms of the wounded impeded the Gauls' advance; more than one stumbled to his death trying to climb over them. They came on.

"Give yourselves up, fools, while there's the most of you alive!" their chieftain yelled to his foes.

"When we said 'no' the first time, did you not believe us?" Marcus shouted back.

The Gaul swung up his sword in challenge. "Maybe after the killing of you, the Roman next in line to your honor will have more sense!"

"Not bloody likely!" Gaius Philippus snarled, but the big Celt was already moving. He cut down one Roman and kicked two more aside. He ducked under a broken spear swung club-fashion, lashing out with his blade to hamstring the swinger. Then he was inside the Roman line and loping at Marcus, longsword at the ready.

A score of legionaries, first among them Gaius Philippus, moved to intercept him, but the tribune waved them back. Fighting died away as, by unspoken common consent, both armies grounded their weapons to watch their leaders duel.

A smile lit the Celt's face when he saw Marcus agree to single combat. He raised his sword in salute and said, "A brave man you are, Roman dear. I'd know your name or ever I slay you."

"I am called Marcus Aemilius Scaurus," the tribune replied. He felt more desperate than brave. The Celt lived for war, where he himself had only played at it, more to further his political ambitions than from love of fighting.

He thought of his family in Mediolanum, of the family name that would fail if he fell here. His parents still lived, but were past the age of childbearing, and after him had three daughters but no son.

More briefly, he thought of Valerius Corvus and how, almost three hundred years before, he had driven a Celtic army from central Italy by killing its leader in a duel. He did not really believe these Gauls would flee even if he won. But he might delay and confuse them, maybe enough to let his army live.

All this sped through his mind as he raised his blade to match the Gaul's courtesy. "Will you give me your name as well?" he asked, feeling the ceremony of the moment.

"That I will. It's Viridovix son of Drappes I am, a chief of the Lexovii." The formalities done, Marcus braced for Viridovix's attack, but the Celt was staring in surprise at his sword. "How is it," he asked, "that a Roman comes by the blade of a druid?"

"The druid who bore it tried to stand against me and found he could not," Marcus replied, annoyed that his enemies, too, found it odd for him to carry a Celtic sword.

"It came of its own free will, did it?" Viridovix murmured, more surprised now. "Well, indeed and it's a brave blade you have, but you'll find mine no weaker." He drifted forward in a fencer's crouch.

Celtic nonsense, the tribune thought; a sword was a tool, with no more will of its own than a broom. But as he brought his weapon to the guard position, he suddenly felt unsure. No trick of the setting sun now made the druids' marks stamped down the length of the blade flicker and shine. They glowed with a hot golden light of their own, a light that grew stronger and more vital with every approaching step Viridovix took.

The Gaul's sword was flaring, too. It quivered in his hand like a live thing, straining to reach the blade the Roman held. Marcus' was also twisting in his hand, struggling to break free.

Awe and dread chased each other down Viridovix' long face, harshly plain in the hellish light of the swords. Marcus knew his own features bore a similar cast.

Men in both armies groaned and covered their eyes, caught in something past their comprehension.

The two blades met with a roar louder than thunder. The charms the druids had set on them, spells crafted to keep the land of the Gauls ever free of foreign rule, were released at their meeting. That one sword was in an invader's hands only powered the unleashing further.

The Celts outside the embattled circle of Romans saw a dome of red-gold light spring from the crossed blades to surround the legionaries. One Gaul, braver or more foolish than his fellows, rushed forward to touch the dome. He snatched his seared hand back with a howl. When the dome of light faded away, the space within was empty.

Talking in low voices over the prodigy they had witnessed, the Celts buried their dead, then stripped the Roman corpses and buried them in a separate grave. They drifted back to their villages and farms by ones and twos. Few spoke of what they had seen, and fewer were believed.

Later that year Caesar came to the land of the Lexovii, and from him not even miracles could save the Gauls. The only magic he acknowledged was that of empire; for him it was enough. When he wrote his commentaries, the presumed massacre of a scouting column did not seem worth mentioning.

Inside the golden dome, the ground faded away beneath the Romans' feet, leaving them suspended in nothingness. There was a queasy feeling of motion and imbalance, though no wind of passage buffeted their faces. Men cursed, screamed, and called on their gods, to no avail.

Then, suddenly, they stood on dirt again; Marcus had the odd impression it had rushed up to meet his sandals. The dome of light winked out. The Romans found themselves once more in a forest clearing, one smaller and darker than that which they had so unexpectedly left. It was dark night. Though Scaurus knew the moon had risen not long before, there was no moon here. There were no massed Celts, either. For that he gave heartfelt thanks.

He realized he was still sword-to-sword with Viridovix. He stepped back and lowered his blade. At his motion, Viridovix cautiously did the same.

"A truce?" Marcus said. The Gaul was part and parcel of the magic that had fetched them to this place. Killing him out of hand would be foolish.

"Aye, the now," Viridovix said absently. He seemed more interested in looking around at wherever this was than in fighting. He also seemed utterly indifferent to the danger he was in, surrounded by his foes. Marcus wondered whether the bravado was real or assumed. In the midst of Gauls, he would have been too terrified to posture.

He glanced from his sword to Viridovix'. Neither, now, seemed more than a length of edged steel.

The Romans milled about, wandering through the open space. To the tribune's surprise, none came rushing up to demand putting Viridovix to death. Maybe, like Scaurus, they were too stunned at what happened to dare harm him, or maybe that confident attitude was paying dividends.

Junius Blaesus came up to Marcus. Ignoring Viridovix altogether, the scout gave his commander a smart salute, as if by clinging to legionary routine he could better cope with the terrifying unknown into which he had fallen. "I don't believe this is Gaul at all, sir," he said. "I walked to the edge of the clearing, and the trees seem more like the ones in Greece, or some place like Cilicia.

"It's not a bad spot, though," he went on. "There's a pond over there, with a creek running into it. For a while I thought we'd end up in Tartarus, and nowhere else but."

"You weren't the only one," Marcus said feelingly. Then he blinked. It had not occurred to him that whatever had happened might have left him and his troops still within land under Roman control.

The scout's salute and his speculation gave the tribune an idea. He ordered his men to form a camp by the pond Blaesus had found, knowing that the routine labor—a task they had done hundreds of times before—would help take the strangeness from this place.

He wondered how he would explain his arrival to whatever Roman authorities might be here. He could almost hear the skeptical proconsul: "A dome of light, you say? Ye-ss, of course. Tell me, what fare did it charge for your passage . . . ?"

Earthworks rose in a square; inside them, eight-man tents sprang up in neat rows. Without being told, the legionaries left a sizeable space in which Gorgidas could work. Not far from where Marcus stood, the Greek was probing an arrow wound with an extracting-spoon. The injured legionary bit his lips to keep from crying out, then sighed in relief as Gorgidas drew out the barbed point.

Gaius Philippus, who had been supervising the erection of the camp, strolled over to Scaurus' side. "You had a good idea there," he said. "It keeps their minds off things."

So it did, but only in part. Marcus and Gorgidas were educated men, Gaius Philippus toughened by a hard life so he could take almost anything in stride. Most legionaries, though, were young, from farms or tiny villages, and had neither education nor experience to fall back on. The prodigy that had swept them away was too great for the daily grind to hold off for long.

The Romans murmured as they dug, muttered as they carried, whispered to one another as they pounded tentpegs. They made the two-fingered sign against the evil eye, clutching the phallic amulets they wore round their necks to guard themselves from it.

And more and more, they looked toward Viridovix. Like the anodyne of routine, his immunity slowly wore away. The mutters turned hostile. Hands started going to swords and spears. Viridovix' face turned grim. He freed his own long blade in its scabbard, though even with his might he could not have lasted long against a Roman rush.

But the legionaries, it seemed, wanted something more formal and awesome than a lynching. A delegation approached Scaurus, at its head a trooper named Lucilius. He said, "Sir, what say we cut the Gaul's throat, to take away the anger of whatever god did this to us?" The men behind him nodded.

The tribune glanced at Viridovix, who looked back, still unafraid. Had he cringed, Marcus might have let his men have their way, but he was a man who deserved better than being sacrificed for superstition's sake.

Scaurus said so, adding, "He could have stood by while his men slew us all, but instead he chose to meet me face-to-face. And the gods have done the same thing to him they did to all of us. Maybe they had their reasons."

Some legionaries nodded, but most were still unsatisfied. Lucilius said, "Sir, maybe they left him with us just so we could offer him up, and they'll be angry if we don't."

But the more he thought about it, the more Marcus hated the idea of deliberate human sacrifice. As a Stoic, he did not believe it would do any good, and as a Roman he thought it archaic. Not since the desperate days a hundred fifty years ago, after Hannibal crushed the Romans at Carthage, had they resorted to it. In even more ancient days, they sacrificed old men to relieve famine, but for centuries they had been throwing puppets made of rushes into the Tiber instead.

"That's it!" he said out loud. Both Viridovix and his own men eyed him, the one warily, the others expectantly. Remembering his fear of what the Gauls would do to his men if they surrendered, he went on, "I won't make us into the savage image of the barbarians we were fighting."

He left everyone unhappy. Viridovix let out an angry snort; Lucilius protested, "The gods should have an offering."

"They will," the tribune promised. "In place of Viridovix here, we'll sacrifice an image of him, as the priests do to mark festivals where the victim used to be a man. If the gods take those offerings, they'll accept this one as well—and in this wilderness, wherever it is, we may need the Gaul's might to fight with us now, not against us."

Lucilius was still inclined to argue, but the practicality of Scaurus' argument won over most of the men. Without backing, Lucilius gave up. To keep from having a disaffected soldier in the ranks, Marcus detailed him to gather cloth and, from the edges of the pond, rushes to make the effigy. Self-importance touched, Lucilius bustled away.

"I thank your honor," Viridovix said.

"He didn't do it for *your* sake," said Gaius Philippus. The senior centurion had stayed in the background, quiet but ready to back Marcus at need. "He did it to hold his leadership over the troops."

That was not altogether true, but Marcus knew better than to dilute Gaius Philippus' authority by contradicting him. He kept quiet. Why the Gaul thought he had saved him did not matter; the result did.

Viridovix looked down his nose at the short, stocky centurion. "And what would you have had him do with me, now? Chop me into dogmeat? The dogs'll feed on more than me if you try that—a deal more, if himself sends runts like you against me."

Scaurus expected Gaius Philippus to fly into a killing rage, but instead he threw back his head and laughed. "Well said, you great hulk!"

"Hulk, is it?" Viridovix swore in Gaulish, but he was grinning too.

"What then?" Marcus said. "Do you aim to join us, at least till we find out where we are? The gods know, you're a warrior born."

"Och, the shame of it, a Roman asking for my comradeship and me saying aye. But these woods are a solitary place for a puir lone Celt, and you Romans are men yourselves, for all that you're dull."

Gaius Philippus snorted.

"There's another score," Viridovix said. "Will your men have me, after my sending more than one of them to the next world?"

"They'd better," the senior centurion said, smacking his vine-stave into a callused palm.

"Dull," Viridovix repeated. "Never the chance to tell your officer be damned to him—and the day you try ordering me about you'll remember forever. Nay, it's always march in line, camp in line, fight in line. Tell me, do you futter in line as well?"

Having done so more than once, the centurion maintained a discreet silence.

The more they snipe, Marcus thought, the sooner they'll grow used to each other. He slapped at a mosquito. He must have missed, because he heard it buzz away.

Lucilius hurried up, carrying in his arms a bundle of rushes tied here and there with linen strips. It did not look much like a man, but again Scaurus had no intention of criticizing. If it satisfied Lucilius, that was good enough.

"What will you do with it, sir?" the trooper asked. "Throw it into the water the way the priests in Rome fling the puppets off the Sublician Bridge into the Tiber?"

Marcus rubbed his chin, thinking briefly. He shook his head. "In view of the color of the dome of light we were in, I think I ought to cast it into the flames instead."

Lucilius nodded, impressed by the tribune's reasoning. "Here, sir." He handed Scaurus the effigy, falling in behind him to make the beginning of a procession. More men joined it as Scaurus walked slowly and ceremoniously toward one of the campfires.

He paused in front of it so more of the legionaries could gather. Others looked up from their tasks to watch. Then he raised the crude rush-puppet high over his head, proclaiming loudly, "Whatsoever god or goddess is responsible for the wonder that has overtaken us, by whatever name or names you wish to be called, accept this offering in propitiation!" He hurled the image into the fire.

The flames leaped as they burned the effigy. "See how the god receives the sacrifice!" Lucilius cried. Marcus hid a smile; it was as if the legionary himself had thought of substituting the puppet for the man.

Yet the tribune wondered for a moment if Lucilius saw something he was missing. An effigy of damp rushes should have burned slowly instead of being consumed like so much tinder.

Marcus scowled, suppressing his superstitious maunderings. One miracle in an evening, he told himself firmly, is enough. He turned his back on the fire and went over to see how Gorgidas was doing with the wounded.

"How does it look like I'm doing?" Gorgidas snarled at him.

"Not well," Scaurus admitted. Gorgidas was rushing from one injured man to the next, bandaging here, suturing there, tossing his head in despair at a head wound he had no hope of treating. The tribune asked, "What help can I give you?"

The Greek looked up, as if just realizing Marcus was there. "Hmm? Let me think. . . . If you order a couple of troopers to work with me, that might help a little. They'd be clumsy, but better than nothing—and sometimes, whether he wants to or not, a man writhes so much he needs to be held."

"I'll take care of it," the tribune said. "What happened to Attilius and Publius Curtianus?"

"My assistants? What do you suppose happened to them?"

His face hot, Marcus beat a hasty retreat. He almost forgot to send the legionaries over to Gorgidas.

Gaius Philippus and Viridovix were still arguing, away from most of the men. The senior centurion drew his sword. Scaurus dashed over to break up the fight. He found none to break up; Gaius Philippus was showing the Gaul the thrusting-stroke.

"All well and good, Roman dear," Viridovix said, "but why then are you spoiling it by using so short a blade?"

The veteran shrugged. "Most of us aren't big enough to handle the kind of pigsticker you swing. Besides, a thrust, even with a *gladius,* leaves a man farther from his foe than a cut from a longsword."

The two lifelong warriors might have been a couple of bakers talking about how to make bread rise highest. Marcus smiled at the way a common passion could make even deadly foes forget their enmity.

One of the junior centurions, a slim youngster named Quintus Glabrio, came up to him and said, "Begging your pardon, sir, could you tell me where this is so I can pass the word along to the men and quiet them down? The talk is getting wild."

"I'm not sure, precisely. From the terrain and the trees, one of the scouts thinks this may be Cilicia or Greece. Come morning we'll send out a detail, track down some peasants, and find out what we need to know."

Glabrio gaped at him. Even in the starlight Marcus could see the fear on his face, fear intense enough to make him forget the pain of a slashed forearm. "Cilicia, sir? Greece? Have you—?" Words failed him. He pointed to the sky.

Puzzled, Marcus looked up. It was a fine, clear night. Let's see, he thought, scanning the heavens, north should be . . . where? Cold fingers walked his spine as he stared at the meaningless patterns the stars scrawled across the sky. Where was the Great Bear that pointed to the pole? Where were the stars of summer, the Scorpion, the Eagle, the Lyre? Where were the autumn groupings that followed them through the night, Andromeda, Pegasus? Where even were the stars of winter, or the strange constellations that peeped above the southern horizon in tropic lands like Africa or Cyrenaica?

Gaius Philippus and Viridovix stared with him, shared his will to disbelieve. The Gaul cursed in his native speech, not as he had at Gaius Philippus, but softly, as if in prayer. "Gods on Olympus," the senior centurion murmured, and Marcus had to fight hysterical laughter. This place was beyond the Olympians' realm. And his own as well; his vision of an angry proconsul blew away in the wind of the unknown.

Few Romans slept much that night. They sat outside their tents, watching the illegible heavens wheel and trying, as men will, to tame the unknown by drawing patterns on it and naming them: the Target, the Ballista, the Locust, the Pederasts.

The naming went on through the night as new stars rose to replace their setting fellows. The east grew pale, then pink. The forest ceased to be a single dark shape, becoming trees, bushes, and shrubs no more remarkable than the ones of Gaul, if not quite the same. The sun rose, and was simply the sun.

And an arrow flashed out of the woods, followed an instant later by a challenge in an unknown tongue.

II

From the way their challenger brushed the bushes aside and strode toward the Romans, Marcus was sure he was no skulking woods-bandit, but a man who felt the full power of his country behind him. It showed in the set of his shoulders, in the watchful suspicion on his face, in the very fact that he dared come out, alone, to defy twelve hundred men.

"You're right enough," Gaius Philippus agreed when the tribune put his thought into words. "He's not quite alone, though—or if I were in his boots, I'd not be so lackwitted as to leave my bow behind. He'll have friends covering him from the woods, I'd wager."

So it seemed, for the warrior stopped well within arrow range of the trees from which he'd come and waited, arms folded across his chest. "Let's see what he has to say," Marcus said. "Gaius, you'll come with me, and you, Viridovix—maybe he understands Celtic. Gorgidas!"

The doctor finished a last neat knot on the bandage he was tying before he looked up. "What do you need *me* for?"

"If you'd rather I relied on my own Greek—"

"I'm coming, I'm coming."

The tribune also picked Adiatun, an officer of the slingers. Like his men, he was from the Balearic Islands off the coast of Spain and had their strange tongue as his birthspeech. One of the legionaries who had served in the east had picked up a bit of Syrian and Armenian. That would have to do, Marcus decided. Any more and the waiting soldier would think them an attack, not a parley.

As it was, he drew back a pace when he saw half a dozen men approaching from the Roman camp. But Marcus and his companions moved slowly, right hands extended before them at eye level, palms out to show their emptiness. After a moment's hesitation, he returned the gesture and advanced. He stopped about ten feet from them, saying something that had to mean, "This is close enough." He studied the new-comers with frank curiosity.

Marcus returned it. The native was a lean man of middle height, perhaps in his mid-thirties. Save for a proud nose, his features were small and fine under a wide forehead, giving his face a triangular look. His olive skin was sun-darkened and weathered; he carried a long scar on his left cheek and another above his left eye. His jaw was outlined by a thin fringe of beard, mostly dark, but streaked with silver on either side of his mouth.

But for that unstylish beard, Marcus thought, by his looks he could have been a Roman, or more likely a Greek. He wore a shirt of mail reaching halfway down his thighs. Unlike the Romans', it had sleeves. Over it was a forest-green surcoat of light material. His helm was a busi-nesslike iron pot; an apron of mail was riveted to it to cover his neck, and a bar nasal protected his face. The spurs on the heels of his calf-length leather boots said he was a horseman, as did the saber at his belt and the small round shield slung on his back.

The soldier asked something, probably, Marcus thought, "Who are you people, and what are you doing here?" The tribune looked to his group of would-be interpreters. They all shook their heads. He answered in Latin, "We have no more idea where we are than you do who we are."

The native spread his hands and shrugged, then tried what sounded like a different language. He had no better luck. The Romans used every tongue at their command, and the soldier seemed to speak five or six himself, but they held none in common.

The warrior finally grimaced in annoyance. He patted the ground, waved his hand to encompass everything the eye could see. "Videssos," he said. He pointed at Marcus, then at the camp from which he had come, and raised his eyebrows questioningly.

"Romans," the tribune answered.

"Are you after including me in that?" Viridovix asked. "The shame of it!"

"Yes, we all feel it," Gaius Philippus told him.

"Enough, you two," Gorgidas said. "I'm no more Roman than you, my mustachioed friend, but we need to keep things as simple as we can."

"Thank you," Marcus said. "Romans," he repeated.

The Videssian had watched the byplay with interest. Now he pointed at himself. "Neilos Tzimiskes."

After echoing him, Scaurus and his companions gave their names. Viridovix grumbled, "A man could choke to death or ever he said 'Tzimiskes,'" but Neilos had no easier time with "Viridovix son of Drappes."

Tzimiskes unbuckled his swordbelt and laid it at his feet. There was a cry of alarm from the woods, but he silenced it with a couple of shouted sentences. He pointed to the sword, to himself, and to Marcus, and made a gesture of repugnance.

"We have no quarrel with you," Scaurus agreed, knowing his words would not be understood but hoping his tone would. He reached into his pack for a ration biscuit, offering it and his canteen, still half-full of wine, to Tzimiskes.

The Videssian nodded and grinned, shedding years as he did so. "Not so happy will he be when he eats what you give him," Adiatun said. "The *bucellum* tastes all too much like sawdust."

But Tzimiskes bit into the hard-baked biscuit without complaint, drank a long swallow of wine with the air of a man who has had worse. He patted himself apologetically, then shouted into the forest again. A few moments later another, younger, Videssian emerged. His equipment was much like that of Tzimiskes, though his surcoat was brown rather than green. He carried a short bow in his left hand and bore a leather sack over his right shoulder.

The young Videssian's name was Proklos Mouzalon. From his sack he brought out dried apples and figs, olives, smoked and salted pork, a hard yellow cheese, onions, and journey-bread differing from the Romans' only in that it was square, not round—all normal fare for soldiers on the move. He also produced a small flask of thick, sweet wine. Marcus found it cloying, as he was used to the drier vintage the Roman army drank.

Before they raised the flask to their lips, the Videssians each spat angrily on the ground, then lifted their arms and eyes to the sky, at the same time murmuring a prayer. Marcus had been about to pour a small libation, but decided instead to follow the custom of the country in which he found himself. Tzimiskes and Mouzalon nodded their approval as he did so, though of course his words were gibberish to them.

By signs, Neilos made it clear there was a town a couple of days' travel to the south, a convenient place to establish a market to feed the Roman soldiers and lodge them for the time being. He sent Mouzalon ahead to prepare the town for their arrival; the clop of hoofbeats down a forest path confirmed the Videssians as horsemen.

While Tzimiskes was walking back to his own tethered mount, Marcus briefed his men on what had been arranged. "I think we'll be able to stay together," he said. "As far as I could understand all the finger-waving, these people hire mercenaries, and they're used to dealing with bodies of foreign troops. The problem was that Tzimiskes had never seen our sort before, and wasn't sure if we were invaders, a free company for hire, or men from the far side of the moon."

He stopped abruptly, mentally cursing his clumsy tongue; he was afraid the Romans were farther from home than that.

Gaius Philippus came to his rescue, growling, "Another thing, you wolves. On march, we treat this as friendly country—no stealing a farmer's mule or his daughter just because they take your fancy. By Vulcan's left nut, you'll see a cross if you bugger that one up. Till we know we have a place here, we walk soft."

"Dull, dull, dull," Viridovix said. The centurion ignored him.

"Are you going to sell our swords to these barbarians?" someone called.

Gaius Philippus glared as he tried to spot the man who had spoken, but Scaurus said, "It's a fair question. Let me answer this way: our swords are all we have to sell. Unless you know the way back to Rome, we're a bit outnumbered." It was a feeble jest, but so plainly true the legionaries nodded to themselves as they began breaking camp.

Marcus was not eager to take up the mercenary's trade, but an armed force at his back lent him bargaining power with the Videssians he would not have had otherwise. It also gave him the perfect excuse for keeping the Romans together. In this strange new land, they had only themselves to rely on.

The tribune also wondered about Videssos' reasons for hiring foreign troops. To his way of thinking, that was for decadent kingdoms like Ptolemaic Egypt, not for healthy states. But Tzimiskes and Mouzalon were soldiers and were also plainly natives.

He sighed. So much to learn—

At Gorgidas' request, Scaurus detailed a squad to cut poles for litters; more than a score of Romans were too badly wounded to walk. "Fever will take some," the Greek said, "but if they get decent food and treatment in this town, most should pull through."

Tzimiskes rode up to the edge of the makeshift earthwork the Romans had made. Atop his horse, he was high enough off the ground to see inside. He seemed impressed by the bustle and the order of the camp.

Though canny enough not to say so, Scaurus was struck by the equipment of the Videssian's saddle and horse. Even at a quick glance, there were ideas there the Romans had never had. For one thing, Neilos rode with his feet in irons shaped to hold them, which hung from his saddle by leather straps. For another, when his mount lifted a forefoot, the tribune saw that its hoof was shod in iron to help protect it from stones and thorns.

"Isn't that the sneakiest thing?" Gaius Philippus said as he strolled up. "The whoreson can handle a sword or a bow—or even a spear—with both hands, and stay on with his feet. Why didn't we ever think of that?"

"It might be a good idea not to let on that we didn't know of such things."

"I wasn't born yesterday."

"Yes, I know," Marcus said. Not a glance had his centurion given to Tzimiskes' gear while he spoke of it. The Videssian, looking from one of them to the other, could have had no clue to what they were talking about.

About an hour's march west along a narrow, twisting woods-path got the Romans free of the forest and into the beginnings of settled country. His horizon widening as he moved into open land, Marcus looked about curiously. The terrain he was passing through was made up of rolling hills and valleys; to the north and northeast real mountains loomed purple against the horizon.

Farmhouses dotted the hillsides, as did flocks of sheep and goats. More than one farmer started driving his beasts away from the road as soon as he caught sight of an armed column of unfamiliar aspect. Tzimiskes shouted reassurance at them, but most preferred to take no chances. "Looks like they've been through it before," Gaius Philippus said. Marcus gave a thoughtful nod.

The weather was warmer and drier than it had been in Gaul, despite a brisk breeze from the west. The wind had a salt tang to it; a gull screeched high overhead before gliding away.

"We'll not be having to take ship to come to this town, will we?" Viridovix asked Marcus.

"I don't think so. Why?"

"For all I've lived by the ocean the whole of my life, it's terrible seasick I get." The Celt paled at the thought of it.

The narrow path they had been following met a broad thoroughfare running north and south. Used to the stone-paved highways the Romans built, Marcus found its dirt surface disappointing until Gaius Philippus pointed out, "This is a nation of horsemen, you know. Horses don't care much for hard roads; I suppose that still holds true with iron soles on their feet. Our roads aren't for animal traffic—they're for moving infantry from one place to another in a hurry."

The tribune was only half-convinced. Come winter, this road would be a sea of mud. Even in summer, it had disadvantages—he coughed as Tzimiskes' horse kicked up dust.

He stepped forward to try to talk with the Videssian, pointing at things and learning their names in Tzimiskes' tongue while teaching him the Latin equivalents. To his chagrin, Tzimiskes was much quicker at picking up his speech than he was in remembering Videssian words.

In the late afternoon they marched past a low, solidly built stone building. At the eastern edge of its otherwise flat roof, a blue-painted wooden spire leaped into the air; it was topped by a gilded ball. Blue-robed men who had shaved their pates but kept full, bushy beards worked in the gardens surrounding the structure. Both building and occupants were so unlike anything Marcus had yet seen that he looked a question to Tzimiskes.

His guide performed the same ritual he had used before he drank wine, spitting and raising his arms and head. The tribune concluded the blue-robes were priests of some sort, though tending a garden seemed an odd way to follow one's gods. He wondered if they did such work full time. If so, he thought, they took their religion seriously.

There was little traffic on the road. A merchant, catching sight of the marching column as he topped a rise half a mile south, promptly turned his packhorses round and fled. Gaius Philippus snorted in derision. "What does he think we can do? Run down his horses, and us afoot?"

"Dinna even think of it," Viridovix said earnestly. "A mess o' blisters bigger than goldpieces, my feet must be. I think you Romans were born so you couldna feel pain in your legs. My calves are on fire, too."

To Scaurus, on the other hand, the day's march had been an easy one. His men were slowed by the litters they bore in teams. Many were walking wounded, and all bone-weary. Four of the soldiers in the litters died that day, as Gorgidas had known they would.

Tzimiskes appeared pleased at the pace the legionaries had been able to keep. He watched fascinated, as they used the last sunshine and the purple twilight to create their square field fortifications. Marcus was proud of the skill and discipline his exhausted troops displayed.

When the sun dipped below the western horizon, Neilos went through his now-familiar series of actions, though his prayer was longer than the one he had made at wine. "That explains the golden ball back down the road," Gorgidas said.

"It does?" Marcus' mind had been elsewhere.

"Of course it does. These people must be sun-worshipers."

The tribune considered it. "There are worse cults," he said. "Reverencing the sun is a simple enough religion." Gorgidas dipped his head in agreement, but Marcus would long remember the naïveté and ignorance behind his remark.

A thin sliver of crescent moon slid down the sky, soon leaving it to the incomprehensible stars. Marcus was glad to see there was a moon, at least, even if it was out of phase with the one he had known. A wolf bayed in the distant hills.

The day had been warm, but after sunset it grew surprisingly chilly. When added to the ripe state of the grainfields he had seen, that made Marcus guess the season to be fall, though in Gaul it had been early summer. Well, he thought, if this land's moon doesn't match my own, no good reason its seasons should, either. He gave it up and slept.

The town's name was Imbros. Though three or four ball-topped blue spires thrust their way into sight, its wall was high enough to conceal nearly everything within. The fortifications seemed sturdy enough, and in good condition. But while most of the gray stonework was old and weathered, much of the northern wall looked to have been recently re-built. The tribune wondered how long ago the sack had taken place and who the foe had been.

He knew the local leaders would not let any large numbers of his men into the town until they were convinced the legionaries could be trusted, but he had expected Imbros would ready a market outside the walls for the Romans' use. Where were the scurrying peasants, the bus-tling merchants, the approaching wagonloads of grain and other sup-plies? The city was not shut up against a siege, but it was not looking to the arrival of a friendly army either.

That could mean trouble. His troops were nearly through the iron rations they carried in their packs, and the fields and farms round Im-bros looked fat. Not even Roman discipline would hold long in the face of hunger.

With his few words and many gestures, he tried to get that across to Tzimiskes. The Videssian, a soldier himself, understood at once; he seemed puzzled and dismayed that the messenger he had sent ahead was being ignored.

"This is good brigand country," Gaius Philippus said. "I wonder if young Mouzalon was bushwhacked on his way here."

Viridovix said, "Wait—is that not the youngling himself, galloping out toward us?"

Mouzalon was already talking as he rode up to Tzimiskes. The lat-ter's answers, short at first, grew longer, louder, and angrier. The word or name "Vourtzes" came up frequently; when at last it was mentioned once too often, Tzimiskes spat in disgust.

"He must be truly furious, to vent his rage by perverting a prayer," Gorgidas said softly to Marcus. The tribune nodded, grateful for the Greek's insights.

Something was happening to Imbros now. There was a stir at the north gate, heralding the emergence of a procession. First came a fat man wearing a silver circlet on his balding head and a robe of maroon brocade. Parasol bearers flanked him on either side. They had to be for ceremony, as it was nearing dusk. Tzimiskes gave the fat man a venomous glance—was this, then, Vourtzes?

Vourtzes, if it was he, was followed by four younger, leaner men in less splendid robes. From their inkstained fingers and the nervous, nearsighted stares they sent at the Romans, Marcus guessed they were the fat man's secretaries.

With them came a pair of shaven-headed priests. One wore a simple robe of blue; the other, a thin-faced man with a graying beard and bright, burning eyes, had a palm-wide circle of cloth-of-gold embroidered on the left breast of his garment. The plain-robed priest swung a brass thurible that gave forth clouds of sweet, spicy smoke.

On either side of the scribes and priests tramped a squad of foot soldiers: big, fair, stolid-looking men in surcoats of scarlet and silver over chain mail. They carried pikes and wicked-looking throwing axes; their rectangular shields had various devices painted on them. Mercenaries, the tribune decided—they looked like no Videssians he had yet seen.

Behind the soldiers came three trumpeters, a like number of flute-players, and a man even fatter than Vourtzes pushing a kettledrum on a little wheeled cart.

Vourtzes stopped half a dozen places in front of the Romans. His honor guard came to a halt with a last stomped step and a loud, wordless shout; Marcus felt his men bristling at the arrogant display. Trumpeters and flautists blew an elaborate flourish. The tubby drummer smote his instrument with such vim that Scaurus waited for it or its cart to collapse.

When the fanfare stopped, the two Videssians with the Roman army put their right hands over their hearts and bent their heads to the plump official who led the parade. Marcus gave him the Roman salute, clenched right fist held straight out before him at eye level. At Gaius Philippus' barked command, the legionaries followed his example in smart unison.

Startled, the Videssian gave back a pace. He glared at Scaurus, who had to hide a grin. To cover his discomfiture, the official gestured his priests forward. The older one pointed a bony finger at Marcus, rattling off what sounded like a series of questions. "I'm sorry, my friend, but I do not speak your language," the tribune replied in Latin. The priest snapped a couple of queries at Tzimiskes.

His reply must have been barely satisfactory, for the priest let out an audible sniff. But he shrugged and gave what Marcus hoped were his blessings to the Romans, his censer-swinging comrade occasionally joining in his chanted prayer.

The benediction seemed to complete a prologue the Videssians felt necessary. When the priests had gone back to their place by the scribes, the leader of the parade stepped up to clasp Marcus' hands. His own were plump, beringed, and sweaty; the smile he wore had little to do with his feelings, but was the genial mask any competent politician could assume at will. The tribune understood that face quite well, for he wore it himself.

With patience and Tzimiskes' help, Scaurus learned this was indeed Rhadenos Vourtzes, *hypasteos* of the city of Imbros—governor by appointment of the Emperor of Videssos. The Emperor's name, Marcus gathered, was Mavrikios, of the house of Gavras. The Roman got the impression Tzimiskes was loyal to Mavrikios, and that he did not think Vourtzes shared his loyalty.

Why, Marcus struggled to ask, had the *hypasteos* not begun to prepare his town for the arrival of the Romans? Vourtzes, when he understood, spread his hands regretfully. The news of their appearance had only come the day before. It was hard to believe in any case, as Vourtzes had no prior reports of any body of men crossing Videssos' border. And finally, the *hypasteos* did not place much faith in the word of an *akrites,* a name which seemed to apply to both Mouzalon and Tzimiskes.

Young Proklos reddened with anger at that and set his hand on the hilt of his sword. But Vourtzes turned his smile to the soldier and calmed him with a couple of sentences. In this case, it seemed, he had been wrong; matters would be straightened out shortly.

Without liking the man who gave it, Marcus had to admire the performance. As for delivery on the promises, he would see.

Gorgidas plucked at the tribune's arm. His thin face was haggard with exhaustion. "Have they physicians?" he demanded. "I need help with our wounded, or at least poppy juice to ease the pain for the ones who are going to die no matter what we do."

"We can find out," Scaurus said. He had no idea of the words to tell Vourtzes what he needed, but sometimes words were unnecessary. He caught the *hypasteos'* eye, led him to the litters. The official's retinue followed.

At the sight of the injured legionaries, Vourtzes made a choked sound of dismay. In spite of the soldiers with him, Marcus thought, he did not know much of war.

To the tribune's surprise, the lean priest who had prayed at the Romans stooped beside a litter. "What's he mucking about for?" Gorgidas said indignantly. "I want another doctor, not spells and flummeries."

"You may as well let him do what he wants," Gaius Philippus said. "Sextus Minucius won't care."

Looking at the moaning legionary, Marcus thought the senior centurion was right. A bandage soaked with blood and pus was wrapped over a spear wound in Minucius' belly. From the scent of ordure, Scaurus knew his gut had been pierced. That sort of wound was always fatal.

Gorgidas must have reached the same conclusion. He touched Minucius' forehead and clicked his tongue between his teeth. "A fever you could cook meat over. Aye, let's see what the charlatan does for him. Poor bastard can't even keep water down, so poppy juice won't do him any good either. With the dark bile he's been puking up, at most he only has a couple of bad days left."

The wounded soldier turned his head toward the sound of the Greek's voice. He was a big, strapping man, but his features bore the fearful, dazed look Marcus had come to recognize, the look of a man who knew he was going to die.

As far as the Videssian priest was concerned, all the Romans but Minucius might have disappeared. The priest dug under the stinking bandages, set his hands on the legionary's torn belly, one on either side of the wound. Scaurus expected Minucius to shriek at the sudden pressure, but the legionary stayed quiet. Indeed, he stopped his anguished thrashing and lay still in the litter. His eyes slid shut.

"That's something, anyhow," Marcus said. "He—"

"Hush," Gorgidas broke in. He had been watching the priest's face, saw the intense concentration build on it.

"Watch your mouth with the tribune," Gaius Philippus warned, but halfheartedly—not being in the chain of command, Gorgidas had more liberty than a simple solider.

"It's all right—" Scaurus began. Then he stopped of his own accord, the skin on his arms prickling into gooseflesh. He had the same sense of stumbling into the unknown that he'd felt when his blade met Viridovix'. That thought made him half draw his sword. Sure enough, the druids' marks were glowing, not brilliantly as they had then, but with a soft, yellow light.

Thinking about it later, he put that down to the magic's being smaller than the one that had swept him to Videssos, and to his being on the edge of it rather than at the heart. All the same, he could feel the energy passing from the priest to Minucius. Gaius Philippus' soft whistle said he perceived it too.

"A flow of healing," Gorgidas whispered. He was talking to himself, but his words gave a better name to what the priest was doing than anything Marcus could have come up with. As with the strange stars here, though, it was only a label to put on the incomprehensible.

The Videssian lifted his hands. His face was pale; sweat ran down into his beard. Minucius' eyes opened. "I'm hungry," he said in a matter-of-fact voice.

Gorgidas leaped at him like a wolf on a calf. He tore open the bandages the priest had disturbed. What they saw left him speechless, and made Scaurus and Gaius Philippus gasp. The great scar to the left of Minucius' navel was white and puckered, as if it had been there five years.

"I'm hungry," the legionary repeated.

"Oh, shut up," Gorgidas said. He sounded angry, not at Minucius but at the world. What he had just witnessed smashed the rational, cynical approach he tried to take to everything. To have magic succeed where his best efforts had been sure failures left him baffled, furious, and full of an awe he would not admit even to himself.

But he had been around Romans long enough to have learned not to quarrel with results. He grabbed the priest by the arm and frogmarched him to the next most desperately hurt man—this one had a sucking wound that had collapsed a lung.

The Videssian pressed his hands to the legionary's chest. Again Marcus, along with his comrades, sensed the healing current pass from priest to Roman, though this time the contact lasted much longer before the priest pulled away. As he did, the soldier stirred and tried to stand. When Gorgidas examined his wound, it was like Minucius': a terrible scar, but one apparently long healed.

Gorgidas hopped from foot to foot in anguished frustration. "By Asklepios, I have to learn the language to find out how he does that!" He looked as though he wanted to wring the answer from the priest, with hot irons if he had to.

Instead, he seized the Videssian and hauled him off to another injured legionary. This time the priest tried to pull away. "He's dying, curse you!" Gorgidas shouted. The cry was in his native Greek, but when Gorgidas pointed at the soldier, the priest had to take his meaning.

He sighed, shrugged, and stooped. But when he thrust his hands under the Roman's bandages, he began to shake, as with an ague. Marcus thought he felt the healing magic begin, but before he could be sure, the priest toppled in a faint.

"Oh, plague!" Gorgidas howled. He ran after another blue-robe and, ignoring the fellow's protests, dragged him over to the line of wounded soldiers. But this priest only shrugged and regretfully spread his hands. At last Gorgidas understood he was no healer. He swore and drew back his foot as if to boot the unconscious priest awake.

Gaius Philippus grabbed him. "Have you lost your wits? He's given you back two you never thought to save. Be grateful for what you have— look at the poor wretch, too. There's no more help left in him than wine in an empty jar."

"Two?" Gorgidas struggled without success against the veteran's powerful grip. "I want to heal them all!"

"So do I," Gaius Philippus said. "So do I. They're good lads, and they deserve better than the nasty ways of dying they've found for themselves. But you'll kill that priest if you push him any more, and then he won't be able to fix 'em at all. As is, maybe he can come back tomorrow."

"Some will have died by then," Gorgidas said, but less heatedly—as usual, the senior centurion made hard, practical sense.

Gaius Philippus went off to start the legionaries setting up camp for the night. Marcus and Gorgidas stood by the priest until, some minutes later, he came to himself and shakily got to his feet.

The tribune bowed lower to him than he had to Vourtzes. That was only fitting. So far, the priest had done more for the Romans.

That evening, Scaurus called together some of his officers to hash out what the legionaries should do next. As an afterthought, he added Gorgidas to Gaius Philippus, Quintus Glabrio, Junius Blaesus, and Adiatun the Iberian. When Viridovix ambled into the tent, he did not chase the Gaul away either—he was after as many different viewpoints as he could find.

Back in Gaul, with the full authority of Rome behind him, he would have made the decision himself and passed it on to his men. He wondered if he was diluting his authority by discussing things with them now. No, he thought—this situation was too far removed from ordinary military routine to be handled conventionally. The Romans were a republican people; more voices counted than the leader's.

Blaesus raised that point at once. "It grates on me, sir, it does, to have to hire on to a barbarian king. What are we, so many Parthians?"

Gaius Philippus muttered agreement. So did Viridovix; to him, even the Romans followed their leaders too blindly. He and the senior centurion looked at each other in surprise. Neither seemed pleased at thinking along with the other. Marcus smiled.

"Did you see the way the local bigwig was eyeing us?" Quintus Glabrio put in. "To him, *we* were the barbarians."

"I saw that too," Scaurus said. "I didn't like it."

"They may be right." That was Gorgidas. "Sextus Minucius would tell you so. I saw him in front of his tent, sitting there mending his tunic. Whatever these Videssians are, they know things we don't."

"Gaius Philippus and I already noticed that," Marcus said, and mentioned the iron riding-aids and horseshoes on Tzimiskes' mount. Glabrio nodded; he had spotted them too. So had Viridovix, who paid close attention to anything related to war. Blaesus and Adiatun looked surprised.

"The other problem, of course, is what happens to us if we don't join the Videssians," Glabrio said. The junior centurion had a gift for going to the heart of things, Scaurus thought.

"We couldn't stay under arms, not in the middle of their country," Gaius Philippus said with a reluctant nod. "I'm too old to enjoy life as a brigand, and that's the best we could hope for, setting up on our own. There aren't enough of us to go conquering here."

"And if we disarm, they can deal with us piecemeal, turn us into slaves or whatever they do to foreigners," Marcus said. "Together we have power, but none as individuals."

Ever since they'd met Tzimiskes, he had been looking for a more palatable answer than mercenary service and failing to find one. He'd hoped the others would see something he had missed, but the choice looked inescapable.

"Lucky we are they buy soldiers," Adiatun said. "Otherwise they would be hunting us down now." As a foreign auxiliary, he was already practically a mercenary; he would not earn Roman citizenship till his discharge. He did not seem much upset at the prospect of becoming a Videssian instead.

"All bets are off if we find out where Rome is, though," Gaius Philippus said. Everyone nodded, but with less hope and eagerness than Scaurus would have thought possible a few days before. Seeing alien stars in the sky night after night painfully reminded him how far from home the legionaries were. The Videssian priest's healing magic was an even stronger jolt; like Gorgidas, the tribune knew no Greek or Roman could have matched it.

Gaius Philippus was the last one to leave Scaurus' tent. He threw the tribune a salute straight from the drill fields. "You'd best start planning to live up to it," he said, chuckling at Marcus' bemused expression. "After all, *you're* Caesar now."

Startled, Marcus burst out laughing, but as he crawled into his bedroll he realized the senior centurion was right. Indeed, Gaius Philippus had understated things. Not even Caesar had ever commanded all the Romans there were. The thought was daunting enough to keep him awake half the night.

The market outside Imbros was established over the next couple of days. The quality of goods and food the locals offered was high, the prices reasonable. That relieved Marcus, for his men had left much of their wealth behind with the legionary bankers before setting out on their last, fateful mission.

Nor were the Romans yet in the official service of Videssos. Vourtzes said he would fix that as soon as he could. He sent a messenger south to the capital with word of their arrival. Scaurus noticed that Proklos Mouzalon disappeared about the same time. He carefully did not remark on it to Tzimiskes, who stayed with the Romans as an informal liaison despite Vourtzes' disapproval. Faction against faction . . .

Mouzalon's mission must have succeeded, for the imperial commissioner who came to Imbros ten days later to inspect the strange troops was not a man to gladden Vourtzes' heart. No bureaucrat he, but a veteran warrior whose matter-of-fact competence and impatience with any kind of formality reminded Marcus of Gaius Philippus.

The commissioner, whose name was Nephon Khoumnos, walked through the semipermanent camp the Romans had set up outside Imbros' walls. He had nothing but admiration for its good order, neatness, and sensible sanitation. When his inspection was done, he said to Marcus, "Hell's ice, man, where did you people spring from? You may know the tricks of the soldier's trade better than we do, you're no folk we've set eyes on before, and you appear inside the Empire without seeming to have crossed the border. How does this happen?"

Scaurus and his officers had been spending every free moment studying Videssian—with Tzimiskes, with Vourtzes' scribes, and with the priests, who seemed surprised the tribune wanted to learn to read and at how quickly he picked up the written language. After working with both the Roman and Greek alphabets, another script held no terrors for him. He found following a conversation much harder. Still, he was beginning to understand.

But he had little hope of putting across how he had been swept here, and less of being believed. Yet he liked Khoumnos and did not want to lie to him. With Tzimiskes' help, he explained as best he could and waited for the officer's disbelief.

It did not come. Khoumnos drew the sun-sign on his breast. "Phos!" he muttered, naming his people's god. "That is a strong magic, friend Roman; you must be a nation of mighty sorcerers."

Surprised he was not being laughed at, Marcus had to disagree. Khoumnos gave him a conspiratorial wink. "Then let it be your secret. That fat slug of a Vourtzes will treat you better if he thinks you may turn him into a newt if he crosses you."

He went on, "I think, outlander, the Imperial Guards could have use for such as you. Maybe you can teach the Halogai"—he named the blond northerners who made up Vourtzes' honor guard, and evidently much of the Emperor's as well,—"that there's more to soldiering than a wild charge at anything you don't happen to like. And I tell you straight out, with the accursed Yezda—may Skotos take them to hell!—sucking the blood from our westlands, we need men."

Khoumnos cocked an eye to the north. Dirty gray clouds were gathering there, harbingers of winter storms to come. He rubbed his chin. "Would it suit you to wait until spring before you come to the city?" he asked Marcus. By the slight emphasis he laid on "the," Scaurus knew he meant the town of Videssos itself. "That will give us time to be fully ready for you . . ."

Time to lay the political groundwork, Marcus understood him to mean. But Khoumnos' proposal suited him, and he said so. A peaceful winter at Imbros would allow his men a full refit and recovery, and let them learn their new land's ways and tongue without the pressure they would face in the capital. When Khoumnos departed, they were on the best of terms.

Rhadenos Vourtzes, Marcus noted, was very polite and helpful the next few days. He was also rather anxious and spent much of the time he was near the Roman looking back over his shoulder. Scaurus liked Nephon Khoumnos even more.

The autumn rains began only a few days after the last of the harvest was gathered in. One storm after another came blustering down from the north, lashing the last leaves from the trees, turning every road and path into an impassable trough of mud, and pointing out all the failures of the Romans' hasty carpentry. The legionaries cursed, dripped, and patched. They scoured the ever-encroaching rust from armor, tools, and weapons.

When the real cold came, the muddy ground froze rock-hard, only to be covered by a blanket of snow that lay in drifts taller than a man. Marcus began to see why, in a climate like this, robes were garments of ceremony but trousers the everyday garb. He started wearing them himself.

In such freezing weather, exercises were not a duty to be avoided, but something avidly sought to put warmth in a man's bones. The Romans trained whenever they could. Gaius Philippus worked them hard. Except when the blizzards were at their worst, they went on a twenty-mile march every week. The senior centurion was one of the oldest men among them, but he fought his way through the snow like a youngster.

He also kept the Romans busy in camp. Once he'd learned enough Videssian to get what he needed, he had the locals make double-weight wicker shields and wooden swords for the legionaries to practice with. He set up pells, against which they continually drilled in the thrusting stroke. Trying to keep the men fresh and interested, he even detailed Adiatun to teach them the fine points of slinging.

The only traditional legionary exercise from which he excused the men was swimming. Even his hardiness quailed at subjecting his men to the freezing water under the ice that covered streams and ponds.

The legionaries did stage mock fights, with the points on their swords and spears covered. At first, they only worked against one another. Later, they matched themselves against the two hundred or so Halogai who made up Imbros' usual garrison.

The tall northerners were skilled soldiers, as befitted their mercenary calling. But, like the Gauls, they fought as individuals and by clans, not in ordered ranks. If their first charge broke the Roman line they were irresistible but, more often than not, the legionaries' large shields and jabbing spears held them at bay until they tired and the Romans could take the offensive.

In the drills Marcus was careful never to cross blades with Viridovix, fearful lest they and all around them be swept away again by the sorcery locked in their swords. His own weapon seemed utterly ordinary when he practiced with his fellow Romans. But when he was working against the garrison troops he left behind such a trail of shattered shields and riven chain mail that he gained a reputation for superhuman strength. The same, he noticed, was true of Viridovix.

The garrison commander was a one-eyed giant of a man named Skapti Modolf's son. The Haloga was not young, but his hair was so fair it was hard to tell silver crept through the gold. He was friendly enough and, like any good fighting man, interested in the newcomers' ways of doing things, but he never failed to make Scaurus nervous. With his long, dour features, rumbling voice, and singleminded concentration on the art of war, he reminded the Roman all too much of a wolf.

Viridovix, though, took to the Halogai. "It's a somber lot they are," he admitted, "and more doomful than I'm fond of, but they fight as men do, and they perk up considerable wi' a drop of wine in 'em, indeed and they do."

That, Marcus found a few days later, was an understatement. After a day and most of a night of drinking, the Gaul and half a dozen northern mercenaries staged a glorious brawl that wrecked the tavern where it happened and most of the participants.

One aftermath of the fight was a visit from Vourtzes to the Roman camp. Marcus had not seen much of him lately and would have forgone this occasion, too, when he learned the *hypasteos* wanted him to pay for all the damage the grogshop had taken. Annoyed, he pointed out that it was scarcely just for him to be saddled with all the charges when only one of his men was involved, as opposed to six or seven under the *hypasteos'* jurisdiction. Vourtzes let the matter drop, but Marcus knew he was unhappy.

"Maybe you should have compromised and saved trouble," Gorgidas said. "If I know our Celtic friend, he raised more than his share of the ruction."

"I shouldn't be a bit surprised. But Vourtzes is the sort to bleed you to death a drop at a time if you let him. I wonder," Marcus mused, "how he'd look as a newt."

Like the rest of the Empire of Videssos, Imbros celebrated the passing of the winter solstice and the turning of the sun to the north once more. Special prayers winged their way heavenward from the temples. Bonfires blazed on street corners; the townsfolk jumped over them for luck. There was a huge, disorderly hockey match on the surface of a frozen pond. Falling and sliding on the ice seemed as much a part of the game as trying to drive the ball through the goal.

A troupe of mimes performed at Imbros' central theater. Marcus saw he was far from the only Roman there. Such entertainments were much like those his men had known in Italy, and the fact that they had no dialogue made them easier for the newcomers to understand.

Venders climbed up and down the aisles, crying their wares: good-luck charms, small roasted birds, cups of hot spiced wine, balls of snow sweetened with syrups, and many other things.

The skits were fast-paced and topical; a couple in particular stuck in Scaurus' mind. One showed an impressive-looking man in a cloth-of-gold robe—the Emperor Mavrikios, the tribune soon realized—as a farmer trying to keep a slouching nomad from running off with his sheep. The farmer-Emperor's task would have been much easier had he not had a cowardly son clinging to his arm and hindering his every move, a fat son in a robe of red brocade . . .

The other sketch was even less subtle. It involved the devastation of Imbros itself, as carried out in a totally inadvertent and unmalicious fashion by a tall, skinny fellow who wore a red wig and had a huge fiery mustache glued over his upper lip.

Viridovix was in the audience. " 'Twas not like that at all, at all!" he shouted to the mummer on stage, but he was laughing as hard as anyone around him.

Venders of food and drink were not the only purveyors to circulate through the crowd. Though exposed flesh would have invited frostbite, women of easy virtue were not hard to spot. Paint, demeanor, and carriage made their calling clear. Marcus caught the eye of a dark-haired beauty in a sheepskin jacket and clinging green gown. She smiled back and pushed her way toward him through the crowd, squeezing between a couple of plump bakers.

She was only a few feet from Scaurus when she abruptly turned about and walked in another direction. Confused, he was about to follow when he felt a hand on his arm. It was the angular prelate who had blessed and healed the Romans when they first came to Imbros.

"A fine amusement," he said. Scaurus was thinking of a better one, but did not mention it. This priest was a powerful figure in the city. The man continued, "I do not believe I have seen you or many of your men at our shrines. You have come from afar and must be unfamiliar with our faith. Now that you have learned something of our language and our ways, would it please you to discuss this matter with me?"

"Of course," Marcus lied. He had a pair of problems as he walked with the hierarch through the frosty, winding streets of Imbros toward its chief temple. First, he was anything but anxious for a theological debate. Like many Romans, he gave lip service to the veneration of the gods, but wasted little serious belief on them. The Videssians were much more earnest about their cult and harsh with those who did not share it.

Even more immediate was his other dilemma; for the life of him, he could not recall his companion's name. He kept evading the use of it all the way to the doorway of Phos' sanctuary, meanwhile flogging his memory without success.

The sweet savor of incense and a choir's clear tones greeted them at the entrance. Scaurus was so bemused he hardly noticed the cleric who bowed as his ecclesiastical superior came in. Then the young priest murmured, "Phos with you, elder Apsimar, and you as well, outland friend." The warmth and gratitude Marcus put into his handclasp left the little shaven-headed man blinking in puzzlement.

A colonnade surrounded the circular worship area, at whose brightly lit center priests served the altar of Phos and led the faithful in their prayers. Apsimar stayed in the semidarkness outside the colonnade. He led Marcus around a third of the circle, stopping at an elaborately carved door of dark, close-grained wood. Extracting a finger-long iron key from the pouch at his belt, he clicked the door open and stood aside to let the Roman precede him.

The small chamber was almost pitch-dark until Apsimar lit a candle. Then Marcus saw the clutter of volumes everywhere, most of them not the long scrolls he was used to, but books after the Videssian fashion, with small, square pages bound together in covers of wood, metal, or leather to form a whole. He wondered how Apsimar could read by candlelight and have any sight left at his age, though the priest had given no sign of failing vision.

The room's walls were as crowded with religious images as its shelves were with books. The dominant theme was one of struggle: here a warrior in armor that gleamed with gold leaf felled his foe, whose mail was black as midnight; there, the same gold-clad figure drove its spear through the heart of a snarling black panther; elsewhere, the disc of the sun blazed through a roiling, sooty bank of fog.

Apsimar sat in a hard, straight chair behind his overloaded desk, waving Scaurus to a more comfortable one in front of it. The priest leaned forward. He said, "Tell me, then, somewhat of your beliefs."

Unsure where to begin, the Roman named some of the gods his people followed and their attributes: Jupiter the king of heaven, his consort Juno, his brother Neptune who ruled the seas, Vulcan the smith, the war god Mars, Ceres the goddess of fertility and agriculture . . .

At each name and description Apsimar's thin face grew longer. Finally he slammed both hands down on the desk. Startled, Marcus stopped talking.

Apsimar shook his head in dismay. "Another puerile pantheon," he exclaimed, "no better than the incredible set of miscegenating godlets the Halogai reverence! I had thought better of you, Roman; you and yours seemed like civilized men, not barbarians whose sole joy in life is slaughter."

Marcus did not understand all of that, but plainly Apsimar thought little of his religious persuasions. He thought for a moment. To his way of looking at things, Stoicism was a philosophy, not a religion, but maybe its tenets would please Apsimar more than those of the Olympian cult. He explained its moral elements: an insistence on virtue, fortitude, and self-control, and a rejection of the storms of passion to which all men were liable.

He went on to describe how the Stoics believed that Mind, which among the known elements could best be equated with Fire, both created and comprised the universe in its varying aspects.

Apsimar nodded. "Both in its values and in its ideas, this is a better creed, and a closer approach to the truth. I will tell you the truth now."

The tribune braced himself for a quick course on the glory of the divine sun, kicking himself for not mentioning Apollo. But the "truth," as Apsimar saw it, was not tied up in heliolatry.

The Videssians, Marcus learned, viewed the universe and everything in it as a conflict between two deities: Phos, whose nature was inherently good, and the evil Skotos. Light and darkness were their respective manifestations. "Thus the globe of the sun which tops our temples," Apsimar said, "for the sun is the most powerful source of light. Yet it is but a symbol, for Phos transcends its radiance as much as it outshines the candle between us."

Phos and Skotos warred not only in the sensible world, but within the soul of every man. Each individual had to choose which he would serve, and on this choice rested his fate in the next world. Those who followed the good would gain an afterlife of bliss, while the wicked would fall into Skotos' clutches, to be tormented forever in his unending ice.

Yet even the eternal happiness of the souls of the deserving might be threatened, should Skotos vanquish Phos in this world. Opinions over the possibility of this differed. Within the Empire of Videssos, it was orthodox to believe Phos would emerge victorious in the ultimate confrontation. Other sects, however, were less certain.

"I know you will be traveling to the city," Apsimar said. "You will be meeting many men of the east there; fall not into their misbelief." He went on to explain that, some eight hundred years before, nomadic barbarians known as the Khamorth flooded into what had been the eastern provinces of the Empire. After decades of warfare, devastation, and murder, two fairly stable Khamorth states, Khatrish and Thatagush, had emerged from the chaos, while to their north the Kingdom of Agder was still ruled by a house of Videssian stock.

The shock of the invasions, though, had caused all these lands to slip into what Videssos called heresy. Their theologians, remembering the long night of destruction their lands had undergone, no longer saw Phos' victory as inevitable, but concluded that the struggle between good and evil was in perfect balance. "They claim this doctrine gives more scope to the freedom of the will." Apsimar sniffed. "In reality, it but makes Skotos as acceptable a lord as Phos. Is this a worthwhile goal?"

He gave Marcus no chance to reply, going on to describe the more subtle religious aberration which had arisen on the island Duchy of Namdalen in the past couple of centuries. Namdalen had escaped domination by the Khamorth, but fell instead, much later, to pirates from the Haloga country, who envied and aped the Videssian style of life even as they wrested away Videssian land.

"The fools were seeking a compromise between our views and the noxious notions which prevail in the east. They refuse to accept Phos' triumph as a certainty, yet maintain all men should act as if they felt it assured. This, a theology? Call it, rather, hypocrisy in religious garb!"

It followed with a certain grim logic that, as any error in belief gave strength to Skotos, those who deviated from the true faith—whatever that happened to be in any given area—could and should be brought into line, by force if necessary. Accustomed to the general tolerance and indeed disregard for various creeds he had known in Rome, Marcus found the notion of a militant religion disturbing.

Having covered the main variants of his own faith, Apsimar spoke briefly and slightingly of others the Videssians knew. Of the beliefs of the Khamorth nomads still on the plains of Pardraya, the less said the better—they followed shamans and were little more than demon-worshippers. And their cousins who lived in Yezd were worse yet; Skotos was reverenced openly there, with horrid rites.

All in all, the Halogai were probably the best of the heathen. Even if incorrect, their beliefs inclined them to the side of Phos by fostering courage and justice. "Those they have in abundance," Apsimar allowed, "but at the cost of the light of the spirit, which comes only to those who follow Phos."

The barrage of strange names, places, and ideas left Marcus' head spinning. To get time to regain his balance, he asked Apsimar, "Do you have a map, so I may see where all these people you mention live?"

"Of course," the priest said. As with his theological discussion, he gave Scaurus more than the tribune had bargained for. Apsimar gestured toward one of the crowded bookshelves. Like a called puppy, a volume wriggled out from between its neighbors and floated through the air until it landed gently on his desk. He bent over it to find the page he wanted.

The tribune needed those few seconds to try to pull his face straight. Never in Mediolanum, never in Rome, never in Gaul, he knew, would he have seen anything to match that casual flick of the hand and what came after it. Its very effortlessness impressed him in a way even the healing magic had not.

To Apsimar it was nothing. He turned the book toward Marcus. "We are here," he said, pointing. Putting his face close to the map, the tribune made out the word "Imbros" beside a dot.

"My apologies," Apsimar said courteously. "Reading by candlelight can be difficult." He murmured a prayer, held his left hand over the map, and pearly light sprang from it, illuminating the parchment as well as a cloudy day.

This time, Scaurus had all he could do not to flee. No wonder, his mind gibbered, eyestrain did not trouble Apsimar. The priest was his own reading lamp.

As the first shock of amazement and fear faded, a deeper one sank into the tribune's bones. The map was very detailed: better, by the looks of it, than the few Marcus had seen in Rome. And the lands it showed were utterly unfamiliar. Where was Italy? No matter how crude the map, the shape of the boot was unmistakable. He could not find it, or any of the other countries he knew.

Seeing the curious outlines of the Empire of Videssos and its neighbors, reading the strange names of the seas—the Sailors' Sea, the Northern Sea, the almost landlocked Videssian Sea, and the rest—drove home to the tribune what he had feared since the two swords swept him and his legionaries here, had suspected since Apsimar's first sorcery. This was a different world from Rome's, one from which he could never go back.

His good-byes to the priest were subdued. Once out in the street, he made for a tavern. He needed a cup of wine, or several, to steady his nerves. The grape worked a soothing magic of its own. And even with magic, he told himself, men were still men. An able one might go far.

He took another pull at the mug. Presently he remembered the business Apsimar had interrupted. He wondered whether he could still find the bright-eyed girl in the green gown. He laughed a little. Men were still men, he thought.

On his way out of the tavern, he wondered for a moment how venery counted in the strife between Phos and Skotos. He decided he did not care and closed the tavern door behind him.

III

AFTER A LAST SERIES OF BLIZZARDS THAT TRIED TO BATTER IMBROS flat, winter sullenly left the stage to spring. Just as they had at the outset of fall, the Empire's roads became morasses. Marcus, anxious for word from the capital, grumbled about the sense of a nation which, to protect its horses' hooves, made those hooves all but worthless over much of the year.

The trees' bare branches were beginning to clothe themselves in green when a mud-splattered messenger splashed his way up from the south. As Nephon Khoumnos had predicted and Marcus hoped, he bore in his leather message-pouch an order bidding the Romans come to *the* city, Videssos.

Vourtzes did not pretend to be sorry to see the last of them. Though the Romans had behaved well in Imbros—for mercenary troops, very well—it had not really been the fat governor's town since they arrived. For the most part they followed his wishes, but he was too used to giving orders to enjoy framing requests.

To Marcus' surprise, Skapti Modolf's son came to bid him farewell. The tall Haloga clasped Scaurus' hand in both his own, after his native custom. Fixing his wintry gaze on the Roman, he said, "We'll meet again, and in a less pleasant place, I think. It would be better for me if we did not, but we will."

Wondering what to make of that, the tribune asked him if he'd had news of the coming summer's campaign.

Skapti snorted at such worry over details. "It will be as it is," he said, and stalked away toward Imbros. Staring at his back, Marcus wondered if the Halogai were as spiritually blind as Apsimar thought.

The march to Videssos was a pleasant week's travel through gently rolling country planted in wheat, barley, olives, and grapevines. To Gorgidas the land, the crops, and the enameled blue dome of the sky were aching reminders of his native Greece. He was by turns sullen with homesickness and rhapsodic over the beauty of the scenery.

"Will you not cease your endless havering?" Viridovix asked. "In another month it'll be too hot for a man to travel by day unless he wants the wits fried out of him. Your grapevine is a fine plant, I'll not deny, but better in the jug than to look at, if you take my meaning. And as for the olive, if you try to eat him his pit'll break your teeth. His oil stinks, too, and tastes no better."

Gorgidas grew so furious working up a reply to this slander that he was his old self for the next several hours. Marcus caught Viridovix grinning behind the irascible doctor's back. His respect for the Celt's wits went up a couple of notches.

The road to Videssos came down by the seaside about a day's journey north of the capital. Villages and towns, some of respectable size, sat athwart the highway at increasingly frequent intervals. After passing through one large town, Gaius Philippus commented, "If these are the suburbs, what must Videssos be like?"

The mental picture Marcus carried of the Empire's capital was of a city like, but inferior to, Rome. In the afternoon of the eighth day out from Imbros, he was able to compare his vision with the reality, and it was the former which paled in the comparison.

Videssos owned a magnificent site. It occupied a triangle of land jutting out into a strait Tzimiskes called the Cattle-Crossing. The name was scarcely a misnomer, either—the opposite shore was barely a mile away, its suburbs plain to the eye despite sea-haze. The closest of those suburbs, the tribune had learned, was simply called "Across."

But with Videssos at which to marvel, the strait's far shore was lucky to get a glance. Surrounded on two sides by water, the capital's third, landward, boundary was warded by fortifications more nearly invulnerable than any Marcus had imagined, let alone seen.

First came a deep ditch, easily fifty feet wide; behind it stood a crenelated breastwork. Overlooking that was the first wall proper, five times the height of a tall man, with square towers strategically sited every fifty to a hundred yards. A second wall, almost twice as high and built of even larger stones, paralleled this outwork at a distance of about fifty yards. The main wall's towers—not all of these were square; some were round, or even octagonal—were placed so that fire from them could cover what little ground those of the outwall missed.

Gaius Philippus stopped dead when he saw those incredible works. "Tell me," he demanded of Tzimiskes, "has this city ever fallen to a siege?"

"Never to a foreign foe," the Videssian replied, "though in our own civil wars it's been taken twice by treachery."

The great walls did not hide as much of the city as had Imbros' fortifications, for Videssos, coincidentally like Rome, had seven hills. Marcus could see buildings of wood, brick, and stucco like those in the latter town, but also some splendid structures of granite and multicolored marble. Many of those were surrounded by parks and orchards, making their pale stone shine the brighter. Scores of shining gilded domes topped Phos' temples throughout the city.

At the harbors, the beamy grainships that fed the capital shared dockspace with rakish galleys and trading vessels from every nation Videssos knew. There and elsewhere in the city, surging tides of people went about their business. Tiny in the distance, to Scaurus they seemed like so many ants, preoccupied with their own affairs and oblivious to the coming of the Romans. It was an intimidating thought. In the midst of such a multitude, how could his handful of men hope to make a difference?

He must have said that out loud. Quintus Glabrio observed, "The Videssians wouldn't have taken us on if they didn't think we mattered." Grateful for Glabrio's calm good sense, the tribune nodded.

Tzimiskes led the Romans past the first two gates that opened into the city. He explained, "An honor guard will escort us into Videssos from the Silver Gate."

Marcus had no idea why the Silver Gate was so called. Its immense portals and spiked portcullis were of iron-faced wood; from their scars, they had seen much combat. Over each wall's entryway hung a triumphant icon of Phos.

"Straighten up there, you shambling muttonheads!" Gaius Philippus growled to the already orderly legionaries. "This is the big city now, and I won't have them take us for gawking yokels!"

As Tzimiskes had promised, the guard of honor was waiting, mounted, just inside the main wall. At its head was Nephon Khoumnos, who stepped up smiling to clasp Scaurus' hand. "Good to see you again," he said. "The march to your barracks is a couple of miles. I hope you don't mind us making a parade of it. It'll give the people something to talk about and get them used to the look of you as well."

"Fine," Marcus agreed. He had expected something like this; the Videssians were inordinately fond of pomp and ceremony. His attention was only half on Khoumnos anyhow. The rest was directed to the troops the imperial officer led.

The three contingents of the honor guard seemed more concerned over watching each other than about the Romans. Khoumnos' personal contingent was a squadron of *akritai*—businesslike Videssians cut in the mold of Tzimiskes or Mouzalon. They wanted to give the Romans their full attention, but kept stealing quick looks to the right and left.

On their left was a band—Marcus rejected any word with a more orderly flavor than that—of nomads from the Pardrayan plains. Dark, stocky men with curly beards, they rode shaggy steppe ponies, wore breastplates of boiled leather and foxskin caps, and carried double-curved bows reinforced with horn. "Foot soldiers!" one said in accented Videssian. He spat to show his contempt. Marcus stared at him until the nomad flushed and jerked his eyes away.

The tribune had a harder time deciding the origin of the escorting party's last group. They were big, solid men in heavy armor, mounted on horses as large as any Marcus had seen, and armed with stout lances and straight slashing swords. They had something of the look of the Halogai to them, but seemed rather less—what was the word Viridovix had used?—doomful than the northern mercenaries. Besides, about half their number had dark hair. They were the first clean-shaven men Scaurus had seen. The only nation that might have spawned them, he decided at last, was Namdalen. There Haloga overlords mixed blood with their once-Videssian subjects, from whom they had learned much.

Their leader was a rugged warrior of about thirty, whose dark eyes and tanned skin went oddly with his mane of wheat-colored hair. He swung himself down from his high-cantled saddle to greet the Romans. "You look to have good men here," he said to Marcus, taking the tribune's hand between his own in a Haloga-style grip. "I'm Hemond of Metepont, out of the Duchy." That confirmed Marcus' guess. Hemond went on, "Once you're settled in, look me up for a cup of wine. We can tell each other stories of our homes—yours, I hear, is a strange, distant land."

"I'd like that," Marcus said. The Namdalener seemed a decent sort; his curiosity was friendly enough and only natural. All sorts of rumors about the Romans must have made the rounds in Videssos during the winter.

"Come on, come on, let's be off," Khoumnos said. "Hemond, your men for advance guard; the Khamorth will take the rear while we ride flank."

"Right you are." Hemond ambled back to his horse, flipping the Videssian a lazy salute as he went. Khoumnos' sudden urgency bothered Marcus; he had been in no hurry a moment before. Could it be he did not want the Romans friendly toward the Namdaleni? Politics already, the tribune thought, resolving caution until he learned the local rules of the game.

A single Videssian with a huge voice led the procession from the walls of the city to the barracks. Every minute or so he bellowed, "Make way for the valiant Romans, brave defenders of the Empire!" The thoroughfare down which they strode emptied in the twinkling of an eye; just as magically, crowds appeared on the sidewalks and in every intersection. Some people cheered the valiant Romans, but more seemed to wonder who these strange-looking mercenaries were, while the largest number would have turned out for any parade, just to break up the monotony of the day.

Eyes front and hands raised in salute, the legionaries marched west. They passed through two large, open squares, by a marketplace whose customers scarcely looked up to notice them, and past monuments, columns, and statues commemorating long-past triumphs and Emperors.

The only bad moment in the procession came near its end. An emaciated monk in a tattered, filthy robe leaped into the roadway in front of the Romans' herald, who perforce stopped. Eyes blazing, the monk screeched, "Beware Phos' wrath, all traffickers with infidels such as these! Woe unto us, that we shelter them in the heart of Phos' city!"

There was a mutter from the crowd, at first confused, then with the beginning of anger in it. Out of the corner of his eye Marcus saw a man bend to pick up a stone. The mutter grew louder and more hostile.

Intent on heading off a riot before it could start, the tribune elbowed his way through the halted Namdalener horsemen to confront the monk. As if he were some demon, the scrawny cleric drew back in horror, sketching his god's sign on his breast. Someone in the crowd yelled, "Heathen!"

Hands empty before him, Scaurus bowed low to the monk, who stared at him suspiciously. Then he drew the sun-circle over his own heart, at the same time shouting, "May Phos be with you!"

The amazement on the monk's face was comical. He ran forward to fold the Roman in a smelly embrace he would have been as glad not to have. For a horrible instant Marcus thought he was about to be kissed, but the monk, after a few quick, babbled prayers, vanished into the crowd, which was now cheering lustily.

Marcus gave himself the luxury of a sigh of relief before he went back to his men. "Quick thinking, outlander," Hemond said as he walked by. "We could all have been in a lot of trouble there."

"Tell me about it," the tribune said feelingly.

"Make way for the valiant Romans!" the herald cried, and the parade advanced once more.

"I did not know you had decided to follow Phos," Tzimiskes said.

"I said nothing at all about me," Marcus replied.

Tzimiskes looked scandalized.

They traversed a last forum, larger than either of the previous two, and passed by a tremendous oval amphitheater before entering a district of elegant buildings set among wide expanses of close-cropped emerald lawn and tastefully trimmed shrubs and vines.

"Another few moments and I'll show you to your barracks," Khoumnos said.

"Here?" Marcus asked, startled. "Surely this is much too fine."

It was the Videssian's turn for surprise. "Why, where else would a unit of the Imperial Guards lodge, but in the Imperial Palaces?"

The buildings devoted to the Emperors of Videssos made up a vast, sprawling complex which itself comprised one of the imperial capital's many quarters. The Romans were billeted some distance from the Emperor's residence proper, in four stuccoed barracks halls set among citrus trees fragrant with flowers.

"I've had worse," Gaius Philippus said with a laugh as he unslung his marching kit and laid it by his fresh straw pallet.

Marcus understood the centurion's way of speaking—he could not remember arrangements to compare with these. The barracks were airy, well lit, and roomy. There were baths nearby, and kitchens better equipped than some eateries. Only the lack of privacy made the long halls less comfortable than an inn or a hostel. If anything, they were too luxurious. "In quarters this fine, the men may lose their edge."

Gaius Philippus gave a wolfish grin. "I'll see to that, never fear." Scaurus nodded, but wondered how well-drilled the rest of the Imperial Guards were.

He had some of his answer within minutes, for cornets blared while the Romans were still stowing their possessions. A plump functionary appeared in the doorway and bawled, "His Highness the Sevastos Vardanes Sphrantzes! His Majesty the Sevastokrator Thorisin Gavras! All abase themselves for his Imperial Majesty, the Avtokrator of the Videssians, Mavrikios Gavras!"

The cornets rang out again. Over them Gaius Philippus yelled, "Whatever you've got, drop it!" The Romans, used to snap inspections, sprang to attention.

Preceded by a dozen Halogai, the rulers of the Empire came into the barracks hall to examine their new warriors. Before they set foot in it, Marcus stole a glance at their guardsmen and was favorably impressed. For all the gilding on their cuirasses, for all the delicate inlaywork ornamenting their axes, these were fighting men. Their eyes, cold as the ice of their northern home, raked the barracks for anything untoward. Only when he was satisfied did their leader signal his charges it was safe to enter.

As they did so, Tzimiskes went to his knees and then to his belly in the proskynesis all Videssians granted their sovereign. Marcus, and his men after his example, held to their stiff brace. It did not occur to him to do otherwise. If the Videssians chose to prostrate themselves before their lord, it was their privilege, but not one the Romans, a republican people for four and a half centuries, could easily follow.

The Haloga captain stared at Scaurus, his face full of winter. But now the tribune had no time to try to face him down, for his attention was focused on the triumvirate in the doorway.

First through it, if they were coming in the order announced, was Vardanes Sphrantzes, whose title of Sevastos was about that of prime minister. Heavyset rather than fat, he wore his gem-encrusted robes of office with a dandy's elegance. A thin line of beard framed his round, ruddy face. His eyes did not widen, but narrowed in surprise when he saw the Romans still on their feet.

He turned to say something to the Emperor, but was brushed aside by Mavrikios' younger brother, the Sevastokrator Thorisin Gavras. In his late thirties, the Sevastokrator looked as if he would be more at home in mail than the silks and cloth-of-gold he had on. His hair and beard were carelessly trimmed; the sword at his side was no ceremonial weapon, but a much-used saber in a sheath of plain leather.

His reaction to the sight of the standing Romans was outrage, not surprise. His bellowed, "Who in Phos' holy name do these baseborn outland whoresons think they are?" cut across Sphrantzes' more measured protest: "Your Majesty, these foreigners fail to observe proper solemnity . . ."

Both men stopped in confusion; Scaurus had the impression they had not agreed on anything in years. From behind them he heard the Emperor's voice for the first time: "If the two of you will get out of my way, I'll see these monsters for myself." And with that mild comment the Avtokrator of the Videssians came in to survey his newest troop of mercenaries.

He was plainly Thorisin's brother; they shared the same long face, the same strong-arched nose, even the same brown hair that thinned at the temples. But at first glance Marcus would have guessed Mavrikios Gavras fifteen years older than his brother. Lines bracketed his forceful mouth and creased his forehead; his eyes were those of a man who slept very little.

A second look told the Roman much of the apparent difference in age between the two Gavrai was illusion. Like the massy golden diadem he wore on his head, Mavrikios bore responsibility's heavy weight, and it had left its mark on him. He might once have shared Thorisin's quick temper and headlong dash, but in him they were tempered by a knowledge of the cost of error.

As the Emperor approached, Tzimiskes rose to stand beside Marcus, ready to help interpret. But Mavrikios' question was direct enough for Scaurus to understand: "Why did you not make your obeisance before me?"

Had Sphrantzes asked that, Marcus might have talked round the answer, but this, he felt instinctively, was a man to whom one gave truth. He said, "It is not the custom in my land to bend the knee before any man."

The Avtokrator's eye roved over the Romans as he considered Scaurus' reply. His gaze stopped on a battered shield; on the stiff peasant face of a young legionary; on Viridovix, who stood out because of his inches and his Celtic panoply.

At last he turned to the waiting Sevastos and Sevastokrator, saying quietly, "These are soldiers." To Thorisin Gavras that seemed to explain everything. He relaxed at once, as did the Haloga guardsmen. If their overlord was willing to let these outlanders keep their rude habits, that was enough for them.

Sphrantzes, on the other hand, opened his mouth for further protest before he realized it would do no good. His eyes locked resentfully with the tribune's, and Marcus knew he had made an enemy. Sphrantzes was a man who could not stand to be wrong or, more to the point, to be seen to be wrong. If he made a mistake, he would bury it . . . and maybe its witnesses, too.

He covered his slip adroitly, though, nodding to Marcus in a friendly way and saying, "At sunset tomorrow evening we have tentatively scheduled a banquet in the Hall of the Nineteen Couches, in honor of your arrival. Would it be convenient for you and a small party of your officers to join us then?"

"Certainly," Marcus nodded back. The Sevastos' smile made him wish he could bring, not his officers, but a food-taster instead.

The Hall of the Nineteen Couches was a square building of green-veined marble not far from the actual living quarters of the imperial family. There had been no couches in it for generations, Marcus learned, but it kept its name regardless. It was the largest and most often used of the palace compound's several reception halls.

When Scaurus and his companions—Gaius Philippus, Quintus Glabrio, Gorgidas, Viridovix, and Adiatun, the captain of slingers, along with Tzimiskes—came to the Hall's double doors of polished bronze and announced themselves, a servitor bowed and flung the doors wide, crying, "Ladies and gentlemen, the Ronams!"

There was a polite spatter of applause from the guests already present. Scaurus suppressed an urge to kick the bungling fool and resigned himself to being called a Ronam for the next year.

The Videssian custom was to talk, nibble, and drink for a time before settling down to serious eating. Marcus took a chilled cup of wine from the bed of snow on which it rested, accepted a small salted fish from a silver tray proffered by the most bored-looking servant he had ever seen, and began to circulate through the crowd.

He soon became aware that four distinct groups were present, each largely—and sometimes pointedly—ignoring the other three.

In the corner by the kitchens, civil servants, gorgeous in their bright robes and colorful tunics, munched hors d'oeuvres as they discussed the fine art of government by guile.

They sent supercilious glances toward the crowd of army officers who held the center of the hall like a city they had stormed. Though these sprang from several nations, they, too, had a common craft. Their shoptalk was louder and more pungent than that of the bureaucrats, whose sneers they returned. "Plague-taken pen-pushers," Marcus heard a young Videssian mutter to a Haloga clutching a mug of mead almost as big as his head. Already half-drunk, the northerner nodded solemnly.

Over half the Roman party vanished into this group. Gaius Philippus and Nephon Khoumnos were talking about drill fields and training
techniques. Glabrio, gesturing as he spoke, explained Roman infantry
tactics to a mixed audience of Videssians, Namdaleni, and Halogai. And
Adiatun was trying to persuade a buckskin-clad Khamorth that the sling
was a better weapon than the bow. The nomad, a better archer than any
Adiatun had imagined, was obviously convinced he'd lost his mind.

If the councilors were peacocks and the soldiers hawks, then the ambassadors and envoys of foreign lands who made up the third contingent
were birds of various feathers. Squat, bushy-bearded Khamorth wore the
wolfskin jackets and leather trousers of the plains and mingled with a
couple of other, more distant, plainsmen whose like Marcus had not seen
before: slim, swarthy, flat-faced men with draggling mustaches and thin,
wispy beards. The tribune learned they were known as Arshaum.

Marcus recognized desert nomads from the southwest, and more
from the distant lands across the Sailors' Sea. There were several envoys
in strange costumes from the valleys of Erzerum, north and west from
Videssos' western borders. There were Haloga princelings, and one man
the tribune would have guessed a Videssian but for his northern clothing
and the perpetually grim expression Scaurus had come to associate with
the Halogai.

A giant in the swirling robes of the desert was so swathed even his
face was obscured. He sipped wine through a straw and moved in a circle
of silence, for even his fellow ambassadors gave him a wide berth. Marcus understood when he found out the man was an emissary out of
Mashiz, the capital of Videssos' deadly western foe, Yezd.

With his insatiable curiosity, Gorgidas had naturally gravitated
toward the ambassadors. He was in earnest conversation with a rabbity
little man who would have made a perfect Videssian ribbon clerk had he
not affected the unkempt facial foliage of the Khamorth.

That takes care of just about all my men, Marcus thought, and when
he turned his head at a burst of laughter to his left he found Viridovix
was rapidly making himself popular with the last group at the banquet:
its women. Looking quite dashing with his cape of scarlet skins flung
back over his wide shoulders, the big Gaul had just finished an uproari-
ously improper tale his brogue only made funnier. A pretty girl was

clinging to each arm; three or four more clustered round him. He caught Scaurus' eye over the tops of their heads and threw him a happy tomcat's smile.

The tribune returned it, but did not feel like emulating the Celt. Nor did the other groups attract him any more. The bureaucrats snubbed soldiers on principle, but Scaurus himself was not enough of a professional warrior to delight in discussing the fine points of honing a broadsword. And unlike Gorgidas, he could not turn his inquisitiveness to distant lands when he was still so ignorant of Videssos. Thus, while he spent a minute here and two more there in polite small talk, he was bored before the evening was very old.

Feeling like the spare wheel on a wagon, he drifted over to get more wine. He had just taken it when a voice behind him asked, "The music tonight is very fine, don't you think?"

"Hmm?" He wheeled so fast the wine slopped in its cup. "Yes, my lady, it's very fine indeed." In fact he had no ear for music and had ignored the small tinkling orchestra, but a "no" would have ended the conversation, and that he suddenly did not want at all.

She was as tall as many of the men there. She wore her straight black hair bobbed just above the shoulder, a far simpler style than the elaborate piles of curls most of the women preferred, but one that suited her. Her eyes were very blue. Her gown was a darker shade of the same color, with a bodice of white lace and wide, fur-trimmed sleeves. A fine-looking woman, Marcus thought.

"You Romans"—He noticed she said the name correctly, despite the botched announcement at the door.—"are from quite far away, it's said. Tell me, is your homeland's music much like what's played here?"

Wishing she would find another topic, Scaurus considered the question. "Not a great deal, my lady—?"

"Oh, I crave your pardon," she said, smiling. "My name is Helvis. You are called Marcus, is that right?"

Marcus admitted it. "From Namdalen, are you not?" he asked. It was a reasonable guess. Her features were less aquiline than the Videssian norm, and she certainly did not bear a Videssian name.

She nodded and smiled again; her mouth was wide and generous. "You've learned a good deal about this part of the world," she said, but then, as the tribune had feared, she returned to her original thought. "In what ways do your music and ours differ?"

Scaurus grimaced. He knew little of Roman music and less of the local variety. Worse, his vocabulary, while adequate for the barracks, had huge holes when it came to matters musical.

At last he said, "We play—" He pantomimed a flute.

Helvis named it for him. "We have instruments of that kind, too. What else?"

"We pluck our stringed instruments instead of playing them with the thing your musicians use."

"A bow," Helvis supplied.

"And I've never seen anything like the tall box that fellow is pounding."

Her eyebrows lifted. "You don't know the clavichord? How strange!"

"He's two days in the city, darling, and you're tormenting him about the clavichord?" The guards' officer Hemond came up to put his arm round Helvis' waist with a casual familiarity that said they had been together for years.

"I wasn't being tormented," Scaurus said, but Hemond dismissed his protest with a snort.

"Don't tell me that, my friend. If you let this one carry on about music, you'll never get your ears back. Come on, love," he said to Helvis, "you have to try the fried prawns. Incredible!" He was licking his lips as they walked off together.

Marcus finished his wine in one long gulp. He was bitter and resentful, the more so because he knew his feelings had no justifiable basis. If Helvis and Hemond were a pair, then they were, and no point worrying about it. It was only that she had seemed so friendly and open and not at all attached . . . and she really was beautiful.

Many Namdalener men, Hemond among them, shaved their scalps from the ears back so their heads would fit their helmets better. It was a remarkably ugly custom, the tribune decided, and felt a little better.

Sphrantzes the Sevastos came in a few minutes later. As if his arrival was a signal—and it probably was—servants leaped forward to remove the tables of hors d'oeuvres and wine, substituting long dining tables and gilded straight-backed chairs.

They worked with practiced efficiency and had just finished putting out the last place setting when the doorman cried, "His Majesty the Sevastokrator Thorisin Gavras and his lady, Komitta Rhangavve! Her Majesty the Princess Alypia Gavra!" Then, in the place his rank deserved, "His Imperial Majesty, Avtokrator of the Videssians, Mavrikios Gavras!"

Marcus expected the entire room to drop to the floor and braced himself to shock everyone in it. But as the occasion was social rather than formal, the men in the hall merely bowed from the waist—the Romans among them—while the women dropped curtsies to the Emperor.

Thorisin Gavras' companion was an olive-skinned beauty with flashing black eyes, well matched to the hot-blooded Sevastokrator. She quite outshone the Princess Alypia, Mavrikios' only surviving child by a long-dead wife. Her lineage was likely the reason Alypia was still unwed—she was a political card too valuable to play at once. She was not unattractive, with an oval face and eyes of clear green, rare among the Videssians. But her attention appeared directed inward, and she walked through the dining hall scarcely seeming to notice the feasters in it.

Not so her father. "The lot of you have been standing around munching while I've had to work," he boomed, "and I'm hungry!"

Scaurus had thought he and his men would be seated with the other mercenary captains, well down the ladder of precedence. A eunuch steward disabused him of the notion. "This festivity was convened in your honor, and it would be less than appropriate were you to take your place elsewhere than at the imperial table."

As his knowledge of elegant Videssian manners was small, the tribune would willingly have forgone the distinction, but, of course, the gently irresistible steward had his way. Instead of soldiers, the tribune found himself keeping company with the leading nobles and foreign envoys in Videssos' court.

The straight-backed chairs were as hard as they looked.

Marcus found himself between the skinny little fellow with whom Gorgidas had been talking and the tall dour man who looked like a Videssian in Haloga clothing. The latter introduced himself as Katakolon Kekaumenos. Going by the name, the tribune asked, "You are of Videssos, then?"

"Nay, 'tis not so," Kekaumenos replied in his archaic accent. "I am his Majesty King Sirelios of Agder's embassy to Videssos; in good sooth, his blood is higher than most in this mongrel city." The man of Agder looked round to see if anyone would challenge his statement. The smaller fragment of the Empire of old had learned more from its Haloga neighbors than wearing snow-leopard jackets: its ambassador spoke with a bluntness rare in the city. He was also taciturn as any northerner, subsiding into moody silence after speaking his piece.

Marcus' other seatmate nudged him in the ribs. "You'd think old Katakolon had a poker up his arse, wouldn't you?" he stage-whispered, grinning slyly. "Ah, you don't know who I am, do you, to get away with such talk? Taso Vones is my name, envoy of Khagan Vologes of Khatrish, and so I have a diplomat's privilege. Besides, Kekaumenos has reckoned me daft for years—isn't that right, you old scoundrel?"

"As well for you I do," Kekaumenos rumbled, but his stern features could not hide a smile. Evidently he was used to making allowances for Vones.

The fast-talking ambassador gave his attention back to Scaurus. "I saw you admiring my beard a few minutes ago."

That was not the emotion Marcus had felt for the untidy growth. "Yes, I—"

"Horrible, isn't it? My master Vologes thinks it makes me look a proper Khamorth, instead of some effete Videssian. As if I could look like that!" He pointed across the table at the emissary of the Khaganate of Thatagush. "Ha, Gawtruz, you butterball, are you drunk yet?"

"Not yet I am," Gawtruz replied, looking rather like a bearded boulder. His Videssian was heavily accented. "But will I be? Haw, yes, to be sure!"

"He's a pig," Taso remarked, "but a pleasant sort of pig, and a sharp man in the bargain. He can also speak perfectly good Videssian when he wants to, which isn't often."

A trifle overwhelmed by the voluble little Khatrisher, Marcus was glad to see the food brought in. The accent was on fish, not surprising in a coastal town like Videssos. There were baked cod, fried shark, lobsters and drawn butter, a tangy stew of clams, crab, and shrimp, as well as divers other delicacies, among them oysters on the half-shell.

Viridovix, a few chairs down from the tribune, took one of these from the crushed ice on which it reposed. After a long, dubious look he gulped it down, but seemed less than pleased he'd done so. With a glance at the girl by his side, he said to Marcus, "If you're fain to be eating something with that feel to it, it's better warm."

Scaurus, *sans* oyster, gulped himself. He was wondering why the Celt had not stopped conversation in its tracks all along the table when the Princess Alypia, who was sitting almost directly across from him, asked, "What does your comrade think of the shellfish?" and he realized Viridovix had spoken Latin.

Well, fool, he said to himself, you thought music a poor topic. How do you propose to cope with *this*? His answer unhesitatingly sacrificed the spirit to the letter: "He said he would prefer it heated, your Highness."

"Odd, such an innocent comment making you start so," she said, but to his relief she did not press him further.

A gray-haired servant tapped the Roman on the shoulder. Setting a small enamelware dish before Marcus, he murmured, "Herrings in wine sauce, my lord, courtesy of his Highness the Sevastos. They are excellent, he says."

Recalling only too vividly his idle thought of the day before, Marcus looked down the table to Vardanes Sphrantzes. The Sevastos raised his glass in genial salute. Scaurus knew he had to take the dainty and yet could not forget the veiled look of menace he had seen in Sphrantzes' eyes.

He sighed and ate. The herrings were delicious.

Alypia noticed his hesitation. "Anyone watching you would say you thought that your final meal," she said.

Damn the observant woman! he thought, flushing. Would he never be able to tell her any truth? It certainly would not do here. "Your Majesty, I could not refuse the Sevastos' gift, but I fear herring and my innards do not blend well. That was why I paused." The tribune discovered he had only told half a lie. The spicy fish *were* making his stomach churn.

The princess blinked at his seeming frankness, then burst into laughter. If the Roman had seen the slit-eyed look Sphrantzes sent his way, he would have regretted the herrings all over again. That it might be dangerous for a mercenary captain to make a princess of the blood laugh had not yet occurred to him.

Although the Sevastokrator Thorisin stayed to roister on, the Emperor and his daughter, having arrived late, left the banquet early. After their departure things grew livelier.

Two of the desert nomads, relegated to a far table by the insignificance of their tribes, found nothing better to do than quarrel with each other. One of them, a ferret-faced man with waxed mustaches, screamed a magnificent guttural oath and broke his winecup over his rival's head. Others at the table pulled them apart before they could go for their knives.

"Disgraceful," Taso Vones said. "Why can't they leave their blood-feuds at home?"

Snatches of drunken song floated up throughout the Hall of the Nineteen Couches. Viridovix began wailing away in Gaulish, loud enough to make the crockery shiver. "If you can't hit the damned notes, at least scare them as they go by," Gaius Philippus growled. The Celt pretended not to hear him.

Several Khamorth were singing in the plains speech. Lifting his face from his cup, Gawtruz of Thatagush looked up owlishly and joined them.

"Disgraceful," Taso said again; he, too, understood the plainsmen's tongue. "You can't have Khamorth at a feast without them getting sozzled and calling on all sorts of demons. Most of them follow Skotos in their hearts, you know; cleaving to the good is too dull to be tolerable."

The wine was starting to go to the Roman's head; he was losing track of how many times he had filled his goblet from the silver decanter in front of him. On his left, Katakolon Kekaumenos had left some time ago. Marcus did not miss him. The strait-laced northerner's disapproving gaze could chill any gathering.

Viridovix was also gone, but not by himself. Scaurus could not remember if he'd left with the talkative brunette who'd sat beside him or the statuesque serving maid who had hovered over him all evening long. A bit jealous, the Roman took a long pull at his wine. His own contacts with women tonight had been less than successful, from any point of view.

He climbed slowly to his feet, filling his glass one last time to keep him warm on the ten-minute walk back to the barracks. Vones stood too. "Let me accompany you," he said. "I'd like to hear more about your leader—Kizar, was it? A fascinating man, from what you've told me."

Marcus hardly remembered what he'd been saying, but Vones was good company. They made their way down toward the end of the imperial table. There someone had spilled something greasy on the mosaic floor; the tribune slipped, his arms waving wildly for balance. He kept his feet, but the wine he was carrying splattered the white robes of Yezd's ambassador.

"I beg your pardon, my lord—" he began, then stopped, confused. "Your pardon twice—I do not know your name."

"Do you not?" A fury the more terrible for being cold rode the Yezda's words. He rose in one smooth motion, to tower over even the Roman's inches. So thick was his veiling that his eyes were invisible, but Scaurus knew he was seen; the weight of that hidden gaze was like a blow. "Do you not, indeed? Then you may call me Avshahin."

Taso Vones broke in with a nervous chuckle. "My lord Avshar is pleased to make a pun, calling himself 'king' in Videssos' language and his own. Surely he will understand my friend meant no offense, but has seen the bottom of his winecup perhaps more often than he should—"

Avshar turned his unseen stare on the Khatrisher. "Little man, this does not concern you. Unless you would have it so . . . ?" His voice was still smooth, but there was menace there, like freezing water under thin ice. Vones, pale, flinched and shook his head.

"Good." The Yezda dealt Marcus a tremendous roundhouse buffet, sending him lurching back with blood starting from the corner of his mouth. "Dog! Swine! Vile, crawling insect! Is it not enough I must dwell in this city of my foes? Must I also be subject to the insults of Videssos' slaves? Jackal of a mercenary, it shall be your privilege to choose the weapon that will be your death."

The feasting hall grew still. All eyes were on the Roman, who abruptly understood Avshar's challenge. In an odd way he was thankful the Yezda had struck him; the blow and the rage that followed were burning the wine from his blood. He was surprised at the steadiness of his voice as he answered, "You know as well as I, I spilled my wine on you by accident. But if you must take it further, sword and shield will do well enough."

Avshar threw back his head and laughed, a sound colder and more cruel than any of the winter blizzards that had howled down on Imbros. "So be it—your doom from your own mouth you have spoken. Mebod!" he shouted, and a frightened-looking Yezda servant appeared at his side. "Fetch my gear from my chambers." He gave the Roman a mocking bow. "The Videssians, you see, would not take it kindly if one who bears them no love were to come armed to a function where their precious Emperor was present."

Taso Vones was plucking at Scaurus' arm. "Have you lost your wits? That is the deadliest swordsman I have ever seen, the winner in a score of duels, and a sorcerer besides. Crave his forgiveness now, before he cuts a second mouth in your throat!"

"I asked his pardon once, but he hardly seems in a forgiving mood. Besides," Marcus said, thinking of the potent blade at his side, "I may know something he doesn't."

Gaius Philippus was so drunk he could hardly stand, but he still saw with a fighting man's knowledge. "The big son of a pimp will likely try to use his reach to chop you to bits from farther out than you can fight back. Get inside and let the air out of him."

Marcus nodded; he had been thinking along those lines himself. "Send someone after my shield, will you?"

"Adiatun is already on his way."

"Fine."

While everyone waited for the fighters' gear to be fetched, a double handful of high-ranking officers, like so many servants, shoved tables around, clearing a space for combat.

Wagers flew thick and fast. From the shouts, Marcus knew he was the underdog. He was pleased, though, when he heard Helvis' clear contralto announce, "Three pieces of gold on the Roman!" Gawtruz of Thatagush covered her bet.

The Sevastokrator Thorisin Gavras called to Vardanes Sphrantzes, "Whom do you like, seal-stamper?"

The dislike on the Sevastos' face covered Gavras, Avshar, and Scaurus impartially. He rubbed his neatly bearded chin. "Though it grieves me to say so, I think it all too likely the Yezda will win."

"Are you a hundred goldpieces sure?"

Sphrantzes hesitated again, then nodded. "Done!" Thorisin exclaimed. Marcus was glad to have the Sevastokrator's backing, but knew the Emperor's brother would have been as quick to favor Avshar if Sphrantzes had chosen him.

A cry rang out when the Yezda ambassador's servant returned with his master's arms. Marcus was surprised that Avshar favored a long, straight sword, not the usual scimitar of the westerners. His shield was round, with a spiked boss. The emblem of Yezd, a leaping panther, was painted on a background the color of dried blood.

Moments later, Adiatun was back with the tribune's *scutum*. "Cut him into crowbait," he said, slapping Scaurus on the shoulder.

The Roman was drawing his blade when something else occurred to him. He asked Taso Vones, "Will Avshar not want me to shed my cuirass?"

Vones shook his head. "It's common knowledge he wears mail himself, under those robes. He's not the envoy of a friendly country, you know."

Marcus spent a last second wishing he had not drunk so much. He wondered how much wine was in Avshar. Then it was too late for such worries. There was only a circle of eager, watching faces, with him and the Yezda in the middle of it—and then he forgot the watchers, too, as Avshar leaped forward to cut him down.

For a man so tall, he was devilishly quick, and strong in the bargain. Marcus caught the first slash on his shield and staggered under it, wondering if his arm was broken. He thrust up at Avshar's unseen face. The Yezda danced back, then came on again with another overhand cut.

He seemed to have as many arms as a spider and a sword in every hand. Within moments Marcus had a cut high up on his sword arm and another, luckily not deep, just above the top of his right greave. His shield was notched and hacked. Avshar wielded his heavy blade like a switch.

Fighting down desperation, Marcus struck back. Avshar turned the blow with his shield. It did not burst as the Roman had hoped, but at the contact Avshar gave back two startled paces. He swung his blade up in derisive salute. "You have a strong blade, runagate, but there are spells of proof against such."

Yet he fought more cautiously after that and, as the hard work of combat helped banish the wine from Scaurus' system, the Roman grew surer and more confident of himself. He began to press forward, blade flicking out now high, now low, with Avshar yielding ground step by stubborn step.

The Yezda, who had kept silent while all around him voices rose in song, began to chant. He sang in some dark language, strong, harsh, and freezing, worse even than his laugh. The torchlight dimmed and almost died in a web of darkness spinning up before Marcus' eyes.

But along the length of the Roman's blade, the druids' marks flared hot and gold, turning aside the spell the wizard had hurled. Scaurus parried a stroke at his face.

The episode could only have taken an instant, for even as he was evading the blow, a woman in the crowd—he thought it was Helvis—called out, "No ensorcelments!"

"Bah! None are needed against such a worm as this!" Avshar snarled, but he chanted no further. And now the tribune had his measure. One of his cuts sheared away the tip of Avshar's shield-boss. The Yezda envoy's robes grew tattered, and red with more than wine.

Screaming in frustrated rage, Avshar threw himself at the Roman in a last bid to overpower his enemy by brute force. It was like standing up under a whirlwind of steel, but in his wrath the Yezda grew careless, and Marcus saw his moment come at last.

He feinted against Avshar's face, then thrust quickly at his belly. The Yezda brought his blade down to cover, only to see, too late, that this too was a feint. The Roman's sword hurtled at his temple. The parry he began was far too slow, but in avoiding it, Scaurus had to turn his wrist slightly. Thus the flat of his blade, not the edge, slammed into the side of Avshar's head.

The Yezda tottered like a lightning-struck tree, then toppled, his sword falling beside him. Scaurus took a step forward to finish him, then shook his head. "Killing a stunned man is butcher's work," he said. "The quarrel was his with me, not mine with him." He slid his blade back into its scabbard.

In his exhaustion afterwards, he only remembered a few pieces of flotsam from the flood of congratulations that washed over him. Gaius Philippus' comment was, as usual, short and to the point. "That is a bad one," he said as Avshar, leaning on his servant, staggered from the hall, "and you should have nailed him when you had the chance."

Her winnings ringing in her hand, Helvis squeezed and kissed the tribune while Hemond pounded his back and shouted drunkenly in his ear.

And Taso Vones, though glad to see Avshar humbled, also had a word of warning. "I suppose," the mousy little man from Khatrish grumbled, "now you think you could storm Mashiz singlehanded and have all the maidens from here to there fall into your arms."

Marcus' mind turned briefly to Helvis, but Vones was still talking. "Don't you believe it!" he said. "A few years ago Avshar was leading a raiding-party along the western marches of Videssos, and a noble named Mourtzouphlos handled him very roughly indeed. The next spring, the biggest snake anyone in those parts had ever seen swallowed Mourtzouphlos down."

"Happenstance," Marcus said uneasily.

"Well, maybe so, but the Yezda's arm is long. A word to the wise, let us say." And he was off, brushing a bit of lint from the sleeve of his brown robe as if amazed anyone could think there was a connection between himself and this outlander rash enough to best Avshar.

IV

WHEN HE RETURNED FOR MARCUS' SHIELD, ADIATUN MUST HAVE wakened the Romans in their barracks. Torches were blazing through the windows, everyone was up and stirring, and by the time Marcus got back to his quarters a good score of legionaries were fully armed and ready to avenge him.

"You don't show much confidence in your commander," he told them, trying to hide how pleased he was. They gave him a rousing cheer, then crowded close, asking for details of the duel. He told the story as best he could, peeling off his belt, corselet, and greaves while he talked. Finally he could not keep his sagging eyelids open any longer.

Gaius Philippus stepped into the breach. "That's the nub of it. The rest you can all hear in the morning—early in the morning," he half threatened. "There's been nothing but shirking the past couple of days while we've got settled, but don't get the notion you can make a habit of it."

As the centurion had known it would, his announcement roused a chorus of boos and groans, but it also freed Scaurus from further questions. Torches hissed as they were quenched. The tribune, crawling under a thick woolen blanket, was as glad of sleep as ever he had been in his life.

It seemed only seconds later when he was shaken awake, but the apricot light of dawn streamed through the windows. Eyes still blurred with sleep, he saw Viridovix, looking angry, crouched above him. "Bad cess to you, southron without a heart!" the Gaul exclaimed.

Marcus raised himself onto one elbow. "What have I done to you?" he croaked. Someone, he noted with clinical detachment, had raced a herd of goats through his mouth.

"What have you done, man? Are you daft? The prettiest bit of fighting since we came here, and me not there to see it! Why did you not send a body after me so I could watch the shindy my own self and not hear about it second hand?"

Scaurus sat up gingerly. While he had made no real plans for the morning, he had not intended to spend the time pacifying an irate Celt. "In the first place," he pointed out, "I had no notion where you were. You had left some little while before I fell foul of Avshar. Besides, unless I misremember, you didn't leave alone."

"Och, she was a cold and clumsy wench, for all her fine chest." It had been the serving maid, then. "But that's not the point at all, at all. There's always lassies to be found, but a good fight, now, is something else again."

Marcus stared at him, realizing Viridovix was serious. He shook his head in bewilderment. He could not understand the Celt's attitude. True, some Romans had a taste for blood, but to most of them—himself included—fighting was something to be done when necessary and finished as quickly as possible. "You're a strange man, Viridovix," he said at last.

"If you were looking through my eyes, sure and you'd find yourself a mite funny-looking. There was a Greek once passed through my lands, a few years before you Romans—to whom it doesn't belong at all—decided to take it away. He was mad to see the way things worked, was this Greek. He had a clockwork with him, a marvelous thing with gears and pullies and I don't know what all, and he was always tinkering with it to make it work just so. You're a bit like that yourself sometimes, only you do it with people. If you don't understand them, why then you think it's them that's wrong, not you, and won't have a bit to do with them."

"Hmm." Marcus considered that and decided there was probably some justice to it. "What happened to your Greek?"

"I was hoping you'd ask that," Viridovix said with a grin. "He was sitting under an old dead tree, playing with his clockwork peaceful as you please, when a branch he'd been ignoring came down on his puir foolish head and squashed him so flat we had to bury the corp of him between two doors, poor lad. Have a care the same doesn't befall you."

"A plague take you! If you're going to tell stories with morals in them, you can start wearing a blue robe. A bloodthirsty Celt I'll tolerate, but the gods deliver me from a preaching one!"

72

After his work of the previous night, the tribune told himself he was entitled to leave the morning drills to Gaius Philippus. The brief glimpse of Videssos the city he'd had a few days before had whetted his appetite for more. This was a bigger, livelier, more brawling town even than Rome. He wanted to taste its life, instead of seeing it frozen as he tramped by on parade.

Seabirds whirled and mewed overhead as he left the elegant quiet of the imperial quarter for the hurly-burly of the forum of Palamas, the great square named for an Emperor nine centuries dead. At its center stood the Milestone, a column of red granite from which distances throughout the Empire were reckoned. At the column's base two heads, nearly fleshless from the passage of time and the attentions of scavengers, were displayed on pikes. Plaques beneath them set forth the crimes they had plotted while alive. Marcus' knowledge of Videssos' written language was still imperfect, but after some puzzling he gathered the miscreants had been rebellious generals with the further effrontery to seek aid for their revolt from Yezd. Their present perches, he decided, were nothing less than they deserved.

The people of Videssos ignored the gruesome display. They had seen heads go up on pikes before and expected these would not be the last.

Scaurus, on the other hand, was anything but ignored. He had thought he would be only one among a thousand foreigners, but the mysterious network that passes news in any great city had singled him out as the man who beat the dreaded Avshar. People crowded forward to pump his hand, to slap his back, or simply to touch him and then draw back in awe. From their reaction to him, he began to realize how great an object of fear the Yezda was.

It was next to impossible to get away. At every stall he passed, merchants and hucksters pressed samples of their wares on him: fried sparrows stuffed with sesame seeds; candied almonds; a bronze scalpel; amulets against heartburn, dysentery, or possession by a ghost; wines and ales from every corner of the Empire and beyond; a book of erotic verse, unfortunately addressed to a boy. No one would hear him say no and no one would take a copper in payment.

"It is my honor, my privilege, to serve the Ronam," declared a ruddy-faced baker with sweeping black mustachioes as he handed the tribune a spiced bun still steaming from his ovens.

Trying to escape his own notoriety, Marcus fled the forum of Palamas for the back streets and alleyways of the city. In such a maze it was easy to lose oneself, and the tribune soon did. His wandering feet led him into a quarter full of small, grimy taverns, homes once fine but now shabby from neglect or crowding, and shops crammed with oddments either suspiciously cheap or preposterously expensive. Young men in the brightly dyed tights and baggy tunics of street toughs slouched along in groups of three and four. It was the sort of neighborhood where even the dogs traveled in pairs.

This was a more rancid taste of Videssos than the tribune had intended. He was looking for a way back toward some part where he could feel safe without a maniple at his back when he felt furtive fingers fasten themselves to his belt. As he was half expecting such attention, it was easy to spin round and seize the awkward thief's wrist in an unbreakable grip.

He thought he would be holding one of the sneering youths who prowled here, but his captive was a man of about his own age, dressed in threadbare homespun. The would-be fingersmith did not struggle in his grasp. Instead he went limp, body and face alike expressing utter despair. "All right, you damned hired sword, you've got me, but there's precious little you can do to me," he said. "I'd have starved in a few days anyways."

He *was* thin. His shirt and breeches flapped on his frame and his skin stretched tight across his cheekbones. But his shoulders were wide, and his hands strong-looking—both his carriage and his twanging speech said he was more used to walking behind a plow than skulking down this alley. He had borne arms, too; Marcus had seen the look in his eyes before, on soldiers acknowledging defeat at the hands of overwhelming force.

"If you'd asked me for money, I would gladly have given it to you," he said, releasing his prisoner's arm.

"Don't want nobody's charity, least of all a poxy mercenary's," the other snapped. "Weren't for you mercenaries, I wouldn't be here today, and I wish to Phos I wasn't." He hesitated. "Aren't you going to give me to the eparch?"

The city governor's justice was apt to be swift, sure, and drastic. Had Scaurus caught one of the street-rats, he would have turned him over without a second thought. But what was this misplaced farmer doing in a Videssian slum, reduced to petty thievery for survival? And why did he blame mercenaries for his plight? He was no more a thief than Marcus was a woodcutter.

The tribune came to a decision. "What I'm going to do is buy you a meal and a jug of wine. Wait, now—you'll earn it." He saw the other's hand already starting to rise in rejection. "In exchange, you'll answer my questions and tell me why you mislike mercenaries. Do we have a bargain?"

The rustic's larynx bobbed in his scrawny neck. "My pride says no, but my belly says yes, and I haven't had much chance to listen to it lately. You're an odd one, you know—I've never seen gear like yours, you talk funny, and you're the first hired trooper I've ever seen who'd feed a hungry man instead of booting him in his empty gut. Phostis Apokavkos is my name, and much obliged to you."

Scaurus named himself in return. The eatery Phostis led them to was a hovel whose owner fried nameless bits of meat in stale oil and served them on husk-filled barley bread. It was better not to think of what went into the wine. That Apokavkos could not afford even this dive was a measure of his want.

For a goodly time he was too busy chewing and swallowing to have much to say, but at last he slowed, belched enormously, and patted his stomach. "I'm so used to empty, I near forgot how good full could feel. So you want to hear my story, do you?"

"More now than I did before. I've never seen a man eat so much."

"If the hole is big, it takes a deal to fill it." He took a pull at his wine. "This is foul, isn't it? I was too peckish to notice before. I grew better grapes than this my own self, back on my farm—

"That's a good place to start, I guess. I had a steading in the province of Raban, not far from the border with Yezd—do you know the country I mean?"

"Not really," Marcus admitted. "I'm new to Videssos."

"Thought you were. Well, then, it's on the far side of the Cattle-Crossing, about a month's foot-travel from here. I should know—I did the hike, fool that I was. Anyway, that farm had been in my family for longer than we could remember any more. We weren't just peasants, either—we'd always been part of the provincial militia. We had to send a man to war if the militia got called and to keep up a horse and gear ready to fight any time, but in exchange we got out of paying taxes. We even got paid sometimes, when the government could afford it.

"That's how my grandfather told it, anyhow. It sounds too good to be real, if you ask me. It was in granddad's day the Mankaphas family bought out about every farm in the village, us included. So we served the Mankaphai instead of the government, but things still weren't bad—they kept the tax collectors off our backs well enough."

Marcus thought of how it was in Rome, with retiring soldiers depending not on the Senate but on their generals for land allotments on mustering out. All too familiar with the turmoil his own land had endured, he could guess Apokavkos' next sentence before it was spoken.

"Of course, the pen-pushers weren't happy over losing our taxes, and the Mankaphai were even less happy about paying in our place now that they owned the land. Five years ago Phostis Mankaphas—I'm named for him—rebelled along with a fair pile of other nobles. That was the year before Mavrikios Gavras raised a ruction big enough to work, and we were swamped," Apokavkos said bleakly; the tribune noted how he took his patron's side without hesitation. He also learned for the first time that the reigning Emperor held his throne thanks to a successful rebellion.

"The pen-pushers broke up the Mankaphas estates and said things would be like they were in granddad's time. Hah! They couldn't trust us for militia no more—we'd fought for the nobles. So in came the taxmen, wanting everything due since the days when Phostis' great-grandfather bought our plot in the first place. I stuck it out as long as I could, but once the bloodsuckers were through, I couldn't keep the dirt under my feet, let alone anything growing on it.

"I knew it was hopeless there and I thought it might not be here, so a year ago I left. Fat lot of good it did me. I'm not much for lying or cheating; all I know is fighting and farming. I commenced to starve just as soon as I got here and I've been at it ever since. I was getting right good at it, too, till you came along."

Scaurus had let Apokavkos spin his tale without interruption. Now that he was through, the Roman found he'd raised as many questions as he'd answered. "Your lord's lands were on the border with Yezd?"

"Near enough, anyway."

"And he rebelled against the Emperor. Did he have backing from the west?"

"From those dung-eaters? No, we fought them at the same time we took on the seal-stampers. That's one of the reasons we lost."

Marcus blinked; the strategy implied was not of the finest. Something else troubled him. "You—and I suppose a good many like you—made up a militia, you said?"

"That's what I told you, all right."

"But when you revolted, the militia was broken up?"

"Say, you did listen, didn't you?"

"But—you're at war with Yezd, or as close as makes no difference," the tribune protested. "How could you disband troops at a time like that? Who took their place?"

Apokavkos gave him an odd look. "You ought to know."

A great many things suddenly became clear to Scaurus. No wonder the Empire was in trouble! Its rulers had seen its own warriors used by power-hungry nobles against the central government and decided native troops were too disloyal to trust. But the Empire still had foreign foes and had to quell revolts as well. So the bureaucrats of Videssos hired mercenaries to do their fighting for them, a cure the tribune was certain would prove worse than the disease.

Mercenary troops were fine—as long as they got paid regularly and as long as their captains did not grow greedy for power rather than money. If either of those things happened . . . the mercenaries had been hired to check the local soldiery, but who would put them down in turn?

He shook his head in dismay. "What a mess! Oh, what a lovely mess!" And we Romans in the middle of it, he thought, disquieted.

"You are *the* most peculiar excuse for a mercenary I ever did see," Apokavkos observed. "Any of them other buggers would be scheming like all get out to see what he could squeeze out of this for him and his, but from the noises you're making, you're trying to figure out what's best for the Empire. I do confess to not understanding."

Marcus thought that over for a minute or two and decided Apokavkos was right. How to explain it, though? "I'm a soldier, yes, but not a mercenary by trade. I never really planned to make a career of war. My men and I are from farther away than you—or I, for that matter—can imagine. Videssos took us in, when we could have been slain out of hand. As much as we have one, the Empire has to be our home. If it goes under, we go under with it."

"Most of that I could follow and I like the sound of it. What do you mean, though, when you're talking of how far you're from? I already said you were a new one on me."

So now for perhaps the twentieth time the tribune told of how the Romans—and a cantankerous Gaul—had come to Videssos. By the time he was through, Apokavkos was staring at him. "You must be telling the truth; no one would make up a yarn like that and figure to be believed. Phos above, there's thousands could tell my story or one about like it, but in all my born days I never heard any to come close to yours." His hand sketched the sun-disc over his breast.

"That's as may be," Scaurus shrugged. "There still remains the problem of what to do with you." He had taken to this strangely met acquaintance, appreciating his matter-of-factness in the face of trouble. Even if he knew it would not be good enough, Apokavkos would give his best. In that, Marcus mused, he's like most of my own men.

The thought gave him his answer; he snapped his fingers in satisfaction. The few seconds of his deliberation had been bad ones for Apokavkos, with new-found hope struggling against the visions of misfortune he had learned to expect.

"I'm sorry," Scaurus said, for all this was painfully clear on the Videssian's face. "I didn't mean for you to worry. Tell me, how would you like to become a Roman?"

"Now I know I don't follow you."

"That's what you will do—follow me. I'll take you back to our barracks, get you some gear, and quarter you with my men. You've soldiered before; the life won't come hard for you. Besides, you haven't done any too well as a Videssian, so what do you have to lose?"

"I'd be a liar if I said I'd be much worse off," Apokavkos admitted. His unhappy stay in the capital had given him a share of big-city cynicism, for his next question was, "What do you get out of the deal?"

Scaurus grinned. "For one thing, a good fighting man—I am a mercenary, remember? There's more to it than that, though. Your scales have got weighted on the wrong side, and it hasn't been your fault. Somehow it seems only fair to even them a little if I can."

The displaced farmer clasped Marcus' hands in a grip that still held the promise of considerable strength. "I'm your man," he said, eyes shining. "All I ever wanted was an even chance and I never came close to one till now. Who would have thought it'd be a foreigner to give it to me?"

After the Roman paid the taverner's score—an outrageous one, for food and drink so vile—he let Apokavkos lead him from the unsavory maze into which he'd wandered. They were not long out of it before the Videssian said, "It's your turn now. That rat's nest is the only part of the city I really know. I never had the money to see the rest."

With some fumbling and the help of passers-by, they made their way back to Palamas' forum. There, to his annoyance, Marcus was promptly recognized again. Apokavkos' mouth fell open when he found his companion had bested the fearsome Avshar with swords. "I saw the son of a snake in action once or twice, leading part of King Wulghash's army against us. He's worth half an army all by his lonesome, 'cause he's as strong as he is sly, which is saying a lump. He beat the boots off us."

The gardens, grounds, and buildings of the palace quarter awed the rustic even more. His comment was, "Now I know what to look forward to, if I'm kindly judged when I die." Another thought struck him. "Phos' light! I'll be bedded down right in the middle of it all! Can you imagine that? Can you?" Marcus was sure he was talking to himself.

When they reached the Roman barracks, they found Tzimiskes and Viridovix outside, a game board between them. Many of the Romans—and the Gaul as well—had become fond of the battle game the Videssians played. Unlike the ones they had known before, it involved no luck, only the skill of the player.

"Glad I am to see you," Viridovix said, sweeping the pieces from the board. "Now I can tell our friend here 'I would have got you in the end' and there's no way for him to make a liar of me."

The tribune had seen how few of his own pieces the Celt had removed, and how many of Tzimiskes'. The Videssian had the game firmly controlled, and all three of them knew it—no, all four, if Apokavkos' raised eyebrows meant anything.

Tzimiskes started to say something, but Viridovix interrupted him. "Where did you come by this scarecrow?" he asked, pointing at Apokavkos.

"There's a bit of a story to that." The Roman turned to Tzimiskes. "Neilos, I'm glad I found you. I want you to take charge of this fellow," he named Apokavkos and introduced him to the other two, "feed him as much as he'll hold, get him weapons—and clothes, too, for that matter. He's our first honorary Roman. He—what is it? You look like you're about to explode."

"Scaurus, I'll do everything you say, and you can tell me the wherefores later. The Emperor has been sending messengers here every hour on the hour since early this morning. Something to do with last night's activities, I gather."

"Oh." That put a different light on matters. Whether or not he was a hero in the city, he realized the Emperor might have to take a dim view of one of his soldiers brawling with a neighboring land's ambassador. "I wonder how much trouble I'm in. Phostis, go with Tzimiskes here. If I have to see the Emperor, I'd best get shaved"—He was still refusing to grow his beard.—"cleaned, and changed."

The next imperial messenger arrived while Marcus was scraping the last whiskers from under his chin. He waited with ill-concealed impatience while the Roman bathed and donned a fresh mantle. "It's about time," he said when Marcus emerged, though he and the tribune both knew how quick the ablutions had been.

He led Scaurus past the Hall of the Nineteen Couches, past the looming Grand Courtroom with its incredible bronzework doors, past a two-story barracks complex—Namdaleni were wandering about here, and Marcus looked for but did not see Hemond—and through a grove of cherry trees thick with sweet, pink blossoms to a secluded building deep within it—the private chambers of the imperial family, Marcus realized.

His worries lessened slightly. If Mavrikios was going to take strong action against him, he would do it publicly, so Yezd's honor could be seen to be satisfied.

A pair of lazy-looking sentries, both Videssians, lounged by the entranceway of the private chambers. They had doffed their helmets so they could soak up the sun; the Videssians deemed a tanned, weathered look a mark of masculine, though not of feminine, beauty.

Scaurus' guide must have been well-known to the guards, who did not offer even a token challenge as he led the tribune inside. It was not his job, though, to conduct Scaurus all the way to the Emperor. Just inside the threshold he was met by a fat chamberlain in a maroon linen robe with a pattern of golden cranes. The chamberlain looked inquiringly at the Roman.

"He's the one, all right," the messenger said. "Took long enough to find, didn't he?" Without waiting for an answer, he was off on his next mission.

"Come with me, if you please," the chamberlain said to Scaurus. His voice was more contralto than tenor, and his cheeks were beardless. Like many of the Videssian court functionaries, he was a eunuch. Marcus presumed this was for the same reason eunuchs were common in the oriental monarchies of his own world; being ineligible for the throne because of their castration, they were thought to be more trustworthy in close contact with the person of the ruler.

Like all such rules, the tribune knew, that one had its dreadful exceptions.

The long corridor down which the chamberlain led him was lit by translucent panes of alabaster set into the ceiling. The milky light dimmed and grew bright as clouds chased across the sun. It was, Marcus thought, a bit like seeing underwater.

And there was much to see. As was only natural, many of the finest gauds of a thousand years and more of empire were displayed for the pleasure of the Emperors themselves. The passageway was crowded with marble and bronze statuary, pottery breathtakingly graceful and painted with elegant precision, busts and portraits of men Scaurus guessed to be bygone Emperors, religious images lavish with gold leaf and polished gems, a rearing stallion as big as Marcus' hand that had to have been carved from a single emerald, and other marvels he did not really see because he had too much pride to swivel his head this way and that like a goatherd on holiday in the city. Even the floor was a bright mosaic of hunting and farming scenes.

In that company, the rusted, dented helmet on a pedestal of its own seemed jarringly out of place. "Why is this here?" he asked.

"That is the helmet of King Rishtaspa of Makuran—we would say 'Yezd' now—taken from his corpse by the Emperor Laskaris when he sacked Mashiz seven hundred and—let me think a moment—thirty-nine years ago. A most valiant warrior, Laskaris. The portrait above the helmet is his."

The painting showed a stern-faced, iron-bearded man in late middle life. He wore gilded scale-mail, the imperial diadem, and the scarlet boots that marked the Emperors of Videssos, but for all that he looked more like a senior centurion than a ruler. His left hand was on the hilt of his sword; in his right was a lance. The spear carried a pennant of sky-blue, with Phos' sun-symbol large on its field.

The chamberlain continued, "Laskaris forcibly converted all the heathen of Makuran to the true faith but, as Videssos proved unable to establish lasting rule over their land, they have relapsed into error."

Marcus thought that over and liked none of his thoughts. War for the sake of religion was a notion that had not crossed his mind before. If the people of Makuran were as resolute about their faith as Videssians were for the worship of Phos, such a struggle would be uncommonly grim.

The eunuch was ushering him into a small, surprisingly spare chamber. It held a couch, a desk, a couple of chairs but, save for an image of Phos, was bare of the artwork crowding the hallway. The papers on the desk had been shoved to one side to make room for a plain earthen jug of wine and a plate of cakes.

Seated on the couch were the Emperor, his daughter Alypia, and a big-bellied man of about sixty whom Marcus had seen but not met the night before.

"If you will give me your sword, sir—" the chamberlain began, but Mavrikios interrupted him.

"Oh, run along, Mizizios. He's not out for my head, not yet, anyway—he doesn't know me well enough. And you needn't stand there waiting for him to prostrate himself. It's against his religion, or some such silly thing. Go on, out with you."

Looking faintly scandalized, Mizizios disappeared.

Once he was gone, the Emperor waved a bemused Scaurus in. "I'm in private now, so I can ignore ceremony if I please—and I do please," Gavras said. This was Thorisin's brother after all; though Thorisin's fiery impetuosity was banked in him, it did not fail to burn.

"You might tell him who I am," the aging stranger suggested. He had an engagingly homely face; his beard was snow streaked with coal and reached nearly to his paunch. He looked like a scholar or a healer, but from his robes only one office could be his; he wore gem-strewn cloth-of-gold, with a large circle of blue silk on his left breast.

"So I might," the Emperor agreed, taking no offense at his aggrieved tone. Here, plainly, were two men who had known and liked each other for years. "Outlander, this tub of lard is called Balsamon. When I took the throne I found him Patriarch of Videssos and I was fool enough to leave him on his seat."

"Father!" Alypia said, but there was no heat in her complaint.

As he bowed, Marcus studied the patriarch's features, looking for the fanaticism he had seen in Apsimar. He did not find it. Wisdom and mirth dominated Balsamon's face; despite his years, the prelate's brown eyes were still keen and among the shrewdest the tribune could recall.

"Bless you, my heathen friend," he said. In his clear tenor the words were a friendly greeting with no trace of condescension. "And do sit down. I'm harmless, I assure you."

Quite out of his depth, Marcus sank into a chair. "To business, then," Gavras said, visibly reassuming part of his imperial dignity. He pointed an accusing finger at the Roman. "You are to know you are reprimanded for assaulting the ambassador of the Khagan of Yezd and offering him gross insult. You are fined a week's pay. My daughter and the patriarch Balsamon are witnesses to this sentence."

The tribune nodded, expressionless; this was what he had expected.

The Emperor's finger dropped and a grin spread across his face. "Having said that, I'll say something else—good for you! My brother came storming in here to wake me out of a sound sleep and show me every thrust and parry. Wulghash sent Avshar here as a calculated insult, and I'm not sorry to see his joke turn and bite him."

He grew sober once more. "Yezd is a disease, not a nation, and I intend to wipe it from the face of the earth. Videssos and what was once Makuran have always fought—they to gain access to the Videssian Sea or the Sailors' Sea, we to take their rich river valleys, and both sides to control the passes, the mines, and the fine fighting men of Vaspurakan between us. Over the centuries, I'd say, honors were evenly divided."

Scaurus chewed on a cake as he listened. It was excellent, full of nuts and raisins and dusted over with cinnamon, and went very well with the spiced wine in the jug. The tribune tried to forget the stale slop he'd drunk before, in the Videssian slums.

"Forty years ago, though," the Emperor went on, "The Yezda from the steppe of Shaumkhiil sacked Mashiz, seized all of Makuran, and rammed their way through Vaspurakan into the Empire. They kill for the sport of it, steal what they can carry, and wreck what they can't. And because they are nomads, they gleefully lay waste all the farmland they come across. Our peasants, from whom the Empire gets most of its taxes, are murdered or driven into destitution, and our western cities starve because no peasants are left to feed them."

"Worse yet, the Yezda follow Skotos," Balsamon said. When Marcus made no reply, the patriarch cocked a bushy gray eyebrow at him in sardonic amusement. "You think, perhaps, this is something I would be likely to say of anyone who does not share my creed? You must have seen enough of our priests to know most of them do not take kindly to unbelievers."

Marcus shrugged, unwilling to commit himself. He had an uneasy feeling the patriarch was playing a game with him and an even more uncomfortable certainty that Balsamon was much the smarter.

The patriarch laughed at his noncommital response. He had a good laugh, inviting everyone within earshot to share the joke. "Mavrikios, it is a courtier, not a solider!"

His eyes still twinkling, he gave his attention back to the Roman. "I am not a typical priest, I fear. Time was when the Makurani gave reverence to their Four Prophets, whose names I forget. I think their faith was wrong, I think it was foolish, but I do not think it damned them or made them impossible to treat with. The Yezda, though, worship their gods with disemboweled victims writhing on their altars and summon demons to glut themselves on the remains. They are a wicked folk and must be suppressed." If anything convinced Marcus of the truth in Balsamon's words, it was the real regret his voice bore . . . that, and the memory of Avshar's chill voice, incanting as they fought.

"And suppress them I shall," Mavrikios Gavras took up the discussion. In his vehemence he pounded right fist into left palm. "The first two years I held the throne, I fought them to a standstill on our borders. Last year, for one reason and another"— He did not elaborate and looked so grim that Marcus dared not ask for details. —"I could not campaign against them. We suffered for it, in raids and stings and torments. This year, Phos willing, I will be able to hire enough mercenaries to crush Yezd once and for all. I read your arrival here as a good omen for that, my proud friend from another world."

He paused, awaiting the Roman's reply. Scaurus recalled his first impression of this man, that giving him the truth served best. "I think," he said carefully, "you would do better to restore the peasant militias you once had than to spend your coin on foreign troops."

The Emperor stared, jaw dropping. Sneaking a glance at Balsamon, Marcus had the satisfaction of knowing he'd managed to startle the patriarch as well. The princess Alypia, on the other hand, who so far had held herself aloof from the conversation, looked at the tribune in appraisal and, he thought, growing approval.

The patriarch recovered before his sovereign. "Be glad this one is on your side, Gavras. He sees things clearly."

Mavrikios was still shaking his head in wonder. He spoke not to Scaurus, but to Balsamon. "What is he? Two days in the city? Three? There are men who have been in the palaces longer than he's been alive who cannot see that far. Tell me, Marcus Aemilius Scaurus"— It pleased but did not surprise the tribune that Gavras knew his full name —"how did you learn so much about our woes so quickly?"

Marcus explained how he had met Phostis Apokavkos. He did not mention the peasant-soldier's name or what he had done about him.

By the time the Roman was done, the Emperor was angry. "May Phos fry all pen-pushers! Until I took the throne, the damned bureaucrats ruled the Empire for all but two years of the last fifty, in spite of everything the nobles in the provinces could do against them. They had the money to hire mercenaries and they held the capital, and that proved enough for the puppet-Emperors they raised to keep their seats. And to ruin their rivals in the power struggle, they turned our militiamen into serfs and taxed them to death so they couldn't fight for their patrons. A plague on every one of them, from Vardanes Sphrantzes on down!"

"It's not as simple as that, Father, and you know it very well," Alypia said. "A hundred years ago the peasantry was really free, not bound to our nobles. When magnates began buying up peasant land and making the farmers their dependents, it cost the central government dear. Would any Emperor, no matter how simple, want private armies raised against him, or want to see the taxes rightfully his siphoned into the hands of men who dream of the throne themselves?"

Mavrikios looked at her with a mixture of exasperation and fondness. "My daughter reads history," he said to Marcus, as if in apology.

The Roman did not think any was necessary. Alypia had spoken well and to the point. There was plainly a keen wit behind her eyes, though she kept it on a short rein of words. The tribune was also grateful for any facts he could get. The Videssos he and his men entered was a maze of interlocking factions more twisted than any Rome had known.

The princess had turned to face her father; Scaurus admired her clean profile. It was softer than Mavrikios' both because of her sex and the influence of her mother's looks, but she was still a distinguished young woman. A cat can look at a king, Marcus thought, but what of a king's daughter? Well, he told himself, no one's yet been killed for thinking, and a good thing too, or the world would be a lonely place.

"Say what you want," the Emperor told Alypia, "about how things were a hundred years ago. Ten years ago, when Strobilos Sphrantzes had his fat fundament on the throne—"

"You'd say 'arse' to anyone but me," Alypia said. "I've heard the word before."

"Probably from my own mouth, I fear." Gavras sighed. "I do try to watch my tongue, but I've spent too many years in the field."

Marcus ignored the byplay. A Sphrantzes ruling Videssos just before Mavrikios forcibly took power? Then what in the name of Jove—or even Phos—was Vardanes Sphrantzes doing as the present Emperor's chief minister?

"Where was I?" Gavras was saying. "Oh yes, that cretin Strobilos. He was a bigger booby than his precious nephew. Fifty thousand peasants on the border of Vaspurakan he converted from soldiers to serfs in one swoop, and overtaxed serfs at that. Is it any wonder half of them went over to the Yezda, foul as they are, on their next raid? There's such a thing, Alypia, as taking too long a view."

Damn it, thought Scaurus, there was no graceful way to ask the question that was consuming him with curiosity. He squirmed in his seat, so busy with unsuccessful tries at framing it that he did not notice Balsamon watching him.

The patriarch came to his rescue. "Your Majesty, before he bursts, will you tell the poor lad why there's still a Sphrantzes in your service?"

"Ah, Scaurus, then there *is* something you don't know? I'd started to wonder. Balsamon, you tell it—you were in things up to your fuzzy eyebrows."

Balsamon assumed a comic look of injured innocence "I? All I did was point out to a few people that Strobilos had, perhaps, not been the ideal ruler for a land in a time of trouble."

"What that means, Roman, is that our priestly crony here broke a hole in the ranks of the bureaucrats you could throw *him* through, which is saying something. Half the pen-pushers backed me instead of the old Sphrantzes; their price was making the younger one Sevastos. Worth it, I suppose, but he wants the red boots for himself."

"He also wants me," Alypia said. "It is not mutual."

"I know, dear, I know. I could solve so many problems if it were, but I'm not sure I'd give you to him even so. His wife died too conveniently last year. Poor Evphrosyne! And as soon as was decent—or before, thinking back on it—there was Vardanes, full of praises for the notion of 'cementing our two great houses.' I do not trust that man."

Marcus decided he too would like to cement Vardanes Sphrantzes—by choice, into the wall of a fortress.

Something else occurred to him. Mavrikios, it seemed, was a man who liked to speak the truth as well as hear it, so the tribune felt he could inquire, "May I ask, my lord, what became of Strobilos Sphrantzes?"

"You mean, did I chop him into chitterlings as he deserved? No, that was part of the bargain Balsamon forged. He lived out his worthless life in a monastery north of Imbros and died a couple of years ago. Also, to his credit, Vardanes swore he would not serve me if I killed his uncle, and I needed him, worse luck for me.

"Here, enough of this—I neglect my hostly duties. Have another cake." And the Emperor of Videssos, like any good host, extended the platter to the Roman.

"With pleasure," Scaurus said, taking one. "They're delicious."

"Thank you," said Alypia. When Marcus blinked, she went on, a bit defensively: "I was not raised in the palaces, you know, with a servant to squirm at every crook of my finger. I learned womens' skills well enough, and after all"—She smiled at her father—"no one can read history all the time."

"Your Highness, I said they were very good cakes before I knew who made them," Marcus pointed out. "You've only given me another reason to like them." As soon as the words were out of his mouth he wished he had not said them. Where his daughter was concerned, Mavrikios could not help but be suspicious of everyone.

Though Alypia dropped her eyes, if the remark annoyed the Emperor he showed no sign of it. "A courtier indeed, Balsamon," he chuckled. As he bowed his way from the imperial audience, Marcus concluded that any soldier of Videssos who had no turn for diplomacy would hardly last long enough to face her foes.

V

MIZIZIOS THE EUNUCH LED THE ROMAN BACK TO THE ENTRANCEWAY of the imperial quarters, then vanished back into the building on some business of his own. The messenger who had led the tribune hither was nowhere to be seen. The Videssians, apparently, took less care over exits than entrances.

Their sentries were also less careful than Marcus found tolerable. When he emerged into the golden sunshine of late afternoon, he found both guards sprawled out asleep in front of the doorway. Their sword belts were undone, their spears lay beside the helmets they had already shed when Scaurus first saw them.

Their sloth infuriated the tribune. With an Emperor worth protecting—and that for the first time in years—these back-country louts could do no better than doze the day away. It was more than the Roman could stand. "On your feet!" he roared. At the same time he kicked their discarded helms, making a fine clatter.

The sentries jerked and scrambled upright, fumbling for the weapons they had set aside. Marcus laughed scornfully. He cursed the startled warders with every bit of Videssian foulness he had learned. He wished Gaius Philippus were at his side; the centurion had a gift for invective. "If you were under my command, you'd be lashed with more than my tongue, I promise you that," he finished.

Under his tirade, the Videssians went from amazement to sullenness. The older one, a stocky, much-scarred veteran, muttered to his companion, "Who does this churlish barbarian think he is?"

A moment later he was on the ground, flat as he'd been while napping. Marcus stood over him, rubbing a sore knuckle and watching the other sentry for any move he might make. Save for backing away, he made none.

Seeing the still-standing guard was safe to ignore, Marcus hauled the man he had felled to his feet. He was none too gentle about it. The sentry shook his head, trying to clear it. A bruise was already forming under his left eye.

"When do your reliefs arrive?" Scaurus snapped at the two of them.

"In about another hour, sir," the younger, milder guard answered. He spoke very carefully, as one might to a tiger which had asked the time of day.

"Very well, then. Tell them what happened to you and let them know someone will be by to check on them sometime during their watch. And may your Phos help them and you if they get caught sleeping!"

He turned his back on the sentries and stalked off, giving them no chance to question or protest. In fact, he did not intend to send anyone to spy on the next watch. The threat alone should be enough to keep them alert.

As he walked back past the barracks hall belonging to the mercenaries from the Duchy of Namdalen, he heard his name called. Helvis was leaning out of a top-story window, holding something in her hand. The Roman was too far away to see what it was until the sun gave back the bright glint of gold—probably some trinket she'd bought with what she'd won betting on him. She smiled and waved.

Grinning himself, he waved back, his anger at the sentries forgotten for the moment. She was a friendly lass, and he had only himself to blame for thinking her unattached the night before. Hemond was a good sort, too; Marcus had liked him from their first meeting at the Silver Gate. His grin turned wry as he reflected that the two women who had interested him most in Videssos both seemed thoroughly unapproachable. It's hardly the end of the world, you know, he told himself, seeing that you've been in the city less than a week.

His mood of gentle self-mockery was suddenly erased by the sight of the tall, white-robed figure of Avshar. His hand reached the hilt of his sword before he knew he had moved it. The envoy of Yezd, though, did not appear to see him in return. Avshar was some distance away in deep conversation with a squat, bowlegged man in the furs and leather of the Pardrayan nomads. The tribune had the feeling he'd seen the plainsman before, but could not recall when or where—maybe at last night's banquet, he thought uncertainly.

He was so intent on Avshar that he forgot to pay attention to where his feet were taking him. The first knowledge he had that he was not alone on his pathway came when he bounced off a man coming in the opposite direction. "Your pardon, I pray!" he exclaimed, taking his eye off the Yezda to see whom he'd staggered.

His victim, a short chubby man, wore the blue robes of the priesthood of Phos. His shaven head gave him a curious ageless look, but he was not old—gray had not touched his beard, and his face was hardly lined. "Quite all right, quite all right," he said. "It's my own fault for not noticing you were full of your own thoughts."

"That's good of you, but it doesn't excuse my clumsiness."

"Don't trouble yourself about it. Am I not right in recognizing you as the leader of the new company of outland mercenaries?"

Marcus admitted it.

"Then I've been wanting to meet you for some time." The priest's eyes crinkled at the corners as he smiled. "Though not so abruptly as this, perhaps."

"You have the advantage of me," the tribune observed.

"Hmm? Oh, so I do—no reason you should know me, is there? I'm called Nepos. I wish I could claim my interest in you was entirely unselfish, but I fear I can't. You see, I hold one of the chairs in sorcery at the Videssian Academy."

Scaurus nodded his understanding. In a land where wizardry held so strong a place, what could be more logical than its taking its place alongside other intellectual disciplines such as philosophy and mathematics? And since the Romans were widely known to have come to Videssos by no natural means, the Empire's sorcerers must be burning with curiosity about their arrival. For that matter, so was he—Nepos might be able to make him better understand the terrifying moment that had whisked him to this world.

He gauged the setting sun. "It should be about time for my men to sit down to supper. Would you care to join us? After we've eaten, you can ask questions to your heart's content."

"Nothing would please me more," Nepos answered, beaming at him. "Lead on, and I'll follow as best I can—your legs are longer than mine, I'm afraid."

Despite his round build, the little priest had no trouble keeping up with the Roman. His sandaled feet twinkled over the ground, and as he walked, he talked. An endless stream of questions bubbled from him, queries not only about the religious and magical practices of Rome and Gaul, but about matters social and political as well.

"I think," the Roman said, wondering at the relevance of some of the things Nepos was asking, "your faith plays a larger part in everything you do than is true in my world."

"I'd begun to reach that conclusion myself," the priest agreed. "In Videssos you cannot buy a cup of wine without being told Phos will triumph in the end, or deal with a jeweler from Khatrish without hearing that the battle between good and evil is evenly matched. Everyone in the city fancies himself a theologian." He shook his head in mock annoyance.

At the Roman barracks Marcus found the sentries alert and vertical. He would have been astounded had it been otherwise.

Far less dangerous for a legionary to face an oncoming foe than Gaius Philippus' wrath, which fell unerringly on shirkers.

Inside the hall, most of the legionaries were already spooning down their evening meal, a thick stew of barley, boiled beef and marrowbones, peas, carrots, onions, and various herbs. It was better food than they would have had in Caesar's barracks, but of similar kind. Nepos accepted his bowl and spoon with a word of thanks.

Marcus introduced the priest to Gaius Philippus, Viridovix, Gorgidas, Quintus Glabrio, Adiatun, the scout Junius Blaesus, and several other Romans. They found a quiet corner and talked while they ate. How many times now, the tribune wondered, had he told some Videssian his tale? Unlike almost all the others, Nepos was no passive audience. His questions were good-natured but probing, his constant effort aimed toward piecing together a consistent account from the recollections of his table companions.

Why was it, he asked, that Gaius Philippus and Adiatun both remembered seeing Scaurus and Viridovix still trading swordstrokes inside the dome of light, yet neither the tribune nor the Gaul had any such memory? Why had it been hard for Gorgidas to breathe, but for no one else? Why had Junius Blaesus felt piercing cold, but Adiatun broken into a sweat?

Gaius Philippus answered Nepos patiently for a time, but before long his streak of hard Roman practicality emerged. "What good does it do you, anyway, to learn that Publius Flaccus farted while we were in flight?"

"None whatever, very possibly," Nepos smiled, taking no offense. "Did he?"

Amid general laughter, the centurion said, "You'd have to ask him, not me."

"The only way to understand anything in the past," Nepos went on in a more serious vein, "is to find out as much as one can about it. Often people have no idea how much they can remember or, indeed, how much of what they think they know is false. Only patient inquiry and comparing many accounts can bring us near the truth."

"You talk like a historian, not a priest or a wizard," Gorgidas said.

Nepos shrugged, as puzzled by the Greek doctor's comment as Gorgidas was by him. He answered, "I talk like myself and nothing else. There are priests so struck by the glory of Phos' divinity that they contemplate the divine essence to the exclusion of all worldly concerns, and reject the world as a snare Skotos laid for their temptation. Is that what you mean?"

"Not exactly." Priest and physician viewed things from such different perspectives as to make communication all but impossible, but each had a thirst for knowledge that drove him to persist.

"To my mind," Nepos continued, "the world and everything in it reflects Phos' splendor, and deserves the study of men who would approach more nearly an understanding of Phos' plan for the Empire and all mankind."

To that Gorgidas could make no reply at all. To his way of thinking, the world and everything in it was worth studying for its own sake, and ultimate meanings, if any, were likely unknowable. Yet he had to recognize Nepos' sincerity and his goodness. "'Countless are the world's wonders, but none more wonderful than man,'" he murmured, and sat back with his wine, soothed as always by Sophokles' verse.

"Being a wizard, what have you learned from us?" Quintus Glabrio asked Nepos; until then he'd sat largely silent.

"Less than I'd have liked, I must admit. All I can tell you is the obvious truth that the two blades, Scaurus' and yours, Viridovix, brought you hither. If there is a greater purpose behind your coming, I do not think it has unfolded yet."

"Now I know you're no ordinary priest," Gorgidas exclaimed. "In my world, I never saw one admit to ignorance."

"How arrogant your priests must be! What greater wickedness than claiming to know everything, arrogating to yourself the privileges of godhood?" Nepos shook his head. "Thanks be to Phos, I am not so vain. I have so very much to learn! Among other things, my friends, I would like to see, even to hold, the fabled swords to which we owe your presence here."

Marcus and Viridovix exchanged glances filled with the same reluctance. Neither had put his weapon in another's hands since coming to Videssos. There seemed no way, though, to decline such a reasonable request. Both men slowly drew their blades from their scabbards; each began to hand his to Nepos. "Wait!" Marcus said, holding out a warning hand to Viridovix. "I don't think it would be wise for our swords to touch, no matter what the circumstance."

"Right you are," the Gaul agreed, sheathing his blade for the moment. "One such mischance cools the appetite for another, indeed and it does."

Nepos took the Roman's sword, holding it up to a clay lamp to examine it closely. "It seems altogether plain," he said to Marcus, some perplexity in his voice. "I feel no surge of strength, nor am I impelled to travel elsewhere—for which I have no complaint, you understand. Save for the strange characters cut into the blade, it is but another longsword, a bit cruder than most. Is the spell in those letters? What do they say?"

"I have no idea," Scaurus replied. "It's a Celtic sword, made by Viridovix's people. I took it as battle spoil and kept it because it fits my size better than the shortswords most Romans use."

"Ah, I see. Viridovix, would you read the inscription for me and tell me what it means?"

The Gaul tugged at his fiery mustache in some embarrassment.

"Nay, I canna, I fear. With my folk letters are no common thing, as they are with the Romans—and with you too, I should guess. Only the druids—priests, you would say—have the skill of them, and never a druid I was, nor am I sorry for it. I will tell you, my own blade is marked as well. Look, if you will."

But when his sword came free of its scabbard the runes set in it were gleaming gold, and those on the other blade sprang to glowing life with them. "Sheathe it!" Marcus shouted in alarm. He snatched his own sword from Nepos' hand and crammed it back into its sheath. There was a bad moment when he thought it was fighting against his grip, but then it was securely back in place. Tension leaked from the air.

Sudden sweat beaded Nepos' forehead. He said to Gorgidas, "Of such a thing as that I was indeed ignorant, nor, to quote your red-haired friend, am I sorry for it." His laugh was shaky and rang loud in the awed and fearful hush that had fallen over the barracks. He soon found an excuse to make an early departure, disappearing after a few quick good-byes.

"There goes a fellow who set his nets for rabbit and found a bear sitting in them," Gaius Philippus said, but even his chuckle sounded forced.

Almost all the Romans, and Marcus with them, sought their pallets early that night. He snuggled beneath his blanket and slowly drifted toward sleep. The coarse wool made him itch, but his last waking thought was one of relief that he still had a blanket—and a barracks, for that matter—over him.

The tribune woke early the next morning to the sound of an argument outside the barracks hall. He flung on a mantle, belted his sword round his middle, and, still rubbing sleep from his eyes, went out to see what the trouble was.

"No, sir, I'm sorry," a Roman guard was saying, "but you cannot see my commander until he wakes." He and his mate held their spears horizontally across their bodies to keep their unwanted guest from entering.

"Phos fry you, I tell you this is urgent!" Nephon Khoumnos shouted. "Must I—oh, there you are, Scaurus. I have to talk to you at once, and your thickskulled sentries would not give me leave."

"You cannot blame them for following their standard orders. Don't worry about it, Gnaeus, Manlius—you did right." He returned his attention to Khoumnos. "If you wanted to see me, here I am. Shall we stroll along the path and give my men a chance to go back to sleep?"

Still fuming, Khoumnos agreed. The Roman sentries stepped back to let their commander by. The path's paving stones were cool on his bare feet. He gratefully sucked in the early morning air. It was sweet after the close, smoky atmosphere inside the hall.

A gold-throated thrush in a nearby tree greeted the sun with a burst of sparkling notes. Even as unmusical a soul as Scaurus found it lovely.

The Roman did not try to begin the conversation. He ambled along, admiring now the delicate flush the early light gave to marble, now the geometric precision of a dew-spangled spiderweb. If Khoumnos had so pressing a problem, let him bring it up.

He did, rising to the bait of Marcus' silence. "Scaurus, where in Phos' holy name do you get the authority to lay your hands on my men?"

The Roman stopped, hardly believing he'd heard correctly. "Do you mean the guards outside the Emperor's dwelling yesterday?"

"Who else could I possibly mean?" Khoumnos snapped. "We take it very ill in Videssos when a mercenary assaults native-born soldiers. It was not for that I arranged to have you come to the city; when I saw you and your men in Imbros, you struck me as being out of the common run of barbarians."

"You take it ill, you say, when a mercenary strikes a native Videssian soldier?"

Nephon Khoumnos gave an impatient nod.

Marcus knew Khoumnos was an important man in Videssos, but he was too furious to care. "Well, how do you take it when your fine Videssian soldiers are snoozing the afternoon away in front of the very chambers they're supposed to guard?"

"What?"

"Whoever was telling you tales out of school," the tribune said, "should have gone through the whole story, not just his half of it." He explained how he had found both sentries napping in the sun as he left his audience with the Emperor. "What reason would I have for setting upon them? Did they give you one?"

96

"No," Khoumnos admitted. "They said they were attacked from behind without warning."

"From above would be more like it." Marcus snorted. "They can count themselves lucky they were your troops, not mine; stripes are the least they could have hoped for in Roman service."

Khoumnos was not yet convinced. "Their stories hang together very well."

"What would you expect, that two shirkers would give each other the lie? Khoumnos, I don't much care whether you believe me or not. You ruined my sleep, and, from the way my guts are churning right now, I'd wager you've ruined my breakfast as well. But I'll tell you this—if those guards were the best men Videssos can offer, no wonder you need mercenaries."

Thinking of Tzimiskes, Mouzalon, Apokavkos—yes, and Khoumnos himself—Scaurus knew how unfair he was being, but he was too nettled to watch his tongue. The incredible gall the sentries had shown—not merely to hide their guilt, but to try to put it on him! He shook his head in wonder.

Anger cloaked by expressionless features, Khoumnos bowed stiffly from the waist. "I will look into what you've told me, I promise you that," he said. He bowed again and strode away.

Watching his rigid back, Marcus wondered if he had made another enemy. Sphrantzes, Avshar, now Khoumnos—for a man who'd aspired to politics, he told himself, you have a gift for the right word at the wrong time. And if Sphrantzes and Khoumnos are both your foes, where in Videssos will you find a friend?

The tribune sighed. As always, it was too late to unsay anything. All he could do now was live with the consequences of what he'd already done. And in that context, he thought, breakfast did not seem such a bad idea after all. He walked back toward the barracks.

Despite his Stoic training, despite his efforts to take things as they came, the rest of that morning and early afternoon were hard for him to wait through. To try to drown his worries in work, he threw himself into the Romans' daily drill with such nervous energy that he flattened everyone who stood against him. At any other time he would have been proud. Now he barked at his men for lying down against their commander.

"Sir," one of the legionaries said, "if I was going to lie down against you, I would have done it sooner." The man was rubbing a bruised shoulder as he limped away.

Scaurus tried to unburden himself to Viridovix, but the big Celt was scant help. "I know it's a bad thing," he said, "but what can you do? Give 'em half a chance and the men'd sooner sleep nor work. I would myself, if there's no fighting or women to be had."

Gaius Philippus had come up during the last part of this speech and listened to it with obvious disagreement. "If your troops won't obey orders you have a mob, not an army. That's why we Romans were conquering Gaul, you know. Man for man, the Celts are as brave as any I've seen, but you can't work together worth a turtle turd."

"Aye, it's not to be denied we're a fractious lot. But you're a bigger fool or ever I thought, Gaius Philippus, if you think your puny Romans could be holding the whole of Gaul in despite of its people."

"Fool, is it?" As with a terrier, there was no room for retreat in the senior centurion. "Watch what you say."

Viridovix bristled back. "Have a care with your own mouth, or I'll cut you a new one, the which you'd not like at all."

Before his touchy comrades heated further, Marcus quickly stepped between them. "The two of you are like the dog in the fable, snapping after the reflection of a bone. None of us here will ever know whether Caesar or the Gauls prevailed. There's not much room for enmity among us, you know—we have enough foes outside our ranks. Besides, I tell you now that before you can go for each other, you'll go through me first."

The tribune carefully did not see the measuring stares both his friends gave him. But he had eased the friction; centurion and Celt, after a last, half-friendly snarl, went about their own affairs.

It occurred to Scaurus that Viridovix had to feel far more lost and alone in their new land than the Romans felt. There were more than a thousand of them to but a solitary Gaul; not a soul in this land even spoke his tongue. No wonder his temper slipped from time to time—the wonder was the Celt keeping up his spirits as well as he did.

At about the time when the Emperor had summoned him to audience the day before, Tzimiskes sought out the tribune to tell him that Khoumnos begged leave to speak with him. There was wonder on the dour Videssian's face as he conveyed the message. "'Begged leave,' he said. I don't think I've heard of Nephon Khoumnos begging leave of anyone. 'Begged leave,'" Tzimiskes repeated, still not believing it.

Khoumnos stood outside the barracks, one square hand scratching his iron-bearded chin. When Marcus walked up to him, he jerked the hand away as if caught doing something shameful. His mouth worked a couple of times before words came out. "Damn you," he said at last. "I owe you an apology. For what it's worth, you have it."

"I accept it gladly," Marcus replied—just how glad he was, he did not want to show the Videssian. "I would have hoped, though, that you'd know I had better things to do than breaking your guardsmen's heads."

"I'd be a liar if I said I wasn't surprised when Blemmydes and Kourkouas came to me with their tale. But you don't go disbelieving your men without some good reason—you know how it is."

Scaurus could only nod; he did know how it was. An officer who refused to back up his troops was useless. Once his men lost confidence in him, he could not rely on their reports, which only made them less confident . . . That road was a downward spiral which had to be stopped before it could start. "What made you change your mind?" he asked.

"After the pleasant little talk I had with you this morning, I went back and gave those two scoundrels separate grillings. Kourkouas cracked, finally."

"The younger one?"

"That's right. Interesting you should guess—you notice things, don't you? Yes, Lexos Blemmydes kept playing the innocent wronged up until the last minute, Skotos chill his lying heart."

"What do you plan to do with the two of them?"

"I've already done it. I may have made a mistake before, but I fixed it. As soon as I knew what the truth was, I had their corselets off their backs and shipped them over the Cattle-Crossing on the first ferry. Between brigands and Yezda, the west country should be lively enough to keep them away. Good riddance, say I, and I'm only sorry such wastrels made me speak hastily to you."

"Don't let it trouble you," Marcus answered, convinced Khoumnos' apology came from mind and heart both. He also realized he had let his anger put him in the wrong with that vicious gibe about Videssian troops. "You weren't the only one who said things he regrets now, you know."

"Fair enough." Khoumnos extended his hand, and the tribune took it. The Videssian's palm was even harder than his own, callused not only from weaponwork but also by years of holding the reins. Khoumnos slapped him on the back and went about his business. Marcus suspected it would be a good long while before the next set of sentries dropped off to sleep before the Emperor's quarters.

His own sleep that night, after tension well relieved, was deep and untroubled for several hours. Ordinary barracks chatter and the noise of men rising to make water or find a snack never bothered his rest. That was as well; if they had, sleep would have been impossible to come by.

The noise that woke him now was no louder than the usual run of nightly sounds. But it was one which did not belong—the soft slide of a booted foot across the flooring. Romans were either barefoot and silent or wore clattering nail-soled sandals. The sound of a footfall neither one nor the other pierced Marcus' slumber and pried his eyelids apart.

Only a couple of torches burned in the hall, giving just enough light to keep the Romans from stumbling over each other in the night. But the crouched figure sneaking between the sleeping soliders was no legionary. The squat silhouette and bushy beard could only belong to a Khamorth; Marcus felt cold fear as he recognized the nomad who had been talking to Avshar the night before. He was coming toward the tribune, a dagger in his hand.

The nomad shook his head, muttering something under his breath. He saw Scaurus as the Roman flung back his blanket and grabbed for his sword. The Khamorth roared and charged.

Naked as a worm, Marcus scrambled to his feet. There was no time to pull his blade from its sheath. He used it as a club to knock aside the Khamorth's first stab, then closed with the shorter man, seizing his assailant's knife-wrist with his left hand.

He caught a glimpse of his foe's face. The nomad's dark eyes were wide with a consuming madness and something more, something the tribune would not identify until some time later as stark terror.

They rolled to the floor, still holding tightly to each other.

There were shouts all through the barracks now—the Khamorth's bellow and the sound of struggle routed the men from their mattresses. It took a few seconds, though, for the sleep-fuzzed soldiers to grasp where the hubbub came from.

Marcus held his grip with all his strength, meanwhile using the pommel of his sword to try to batter the nomad into submission. But his enemy seemed to have a skull hard as rock. For all the blows he took, he still writhed and twisted, trying to plant his knife in the tribune's flesh.

Then a second strong hand joined Marcus' on the nomad's wrist. Viridovix, as naked as Scaurus, squeezed down on the Khamorth's tendons, forcing his fingers to open. The knife dropped to the floor.

Viridovix shook the Khamorth like a great rat. "Why would he be after having a grudge against you, Roman dear?" he asked. Then, to his prisoner, "Don't wriggle, now!" He shook him again. The Khamorth, eyes riveted on the fallen dagger, ignored him.

"I don't know," Marcus answered. "I think he must be in Avshar's pay, though. I saw them walking together yesterday."

"Avshar, is it? The why of that omadhaun's misliking for you everyone knows, but what of this kern? Is he a hired knife, or did you do something to raise his dander, too?"

Some of the Romans gathered round grumbled at the Gaul's tone of voice, but Marcus waved them to silence. He was about to say he had only seen the Khamorth that once with Avshar, but there was still a nagging familiarity about him, about the way he kept his gaze fixed on the knife he no longer held.

Scaurus snapped his fingers. "Remember the plainsman at the Silver Gate who tried to stare me down when we came into Videssos?"

"I do that," Viridovix said. "You mean—? Hold still, blast your hide!" he snapped at the prisoner, who was still struggling to break free.

"There's no need to hold him all night," Gaius Philippus said. The senior centurion had found a length of stout rope. "Titus, Sextus, Paulus, give me a hand. Let's go get our bird trussed."

It took all four Romans and the big Gaul to bind the Khamorth. He fought the rope with more fury than he had shown against Scaurus himself, shrieking and cursing in his harsh native tongue. So frenziedly did he kick, scratch, and bite that none of his captors was left unmarked, but in the end to no avail. Even after the ropes were tight around him, he still thrashed against their unyielding grip.

No wonder, the tribune thought, Avshar had chosen to use this man against him. The nomad's already-existing contempt for infantry of any sort must have become a personal hatred when Scaurus won their battle of wills at the city gate. As Viridovix had said, the Khamorth had a reason for furthering the schemes of the envoy of Yezd.

But still—at the Silver Gate the plainsman had been in full control of his faculties, while now he acted for all the world like a madman. Had Avshar given him a drug to heighten his fury? There might be a way to find out. "Gorgidas!" he called.

"What is it?" the Greek answered from the fringes of the crowd around the tied-up Khamorth.

Marcus explained his idea to the doctor, adding, "Can you examine him and find out why his nature has changed so greatly since the last time we saw him?"

"What do you think I've been trying to do? But all these gawkers here are too tightly packed to let me through." The physician was too slight to have much luck elbowing his way into a crowd.

"Let him by. Make way, there," the tribune ordered, moving his men out of the way so Gorgidas could reach the nomad, who lay across Scaurus' own pallet. The physician knelt beside him, touching his forehead, peering into his eyes, and listening to his breathing.

When he stood, his face was troubled. "You were right, sir," he said. Marcus knew how concerned he was when he used the title of respect; Gorgidas was a man with no time for formality. "The poor devil is at the point of death, from some toxic potion, I would say."

"At the point of death?" Scaurus said, startled. "He was lively enough a few minutes ago."

Gorgidas made an impatient gesture. "I don't mean he's liable to die in the next hour, maybe even not in the next day. But die he will—his eyes are sunk in his head, and one pupil is twice the other's size. He breathes like a delirious man, deep and slow. And between his bellows you can hear him grinding his teeth fit to break them. As anyone who has read the writings of Hippokrates will tell you, those are fatal signs."

"Yet he has no fever," the doctor continued, "and I see no sores or pustules to indicate some disease has him in its clutches. Therefore, I must conclude he has been drugged—poisoned would be a better word."

"Can you cure him, do you think?" Marcus asked.

Gorgidas tossed his head in an imperious Greek negative. "I've told you before, I am a doctor, not a worker of miracles. Without knowing what hell-brew is in him, I wouldn't know where to start, and, if I did, it would probably still be useless."

"'Worker of miracles,' your honor said?" Viridovix put in. "Could it be the priests of Phos might save him, where you canna?"

"Don't be ridi—" Gorgidas began, and then stopped in confusion. Marcus had to admire the way he faced up to an idea he did not like. He reluctantly admitted, "That might not be foolish after all. Some of them can do what I'd not have believed—isn't that right, Minucius?"

The legionary a priest had saved outside of Imbros was a stalwart young man whose stubbly whiskers were black almost to blueness. "So you keep telling me," he answered. "I don't recall a bit of it—the fever must have made my wits wander."

"That Nepos fellow you brought over last night seemed a man of sense," Gorgidas suggested to Marcus.

"I think you're right. Nephon Khoumnos will have to know of this, too, though I wouldn't blame him for thinking I'm trying to tear down Videssos' army from the inside out."

"If this sort of garbage goes on, I'd say the Videssian army could use some tearing down," Gaius Philippus said. Privately, his superior officer was beginning to agree with him, but Scaurus had already found that was not something he could tell the Videssians.

The tribune bent to pick up the dagger forced from the Khamorth. He misliked the blade even before he touched it. The pommel was carved into a leering, evil cat's-face, while the hilt was covered by a green, velvety leather that must have come from the skin of a serpent. The blade itself was badly discolored, as if it had been tempered too long or too often.

No sooner had Marcus' fingers folded round the hilt than he dropped the weapon with a cry of alarm. The discolored blade had begun to gleam, not an honest red-gold like the Druids' marks on his sword and

Viridovix', but a wavering yellowish green. The tribune was reminded of some foul fungus shining with the sickly light of decay. He sniffed . . . no, it was not his imagination. A faint corrupt reek rose from the dagger.

He thanked every god he knew that the baneful weapon had not pierced his flesh; the death it would have dealt would not have been clean.

"Nepos must see this at once," Gorgidas said. "Magic is his province."

Marcus agreed, but could not nerve himself to pick up the wicked blade again. Magic was no province of his.

"It came to life when you touched it," Gorgidas said. "Was it glowing when the nomad assailed you?"

"Truth to tell, I have no idea. I had other things on my mind at the moment."

Gorgidas sniffed. "Well, I suppose you can't be blamed," he said, but his tone belied his words. The Greek was a man who, if it befell him to lose his head, would notice the color of the headsman's eyes behind his mask.

Now he stooped down to take the vicious dagger gingerly by the handle. The blade flickered uncertainly, like a half-asleep beast of prey. The doctor tore a strip of cloth from a solider's mantle and wrapped it several times round the dagger's hilt, tying it with an elegant knot he usually used to finish a bandage on an arm or leg.

Only when the knot was done did he touch the hilt with his bare hand. He grunted in satisfaction as the blade remained dark. "That should keep it safe enough," he said, carefully handing the weapon to Scaurus, who took it with equal caution.

Holding the knife well away from his body, Scaurus started for the door, only to be stopped by a guffaw from Viridovix. "Would your honor not think it a good idea to put on a cloak, ere he scandalize some early-rising lass?"

The tribune blinked; he had had too much else to worry about in the commotion to think of clothes. Not sorry to be rid of it, he put the dagger down for a moment to wrap himself in a mantle and strap on his sandals. Then he picked it up again with a sigh and stepped out into the crisp sunrise coolness.

As soon as he reached the door, he discovered how the nomad had been able to get into the barracks without the Roman sentries stopping him or raising the alarm. Both of them were lying in front of the entrance, fast asleep. Amazed and furious, Marcus prodded one none too gently with his foot. The man murmured faintly but would not wake, even after another, harsher, prod. Nor could his fellow guard be roused. Neither seemed harmed in any way, but they could not be brought to consciousness.

When Marcus summoned Gorgidas, the Greek physician was also unable to make the guards stir. "What's happened to them, do you think?" the tribune asked.

"How in blazes do I know?" Gorgidas sounded thoroughly harried. "In this bloody country you have to be a he-witch as well as a doctor, and it puts me at a disadvantage. Go on, go on, fetch Nepos—they're breathing well and their pulses are strong. They won't die while you're gone."

The sun's first rays were just greeting the tops of the city's taller buildings when the tribune began his walk to the Videssian Academy, which was on the northern edge of the palace complex. He did not know whether he would find Nepos there so early, but could think of no better place to start looking for the priest.

As he walked, he watched the sun creep down the walls of the structures he passed by, watched it caress the flowering trees in the palace gardens and orchards, watched their blossoms begin to unfold under its light. And as he walked out from behind the long blue shadow of a granite colonnade, the sun reached him as well.

The dagger he carried was suddenly hot in his hand. At the sun's first touch the blade began to burn, giving off clouds of acrid yellow smoke. The Roman threw it to the ground and backed away, coughing and gasping for breath—the smoke felt like live coals in his lungs.

He thought he heard the metal wail as if in agony and resolved to clamp down on a runaway imagination.

The fire was so furious it soon burned itself out. After the breeze had dispersed the noxious fumes, Marcus warily approached the sorcerous weapon. He expected to see only a lump of twisted, fused metal, but found to his dismay that hilt, pommel, and even Gorgidas' wrappings were still intact, as was a thin rod of steel extending the length of what had been the blade.

A cautious touch revealed the dagger to be cool enough to handle. Fighting back a shudder, the tribune picked it up and hurried on to the Academy.

A four-story building of gray sandstone housed the Videssian center of learning. Though both secular and religious knowledge were taught there, a spire and golden sphere surmounted the structure; here as elsewhere in the Empire, its faith had the last word.

The doorman, half-asleep over his breakfast of bread and hot wine, was surprised his first guest should be a mercenary captain, but polite enough to try to hide it. "Brother Nepos?" he said. "Yes, he's here—he's always an early riser. You'll probably find him in the refectory, straight down this hall, the third door on your right."

This early in the day, the Academy hallway was almost deserted. A young blue-robe looked intrigued as the Roman strode past him but, like the doorman, offered no comment.

Sunlight streamed through the tall, many-paned windows of the refectory and onto its battered tables and comfortably dilapidated chairs. But somehow, instead of accenting their shabbiness, the warm light gave the old furniture the effect of being freshly varnished and newly reupholstered.

Except for the fat, unshaven cook sweating behind his pots, Nepos was alone in the room as Marcus stepped in. The priest stopped with a steaming spoonful of porridge halfway to his mouth. "You look like grim death," he told the tribune. "What has brought you here so early?"

By way of answer, Scaurus dropped what was left of the Khamorth's dagger with a clank onto the priest's table. Nepos' reaction could not have been more emphatic had it been a fat viper in front of him. Forgetting the spoon in his hand, he shoved his chair back as fast as he could. Porridge splattered in all directions. The priest went first red, then pale, to the crown of his shaven head. "Where did you come by this?" he demanded; the sternness his light voice could assume was amazing.

His round face grew more and more grave as the Roman told his tale. When at last Marcus was done, Nepos sat silent for a full minute, his chin cupped in the palms of his hands. Then he bounced to his feet, crying, "Skotos is among us!" with such fervor that the startled cook dropped his spoon into a pot and had to fish for it with a long-handled fork.

"Now that you've been informed," Marcus began, "I should also pass my news on to Nephon Khoumnos so he can question—"

"Khoumnos question?" Nepos interrupted. "No! We need subtlety here, not force. I will put the question to your nomad myself. Come!" he snapped, scooping up the dagger and moving for the door so quickly Marcus had to half trot to catch him up.

"Where are you going, your excellency?" the Academy doorman asked the priest as he hurried by. "Your lecture is to begin in less than an hour, and—"

Nepos did not turn his head. "Cancel it!" Then, to Marcus, "Hurry, man! All the freezing furies of hell are at your back, though you know it not!"

When they got back to the barracks, the bound Khamorth screamed in despair as he saw the consumed weapon Nepos carried. The prisoner shrank in upon himself, drawing his knees up against his belly and tucking his head down into the hollow of his shoulder.

Gaius Philippus, a firm believer in the saving value of routine, had already sent most of the Romans out to the drill field. Now Nepos cleared the barracks of everyone save himself, the nomad, the two unconscious Roman sentries, and Gorgidas, allowing the doctor to act as his assistant.

"Go on, go on," he said, shooing them out before him. "You can do nothing to help me, and a word at the wrong moment could do great harm."

"Sure and he's just like a druid," Viridovix grumbled, "always thinking he knows twice as much as anyone else."

"I notice you're out here with the rest of us," Gaius Philippus said.

"That I am," the Celt admitted. "All too often, your druid is right. It's a rare chancy thing, going against one."

Only a few minutes passed before the sentries came out of the barracks hall. They seemed none the worse for what they had undergone, but had no memory of how their unwilled sleep had begun. As far as they knew, one moment they were on guard, while in the next Nepos was bending over them in prayer. Both of them were angry and embarrassed at failing in their duty.

"Don't trouble yourselves about it," Marcus told them. "You can't be blamed for falling victim to wizardry." He sent them on to exercise with their comrades, then settled back to wait for Nepos to emerge.

And wait he did; the fat little priest did not come forth for another two hours and more. When he appeared at last, Scaurus bit back a shocked exclamation. Nepos' gait was that of a man in the last throes of exhaustion; he clutched Gorgidas' elbow as a shipwreck victim clings to a plank. His robe was soaked with sweat, his eyes black-circled. Blinking at the bright sunlight, he sank gratefully onto a bench. There he sat for several minutes, gathering his strength before he began to speak.

"You, my friend," he told Marcus wearily, "have no notion of how lucky you were to wake, and how much luckier still not to be touched by that accursed knife. Had it pierced you, had it even pricked you, it would have drawn the soul from your body into the deepest pits of hell, there to lie tormented for all eternity. A demon was bound in that blade, a demon to be set free by the taste of blood—or destroyed by Phos' sun, as in fact befell."

In his own world, the tribune would have taken all that as a metaphor for poison. Here he was not so sure . . . and suddenly more than half believed, as he remembered how the dagger had shrieked when struck by sunlight.

The priest continued, "You were right in blaming Avshar for setting upon you the poor, damned nomad inside your hall. Poor lost soul—the wizard linked his life to that of the demon he bore, and when it failed, he began to gutter out, like a candle in air unable to sustain a flame. But the destruction of the demon severed the hold Avshar had on him, and I learned much before his flame fell into nothingness."

"Is your honor saying he's dead?" Viridovix said. "Hardly hurt, he was, in the taking of him."

"He's dead," Gorgidas said. "His soul, his will to live—call it what you like—there was none in him, and he died."

Marcus recalled the doom-filled cry on the Khamorth's lips when he saw the ruin of the weapon he had carried, recalled how he had crumpled in on himself. "Can you trust the knowledge you get from a dying man who was your foe's tool?" he asked Nepos.

"A good question," the priest nodded. Little by little, as he sat, his voice and manner were losing their haggard edge. "The chains the Yezda put on him were strong—I would curse him, but he has cursed himself beyond my power to damn. Nonetheless, Phos has granted those who follow him a means of cutting through such chains—"

"A decoction of henbane is what we used," Gorgidas put in, impatient at Nepos' elliptical phrasing. "I've used it before, Phos notwithstanding. It dulls pain and frees the guard on a man's tongue. You have to be careful, though—too high a dose, and you've put your patient out of pain forever."

The priest plainly did not care for Gorgidas' casual revelation of a secret of his magical craft. But, impelled by larger concerns, he kept his temper, saying, "It is enough that we know two things: Avshar loosed this treacherous assault on you; and he is a sorcerer more powerful in his wickedness than any we have met for years uncounted. Yet by the first action I named, he forfeited the protections all envoys, no matter how evil, enjoy."

A smile of anticipation flitted across Nepos' face as he went on, "So, my outland friends, the fiend has delivered himself into our hands! *Now* we send for Nephon Khoumnos!"

VI

Tʜᴇ ᴛʜᴏᴜɢʜᴛ ᴏꜰ Aᴠꜱʜᴀʀ'ꜱ ʜᴇᴀᴅ ɢᴏɪɴɢ ᴜᴘ ᴏɴ ᴛʜᴇ Mɪʟᴇꜱᴛᴏɴᴇ ʜᴀᴅ so ferocious an appeal to Marcus that he charged away from the barracks hall before he realized he was not sure where to find Khoumnos. Neither was Nepos, who puffed along gamely beside him. "I know of the man, you understand," he said to the Roman, "but I do not know him personally."

Scaurus was not overly worried at his ignorance. He felt sure any soldier in Videssos for longer than a week could give him the directions he needed. The first group he saw was a squad of Namdaleni returning from the practice field. At their head was Hemond of Metepont, his conical helm tucked under his arm. He had seen the tribune, too—he waved his men to a halt and sauntered over to Scaurus.

"For a newly come mercenary, you make the oddest set of acquaintances," he observed with a smile. "It's a long road to travel from the wizard-envoy of Yezd to a priest of the Academy."

Nepos' robes were no different from those of any other priest of similar rank; Hemond, Marcus thought, was uncommonly well informed.

The Namdalener acknowledged his introduction of Nepos with a friendly nod. "Actually," Scaurus continued, "you can do us a favor, if you will."

"Name it," Hemond said expansively.

"We need to see Nephon Khoumnos as quickly as we can, and neither of us is sure where he might be."

"Ho-ho!" Hemond laid a finger alongside his nose and winked. "Going to twist his beard some more over his sleepy sentries, are you?"

Uncommonly well informed indeed, Marcus thought, but this time not quite well enough. He considered for a moment. Remembering that

Hemond and Helvis had backed him against Avshar, he decided he could tell the Namdalener his story. "It's not that—" he began.

When he was done, Hemond rubbed the shaven back of his head and swore in the broad dialect of his homeland. "The snake has really over-reached himself this time," he said, more to himself than to Marcus or Nepos. His face suddenly was that of a hunter about to bag his prey. "Bors! Fayard!" he snapped, and two of his men stiffened to attention. "Get back to quarters and let the men know the rest of us will be de-layed." As the soldiers hurried away, their captain turned back to the Roman. "I'd have given a year's pay to drag that losel down, and here you offer me a free chance!"

He grabbed Scaurus' hand in his double clasp, barked to his troop-ers, "First for Khoumnos and some help, then we peg out Avshar the wizard over a slow fire!" Their full-throated shout of approval made Marcus see again how widely the Yezda was detested.

Hemond may have preferred to fight on horseback, but there was nothing wrong with his legs. He set a pace Marcus was hard pressed to match, one that had Nepos in an awkward half-trot to keep up.

Ten minutes and three expostulating sentries later, they were in Khoumnos' office, a well-lit room attached to the Grand Courtroom of the palace complex. The Videssian looked up from the paperwork he had been fighting. His heavy brows lowered to see Scaurus and Nepos with Hemond and his squad. "You keep odd company," he said to the tribune, unconsciously paraphrasing the easterner he mistrusted.

"That's as may be," the Roman shrugged. "They helped me find you, though, when I needed to." And he told Khoumnos the same tale he had spun out to Hemond shortly before.

Long before he was through, the same predatory eagerness that gripped him and Hemond had communicated itself to the Videssian. A triumphant grin spread over his face; he slammed his fist down onto his desk. Ink slopped out of its pot to mar the sheets over which he had been working. He did not care.

"Zigabenos!" he shouted, and his aide appeared from another room. "If there's not a squad here double-quick, you'll find out if you remember which end of a plow you stand behind."

Zigabenos blinked, saluted, and vanished.

"My men and I want a piece of the wizard," Hemond warned.

"You'll have it," the Videssian officer agreed. Marcus had expected Khoumnos to argue, but if the Videssian was unsure of the Namdaleni's loyalty to the Empire, he had no doubt they hated Avshar more.

Khoumnos was still buckling on his swordbelt when a sweating Zigabenos led a squad of *akritai* into his superior's office. Their arrival filled it almost to overflowing. The native Videssian troops sent suspicious looks at Hemond's mercenaries.

But Khoumnos was master of the situation. He knew he had a cause bigger than any rivalry within the imperial army. A single sentence was enough to electrify his men: "What we and the islanders are going to do, boys, is march over to the Hall of the Ambassadors, winkle our *dear* friend Avshar the Yezda out of his hole, and clap him in irons."

After a second's disbelieving silence, the Videssians burst into cheers. Hemond and his Namdaleni, although they had already cheered once, were more than willing to do so again. In the confined space, the noise was deafening. All dissension forgotten, the double squad—and Nepos and Marcus with it—rushed for the Hall of the Ambassadors like hounds upon a leopard's den.

The Hall, as was only natural, lay close by the Grand Courtroom, so foreign envoys could attend the Emperor at their mutual convenience. Above it flapped, fluttered, or simply hung the emblems of twoscore nations, tribes, factions, and other political entities less easily defined; among them was the leaping panther of Yezd.

The diplomatic calm ambassadors cultivate was not altogether proof against two dozen armed men swarming toward Avshar's dwelling-place. Taso Vones of Khatrish was on the Hall's steps discussing trade in spices and furs with a nomad from the far western plains of Shaumkhiil when he heard the troopers clattering toward him. He looked up, saw the source of the pother, murmured to the Arshaum, "You will excuse me, I hope," and ran for his life.

The nomad ran, too—for the bow he kept in his chamber, to sell himself as dearly as he could.

But the warriors ignored him, just as they ignored the shouts of alarm that rang out in the Hall's lobby as they rushed through it behind

Nephon Khoumnos. The Videssian led them up the wide stairway of polished marble at the lobby's back. As they climbed, he panted, "The whoreson's suite is on the second story. More than once I've been here to ransom prisoners—this is a job I'd rather do!" The men with him yelled their agreement.

Gawtruz of Thatagush was carrying a silver tray loaded with fried meats and candied fruits back to his own suite of rooms when the stairs erupted soldiers behind him. Though fat and past fifty, he still had a warrior's reflexes. He hurled his tray, food and all, at what he thought were his attackers.

Hemond knocked the spinning tray aside with his shield. A man or two cried out as they were hit by hot meat. Another tripped over the trail of grease a skidding fowl had left behind and went sprawling.

"Phos!" Khoumnos muttered. He cried to Gawtruz, "Mercy, valiant lord! We have no quarrel with you—it's Avshar we seek."

At his words, Gawtruz lowered the knife he had drawn from his belt. His eyes widened. "The man of Yezd? He and you are enemies, yes, but he is an embassy and cannot be assailed." Marcus noted Taso Vones had been correct at the ill-fated banquet a few days before—at need, Gawtruz' Videssian was perfect, polished, and unaccented.

"Ambassadors who live within the law of nations enjoy its protections," Khoumnos returned. "Sorcerers who hire knives in the night do not." His men and Hemond's were already gathered before a stout door on which stood Yezd's panther. Khoumnos ordered, "Rap gently once. I would not have it said we invaded the suite without giving warning."

The warning rap was scarcely gentle; a dozen heavy fists slammed into the door. There was no response. "Break it down!" Khoumnos snapped. But the portal so staunchly resisted shoulders and booted feet that Scaurus wondered whether it was merely a strong bar or magic which held it closed.

"Enough of this foolery! Out of my way!" One of the Namdaleni, a dark-haired giant with tremendous forearms, preferred the axe of his Haloga cousins. Men scurried back to give him room to swing. Chips flew and boards split as his axe buried itself helve-deep.

Within a dozen strokes, the door sagged back in defeat. The troopers stepped into their enemy's chambers, weapons at the ready. Khoumnos stood outside the door, repeatedly explaining to the startled, frightened, or angry diplomats who threw questions at him why the Videssians had come.

Marcus' first thought was that, while Avshar's lusts for power and destruction were boundless, he had no corresponding desire for personal luxury. Except for a Videssian desk, the embassy of Yezd was furnished nomad-style. Pillows took the place of chairs, and tables were low enough for men sitting on the ground to use. Cushions and tables alike were black, the walls of the room a smoky gray.

The door between Yezd's public offices and Avshar's private quarters was locked, but a few strokes of the axe dealt with that. But Avshar was no more to be found in his chambers than in the embassy portion of Yezd's suite. Marcus was not surprised; the rooms had a dead feel, a feel of something discarded and forgotten. The Videssians had come too late.

The Yezda's room was as sparely equipped as the office: more black-lacquered low tables, pillows, and a sleeping mat of felt stuffed with horsehair. Above the mat hung the image of a fierce-faced warrior dressed all in black and hurling a livid blue thunderbolt. He strode against the fleeing sun over a pile of naked, bloody victims. "Skotos!" the Videssian soldiers murmured to themselves; their fingers moved in signs against evil.

On one of the tables stood a small brazier and another icon of the dark god Yezd followed. Beside the icon lay the pitiful figure of a white dove with its neck wrung. The brazier was full of ashes; Avshar had left not intending to return and burned those papers he did not wish his foes to see.

Neither Videssians nor Namdaleni would go near that table, but when Marcus walked around it he saw on the floor a scrap of parchment scorched at one edge; it must have fallen from the brazier before the fire could sieze it. He bent to pick it up and shouted in sudden excitement: it was a sketch-map of the city and its walls, with a spidery red line leading from the Hall of the Ambassadors to a tower by the sea.

His companions crowded round him at his yell, peering over his shoulder and asking what he'd found. Their letdown at not trapping Avshar in his lair disappeared when they understood what the Roman was holding. They shook his hand and slapped his back in congratulations. "A second chance!" Hemond whooped. "Phos is truly with us today!"

"There's still no time to lose," Nepos said. "We should celebrate after we catch the Yezda, not before."

"Well said, priest," Hemond agreed. Leaving a couple of his men and a like number of Videssians to search the embassy quarters further, he led the rest out past Nephon Khoumnos, who was still justifying the soldiers' presence to the diplomats crowding around him.

Marcus stuck the fragment of parchment under his nose. Khoumnos' eyes crossed as he snatched it from the Roman's hands and tried to focus on it. "The game is still in play, then!" he exclaimed. He bowed to the envoys and their aides, saying, "Gentles, further explanations must wait on events." He pushed his way through the crowd, shouting to his men, "Wait, fools, I have the map!"

The tower Avshar's sketch had shown was at Videssos' northwest corner, where the city jutted furthest into the strait called the Cattle-Crossing. It was about half a mile north and slightly west of the Hall of the Ambassadors, through the palace complex and the streets of the town, and it seemed mostly uphill.

The tribune felt his heart race and the sweat spring from his brow as he trotted through the city. The troopers with him suffered far more than he, for he was in mantle and sandals while they loped along fully armored. One Namdalener could not stand the pace and fell back, his face flushed lobster-red.

As he ran, Scaurus was spurred on by the knowledge that so cold-blooded a calculator as Avshar could blunder—and blunder badly. Not only had his attempt at assassination gone for nought, but when he set about destroying his papers the most crucial one of all, the route of his escape, failed to burn and gave his pursuers another chance at him. If only he knew, Marcus thought—he'd gnash his teeth behind those veils of his.

The path turned down, bringing the sea wall of Videssos into sight. "That one!" Khoumnos panted, pointed at the square tower straight ahead. But when he sucked in wind, the middle-aged officer had enough breath to shout, "Ho the tower guards! Any sign of Avshar the Yezda?"

No answering shout came. When the soldiers wove their way through the last of the buildings between themselves and the wall, they saw the four-man watch contingent lying motionless in front of the guard tower's open gate. Khoumnos swore horribly. To Marcus he said, "The past five years I can recall no dozing sentries. Now I find them twice in two days, and you as witness both times. In Phos' holy name, I stand ashamed before you."

But the sprawled-out guards suggested only one thing to the tribune—the magic Avshar's nomad tool had used to get into the Roman barracks. He explained quickly, adding, "I don't think they are asleep through any fault of their own; it's some spell the westerner knows. His map did not lie—there may still be time to catch him before he can get down the seaward side of the wall."

Nephon Khoumnos reached out to press his arm. "Outlander, you are a man of honor."

"Thank you," Marcus said, surprised and touched.

"Come on, the two of you!" Hemond exclaimed, tugging his straight sword free of its scabbard. "Time enough for pretty speeches later!" He charged toward and through the gate, the rest of the warriors close behind. Nepos fell behind for a moment to revive the guardsmen Avshar had entranced.

Marcus was almost blind for a few seconds in the sudden gloom of the tower's interior. He stumbled up the tight spiral staircase; the only light in the stairwell came from small arrow slits let into the wall.

"Hold up!" Hemond called from above him. Men cursed as they bumped and tripped trying to stop quickly.

"What is it?" asked Khoumnos, who was several men below the Namdalener.

"I'm at the mouth of a corridor," Hemond replied. "It must lead to a weapons store, or something like that—and, square in the strip of sun from a firing slit, there's a scrap of white wool, just what might get torn from a nomad's robes if he ran past something stickery. We have the bastard hooked!" He laughed aloud in sheer exultation.

An excited hum ran up and down the spiral line of hunters. More swords slid from their scabbards. One by one, the men stepped into the passage Hemond had found.

The narrow corridor within the wall ran about fifty feet before ending in a single doorway. Clutching his sword hilt, Marcus moved forward with the rest of the warriors. He no longer saw Avshar as the dreaded evil mage Nepos had depicted, but as a wicked, frightened fool who had slipped at every turn in his escape attempt and, at the end, managed to close himself in a chamber with but one entrance. He could nearly pity the trapped Yezda on the other side of the door.

Hemond gave that door a tentative push. It swung open easily. The mercenary had been right in his guess at the chamber's function; it was indeed an armory. Through the doorway Marcus could see neat sheaves of arrows, piled spears, rows of maces and swords, and, as he came nearer and gained a wider view, the tip of an outstretched foot upon the floor.

Along with the rest of the soldiers, Scaurus pushed into the storeroom to see better. Unlike most of them, he recognized the dead man lying by the back wall—it was Mebod, Avshar's ever-frightened body servant. His head was twisted at an impossible angle, his neck broken like that of the dove on Skotos' altar in the Yezda's private chamber.

The senselessness and wanton cruelty of slaying this inoffensive little man bewildered the tribune. So did something else—Avshar had surely been here, but was no longer. There was no place to hide among the glittering weapons. Where, then, was the fugitive emissary of Yezd?

At nearly the same moment that thought crossed his mind, the door slammed shut behind them. Though it had opened invitingly to Hemond's lightest touch, now it would not yield to the frantic tugging of all the warriors caught behind it. Suddenly trapped instead of trapper, Marcus felt dread course through his veins.

"Ah, how pleasant. My guests have arrived." At the sound of that deep voice, full of chilly hate, the soldiers' hands fell from the bronze doorlatch. They turned as one, in disbelief and terror. Head still lolling on its right shoulder, eyes blind and staring, the corpse of Mebod was on its feet, but through its dead lips came Avshar's voice.

"You were so kind—and so clever—to answer the invitations I left for you," the wizard went on, bending his servant to his will in death as in life, "that I thought I should prepare fitting hospitality for you." With the jerky grace of a stringed puppet, what had been Mebod threw its hands wide. At their motion the weapons of the armory came alive, flying against the stunned men who, minutes before, had thought themselves about to seize Yezd's wizard-envoy.

One of the Videssians fell at once, a spear driven through chain mail and flesh alike. An instant later a Namdalener was on the ground beside him, his neck pierced from behind by a dagger. Another screamed in fear and pain as a mace laid open his arm.

Never had Marcus imagined—never had he wanted to imagine—a fight like that one, men against spears and swords that hovered in the air and struck like giant angry wasps. It did no good to strike back against them; there was no wielder to lay low. Worse, there was no shuffle of foot, no telltale shift of eye, to give a clue where the next blow would fall. The warriors were reduced to a purely defensive fight and, thus constrained in their very thoughts, suffered wounds from strokes they would have turned with ease had a body been behind them.

With his usual quickness of thought, Hemond slashed at Mebod's animate lich, but his blow did no good—the weapons still came on.

At first clash of enchanted steel, the druids' marks on Scaurus' blade flamed into fiery life. The sword his brand had met clattered to the floor and did not rise again. The same things happened again and yet again. So many blades were hovering for a chance to bite, though, that the unarmored Roman had all he could do to stay alive. He gave the best protection he could to his mates, but when he tried to follow Hemond's lead and strike down Mebod with his potent sword, the disembodied weapons kept him at bay and drove him back, bleeding from several cuts.

Someone was pounding on the door from the outside. Marcus shouted a warning to whoever it was, but his shout was drowned by a bellow of anguish from Hemond. A sword stood hilt-deep in the Namdalener's chest. His hands grabbed at the hilt, then fell limply to his side as he went down.

From the other side of the door came a cry louder even than Hemond's. "Open, in Phos' holy name!" Nepos roared, and the portal sprang back as if kicked. The priest-mage bounded into the weapons store, his arms upraised. He was a short man, but the power crackling from his rotund frame seemed to give him inches he did not possess.

Recognizing the danger in Nepos, Avshar's swooping armory abandoned the mere men-at-arms to dart at this new foe. But the priest was equal to them. He moved his hands in three swift passes, shouting a fraction of prayer or spell with each. Before the blades could touch him, they fell, inert, to the floor. As they did so, Mebod's body sank with them, to become again nothing more than a corpse.

It was like waking from a nightmare. The soldiers still on their feet held their guard for several seconds, hardly daring to believe the air empty and quiet. But quiet as it was, the weapons strewn like jackstraws and the bodies on the ground showed it had been no dream.

As the dazed survivors of the sorcerous assault bent to the fallen, they learned four were dead: the Videssian killed in the first instant of attack and three Namdaleni, Hemond among them. The mercenary officer had died as rescue stood outside the door. Marcus shook his head as he closed Hemond's set eyes. Had he not happened on the Namdalener in his search for Nephon Khoumnos, a good soldier who was becoming a good friend would still be alive.

Still looking down at Hemond's body, the tribune flinched when someone touched his arm. It was Nepos, his chubby features haggard and drawn. "Let me tie those up for you," he said.

"Hmm? Oh, yes, go ahead." Lost in his thoughts, Scaurus had almost forgotten his own wounds. Nepos bandaged them with the same dexterity Gorgidas might have shown.

As the priest worked, he talked, and Marcus learned he was not the only one carrying a burden of self-blame. Nepos could have been talking to anyone or no one; as it happened, the Roman heard his struggle to understand the why of what had taken place.

"Had I not paused to end a small enchantment," the priest said bitterly, "I could have checked this far more wicked one. Phos knows his own ways, but it is an untasty thing to rouse four men from sleep only to see four others die."

"You did what was in your nature, to help wherever you first saw it needed," Marcus told him. "You could not be what you are and have done otherwise. What happened afterwards could not be helped."

Nepos did not agree. "You feel as do the Halogai, that there is a fate no man can hope to escape. But we who follow Phos know it is our god who shapes our lives and we seek to make out his purposes. There are times, though, when those are hard, hard to understand."

Moving slowly, as if still caught up in the bad dream from which they had just escaped, the warriors bound one another's wounds. Almost in silence, they lifted their fallen comrades' bodies—and that of Mebod as well—and awkwardly brought them down the watchtower's spiral stair and out into the sunlight once more.

The sentries Nepos had awakened met them there. One of the watchmen, alarm on his face, said to Marcus, "Please do not blame us for failing, sir. One moment we were all standing to arms, and the next this priest was bending over us, undoing the magic that laid us low. We didn't doze by choice."

At any other time the Roman would have been gladdened by the way his reputation had shot through the Videssian army. As it was, he could only say tiredly, "I know. The wizard who tricked you gulled us all. He got clean away, and I don't doubt many throughout the Empire will have cause to regret it."

"The son of nobody's not safe yet," Nephon Khoumnos declared. "Though he's crossed the strait, he has five hundred miles of travel through our western provinces before he reaches his accused borders. Our fire-beacons can flash word to seal the frontiers long before even a wizard could reach them. I'll go have the beacons fired now; we'll see what kind of welcome our *akritai* ready for that fornicating sorcerer!" And Khoumnos was off, shoulders hunched forward like a determined man walking into a gale.

Scaurus could only admire his tenacity, but did not think much would come of it. If Avshar could get free of the most strongly fortified city this world knew, the Roman did not believe Videssos' border troops, no matter how skilled, would keep him from slipping across the frontier into his own dark land.

He turned to the Namdaleni. Though he shrank from it, there was something he felt he had to do, something for which he needed the good will of these men. He said, "It was an unlucky chance that led me to you this morning. Now three of you have died, thanks to that unlucky chance. I had not known him long, but I was happy to call Hemond my friend. If it is not against your customs, it seems only right for me to be one of those who carries news of his loss to his lady. I bear the blame for it."

"A man lives as long as he lives and not a day more," said one of the men of the Duchy. Whether or not he followed the cult of Phos, some of the ways of his Haloga ancestors still lived in him. The Namdalener went on, "You were doing the best you could for the state that bought your sword. So were we. Service honorably done may cause hurt, but it is no matter for blame."

He paused for a moment to read his countrymen's eyes. Satisfied by what he saw, he said, "There is nothing in our usages to keep you from being the man who brings Hemond's sword to Helvis." Seeing Scaurus' lack of understanding, he explained, "That is our way of saying without word what words are too painful to carry. No blame rests with you," the mercenary repeated, "but were it there, what you are doing now would erase it. I am called Embriac Rengari's son and I am honored to know you."

The other six Namdaleni nodded soberly; one by one, they spoke their names and gave the tribune the two-handed clasp all men of northern descent seemed to share. That brief formality over, they lifted their burdens once more and began the somber journey back to their quarters.

News of what had happened spread like windblown fire, as always in Videssos. Before the soldiers had finished half their short course, the first cries of "Death to Yezd!" began ringing through the city. Scaurus saw a band of men armed with clubs and daggers dash down an alley after some foreigner or other—whether a Yezda or not, he never knew.

As he trudged toward the palace complex, the dead weight of Hemond's body made the tribune's shoulders ache, though he shared it with a Namdalener. He and his companions were all wounded. They slowly made their way to the mercenaries' barracks, pausing more than once to lay down the bodies of the dead and rest for a moment. Their load seemed heavier after each halt.

Marcus kept turning over in his mind why he had taken on himself the task of telling Hemond's woman of his death. What he had said to the Namdalener was true, but he was uneasily aware it was not the entire truth. He remembered how attractive he had found Helvis before he knew she was attached and had a guilty suspicion he was letting that attraction influence his behavior.

Stop it, lackwit, he told himself, you're only doing what has to be done. But . . . she was very beautiful.

The barracks of the Namdaleni were an island of ironic peace in the ferment rising in Videssos. Because they were outlanders and heretics, the men of the Duchy had few connections with the city's ever-grinding rumor mill and had no notion of the snare Avshar had sprung on their countrymen. A couple of men were wrestling outside the barracks. A large crowd cheered them on, shouting encouragements and bets. Two other soldiers practiced at swords, their blades clanging off one another. From a nearby smithy, Marcus heard the deeper ring of a hammer on hot steel. Several islanders were on their knees or haunches shooting dice. It occurred to Marcus that he had seen dicing soldiers whenever he passed their barracks, and they were quick to bet on almost anything. Gambling appealed to them, it appeared.

Someone in the back of the crowd looked up from the half-naked wrestlers and saw the approaching warriors and their grim burden. His startled oath lifted more eyes; one of the fencers whipped his head around and dropped his sword in surprise and shock. His opponent's blade was beginning its victory stroke when its owner, too, caught sight of the bodies the returning troopers bore. The stroke went undelivered.

The Namdaleni rushed up, crying out questions in the broad island patois they spoke among themselves. Marcus could hardly make out their dialect at the best of times; now he was too full of his own misery to make the effort. He and the mercenary who had helped him carry Hemond put down their burden for the last time. The Roman freed Hemond's sword and scabbard from his belt and made his way through the Namdaleni toward their barracks.

Most of the mercenaries stood back to let him pass when they saw what he bore, but one came up and grasped his arm, shouting something in his own speech. Scaurus could not catch more than a word or two, but Embriac replied, "He took it on himself, and his claim to it is good." He spoke in clear Videssian so his countryman and the tribune could both understand him. The islander nodded and let Marcus go.

The barracks of the Namdaleni were, if anything, even more comfortable than the Romans' quarters. Part of the difference, of course, was that there had been a Namdalener contingent in the Videssian army for many years, and over those years the men of the Duchy had lavished much labor on making their dwelling as homelike as they could. By contrast, the Romans had not yet made their hall their own.

Because many of the mercenaries spent a large portion of their lives in Videssian service, it was not surprising that they formed families in the capital, either with women of the Empire or with wives or sweethearts who had accompanied them from Namdalen. Their barracks reflected this. Only the bottom floor was a common hall like that of the Romans, a hall in which dwelt warriors who had formed no household. The upper story was divided into apartments of varying size.

Remembering Helvis waving to him from a window above—was it only a couple of days before?—Marcus climbed the stairway, a wide, straight flight of steps nothing like the spiral stair that had led to Avshar's trap. He felt more misgivings now than he had on the wizard's trail; Hemond's sword in his hand was heavy as lead.

Thanks to his memory of Helvis displaying for him the jewelry she'd brought with her winnings, the tribune knew about which turns to take through the upper story's corridors. From an open doorway ahead, he heard a clear contralto he knew. "Now stay there for a few minutes," Helvis was saying firmly. "I want to find out what the commotion down below is all about."

He and she came into the doorway at the same moment. Helvis drew back a pace, laughing in surprise. "Hello, Marcus!" she said. "Are you looking for Hemond? I don't know where he is—he should have been back from the drillfield some time ago. And what's going on outside? My window won't let me see."

She came to a halt, really seeing him for the first time. "Why so grim? Is anything the . . ." Her voice faltered as she finally recognized the sheathed blade he carried. "No," she said. "No." The color faded from her face; her knuckles whitened as her hand clutched at the doorlatch, seeking a support it could not give her.

"Who is this man, Mama?" A naked boy of about three came up to peer at Scaurus from behind Helvis' skirts. He had her blue eyes and Hemond's shock of blond hair. Marcus had not imagined he could be more wretched, but then he had not known Hemond had a son. "Aren't you going downstairs?" the tot asked his mother.

"Yes. No. In a minute." Helvis searched the tribune's features, her eyes pleading with him to give her some other, any other explanation than the one she feared for Hemond's sword in his hands. He bit his lip until the pain made him blink, but nothing he could say or do would erase his mute message of loss.

"Aren't you going downstairs, Mama?" the child asked again.

"Hush, Malric," Helvis said absently. "Go back inside." She stepped into the hall, closing the door behind her. "It's true, then?" she said, more wonder in her voice than anything else. Though she said the words, it was plain she did not believe them.

Marcus could only nod. "It's true," he answered as gently as he could.

Not looking at the tribune, moving in a slow, dreamlike fashion, she took Hemond's sword from his hands into her own. She caressed the blade's worn, rawhide-wrapped hilt. Her hand, Marcus noticed in one of those irrelevant flashes he knew he would remember forever, though large for a woman's, was much too small for the grip.

Her head still bent, she leaned the sword against the wall by the closed door of her rooms. When at last she looked at the tribune, tears were running down her cheeks, though he had not heard her start to weep. "Take me to him," she said. As they walked down the hall, she clasped his arm like a drowning man seizing a spar to keep himself afloat a few minutes longer.

She was still looking for small things she did not understand to keep from facing the great incomprehensibility that lay, cold and stiffening, outside the barracks. "Why did you bring me his sword?" she asked the tribune. "I mean no harm, no insult, but you are not of our people or our ways. Why you?"

Scaurus heard the question with a sinking feeling. He would have given a great deal for a plausible lie but had none ready; in any case, such false kindness was worse than none. "It seemed only right I should," he said, "because it is all too much my fault he fell."

She stopped as short as if he had struck her; her nails were suddenly claws digging into his flesh. Only by degrees did the misery on the Roman's face and in his voice reach her. Her face lost the savage look it had assumed. Her hand relaxed; Marcus felt blood trickle down his arm from where her nails had bitten him.

"Tell me," she said, and as they walked down the stairs he did so, hesitantly at first but with growing fluency as the tale went on.

"The end was very quick, my lady," he finished lamely, trying to find such consolation as he could. "He could hardly have had time to feel much pain. I—" The upwelling futility of any apology or condolence he might make silenced him effectively as a gag.

Helvis' touch on his arm was as gentle as it had been fierce a minute before. "You must not torment yourself for doing what was only your duty," she said. "Had your roles been reversed, Hemond would have asked the same of you. It was his way," she added softly, and began to cry again as the truth of his death started forcing its way past the defenses she had flung up.

That she could try to comfort him in her own anguish amazed Marcus and made him feel worse at the same time. Such a woman did not deserve to have her life turned upside down by a chance meeting and a wizard's scheme. Another score against Avshar, he decided, as if more were needed.

After the dimness of the interior of the barracks, the bright sun outside dazzled the Roman. Seeing the crowd still ringing the bodies of Hemond and his squadmates, Helvis dropped Scaurus' arm and ran toward them. Suddenly alone among strangers, the tribune felt another burst of empathy for Viridovix' plight. As quickly as he could, he found an excuse to get away and, wishing he had this day back to live over in some other way, went back to the Roman barracks.

As he stood sweating in his full regalia on the elevated central spine of Videssos' amphitheater, Scaurus decided he had never seen such a sea of people gathered together in one place. Fifty thousand, seventy thousand, a hundred twenty thousand—he had no way to guess their numbers. For three days criers ran through the city to proclaim the Emperor would speak this noon; the great arena had begun to fill at dawn and now, a few minutes before midday, almost every inch of it was packed with humanity.

The only clear spaces in all that crush were a lane leading from the Emperor's Gate at the western end of the amphitheater's long oval to its spine and that spine itself. And the clearing of that latter was only relative. Along with statues of marble, bronze, and gold, along with a needle of gilded granite reaching for the sky, the spine held scores of Videssian functionaries in their gaudy robes of state, priests of various ranks in blue regalia, and contingents of troops from every people who soldiered for the Empire. Among them, Scaurus and the maniple he led had pride of place this day, for they stood just below the elevated rostrum from which Mavrikios Gavras would soon address the throng.

To either side of the Romans were squadrons of tall Halogai, unmoving as the statuary they fronted. All the discipline in the world, though, could not keep resentment from their faces. The place of honor the Romans were usurping was at most times theirs, and they were not happy to be displaced by these newcomers, men who would not even show proper respect for the Emperor they served.

But today that central place was rightfully the Romans'; they, indeed, were the reason this assemblage had been called. News of Avshar's sorcerous assault on Scaurus and the deadly snare he had set to make good this escape had raced through the city like fire through parched woodlands. The mob Marcus saw chasing a fleeing foreigner was but the start of troubles. Many Videssians concluded that, if Yezd could reach into their capital to assail them, it was their Phos-given right to take vengeance on anyone they imagined a Yezda—or, at a pinch, on any other foreigners they could find.

Nearly all the folk from what was now Yezd who lived in Videssos were of trading houses that had been in the capital since the days when the Empire's western neighbor was still called Makuran. They hated their ancestral homeland's nomadic conquerors more bitterly than did the people of the Empire. Their hatred, however, was of no avail when the Videssian rabble came roaring up to loot and burn their stores. "Death to the Yezda!" was the mob's cry, and it did not ask questions of its victims.

It had taken troops to quell the riots and douse the flames—native Videssian troops. Knowing his people, the Emperor had known the sight of outlanders trying to quell them would only inflame them further.

And so the Romans, the Halogai, the Khamorth, and the Namdaleni kept to their barracks while Khoumnos used his *akritai* to restore order to the city. Marcus gave him credit for a good, professional job. "Well, why not?" Gaius Philippus had said. "He's probably had enough practice at it."

Those three days had not been altogether idle. An imperial scribe came to record depositions from all the Romans who had been a part of subduing Avshar's luckless pawn of a plainsman. Another, higher-ranking scribe questioned Marcus minutely over every tiny detail he could recall about the nomad, about Avshar himself, and about the spell the Yezda had unleashed in the sea-wall armory. When the tribune asked what point the questions had, the scribe shrugged, blandly said, "Knowledge is never wasted," and returned to the interrogation.

The gabble in the amphitheater rose suddenly as a pair of parasol-carriers stepped from the shadows behind the Emperor's Gate into the sight of the crowd. Another pair emerged, and another, and another, until twelve silk flowers of varied hues bloomed in the narrow passage which twin lines of *akritai* kept open. Rhadenos Vourtzes had been proud of the two sunshades to which his provincial governor's rank entitled him; the imperial retinue was more splendid by six-fold.

The cheering which had begun at first glimpse of the parasol bearers rose to a crescendo of shouting, clapping, and stamping as the Emperor's party proper came into view. Marcus felt the arena's spine quiver beneath his feet; the noise the crowd put forth transcended hearing. It could only be felt, stunning the ears and the mind.

First behind the escort was Vardanes Sphrantzes. It might have been Marcus' imagination, but he did not think many of the cheers went to the Sevastos. Far more beloved by the people was their patriarch Balsamon. In matters of ceremony he outranked even the prime minister, and thus had his place between Sphrantzes and the imperial family itself.

The fat old priest flowered in adulation like a lilac in the sun. His shrewd eyes crinkled into a mischievous grin; he beamed out at the crowd, his hands raised in blessing. When people reached between the tight ranks of guardsmen to touch his robes, more than once he stopped to take hold of their hands for a moment before moving on.

Thorisin Gavras, too, was popular in the city. He was everyone's younger brother, with all the amused toleration that went with that status. Had the Emperor brawled in a tavern or tumbled a serving wench, he would have forfeited all respect due his office. The Sevastokrator, without his brother's burdens, could—and did—enjoy himself to the fullest. Now he strode along briskly, with the air of a man fulfilling an important task he nonetheless found boring and wanted to finish quickly.

His niece, Mavrikios' daughter Alypia, came just before her father. From her demeanor, the amphitheater might as well have been still and empty, not packed to its rearmost benches with screaming citizens. The same air of preoccupation she had shown entering the banquet held her now. Marcus wondered if shyness was at its root rather than indifference; she had been far less reserved in the closer setting of the banquet table and in the imperial chambers.

Several times now the tribune had thought the tumult in the arena could not grow greater, and several times was wrong. And with the entrance of the Emperor, he found himself mistaken once more. The noise was a real and urgent pain, as if someone were driving dull rods through his ears and into his brain.

Mavrikios Gavras was not, perhaps, the ideal Emperor for a land in turmoil. No long generations strengthened his family's right to the throne; he was but a usurping general more successful than his predecessors. Even as he ruled, his government was divided against him, with his highest civil ministers standing to profit most from his fall and doing their best to stifle any reforms which might weaken their own positions.

But ideal or not, Mavrikios was what Videssos had, and in the hour of crisis its people rallied to him. With every step he took, the crescendo of noise rose. Everyone in the amphitheater was standing and screaming. A group of trumpeters followed the Emperor, but in the bedlam they must have been inaudible even to themselves.

Behind the Sevastos, the patriarch, and his family, the Emperor mounted the twelve steps up onto the arena's spine. Each company of soldiers presented arms to him as he passed, the Khamorth and native Videssians drawing empty bows, the Halogai lifting their axes in salute, and the Namdaleni and at last the Romans holding their spears out at arm's length before them.

Thorisin Gavras gave Marcus an eager, predatory grin as he walked by. His thoughts were easy to read—he wanted to fight Yezd, Scaurus had furnished a valid reason for fighting, and so the Roman stood high in his favor. Mavrikios was more complex. He said something to Scaurus, but the crowd's din swept it away. Seeing he could not hope to make himself understood, the Emperor shrugged almost sheepishly and moved on.

Gavras halted for a few seconds at the base of his speaking platform while his retinue, parasols bobbing, arranged themselves around it. And when the Emperor's foot touched its wooden step, Marcus wondered whether Nepos and his wizardly colleagues had worked a potent magic or whether his ill-used ears had given out at last. Sudden, aching silence fell, broken only by the ringing in his head and the thin shout of a fishmonger outside the arena: "Fre-esh squi-id!"

The Emperor surveyed the crowd, watching it settle back into its seats. The Roman thought it hopeless for one man to be heard by so many, but he knew nothing of the subtlety Videssian craftsmen had invested in their amphitheater. Just as the center of the spine was the focus where every sound in the arena reverberated, so words emanating from that one place were plain throughout.

"I'm not the man for fancy talk," the Emperor began, and Marcus had to smile, remembering how, in a Gallic clearing not so long ago, he had used a disclaimer like that to start a speech.

Mavrikios went on, "I grew up a soldier, I've spent all my life among soldiers, and I've come to prize a soldier's frankness. If it's rhetoric you're after, you don't have far to look today." He waved his hand to take in the rows of seated bureaucrats. The crowd chuckled. Turning his head, Scaurus saw Vardanes Sphrantzes' mouth tighten in distaste.

Though unable to resist flinging his barb, the Emperor did not sink it deeply. He knew he needed such unity as he could find in his divided land and spoke next in terms all his subjects could understand.

"In the capital," he said, "we are lucky. We are safe, we are well fed, we are warded by walls and fleets no land can match. Most of you are of families long-settled in the city and most of you have lacked for little in your lives." Marcus thought of Phostis Apokavkos, slowly starving in Videssos' slums. No king, he reflected, not even one so recent and atypical as Mavrikios, could hope to learn of all his country's troubles.

The Emperor was only too aware of some of them, however. He continued, "In our western lands, across the strait, they envy you. For a man's lifetime now, Yezd's poisons have spilled into our lands, burning our fields, killing our farmers, sacking and starving cities and towns, and desecrating the houses of our god.

"We've fought the followers of Skotos whenever we could catch them laden with their plunder. But they are like so many locusts; for every one that dies, two more spring up to take his place. And now, in the person of their ambassador, they spread their canker even into Videssos itself. Avshar the Phos-forsaken, unable to withstand one soldier of the Empire in honest combat, cast his web of deception over another and sent him like a viper in the night to murder the man he dared not face in open battle."

The multitude he addressed growled ominously, a low, angry sound, like the rumble just before an earthquake. Mavrikios let the rumble build a moment before raising his arms for silence.

The anger in the Emperor's voice was real, not some trick of speech-making. "When his crime was found out, the beast of Yezd fled like the coward he is, with more of his unclean magic to cover his trail—and to once more kill for him so he need not face danger himself!" This time the crowd's ire did not subside at once.

"Enough, I say, enough! Yezd has struck too often and taken too few blows in return. Its brigands need a lesson to learn by heart: that while we are patient with our neighbors, our memory for wrongs is also long. And the wrongs Yezd has given us are far beyond forgiveness!" His last sentence was almost drowned by the rancor of the crowd, now nearly at the boil.

Scaurus' critical side admired the way the Emperor had built up his audience's rage step by step, as a mason erects a building with course after course of bricks. Where the Roman had drawn on the speeches he made before becoming a soldier to hearten his troops, Gavras was using his memory of field orations to stir a civilian crowd. If the bureaucrats were the models the people of the city were used to, Mavrikios' gruff candor made for an effective change.

"War!" the assemblage shouted. "War! War!" Like the savage tolling of an iron bell, the word echoed and re-echoed in the amphitheater. The

Emperor let the outcry last as long as it would. Perhaps he was enjoying to the fullest the rare concord he had brought into being; perhaps, thought Marcus, he was trying to use this outpouring of hatred for Yezd to overawe the bureaucrats who opposed his every action.

At last the Emperor raised his hands for quiet, and slowly it came. "I thank you," he told the throng, "for bidding me do what is right in any case. The time for half-measures is past. This year we will strike with all the strength at our command; when next you see me here, Yezd will be a trouble no more!"

The arena emptied after a last rousing cheer, people still buzzing with excitement. Only after the last of them had gone could the guard units, too, stand down and return to their more usual duties.

"What did you think?" Scaurus asked Gaius Philippus as they marched back toward the barracks.

The senior centurion rubbed the scar on his cheek. "He's good, there's no doubt of that, but he's not Caesar, either." Marcus had to agree. Mavrikios had fired the crowd, yes, but Scaurus was sure the Emperor's foes within the government had neither been convinced by his words nor intimidated by the passions he had roused. Such theatrics meant nothing to cold calculators like Sphrantzes.

"Besides," Gaius Philippus unexpectedly added, "it's foolhardy to speak of your triumphs before you have them in hand." And to that thought, too, the tribune could take no exception.

VII

"THERE'S A NAMDALENER OUT FRONT WANTS TO SEE YOU," PHOSTIS
Apokavkos told Scaurus on the morning of the second day after the Emperor's declaration of war. "Says he's Soteric somebody's son."

The name meant nothing to Marcus. "Did he say what he wanted
of me?"

"No; didn't ask him, either. Don't much like Namdaleni. Far as I can
see, the most of them aren't any more than so many—" and Apokavkos
swore a ripe Latin oath.

The ex-farmer was fitting in among the Romans even better than
Marcus could have hoped when he plucked him from his miserable life
in Videssos' thieves' quarter. His face and frame were losing their gaunt-
ness, but that was only to be expected with regular meals.

It was, however, the least of his adaptation. Having been rejected by
the nation that gave him birth, he was doing everything he could to become a full part of the one that had taken him in. Even as the Romans
had learned Videssian to make life within the Empire easier, Phostis was
picking up Latin to blend with his new surroundings. He was working
hard with the thrusting-sword and throwing-spear, neither of them
weapons he was used to.

And . . . Marcus' brain finally noticed what his eyes had been telling
him. "You shaved!" he exclaimed.

Apokavkos sheepishly rubbed his scraped jaw. "What of it? Felt right
odd, being the only hairy-cheeks in the barracks. I'll never be pretty,
with whiskers or without. Can't see why you people bother, though—
hurts more than it's worth, if you ask me. But my naked chin isn't what I
came to show you. Are you going to talk to that damned Namdalener, or
shall I tell him to take himself off?"

"I'll see him, I suppose. What was it that priest said a few days ago?

'Knowledge is never wasted.'" Just listen to you, he thought; anyone would think it was Gorgidas talking.

Leaning comfortably against the side of the barracks hall, the mercenary from the eastern islands did not seem much put out at having had to wait for Scaurus. He was a solidly built man of middle height, with dark brown hair, blue eyes, and the very fair skin that bespoke the northern origins of the Namdaleni. Unlike many of his countrymen, he did not shear the back of his head, but let his hair fall in long waves down to the nape of his neck. Marcus doubted he could be more than a year or two past thirty.

When he recognized the tribune, he straightened and came up to him, both hands extended for the usual Namdalener clasp. Scaurus offered his own, but had to say, "You have the better of me, I'm afraid."

"Do I? I'm sorry; I gave your man my name. I'm Soteric Dosti's son, from Metepont. In the Duchy, of course."

Apokavkos had forgotten Soteric's patronymic, but the mercenary's name meant no more to Scaurus with it. But the Roman had heard of his native town somewhere before. "Metepont?" he groped. Then he found the memory. "Hemond's home?"

"The same. More to the point, Helvis' as well. She's my sister, you see."

And Marcus did see, once he knew of the relationship. Helvis had not mentioned her brother in his hearing, or her father's name to let him guess the kinship, but now it was easy to pick out Soteric's resemblance to her. That their coloring was alike was not enough; many Namdaleni had similar complexions. But Soteric had a harder version of Helvis' ample mouth, and his face, like hers, was wide with strong cheekbones. His nose, on the other hand, was prominent enough to make any Videssian proud, where hers was short and straight.

He realized he was staring rudely. "Your pardon. Will you come in and tell me your business over an early mug of wine?"

"Gladly." Soteric followed the tribune into the barracks; Scaurus introduced him to the legionaries they passed. The Namdalener's greetings were friendly, but Marcus noticed he was unobtrusively taking the measure both of the Romans and of the hall in which they lived. It did not upset the tribune—he would have done the same.

When they sat, Soteric picked a chair whose back faced no doors. With a smile, Marcus said, "Now that you're quite sure you won't be suddenly killed, will you risk a glass of red with me? I think it's too sweet, but everyone hereabouts swears by it."

Soteric's clear skin made his flush easy to see. "Am I as easy to read as that?" the Namdalener asked, shaking his head ruefully. "I've been long enough among the Videssians to mistrust my own shadow, but not long enough, it seems, to keep the fact to myself. Yes, the red will do excellently, thank you."

They sipped awhile in silence. The barracks hall was almost empty, as most of the Romans were at their exercises. As soon as he saw the Namdalener come in the front way, Phostis Apokavkos had vanished out the back, wanting nothing more to do with the mercenary.

Finally Soteric put down his wine and looked at Marcus over his steepled fingertips. "You aren't what I thought you'd be," he said accusingly.

"Ah?" To a statement of that sort, no real answer seemed possible. The Roman lifted his glass to his lips once more. The wine, he thought, really was sticky.

"Hemond—Phos rest him—and my sister both claimed you had no patience for the poisonous subtlety the Empire so loves, but I own I didn't believe them. You were too friendly by half with the Videssians and too quick to win the Emperor's trust. But having met you, I see they were right after all."

"I'm glad you think so, but in fact my subtlety is so great you take it for frankness."

Soteric flushed again. "I had that coming."

"You would know better than I. Don't think too little of your own delicacy, either; it's half an hour now, and I have no more idea of why you're here than when I first set eyes on you."

"Surely you must know that—" the Namdalener began, but then he saw he was judging Marcus by the standards of his own people. "No, there's no reason why you should," he decided, and explained, "Our custom is to offer formal thanks to the man who brings a slain warrior's sword back to his family. Through Helvis, I am Hemond's closest male kin here, so the duty falls on me. Our house is in your debt."

"You would be deeper in my debt if I hadn't seen Hemond that morning," Marcus said bitterly. "You owe me no debt, but rather I one to you. Thanks to that unlucky meeting, a man who was becoming my friend is dead, a fine woman widowed, and a lad I didn't even know existed is an orphan. And you speak of debts?"

"Our house is in your debt," Soteric repeated, and Marcus realized the obligation was real to him, whatever the circumstances. He shrugged and spread his hands, unwillingly accepting it.

Soteric nodded, his part in the Namdalener usage satisfactorily completed. Marcus thought he would now rise and take his leave, but he had other things on his mind besides his custom-assumed debt.

He poured himself a second glass of wine, settled back in his seat, and said, "I have some small rank among my countrymen, and I speak for all of us when I tell you we've watched your men on the practice field. You and our cousins the Halogai are the only folk we know who prefer to fight on foot. From what we've seen, your style of war is different from theirs, and a good deal more precise. Would you be interested in exercising your men against ours and showing us some of what you know? We're horsemen by choice, true, but there are times and terrains where fighting has to be on foot. What say you?"

Here was a proposal to which the tribune could agree with pleasure. "We might learn something from you as well," he said. "Your warriors, from the little I know of them, are brave, well armed, and better ordered than most of the troops I've seen here."

Soteric dipped his head, acknowledging the compliment. After a few minutes of discussion to find a time and day suitable to Romans and Namdaleni alike, they arranged to meet three days hence, three hundred men to a side. "Would you care to lay a stake on the outcome?" Soteric asked. Not for the first time, Marcus thought that the Namdaleni seemed fond of betting.

"Best keep it a small one, lest tempers in the skirmish flare higher than they should," he said. He thought briefly. "What do you say to this: let the losing side treat the winners to a feast at their barracks—food and drink both. Does that sound fair?"

"Outstandingly so," Soteric grinned. "It's better than a money bet, because it should cure any ill feelings left from the fight instead of letting them fester. By Phos' Wager, Roman, I like you."

The oath puzzled Marcus for a moment. Then he remembered Apsimar's slighting reference to the Namdalener belief that, though the battle between good and evil was of unsure result, men should act as though they felt good would win. With a theology of that sort, the tribune thought, no wonder the men of the Duchy enjoyed gambling.

Soteric emptied his glass and started to rise, then seemed to think better of it. "There is one other message I bear," he said slowly.

He was quiet so long Marcus asked, "Do you intend to give it to me?"

The islander surprised him by saying, "When I was coming here, I did not. But, as I said before, you Romans—and you yourself—are not what I'd pictured you to be, and so I can pass it on. It comes from Helvis, you see."

That was enough to gain Scaurus' complete attention. With no idea what to expect, he did his best to keep everything but polite interest from his face. Soteric went on, "She asked me, if I thought it suitable, to tell you that she bears no grudge against you for what befell, and that she feels the sword-bringer's debt extends to her as well as to me."

"She is gracious, and I'm grateful," Marcus replied sincerely. It would have been all too easy, after a few days of bitter reflection, for Helvis to grow to hate him for his part in Hemond's death.

At drill, the Romans proved as eager to scrimmage with the Namdaleni as Scaurus had thought they would. They did their best to catch an officer's eye for inclusion in the select three hundred, working harder than they had in weeks. Marcus' wager touched their pride; in their skirmishes at Imbros they had become convinced they were better soldiers than any other infantry the Empire had. They were keen to prove it again at the capital.

"You'd not be leaving me out of the shindy for misliking fighting in line, now would you?" Viridovix asked anxiously as they trudged back through the city from the field.

"I wouldn't think of it," Scaurus assured him. "If I tried to, you'd come after me with that sword of yours. Better you should use it on the Namdaleni."

"All right, then."

"Why this passion for carving up your fellow man?" Gorgidas asked the Celt. "What satisfaction do you take from it?"

"For all your bark, my Greek friend, you're a cold-blooded man, I ween. Fighting is wine and women and gold all rolled up into one. Never do you feel more alive than after beating your foe and seeing him drop before you."

"And never more dead than when he beats you," Gorgidas retorted. "It would open your eyes to see war from a doctor's view—the filth, the wounds, the pus, the arms and legs that will never be sound again, the face of a man dying over days with a stab in his belly."

"The glory!" Viridovix cried.

"Tell it to a bloodsoaked boy who's just lost a hand. Don't speak to me of glory; I patch the bodies you build it on." The physician stamped off in disgust.

"If you'd lift your face from the muck you'd see more!" Viridovix called after him.

"Were you not strewing corpses through it, the muck and I would never meet."

"He hasn't the proper spirit at all, at all," Viridovix sadly told Scaurus.

The tribune's thoughts kept slipping back to Hemond. "Hasn't he? I wonder." The Gaul stared at him, then moved away as if afraid he might have something catching.

Nepos was waiting for them back at the barracks. The fat priest's face was too jowly to grow truly long, but he was not a happy man. After polite greetings, his voice became beseeching as he asked Marcus, "Tell me, have you recalled anything of any relevance whatever to Avshar in the time since the Emperor's investigators questioned you? Anything at all?"

"I don't think I'll ever recall any more of Avshar than they pulled out of me," Marcus said, remembering the interrogation he had undergone. "They couldn't have wrung more from me with pincers and red-hot irons."

Nepos' shoulders slumped. "I feared you would say as much. Then we are stymied, and the accursed Yezda—may Phos turn his countenance from him—has won another round. Like a weasel, he slips through the tiniest holes."

The Roman had thought that, once Avshar reached the western shore of the Cattle-Crossing, any chance of laying hold of him was gone. He put no faith in Khoumnos' fire-beacons to the frontier; the border was too long, too weakly held, and too often punctured by raiders—and even armies—out of Yezd. But from Nepos' disappointment, it seemed the priest had held real hopes of locating the wizard, hopes now dashed. When Scaurus asked him about this, he got a dispirited nod as answer.

"Oh, indeed. There should have been nothing easier than to trace him. When he fled the Hall of the Ambassadors, he had to leave nearly all his gear behind, not least the smoking altar to his dark god. What was once his, of course, retains its affinity for him, and through the possessions, our mages have the skill to find their owner. Or so they should, at any rate. But there was only a great emptiness awaiting their search, a void as wide as the land where Avshar could be hiding. He has baffled seven of our most potent wizards, your servant among them. His sorcery keeps to none of the scruples that those who follow good needs must observe, and the fiend is strong, strong."

Nepos looked so gloomy Marcus wanted to cheer him in some way, but he could find nothing cheerful to say. Like a giant pursued by pygmies, Avshar had shaken loose of those who would check him and was free to unleash whatever blows against the Empire his foully fertile mind could devise.

"In the days before the Yezda swallowed them down," Nepos said, "the folk of Makuran had a favorite curse: 'May you live in interesting times.' Until you and yours came to Videssos, my friend from far away, it never struck me what a potent curse that could be."

The field where Videssos' soldiers trained for war was just outside the southern end of the great city wall. Looking southeast, it was easy to see the island the Videssians called the Key, a purple mass on the gray horizon. Lying between the Empire's eastern and western dominions, it also commanded the approach to the capital from the Sailors' Sea. It was, Marcus knew, second only to the city itself as center for the imperial fleets.

But the tribune's thoughts were not really on the distant Key, not when more urgent matters were so much closer. His handpicked band of three hundred legionaries was eyeing the Namdaleni limbering themselves up at the far end of the drillfield. Gorgidas had wanted to call the troop "the Spartans," for their numbers were the same as those of the gallant company which had faced Xerxes' Persians at Thermopylae.

Scaurus demurred, saying, "I know they are part and parcel of your Greek pride, but we need a name of better omen—as I recall, none of those men survived."

"No, two did live, it's said. One made up for it with a brave fight at Plataia the next year; the other hanged himself for shame. Still, I take your point."

As he watched the Namdaleni stretch and twist, the tribune thought, not for the first time, how physically impressive they were. At least as much taller than the Romans as were the Celts, their height was made still more intimidating by the conical helms they preferred. They were wider in the shoulder and thicker in the chest than the Gauls, too, and wore heavier armor. That, though, was partly because they liked to fight from horseback; afoot, so much mail might tire them quickly.

Between the Namdaleni and Romans paced a score of umpires, Videssians and Halogai of known integrity. They bore whistles made of tin and white wands. It was easy for the combatants to carry spears without points, but swordplay, even in sport, could grow bloody unless controlled.

Marcus was getting used to the way rumors of all sorts flashed through Videssos, but he was still surprised by the crowd round the drill field's edge. There were Romans and Namdaleni in plenty, of course, and officers and men from Videssos' native soldiery as well. But how had the colorfully dressed civil servants and the large numbers of ordinary city folk learned of the impending match? And the last time Scaurus had seen the skinny envoy of the Arshaum, he was running for his bow at the Hall of the Ambassadors. How had he heard of this meeting?

The tribune had his answer to that, at least, within moments. The nomad shouted something in the Romans' direction and Viridovix replied with a wave. The tall, fair Gaul and swarthy little plainsman were odd to think of as a pair, but they had plainly come to know and like each other.

The chief umpire, a Haloga commander called Zeprin the Red, beckoned the two leaders to the center of the field. The burly Haloga took his name not from his hair, which was blond, but from his complexion. Atop a thick neck, his face was almost the color of poached salmon. Gorgidas would have called him a good candidate for apoplexy, but he was not a man to argue with.

Marcus was pleased to see Soteric as his opposite number. There were higher-ranking Namdaleni, true, but Dosti's son had the privilege of heading the men of the Duchy because he had arranged their meeting with the Romans.

Zeprin looked sternly from one leader to the other. His slow, drawling Haloga accent lent his words gravity. "This frolic is for pride and for sport. You know that, and your men know it—now. See they remember it after they take a spearshaft in the ribs. We want no riots here." He flicked his eyes about to see if any of his Videssian colleagues were close enough to hear. Satisfied, he lowered his voice to resume, "I've no real fears—there's not a city man among you. Have fun—I only wish I had a sword in my hand to join you, not this puny wand."

Scaurus and Soteric trotted back to their troops. The Romans were aligned in three maniples, two side by side at the fore and the third in reserve behind them. Their opponents formed in a single deep column with a forward fence of spears. Soteric was in the center of the first rank.

When he was sure both sides were ready, Zeprin swung his wand in a circle over his head. His fellow umpires scrambled out of the way as the Romans and Namdaleni bore down on each other.

Just as the chief umpire had said, it was hard to remember this was not real combat. The faces of the Namdaleni were set and grim under their bar nasals. The forward thrust of their bodies, their white-knuckled hands tight on their long spears—*poles*, the tribune reminded himself—their yells to terrify their foes—only the cold glint of steel from their spearheads was missing.

Closer and closer they came. "Loose!" the tribune shouted, and his front rank flung their dummy *pila*. Most bounced harmlessly from the shields of the Namdaleni. That was not as it should be; with their points and soft-iron shanks, real *pila* would have fouled the islanders' bucklers and forced the mercenaries to discard them.

Here and there a spear thudded home against mail or flesh. Umpires tooted frantically and waved their wands, ordering "killed" warriors to the sidelines. One islander, who felt his armor would safely have turned the spear, screamed abuse at the referee who had declared him dead. The umpire was a Haloga half a head taller than the incensed man of the Duchy. He listened for a few moments, then planted a huge hand on the Namdalener's chest and shoved. His attention was back to the skirmish before the mercenary hit the ground.

The Namdaleni did not use their pikes as throwing weapons. Standing up under the Roman volleys, they accepted their mock casualties until they could close with the legionaries. The weight of their phalanx and the length of their thrusting-spears began to tell then. Unable to get close enough to their foes to use their swords with any effect, the Romans saw their line begin to sag in the middle. More and more now, the whistles and the waving, tapping wands of the umpires ushered Scaurus' men from the field.

The men of the Duchy shouted in anticipated victory. Gaius Philippus was beset by two Namdaleni at once. His sword darted like an adder's tongue as he desperately held them off. Then Viridovix came rampaging up behind the easterners. One he flattened with a brawny fist; he traded sword strokes with the other for a few hot seconds, then, delicate as a surgeon, barely touched the islander's neck with the edge of his blade. Ashen-faced, the Namdalener staggered away. He heard the umpire's whistle with nothing but relief. The Romans—and some of the Namdaleni as well—yelled applause for the Celt's swordplay.

More than one man had really fallen; even without their points, the spearshafts both sides used were effective weapons. Here a man staggered away clutching a broken arm, there another was stretched full length on the ground, stunned or worse by a blow to the side of the head. A couple on each side had real sword wounds, too. The men were doing their best to use the flats of their blades instead of edges or points, but accidents had to happen.

Marcus paid scant heed to the casualties. He was too busy trying to keep the Namdaleni from splitting his wider battle line and beating the Romans in detail. Also, thanks to his high-crested helm and red cape of rank, he was a primary target for the islanders. Some fought shy of his already fabled sword, but to the bravest of the brave it was challenge, not deterrent.

Soteric had leaped for him at the outset, high glee on his face. The Roman ducked the lunge of his spear. Before he could reply with his own shorter weapon, the swirl of fighting swept them apart. Another Namdalener clouted him with a broken spearshaft. The tribune saw stars and waited for wand or whistle to take him out of action, but none of the referees spotted the stroke.

Scaurus fought his way through the press to his senior centurion, who had just sent an islander from the fray by slipping past his thrust and thumping him on the chest with his sword. The tribune bellowed his plan at the top of his lungs. Some of the Namdaleni must have heard him, but he did not care—where in this world would they have learned Latin?

When he was through, Gaius Philippus raised a startled eyebrow. "You're sure?"

"I'm sure. They're certain to beat us if we keep fighting on their terms."

"All right." The centurion brushed the sweat from his forehead with his sword arm. "This puts it all on one throw, doesn't it? But I think you're right—we've got nothing to lose. The bastards are just too big to deal with, straight up. You want me to lead it, I hope?"

"No one else. Take the Gaul along, too, if you find him."

Gaius Philippus grinned wolfishly. "Aye, if it works he'd be just the man I want. Wish me luck." He slipped back through the Roman ranks, shouting orders as he went.

The third, rearmost, maniple had not yet been entirely committed to the fighting, despite the pressure at the front. Gaius Philippus pulled about thirty men from the last couple of ranks and led them at a fast trot round the left side of the Romans' line. As he ran, he caught Viridovix's eye and waved for him to join them.

"Good-bye to you, now," the Celt told the man he was fighting; he checked his slash inches from the flinching Namdalener's face. Before a nearby umpire could tap his victim, Viridovix was free of the crush and loping after the centurion and his flanking party.

The next minute or two would tell the story, Marcus knew. If the Namdaleni could break through his suddenly thinned line before Gaius Philippus took them in flank, it would be all over. If not, though, he would have built himself a miniature Kynoskephalai. Just as Flaminius had against King Philip of Macedon's phalanx one-hundred-forty years before, he was using his troops' ability to maneuver and fight in small units to overcome a more heavily-armed, less wieldy foe.

Learning Greek was good for something after all, he thought irrelevantly. If it hadn't been for Polybios, I might never have thought of this.

It was going to be very close, though. The Roman center was stretched almost to the breaking point. There in the very heart of the fire stood the legionary Minucius like a stone wall. His helmet was jammed down over one ear by some blow he had taken and his shield was almost beaten to bits, but he was holding the Namdaleni at bay. Other Romans, driven back by the men of the Duchy, rallied to him and kept the line intact.

Then the pressure on them suddenly eased as Gaius Philippus and his little band crashed against the easterners' flank. The pikes which had given the Romans so much trouble now proved the bane of the islanders. Hampered by their long shafts, the Namdaleni could not spin to meet the new threat without fouling each other and throwing their lines into chaos. Yelling their own victory paean, the Romans slid into the gaps thus exposed and worked what would have been a ghastly slaughter. Behind them came sweating, panting referees to reckon up their victims.

In this sort of fight, with all order fallen by the wayside, Viridovix was at his best. Like some runaway engine of destruction, he howled through the disintegrating Namdalener ranks, smashing pikeshafts to kindling and caving in shields with blows of his mighty sword. His long red locks streamed from under his helmet, a private battle banner.

As the Namdaleni faltered, the Romans' main line surged forward too, completing the work the flanking column had begun. The demoralized islanders could not stand against them. Soon those whose dooms the umpires had not decreed were a small, struggling knot almost surrounded by their conquerors.

Soteric was still there, fighting with the best of them. When he saw Marcus prowling round the Namdaleni looking for an opening, he cried with a laugh, "Vile foe, you'll not take me alive!" He rushed at the tribune, sword held high over his head. Grinning in return, Scaurus stepped up to meet him.

Helvis' brother was quick and strong and as skillful a user of the slashing style as any Marcus had faced. The Roman had all he could do to keep himself untouched, parrying with his own blade and blocking Soteric's cuts with his shield. He was panting at once, as was the islander—mock-fighting, it seemed, was about as tiring as the real thing.

A legionary ran up to help his commander. Distracted by the new threat, Soteric left himself unguarded for an instant, and Marcus' blade snaked past his shield to ring off his breastplate. Zeprin the Red tooted his whistle and pointed at the Namdalener with his wand.

Soteric threw both hands in the air. "Beset by two at once, your valiant leader falls," he shouted to his men. "The time has come to ask the enemy for mercy." Quite realistically, he tumbled to the ground. The few easterners still in the fray doffed their helmets in token of surrender.

"A cheer for our enemies in this fight, our friends in the next!" Marcus called, and the Romans responded with a will. The Namdaleni gave back the compliment. The two groups left the field as one. Marcus saw a man of the Duchy help a hobbling Roman along, watched one of his legionaries demonstrating the thrusting stroke to a pair of easterners, and decided the morning's work had been a great success.

Miraculously risen from the slain, Soteric caught up with the tribune. "Congratulations," he said, taking the Roman's hand. "I have to ask your indulgence in putting off payment of our stake for a day or two. I felt so sure we would win, I fear I laid in no supplies for a feast I didn't think we'd have to give."

"No hurry," Marcus said. "Your men fought very well." He meant it; the Namdaleni, not natural foot soldiers, had given the Romans all they wanted.

"Thank you. I thought we were going to push straight through you until you sprang that flanking maneuver on us. That was quick thinking."

"The idea wasn't altogether mine, I'm afraid." He explained how he had borrowed Flaminius' solution to a similar tactical problem.

Soteric nodded thoughtfully. "Interesting," he commented. "You're drawing on knowledge of war no one here can match. That could be precious one day."

It was the Roman's turn to nod; the same thought had crossed his mind. And because his nature was one to grapple with all sides of a question, he also wondered what the Videssians and their neighbors knew of war that Rome had never learned . . . and what price he would have to pay for instruction.

Torches, lamps, and fat beeswax candles kept the courtyard in front of the Namdalener barracks bright as day, though by now the sun was a couple of hours gone. The courtyard, most of the time a pleasant open place, was full of splintery benches and tables hastily made by throwing boards over trestles. The benches were full of feasters and the tables piled high with food.

Except for an unlucky handful who had drawn sentry duty, all the Romans were there to collect the prize they'd won from the Namdaleni. They and the easterners seemed to have nothing but respect for each other. Seating arrangements intermingled the two groups, and those on both sides who had been in the bout three days before swapped stories and proudly displayed their bandages to their admiring comrades.

Roast pork, beef, mutton, and goat were the main courses, eked out with fowl and the fish and other seafood so easily available in the city. To the dismay of the Namdaleni, most of the Romans gave everything a liberal dousing with the spicy sauce of fermented fish the Videssians loved. The men of the Duchy kept the puritan palates of their northern ancestors, but to the Romans liquamen was a condiment known and loved for many years.

"I suppose you like garlic, too," Soteric said with a shudder.

"Don't you?" Marcus replied, amazed anyone could not.

Wine, ale, and mead flowed like water. Thanks to the sweetness of the local wines, the tribune found he was developing a real taste for the thick, dark ale the Videssians brewed. But when he said that to Soteric, it was the islander's turn for surprise. "This bilgewater?" he exclaimed. "You should come to the Duchy, my friend, where you drink your ale with a fork."

Viridovix, an earthenware mug in his hand, said, "Why anyone would drink ale—with a fork or no, mind you—when there's the blood of the grape to be had is past my understanding. In the land where I was born, ale was a peasant's drink. For the chiefs, now, it was wine, when we could get it and when we could afford it. A dear thing it was, too, that I'll tell you."

Some fine wines came from Narbonese Gaul, with its warm Mediterranean climate, but Marcus realized he had seen no vines in Viridovix's northern homeland. Like most Romans, the tribune had drunk wine from childhood and took it very much for granted. For the first time, it occurred to him how precious it could be when hard to come by.

At the Celt's right hand sat his nomad friend from the far northwest; the Arshaum had given his name as Arigh, son of Arghun. The night was mild, but he wore a wolfskin jacket and a hat of red fox. His hard, lean frame and the lithe, controlled intensity of his movements reminded Scaurus of a hunting hawk. Until now he had been too busy with heroic eating to say much, but the talk of drink gained his interest.

"Ale, mead, wine—what difference does it make?" he said. He spoke Videssian fairly well, with a clipped, quick accent in perfect accord with the way he carried himself. "Kavass, now, is a man's drink, made from his horses' milk and with a kick as strong."

The stuff sounded ghastly, Marcus thought. He also noticed that Arigh's derisive comment about the drinks before him was not keeping him from downing quite a lot of them.

At the rate food was vanishing, it was no easy task to keep the tables loaded. Almost as if they were a bucket brigade battling a fire, the Namdalener women made never-ending trips from the kitchens with full platters and pitchers and back to them with empties. Marcus was surprised to see that Helvis was one of them. When he remarked on it, Soteric said with a shrug, "She told me she would sooner distract herself than sit alone and ache. What could I say to that?"

The servers were, most of them, much like the soldiers' women Scaurus had known in Rome's dominions. They thought nothing of trading bawdry with the men they were attending; pats and pinches brought as many laughs as squeaks of outrage. Through all that Helvis passed unaffronted; she wore her mourning like invisible armor. Her look of quiet sorrow and her air of remoteness, even when bending over a man's shoulder to fill his winecup, were enough to deter the most callous wencher.

More and more drink was fetched as time went by, and less and less food. Never sedate to begin with, the feast grew increasingly boisterous. Romans and Namdaleni learned each other's curses, tried to sing each other's songs, and clumsily essayed each other's dances. A couple of fights broke out, but they were instantly quelled by the squabblers' neighbors— good feelings ran too high tonight to give way to quarrels.

More than a few people wandered into the courtyard to see what the racket was about, and most of them liked what they found. Scaurus saw Taso Vones several tables away, a mug of wine in one hand and a partridge leg in the other. He waved to the ambassador of Khatrish, who made his way through the crowd and squeezed in beside him.

"You're kind to want anything to do with me," he said to the tribune, "especially if you recall that the last time I set eyes on you, I did nothing but flee."

Marcus had drunk enough wine and ale to make him brush aside such trifles. "Think nothing of it," he said grandly. "It was Avshar we were after, not you." That, though, served to remind him of the pursuit and its grievous outcome. He subsided, feeling like a blockhead.

Vones cocked his head to the side and watched the Roman out of one eye, for all the world like some bright-eyed little sparrow. "How curious," he said. "You of all people are the last I'd expect to find hobnobbing with the Namdaleni."

"Why don't you shut up, Taso?" Soteric said, but from his resigned tone he felt it would do no good. Evidently he knew the Khatrisher and, like so many, was used to giving him leeway. "I think you talk for the sake of hearing yourself."

"What better reason?" Vones returned with a smile.

He would have said more, but Marcus, his curiosity fired by Vones' comment, interrupted him. "What's wrong with these folk?" he asked, waving to encompass the courtyard and everyone in it. "We get on well with them. Is something amiss in that?"

"Easy, easy." The ambassador laid a warning hand on his arm, and he realized how loudly he'd spoken. "Why don't we take an evening stroll? The night-blooming jasmine is particularly sweet this time of year, don't you think?" He turned to Soteric. "Don't worry, my island friend. I shan't pick his pocket—I can guess what you have planned for later."

Soteric shrugged; he had gotten involved in a conversation with the Namdalener on his left, who was making a point about hunting dogs. "I don't like the hook-nosed breed," the man was saying. "It makes their mouths too small to hold the hare. And if they have gray eyes, too, so much the worse—they can't see to grab the beast in the first place."

"About that I'm not so sure," Soteric said, swigging. The more he drank, the more his island drawl came to the fore; his last word had sounded like "shoo-ah." He went on, "Gray-eyed hounds have keen noses, they say."

With scant interest in hunting dogs, gray-eyed or otherwise, Marcus was willing to follow Taso Vones as he sauntered out toward the darkness beyond the courtyard. The emissary kept up a nonstop chatter about nightflowers and other matters of small consequence until they had cleared the press. When he was satisfied no one could overhear, his manner changed. Giving the Roman more of that one-eyed study, he said, "I have yet to decide if you are the cleverest man or the greatest fool I've met lately."

"Do you always speak in riddles?" Marcus asked.

"Most of the time, actually; it's good practice for a diplomat. But forget me for the moment and look at yourself. When you met Avshar with swords, I felt sure our acquaintance would be short. But you won, and it seemed you knew what you were all about after all. And now this!"

"Now what?" the tribune wondered, thoroughly bewildered.

"You and your men beat the Namdaleni in your exercise. Well and good. You must have made Nephon Khoumnos proud and likely brightened the Emperor's day as well. The men of the Duchy are very good troops; Mavrikios will be glad to know he has loyal men who can stand against them at need."

He shot an accusing finger at Scaurus. "Or are you loyal? Having beaten them, what do you do? Boast of it? Hardly. You crack a bottle with them as if you and they were the best of friends. Are you trying to make the Emperor nervous? Or do you think the Sevastos will like you better now? After those herrings, I doubt it—yes, I saw you pause, and your stomach seems sound enough to me."

"What has Sphrantzes to do with—" Scaurus began. His mouth snapped shut before the question was done, for he knew the answer. The Namdaleni were mercenaries, of course, but what that meant had not struck him until now. It was not the present Emperor or his backers who employed foreign troops. That had been the policy of the bureaucrats of the capital, who used their hired swords to keep Gavras and his ilk in check while they ran the Empire for their own benefit. . . . And at their head was Vardanes Sphrantzes.

He swore, first in Videssian for Taso Vones' benefit, then in Latin to relieve his own feelings. "I see you understand me now," Vones said.

"This is nothing more than settling up a bet," Scaurus protested. Taso Vones lifted an eloquent eyebrow. No other comment was needed. The Roman knew how easy it was to judge a man by the company he kept. Caesar himself, in his younger days, had fallen into danger through his association with Marius' defeated faction.

Besides, there was no denying he did like the Namdaleni. They had a workmanlike approach to life, one rather like the Romans'. They did not show the Videssians' touchy pride and deviousness, nor yet the dour fatalism of the Halogai. The men of the Duchy did the best with what they had, an attitude that marched well with the tribune's Stoic background. There are other reasons, too, he whispered deep inside himself.

He remarked, "It's rather too late to worry about it now, wouldn't you say?" Then he asked, "Why bother warning me? We hardly know each other."

Vones laughed out loud; like the patriarch Balsamon's, his laugh had real merriment in it. He said, "I've held my post in the city eight years now and I'm scarcely the oldest hand here—Gawtruz has been an ambassador for twice that long and more. I know everyone, and everyone knows me. We know the games we play, the tricks we try, the bargains we drive—and most of us, I think, are bloody bored. I know I am, sometimes.

"You, though, you and your Ronams"—He watched Marcus flinch, —"are a new pair of dice in the box, and loaded dice at that. It's whether you throw ones or sixes that remains to be seen." He scratched his fuzzy-bearded chin. "Which reminds me, we probably should be wandering back. Soteric won't talk about hook-nosed hounds forever, I promise you that."

When the tribune pressed him to explain himself, he refused, saying, "You'll see soon enough, I suspect." He headed toward the court-yard, leaving Scaurus the choice of staying behind by himself or following. He followed.

Taso Vones grunted in satisfaction when they rounded the last corner. "A little early," he said, "but not bad. Too early is better than too late, else we'd not find room at the games we favor—not for stakes we can afford, at any rate." Gold and silver clinked as he dug in his pouch for coins.

As he stared at the scene before him, Marcus wondered about his earlier analysis of Namdalener character. Were they fond of gambling because they believed in Phos' Wager, or had their theologians concocted the Wager because they were gamblers born? At the moment, he would have bet on the latter—and likely found an islander to cover his stake.

Most of the tables and benches had disappeared. In their places were circles chalked on the ground for dice-throwing, wheels of fortune, boards for tossing darts, others for hurling knives, a wide cleared space with a metal basin set in its center for throwing the dregs from winecups—as he expected, Scaurus saw Gorgidas there; the Greek was a dab hand at kottabos—and other games of skill or chance the tribune did not immediately recognize.

He rummaged in his own pouch to see what money he had. It was about as he had thought—some bronze pieces of irregular size and weight, some rather better silver, and half a dozen goldpieces, each about the size of his thumbnail. The older, more worn coins were fine gold, but the newer ones were made pale by an admixture of silver or blushed red with copper. With its revenues falling, the government, as governments will, had resorted to cheapening the currency. All its gold coinage, of whatever age, was nominally of equal value, but in the markets and shops the old pieces took a man further.

Videssian rules at dice, he had learned during the long winter at Imbros, were different from those at Rome. They used two dice here, not three, and Venus—a triple six, the best throw in the game he knew—would only have brought a hoot of derision even with a third dice allowed. A pair of ones—"Phos' little suns," they called them—was the local goal. You kept the dice until you threw their opposite—"the demons," a double six—in which case you lost. There were side bets on which you would roll first, how many throws you would keep the dice, and anything else an ingenious gambler could find to bet on.

The first time the dice came his way, Scaurus threw the suns three times before the demons turned up to send the little bone cubes on to the Namdalener at his left. That gave him a bigger stake to play with, one he promptly lost in his next turn with the bones—on his very first cast, twin sixes stared balefully up at him.

Shouts and applause came from the circle round the kottabos basin. Marcus looked up from his own play for a moment, to find it was just as he'd thought; with that deadly wristflick of his, Gorgidas was making the basin ring like a bell, flicking in the lees from farther and farther away. If he didn't get too drunk to stand, he'd own half the Namdaleni before the night was through.

Scaurus' own luck was mixed; he would win a little before dropping it again, get behind and make it up. His area of attention shrank to the chalked circle before him—the money in it, the dice spinning through, the men's hands reaching in to pick up the cubes, gather in their winnings, or lay new bets.

Then, suddenly, the hand that took the dice was not masculine at all, but a smooth, slim-wristed lady's hand with painted nails and an emerald ring on the forefinger. Startled, Marcus looked up to see Komitta Rhangavve, with Thorisin Gavras beside her. The Sevastokrator wore ordinary trousers and tunic and could have been in the game an hour ago, for all Scaurus had noticed.

Komitta slightly misinterpreted his surprise. Smiling prettily at him, she said, "I know it's against custom, but I so love to play myself. Do you mind?" Her tone warned that he had better not.

That he really did not care made it easier. "Certainly not, my lady." On the other hand, even if he had minded, he could scarcely say so, not to the Sevastokrator's woman.

She won twice in quick succession, letting her stake ride each time.

When her third series of rolls ended by wiping her out, she angrily hurled the dice away and cursed with unladylike fluency. The gamblers snickered. Someone found a new pair of dice and from that moment she was an accepted member of the circle.

With his landed wealth, Thorisin could easily have run the other dicers from the game by betting more than they could afford to cover. Remembering his hundred goldpiece bet with Vardanes Sphrantzes, Marcus knew the Sevastokrator was not averse to playing for high stakes. But, matched against men of limited means, he was content to risk now a goldpiece, now two, or sometimes a handful of silver. He took his wins and losses as seriously as if he were playing for provinces—whatever he did, he liked to do well. He was a canny gambler, too; before long, a good-sized pile of gold and silver lay before him.

"Did you get that at swordpoint, or are they losing on purpose to curry favor with you?" someone asked the Sevastokrator, and Marcus was amazed to see Mavrikios Gavras standing over his brother. The Emperor was no more regally dressed than the Sevastokrator and attended only by a pair of Haloga bodyguards.

"You don't know skill when you see it," Thorisin retorted. "Hah!" He raked in another stake as the Namdalener across from him rolled the demons.

"Move over and let your elder show you how it's done. I've been listening to accountants since this morning and I've had a gutful of, 'I'm most sorry, your Imperial Majesty, but I cannot advise that at the present time.' Bah! Sometimes I think court ceremonial is a slow poison the bureaucrats invented to bore usurpers to death so they can sneak back into power themselves." He grinned at Marcus. "My daughter insists it's otherwise, but I don't believe her anymore."

With a murmured, "Thank you, sweetheart," he took a cup from a passing girl. The lass whirled in surprise as she realized whom she'd served. Mavrikios might not trust the Namdaleni where his Empire was concerned, Scaurus thought, but he certainly had no fears for his own person among them.

The Gavrai, naturally, were on opposite sides of every bet. As he'd been doing most of the evening, Thorisin won several times in a row after his brother sat down. "Go back to your pen-pushers and leave dicing to people who understand it," he said. "You'll get a fart from a dead man before you collect a copper from me."

Mavrikios snorted. "Even a blind hog stumbles across an acorn now and then. There we go!" he exclaimed. Marcus had just thrown suns, and Thorisin had bet against him. The Emperor turned to his brother, palm out. With a shrug, Thorisin passed the stake to him.

Marcus soon decided these were two men who should not gamble against each other. Both were such intense competitors that they took losing personally, and the good humor in their banter quickly disappeared. They were tight-lipped with concentration on the dice; their bets against each other were far greater than any others round the circle. Thorisin's earlier winnings vanished. When Mavrikios rolled the suns yet another time, his brother had to reach into his pouch to pay.

Mavrikios stared at the coins he produced. "What's this?" he said, flinging half of them to the ground. "You'd pay me with money from Yezd?"

Thorisin shrugged once more. "They look like gold to me, and finer than what we mint these days, for that matter." He scooped them up and tossed them far into the crowd. Glad cries said they were not lost for long. Seeing his brother's expression, Thorisin said, "If it won't pay my scot, what good is money to me?" Mavrikios slowly turned a dull red.

Everyone who saw or heard the exchange between the two brothers did his best to pretend he had not. Nevertheless, the camaraderie the dicing circle had enjoyed was shattered, and Marcus was not sorry to see the game break up a few minutes later. It could only bode ill for Videssos when the Emperor's brother showed him up in public, and he knew the story would do nothing but grow in the telling.

Climbing a stairway in the great building that housed the Grand Courtroom—the opposite side of the building from Nephon Khoumnos' workplace—Marcus wondered how much the story had grown in the past few days. Ahead of him on the stair was the thin clerk who had brought the tribune the invitation to this meeting, and ahead of *him* was a destination to which Scaurus had never thought to be bidden—the offices of Vardanes Sphrantzes.

"This way, if you please," the clerk said, turning to his left as he reached the top of the stairs. He led the Roman past a series of large rooms, through whose open doors Scaurus could see whole maniples of men busy with stylus and waxed tablet, pen, ink, and parchment, and the trays of reckoning beads with which skilled Videssians could calculate magically fast. The tribune was far more at home with the power of the barracks hall, but, watching the bureaucrats at work in this nerve center of Empire, he could not deny that power dwelt here too.

A pair of stocky nomads from the plains of Pardraya stood sentry at the door the clerk was approaching. Their faces, blank with boredom before, turned alert when they spied him and stormy when they recognized the Roman behind him. Scaurus had neither wanted nor had much to do with the Khamorth since coming to Videssos, but it was plain they felt he had brought disgrace down on them by exposing one of their number as Avshar's tool.

From the black looks they were giving him, Marcus got the notion they would have much preferred it if their countryman had succeeded in driving his demon-haunted blade hilt-deep in the Roman.

"The boss wants to see this?" one of them asked the tribune's guide, jerking his thumb at Scaurus in a deliberately offensive way. "You're sure?"

"Of course I'm sure," the clerk snapped. "Now stand aside, will you? You'll win no thanks for interfering in his business."

Insolently slow, the Khamorth gave way. As Scaurus stepped past them, one made a ghastly gurgle, like the dying gasp of a man with a slit throat. It was so horribly authentic the tribune whipped his head around before he could stop himself. The plainsman grinned nastily.

Furious at losing face before the barbarian, Scaurus cranked his defenses to the highest pitch of readiness as he walked into the Sevastos' office. When the functionary who led him announced his name, he bowed with the same punctiliousness he would have shown the Emperor—not by any act of omission would he give Sphrantzes a moral advantage over him.

"Come in, come in, you are most welcome," the Sevastos said. As always, his smooth, deep voice revealed nothing but what he wanted in it; at the moment, a cultured affability.

Before Marcus could fully focus his suspicions on the Sevastos, the office's other occupant, a gangling, scraggly-bearded fellow in his early twenties, bounced up from his seat to shake the tribune's hand. "A brilliant martial display, truly brilliant!" he exclaimed, adding, "I saw you beat the Namdaleni. Had it been crimson-handed war and not mere sport, the ground would have been a thirsty sponge to drink their blood. Brilliant!" he said again.

"Er—yes, of course," Scaurus muttered, at a loss to reconcile this unwarlike-seeming youth with his gore-filled talk.

Vardanes Sphrantzes coughed drily. "One of the reasons I asked you here, my outland friend, was to present you to my nephew, the spatharios Ortaias Sphrantzes. Since your victory over the easterners, he's done nothing but pester me to arrange the meeting."

While spatharios had the literal meaing of "sword-bearer," it was a catch-all title, often with little more real meaning than "aide." In young Ortaias' case, that seemed just as well; he looked as if the effort of toting a sword would be too much for him.

He was, though, nothing if not an enthusiast. "I was fascinated to see you successfully oppose the Namdaleni on foot," he said. "In his *Art of Generalship* Mindes Kalokyres recommends plying them with arrows from afar and strongly implies they are invincible at close quarters. It's a great pity he is a century in his grave; I should have like to hear his comments on your refutation of his thesis."

"That would be interesting, I'm sure, your excellency," Scaurus agreed, wondering how much of Ortaias' speech he was understanding. The young noble spoke very quickly; this, coupled with his affected accent and his evident love for long words, made following his meaning a trial for someone with the tribune's imperfect grasp of Videssian.

"Kalokyres is our greatest commentator on things military," Ortaias' uncle explained courteously. "Do sit down, both of you," he urged. "Scaurus,"—In Videssian it sounded more like Scavros—"take some wine if you will. It's a fine vintage, from the western province of Raban, and rather hard to come by in these sorry times."

The pale wine poured silkily from its elegant alabaster carafe. Marcus sipped once for politeness' sake, then a second time with real appreciation; this was more to his liking than any wine he'd yet sampled in Videssos.

"I thought you would enjoy it," Vardanes said, drinking with him. "It's a touch too piquant for me to favor ordinarily, but it is a pleasant change of pace." Scaurus gave the Sevastos his reluctant admiration. It could hardly have been easy for him to learn the Roman's taste in wine and then to meet it. The obvious effort Sphrantzes was making to put him at his ease only made him wonder further what the real object of this meeting might be.

Whatever it was, the Sevastos was in no hurry to get around to it. He spoke with charm and wit of bits of gossip that had crossed his path in the past few days and did not spare his fellow bureaucrats. "There are those," he remarked, "who think the mark for a thing in a ledger is the thing itself." Raising his cup to his lips, he went on, "It takes but a taste of the wine to see how foolish they are."

The tribune had to agree, but noted how possessively Sphrantzes' hand curled over the polished surface of the cup.

The Sevastos' office was more richly furnished than Mavrikios Gavras' private chambers, with wall hangings of silk brocade shot through with gold and silver threads and upholstered couches and chairs whose ebony arms were inlaid with ivory and semiprecious stones. Yet the dominant impression was not one of sybaritic decadence, but rather of a man who truly loved his comforts without being ruled by them.

In Rome Marcus had known men who enjoyed having fish ponds set in their villas' gardens, but he had never seen a decoration like the one on Sphrantzes' desk—a globular tank of clear glass with several small, brightly colored fish darting through waterplants rooted in gravel. In a strange way, it was soothing to watch. The tribune's eyes kept coming back to it, and Sphrantzes gazed fondly at his little pets in their transparent enclosure.

He saw Scaurus looking at them. "One of my servants has the duty of catching enough gnats, flies, and suchlike creatures to keep them alive. He's certain I've lost my wits, but I pay him enough that he doesn't say so."

By this time the Roman had decided Sphrantzes' summons masked nothing more sinister than a social call. He was beginning to muster excuses for leaving when the Sevastos remarked, "I'm glad to see no hard feelings exist between yourselves and the Namdaleni after your recent tussle."

"Indeed yes! That is most fortunate!" Ortaias said enthusiastically. "The tenacity of the men of the Duchy is legendary, as is their fortitude. When linked to the specialized infantry skills you Ronams—"

"Romans," his uncle corrected him.

"Your pardon," Ortaias said, flushing. Thrown off his stride, he finished with the simplest sentence Scaurus had heard from him. "You'll fight really well for us!"

"I hope so, your excellence," Marcus replied. Interested by Vardanes' mention of the islanders, he decided to stay a bit longer. Maybe the Sevastos would be forthcoming after all.

"My nephew is right," the elder Sphrantzes said. "It would be unfortunate if there were a lasting grudge between yourselves and the Namdaleni. They have served us well in the past, and we expect the same of you. There is already too much strife within our army, too much talk of native troops as opposed to mercenaries. Every soldier is a mercenary, but with some, paymaster and king are one and the same."

The tribune steepled his fingers without replying. The Sevastos' last statement, as far as he was concerned, was nonsense, and dangerous nonsense at that. Nor did he think Sphrantzes believed it any more than he did—whatever else he was, Vardanes Sphrantzes was no fool.

He also wondered how Vardanes was using his "we" and "us." Did he speak as head of the bureaucratic faction, as prime minister of all the Empire, or with the royal first person plural? He wondered if Sphrantzes knew himself.

"It's regrettable but true," the Sevastos was saying, "that foreign-born troops do not have the fairest name in the Empire. One reason is that they've so often had to be used against rebels from the back of beyond, men who, even on the throne, find no more dignity than they did in the hayseed robbers' nests from which they sprang." For the first time, his disdain rang clear.

"They have no breeding!" Ortaias Sphrantzes was saying. "None! Why, Mavrikios Gavras' great-grandfather was a goatherd, while we Sphrantzai—" The cold stare Vandanes sent his way stopped him in confusion.

"Forgive my nephew once more, I beg you," the Sevastos said smoothly. "He speaks with youth's usual exaggeration. His Imperial Majesty's family has been of noble rank for nearly two centuries." But by the irony still in his voice, he did not find that long at all.

The conversation drifted back toward triviality, this time for good. A curiously indecisive meeting, Marcus thought on his way back to the barracks. He had expected the Sevastos to show more of his mind but, on reflection, there was no reason why he should do so to a man he felt to be of the opposite side. Then too, with one slip of the tongue his nephew probably had revealed a good deal more than the senior Sphrantzes wanted known.

Two other things occurred to the tribune. The first was that Taso Vones was a lucky acquaintance. The little Khatrisher had an uncanny knowledge of Videssian affairs and was willing to share it. The second was a conclusion he reached while wondering why he still distrusted Vardanes Sphrantzes so much. It was utterly in character, he decided, for the Sevastos to delight in keeping small, helpless creatures in a transparent cage.

VIII

As the weeks passed after Mavrikios Gavras' ringing declaration of war against Yezd, Videssos began filling with warriors mustered to wage the great campaign the Emperor had planned. The gardens, orchards, and other open spaces which made the imperial capital such a delight saw tent cities spring up on them like mushrooms after a rain. Every street, it seemed, had its contingent of soldiers swaggering along, elbowing civilians to one side, on the prowl for food, drink, and women . . . or simply standing and gaping at the wonders Videssos offered the newcomer's eye.

Troops flowed in day after day. The Emperor pulled men from garrisons in towns he reckoned safe, to add weight to his striking force. A hundred men came from here, four hundred more from there, another two hundred from somewhere else. Marcus heard that Imbros' troops had arrived and wondered if Skapti Modolf's son was among them. Even the saturnine Haloga would be hard pressed to call the city a less pleasant place than Imbros.

The Empire's own soldiers were not the only ones to swell Videssos to the bursting point. True to his promise, Mavrikios sent his neighbors a call for mercenaries against Yezd, and the response was good. Videssian ships sailing from Prista, the Empire's watchport on the northern coast of the Videssian Sea, brought companies of Khamorth from the plains, and their steppe-ponies with them. By special leave, other bands of nomads were permitted to cross the Astris River. They came south to the capital by land, paralleling the seacoast and, in the latter stage of their journey, following the route the Romans had used from Imbros. Parties of Videssian outriders made sure the plainsmen did not plunder the countryside.

Khatrish, whose border marched with Videssos' eastern frontier, sent the Empire a troop of light cavalry. In gear and appearance they were about halfway between imperials and plainsdwellers, whose bloods they shared. Most of them seemed to have the outspoken cheeriness of Taso Vones. Scaurus had a chance to get acquainted with a fair number of them at a heroic feast the Khatrisher ambassador put together. Viridovix made the night memorable by throwing a Khamorth clear through a very stout wineshop door without bothering to open it first. Vones paid the repair costs out of his own pocket, declaring, "Strength like that deserves to be honored."

"Foosh!" the Celt protested. "The man was a natural-born damn fool, the which is proven by the hardness of his head. For no other reason did he make so fine a battering ram."

The Namdaleni also heeded the Empire's rallying cry. The Duchy's lean square-riggers brought Videssos two regiments to fight the Yezda. Getting them into the capital, however, was a tricky busines. Namdalen and the Empire were foes too recent for much trust to exist on either side. Mavrikios, while glad of the manpower, was not anxious to see Namdalener warships anchored at Videssos' quays, suspecting the islanders' piratical instincts might get the better of their good intentions. Thus the Namdaleni transshipped at the Key and came to the city in imperial hulls. The matter-of-fact way they accepted the Emperor's solution convinced Marcus that all Gavras' forebodings were justified.

"How right you are," Gaius Philippus agreed. "They don't so much as bother pretending innocence. If they got a quarter of a chance they'd jump Mavrikios without even blinking. He knows it, and they know he knows it. And on those terms they can deal with each other."

For the Romans, spring and early summer were a time of adjustment, a time to find and to make their place in their new homeland. Their position in the army was never in doubt, not after the win over the men of the Duchy in their mock-combat. Marcus became the oracle of infantry. Almost daily, high-ranking Videssians or mercenary officers would appear at the Roman drills to watch and question. The tribune found it flattering and ironically amusing, as he knew he was but an amateur soldier.

When other business kept him from leading the exercises, the duty of coping with observers fell on Gaius Philippus. The senior centurion got on well with fellow professionals, but did not suffer fools gladly. After one such meeting, he asked Scaurus, "Who's the lanky half-shaved whiffet always hanging about? You know, the fellow with the book under one arm."

"Ortaias Sphrantzes?" Marcus asked with a sinking feeling.

"That's the one. He wanted to know how I heartened the men before a battle; and before I could get a word out of my mouth, he started a harangue he must have written himself, the stupid puppy. To win a battle after that speech, he'd need to be leading a crew of demigods."

"You didn't tell him so, I hope?"

"Me? I told him he should save it for the enemy—he'd bore them to death and win without a fight. He went away."

"Oh." For the next few days the tribune kept expecting poison in the radishes, or at least a summons from Ortaias' uncle. But nothing happened. Either the young Sphrantzes had not told the Sevastos of his embarrassment, or Vardanes was resigned to his nephew stubbing his toes every now and again. Marcus judged it was the former; resignation was not an expression he could easily see on Vardanes Sphrantzes' face.

Just as the Romans changed Videssian notions of military practice, the Empire's way of life had its effect on them. To the tribune's surprise, many of his men began to follow Phos. While he had nothing against Videssos' faith, it also had no appeal for him. He worried lest the legionaries' adoption of the Empire's god was the first step in forgetting Rome.

Gaius Philippus shared his concern. "It's not right, hearing the lads go, 'Phos fry you!' when someone trips over their feet. We should order them to stop that nonsense right now."

Looking for more disinterested advice, the tribune put the question to Gorgidas. "An order? Don't be absurd. You can tell a man what to do, but even your iron-fisted centurion can't tell him what to think. They'll only disobey if he tries. And if they don't follow the one command, who's to say they'll follow the next? It's easiest to ride a horse in the direction he's already going."

Scaurus felt the sense of the doctor's words; the Greek articulated the conclusion he was reaching himself. But the certainty in Gorgidas' next remark rocked him back on his heels. "Of course we'll forget Rome—and Greece, and Gaul."

"What? Never!" Marcus said with unthinking rejection.

"Come now, in your head you know I'm right, say your heart what it will. Oh, I don't mean every memory of the world we knew will disappear; that's truly impossible. But as the years pass, Videssos will lay its hand on us all, gently, yes, but the day will come when you discover you've forgotten the names of half your parents' neighbors . . . and it won't really bother you." Gorgidas' eyes were far away.

The tribune shivered. "You see a long way ahead, don't you?"

"Eh? No, a long way behind. I tore my life up by the roots once before, when I left Elis to ply my trade at Rome. It gives me a sense of proportion you may not have.

"Besides," the Greek went on, "eventually we'll have a good many Videssians in our own ranks. Apokavkos is doing well, and we'll not find more Romans to make up the losses we'll take."

Scaurus did not reply; Gorgidas had a gift for bringing up things he would rather not think about. He did resolve to fix his every memory so firmly it could never escape. Even as he made the resolution, he felt the cold wind of futility at his back. Well, then, the best you can, he told himself, and was satisfied. Failure was no disgrace; indifference was.

Videssian usages also began to change what Marcus had thought a fundamental part of Roman military thinking—its attitude toward women. The army of Rome was so often on campaign that marriage during legionary service was forbidden as being bad for discipline. Neither the Videssians nor their mercenary soldiers followed that rule. They spent much of their time in garrison duty, which gave them the chance to form long-lasting relationships that could not have existed in a more active army.

As with the worship of the Empire's god, the tribune knew he could not keep his men from uniting with Videssos' women. He would have faced mutiny had he tried, the more so as the local soldiers enjoyed the privilege the legionaries were seeking. First one and then a second of the four barracks halls the Romans used was transformed by hastily erected partitions of wood and cloth into quarters where privacy could be had. Nor was it long before the first proud Romans could boast that they would be the fathers of fine sons—or so they hoped—to take their places.

Gaius Philippus grumbled more than ever. "I can see us in a few years' time—brats squalling underfoot, troopers brawling because their queans had a spat. Mars above, what are we coming to?" To forestall the evil day, he worked the legionaries harder than before.

Scaurus had reservations too, but he noted that while most of the Namdaleni had women, it did not seem to blunt their edge. In a way, he could even see it as an advantage—with such an intimate stake in Videssos' survival, the legionaries might fight harder for the Empire.

Yet he also realized that acquiring mates was another tap on the wedge Videssos was driving into the souls of his men, another step in their absorption into the Empire. Every time the tribune saw a Roman walk by with his attention solely on the woman whose waist his arm encircled, he felt again the inevitability of Gorgidas' words. The Romans were a drop of ink fallen into a vast lake; their color had to fade with time.

Of all the peoples they came to know in the capital, the legionaries seemed to blend best with the Namdaleni. It embarrassed Scaurus, who reserved his loyalty for the Emperor and knew the men of the Duchy would cheerfully gut Videssos if ever they saw their chance. But there was no getting around it—Roman and Namdalener took to one another like long-separated relatives.

Maybe the skirmish and feast they had shared made friendship easier; maybe it was simply that the Namdaleni were less reserved than Videssians and more willing to meet the Romans halfway. Whatever the reason, legionaries were always welcome in taverns that catered to the easterners, and constant traffic flowed between the islanders' barracks and those housing the Romans.

When Marcus worried his soldiers' fondness for the men of the Duchy would undermine the friendships he'd built up with the Videssians, Gaius Philippus put an arm round his shoulder. "You want friends everywhere," he said, speaking like a much older brother. "It's your age, I suppose; everyone in his thirties thinks he needs friends. Once you reach your forties, you find they won't save you any more than love did."

"To the crows with you!" Marcus exclaimed, appalled. "You're worse than Gorgidas."

One morning, Soteric Dosti's son came to invite several of the Roman officers to that day's Namdalener drill. "Aye, you bettered us afoot," he said, "but now you'll see us at our best."

Marcus had watched the Namedaleni work before and had a healthy respect for their hard-hitting cavalry. He also approved of their style of practice. Like the Romans, they made their training as much like battle as they could, so no one would be surprised on the true field of combat. But from the smug grin Soteric was trying to hide, this invitation was to something special.

A few Khamorth were practicing archery at the drillfield's edge. Their short, double-curved bows sent arrow after arrow *whocking* into the straw-stuffed hides they had set up as targets. They and the party Marcus led were the only non-Namdaleni on the field that day.

At one end stood a long row of hay bales, at the other, almost equally still, a line of mounted islanders. The men of the Duchy were in full caparison. Streamers of bright ribbon fluttered from their helms, their lances, and their big horses' trappings. Each wore over his chain mail shirt a surcoat of a color to match his streamers. A hundred lances went up in salute as one when the easterners caught sight of the Romans.

"Och, what a brave show," Viridovix said admiringly. Scaurus thought the Gaul had found the perfect word; this was a show, something prepared specially for his benefit. He resolved to judge it on that basis if he could.

The commander of the Namdaleni barked an order. Their lances swung down, again in unison. A hundred glittering leaf-shaped points of steel, each tipping a lance twice the length of a man, leveled at the bales of hay a furlong from them. Their leader left them thus for a long dramatic moment, then shouted the command that sent them hurtling forward.

Like an avalanche thundering down an Alpine pass, they started slowly. The heavy horses they rode were not quick to build momentum, what with their own bulk and the heavily armored men atop them. But they gained a trifle at every bound and were at full stride before halfway to their goal. The earth rolled like a kettledrum under their thuttering hooves; their iron-shod feet sent great clods of dirt and grass flying skywards.

Marcus tried to imagine himself standing in a hay bale's place, watching the horses thunder down on him until he could see their nostrils flaring crimson, staring at the steel that would tear his life away. The skin on his belly crawled at the thought of it. He wondered how any men could nerve themselves to oppose such a charge.

When lances, horses, and riders smashed through them, the bales simply ceased to be. Hay was trampled underfoot, flung in all directions, and thrown high into the air. The Namdaleni brought their horses to a halt; they began picking hay wisps from their mounts' manes and coats and from their own surcoats and hair.

Soteric looked expectantly to Scaurus. "Most impressive," the tribune said, and meant it. "Both as spectacle and as a show of fighting power, I don't think I've seen the like."

"Sure and it's a cruel hard folk you Namdaleni are," Viridovix said, "to beat poor hay bales all to bits, and them having done you no harm."

Gaius Philippus added, "If that was your way of challenging us to a return engagement on horseback, you can bloody well think again. I'm content to rest on my laurels, thank you very kindly." The veteran's praise made Soteric glow with pride, and the day, the islanders agreed, was a great success.

But the centurion was in fact less overawed than he let the Namdaleni think. "They're rugged, don't misunderstand me," he told Scaurus as they returned to their own quarters after sharing a midday meal with the easterners. "Good steady foot, though, could give them all they want. The key is keeping their charge from flattening you at the start."

"Do you think so?" Marcus asked. He'd paid Gaius Philippus' words less heed than he should. It must have shown, for Viridovix looked at him with mischief in his eye.

"You're wasting your breath if you speak to the lad of war, I'm thinking," he said to the centurion. "There's nothing in his head at all but a couple of fine blue eyes, sure and there's not. She'a a rare beauty lass, Roman; I wish you luck with her."

"Helvis?" Marcus said, alarmed his feelings were so obvious. He covered himself as best he could. "What makes you think that? She wasn't even at table today."

"Aye, that's true—and weren't you the disappointed one now?" Viridovix did his best to assume the air of a man giving serious advice, something of a wasted effort on his naturally merry face. "You're about it the right way, I'll say that. Too hard and too soon would do nothing but drive her from you. But those honied plums you found for her boy, now—you're a sly one. If the imp cares for you, how could the mother not? And giving them to Soteric to pass along will make him think the better of you too, the which canna hurt your chances."

"Oh, hold your peace, can't you? With Helvis not there, who could I give the sweets to but her brother?" But quibble as he would over details, in broad outline he knew the Celt was right. He was powerfully drawn to Helvis, but that was complicated by his guilt over his role, accidental though it was, in Hemond's death. Still, in the few times he had seen her since that day, she bore out her claim that she had no ill will toward him. And Soteric, for his part, would have had to be blind not to have noticed the attention Scaurus paid his sister, yet he raised no objections—a promising sign.

But that his feelings should be common knowledge, maybe—no, certainly—the subject of gossip through Videssos' community of soldiers, could only dismay the tribune, who did not much care to reveal himself to any but his friends.

He was relieved when Gaius Philippus returned to the conversation's original subject. "Stiffen your line with pikemen and give them a good volley of *pila* as soon as they come into range, and your fine Namdalener horsemen will have themselves a very warm time indeed. Horses know better than to run up against anything sharp."

Viridovix gave the centurion an exasperated glance. "You are the damnedest man for holding on to a worthless idea I ever did see. Here we could be making himself squirm like a worm in a mug of ale, and you go maundering on about nags, Epona preserve them." He named the Gallic horse-goddess.

"One day, maybe, it'll be you in the alepot," Gaius Philippus said, looking him in the eye. "Then we'll see if you're glad to have me change the subject."

While Mavrikios readied his stroke to put an end to Yezd once for all, the Empire's western enemy did not stand idle. As always, there was a flow of wild nomads down off the steppe, over the Yegird River, and into the northwest of what had been the land of Makuran. Thus had the Yezda entered that land half a century before. Khagan Wulghash, Marcus thought, was no one's fool. Instead of letting the newcomers settle and disrupt his state, he shunted them eastward against Videssos, urging them on with promises of fighting, loot, and the backing of the Yezda army.

The nomads, more mobile than the foe they faced, slid through Vaspurakan's mountain valleys and roared into the fertile plains beyond them, spreading atrocity, mayhem, and rapine. The raiders were like so much water; if checked at one spot, they flowed someplace else, always probing for weak spots and all too often finding them.

And at their head was Avshar. Marcus cursed and Nephon Khoumnos swore the first reports of him were lies, but soon enough they had to admit the truth. Too many refugees, straggling into Videssos with no more than they could carry, told a tale that left no room for doubt. Yezd's wizard-chieftain did not try to hide his presence. On the contrary, he flaunted it, the better to terrify his foes.

With the white robes he always wore, he chose to ride a great black charger, half again the size of his followers' plains-ponies. His sword hewed down the few bold enough to stand against him, and his mighty bow sent shafts of death winging farther than any normal man, any human man, could shoot. It was said that any man those arrows pierced would die, be the wound ever so tiny. It was also said no spear or arrow would bite on him, and that the mere sight of him unstrung even a hero's courage. Remembering the spell his good Gallic blade had turned aside, Marcus could well believe the last.

High summer approached and still the Emperor gathered his forces. Local levies in the west fought the Yezda without support from the host building in the capital. None of the Romans could understand why Mavrikios, certainly a man of action, did not move. When Scaurus put the question to Neilos Tzimiskes, the borderer replied, "Too soon can be worse than too late, you know."

"Six weeks ago—even three weeks ago—I would have said aye to that. But if matters aren't taken in hand soon, there won't be much of an Empire left to save."

"Believe me, my friend, things aren't as simple as they seem." But when Marcus tried to get more from Tzimiskes than that, Neilos retreated into vague promises that matters would turn out for the best. It was not long before the Roman decided he knew more than he was willing to say.

The next day, Scaurus kicked himself for not seeking what he needed to know from Phostis Apokavkos. The truth was, the former peasant had blended so well into the Roman ranks that the tribune often forgot he had not been with the legionaries in the forests of Gaul. His new allegiance, Marcus reasoned, might make him more garrulous than Tzimiskes.

"Do I know why we're not out on campaign? You mean to tell me you don't?" Apokavkos stared at the tribune. He plucked the air where his beard had been, then laughed at himself. "Still can't get used to this shaving. Answer to your question's a simple thing: Mavrikios isn't about to leave the city until he's sure he'll still be Emperor when he gets home."

Marcus thumped his forehead with the heel of his hand. "A pox on faction politics! The whole Empire is the stake, not who sits the throne."

"You'd think a mite different if it was your backside on it."

Scaurus started to protest, then thought back on the last decades of Rome's history. It was only too true that the wars against King Mithridates of Pontus had dragged on long after that monarch should have been crushed, simply because the legions opposing him were sometimes of Sulla's faction, sometimes of the Marians'. Not only was cooperation between the two groups poor; both kept going back to Italy from Asia Minor to fight another round of civil war. The Videssians were men like any others. It was probably too much to ask of them not to be fools like any others.

"You're getting the idea, all right," Apokavkos said, seeing Marcus' grudging agreement. "Besides, if you doubt me, how do you explain Mavrikios staying in the city last year and not going out to fight the Yezda? Things were even tighter then than they are now; he plain didn't dare leave."

The adopted Roman's comment made clear something Scaurus had puzzled over for some time. No wonder Mavrikios looked so bleak when he admitted his earlier inability to move against Yezd! The past year had seen the Empire's power vastly increase and, in the face of the Yezda threat, its unity as well. The tribune better understood Mavrikios' pouched, red-veined eyes; it was strange he dared sleep at all.

Yet power and unity still did not walk hand in hand in Videssos, as Marcus discovered a few mornings later. The tribune had urged Apokavkos to keep the street connections he'd made in the city. Marcus saw how the Namdaleni were excluded from the news and rumors always seething, and did not want his Romans similarly deprived. The report Phostis brought made him thankful for his forethought.

"If it didn't have us in it, too, I likely wouldn't tell you this," Apokavkos said, "but I think it'd be smart for us to walk small the next few days. There's trouble brewing against the damned easterners, and too many in town put us and them in the same wagon."

"Against the Namdaleni?" Marcus asked. At Phostis' nod, he said, "But why? They've quarreled with the Empire, true, but every one of them in the city now is here to fight Yezd."

"There's too many of 'em here, and they're too proud of themselves, the swaggering rubes." Phostis' conversion to Roman tastes did not stretch to the men of the Duchy. "Not only that, they've taken over half a dozen shrines for their own services, the damned heretics. Next thing you know, they'll start trying to convert decent folk to their ways. That won't do."

Marcus suppressed a strong impulse to scream. Would no one in this god-ridden world forget religion long enough to do anything needful? If the followers of Phos as sure victor over evil fought those who believed in Phos' Wager, then the only winners would be Skotos-worshippers. But when the Roman suggested that to Apokavkos, his answer was, "I don't know but what I'd sooner see Wulghash ruling in Videssos than Duke Tomond of Namdalen."

Throwing his hands in the air, Scaurus went off to pass the warning to Soteric. The islander was not in his usual billet on the ground floor of the barracks. "He's with his sister, I think. You can probably find him there," offered one of the men whose bed was nearby.

"Thanks," the tribune said, heading for the stairway. As usual, the prospect of seeing Helvis made him skittish and eager at the same time. He was aware that more than once he'd invented excuses to visit Soteric in the hope of encountering his sister. This time, though, he reminded himself, his business with the Namdalener was real and urgent.

"By the Wager!" Soteric exclaimed when he saw who was knocking on Helvis' door. "Talk about someone and just see if he doesn't show up." That was an opening to take Scaurus clean out of play, especially since the Namdalener declined to follow it up and left Marcus guessing.

"Would you care for some wine, or some bread and cheese?" Helvis asked when the Roman was comfortable. She was still far from the vibrant lady who had caught his fancy a few weeks before, but time, as it always does, was beginning its healing work. The pinched look of pain that sat so wrongly on her lively features was not so pronounced now; there were times again when her smile would reach her eyes.

Malric darted into the livingroom from the bedchamber beyond. He was carrying a tiny wooden sword. "Kill a Yezda!" he announced, swinging his toy blade with three-year-old ferocity.

Helvis caught up her son and swung him into the air. He squealed in glee, dropping his play weapon. "Again!" he said. "Again!" Instead, his mother squeezed him to her with fierce intensity, remembering Hemond in him.

"Run along, son," Soteric said when his nephew was on his feet again. Grabbing up his sword, the boy dashed away at the same breakneck speed he'd used to come in. Recalling his own younger sisters growing up, Scaurus knew all small children were either going at full tilt or asleep, with next to nothing in between.

Once Malric was gone, the tribune told Soteric the story he had heard from Phostis Apokavkos. The islander's first reaction was not the alarm Marcus had felt, but rather smoldering eagerness. "Let the rabble come!" he said, smacking fist into palm for emphasis. "We'll clean the bastards out, and it'll give us the excuse we need for war on the Empire. Namdalen will inherit Videssos' mantle soon enough—why not now?"

Scaurus gaped at him, flabbergasted. He knew the men of the Duchy coveted the city and the whole Empire, but Soteric's arrogance struck him as being past sanity. Helvis was staring at her brother, too. As softly as he could, Marcus tried to nudge him back toward sense. "You'll take and hold the capital with six thousand men?" he asked politely.

"Eight thousand! And some of the Khamorth will surely join us—their sport is plunder."

"Quite true, I'm sure. And once you've disposed of the rest of the plainsmen, the Emperor's Haloga guards, and the forty thousand or so Videssian warriors in the city, why then all you need do is keep down the whole town. They'd hate you doubly—for being heretics and conquerors both. I wish you good fortune, for you'll need it."

The Namdalener officer looked at him as Malric would if he'd snapped the boy's toy sword over his knee. "Then you didn't come to offer your men as allies in the fight?"

"Allies in the fight?" If it came to a fight such as Soteric envisioned, Scaurus hoped the Romans would be on the other side, but he guessed the islander would be more furious than chastened to hear that. The tribune was still marveling at Soteric's incredible . . . there was no word in Latin for it. He had to think in Greek to find the notion he wanted: *hubris.* What tragedian had written, "Whom the gods would destroy, they first make mad"?

Gorgidas would know, he thought.

Some of the ravening glitter in Soteric's eye faded as he saw Marcus' rejection. He looked to his sister for support, but Helvis would not meet his glance. She was as ardent a Namdalener as her brother, but too firmly rooted in reality to be swept away by a vision of conquest, no matter how glowing.

"I came to stop a riot, not start a war," Marcus said into the silence. He looked for some reason he could use to draw Soteric from his dangerous course without making him lose face. Luckily, one was close at hand. "With Yezd to be dealt with, neither you nor the Empire can afford secondary fights."

There was more than enough truth in that to make Soteric stop and think. The smile on his face had nothing to do with amusement; it was more like a stifled snarl. "What would you have us do?" he asked at last. "Hide our beliefs? Skulk like cowards to keep from firing the rabble? The

Videssians have no shame over throwing their creed in our faces. I'd sooner fight than kowtow to the street mob, and damn the consequences, say I!" But mixed with the warrior's pride in his speech was the frustrated realization that the outcome of such a fight likely would not be what he wished.

Marcus tried to capitalize on the islander's slowly emerging good sense. "No one would expect you to knuckle under," he said. "But a little restraint now could stop endless trouble later."

"Let the bloody Cocksures show restraint," Soteric snapped, using the Duchy's nickname for the orthodox of Videssos.

Continued contact with the Namdalener's hot temper was beginning to fray Scaurus' own. "There's the very thing I'm talking about," he said. "Call someone a 'Cocksure' once too often and you can be sure you'll have a scramble on your hands."

Up to this time Helvis had listened to her brother and the Roman argue without taking much part. Now she said, "It seems to me the two of you are only touching one part of the problem. The city people may like us better if we're less open about some things they don't care for, but what we do can only go so far. If Videssos needs our service, the Emperor—or someone—should make the people know we're important to them and should not be abused."

"Should, should, should," Soteric said mockingly. "Who would put his neck on the block for a miserable band of mercenaries?"

It was plain he did not think his sister would have a good answer for him. Thinking of the government leaders he knew, Marcus did not find it likely either. Mavrikios or Thorisin Gavras would sacrifice the men of the Duchy without a qualm if they interfered with the great campaign against Yezd. Nephon Khoumnos might sacrifice them anyway, on general principles. True, the Namdaleni were part of the power Vardanes Sphrantzes wielded against the Gavrai, but the Sevastos, Scaurus was sure, was too unpopular in the city to make his words, even if given, worth much.

But Helvis did have a reply, and one so apt Marcus felt like a blockhead for not finding it himself. "What of Balsamon?" she asked. "He strikes me as a good man, and one the Videssians listen to."

"The Cocksures' patriarch?" Soteric said incredulously. "Any Videssian blue-robe would send us all to the eternal ice before he'd lift a finger for us."

"Of most of them I would say that's true, but Balsamon has a different feel to him. He's never harassed us, you know," Helvis said.

"Your sister's right, I think," Marcus said to Soteric. He told him of the startling tolerance the prelate of Videssos had shown in the Emperor's chambers.

"Hmm," Soteric said. "It's easy enough to be tolerant in private. Will he do it when it counts? There's the rub." He rose to his feet. "Well, what are the two of you waiting for? We'd best find out—myself, I'll believe it when I hear it."

The ruthless energy Soteric had wanted to turn on Videssos now was bent against his sister and the tribune. Helvis paused only to pick up her son—"Come on, Malric, we're going to see someone."—and Marcus not at all, but they were not quick enough to suit Soteric. Scoffing at Helvis' idea at the same time as he pushed it forward, her brother had her and Scaurus out of the Namdalener barracks, out of the palace complex, and into the hurly-burly of the city almost before the Roman could blink.

The patriarchal residence was in the northern central part of Videssos, on the grounds of Phos' High Temple. The Roman had not cared to visit that, but some of his men who had taken to Phos marveled at its splendor. The High Temple's spires, topped with their gilded domes, were visible throughout the city; the only problem in reaching them was picking the proper path through Videssos' maze of roads, lanes, and alleys. Soteric led the way with assurance.

More by what did not happen than by what did, Marcus got the feel of how unwelcome foreigners had become in the capital. It was as if the city dwellers were trying to pretend they did not exist. No merchant came rushing out of his shop to importune them, no peddler approached to ply his wares, no small boy came up to offer to lead them to his father's hostel. The tribune wryly remembered how annoyed he had been at not achieving anonymity after his fight with Avshar. Now he had it, and found he did not want it.

Malric was entranced by the colors, sounds, and smells of the city, so different from and so much more exciting than the barracks he was used to. Half the time he walked along among Helvis, Soteric, and Marcus, doing his short-legged best to keep up; they carried him the rest of the way, passing him from one to the next. His three constant demands were, "Put me down," "Pick me up," and, most of all, "What's that?" Everything drew the last query: a piebald horse, a painter's scaffold, a prostitute of dubious gender.

"Good question," Soteric chuckled as the quean sauntered past. His nephew was not listening—a scrawny black puppy with floppy ears had stolen his interest.

The High Temple of Phos sat in lordly solitude at the center of a large enclosed courtyard. Like the arena by the palace complex, it was one of the city's main gathering points. At need, lesser priests would speak to the masses assembled outside the Temple while the prelate addressed the smaller, more select audience within.

The residence of the patriarchs of Videssos stood just outside the courtyard. It was a surprisingly unassuming structure; many moderately wealthy traders had larger, more palatial quarters. But the modest building had a feeling of perpetuity to it that the houses of the newly wealthy could not hope to imitate. The very pine trees set round it were gnarled and twisted with age, yet still green and growing.

Coming from young Rome, whose history was little more than legend even three centuries before his own time, Marcus had never quite gotten over the awe Videssos' long past raised in him. To him, the ancient but vigorous trees were a good metaphor for the Empire as a whole.

When he said that aloud, Soteric laughed mirthlessly, saying, "So they are, for they look as if the first good storm would tear them out by the roots."

"They've weathered a few to come this far," Marcus said. Soteric brushed the comment away with a wave of his hand.

The door opened before them; a high-ranking ecclesiastic was ushering out a Videssian noble in white linen trousers and a tunic of lime-green silk. "I trust his Sanctity was able to help you, my lord Dragatzes?" the priest asked courteously.

"Yes, I think so," Dragatzes replied, but his black-browed scowl was not encouraging. He strode past Marcus, Helvis, and Soteric without seeming to notice them.

Nor did the priest pay them any heed until his gaze, which was following Dragatzes' retreating back, happened to fall on them. "Is there something I can do to help you?" he said. His tone was doubtful; Helvis and her brother were easy to recognize as Namdaleni, while Marcus himself looked more like a man of the Duchy than a Videssian. There was no obvious reason for folk such as them to visit the head of a faith they did not share.

And even after Marcus asked to speak with Balsamon, the priest at the door made no move to step aside. "As you must know, his Sanctity's calendar is crowded. Tomorrow would be better, or perhaps the next day . . ." Go away and don't bother coming back, Marcus translated.

"Who is it, Gennadios?" the patriarch's voice came from inside the residence. A moment later he appeared beside the other priest, clad not in his gorgeous patriarchal regalia but in a none too clean monk's robe of simple blue wool. Catching sight of the four outside his door, he let loose his rich chuckle. "Well, well, what have we here? A heathen and some heretics, to see me? Most honored, I am sure. Come in, I beg of you." He swept past the spluttering Gennadios to wave them forward.

"But, your Sanctity, in a quarter hour's time you are to see—" Gennadios protested, but the patriarch cut him off.

"Whoever it is, he'll wait. This is a fascinating riddle, don't you think, Gennadios? Why should unbelievers care to see me? Perhaps they wish to convert to our usages. That would be a great gain for Phos' true faith, don't you think? Or perhaps they'll convert *me*—and wouldn't that be a scandal, now?"

Gennadios gave his superior a sour look, clearly finding his humor in questionable taste. Soteric was staring at the patriarch in disbelief, Helvis in delight. Marcus had to smile, too; remembering his last meeting with Balsamon, he knew how much the prelate relished being outrageous.

Malric was in his mother's arms. As she walked by Balsamon, her son reached out for two good handsful of the patriarchal beard. Helvis stopped instantly, as much in alarm at what Balsamon might do as to keep him from being tugged with her.

Her fright must have shown, for the patriarch laughed out loud. "You know, my dear, I don't eat children—at least not lately." He gently detached Malric's hands from their hold. "You thought I was an old billy goat, didn't you?" he said, poking the boy in the ribs. "Didn't you?" Malric nodded, laughing in delight.

"What's your name, son?" the patriarch asked.

"Malric Hemond's son," Malric answered clearly.

"Hemond's son?" The smile slipped from Balsamon's face. "That was a bad business, a very bad business indeed. You must be Helvis, then," he said to Malric's mother. As she nodded, Marcus was impressed—not for the first time—with the patriarch's knowledge and memory of detail. Balsamon turned to Helvis' brother. "I don't think I know you, sir."

"No reason you should," Soteric agreed. "I'm Soteric Dosti's son; Helvis is my sister."

"Very good," Balsamon nodded. "Come with me, all of you. Gennadios, do tell my next visitor I'll be somewhat delayed, won't you?"

"But—" Realizing the uselessness of any protest he might make, Gennadios gave a sharp, short nod.

"My watchdog," Balsamon sighed as he led his visitors to his chambers. "Strobilos set him on me years ago, to keep an eye on me. I suppose Mavrikios would take him away if I asked, but somehow I've never bothered."

"It must amuse you to bait the ill-humored fool, besides," Soteric said. Marcus had thought the same thing, but not in the cruel way the Namdalener said it.

Helvis laid her hand on her brother's arm, but Balsamon did not seem disturbed. "He's right, you know," the patriarch told her. He looked musingly at Soteric, murmuring, "Such a pretty boy, to have such sharp teeth." Soteric flushed; Marcus was reminded that the patriarch could care for himself in any battle of wits.

Balsamon's audience room was even more crowded with books than Apsimar's had been back at Imbros, and far less orderly in the bargain. Volumes leaned drunkenly against the shabby chairs that looked like castoffs from the Academy's refectory. Others jammed shelves, swallowed tables, and did their best to make couches unusable for mere human beings.

Peeping out from the few spaces parchment did not cover was a swarm of ivories, some no bigger than a fingernail, others the size of a big man's arm. They were comical, ribald, stately, furious, what have you, and all carved with a rococo extravagance of line alien to the Videssian art Scaurus had come to know.

"You've spied my vice, I fear," Balsamon said, seeing the tribune's eye roam from one figurine to the next, "and another, I admit unjust, cause for my resentment against Yezd. These are all the work of the Kingdom of Makuran that was; under its new masters, the craft does not flourish. Not much does, save only hatred."

"But you didn't come to hear me speak of ivories," the patriarch said, clearing things enough for them to sit. "Or if you did, I may indeed become a Gambler, from sheer gratitude." As usual, what would have been a provoking name in another's mouth came without offense from his. His hands spread in a gesture of invitation. "What do you think I can do for you?"

Helvis, Soteric, and Marcus looked at each other, none of them anxious to begin. After a few seconds of silence, Soteric took the plunge, blunt as always. "We've had reports the people of Videssos are thinking of violence against us because of our faith."

"That would be unfortunate, particularly for you," Balsamon agreed. "What am I to do about it? And why ask me to do anything, for that matter? Why should I? After all, I am hardly of your faith." He pointed at the patriarchal robe draped untidily over a chair.

Soteric drew in a breath to damn the prelate for being the stiff-necked fool he'd thought him, but Helvis caught the gleam of amusement in Balsamon's eye her brother missed. She, too, waved at the crumpled regalia. "Surely your flock respects the office you hold, if nothing else," she said sweetly.

Balsamon threw back his head and laughed till the tears came, clutching his big belly with both hands until his wheezes subsided. "One forgets what a sharp blade irony has—until stuck with it, that is," he said, still chuckling. "Yes, of course I'll pour water on the hotheads; I'll give them ecumenism enough to choke on. For your presumption, if nothing else, you deserve that much. We have worse enemies than those who could be our friends."

The patriarch turned his sharp black stare on Marcus. "What are you, the silent partner in this cabal?"

"If you like." Unlike either of the Namdaleni, Scaurus had no intention of being drawn into a verbal duel with Balsamon, knowing it could only have one outcome.

Helvis thought he had little to say out of modesty, not policy, and came to his defense. "Marcus brought us word of trouble brewing," she said.

"You have good sources, my quiet friend," Balsamon told the Roman, "but then I already know that, don't I? I thought that was your role here—it's too soon for externs like the islanders to have caught the smell of riot. I haven't been working on this sermon more than a day or two myself."

"What?" Marcus shouted, jolted from the calm he'd resolved to maintain. Soteric and Helvis simply gaped. Malric had been almost asleep in his mother's arms; startled by the sudden noise, he began to cry. Helvis calmed him automatically, but most of her attention was still on Balsamon.

"Give me some credit for wits, my young friends." The patriarch smiled. "It's a poor excuse for a priest who doesn't know what his people are thinking. More than a few have called me a poor excuse for a priest, but that was never why."

He rose, escorting his astounded guests to a door different from the one they'd used to enter. "It would be best if you left this way," he said. "Gennadios was right, as he all too often is—I do have another visitor coming soon, one who might blink at the company some of you keep."

Thick hedges screened the side door from the front of the patriarchal residence. Peering through the greenery, Marcus saw Gennadios bowing to Thorisin Gavras. Balsamon was right—the Sevastokrator would not be pleased to see the tribune with two Namdaleni.

"Right?" Soteric exclaimed when Scaurus remarked on it. The islander was still shaking his head in wonder. "Is he ever wrong?"

The tribune elbowed his way through the thick-packed crowd surrounding Phos' High Temple. In his hand was a small roll of parchment entitling him to one of the coveted seats within the Temple itself to hear the patriarch Balsamon's address. A priest had delivered it to the Roman barracks the day before; it was sealed with the sky-blue wax that was the prerogative of the patriarch alone.

In his outland gear, Marcus drew some hard looks from the Videssians he pushed by. A disproportionate number of them seemed to be city toughs of the sort Scaurus had seen on the day he first met Phostis Apokavkos. They did not take kindly to foreigners at the best of times, but the sight of the Roman's blue-sealed pass was evidence enough for them that he stood high in the regard of their well-loved prelate, and he had no real trouble making headway.

Videssian soldiers at the bottom of the broad stairways leading up the Temple kept the mob from crowding rightful seatholders out of their pews. They were nonplussed to find a mercenary captain with a token of admission, but stood aside to let him pass. At the top of the stairs a priest relieved him of his parchment and lined through his name on a roll of expected attenders. "May the words of our patriarch enlighten you," the priest said.

"He enlightens me every time I hear him," Marcus replied. The priest looked at him sharply, suspecting derision from this manifest unbeliever, but the Roman meant what he said. Seeing that, the priest gave a curt nod and waved him into the High Temple.

From the outside, Marcus had found the Temple rather ugly, impressive for no other reason than sheer size. He was used to the clean, spare architecture the Romans had borrowed from Greece and found the Temple's heavy projecting buttresses clumsy, cluttered, and ponderous. Inside, though, its architects had worked a miracle, and the tribune stood spellbound, wondering if he had been suddenly whisked to the heaven Phos' followers looked to in the life to come.

The structure's basic plan was like that of Phos' main temple in Imbros: at its heart was a circular worship-area, surmounted by a dome, with rows of benches projecting off in each of the cardinal directions. But Imbros' shrine was the work of a not very gifted child when compared to this great jewel of a building.

First and most obvious, the craftsmen of the imperial capital had the advantage of far greater resources to lavish on their creation. The High Temple's benches were not of serviceable ash but sun-blond oak, waxed and polished to glowing perfection and inset with ebony, fragrant red sandalwood, thin layers of semi-precious stones, and whole sheets of shimmering mother of pearl. Gold leaf and silver foil ran riot through the Temple, reflecting soft sheets of light into its furthest recesses. Before the central altar stood the patriarch's throne. For Balsamon that throne alone should have made the High Temple a place of delight, for its tall back was made up of a score of relief-carved ivory panels. Scaurus was too far away to see their detail but sure only the best was tolerated in this place.

He tried to calculate what sum the erection of this incredible edifice must have consumed. His mind, however, dazzled by this Pelion on Ossa of wonders, could make no coherent guess, but only continue to marvel at the prodigies his eyes reported.

Dozens of columns, sheathed in glistening moss agate, lined the Temple's four outthrusting wings. Their acanthus capitals, while more florid than the ones Marcus was familiar with, were in keeping with the extravagance of the Temple as a whole. Its interior walls were of purest white marble, turquoise, and, at east and west, pale rose quartz and orange-red sard, reproducing the colors of Phos' sky.

Halfway up the eastern wall was a niche reserved for the imperial family. A screen of elaborate filigreework drawn around the enclosure allowed Emperors and their kin to see without being seen themselves.

For all the treasure lavished on the Temple, it was its splendid design that emerged triumphant. Columns, walls, arches, ancillary semidomes—all smoothly led the eye up to the great dome, and that was a miracle in itself.

It seemed to float in midair, separated from the real world echoingly far below by flashing beams of sunlight streaming in through the many windows which pierced its base. So bulky from the outside, it was light, soaring, graceful—almost disembodied—when seen from within. It took a distinct effort of will to think of the tremendous weight that free-standing dome represented, and of the massive vaults and piers on which it rested. Easier by far to believe it light as a soap-bubble, and so deli-cately attached to the rest of the Temple that the faintest breeze might send it drifting away and leave Phos' shrine open to the air.

The play of light off the dome's myriad tesserae of gold-backed glass further served to disembody it, and further emphasized the transcen-dence of Phos' image at its very zenith. The Videssians limned their god in many ways: kind creator, warrior against the darkness, bright youth, or, as here, severe almighty judge. This Phos watched over his congregation with a solemn yet noble face and eyes so all-seeing they seemed to follow Scaurus as he moved beneath them. Videssos' god held his right hand upraised in blessing, but in his left was the book wherein all good and evil were recorded. Justice he would surely mete out, but mercy? The tribune could not find it in those awesome eyes.

More than a trifle daunted, he took a seat. He could not help sneaking glances toward the stern omnipotence high above and noted hard-faced Videssian nobles, who must have seen that Phos hundreds of times, doing the same thing. It was, quite simply, too powerful to ignore.

The Temple filled steadily; latecomers grumbled as they slid into seats far from the central altar. Yet the floor sloped almost imperceptibly down toward the center, and no one was denied a view.

Soteric strode in, wearing his dignity as proudly as the wolfskin cape and tight breeches that marked him for a Namdalener. Catching Scaurus' eye, he sketched a salute. But even his sangfroid showed signs of cracking when he locked eyes with the god in the dome. Under the weight of that gaze his shoulders' proud set lowered a touch, and he sat with evident relief. Marcus did not think less of him for it; he would have been beyond humanity's pale to remain unmoved by first sight of that omniscient, commanding frown.

The low mutter of conversation in the Temple died away as a choir of blue-robed monks filed in to range themselves round the altar. Joined by their audience and the pure tones of handbells from behind the tribune, they sang a hymn in praise of Phos.

Marcus had to content himself with listening, as he did not know the words. Nor did listening profit him much, for the canticle was in so archaic a dialect of Videssian that he could understand only a word here and there. A trifle bored, he wanted to crane his neck rudely to watch the bell players perform; he forbore only with reluctance. They were wonderfully skilled, their music clean and simple enough to appeal even to the tribune.

The High Temple's thick walls had muffled the noise of the crowd outside. As the hymn's last sweet notes faded, the throng's clamor swelled, growing like the roar of the surf when the tide walked up the beach. All questions as to the reason for the increasing uproar disappeared when Balsamon, preceded by a pair of censer-swinging acolytes, came into the Temple. His face was wreathed in smiles as he made his way toward the altar.

Everyone rose at first sight of the patriarch. Out of the corner of his eye Marcus caught a flicker of motion from behind the screen guarding the imperial family's box. Even the Emperor paid homage to Phos' representative, at least here in the Temple, the heart of Phos' domain on earth.

The tribune would have sworn Balsamon winked at him as he walked past. He doubted himself a second later; with every step the patriarch took toward his throne, he assumed a heavier mantling of distinction. He did not contradict the figure he cut in private, but there was more to him than his private self.

He sank into the patriarchal throne with a silent sigh. Marcus had to remind himself that Balsamon was not a young man. The patriarch's mind and spirit were so vital it was hard to remember his body might not always answer.

Balsamon pushed himself up out of the throne in less than a minute; the packed Temple had remained on its feet for him. He raised his hands to the mighty image of his god on high and, joined by his entire congregation, intoned the prayer Marcus had first heard from the lips of Neilos Tzimiskes northeast of Imbros, though of course he had not understood it then: "We bless thee, Phos, Lord with the right and good mind, by thy grace our protector, watchful beforehand that the great test of life may be decided in our favor."

Through the murmured *Amens* that followed, Scaurus heard Soteric firmly add, "On this we stake our very souls." Glares flashed at the Namdalener from throughout the Temple, but he stared back in defiance— that the men of the Empire chose to leave their creed incomplete was no reason for him to do likewise.

Balsamon lowered his arms; the worshippers took their seats once more, though necks still turned to catch sight of the bold heretic in their midst. Marcus expected the patriarch, no matter how forbearant his personal beliefs were, to take some public notice of Soteric's audacity.

And so, indeed, he did, but hardly in the way the Roman had looked for. Balsamon looked to the Namdalener almost in gratitude. "'On this we stake our very souls,'" he repeated quietly. His eyes darted this way and that, taking the measure of those who had stared hardest at Soteric. "He's right, you know. We do."

The patriarch tapped gently on the top of his throne's ivory back; his smile was ironic. "No, I am not speaking heresy. In its most literal sense, the Namdalener's addition to our creed is true. We have all staked our souls on the notion that, in the end, good shall triumph over evil. Were that not so, we would be as one with the Yezda, and this Temple would not be a place of quiet worship, but a charnel house where blood would flow as does our wine and, instead of incense, the stinking smoke of scorched flesh would rise to heaven."

He looked about him, defying anyone to deny his words. Some of his listeners shifted in their seats, but no one spoke. "I know what you are thinking but will not say," the patriarch continued: "'That's not what the cursed barbarian means by it!'" He brought his voice down to a gruff baritone, a parody of half the Videssian officers in the audience.

"And you're right." His tones were his own again. "But the question still remains: When we and the men of the Duchy quarrel at theology, when we damn each other and fling anathemas across the sea like stones, who gains? The Phos we all revere? Or does Skotos, down there in his frozen hell, laugh to see his enemies at strife with one another?

"The saddest part of the disagreement between us is that our beliefs are no further apart than two women in the streets. For is it not true that, while orthodoxy is indeed my doxy, heterodoxy is no more than my neighbor's doxy?" Balsamon's listeners gaped in horror or awestruck admiration, each according to his own temperament.

The patriarch became serious once more. "I do not hold to the Wager of Phos, as do the islanders—you all know that, even those who like me none too well. I find the notion childish and crude. But by our standards, the Namdaleni *are* childish and crude. Is it any wonder they have a doctrine to fit their character? Merely because I think them mistaken, must I find them guilty of unpardonable crimes?"

His voice was pleading as he looked from one face to the next. The noise of the crowd outside the Temple had died away; Marcus could hear a great-voiced priest reading the patriarch's words to the multitude.

Balsamon resumed, "If the men of the Duchy have their faith founded on true piety—and that, no reasonable man could doubt—and if they grant us our customs in our own land, what cause have we to worry? Would you argue with your brother while a thief was at the door, especially if he'd come to help hold that thief at bay? Skotos is welcome to the man who'd answer yes.

"Nor are we Videssians without blame in this senseless squabble over the nature of our god. Our centuries of culture have given us, I fear, conceit to match our brilliance. We are splendid logic-choppers and fault-finders when we think we need to criticize our neighbors, but oh! how we bawl like branded calves when they dare return the favor.

"My friends, my brothers, my children, if we stretch out our arms in charity, even so little charity as would hardly damage the soul of a tax-collector"—No matter how solemn the moment, Balsamon would have his joke, and the sudden, startled laughter from outside when the reader reached it showed it had struck its intended audience—"surely we can overlook disagreements and build goodwill. The seeds are there—were it otherwise, why would the men of Namdalen sail from overseas to aid us against our foe? They deserve our grateful thanks, not tumult readied against them."

The patriarch looked about one last time, begging, willing his listeners to reach for something bigger than themselves. There was a moment of stony silence before the applause began. And when at last it came, it was not the torrent Balsamon—and Scaurus—would have wished for. Here a man clapped, there another, off to one side several more. Some looked sour even as they applauded, honoring the patriarch but at best tolerating the message for the sake of the man.

Mavrikios was not one of those. He had risen and pushed aside the ornamental grill work, loudly acclaiming Balsamon. At his side, also clapping, was his daughter Alypia. Thorisin Gavras was nowhere to be seen.

Marcus found a moment to worry over the Sevastokrator's absence. He could not recall seeing the two Gavrai together since their unfortunate meeting at dice. One more thing to plague the Emperor, he thought. It was a dreadful time for Mavrikios to be at odds with his peppery brother.

And not even the Emperor's open approval could make the notables in the High Temple warm to Balsamon's sermon. The same confused, halfhearted applause came from the larger audience outside. Marcus remembered what Gorgidas had said; even the patriarch had trouble turning the city from the direction it had chosen.

He did win some measure of success. When Soteric emerged from the High Temple, no one snarled at him. Indeed, a couple of people seemed to have taken Balsamon's words to heart, for they shouted "Death to the Yezda!" at the mercenary. Soteric grinned savagely and waved his sword in the air, which won him a few real cheers.

Such lukewarm victory left him dissatisfied. He turned to Scaurus, grumbling, "I thought that when the patriarch spoke, everyone leaped to do as he said. And by what right does he call the men of the Duchy children? One fine day, we'll show him the sort of children we are."

Marcus soothed his ruffled feathers. Having expected no improvement in the situation, the tribune was pleased with whatever he got.

Back at the Roman barracks that night, Scaurus did some hard thinking about Soteric. Helvis' brother could be alarming. He was, if anything, more headstrong than Thorisin Gavras—and that was saying something. Worse, he lacked the Sevastokrator's easy charm. Soteric was always in deadly earnest. Yet there was no denying his courage, his energy, his military skill, or even his wit. The tribune sighed. People were as they were, not as he wished they'd be, and it was stupid—especially for someone who thought himself a Stoic—to expect them to be different.

Nevertheless, he recalled the adage he'd mentally applied to Soteric when the islander proposed seizing Videssos in despite of the whole imperial army. He sought Gorgidas. "Who was it," he asked the Greek, "who said, 'Whom the gods would destroy, they first make mad'? Sophokles?"

"Merciful Zeus, no!" Gorgidas exclaimed. "That could only be Euripides, though I forget the play. When Sophokles speaks of human nature, he's so noble you wish his words were true. Where Euripides finds truth, you wish he hadn't."

The tribune wondered whose play he'd watched that afternoon.

IX

THE FELLOW-FEELING BALSAMON LABORED SO VALIANTLY TO CREATE crumbled, as things would have it, under the fury of an outraged section of his own clergy—the monks. All too few had Nepos' compassion or learning; most were arrogant in their bigotry. From their monasteries they swarmed forth like angry bees to denounce their patriarch's call for calm and to rouse Videssos once more to hatred.

Marcus was leading a couple of Roman maniples back from the practice field when he found his way blocked by a large crowd avidly taking in one such monk's harangue. The monastic, a tall thin man with a pocked face and fiery eyes, stood on an upended crate in front of a cheese merchant's shop and screamed out his hatred of heresy to everyone who would listen.

"Whoever tampers with the canons of the faith sells—no, gives!—his soul to the ice below! It is Phos' own holy words the foul foreigners pervert with their talk of wagers. They seek to seduce us from the way of truth into Skotos' frigid embrace, and our great patriarch"—In his rage, he fairly spat the word—"abets them and helps the demon spread his couch.

"For I tell you, my friends, there is, there can be, no compromise with evil. Corrupters of the faith lead others to the doom they have chosen for themselves, as surely as one rotten pear will spoil the cask. Balsamon prates of toleration—will he next tolerate a temple to Skotos?" The monk made "tolerate" into an obscenity.

His voice grew shriller yet. "If the eastern barbarians will not confess the truth of our faith, drive them from the city, I say! They are as much to be feared as the Yezda—more, for they wear virtue's mask to hide their misbelief!"

The audience he had built up shouted its agreement. Fists waved in the air; there were cries of "Dirty barbarians!" and "The pox take Nam-dalen!"

"We may be having to break their heads to get through, if himself pushes the fire up any more," Viridovix said to Marcus.

"If we do, we'll set the whole city ablaze," the tribune answered. But he could see his men loosening swords in their scabbards and taking a firmer grip on the staves they were carrying in lieu of spears.

Just then the monk looked over the heads of the throng before him and caught sight of the Romans' unfamiliar gear. He probably would not have recognized a true Namdalener had he seen one, but in his passion any foreigner would serve. He stretched out a long bony finger at the legionaries, crying, "See! It is the men of the Duchy, come to cut me down before my truth can spread!"

"No, indeed!" Marcus shouted as the crowd whirled to face the Romans. Behind him he heard Gaius Philippus warning, "Whether the mob does or not, I'll have the head of the first man who moves without orders!"

"What then?" the monk asked Scaurus suspiciously. The crowd was spreading out and edging forward, readying itself for a rush.

"Can't you tell by looking? We're the surveying party for that temple to Skotos you were talking about—do you know where it's supposed to go?"

The monk's eyes bulged like a freshly boated bream's. The members of the would-be mob stopped where they stood, gawping at the Roman's insolence. Scaurus watched them closely—would they see the joke or try to tear the Romans to pieces for blasphemy?

First one, then another, then three more in the crowd burst into guffaws. In an instant the whole fickle gathering was shrieking with laughter and running forward, not to attack the legionaries, but to praise their leader's wit. Suddenly deserted by his audience, the monk, with a last malice-filled glance at Scaurus, clambered down from his makeshift podium and disappeared—to spread his hatred elsewhere, Marcus was sure.

That, though, left his former throng discontented. The monastic had entertained them, and they expected the same from Scaurus. The silence stretched embarrassingly; with the tribune's one quip gone, his mind seemed blank.

Viridovix filled the breach in magnificent style, bursting into a borderer's song about fighting the cattle-thieves from Yezd. Only Marcus' thorough lack of interest in music had kept him from noticing what a fine voice Viridovix owned. Even his Gallic accent brought song to his speech. Someone in the crowd had a set of pipes; the Celt, the Videssians, and those Romans who knew the tune's words sang it through at the top of their lungs.

When it was done, one of the city men began another ditty, a ribald drinking song everyone in the crowd seemed to know. More legionaries could sing along with this one; Marcus himself had spent enough time in taverns to learn the chorus: "The wine gets drunk, but you get drunker!"

After two or three more songs it seemed as if the Romans and Videssians had been friends forever. They mingled easily, swapping names and stories. Marcus had no trouble continuing back to the barracks. A couple of dozen Videssians walked most of the way with the legionaries; every few blocks someone would think of a new song, and they would stop to sing it.

Once inside their hall at last, four of Scaurus' men discovered their belt pouches had been slit. But even Gaius Philippus, who under most conditions would have gone charging back into the city after the thieves, took the loss philosophically. "It's a small enough price to pay for dousing a riot," he said.

"Small enough for you, maybe," one of the robbed legionaries muttered, but so softly the centurion could not tell which. He snorted and gave them all an impartial glare.

"Sure and that was quick of you, to stop the shindy or ever it started," Viridovix said to Scaurus. "Was your honor not afraid it might set the spalpeens off altogether?"

"Yes," Marcus admitted, "but I didn't think we would be much worse off if it did. There wasn't time to reason with them, or much hope of it, for that matter—not with that madman of a monk egging them on. I thought I had to shock them, or make them laugh—by luck, I managed to do both at once. You helped a bit yourself, you know; you sing very well."

"Don't I, now?" the Celt agreed complacently. "Aye, there's nothing like a good tune to make a man forget the why of his ire. There's some fine songs in this Videssian tongue, too. That first one I sang reminds me of a ditty I knew at home—kine-stealing's almost a game with us, for pride and honor's sake, and we're fond of singing over it.

"Or we were," he added bleakly. For a rare moment, he let Marcus see the loneliness he usually hid so well.

Touched, the tribune reached out to clasp his shoulder. "You're among friends, you know," he said. It was true—there was not a Roman who had anything but liking for their former foe.

Viridovix knew that, too. "Aye," he said, tugging at his long mustaches, "and glad I am of it, but there's times when it's scarce enough." He said something in his own tongue, then shook his head. "Even in my ears the Celtic speech grows strange."

The riots against Namdalen began in earnest the next day, incited, as Marcus had feared, by the monks. The day was one sacred to Phos. Processions of worshippers marched through the streets carrying torches and gilded spheres and discs of wood as they hymned their god. As the tribune learned much later, one such parade was wending its way down Videssos' chief thoroughfare—the locals, with their liking for simple names, called it Middle Street—when it happened to pass a small temple where the Namdaleni were celebrating the holiday with their own rites.

Seeing a party of islanders enter the schismatic chapel infuriated the monks heading the procession. "Root out the heretics!" they cried. This time no jests or soft words distracted their followers. Phos' torches torched Phos' temple; believer slew believer, believing him benighted. And when the Namdaleni sallied forth from their smoke, as brave men would, Videssian blood, too, crimsoned the cobbles of Middle Street.

The mob, made brave only by numbers, was rabid when a few from among those numbers fell. "Revenge!" they screamed, ignoring their own guilt, and went ravening through the city for Namdaleni to destroy. As riots will, this one quickly grew past its prime purpose. Burning, looting, and rape were sports too delightful to be reserved for the islanders alone; before long, the swelling mob extended their benefits to natives of the city as well. Nevertheless, the men of the Duchy remained chief targets of the rioters' attention.

The mob's distant baying and the black pillars of smoke shooting into the sky brought news of the tumult to the Romans. Scaurus was always thankful the city did not erupt until noon, Phos' most auspicious hour. The early-rising legionaries had already finished their drill and returned to the palace complex before the storm broke. It could have gone hard for them, trapped in a labyrinth the Videssian rioters knew far better than they.

At first Scaurus thought the outbreak minor, on the order of the one that had followed his own encounter with Avshar's necromancy. A few battalions of native soldiers had sufficed to put down that disturbance. The tribune watched the Videssians tramping into action, armed for riot duty with clubs and blunt-headed spears. Within two hours they were streaming back in disarray, dragging dead and wounded behind them. Their smoke-blackened faces showed stunned disbelief. Beyond the palace complex, Videssos was in the hands of the mob.

Sending inadequate force against the rioters proved worse than sending none. The howling pack, buoyed up by the cheap victory, grew bolder yet. Marcus had gone up onto the roof of the Roman barracks to see what he could of the city and its strife; now he watched knots of ill-armed men pushing through the lush gardens of the palace quarter itself, on the prowl for robbery or murder.

Still far away but terribly clear, he could hear the mob's battle cry: "Dig up the bones of the Namdaleni!" The call was a bit of lower-class city slang; when Videssos' thieves and pimps were displeased with someone, they wished him an unquiet grave. If the Roman needed further telling, that rallying-cry showed him who the rioters were.

Scaurus put a maniple of battle-ready legionaries around his soldiers' barracks. Whether the bared steel they carried deterred the mob or the Videssians simply had no quarrel with the Roman force, no rioters tested them.

Sunset was lurid; it seemed grimly appropriate for Phos' symbol to be reduced to a ball of blood disappearing through thick smoke.

Like dragons' tongues, flames licked into the night sky. In their island of calm the Romans passed the hours of darkness at full combat alert. Marcus did not think the Videssians would use his men against the rioters, judging from their past practice, but he was not nearly so sure the mob would keep giving immunity to the legionaries.

The tribune stayed on his feet most of the night. It was long after midnight before he decided the barracks probably would not be attacked. He sought his pallet for a few hours of uneasy sleep.

One of his troopers roused him well before dawn. "What is it?" he asked blearily, only half-awake. Then he jerked upright as full memory returned. "Are we under assault?"

"No, sir. It's almost too quiet, what with the ruction all around us, but there's no trouble here. Nephon Khoumnos says he needs to speak with you; my officer thinks it sounds important enough for me to get you up. If you like, though, I'll send him away."

"Who's out there? Glabrio?"

"Yes, sir."

Marcus trusted that quiet young centurion's judgment and discretion. "I'll see Khoumnos," he said, "but if you can, hold him up for a couple of minutes to let me get my wits together."

"I'll take care of it," the legionary promised and hurried away. Scaurus splashed water on his face from the ewer by his bed, ran a comb through his sleep-snarled hair, and tried to shake a few of the wrinkles from his cloak before putting it on.

He could have omitted his preparations, sketchy as they were. When the Roman guardsman led Nephon Khoumnos into the barracks hall, a glance was enough to show that the Videssian officer was a man in the last stages of exhaustion. His usual crisp stride had decayed into a rolling, almost drunken gait; he seemed to be holding his eyes open by main force. With a great sigh, he collapsed into the chair the Romans offered him.

"No, no wine, thank you. If I drink I'll fall asleep, and I can't yet." He yawned tremendously, knuckling his red-tracked eyes at the same time. "Phos, what a night!" he muttered.

When he sat without elaborating, Marcus prompted him, "How are things out there?"

"How do you think? They're bad, very bad. I'd sooner be naked in a wood full of wolves than an honest man on the streets tonight. Being robbed is the best you could hope for; it gets worse from there."

Gaius Philippus came up in time to hear him. Blunt as always, he said, "What have you been waiting for? It's only a mob running wild, not an army. You have the men to squash it flat in an hour's time."

Khoumnos twisted inside his shirt of mail, as if suddenly finding its weight intolerable. "I wish things were as simple as you make them."

"I'd better turn around," Gaius Philippus said, "because I think you're about to bugger me."

"Right now I couldn't raise a stand for the fanciest whore in the city, let alone an ugly old ape like you." Khoumnos drew a bark of laughter from the senior centurion, but was abruptly sober again. "No more could I turn the army loose in the city. For one thing, too many of the men won't try very hard to keep the mob from the Namdaleni—they have no use for the islanders themselves."

"It's a sour note when one part of your fornicating army won't help the next," Gaius Philippus said.

"That's as may be, but it doesn't make it any less true. It cuts both ways, though: the men of the Duchy don't trust Videssian soldiers much further than they do any other Videssians."

Scaurus felt like turning around himself; he had caught Nephon Khoumnos' drift, and did not like it. The imperial officer confirmed the tribune's fears with his next words. "In the whole capital there are only two bodies of troops who have the respect of city-folk and Namdaleni alike: the Halogai, and your men. I want to use you as a screen to separate the mob and the easterners, while Videssian troops bring the city as a whole under control. With you and the Halogai keeping the main infection cordoned off, the riot should lose force quickly."

The tribune was anything but eager to use his troops in the street-fighting that wracked Videssos. He had already learned the mercenary commander's first lesson: his men were his capital, and not to be spent lightly or thrown away piecemeal in tiny, meaningless brawls down the city's back alleys. Unfortunately, what Khoumnos was proposing made sense. Without the excitement of heretic-hunting, riot for the sake of riot would lose much of its appeal. "Are you ordering us into action, then?" he demanded.

Had Nephon Khoumnos given him an imperious yes, he probably would have refused him outright—in the city's confusion, Khoumnos could not have enforced the order. But the Videssian was a soldier of many years' standing and knew the ways of mercenaries better than Scaurus himself. He had also come to know the tribune accurately.

"Ordering you?" he said. "No. Had I intended to give you orders, I could have sent them through a spatharios. I came to ask a favor, for the Empire's sake. Balsamon put it better than I could—the fight against Yezd makes everything else trivial beside it. No matter what the idiot monks say, that's true. That fight can't go forward without peace here. Will you help bring it?"

"Damn you," Scaurus said tiredly, touched on the weak spot of his sense of duty. There were times, he thought, when a bit of simple selfishness would be much sweeter than the responsibility his training had drilled into him. He considered how much of his limited resources he could afford to risk.

"Four hundred men," he decided. "Twenty squads of twenty. No units smaller than that, unless my officers order it—I won't have a solitary trooper on every corner for the young bucks to try their luck with."

"Done," Khoumnos said at once, "and thank you."

"If I said you were welcome, I'd be a liar." Shifting into Latin, Scaurus turned to Gaius Philippus. "Help me find the men I'll need. Keep things tightly buttoned here while we're gone and in the name of the gods don't throw good men after bad if we come to grief. Even if we should, you'd still have better than a cohort left; that's a force to reckon with, in this world of useless infantry."

"Hold up, there. What's this talk about you not coming back, and what I'd have if you didn't?" the centurion said. "I'm going out there myself."

Marcus shook his head. "Not this time, my friend. I have to go—it's by my orders we're heading into this, and I will not send men into such a stew without sharing it with them. Too many officers will be out in the city as is; someone here has to be able to pick up the pieces if a few of us don't come back. That's you, I fear. Curse it, don't make this harder than it is; I don't dare risk both of us at once."

On Gaius Philippus' face discipline struggled with desire and finally threw it to the mat. "Aye, sir," he said, but his toneless voice accented instead of concealed his hurt. "Let's get the men picked out."

The colloquy between Khoumnos, the tribune, and Gaius Philippus had been low-voiced, but once men were chosen to go out into Videssos and they began to arm themselves, all hope for quiet vanished. As Scaurus had feared, Viridovix woke up wildly eager to go into the city and fight.

The tribune had to tell him no. "They want us to stop the riot, not heat it further. You know your temper, Viridovix. Tell me truly, is that the task you relish?"

Marcus had to give the big Gaul credit; he really did examine himself, chewing on his mustaches as he thought. "A plague on you for a cruel, hard man, Marcus Aemilius Scaurus, and another for being right. What a cold world it is, where a man knows himself too hot-blooded to be trusted with the breaking of heads."

"You can stay here and wrangle with me," Gaius Philippus said. "I'm not going either."

"What? You?" Viridovix stared at him. "Foosh, man, it'd be the perfect job for you—for a good soldier, you're the flattest man ever I've met."

"Son of a goat," the centurion growled, and their long-running feud was on again. Scaurus smiled inside himself to hear them; each, he knew, would take out some of his disappointment on the other.

When the selection was done, and while the legionaries chosen were readying themselves for action, the tribune asked Khoumnos, "Where are you sending us?"

The Videssian officer considered. "There's a lot of newly come Namdaleni in the southern harbor district, especially round the small harbor; you know, the harbor of Kontoskalion. My reports say the fighting has been vicious there—city people murdering islanders, and islanders murdering right back when the odds are in their favor. It's a running sore that needs closing."

"That's what we'll be there for, isn't it?" Marcus said. He made no effort to pretend an enthusiasm he did not feel. "The harbor district, you say? Southeast of here, isn't it?"

"That's right," Khoumnos agreed. He started to say more, but the tribune cut him off.

"Enough talk. All I want is to get this worthless job over. Soonest begun, soonest done. Let's be at it." He strode out of the barracks into the predawn twilight.

As the legionaries came to attention, he walked to the head of their column. There were a couple of warnings he felt he had to give his men before he led them into action. "Remember, this is riot duty, not combat—I hope. We want the least force needed to bring order, not the most, lest the riot turn on us. Don't spear someone for throwing a rotten cabbage at you.

"That's one side of things. Here's the other: if your life is on the line, don't spend it; if the choice is between you and a rioter, you count ten thousand times as much, so don't take any stupid chances. We're all the Romans there are here and all the Romans who ever will be here. Do your job, do what you have to do, but use your heads."

He knew as he gave it the advice was equivocal, but it accurately reflected his mixed feelings over the mission Khoumnos had given him. As the sun rose red through the city's smoke, he said, "Let's be off," and marched his men away from their barracks, out of the palace complex, and into the strife-torn heart of the city.

Most times he savored Videssos' early mornings, but not today. Smoke stung his eyes and stank in his nostrils. Instead of the calls of gulls and songbirds, the dominant sounds in the city were looters' cries, the crack of glass and splintering of boards as houses and shops were plundered, and the occasional sliding rumble of a fire-gutted building crashing down.

The legionaries stayed in a single body on their way to the harbor of Kontoskalion. Scaurus did not intend to risk his men before he had to and reckoned the sight of four hundred armored, shielded warriors tramping past would be enough to make any mob think twice.

So it proved; aside from curses and a few thrown stones, no one interfered with the Romans as they marched. But theirs was a tiny, moving bubble of order drifting through chaos. Videssos, it seemed, had abandoned law's constraints for an older, more primitive rule: to the strong, the quick, the clever go the spoils.

Where there were few Namdaleni to hunt, the riot lost part of its savagery and became something of a bizarre carnival. Three youths pulled velvet-covered pillows from a shop and tossed them into the arms of a waiting, cheering crowd. Marcus saw a middle-aged man and woman dragging a heavy couch down a sidestreet, presumably toward their home.

A younger pair, using their clothes for padding, made love atop a heap of rubble; they, too, were cheered on by a rapt audience. The Romans passing by stared and shouted with as much enthusiasm as any Videssians. They clattered their shields against their greaves to show their enjoyment. When the couple finished, they sprang to their feet and scampered away, leaving their clothes behind.

In madness' midst, the occasional island of normality was strange in itself. Marcus bought a pork sausage on a bun from a vender plying his trade as if all were peaceful as could be. "Haven't you had any trouble?" the tribune asked as he handed the man a copper.

"Trouble? Why should I? Everyone knows me, they do. Biggest problem I've had is making change for all the gold I've got today. A thing like this is good for the city now and again, says I—it stirs things up, a tonic, like." And he was off, loudly crying his wares.

Two streets further south, the Romans came upon a double handful of corpses sprawled on the cobbles. From what could be seen through the blackened, congealed blood that covered them, some were Namdaleni while others had been city men. They were covered in little more than their blood; all the bodies, alien and citizen alike, had been stripped during the night.

Soon the sound of active combat came to the Romans' ears. "At a trot!" Scaurus called. His men loped forward. They rounded a corner to find four Namdaleni, two of them armed only with knives, trying to hold off what must have been three times their number of attackers. Another easterner was on the ground beside them, as were two shabbily dressed Videssians.

Their losses made the rioters less than enthusiastic about the fight they had picked. While the ones to the rear yelled, "Forward!" those at the fore hung back, suddenly leery of facing professional soldiers with weapons to hand.

The Videssians cried out in terror when they saw and heard the Romans bearing down on them. They turned to flee, throwing away their weapons to run the faster.

The men of the Duchy joyfully greeted their unexpected rescuers. Their leader introduced himself as Utprand Dagober's son. He was not a man Marcus had seen before; the tribune guessed he must be one of the newly come Namdalener mercenaries. His island accent was so thick he sounded almost like a Haloga. But if the tribune had trouble with his shades of meaning, there was no mistaking what Utprand wanted.

"Are you not after the devilings?" he demanded. "T'ree of my stout lads they kill already—we had the misfortune to be near their High Temple when they set on us and we've crawled through stinking alleys since, trying to reach our mates. Do for them, I say!" The other islanders still on their feet snarled agreement.

After some of the things he had seen in Videssos, Marcus was tempted to turn his men loose like so many wolves. Though it would do no good—and in the long run endless harm—it would be so satisfying. In this outburst the city folk had forfeited a great part of the respect he had come to feel for their state. He could also see the legionaries trembling to be unleashed.

He shook his head with regret, but firmly. "We were sent here to make matters better, not worse, and to form a cordon between you and the Videssians to let the riot burn itself out. It has to be so, you know," he said, giving Utprand the same argument he had used against Soteric. "If the imperial army moves against you with the mob, you're doomed, do what you will. Would you have us incite them to it?"

Utprand measured him, eyes pale in a gaunt, smoke-blackened face. "I never thought I could want to hate a clear-thinking man. Curse you for being right—it gripes my belly like a green apple that you are."

He and two of his men took up their fallen comrade and the dagger he had used in vain to defend himself. Marcus wondered where the dead man's sword might be and who would take the dagger to his kin. The three started toward their camp by the harbor. The fourth islander, Grasulf Gisulf's son, stayed behind with the Romans to point out the best places to seal off the harbor of Kontoskalion from the rest of the city.

The tribune posted his double squads where Grasulf recommended;

most of them were stationed along major streets leading north and south. Scaurus had no reason to complain of Grasulf's choices. The Namdalener had an eye for a defensible position.

As he'd known he might have to, Marcus gave his underofficers leave to split their commands in half to cover more ground. "But I want no fewer than ten men together," he warned them, "and if you do divide your forces, stay in earshot of each other so you can rejoin quickly at need."

The Romans worked their way steadily west. They passed from a district of small shops, taverns, and cramped, untidy houses into a quarter inhabited by merchants who had made their fortunes at Videssos' harbors and still dwelt nearby. Their splendid homes were set off from the winding streets by lawns and gardens and warded further with tall fences or hedges of thorn. These had not always saved them from the mob's fury. Several were burned, looted wrecks. Others, though still standing, had hardly a pane of glass left in their windows. Many had an unmistakable air of desertion about them. Their owners, knowing how easily rioters' anger could turn from the foreign to the merely wealthy, had taken no chances and left for safety in the suburbs or on the western shore of the Cattle-Crossing.

By the time he had penetrated most of the way into this section of the city, Marcus had only a couple of units of legionaries still with him. He placed one between a temple of Phos built solidly enough to double as a fortress and a mansion's outreaching wall. Along with Grasulf and his last twenty men, he pressed on to find a good spot to complete the cordon. The sound of the sea, never absent in Videssos, was sharp in his ears; a final good position should seal Videssians and Namdaleni from each other.

A spot quickly offered itself. Sometime during the night, the rioters had battered a rich man's wall to rubble and swarmed in to plunder his villa. The prickly hedge on the other side of the street still stood, unchallenged. "We can throw up a barricade here," the tribune said, "and stand off troubles from either side."

His men fell to work with the usual Roman thoroughness; a breastwork of broken brick and stone soon stretched across the roadway. Marcus surveyed it with considerable pride. Fighting behind it, he thought, the legionaries could stop many times their numbers.

That thought loosed another. The position the Romans had just made was so strong it did not really need twenty men to hold it. He could leave ten behind and push closer yet to the sea. It would be safe enough, he thought. This part of the city, unlike the turbulent portion he'd gone through before, seemed to be a no man's land of sorts. Most of the property owners had already fled, and, after the storm of looting passed by, neither the men of the city nor those of the Duchy were making much use of these ways to reach each other.

Taking heart in that observation, Marcus divided his small force in two. "I know just the place for you," Grasulf told him. He led the Romans to a crossroads between four mansions, each of them with strong outwalls at the edge of the street. The sea was very close now; along with its constant boom against the seawall, the tribune could hear individual waves slap-slapping against ships and pilings in the harbor of Kontoskalion.

The city was still troubled. New smokes rose into the noonday sky, and from afar came the sound of fighting. Scaurus wondered if the mob was battling Namdaleni, the Videssian army, or itself. He also wondered how long and how much it would take before Nephon Khoumnos—or, by rights, the Emperor himself—decided to teach the city's explosive populace a lesson it would remember.

In this momentary backwater it was easy to forget such things. The Romans stood to arms for the first couple of hours at their post, but when nothing more frightening came by than a stray dog and a ragpicker with a great bag of scraps slung over his back, the tribune did not see anything amiss in letting them relax a bit. While three men took turns on alert, the others sat in the narrow shade of the southern wall. They shared food and wine with Grasulf. The Namdalener puckered his lips at their drink's bite, though to Scaurus it was still too sweet.

Shadows were beginning to lengthen when the distant commotion elsewhere in Videssos grew suddenly louder. It did not take Marcus long to decide the new outbreak was due east of his position—and, from its swelling volume, heading west at an uncomfortable clip.

His men climbed to their feet at his command, grumbling over leaving their shadows for the sunshine's heat. As any good soldiers would, they quickly checked their gear, making sure their short swords were free in their scabbards and their shield straps were not so frayed as to give in action.

Videssos' twisting, narrow streets distorted sound in odd ways. The mob's roar grew ever closer, but until it was all but on him Scaurus did not think he was standing in its path. He was ready to rush his men to another Roman party's aid when the first rioters turned the corner less than a hundred yards away and spotted his little detachment blocking their path.

They stopped in confusion. Unlike the monk a few days before, they knew the warriors in front of them were not Namdaleni and had to decide whether they were foes.

Taking advantage of their indecision, Marcus took a few steps forward. "Go back to your homes!" he shouted. "We will not harm you if you leave in peace!" He knew how colossal the bluff was, but with any luck the mob would not.

For a heady second he thought he had them. A couple of men at the head of the throng, plump middle-class types who looked badly out of place among the rioters, turned as if to retreat. But then a fellow behind them, a greasy little weasel of a man, recognized Grasulf for what he was. "An islander!" he yelled shrilly. "They're trying to keep him from us!" The rioters rushed forward in a ragged battle line, brandishing a motley collection of makeshift or stolen weapons.

"Oh, bugger," one of the legionaries beside Marcus muttered as he drew his sword. The tribune had a sinking feeling in the pit of his stomach. More and more Videssians kept rounding that cursed corner. The Romans were professional soldiers, true, but as a professional Scaurus knew enough to mislike odds of seven or eight to one against him.

"To me, to me!" he shouted, wondering how many Romans he could draw to his aid and whether they would come too late and be swallowed up band after band by the mob.

Grasulf touched his arm. "Bring my sword home, if you can," he said. And with a wild cry the Namdalener charged forward against the mob. His blade swung in two glittering arcs; a pair of heads bounced from rioters' shoulders to the ground. Had his success gone on, he might have singlehandedly cowed his foes. But the same little sneakthief who had first spied him now darted up to plunge his dagger through the Namdalener's mail shirt and into his back. Grasulf fell; howling in triumph as they trampled his corpse, the mob stormed into the Romans.

The legionaries were well trained and heavily armed. They wore chain mail and greaves and carried their metal-faced semicylindrical shields. But their foes had such weight of numbers pushing them on that the Roman line, which by the nature of things could only be three men deep here, cracked almost at once. Then the fighting turned into a series of savage combats, in each of which one or two Romans were pitted against far too many opponents.

In his place at the legionaries' fore, Marcus had three men slam into him at once. One was dead as he hit, the tribune's sword twisting in his guts to make sure of the kill. But his momentum and that of his two living comrades bowled Scaurus to the ground. He pulled his shield over him and saved himself from the worst of the trampling as the mob passed over him, but it was only luck that no one aimed anything more deadly at him than a glancing blow from a club.

Striking out desperately in all directions with his sword, he managed to scramble to his feet after less than a minute on the cobblestones, to find himself alone in the midst of the mob. He slashed his way toward a wall that would cover his back. To judge from the noise and the flow of the action, the other Romans yet on their feet were doing the same.

A Videssian armed with a short hunting spear lunged at the tribune. His thrust was wide; its impetus propelled him into the Roman's shield. Marcus shoved as hard as he could. Taken off balance, the rioter stumbled backwards to trip up another of his fellows. Scaurus' sword made them both pay for the one's clumsiness.

Not all the rioters, luckily, were staying to fight the Romans. Some kept pressing west, in the hopes of finding Namdaleni to slaughter. Before long, only the mob's tail was still assailing the tribune. As the pressure against him eased, he began to hope he would live.

Through the din of fighting he heard the shouts and clatter of more Romans charging to the aid of the beleaguered squad. The rioters, without the discipline of real warriors, could not stand against their rush.

Marcus started to call out to his men, but at that moment a stone rang off the side of his helmet, filling his head with a shower of silver sparks. As he staggered, his sword slipped from his hand. A rioter bent, snatched it up, and fled; newly armed or not, he had seen enough combat for this day.

Panic's chill wind blew through Marcus' brain. Had it been an ordinary Roman shortsword, he would have been glad enough to let the thief keep his booty. But this was the blade whose magic had brought him to this very world, the blade that stood against Avshar and all his sorceries, the blade that lent him strength. He threw his shield aside, drew his long-unused dagger, and gave chase.

He thanked his gods the fighting had almost passed him by. His hurled *scutum* decked one Videssian, a slash on his arm sent another reeling back. Then Scaurus was free of the crush and pounding after the sword-thief.

His pulse thudded in his ears as he ran; he would gladly have foregone the weight of his armor and his heavy boots. But his long strides were still closing the gap. The man bouncing along ahead of him was a short, fat fellow who seemed too prosperous to need to riot. Hearing himself pursued, he looked back over his shoulder and almost ran full tilt into a wall. He saved himself at the last instant and scurried down an alleyway, Marcus ten yards behind.

Strain as he would, the tribune could get no closer. Nor could his quarry shake free, though his zigzagging dash through backstreets and by-roads lost Scaurus in Videssos' maze.

The thief's knowledge of the city's ways was no more perfect than Marcus'. He darted halfway down an alley without realizing it was blind. Before he could mend his error, the tribune came panting up to cork the entrance.

Wiping the sweat from his face, the rotund thief brought his stolen sword up to the guard position. The awkward set of his feet and his tentative passes with the blade said he was no swordsman. Scaurus approached with caution anyhow. His opponent, after all, had three times his length of blade, clumsy or not.

He took another pace forward, saying, "I don't want to have to fight you. Lay my sword down and you can go, for all of me."

Scaurus never learned whether the other thought he spoke from cowardice and was thus emboldened, or whether he simply was afraid to be weaponless before the Roman. He leaped at Marcus, swinging the tribune's sword with a stroke that confirmed his ineptness. But even as Marcus' mind realized he was facing a tyro, his body responded with the motions long hours on the practice field had drilled into it. He ducked under the amateurish slash and stepped forward to drive his knife into his foe's belly.

The plump thief's mouth shaped a voiceless "Oh." He dropped the Roman's blade to clutch his wound with both hands. His eyes went wide, then suddenly showed only white as he sagged to the ground.

Marcus stooped to recover his sword. He felt no pride in his victory, rather self-disgust at having killed an opponent so little a match for him. He looked reproachfully down at the crumpled corpse at his feet. Why hadn't the fat fool had enough sense to bar his door and stay behind it, instead of playing at what he knew nothing about?

The tribune thought he could let his ears lead him back to the brawl between his man and the rioters, but retracing his path was not so simple. The winding streets kept leading him away from the direction in which he needed to go, and that direction itself seemed to shift as he moved. The homes he walked by offered few clues to guide him. Their outer walls and hedges were so much alike that only a longtime resident of the neighborhood could have steered by them.

He was passing another not much different from the rest when he heard a scuffle from the far side of the wall. Scuffles today were a copper a handful; worrying about finding his way back to the Romans, Scaurus was on the point of ignoring this one until it was suddenly punctuated by a woman's scream.

The sound of a blow cut across it. "Quiet, bitch!" a rough male voice roared.

"Let her bleat," another replied, coldly callous. "Who's to hear, anyway?"

The wall was too high to see over and too high for a man encumbered by armor to hope to climb. Marcus' eye flashed to its gate. He ran at it, crashing into it with an iron-clad shoulder. It flew open, sending the tribune stumbling inside onto a wide expanse of close-trimmed grass.

The two men holding a woman pinned to that grass looked up in amazement as their sport was interrupted. One had hold of her bare shoulders; a ripped tunic lay nearby. The other was between her thrashing white legs, hiking her heavy skirt up over her waist.

The second man died as he was scrambling to his feet, Marcus' blade through his throat. The tribune had a moment's regret at giving him so easy an end, but then he was facing the dead man's comrade, who was made of sterner stuff. Though he looked a street ruffian, he carried a shortsword instead of a dagger, and from his first cut Scaurus saw he knew how to use it.

After that first slash failed to fell the Roman, his enemy chose a purely defensive fight and seemed to be looking for a chance to break and run. But when he tried to flee, the woman he had been holding down snaked out a wrist to trip him. Marcus ran the falling man through. Where he had regretted killing the miserable little fellow who ran off with his sword, now he felt nothing but satisfaction at ridding the world of this piece of human offal.

He knelt to wipe his blade on the dead man's shirt, then turned, saying, "Thank you, lass, the whoreson might have got away if you—" His mouth stayed open, but no more words emerged. The woman sitting up was Helvis.

She was staring at him, too, seeing for the first time who her rescuer was. "Marcus?" she said, as if in doubt. Then, sobbing wildly in reaction to the terror of a moment before, she ran to him. Of themselves, his arms tightened around her. The flesh of her back was very smooth and still cool from the touch of the grass to which she had been forced. She trembled under his hands.

"Thank you, oh, thank you," she kept repeating, her head pressed against his corseleted shoulder. A moment later she added, "There's so much metal about you—must you imprison me in an armory?"

Scaurus realized how tightly he was holding her to his armored front. He eased his grip a bit; she did not pull away, but still clung to him as well. "In the name of your Phos, what are you doing here?" the tribune demanded roughly. The stress of the moment made his concern sound angry. "I thought you safely back at your people's barracks by the palaces."

It was precisely because of Phos, he learned, that she was not at the Namdalener barracks. She had chosen to celebrate her god's holiday— was it only yesterday? Marcus wondered; that seemed impossible—by praying not at the temple near the barracks, but at another one here in the southern part of Videssos. It was a shrine popular with the Namdaleni, for it was dedicated to a holy man who had lived and worked on the island of Namdalen, though he was three hundred years dead before the northerners wrested his native land from the Empire.

Helvis continued, "When the riots started and the crowds were screaming, 'Dig up the Gamblers' bones!' I had no hope of getting back to my home through the streets. I knew my countrymen had an encampment by the harbor and decided to make for that. Last night I spent in a deserted house. When I heard the mob screaming down toward the harbor, I thought I should hide again.

"The far gate over there was open," she said, pointing. She ruefully went on, "I found out why all too soon. Those—" No word sufficed; she shuddered instead "—were ransacking the place, and I was just another lucky bit of loot."

"It's all right now," Scaurus said, stroking her tangled hair with the same easy motion he would have used to gentle a frightened horse. She sighed and snuggled closer. For the first time, he was actually aware of her half-clothed state and that their embrace was changing from one sort of thing to another altogether.

He bent his head to kiss the top of hers. Her hands stroked the back of his neck as he tilted her face up to his. He kissed her lips, her ear; his mouth trailed down her neck toward her uncovered breasts. Her skirt rustled as it slid over her hips and fell to the ground. His own coverings were more complicated, but he was free of them soon enough. He had a brief second of worry for his embattled men, but this once not all his discipline could have stopped him from sinking to the grass beside the woman waiting for him there.

There is almost always a feeling among first-time lovers, no matter how much they please each other, that their love will grow better as they come to know each other more. So it was here; there was fumbling, some awkwardness, as between any two people unsure of one another's likes. Despite that, though, for the tribune it was far sweeter than he had known before, and he was so close to his own time of joy he nearly did not notice the name Helvis cried as her nails dug into his back was not his own.

Afterward he would have liked nothing better than to lie beside her forever, wholly at peace with the world. But now the tuggings of his conscience were too strong to ignore. Already he felt guilt's first stir over the time he had spent pleasuring himself while his troopers fought. He tried to drown it with Helvis' lips but, as is ever the way, only watered it instead.

His armor had never felt more confining than when he redonned it now. He handed Helvis her slain attacker's shortsword, saying, "Wait for me, love. You'll be safer here, I think, even alone, than on the streets. I won't be long, I promise."

Another woman might have protested being left behind, but Helvis had seen combat and knew what Marcus was going to. She rose, ran her finger down his cheek to the corner of his mouth. "Yes," she said. "Oh, yes. Come back for me."

Like a man recovering from a debilitating fever, Videssos slowly came back to its usual self. The riots, as Khoumnos had predicted, died away after the Romans and Halogai succeeded in cordoning off the Namdaleni who were their focus. By the time a week had gone by, the city was nearly normal once more, save for the uncleared piles of rubble that showed where the mob had struck. Small, stubborn columns of smoke still rose from some of these, but the danger of great conflagrations was past.

Where the city was almost itself again, Scaurus' life changed tremendously in the couple of weeks following the riots. He and a party of his men had taken Helvis first to the Namdaleni based by the harbor of Kontoskalion and then, as Videssos began to calm, she was able to return to the islanders' barracks in the palace complex.

She did not stay there long, however. Their first unexpected union did not slake, but whetted, her appetite and the tribune's. It was only days before she and Marcus—and Malric—took quarters in one of the two halls the Romans reserved for partnered men.

While he was more eager to share her company than he had ever been for anyone else's, a few concerns still gave him pause. First and foremost in his mind was the attitude Soteric would take. The tribune had seen more than once how prickly Helvis' brother could be when he thought his honor touched. How would he react to the Roman's first taking his sister and then taking her away?

When he raised the question to Helvis, she disposed of it with a woman's practicality. "Don't trouble yourself over it. If anything needs saying, I'll say it; I doubt it will. You hardly seduced a blushing virgin, you know, and had you not been there, the dogs who had me likely would have slit my throat when they were too worn to have any other use for me. Dearest, your saving me will count for more with Soteric than anything else—and so it should."

"But—" Helvis stopped his protest with a kiss, but could not quiet his fretting so easily. Still, events proved her right. Her brother's gratitude for her rescue carried over to the rescuer as well. He treated Marcus like a member of his family, and his example carried over to the rest of the Namdaleni. They knew what the Romans had done for them in Videssos' turmoil; when the legionaries' commander fell in love with one of their women, it was yet another reason to treat him as one of themselves.

That problem solved, Marcus waited for the reaction of his own men to the new situation. There was some good-natured chaffing, for the Romans knew his acquiescence to their taking companions had been grudging, and here he was with one himself.

"Pay them no mind," Gaius Philippus said. "No one will care if you're bedding a woman, a boy, or a purple sheep, so long as you think with your head and not with your crotch." And after that bit of pungent but cogent advice the centurion went off to hone his troops once more.

It was, Scaurus found, a suggestion easier to give than to follow. He found himself wallowing in sensuality in a way unlike any he had known. Before, he was always moderate in venery—in vanished Mediolanum, in Caesar's army, and since his arrival in Videssos. When he needed release he would buy it, and he did not often seek the same woman twice. Now, with Helvis, he found himself making up for long denial and growing greedier of her with every night that passed.

She, too, took ever-increasing delight from their love. Hers was a simple, fierce desire; though she had looked at no man since Hemond's death, her body nonetheless craved what it had become accustomed to and reacted blissfully to its return. Marcus found he was sleeping more soundly than he had since he was a boy. It was lucky, he thought once, that Avshar's Khamorth had not come seeking him after he found Helvis. He surely would never have wakened at the nomad's approach.

Scaurus had wondered how Malric would adjust to the change in his life, but Helvis' son was still young enough to take almost anything in his stride. Before long he was calling the tribune "Papa" as often as "Marcus," which gave the Roman an odd feeling, half pride, half sorrow it was not so. The lad instantly became the legionaries' pet. There were few children around the barracks, and the soldiers spoiled them all. Malric picked up Latin with the incredible ease small children have.

There were days when the tribune almost forgot he was in a city arming for war. He wished there could be more of them; he had never been happier in his life.

X

"It's bloody well time," Gaius Philippus said when the summons to the imperial council of war came. "The campaign should have started two months ago and more."

"Politics," Marcus answered. He added, "The riots didn't help, either. But for them, I think we'd be under way by now." With faint irony, he heard himself justifying the delays he had complained about not long before. He was much less anxious to begin than he had been then and knew why only too acutely. At the moment, it was as well such matters were not under his control.

The tribune had not been in the Hall of the Nineteen Couches since the night of his duel with Avshar. As always, the reception hall was couchless. A series of tables was joined end-to-end to form a line down its center. Atop the tables were maps of the Videssian army's proposed line of march; along them sat the leaders from every troop contingent in that army: Videssians, Khatrishers, nomadic Khamorth chieftains, Namdalener officers, and now the Romans too.

Mavrikios Gavras, as was his prerogative, sat at the head of the tables. Marcus was glad to see Thorisin at his brother's right hand. He hoped it meant their rift was healing. But the other two people by the Emperor made Scaurus want to rub his eyes to make sure they were not tricking him.

At Mavrikios' left sat Ortaias Sphrantzes. For all the young aristocrat's book-learning about war, Marcus would not have thought he had either the knowledge or the mettle to be part of this council, even if he was a member of the Emperor's faction instead of the nephew of Gavras' greatest rival. Yet here he was, using the point of his ornately hilted dagger to trace a river's course. He nodded and waved when he spied the entering Romans. Marcus nodded back, while Gaius Philippus, muttering something unpleasant under his breath, pretended not to see him.

The Emperor's daughter was on Thorisin Gavras' right, between him and Nephon Khoumnos. Alypia was the only woman at the gathering and, as was usually her way, doing more listening than talking. She was jotting something on a scrap of parchment when the Romans came into the Hall of the Nineteen Couches and did not look up until a servant had taken them to their assigned place, which was gratifyingly close to the table's head. Her glance toward Scaurus was cool, measuring, and more distant than the tribune had expected; he suddenly wondered if she knew of his joining with Helvis. Her face was unreadable, a perfect mask to hide her thoughts.

Marcus took his seat with some relief. He bent his head to study the map before him. If he read the spidery Videssian writing aright, it represented the mountains of Vaspurakan, the border land whose passes offered tempting pathways between the Empire and Yezd.

As had Apsimar's, the map looked marvelously precise, far more so than any the Romans made. Peaks, rivers, lakes, towns—all were portrayed in meticulous detail. Nevertheless, Scaurus wondered how trustworthy a chart it was. He knew how even well-intentioned and usually accurate men could go wrong. In the third book of his history, Polybios, as careful an investigator as was ever born, had the Rhodanus River going from east to west before it flowed south through Narbonese Gaul and into the Mediterranean. Having tramped along almost its entire length, the Roman was wearily certain it ran north and south throughout.

Mavrikios did not formally begin the council until an hour after the Romans arrived. Only when the last latecomers—Khamorth, most of them—were seated did he break his quiet conversation with his brother and raise his voice for the entire room to hear.

"Thank you for joining us this morning," he said. The hum of talk running along the tables as the gathered soldiers discussed their trade died away. He waited until it was quite gone before continuing, "For those who have marched and fought in the westlands before, much of what you'll hear today will be stale news, but there are so many newcomers I thought this council would be worthwhile for their sakes alone."

"Fewer new men are here than should be, thanks to your cursed monks," someone called, and Marcus recognized Utprand son of Dagober. The Namdalener still wore the same look of cold fury he'd had when the tribune rescued him from the riots; here, Scaurus judged, was a man not to be easily deflected from his purposes. Growls of agreement came from other easterners. Marcus saw Soteric well down at the junior end of the tables, nodding vehemently.

Ortaias Sphrantzes and Thorisin Gavras looked equally offended at Utprand's forthrightness. Their reasons, though, were totally different. "Blame not our holy men for the fruit of your heresy," Ortaias exclaimed, while the Sevastokrator snapped, "Show his Imperial Majesty the respect he deserves, you!" Up and down the tables, Videssians assented to one or the other—or both—of those sentiments.

The Namdaleni stared back in defiance. "What respect did we get when your holy men were murdering us?" Utprand demanded, answering both critics in the same breath. The temperature in the Hall of the Nineteen Couches shot toward the boiling point. Like jackals prowling round the edge of a fight, the Khamorth shifted in their seats, ready to leap on the battler they thought weaker.

Marcus felt the same growing despair he had known many times before in Videssos. He was calm both by training and temperament, and found maddening the quarrels of all the touchy, excitable people the Empire and its neighbors bred.

Mavrikios, it seemed, was cast from a similar mold. He laid one hand on his brother's shoulder, the other on that of Ortaias Sphrantzes. Both subsided, though Thorisin moved restively. The Emperor looked down the tables to Utprand, his brown eyes locking with the Namdalener's wolf-gray ones. "Fewer of you *are* here than should be," he admitted, "nor is the fault yours." Now it was Sphrantzes' turn to squirm.

The Emperor ignored him, keeping all his attention on Utprand. "Do you remember why you are here at all?" he asked. His voice held the same urgency Balsamon's had carried in the Great Temple when he requested of Videssos a unity it would not grant him.

As Marcus had already seen, Utprand recognized truth when he heard it. The Namdalener thought for a moment, then gave a reluctant nod. "You're right," he said. For him that was enough to settle the matter.

He leaned forward, ready to take part in the council once more. When a few hotheaded young Namdaleners wanted to carry the argument further, the ice in his eyes quelled them faster than anything the Videssians might have done.

"There is one hard case," Gaius Philippus whispered admiringly.

"Isn't he, though? I thought the same when I met him during the riots," Scaurus said.

"He's the one you talked of, then? I can see what you meant by—" The centurion broke off in mid-sentence, for the Emperor was speaking.

Calm as if nothing untoward had happened, Mavrikios said to Ortaias Sphrantzes, "Hold up that map of the westlands, would you?" The spatharios obediently lifted the parchment so everyone could see it.

On the chart, Videssos' western dominions were a long, gnarled thumb of land stretching toward the imperial capital and separating the almost landlocked Videssian Sea in the north from the great Sailors' Sea to the south.

The Emperor waited while a couple of nearsighted officers traded seats with colleagues near the map, then began abruptly, "I want to leave within the week. Have your troops ready to go over the Cattle-Crossing within that length of time, or be left behind." He suddenly grinned a most unpleasant grin. "Anyone who claims he cannot be ready by then will find himself ordered to the hottest, most Phos-forsaken garrison I can think of—he'll wish he were fighting the Yezda, I promise you that."

Mavrikios waited to let the sudden excited buzz travel the length of the tables. Marcus had the same eager stirring the Emperor's other officers felt—a departure date at last, and a near one, too! The tribune did not think Gavras would have to make good on his threat.

"For those of you who don't know," the Emperor resumed, "our western frontier against the Yezda is about five hundred miles west of the city. With an army as large as the one we've mustered here, we should be through Vaspurakan and into Yezd in about forty days." At a pinch, Scaurus thought his Romans could halve that time, but the Emperor was probably right. No army could move faster than its slowest members, and with a force of this size, the problem of keeping it supplied would slow it further.

Gavras paused for a moment to pick up a wooden pointer, which he used to draw a line southwest from Videssos to the joining of two rivers. "We'll make the journey in four stages," he said. "The first one will be short and easy, from here to Garsavra, where the Eriza flows into the Arandos. We'll meet Baanes Onomagoulos there; he'll join us with his troops from the southern mountains. He would be bringing more, but the fornicating pen-pushers have taxed too many of them into serfdom."

The map Ortaias Sphrantzes was holding did not let Scaurus see his face. That was a pity; he would have given a good deal to learn how the young aristocrat was reacting to the ridicule heaped on his family's policy. That map was beginning to quiver, too—it could not be comfortable for Ortaias, the tribune realized, sitting there with his arms out at full length before him. Sure enough, the Emperor was finding ways to put him in his place.

"From Garsavra we'll head west along the Arandos to Amorion, up in the plateau country. That's a longer stage than the first one, but it should be no harder." Marcus saw one of Alypia's eyebrows quirk upward, but the princess made no move to contradict her father. She scribbled again on her piece of parchment.

"There will be supply caches all along the line of march," Gavras went on, "and I'll not have anyone plundering the peasants in the countryside—or robbing them for the sport of it, either." He stared down the twin lengths of officers before him, especially pausing to catch the eyes of the Khamorth chieftains newly come from the plains. Not all of them spoke Videssian; those who did murmured translations of the Emperor's words for their fellow nomads.

One of the men from the Pardrayan steppe looked a question back at Mavrikios, who acknowledged him with a nod. "What is it?"

"I am Firdosi Horse-breaker," the nomad leader said in labored Videssian. "I and mine took your gold to fight, not to play the robber. Slaying farmers is woman's work—are we not men, to be trusted to fight as men?" Other Khamorth up and down the tables bowed their heads to their chests in their native gesture of agreement.

"That is well said," the Emperor declared. Without troops at his back, Marcus would not have trusted Firdosi or any of the other steppe-dwellers and was sure Mavrikios felt the same. But, he thought, this was hardly the time to stir up trouble.

Then Thorisin Gavras added lazily, "Of course, what my brother said should not be taken to apply only to our allies from the north; all foreign troops should bear it in mind." And he looked, not at the Khamorth, but at the Namdaleni.

They returned his mocking glance with stony silence, which filled the hall for a long moment. Mavrikios' nostrils dilated in an anger he could not release before his watching officers. As they had at Soteric's gambling party, men looked here and there to try to cover their discomfiture. Only Alypia seemed indifferent to it all, watching her father and uncle with what looked to Scaurus like amused detachment.

Making a visible effort, Mavrikios brought his attention back to the map Ortaias was still holding. He took a deep breath before carrying on. "At Amorion another detachment will meet us, this one headed by Gagik Bagratouni. From there we will move northwest to Soli on the Rhamnos River, just east of the mountain country of Vaspurakan, the land of princes—or so they claim," he added sardonically.

"That may be a hungry march. The Yezda are loose there, and I need not tell anyone here what they do in farming country, Phos blight them for it. If the earth does not produce its fruits, everyone—peasant, artisan, and noble alike—must perish."

Marcus saw two of the nomads exchange disdain-filled glances. With their vast herds and flocks, they had no need for the products of agriculture and felt the same hostility toward farmers as did their Yezda cousins. Firdosi had said it plainly—to the plainsmen, peasants were beneath contempt, and even to be killed by a true man was too good for them.

"After Soli we'll push into Vaspurakan itself," the Emperor said. "The Yezda will be easier to trap in the passes than on the plain, and the loot they'll be carrying will slow them further. The Vaspurakaners will help us, too; the princes may have little love for the Empire, but the Yezda have raped their land time and again.

"And a solid win or two against Avshar's irregulars will make Wulghash himself come out from Mashiz with his real army; either that, or have the wild men turn on him instead." Anticipation lit Mavrikios' face. "Smash that army, and Yezd lies open for cleansing. And smash it we shall. It's been centuries since Videssos sent out a force to match the one we have here today. How can any Skotos-loving bandit lord hope to stand against us?"

More with his soldiers than with the crowd in the amphitheater, Mavrikios succeeded in firing imaginations—made his officers truly see Yezd prostrate at their feet. The prospect pleased them all, for whatever reason, political gain, religious purification, or simply finding any booty in plenty.

When Ortaias Sphrantzes understood the Emperor was through at last, he put the map down with relief.

Marcus shared the officers' enthusiasm. Mavrikios' plan was in keeping with what the Roman had come to expect of Videssian designs—ponderous, but probably effective. He seemed to be leaving little to chance. That was as it should be, with so much soldiering in his past. All that remained was to convert plan to action.

As with everything else within the Empire, ceremony surrounded the great army's preparations for departure. The people of Videssos, who not long before had done their best to tear that army apart, now sent heavenward countless prayers for its success. A solemn liturgy was scheduled in the High Temple on the night before the troops were to leave.

Scaurus, as commander of the Romans, received the stamped roll of heavy parchment entitling him to a pair of coveted seats at the ritual. "Whom do you suppose I can give these to?" he asked Helvis. "Do you have any friends who might want them?"

"If that's meant as a joke, I don't find it funny," she replied. "We'll go ourselves, of course. Even though I don't fully share the Videssian creed, it would be wrong to start so important an undertaking without asking Phos' blessing on it."

Marcus sighed. When he asked Helvis to share his life, he had not anticipated how she would try to shape it into a pattern she found comfortable. He did not oppose the worship of Phos but, when pushed in a direction he did not want to take, his natural reaction was to dig in his heels.

Nor was he used to considering anyone else's wishes when planning his own actions. Since reaching the age of manhood he had steered his own course and ignored advice he had not sought. But Helvis was used to having her opinions taken into account; Scaurus remembered how angry she had been when he was close-mouthed over what the council of war decided. He sighed again. Nothing, he told himself, was as simple as it looked to be at its beginnings.

He held firm in his plans to avoid the service at the High Temple until he saw Neilos Tzimiskes' horror when he offered the Videssian the chance to go in his place. "Thank you for the honor," the borderer stammered, "but it would look ill indeed if you did not attend. All the great captains will be there—even the Khamorth will come, though they have scant use for Phos."

"I suppose so," Scaurus grumbled. But put in those terms, he could see the need for appearing; no less than Balsamon's unsuccessful sermon had been, this was an occasion for a public display of unity. And, he thought, it would certainly help the unity of his new household. There, at least, he was not mistaken.

That was as well; preparations for the coming campaign were leaving him exhausted and short-tempered at the end of every day. Roman discipline and order were still intact, so having his men ready was no problem. They could have left the day after Mavrikios' council—or the day before. But Videssian armies marched in greater luxury than a Caesar would have tolerated. As was true in the oriental monarchies Rome had known, great flocks of noncombatants accompanied the soldiers, including their women. And trying to get them in any sort of traveling order was a task that made Marcus understand the doom ordained for Sisyphos.

By the night of the liturgy, the tribune was actually looking forward to it and wondering how Balsamon would manage to astound his listeners this time. When he entered the High Temple, Helvis clinging proudly to his arm, he found she and Tzimiskes had been right—he could not have afforded to miss the gathering. The Temple was packed with the high officers and functionaries of every state allied against Yezd and with their ladies. It was hard to say which sex made a more gorgeous display, the men in their burnished steel and bronze, wolfskin and leather, or the women showing off their gowns of linen and clinging silk and their own soft, powdered flesh.

Men and women alike rose as the patriarch of Videssos made his way to his ivory throne. When he and his flock offered Phos their fundamental prayer, tonight there were many Namdaleni to finish the creed with their own addition: "On this we stake our very lives." At Marcus' side Helvis did so with firm devotion and looked about defiantly to see who might object. Few Videssians seemed offended; on this night, with all kinds of heretics and outright unbelievers in the Temple, they were willing to overlook outlanders' barbarous practices.

When the service was done, Balsamon offered his own prayer for the success of the enterprise Videssos was undertaking and spoke at some length of the conflict's importance and the need for singleness of purpose in the face of the western foe. Everything he said was true and needed saying, but Marcus was still disappointed at his sermon. There was little of Balsamon's usual dry wit, nor did his delivery have its normal zest. The patriarch seemed very tired and halfhearted about his sermon. It puzzled Scaurus and concerned him, too.

But Balsamon grew more animated as his talk progressed and ended strongly. 'A man's only guide is his conscience—it is his shield when he does well and a blade to wound him if he falters. Now take up the shield of right and turn back evil's sword—bow not to wickedness' will, and that sword can never harm you!"

As his listeners applauded his words and calls of "Well said!" came from throughout the Temple, above them rose the massed voices of the choir in a triumphant hymn to Phos, and with them the bell players whose music had intrigued Scaurus before. Now he was sitting at an angle that let him watch them work, and his fascination with them was enough to wipe away a good part of the letdown at Balsamon's pedestrian address.

The twoscore players stood behind a long, padded table. Each had before him some half dozen polished bells of various sizes and tones. Along with their robes, the players wore kidskin gloves to avoid smudging the bright bell metal. They followed the direction of their bellmaster with marvelous speed and dexterity, changing and chiming their bells in perfect unison. It was, Marcus found, as entrancing to watch as to hear.

The bellmaster was a show in himself. A dapper little man, he led his charges with slightly exaggerated, theatrical gestures, his body swaying to the hymn he was conducting. His face wore a look of exaltation, and his eyes never opened. It was several minutes before Scaurus realized he was blind; he hardly seemed to need to see, for his ears told him more than most men's eyes ever would.

If the music of the bells impressed the unmusical tribune, it delighted Helvis, who said, "I've heard the Temple's bell players praised many times, but never had the chance to listen to them before. They were another reason I wanted to be here tonight." She looked at Marcus quizzically. "If I'd known you liked them, I would have used them as an argument for coming."

He had to smile. "Probably just as well you didn't." He found it hard to imagine being persuaded to go anywhere by the promise of music. Still, there was no doubt the bell players added spice to what otherwise would have been an unsatisfying evening.

The Emperor ordered criers through the streets to warn the people of Videssos to spend the following day at home. The major thoroughfares were packed tight with soldiers in full kit, with nervous horses and braying donkeys, wagons carrying the warriors' families and personal goods, other wagons driven by sutlers, and still others loaded with every imaginable sort of military hardware. Tempers shortened more quickly than the long files of men, animals, and wains inching toward the quays where ships and boats waited to take them over the Cattle-Crossing to the Empire's westlands.

The Romans, as part of Mavrikios' Imperial Guard, had little waiting before they crossed. Everything went smoothly as could be, except for Viridovix. The luckless Celt spent the entire journey—fortunately for him, one of less than half an hour—leaning over the galley's rail, retching helplessly.

"Every time I'm on the water it happens to me," he moaned between spasms. The usual ruddiness had faded from his features, leaving him fishbelly pale.

"Eat hard-baked bread crumbled in wine," Gorgidas recommended, "or, if you like, I have a decoction of opium that will help, though it will leave you drowsy for a day."

"Eat—" The very word was enough to send the Gaul lurching toward the rail. When he was through he turned back to Gorgidas. Tears of misery stood in his eyes. "I thank your honor for the advice and all, but it'd be too late to do me the good I need. Dry dirt, bless it, under my feet will serve me better than any nostrum ever you made." He cringed as another wavelet gently lifted the ship's bow.

With their small harbors, Videssos' suburbs on the western shore of the Cattle-Crossing could not hope to handle the avalanche of shipping descending on them. The capital was the Empire's chief port and, jealous of its status, made sure no other town nearby could siphon business from it.

Nevertheless, the armada of sharp-beaked slim galleys, merchantmen, fishing boats, barges, and various motley small craft did not have to stand offshore to disembark its host. Videssian ships, like the ones the Romans built, were even at their biggest small and light enough to stand beaching without damage. For several miles up and down the coast, oars drove ships ashore so men and beasts could splash through the surf to land. Sailors and soldiers cursed together as they labored to empty hulls of supplies. That also lightened the beached craft and made them easier to refloat.

Viridovix was so eager to reach land that he vaulted over the rail before the ship was quite aground and came down with a splash neck-deep in the sea. Cursing in Gaulish, he floundered onto the beach, where he lay at full length just beyond the reach of the waves. He hugged the golden sand as he would a lover. Less miserable and thus more patient, the Romans followed him.

The imperial galley came ashore not far from where they were disembarking. First out of it were Mavrikios' ever-present Haloga guardsmen. Like the Romans, they left their vessel by scrambling down rope ladders and nets cast over the side. Then, watchful as always, they hurried to take up positions to ward off any sudden treachery.

For an Emperor, however, even one who set as little store in ceremony as Mavrikios Gavras, clambering down a rope would not do. As soon as his guards were in place, a gangplank of gilded wood was laid from ship to beach. But when the Emperor was about to step onto the sand, his booted foot came down on the hem of his long purple robe. He tripped and went to all fours on the beach.

Romans, Halogai, and Videssian seamen alike stared in consternation. What omen could be worse for a campaign than to have its leader fall before it began? Someone made a sign to avert evil.

But Mavrikios was equal to the occasion. Rising to his knees, he held aloft two fistsful of sand and said loudly, "Videssos, I have tight hold of you!" He got to his feet and went about his business as if nothing out of the ordinary had happened.

And, after a moment or two, so did the men who had witnessed the mishap. The Emperor's quick wits had succeeded in turning a bad omen into a good one. Discussing it that evening, Gaius Philippus gave Mavrikios his ultimate accolade. "Caesar," he declared, "couldn't have done it better."

Like a multitude of little streams running together to form a great river, the Videssian army gathered itself on the western shore of the Cattle-Crossing. The transfer from the capital had been far easier than Marcus had expected. There were, it seemed, some advantages after all to the minute organization that was such a part of life in the Empire.

That organization showed its virtue again as the march to Garsavra began. Scaurus doubted if Rome could have kept so huge a host fed without its pillaging the countryside and gave his men stern orders against foraging. But plundering for supplies never came close to being necessary. No Yezda had yet come so far east, and the local officials had no trouble providing the army and its hangers-on with markets adequate for their needs. Grain came by oxcart and rivercraft, along with herds of cattle and sheep for meat.

Hunters added to the meat bag with deer and wild boar. In the case of the latter, there were times when Scaurus was not sure the pig was truly wild. Videssian hogs shared with their boarish cousins a lean, rangy build, a strip of bristly hair down their backs, and a savage disposition.

Stealing one of them could give a hunting party as lively a time as going after a wild boar. The tribune enjoyed gnawing the fat-rich, savory meat from its bones too much to worry over its source for long.

The first leg of the march from the city was a time of shaking down, a time for troops too long in soft billets to begin to remember how they earned their pay. For all the drills and mock fights Gaius Philippus had put the Romans through, they were not quite the same hard-bitten, hungry band who had fought in Gaul. Their belts had gone out a notch or two and, most of all, they were not used to a full day's march, even one at the slow pace of the army they accompanied.

At the end of each of the first few days out of the capital, the legionaries were glad to collapse and try to rub some life back into their aching calves and thighs. Gorgidas and the other medics were busy treating blisters, laying on a thick ointment of lard mixed with resin and covering the sores with bandages of soft, fluffy wool well sprinkled with oil and wine. The troopers cursed the medicine's astringent bite, but it served them well until their feet began to harden once more.

Marcus had expected all that sort of thing and was not put out when it happened. He had not really anticipated, however, how resentful his Romans would be when called on to create a regular legionary camp every night. Throwing up daily earthworks did not appeal to them after their comfortable months in the permanent barracks of Videssos.

Gaius Philippus browbeat the troops into obedience the first three nights on march, but an ever more sullen, halfhearted obedience. By the third night he was hoarse, furious, and growing desperate. On the next day a deputation of legionaries came to see Scaurus with their grievances. Had they been shirkers or men of little quality, he would have dealt with the matter summarily, punishing them and not listening for an instant. But among the nine nervous soldiers—one from each maniple—were some of his finest men, including the stalwart Minucius. He decided to hear them out.

For one thing, they said, none of the other contingents of the imperial army made such a production of their nightly stopping places. They knew they were deep in Videssian territory and altogether safe, and their tents went up in a cheerful, casual disarray wherever their officers happened to feel like pitching them. Worse yet, in a proper Roman camp there was no place for women, and many of the legionaries wanted to spend their nights with the partners they had found in Videssos.

The tribune could find no sympathy with the first of these points. He said, "What the rest of the army does is its own concern. It's too simple to go slack when things are easy and then never bother to tighten up again—until it costs you, and then it's too late. The lot of you are veterans; you know what I'm saying is true."

They had to nod. Minucius, his booming voice and open manner subdued by the irregular situation in which he'd put himself, said timidly, "It's not the work we mind so much, sir. It's just that well . . . once camp is made, it's like a jail, with no escape. My woman's pregnant, and I worry about her." His comrades muttered agreement; looking from one of them to another, Marcus saw they were almost all coupled men.

He understood how they felt. He had slept restlessly the past couple of nights, knowing Helvis was only a few hundred yards away but not wanting to give his troopers a bad example by breaking discipline for his private gratification.

He thought for a few seconds; less than a third of the Romans had women with them. If a party of about a hundred got leave each night, each soldier could see his lover twice a week or so. The improvement in morale would probably be worth more than the slightly loosened control would cost.

He gave the legionaries his decision, adding, "Leave will only be granted after all required duties are complete, of course."

"Yes, sir! Thank you sir!" they said, grinning in relief that he had not ordered them clapped in irons.

He knew they must not be allowed to think they could violate the proper chain of command on every whim. He coughed dryly, and watched the grins fade. "The lot of you are fined two weeks' pay for bringing this up without your officers' permission," he said. "See that it doesn't happen again."

They took the fine without a murmur, still afraid he might condemn them to far worse. Under the law of the legions he could confiscate their goods, have them flogged, or give them over to the *fustuarium*—order them clubbed, beaten, and stoned to death by their fellow soldiers. When he snapped, "Get out!" they fell over themselves scrambling from his tent. In some ways, Roman discipline still held.

The order duly went out, and the grumbling in the ranks vanished or was transmuted into the ordinary grousing that has existed in every army since time began. "I suppose you had to do it," Gaius Philippus said, "but I still don't like it. You may gain in the short run, but over the long haul anything that cuts into discipline is bad."

"I thought about that," Scaurus admitted, "but there's discipline and discipline. To keep the vital parts, you have to bend the ones that aren't. The men have to keep thinking of themselves as Romans and *want* to think that way, or they—and we—are lost. If they decide they'd rather slip off and be peasants in the countryside, what can we do? Where can we find the legions, the generals, the Senate to back up our Roman discipline? Do you think the Videssians give a damn about our ways? I can't order us to feel like Romans; it *has* to come from within."

Gaius Philippus looked at him like a Videssian suddenly confronted with heresy. The centurion had kept himself—and, to a large measure, the rest of the legionaries, too—going by ignoring, as far as he could, the fact that Rome was gone forever. It rocked his world for Scaurus to speak openly of what he tried not even to think about. Shaking his head, he left the tribune's tent. A few minutes later Marcus heard him blistering some luckless soldier over a speck of rust on his greave. Scaurus made a wry face. He wished he could work off his own concerns so easily.

Letting the Romans out of camp at night proved to have one advantage the tribune had not thought of when he decided to allow it. It put them back in the mainstream of army gossip, as much a constant as that of the capital. The women heard everything, true or not, and so did the legionaries while with them. Thus it was that Scaurus learned Ortaias Sphrantzes was still with the army. He found it almost impossible to believe, knowing the mutual loathing the Gavrai and Sphrantzai had for one another, but on his way to see Helvis a night later he proved its accuracy by almost bumping into the spatharios.

"Your pardon, I beg," the young Sphrantzes said, stepping out of his way. As he had when Gaius Philippus rated him while he watched the

Romans drill, he had a fat volume under his arm. "Yes, it's Kalokyres on generalship again," he said. "I have so much to learn and so little time to learn it."

The idea of Ortaias Sphrantzes as a general was enough to silence the tribune. He must have raised an eyebrow, though, for Ortaias said, "My only regret, my Roman"—He pronounced the word carefully—"friend, is that I'll not have your formidable infantry under my command."

"Ah? What command is that, my lord?" Marcus asked, thinking Mavrikios might have given the youth a few hundred Khamorth to play with. The answer he got shook him to his toes.

"I am to lead the left wing," Sphrantzes replied proudly, "while the Emperor commands the center and his brother the right. We shall make mincemeat of the foe! Mincemeat! Now you must forgive me; I am studying the proper way to maneuver heavy cavalry in the face of the enemy." And the newly minted field marshal vanished into the warm twilight, paging through his book to the place he needed.

That night, Helvis complained Scaurus' mind was somewhere else.

The next morning the tribune told Gaius Philippus the ghastly news. The senior centurion held his head in his hands. "Congratulations," he said. "You just ruined my breakfast."

"He seems to mean well," Marcus said, trying to find a bright side to things.

"So does a doctor treating somebody with the plague. The poor bastard'll die all the same."

"That's not a good comparison," Gorgidas protested. "True, the plague is past my power to treat, but at least I'm skilled in my profession. After reading one book of medicine, I wouldn't have trusted myself to treat a sour stomach."

"Neither would anyone else with sense," Gaius Philippus said. "I thought Mavrikios had too much sense to give the puppy a third of his army." He pushed his barley porridge aside, saying to the Greek doctor, "Can you fix *my* sour stomach? The gods know I've got one." Gorgidas grew serious. "Barley after you're used to wheat will give you distress, or so says Hippokrates."

"It never did before," Gaius Philippus said. "I'm disgusted, that's all. That bungling twit!"

The "twit" himself appeared later that day, apparently reminded of the Romans' existence by his encounter with Marcus. Sphrantzes looked dashing as he rode up to the marching legionaries; his horse had the mincing gait of a Videssian thoroughbred. His breastplate and helm were gilded to show his rank, while a deep-blue cape streamed out behind him. The only flaw in his image of martial vigor was the book he still carried clamped under his left arm.

Sphrantzes reined his horse in to a walking pace at the head of the Roman column. He kept looking back, as if studying it. Gaius Philippus' hostile curiosity soon got the better of him. He asked, "What can we do for you today, sir?" His tone belied the title of respect he'd granted Sphrantzes.

"Eh?" Ortaias blinked. "Oh, yes—tell me, if you would, are those the standards under which you fight?" He pointed at the nine tall manipular *signa* the standard-bearers proudly carried. Each was crowned by an open hand ringed by a wreath, representing faithfulness to duty.

"So they are. What of it?" Gaius Philippus answered shortly.

Marcus understood why the subject was a sore one. He explained to Sphrantzes, "We were only a detachment of a larger unit, whose symbol is the eagle. We have no eagle here, and the men miss it dearly."

That was an understatement, but no Videssian could hope to understand the feeling each legion had for its eagle, the sacred symbol of its very being. During the winter at Imbros there had been some talk of making a new eagle, but the soldiers' hearts were not in it. Their *aquila* was in Gaul and lost to them forever, but they wanted no other. The lesser *signa* would have to do.

"Most interesting," Ortaias said. His concern with the Romans' standards, however, was for a different reason. "Is your custom always to group like numbers of soldiers under each ensign?"

"Of course," Scaurus replied, puzzled.

"And why not?" his centurion added.

"Excuse me a moment," Sphrantzes said. He pulled out of the Roman line of march so he could stop his horse and use both hands to go through his tactical volume. When he found what he wanted, he sent the beast trotting back up to the Romans.

"I quote from Kalokyres," he said: "The first book, chapter four, part six: 'It is necessary to take care not to make all companies exactly equal in number, lest the enemy, counting one's standards, form an exact idea of one's numbers. Take heed in this matter: as we said, the companies should not be more than four hundred men, nor less than two hundred.' Of course, your units are smaller than the ones Kalokyres uses, but the principle, I should say, remains the same. Good day to you, gentlemen." He rode away, leaving the Romans speechless behind him.

"Do you know," Gaius Philippus said, "that's not a bad notion?"

"So it isn't," Marcus said. "In fact, it's a very good one. How in the world did Ortaias Sphrantzes ever come up with it?"

"It's not as if he thought of it himself," the centurion said, looking for a way out of his discomfiture. "This Kalo-what's-his-name must have had his wits about him. Yes." He tried to console himself with that thought, but still looked rattled.

Viridovix had watched the entire exchange with high glee. "Sure and there he is, the man who sucked in soldiering with his mother's milk—a centurion she was herself, I have no doubt—all tossed in a heap by the biggest booby ever hatched. It all goes to prove the Celtic way of fighting is the best—get in there and do it, for the more you think, the more trouble you're in."

Gaius Philippus was too graveled even to argue. "Oh, shut up," he muttered. "Where'd Gorgidas get to? My stomach's hurting again."

The coastal plain between the suburbs across from Videssos and the city of Garsavra was some of the most fertile land the Romans had ever seen. The soil was a soft black loam that crumbled easily in the hand and smelled rich, almost meaty, in its promise of growth. Scores of rivers and lesser streams ran down from the central plateau so that the soil could fulfill its promise. The warm rain fetched by the constant breeze off the Sailors' Sea watered those few stretches flowing water did not touch.

Viridovix' dire predictions about the weather, made months before, came true with a vengeance. It was so hot and humid the ground steamed each morning when the sun came up. The pale Halogai, used to the cool, cloudy summers of their northern home, suffered worse than most; day after day, they fainted in their armor and had to be revived with helmets-ful of water.

"Red as a boiled crayfish, he was," Viridovix said of one sunstruck northerner.

Gorgidas cocked an eye at him. "You don't look any too good your-self," he said. "Try wearing a soft hat instead of your helmet on march."

"Go on with you," the Celt said. "It takes more than a bit of sun to lay me low." But Scaurus noticed he followed the physician's advice.

With fine soil, abundant water, and hot sun, no wonder the bread-basket of the Empire lay here. The land was clothed with the various greens of growing plants. There were fields of wheat, millet, oats, and barley, and others growing flax and cotton, which Gorgidas insisted on calling "plant wool." Orchards grew figs, peaches, plums, and exotic cit-rus fruits. As none of these last had been common in the western Medi-terranean, Marcus had trouble telling one from the next—until the first time he bit into a lemon, thinking it an orange. After that he learned.

Vineyards were rare here; the soil was too good, and water too plen-tiful. Nor did Scaurus see many olive trees until the land began to rise toward the plateau a day or so outside of Garsavra.

The folk who farmed the fertile plain were as much a revelation to the tribune as their land. They were quiet, steady, and as industrious as any people he had seen. He was used to the tempestuous populace of Videssos the city, with their noisy, headlong pace, their arrogant as-sumption of superiority over all the rest of mankind, and their fickle swings of mood. He'd wondered more than once how the Empire had managed to prosper for so many centuries with such truculent material on which to build.

Gorgidas laughed at him for saying that one night. The Greek physi-cian was always a part of the unending talk round the Roman watchfires. He seldom left camp after dusk had fallen. Scaurus knew he had no sweetheart, but used the company of men to hold loneliness at bay.

Now he commented, "You might as well judge Italy by the hangers-on at the lawcourts in Rome. For as long as Videssos has had its empire, the Emperors have spoiled the people of the capital to win their favor. You can hardly blame them, you know—reckoning by the riots a few weeks ago, their necks would answer if they didn't keep them happy.

Don't forget, the Empire has lasted a long time; the city people think luxury their rightful due."

The tribune remembered Cato's complaint of over a century before his own time, that a pretty boy could cost more than a plot of land, and a jar of imported liquamen more than a plowman. Rome had not become less fond of pleasure in the intervening years. What was the joke about Caesar?—every woman's husband and every man's wife. Scaurus shook his head, wondering what his native capital would be like after hundreds of years as an imperial capital.

Garsavra, which the army reached on the ninth day out of Videssos, was a long way from imperial status. The town was, in fact, smaller than Imbros. Thanks to its river-junction site, it was a trade center for a good part of the westlands. Nevertheless, when the expeditionary force camped round the city, it more than doubled Garsavra's population.

There was something wrong with the town's outline as the Romans came up to it, but Marcus could not put his finger on its oddness. Gaius Philippus had never a doubt. "I will be damned," he said. "The bloody place is without a wall!"

He was right; Garsavra's houses, shops, and public buildings were open to the surrounding world, unprotected from any attack. More than anything else he had seen in the Empire, that brought home to Marcus Videssos' accomplishment. Imbros, even the capital itself, had to ward off barbarians from the north, but the land they shielded had known peace so long it had forgotten even fortcraft.

With his predator's mind, Viridovix was quick to see the other side of the coin. "Wouldn't the Yezda have a lovely time now, swooping down on a town so naked and all? They'd fair break their poor horses' backs with the booty they'd haul off."

The thought of Avshar's wolves laying waste this peaceful, fertile land was nearly enough to make Scaurus physically sick. Like vicious children loose in a pottery, they could wreck in minutes what had taken years to create and take only delight in the wrecking.

"That's why they pay us," Gaius Philippus said, "to do the dying so they can stay happy and fat."

Marcus found that notion little more appetizing than Viridovix'. It was not strictly fair, either; Videssians made up much the greatest part of Mavrikios' army, and several thousand more native troops were already here awaiting the Emperor's arrival.

There was, however, a grain of truth behind the centurion's cynical words. The men Baanes Onomagoulos had called up from the soldier-peasants of the countryside were all too plainly less soldier than peasant. Their mounts were a collection of crowbait, their gear old and scanty, and their drill next to nonexistent.

Their commander was something else again, a general out of the same school from which Mavrikios Gavras had come. Scaurus got a good look at him during the review the Emperor called to welcome the new contingent into his forces. Onomagoulos rode past the Romans on his way to Mavrikios; now and again he touched his spurs to his horse's flank to make the beast rear. He was not a very big man, but the way he sat his horse and the set of his hawk-nosed face proclaimed him a seasoned warrior nevertheless. He was well past forty; the years had swept most of the hair from his crown, but neither its remnants nor his pointed beard were frosted with gray.

Protocol demanded that he rein in, dismount, and perform a proskynesis before addressing the Emperor. Instead, he rode straight up to Mavrikios, who was also mounted, and cried, "Gavras, you old bastard, how have you been?"

Marcus waited for the world to fall to ruins, or at least for the Halogai at the Emperor's side to tear the offender limb from limb. Some of the younger guardsmen reached for their swords, but Zeprin the Red was watching Mavrikios. Seeing the Emperor was not angry, the mercenary officer made a quick hand signal, and his men relaxed.

Gavras smiled thinly. "I manage to keep busy—too busy, usually. Maybe you should have had the job after all." He brought his horse forward and slapped Onomagoulos on the back. Onomagoulos threw a lazy phantom punch at the Emperor, who ducked, his smile wider now.

The tribune suddenly understood a great deal. For Baanes Onomagoulos, Mavrikios Gavras was no distant omnipotent sovereign, but a fortunate equal, like a man who was lucky in love—and Scaurus thought of Helvis with a brief, warm glow. He wondered how long these two leaders had known each other and what they had seen together, for their friendship to survive the challenge of Mavrikios' imperial rank.

Baanes looked to Thorisin, asking, "And how are you, pup?"

"Well enough," the Sevastokrator answered. His tone was not as warm as his brother's. Marcus noted he made no move to join Baanes and Mavrikios.

"'Pup,' is it?" Viridovix breathed into Scaurus' ear. "Sure and it's a rare bold man to be calling Thorisin Gavras a name like that, with himself so feisty and all."

"Onomagoulos has likely known him since before he could walk," the Roman whispered back.

"All the more reason for the name to rankle now. You have no older kin, I'm thinking?"

"No," Scaurus admitted.

"There's no one worse than your elder brother's friends. The first they see of you is a wee pulling lad, and they never forget it, not when you're taller than the lot of them." There was an edge to the Celt's voice Marcus had seldom heard; when he looked round, Viridovix was thoroughly grim, as if chewing on a memory whose taste he did not like.

The Arandos River bounced down from the plateau into the flatlands over a series of cataracts, past which the army marched as it made its way westward. Churning down over the great boulders in the streambed, the Arandos hurled rainbow-catching spray hundreds of feet to either side of the riverbanks. The fine droplets drying on the faces of the soldiers slogging west were almost the only relief they got from the burning heat.

The central highlands were a very different place from the lush coastal plain. The land was baked a dirty gray-brown by the sun and crisscrossed by gullies, dry nine parts of the year but rampaging torrents the tenth. Wheat grew here too, but only with reluctance when compared to the riot of fertility to the east.

Long stretches of land were too poor for agriculture of any sort, supporting only a thin cover of grass and spikey shrubs. Herdsmen drove vast flocks of sheep, cattle, and goats across the rugged terrain, their way of life more akin to that of the nomadic Khamorth than to that practiced elsewhere in the Empire.

For the first time, the supply problems Marcus had feared began showing up. Bread from the lowlands still followed the army up the Arandos, portaged past the rapids. It helped, for local deliveries of flour and grain were spotty and small. Some of the shortfall was made up from the herds, which gave the Romans something new to gripe about. On campaign they preferred a largely vegetarian diet, feeling that eating too much meat made them hot, heavy, and slow.

Most of the Videssians, used to a climate like Italy's, had similar frugal tastes. The Halogai and their Namdalener cousins, on the other hand, gorged themselves on roast mutton and beef—and, as always, suffered more from the heat than did the rest of the army.

The Khamorth ate everything edible and did not complain.

Marcus grew more thankful for the Arandos with every day that passed. Without it and its occasional tributaries, the plateau would have been a desert in which nothing could survive. Its water was blood-warm and sometimes muddy, but never failed or slackened. The tribune found nothing more exquisite on a scorching afternoon than dipping up a helmetful and pouring it over his head. So thirsty was the air for moisture, though, that half an hour later he would have to do it again.

By the middle of the third week of the march, the army was beginning to become a real unit, not the motley collection of forces that had set out from Videssos. Mavrikios sped the process with a series of drills, rushing the men from column formation into line of battle, now ordering them to defend against the front, now the right, and again the left.

The maneuvers were exhausting when carried out in that heat, but the men started to know each other and to know what they could expect in battle from their comrades: the iron courage of the Halogai, the Romans' steadiness, the overwhelming charges of the Namdaleni, the dash of the little company of light horse from Khatrish, the Khamorth bands' speed and ferocity, and the all-around competence of most of the Videssian majority—though not so specialized in their techniques as their allies, the Videssians were more versatile than any other troops.

The army's left wing seemed no slower to deploy than the right or the center and no clumsier in its evolutions. Marcus began to think he had done Ortaias Sphrantzes an injustice. Then one day he heard Nephon Khoumnos' bull voice roaring out on the left, overriding Sphrantzes' reedy tones but careful to preface each command with, "Come, on, you lugs, you heard the general. Now—" and he would shout out whatever was needed.

Gaius Philippus heard him too, and said, "There's a relief. At least now we know things won't fall apart on our flank."

"True enough," Scaurus agreed. His solid respect for Mavrikios' wits increased once more. The Emperor had managed to give the young scion of the rival faction a position that seemed powerful, but no authority to go with his rank. Sometimes Videssian subtlety was not to be despised.

As he and his men were slowly making their way to the Roman position in column after an exercise, the tribune caught sight of a familiar plump figure atop a donkey. "Nepos!" he called. "I didn't know you were with us."

The fat little priest steered his mount over to the Romans. A conical straw hat protected his shaven pate from the sun's wrath. "There are times I'd sooner be lecturing at the Academy," he admitted. "My fundament was not designed for days on end in the saddle—oh, a horrid pun there. I crave pardon—it was unintentional." He shifted ruefully, continuing, "Still, I was asked to come and so here I am."

"I would have thought the Emperor could find enough priests to take omens, hearten the men, and suchlike without pulling you away from your research," Gorgidas said.

"And so there are," Nepos said, puzzled at the physician's slowness. "I do such things, to be sure, but they are hardly my reason for being here."

"What then, your honor?" Viridovix asked with a sly grin. "Magic?"

"Why, of course," Nepos replied, still surprised anyone needed to put the question to him. Then his brow cleared as he remembered. "That's right—in your world, magic is more often talked of than seen, is it not? Well, my friends, answer me this—if not for magic, how and why would you be marching through some of the least lovely land in the Empire of Videssos? How would you be talking with me now?"

232

Viridovix, Gorgidas, and the Romans in earshot looked uncomfortable. Nepos nodded at them. "You begin to understand, I see."

While his mates were still wrestling with Nepos' words, Gaius Philippus drove to the heart of the problem. "If you use magic in your fighting, what can we poor mortals expect? Hordes of demons shrieking out of the sky? Man-sized fireballs shot from miles away? Gods above, will the very earth crack under our feet?"

Nepos frowned at the centurion's oath, but saw from his listeners' faces how alarming the prospect of the unknown was. He did his best to reassure them. "Nothing so dramatic, I promise you. Battle magic is a very chancy thing—with men's minds and emotions at the pitch of combat, even the most ordinary spells often will not bite. For that matter, sorcerers are often too busy saving their own skins to have the leisure they need for magecraft.

"And you must bear in mind," the priest went on, "that both sides will have magicians with them. The usual result is that they cancel each other's work and leave the result to you armored ruffians. In short, you have little to fear. I think my colleagues of the Academy and I should be able to keep our sorcerous friend Avshar quite well checked and perhaps give him more than he bargained for."

Nepos sounded confident. Yet for all the priest's assurances of wizardry's small use in battle, Marcus could not help remembering the talking corpse in the armory of Videssos' seawall, could not stop himself from recalling the black rumors swirling round Avshar's name in the fighting thus far. His hand slid to the hilt of his good Gallic sword. There, at least, was something to be counted on to hold dire sorceries at bay.

XI

THE FIRST SIGNS VIDESSOS WAS A LAND UNDER ATTACK SHOWED THEM-
selves several days' march east of Amorion. A string of plundered,
burned-out villages said more clearly than words that Yezda raiders had
passed this way. So did abandoned farms and a gutted monastery with
its ravaged fields. Some of the destruction was very fresh; a pair of starving hounds still prowled round the monastery, waiting for masters who
would not return.

The damage the nomads had done elsewhere was not much worse
than any land could expect in wartime. For the Empire's god, though,
the Yezda reserved a special fury. The small chapel by the monks' living
quarters was viciously desecrated. The images on its walls were ripped to
bits, and the altar chopped up and used for stovewood. As a final act of
insult, the bandits had stabled their horses there.

If the Yezda thought to strike terror into their enemies by such tactics, they failed. The Videssians already had good cause to hate their
western neighbors. Now the same hatred was inculcated in the mercenaries who followed Phos, for Mavrikios made sure all his soldiers looked
inside the profaned chapel. The Emperor made no comment about what
they saw. None was needed.

The devastation upset Marcus for another reason. He had long since
decided Yezd was a foe worth fighting. Any land that placed one such as
Avshar high in its councils was not one with which decent men could
hope to live at peace.

What the tribune had not realized was how strong Yezd was. The
imperial army was not much more than halfway to Videssos' western
frontier, yet already the land bore the marks of the strokes the nomads
were hurling at the Empire. And what they were seeing today was but the

weakest, furthest touch of the Yezda. What would the land be like five days further west, or ten? Would anything grow at all?

That night there were no complaints over setting up the usual Roman field fortifications, with ditch, earth breastwork, and palisade of stakes. Not a Yezda had been seen, but the entire imperial force made camp as if in hostile country.

Scaurus was glad it was the turn of his group of legionaries to visit their women. As he and his men strolled from their camp to that of the women, he looked askance at local notions of what a fortified camp should be. He always did.

True, the women's tents were surrounded by a palisade of sorts, but it was no better than other Videssian productions. There were too many large, haphazardly trimmed tree trunks—as soon as two or three foes could combine to pull one away from its fellows, the palisade was breached. The Romans, on the other hand, each carried several stakes, which they set up each night with their branches intertwining. They were hard to uproot, and even if one was torn free, it did not leave a gap big enough for a man to enter. He'd mentioned the matter to the Videssians several times; they always sounded interested, but did nothing.

Nervous sentries challenged the Romans half a dozen times in the five-minute walk. "Use your wits, fool!" Marcus snapped to the last of the challengers. "Don't you know the Yezda fight on horseback?"

"Of course, sir," the sentry answered in injured tones. Scaurus hesitated, then apologized. Any sort of ruse was possible, and the last thing he should do was mock a man's alertness. He was more on edge than he'd thought; tonight he badly needed the peace Helvis could bring him.

Yet it was not easy for him to find that peace, though Helvis sent Malric to sleep with some friends he had made on the march. Scaurus was so long out of the habit of unburdening himself to anyone—and perhaps especially to a woman—that he spoke not of his concerns, but merely of the day's march and other matters of little importance. Not surprisingly, Helvis sensed something was wrong, but the tribune's shield was up so firmly she could not tell what it was.

Even their love that night could not give the Roman the relief he sought. He was too much within himself to be able to give much, and what passed for lovemaking had a hesitance and an incompleteness it had not known before. Feeling all the worse because he had hoped to feel better, the tribune slipped into uneasy sleep.

The next he knew, he was in a Gallic clearing he remembered only too well, in the midst of his little band of legionaries as the Celts began their massacre. He stared wildly about him. Where was Videssos, the Emperor, the baking plain he and the survivors of this very night had been crossing? Or were there any survivors? Was the Empire but a fantasy of a man driven from his wits by fear?

Here came Viridovix, swinging the long blade that was twin to Scaurus' own. The tribune raised his sword to parry, or so he thought, but the hand he brought up over his head was empty. The Celt's blade hurtled down—

"What is it, darling?" The touch on his cheek was not the bite of a blade, but Helvis' hand. "Your thrashing woke me, and then you cried out loud enough to rouse half the camp."

Marcus lay on his back for several seconds without answering. The night was nearly as hot as the day had been, but there was cold sweat on his chest and shoulders. He looked up to the ceiling of the tent, his mind still seeing torchlight glittering off a Celtic sword.

"It was a dream," he said, more to himself than to Helvis.

"Of course it was," she answered, caressing his face again. "Just a bad dream."

"By the gods, how real it felt! I was in a bad dream inside a nightmare, dreaming Videssos was but a dream, and me about to die in Gaul—as I should have, by any sane man's rules.

"How real it was!" he said again. "Was that the dream, or is this? What am I doing here, in this land I never imagined, speaking its tongue, fighting its wars? Is Videssos real? Will it—oh, the dear gods, will you—vanish, too, one day, like a soap-bubble when a needle pricks it? And am I doomed to soldier on, then, for whatever new king I find, and learn his ways as well?"

He shuddered; in the hours when one day was long dead and the next far from born, the vision had a terrifying feel of probability to it.

Helvis pressed her warm naked length against him. "The nightmare is gone when you wake. This is real," she said positively. "You see it, you feel it, you taste it—what more could there be? I am no one's dream but my own—though it gives me joy you share it." In the darkness her eyes were enormous.

"How tight you are," she said, her fingers exploring his chest, the side of his neck. "Roll over!" she ordered, and Scaurus turned obediently on his belly. She straddled his middle; he grunted in pleasure as her strong hands began to knead the tension from his back. Her massage always made him want to purr like a kitten, never more so than now.

After a few minutes he rolled to his back once more, careful not to dislodge her from atop him. "What are you doing?" she asked, but she knew the answer. He raised himself on his elbows to kiss her more easily. A strand of her hair was between them; she brushed it aside with a laugh. Her breath sighed out as she lowered herself onto him.

"*This* is real, too," she whispered as she began to move. The tribune could not argue, nor did he want to.

Three days later the army saw its first live Yezda, a small band of raiders silhouetted against the sky to the west. The Emperor gave chase with a squadron of Videssian horse, but the nomads on their steppe ponies eluded the hunters.

Ortaias Sphrantzes was intemperate in his criticism of Mavrikios' choice. He told everyone who would listen, "Kalokyres plainly states that only nomads should be employed in the pursuit of other nomads since, being accustomed to the saddle from infancy, they are superior horse-men. Why have we Khamorth with us, if not for such a purpose as this?"

"If himself doesna cease his havering anent his precious book, the Gavras will be after making him eat it one fine day," Viridovix said. Marcus thought the same, but if the Emperor was displeased he gave no immediate sign.

The morning after the Yezda were spotted, Scaurus was returning to the Roman camp from the women's quarters when someone called his name. He turned to find Thorisin Gavras behind him. The Sevastokrator was swaying slightly; he looked to have had quite a night of it.

"Good morning, your Highness," Scaurus said.

Thorisin raised a mocking eyebrow. "'Good morning, your highness,'" he mimicked. "Well, it's good to see you can still be polite to the hand that feeds you, even if you do sleep with an island wench."

Marcus felt his face grow hot; the flush was all too noticeable with his fair skin. Catching sight of it, Thorisin said, "Nothing to be ashamed about. The lass is far from homely, I give you that. She's no fool, either, from what I've heard, whether or not her brother eats nails every morning."

"That sounds like Soteric." Marcus had to smile, struck by the aptness of Thorisin's description.

Gavras shrugged. "Never trust a Namdalener. Deal with them, yes, but trust? Never," he repeated. He walked slowly up to Scaurus and then around him, studying the bemused Roman as he might a horse he was thinking of buying. Marcus could smell the wine on the Sevastokrator's breath. Thorisin considered silently as he walked, then burst out, "So what's wrong with you?"

"Sir?" When faced with a superior in an unpredictable mood, least said was best. The tribune knew that lesson as well as the lowliest of his troopers.

"What's wrong with you?" It seemed Thorisin could only keep track of his thoughts by saying them over again. "You damned Romans keep company with the islanders by choice; Skotos' frozen beard, you take to them like flies to dead meat." Despite the unflattering simile, there was no rancor in the Sevastokrator's voice, only puzzlement. "By rights, then, you should be bubbling with seditions, rebellions, and plots to put one Scaurus on my brother's throne, with his skull for a drinking goblet."

Now genuinely alarmed, the Roman started to protest his loyalty. "Shut up," Thorisin said, with the flat authority power and drink can sometimes combine to put in a voice. "You come with me," he added, and started back to his own tent, not looking to see whether the tribune was following.

Marcus wondered if he should disappear and hope the Sevastokrator would forget their meeting once sober. He could not take the chance, he decided; Thorisin was too experienced a drinker to go blank that way. Feeling nothing but trepidation, he trailed along after Mavrikios' brother.

Gavras' tent was of blue silk, but not a great deal larger than the canvas and wool shelters of the Videssian army's common soldiers. The Sevastokrator was too much a warrior to care for extravagance in the field. Only the pair of Haloga bodyguards in front of the opening gave any real indication of his rank. They snapped to attention when they caught sight of their master. "Sir," said one, "the Lady Komitta has been asking for you for the past—"

Komitta Rhangavve herself chose that moment to poke her head out of the tent. Her lustrous black hair was pulled back from her face, accenting her aquiline features. She looked, in fact, like a barely tamed angry falcon, and the tirade she loosed at Thorisin did nothing to lessen the resemblance.

"Where have you been, you worthless rutting tinpot?" she shrilled. "Out swilling again, from the look of you, with the mountain men and the goatherds, and tumbling their women—or their goats! I am of noble kin—how dare you subject me to this humiliation, you—" and she swore with the same aptness Scaurus had heard from her when she gambled with the Namdaleni.

"Phos' little suns," Thorisin muttered, giving back a pace under the blast. "I don't need this, whether she's right or not. My head hurts already."

The two guards stood rigid, their blank faces caricatures of unhearingness. The Roman's efforts along the same line were not so successful, but then, he thought, the poor guards likely got more practice.

He had to admire the way the Sevastokrator pulled himself together and returned his irascible mistress' barrage. "Don't bite the thumb at me, slattern!" he roared, his baritone pounding through her soprano curses. "Give me peace, or I'll warm your noble backside!"

Komitta kept on at full bore for another few seconds, but when Thorisin Gavras stalked toward the tent with the evident intention of carrying out his threat, she turned and ducked back inside, only to emerge a moment later. Proud as a cat, she strode stiff-backed past Thorisin. "I shall be with my cousins," she informed him with icy hauteur.

"Good enough," he replied amicably; Marcus thought his anger mostly assumed. Gavras suddenly seemed to remember the Roman standing by his side. "True love is a wonderful thing, is it not?" he remarked with a sour grin. A few seconds later he added, "If you pray to Phos, outlander, tack on a prayer that he deliver you from a taste for excitable women. They're great fun, but they wear . . . oh, they wear."

The Sevastokrator sounded very tired, but he was brisk again when he said to one of his bodyguards, "Ljot, fetch my brother for me, will you? We have a few things to discuss with this lad here." He stabbed a thumb at Marcus. Ljot, who proved to be the guard on the right, hurried away.

Thorisin pulled the tent flap back for the Roman to precede him. "Go on," he said, returning to the ironic tone with which he'd begun the encounter. "If not the Avtokrator's throne, will the Sevastokrator's mats please your excellency?"

Scaurus stooped to enter the tent; the air inside was still musky with Komitta's perfume. He sank to the silk-lined mat flooring, waiting for the Sevastokrator to follow. Thorisin's gamesome mood, his half-threats and sardonic compliments, only served to make the tribune jittery. As he had in the Emperor's chambers, he felt caught up in an elaborate contest whose rules he did not understand, but where the penalty for a misplay could be disastrous.

The Sevastokrator and the Roman had waited only a couple of minutes when the guardsman Ljot returned. "His Majesty asked me to tell you he will be delayed," the Haloga reported. "He is at breakfast with Baanes Onomagoulos and will join you when they are through."

If Thorisin Gavras had put on anger to match Komitta's, there was no mistaking his real wrath now. "So I'm less important than that bald-headed son of a smith, am I?" he growled. "Ljot, you take your arse back to Mavrikios and tell him he and his breakfast can both climb right up it."

The Emperor's own head appeared inside the tent, a wide grin on his face. "Little brother, if you're going to commit lese majesty, never do it by messenger. I'd have to execute him too, and it's wasteful."

Thorisin stared, then started to laugh. "You are a bastard," he said. "Come on, set that stringy old carcass of yours down here." Mavrikios did so; the tent was a bit cramped for three but, thanks to its thin silk walls, not unbearably stuffy.

Opening a battered pine chest no finer than any private soldier might have owned, Thorisin produced an earthenware jug of wine, from which he swigged noisily. "Ahh, that's good. Phos willing, it will make my headache go away." He drank again. "Seriously, brother, you shouldn't use Baanes to twit me—I remember too well how jealous of him I was when I was small."

"I know, but the chance to listen to you fume was too good to pass up." Mavrikios sounded half-contrite, half-amused at his practical joke's success.

"Bastard," Thorisin said again, this time with no heat.

Marcus looked from one of the brothers Gavras to the other; though he'd had nothing to drink, he could feel the world starting to spin. Much of what he'd thought he understood of Videssian politics had just fallen to pieces before his eyes. Where was the feud that had the Gavrai so at odds with each other they rarely spoke?

"Oh dear," Mavrikios said, spying the bewilderment Scaurus was doing his best to hide. "I'm afraid we've managed to confuse your guest."

"Have we, now? Well, I'm damned if I'll apologize to any Namdalener-loving barbarian." Thorisin's words were fierce enough to make the tribune start up in fright, but he accompanied them with an unmistakable wink. Marcus sagged back to his haunches, altogether muddled.

"Only right he should be confused," the Sevastokrator went on, warming to his theme. "He and his whole crew like the easterners so bloody well this whole camp should be buzzing with talk they're ganging together to kill us all. Phos knows we've paid enough good gold to sniff out the rumors."

"We didn't find any, either," Mavrikios said accusingly. "Which leads to one of two conclusions: either you're clever beyond compare, or else you may be loyal in spite of your perverse choice of friends."

"I don't think he looks all that bright, Mavrikios," Thorisin said.

"You don't look any too well yourself, little brother," the Emperor retorted, but again the tone of the badinage was what would be expected from two brothers who liked each other well.

With the persistence too much wine can bring, Thorisin said, "If he's not so smart as to be able to fool us all, he's most likely loyal. Who would have thought it, from a friend of the Namdaleni?" He shook his head in amazement, then belched softly.

"The gods be thanked," Marcus murmured to himself. When both Gavrai eyed him questioningly, he realized he'd spoken Latin. "I'm sorry you had any reason to doubt me," he told them, returning to Videssian, "and very glad you don't any longer."

His relief was so great all of his defenses slid down at once, along with the guards on his tongue. "Then the two of you aren't quarreling with each other?" he blurted, then stopped in worse confusion than before.

The brothers Gavras suddenly looked like small boys whose secret has been discovered. Mavrikios plucked a hair from his beard, looked at it musingly, and tossed it aside. "Thorisin, he may be smarter than he seems."

"Eh?" Thorisin said blurrily. "I should hope so." He was sprawled out on his side and fighting a losing battle with sleep.

"Lazy good-for-nothing." Mavrikios smiled. He turned back to Scaurus. "You're quite right, outlander. We are having a little play, and to a fascinated audience, I might add."

"But I was there when you first quarreled, gambling against each other," the tribune protested. "That couldn't have been contrived."

The Emperor's smile slipped a notch. He looked at his brother, but Thorisin was beginning to snore. "No, it was real enough," he admitted. "Thorisin's tongue has always been more hasty than is good for him, and I own he made me spleenish that night. But next morning we made it up—we always do."

Mavrikios' smile broadened again. "This time, though, my contrary brother chose to make a donkey of himself in front of a hundred people. It was less than no time before the vultures started gathering over the corpse of our love." He cocked an eyebrow at the Roman. "Some of them flapped near you, I've heard."

"So they did," Scaurus agreed, remembering the odd meeting he'd had with Vardanes Sphrantzes.

"You know what I mean, then." Mavrikios nodded. "You were far from the only one sounded, by the way. It occurred to Thorisin and me that if we lay very still and let the vultures land, thinking they were about to pick our bones, why then we might have the makings of a fine buzzard stew for ourselves."

"I can follow all that," Marcus allowed. "But why, having laid your trap, did you give Ortaias Sphrantzes the left wing of your army, even with Khoumnos to keep him in check?"

"He is an imbecile, isn't he?" the Emperor chuckled. "Nephon has his eye on him, though, so have no fear on that score."

"I've noticed that. But why is he here at all? Without his precious book he knows less about soldiering than his horse does, and with it he's almost more dangerous, because he thinks he knows things he doesn't."

"He's here for the same reason he has his worthless command: Vardanes asked them of me."

Marcus was silent while he tried to digest that. At last he shook his head; the crosscurrents of intrigue that could make the Sevastos request such a thing and the Emperor grant it were too complex for him to penetrate.

Mavrikios Gavras watched him struggle and give up. "It's good to find there are still some things you don't understand," he said. "You have more skill at politics than most mercenary soldiers I know."

Thinking of the ruling Roman triumvirate of Caesar, Crassus, and Pompey—each of whom gladly would have torn the hearts from the other two could he have done so without plunging his country into civil war— Scaurus said, "I know something of faction politics, but yours, I think, are worse." He waited to see if Mavrikios would solve the riddle for him.

The Emperor did, with the air of a professor giving a demonstration for an inexperienced student who might have talent. "Think it through. With Ortaias here, Vardanes gets an eye in the army—not the best of eyes, perhaps, because I know it's there, but an eye just the same. And who knows? Even though Khoumnos has the real power on the left, Ortaias may eventually learn something of war and become more useful to his uncle in that way. Clear so far?"

"Clear enough, anyway."

"All right. If I'd said no to Vardanes, he wouldn't have stopped plotting against me—he could no more do that than stop breathing. I thought it safer to have Ortaias here where I could keep an eye on him than involved in Phos knows what mischief back in the city."

"I follow the logic well enough. From what little I've seen of Vardanes Sphrantzes, I'd say it was sound, but you know him far better than I."

"He's a serpent," Mavrikios said flatly. His voice grew grim. "There's one other reason to let Ortaias come along. If worse comes to worse, he's worth something as a hostage. Likely not much, when I recall how conveniently Evphrosyne died, but something." Still in the role of instructor, he spread his hands, palms out, as if he had just proven two lines in a complex figure parallel after all.

His, though, were not the pale soft hands of a sheltered don. Spear, sword, and bow had scarred and callused them, and sun and wind turned them brown and rough. They were the hands of a warrior, yes, but a warrior who also showed his skill in another arena, one where the weapons were the more deadly for being invisible.

The Emperor saw Scaurus' admiration, dipped his head in acknowledgment of it. "Time the both of us got back to work," he said. "Look angry when you come out. I've dressed you down, and Thorisin and I have been snapping at each other again. It would never do for people to think we like each other."

"Are you odd-looking people, uh, Romans?" The speaker was a smilingly handsome, swarthy young man on a stocky, fast-looking horse. A girl of about his own age, her silver-braceleted arms round his middle, rode behind him.

Both were in typical Videssian horseman's gear, a light, long-sleeved tunic over baggy woolen trousers tucked into boots. Each of them wore a sheathed saber; he had a bow and a felt quiver slung over his back.

They led a packhorse loaded with gear, prominent among it a wickerwork helmet, a bundle of javelins, and a fine pandoura, its soundbox decorated with elaborate scrollwork and inlays of mother-of-pearl.

The young fellow's Videssian had a slight guttural accent. He wore a leather cap with three rounded projections toward the front, a broad neckflap and several streamers of bright ribbon trailing off behind. Marcus had seen a good many Vaspurakaners with such headgear—quite a few of them had settled in these lands not far from their ancestral home. On most of them the cap seemed queer and lumpy, but the stranger somehow gave it a jaunty air.

His flashing smile and breezy way of speech were wasted on Gaius

Philippus, who frowned up at him. "You don't look any too good your-self," he growled, unconsciously echoing Mavrikios speaking to Thori-sin. "If we are Romans, what do you want with us?"

The centurion's sour greeting did not put off the horseman. He an-swered easily, "You may as well get used to me. I am to be your guide through the passes of my lovely homeland. I am Prince Senpat Sviodo of Vaspurakan." He drew himself up in the saddle.

Marcus was pleased he'd guessed the young man's people, but more alarmed than anything else at the prospect of having to deal with a new and unfamiliar royalty. "Your Highness—" he began, only to stop, non-plused, when Senpat Sviodo and his companion burst into gales of laugh-ter.

"You *are* from a far land, mercenary," he said. "Have you never heard Vaspurakan called the princes' land?"

Thinking back, the tribune did recall some slighting reference of Mavrikios' during the briefing before the imperial army left Videssos. Of its significance, however, he had no idea, and said so.

"Every Vaspurakaner is a prince," Sviodo explained. "How could it be otherwise, since we are all descendants of Vaspur, the first and most noble of the creations of Phos?"

Scaurus was instantly sure the Videssians did not take kindly to that theology. He had little time to ponder it, though, for the girl was nudging Senpat, saying, "Half-truths, and men's half-truths at that. Without the princesses of Vaspurakan, there would be no princes."

"A distinct point," Senpat Sviodo said fondly. He turned back to the Romans. "Gentlemen," he said, looking at Gaius Philippus as if giving him the benefit of the doubt, "my wife Nevrat. She knows Vaspurakan and its pathways at least as well as I do."

"Well, to the crows with *you*, then," someone called from about the third rank of Romans. "I'd follow her anywhere!" The legionaries who heard him whooped agreement. Marcus was relieved to see Senpat Sviodo laugh with them, and Nevrat too. She was a comely lass, with strong sculptured features, a dark complexion like her husband's, and flashing white teeth. Instead of Senpat's distinctive Vaspurakaner cap, she wore a flower-patterned silk scarf over her black, wavy hair.

Lest the next gibe have a less fortunate outcome, the tribune made haste to introduce some of his leading men to the Vaspurakaners. Then he asked, "How is it you are in Videssos' service?"

Senpat Sviodo told his story as they traveled west; it was not much different from what Scaurus had expected. The young man was of a noble house—his fine horse, his elegant pandoura, and the silver Nevrat wore had already made the tribune sure he was no common soldier.

"Being a noble in Vaspurakan these past few years was not an un-mixed blessing," he said. "When the Yezda came sweeping through, our peasants could flee, having little to lose by taking shelter here inside the Empire. But my family's estates had rich fields, wealth besides from a small copper mine, and a keep as strong as any. We chose to fight to hold them."

"And well, too," Nevrat added. "More than once we drove the raiders off our lands licking their wounds." Her slim hand touched the hilt of her saber in a way that told Marcus she meant "we" in the most literal sense.

"So we did," Senpat agreed with a smile. But that smile faded as he thought of the grinding fight he had waged—and lost. "We never drove them far enough, though, or hard enough. Season by season, year by year, they wore us down. We couldn't farm, we couldn't mine, we couldn't go more than a bowshot from the keep without being attacked. Two years ago a Videssian regiment passed by our holding chasing Yezda, and Senpat Sviodo, prince of Vaspurakan, became Senpat Sviodo, imperial scout. There are worse fates." He shrugged.

He tugged at the rope by which he led his packhorse. When the beast came forward, he plucked the pandoura from its back and struck a fiery chord. "Worse fates indeed!" he shouted, half singing. "Wolves of the west, beware! I come to take back what is mine!" Nevrat hugged him tightly, her face shining with pride.

The Romans thought well of his display of spirit, but it had a special purport for Gorgidas. Familiar with the strife-torn politics of Greek cities, he said, "That one and his wife will do well. It's so very easy for an exile to leave hope behind along with his home. The ones who somehow bring it with them are a special breed."

As the army halted for the night, Senpat Sviodo and his wife, like so many before them in the Empire of Videssos, walked up to observe with unfeigned admiration as the Romans created their camp. "What a good notion!" he exclaimed. "With fieldworks like these, it would be easy to stand off attackers."

"That's the idea behind them," Scaurus agreed, watching his men toss the dry, reddish-brown plateau soil up from the ditch they were digging to form the camp's breastwork. "You'll have officer's status among us, so your tent will be one of those in front of mine, along the *via principalis*—" At Senpat's blank expression, he realized he'd used the Latin name and hastily translated: "The main road, I should say."

"Well enough, then," the Vaspurakaner said. Lifting the three-peaked cap from his head, he used a tunic sleeve to wipe caked sweat and dust from his forehead. "I could use a good night's sleep—my behind isn't sorry to be out of the saddle."

"Yours?" Nevrat said. "At least you had a saddle to be out of—I've been astride a horse's bumpy backbone all day, and my stern is petrified." She gave her husband a look full of meaning. "I hope you don't plan on being out of the saddle the whole night long."

"Dear, there are saddles, and then there are saddles," Senpat grinned. His arm slid round her waist; she nestled happily against him.

Seeing their longing for each other, Scaurus muttered a Latin curse— Videssian was too new in his mouth for comfortable swearing. Until that moment he had forgotten the rule he'd imposed against women in the camp. If it stood for his own men, he could hardly break it for these newcomers. As gently as he could, he explained his edict to the Vaspurakaners.

They listened in disbelief, too amazed to be really angry. Finally Senpat said, "Watching your soldiers building this camp convinced me you were men of no common discipline. But to enforce that kind of order and have it obeyed—" He shook his head. "If your Romans are fools enough to put up with it, that's their affair and yours. But I'm damned if we will. Come on, love," he said to Nevrat. And their tent went up, not within the Roman stockade, but just outside it, for they preferred each other's company to the safety of trench, earthwork, and palisade. Alone inside his tent later that evening, Marcus decided he could not blame them.

His own sleep came slowly. It occurred to him that Phostis Apoka-vkos might well be able to tell him much more than he already knew about the strong-willed folk who came out of Vaspurakan. Apokavkos was from the far west and presumably had dealt with Vaspurakaners before.

The adopted Roman was not sleeping either, but throwing knucklebones with a double handful of men from his maniple. "You looking for me, sir?" he asked when he saw Marcus. "Won't be sorry if you are—I've got no luck tonight."

"If you're after an excuse to get out of the game, your luck just turned," the tribune said. He spoke in his own language, and Apokavkos had no trouble understanding him; when the onetime peasant-soldier tried to speak Latin, though, his lisping Videssian accent still made him hard to follow. But he stuck with it doggedly, and his progress was easy to see.

Scaurus took him back to his own tent and asked him, "Tell me what you know of Vaspurakan and its people." Recalling Apokavkos' dislike of the Namdaleni for their heterodox beliefs, he made himself ready to discount as prejudiced some of what the other would reply.

"The 'princes'?" Phostis said. "About their land I can't tell you that much—where I grew up, it was no more than mountains on the northern horizon. Beastly cold in winter, I've heard. They raise good horses there, but everybody knows that."

Even Scaurus had heard good things about Vaspurakaner horseflesh, and he had the traditional Roman attitude toward the equestrian art—that it was a fine skill, for other people. He was intellectually aware that the use of stirrups made horsemanship a very different thing from the one he knew, but still found it hard to take the idea seriously.

Apokavkos proceeded to surprise him, for he spoke of the Vaspurakaners themselves, not with suspicion, but with genuine and obvious respect. "It's said three 'princes' working together could sell ice to Skotos, and I believe it, for work together they would. I don't know where they learned it, unless being stuck between countries bigger'n they are taught it to them, but they take care of their own, always. They'll fight among themselves, aye, but let an outsider meddle in their affairs and they're tight as trap jaws against him."

To Marcus that seemed such plain good sense as hardly to be worth comment, but Phostis Apokavkos' voice was full of wistful admiration.

"You—*we*, I mean—Romans are like that too, but there's plenty of Videssians who'd hire on Skotos himself, if it meant paying their enemies back one."

The tribune's thoughts went to the decayed heads he had seen at the foot of the Milestone in Videssos, generals who rebelled with Yezda backing, both of them. He also thought, uneasily, of Vardanes Sphrantzes. Apokavkos had a point.

Trying to shake the worrisome pictures from his mind, Scaurus decided to tease Phostis a bit, to see what he would do. "How can you speak so well of heretics?" he asked.

"Because they're good people, religion or no," Apokavkos said at once. "They aren't like your precious islanders—begging your pardon, sir—always chipping away at other people's ideas and changing their own whenever the wind shifts. The 'princes' believe what they believe and they don't care a horseturd whether you do or not. I don't know," he went on uncomfortably, "I suppose they're all damned—but if they are, old Skotos had better watch himself, because enough Vaspurakaners in his hell and they might end up taking it away from him."

The first raid on the imperial army came two days before it got to Amorion. It was a pinprick, nothing more—a handful of Yezda waylaying a Videssian scout. When he was missed, his comrades searched until they found his body. The Yezda, of course, had plundered it and stolen his horse.

There was a slightly larger encounter the next day, when a small band of Khamorth traded arrows with the Yezda until reinforcements drove the enemy away. Trivial stuff, really, Marcus thought, until he remembered the Emperor promising the journey from Garsavra to Amorion would be as easy as that from the capital to Garsavra. More invaders were loose in the Empire than Mavrikios had thought.

And Amorion, when the army reached it, proved to have suffered badly. Lying on the northern bank of the Ithome, a tributary of the Arandos River, Amorion, like most towns in Videssos' westlands, had long ago torn down its walls for their building stone. Yezda raiders took full advantage of the city's helplessness, ravaging its suburbs and penetrating almost to the river bank in several places. As the army approached, the plundered areas were barren and rubble-strewn, in stark contrast to the fertility the river brought neighboring districts.

The contingent Gagik Bagratouni had gathered to reinforce Mavrikios was not as large as the one under Baanes Onomagoulos, but it was, Marcus soon decided, made up of better men. Most were Vaspurakaners like their commander—dark, curly-haired men with bushy beards, usually heavier of build than the Videssians they lived among. They wore scale-armor; many had helmets of wicker like Senpat Sviodo's, often ornamented with plaited horns or wings. Almost all of them looked like veterans.

"So we should," Senpat Sviodo said when Marcus remarked on this. "At least as much as the Empire's *akritai*, we have stood in Yezd's way these past years and been Videssos' shield. Believe me, it was not what we wanted, but being set where Phos chose to place his princes in this world, we had no choice."

He shrugged, then went on, "My people tell a fable about a little lark who heard the sky was about to fall. She turned on her back with her legs in the air to catch it. 'Have you become a tree, then?' all the other animals asked. 'No,' she answered, 'but still I must do all I can.' So did she, and so do we."

Just as it had for Onomagoulos, the army arranged itself in review to honor Gagik Bagratouni. As the general rode up on a roan stallion, Scaurus found himself impressed by the man's sheer physical presence. If Caesar had been a bird of prey, a human expression of Rome's eagle, Gagik Bagratouni was a lion.

His tawny skin, his mane of coal-black hair, and the thick dark beard that covered his wide, high-cheekboned face almost to the eyes were enough in themselves to create that impression. The steady gaze from those eyes, a hunter's look, added to the image, as did the thrust of his nose—it was thicker and fleshier than the typical Videssian beak, but no less imperious. He even sat his horse strikingly, as if posing for an equestrian statue or, more likely, conscious that many eyes were on him.

Bagratouni held that impassive seat as he walked his horse past unit after unit. The only acknowledgment the troops got that he was so much as aware of their presence was a flick of his eyes across their ranks, the slightest dip of his head as he passed by each commander. Mavrikios himself was not nearly so imperial of demeanor, yet it was plain Gagik Bagratouni meant no slight to the Emperor, but was merely acting as he always did.

When he came to the Romans, drawn up next to the Emperor's Haloga guard, Bagratouni's thick brows rose—these were men whose like he had not seen. He looked them over appraisingly, studying their equipment, their stance, their faces. Whatever his judgment was, he did not show it. But when he saw Senpat and Nevrat Sviodo standing with the Romans' officers, his heavy features lit in the first smile Scaurus had seen from him.

He shouted something in his own tongue. His voice was in keeping with the rest of him, a bass roar. Senpat answered in the same speech; though altogether ignorant of it, Marcus heard the name "Sviodo" several times. Gagik Bagratouni cried out again, then jumped down from his horse and folded Senpat Sviodo in a bearhug, kissing him on each cheek. He did the same to Nevrat, with a different kind of gusto.

"Sahak Sviodo's son!" he said in thickly accented Videssian, switching languages out of courtesy to the Romans around him, "and with such a lovely bride, too! Lucky you are, both of you! Sahak was a great one for pulling Yezd's beard, yes, and the Emperor's too, when in our affairs he stuck it. You have the very look of home—I knew him well."

"I wish I could say the same," Senpat answered. "He died before my beard sprouted."

"So I heard, and a great pity it was," Bagratouni said. "Now you must tell me—who are these strange men you travel with?"

"Have you noticed, Scaurus darling," Viridovix said, "that every one of these Vaspurakaner omadhauns who sets eyes on you and yours is after calling you funny-looking? Right rude it is, I'm thinking."

"Likely they saw you first," Gaius Philippus put in, drawing a glare from Viridovix.

"Enough, you two," Marcus said. Perhaps luckily, the Gaul and the centurion preferred Latin as a language for bickering, and the Vaspurakaners could not understand them. Scaurus named his men for Bagratouni, introduced some of his officers and, as he had done so often by now, briefly explained how they had come to Videssos.

"That is most marvelous," Gagik Bagratouni said. "You—all of you"—His expansive gesture took in everyone the tribune had presented to him—"must to my home come this evening for a meal, and more of your tale to tell me. I would have it now, but things are piling up behind me."

He spoke the truth there; the procession he headed, which was made up of his contingent's officers and some of the leading officials and citizens of Amorion, had halted in confusion when he dismounted. Its members were variously standing about or sitting on horseback while waiting for him to continue. One of them in particular, a tall harsh-faced priest who had a fierce hound on a lead of stout iron chain, was staring venomously at Bagratouni. The Vaspurakaner affected not to notice, but Scaurus stood near enough to hear him mutter, "Plague take you, Zemarkhos, you shave-pated buzzard."

Bagratouni remounted, and the army of functionaries moved on toward the Emperor. When the priest started forward once more, his dog balked, setting itself on its haunches. He jerked at its chain. "Come on, Vaspur!" he snapped, and the beast, choked by its collar, yelped and followed him.

Marcus was not sure he believed his ears. Clearly, not all Videssians shared the liking Phostis Apokavkos had for the folk of Vaspurakan—not when a priest would name his dog for the Vaspurakaners' eponymous ancestor. Senpat Sviodo stood tight-lipped beside Scaurus, plainly feeling the insult's sting. The Roman wondered how Gagik Bagratouni put up with such calculated insolence.

Unlike Baanes Onomagoulos at Garsavra, Bagratouni dismounted and performed a full proskynesis before the Emperor, followed by everyone accompanying him. Even in the formal act of submission to his overlord he was still a commanding figure, going to his knees and then to his belly with feline dignity and grace. Scaurus noted with amusement that, by comparison, the churlish priest Zemarkhos looked a poorly built stick man.

After Mavrikios' brief speech of thanks for the men Bagratouni had collected, the Vaspurakaner general and his party performed the proskynesis once more, then retired from the imperial presence. He held up their withdrawal for a moment to give Senpat Sviodo and Scaurus directions to his dwelling. Zemarkhos had never seen Romans before, but, from the look he gave them, their willingness to be a Vaspurakaner's guests was enough to brand them agents of Skotos.

When Senpat Sviodo and his wife met the Romans who were going with them to Bagratouni's, they had exchanged their traveling garb for more elegant attire. He wore a spotless white tunic coming almost to his knees, baggy trousers of reddish-brown wool, and sandals with golden clasps. On his head was the familiar Vaspurakaner cap; his pandora was slung across his back.

Nevrat was in a long gown of light blue linen, its cut subtly different from Videssian designs. The dress set off her dark skin magnificently, as did her massy silver bracelets, necklace, and earrings.

Senpat stared at the Romans in amazement. "What matter of men have I fallen in with?" he cried. "Do you satisfy each other? Where are your women, in Phos' sacred name?"

"It's not our usual custom to bring them, unbidden, to a feast," Marcus answered, but he shared an apprehensive look with Quintus Glabrio. The junior centurion was partnered to a fiery-tempered Videssian girl named Damaris. She and Helvis would not be pleased to learn they had been excluded from a function which they could have attended.

The rest of the Roman party was more sanguine about being by themselves. "Sure and there'll be a lass or three fair famished for the sight of a Celtic gentleman," Viridovix said. "It's not as if I'm thinking to return alone."

Gaius Philippus was in most ways an admirable man but, as Marcus knew, women were of no use to him out of bed. He looked back at Senpat Sviodo with as much incomprehension as the Vaspurakaner directed toward him.

"Are you looking at me?" Gorgidas asked Senpat. "I hold with the idea of Diogenes, a wise man of my people. When he was asked the right time for marriage, he said, 'For a young man, not yet; for an old man, never.'"

"What of you, though?" Senpat asked. "You're neither one nor the other."

"I manage," Gorgidas said shortly. "Right now, I manage to be hungry. Come on, shall we?"

Gagik Bagratouni's home was half villa, half fortress. Its grounds were spacious and well kept, with little groves of citruses, figs, and date palms placed artfully among flowerbeds full of bright blooms. But the main house was a thick-walled stronghold seemingly transplanted from Vaspurakan's hills, set behind outworks that would have delighted the commander of any border keep.

As he greeted his guests by the massive, metal-clad gate, Bagratouni noticed the tribune taking the measure of the place and Gaius Philippus' frank stare of professional appraisal. "This is not what I would want," he said, waving at the forbidding gray stone walls. "But I fear too many in Amorion delight not in seeing prosper the princes. But prosper I do, and I am able for myself to care."

That, if anything, was an understatement, for Gagik Bagratouni did not rely on walls alone for protection. His personal guard manned them, a picked group of young Vaspurakaners as formidable as any band of warriors Scaurus had seen.

"Do not worry about such things," the general said. "Come into my courtyard; eat, drink, talk, laugh."

Bagratouni's house was laid out in a basic style Marcus knew well, for it was popular among the wealthy in Italy. Instead of facing out onto the world, the home's focus was directed inward to a central court. But the structure was more a bastion than any Roman home Marcus knew. Only a few windowslits were directed outward, and those as much for arrow-fire as for view. The gates that led from the outer grounds into the court-yard were almost as stoutly made as those protecting the estate as a whole.

Lanterns hung from trees inside the courtyard. Their glass panes were of many colors; as twilight deepened, beams of gold and red, blue and green danced in the foliage. The main tables in the courtyard's center, though, were brightly lit, to call attention to the feast they bore.

Vaspurakaner cookery was nothing like Videssian cuisine, which emphasized seafood and sauces of fermented fish. The main course was a roasted kid, spiced with a glaze of tarragon, mint, and lemon, and garnished with shreds of sharp yellow cheese. There was also a stew of ground lamb and hard-boiled eggs, made flavorful with onion, coriander, and cinnamon, and extended with chickpeas. Both dishes made the eyes water along with the mouth, but both were delicious.

"Whoo!" Viridovix said, fanning his face with his hand. "There's a lot going on in there." To quell the flames, he downed his winecup and reached for the decanter before him. Of all Bagratouni's guests, the big Celt probably felt the food's tang the most. Beyond vinegar, honey, and a few pale-flavored herbs, northern Gaul had little to offer in the way of spices.

Scaurus sat at Gagik Bagratouni's right, between the general and his chief aide, a man of early middle years named Mesrop Anhoghin, who was even more thickly bearded than his commander. At Bagratouni's left, confirming Senpat Sviodo's words, was the general's wife Zabel, a plump, comfortable lady whose few words of Videssian were mostly an apology for not knowing more. Anhoghin's command of the imperial tongue was not much better. As a result, Gagik Bagratouni had the tribune's conversation almost entirely to himself, something Marcus soon began to suspect he had arranged deliberately.

The general—*nakharar,* he styled himself in his own language; it meant warrior-prince—had a hunger for knowledge of the world's far reaches that rivaled Gorgidas'. Perhaps, thought Scaurus, it sprang from his effort to grow beyond the limits of the isolated land in which he'd come to manhood. Whatever the reason, he bombarded the Roman with questions not only touching on matters military, but also about his native land, its people, what the city of Videssos was like, even what it was like to see the ocean. "Never have I seen it," he remarked sadly. "Rivers, yes, lakes, those yes, too, but never the sea."

"Did I see his honor ask you about the sea?" asked Viridovix, who was a few seats away. At Marcus' nod, the Gaul said earnestly, "Tell him it's a fit province for lunatics, and precious little else. A boat's no more than a prison, with the risk of drowning besides."

"Why says he that?" Gagik asked. "On rivers and lakes I enjoy to fish in a boat."

"He suffers from seasickness," Scaurus answered, and then had to explain the concept to Bagratouni. The Vaspurakaner tugged his beard as he considered the Roman's words; Marcus wondered if he thought he was being made sport of.

Dessert consisted of fruit and some interesting pastry balls, a mixture of wheat flour, ground dates, and minced almonds, covered over

255

with powdered sugar. This last was a discovery for the Romans, for the Videssians sweetened with honey, even as they did themselves. Reaching for about his fourth, Gorgidas remarked, "It's as well I don't see these more often, lest I bulge with lard."

"Bah!" Gaius Philippus said. "Why is it always the skinny ones who complain?" Only the hard life he led kept the centurion from losing the battle with his belly.

"Not only are they very good," said Quintus Glabrio, licking his fingers, "but they look as if they'd keep well, and they're so rich a few would feed a man for some time. They'd be good travelers' fare."

"So they would and so they are. You are one who sees the importance in things, then? That is good," Bagratouni rumbled approvingly. "We of Vaspurakan often on journeys carry them."

"The Videssians do, too," Senpat Sviodo told him with a grin. "They call them 'princes' balls.'" The Romans and most of the Vaspurakaners snorted; Gagik Bagratouni looked blank. Senpat translated the pun into his native language. The *nakharar* blinked, then he and his wife began to laugh at the same time. When Zabel laughed it was easy to see how the lines had come to crease her features; her face was made for laughter. Gagik smiled at her fondly. She was far from beautiful, but in her own way lovely.

"Do they indeed?" her husband chuckled. "Do they indeed?"

After the dessert was finished, someone called to Senpat, "Give us a tune, there, since you've brought your pandoura along."

"Fair enough," he said. "Who's with me?" One of the Vaspurakaners had a flute; a quick search of the house turned up a small hand-drum for another volunteer. And with no more ado than that they struck up a song of their mountain homeland. All the Vaspurakaners seemed to know the words and clapped out the beat with their hands. Senpat's fingers danced over the strings of his instrument; his strong clear tenor helped lead the singers. Gagik Bagratouni sang with enthusiasm and great volume, but even Marcus could tell that the *nakharar* could not carry a tune in a bucket.

The tribune felt isolated, both by his indifference toward music in general and his ignorance of this music in particular. He wondered what Helvis would make of it and had another twinge of conscience over not bringing her with him. To his untrained ear, most of the songs had a defiant air to them, as befit the resilient folk who gave them birth.

As the musicians played on, the Vaspurakaners got up from the table one by one and began to dance, either with the ladies who accompanied them or with some of Gagik Bagratouni's servinggirls. The slates of the courtyard rang to boot heels stamping in intricate rhythms. Bodies swayed, sinuous and sinewy at the same time. The dancers were a physical expression of what they heard, Marcus thought with surprise, and began to understand the grip strong music could take, even if he failed to feel it himself.

Viridovix, now, was taken hard by it, watching and listening as if in a trance. When at length Senpat and his fellows struck up a particularly sprightly tune, the Celt could stand—or rather sit—no more. He rose to join the dancers.

He did not try to imitate their steps, dancing instead in his native Gallic style. Where their upper bodies shifted to the music, he was almost still above the waist, his arms motionless at his sides while his legs and feet twinkled in the complex figures of his dance. He leaped, spun, checked himself seemingly in midair, spun in the other direction, leaped again. His movements were utterly dissimilar to those of the dancers round him, yet strangely complementary as well.

A few at a time, the Vaspurakaners formed a circle around Viridovix, clapping him on. The musicians played faster and faster, but the Gaul was equal to the challenge, whirling and capering like a man possessed. As the music reached a fiery pitch, he capped his dance by springing almost his own height into the air. He let out a great shout at the top of his leap and came back to earth with a final splendid flourish.

The clapping turned from time-keeping to applause, in which all those still in their seats heartily joined. "Marvelous, marvelous!" Gagik exclaimed. "That step I should like to learn, were I less stiff in knee and thick of belly. Marvelous!" he repeated.

"I thank your honor," Viridovix panted; his exertions had deeply flushed his fair skin. He brushed sweat from his forehead. "Thirsty work it is, too. Would you be so kind as to fetch me a cup of wine, love?" he asked one of the serving-maids in the circle around him. Marcus noticed he chose a girl who had hardly been able to keep her eyes off him as he danced. The big Celt might be slipshod about some things, but where wenching was concerned he noted every detail.

"Thank you, lass," the Gaul purred as the girl brought his drink. He slipped an arm around her in what could have passed for no more than thanks, but when she moved closer to him instead of away he gathered her in with practiced efficiency.

"Your friend is as good as his word," Senpat Sviodo remarked to the tribune.

"I was thinking the same thing myself," Marcus laughed.

One of Bagratouni's retainers came trotting into the courtyard with some word for his master. He spoke in throaty Vaspurakaner, so Scaurus, sitting by the *nakharar*, could not understand what he said, but the Roman did catch the name Zemarkhos mentioned several times. Gagik Bagratouni's black brows lowered in anger. He asked a curt question of his guardsman, who nodded.

Bagratouni's scowl grew darker yet. He sat a moment in thought, his hands tangled in his thick beard. Then he snapped out a string of quick orders. The guard, startled, repeated the first one in a questioning voice, then broke into a toothy grin as Gagik explained. The man hurried away.

"Forgive me my rudeness, I pray you," the *nakharar* said, turning back to Scaurus. "When rises my temper, I forget the Empire's speech."

"So do I," the tribune admitted. "You've shown me much kindness tonight. I heard your man name the priest who hates you. Can I help you in your trouble? I think the Emperor would hear me if I asked him to make the man leave you at peace—Mavrikios is not one to sacrifice the Empire's unity for the sake of a priest's feelings."

"I need no man to fight my battles for me," was Gagik's instant response, and Scaurus was afraid he had offended the proud *nakharar*. But Bagratouni was hesitating, embarrassment on his leonine face—an expression that did not sit well there. "But by bad luck this foul priest wants not to speak with me, but with you and yours."

"With me? Why?" The prospect was alarming; Marcus had seen enough fanatical priests in Videssos to last him a lifetime.

"To read the mind of a cur, one must a cur be. It is better not to try. Do you wish to have words with him?"

The tribune's first impulse was to say no at once and have done. But to do so might leave his host in the lurch. "Whatever would serve you best," he replied at last.

"You are a good man, my friend. Let me think." The *nakharar* rubbed his forehead, as if trying to inspire wisdom.

"It might be better if you saw him," he decided. "Otherwise this Zemarkhos can claim I kept you from him. To me this matters not so much, for I shall Amorion be leaving with you and the Emperor. But for my people who stay behind, no end of trouble could he cause."

"All right, then." Marcus quickly rounded up Gaius Philippus, Quintus Glabrio, and Gorgidas, but Viridovix had contrived to disappear. Looking around, Scaurus also failed to see the serving wench the Celt had chosen as his quarry for the evening. He decided not to go chasing after Viridovix; he did not judge it likely that Zemarkhos knew the exact nature of the Roman party.

"I'd gladly trade places with the Gaul, sir," Glabrio grinned.

"I'm senior to you, puppy," Gaius Philippus said. "You wait your turn."

Ignoring their byplay, Gorgidas asked Scaurus, "What does the priest want with us?"

"To tell us we're all damned, I suppose. I'm glad you're here tonight; you're good at theological arguments."

"My favorite amusement," Gorgidas said, rolling his eyes in despair. "Oh, well, we'd best get this over with, I suppose—our host is growing impatient." That was true enough; like a caged hunting-beast, the *nakharar* was pacing up and down the courtyard, now and again smacking fist into palm.

When he saw the Romans finally ready, Bagratouni led them out through his fragrant gardens to the front gates of his estate. On their way to the gates, they were joined by the retainer who had brought Bagratouni word of Zemarkhos' arrival. Heavy leather gauntlets sheathed the man's arms, which were full of what looked like canvas sheeting. His face bore an expression of anticipation.

The gates were closed, as against any enemy. At the *nakharar*'s impatient gesture, his men unbarred them and swung them wide. And, as if entering a conquered city in triumph, Zemarkhos strode onto the Vaspurakaner's land, his hound at his side.

He caught sight of Gagik Bagratouni before noticing the Romans behind him. "So," he said, "you dare not let these ignorant foreigners learn the truth, but seek only to enmesh them in your evil schemes?"

Bagratouni almost visibly swelled with wrath. Fists clenched, he stepped toward the priest. Zemarkhos' dog growled in warning; the hair stood up along its back. Zemarkhos took a tighter grip on the leash. "Stay, Vaspur!" he ordered, but that command was hardly one to make him better loved by the man he confronted.

Trying to avert the explosion, Marcus hastily brought his companions up past the *nakharar* so Zemarkhos could see them. "We are here, as you asked," he told the priest, "and at our kind host's urging as well. What do you have to say that would be of such importance for men you never met?"

"From your strange gear and now from your speech, I see you are a foreigner and know no better than to enter into this house of iniquity. My duty to your soul and those of your men has brought me to rescue you from the clutches of the infamous heretic who lured you here."

The tribune reluctantly admired Zemarkhos' misplaced courage. No faintheart would speak so boldly at his foe's very threshold. But, as with too many clerics Scaurus had met in Videssos, the priest's dogmas blinded him to the worth of any man who did not share them.

He answered as politely as he could. "As we did not discuss religious matters, the subject of heresy never came up."

"Oh, he is a sly one, cunning as the fox, hungry as the jackal. The ice will take him even so." Bagratouni's men muttered angrily as they listened to Zemarkhos revile their overlord, but the *nakharar* stood still and silent, as if carved from stone. His face was thunderous, but he did not answer the priest.

Gorgidas spoke up. His passionate interest in everything he came across had led him to examine Videssos' sacred writings as soon as he could read them, even if he could not accept their precepts. Now, with his facility for an apt quotation, he asked Zemarkhos, "Is it not written in the forty-eighth chapter: 'Let fury be suppressed! Put down violence, you who would assure yourselves, through righteousness.'?"

But quoting holy scriptures to the priest was letting him fight on ground of his own choosing. His reply was quick and sure. "Aye, and it is also written in the thirty-third chapter, 'Whoever works evil on the wicked pleases Phos and fulfills his will.' The Emperor may think he is doing a great thing in sallying forth against the heathen of Yezd. He could do better inside Videssos itself, by purifying it of the poisonous misbelievers within our borders!"

Bagratouni shoved past the Romans. "Priest, hatred you spew like a drunk his dinner. All this on my land you have done. Give I my men leave, and they treat you as you deserve."

Zemarkhos touched his dog's lead. In an instant the beast was leaping at Bagratouni, only to be brought up short by the leash. It snapped viciously, a growl rumbling in its throat. The priest laughed. "Send your dogs against mine—they'll have their tails between their legs soon enough."

"Why did you name that beast Vaspur? Tell me this," Bagratouni asked, tone deceptively mild.

"Why?" the priest jeered. "What better name for a dog?"

With that last insult, all Gagik Bagratouni's patience blew away. His voice was lion's roar indeed as he bellowed a command in his birth-tongue at the warrior who carried the roll of canvas. Deft as a net-wielding gladiator, the man jumped forward to pop his huge bag of heavy cloth over Zemarkhos' head. Screeching curses, the priest fell thrashing to the ground.

The hound Vaspur sprang snarling to protect its master. But Bagra-touni's retainer was ready for the dog. Though tumbled about by its charge, he lodged one gauntleted arm between its gaping jaws while hugging the beast to his armored chest with the other. The snarl turned to a half-throttled whine.

The Vaspurakaner stooped to lift up the open end of the sack, which was now, of course, around Zemarkhos' flailing feet. Dodging a fusillade of kicks, he pushed the dog into the bag with its owner, then dropped the flap once more.

Zemarkhos' shrieks took on a sudden, desperate urgency as Vaspur, crazed with fear, began snapping wildly at everything near it—which, at the moment, consisted almost entirely of the priest. Great satisfaction on his face, Bagratouni came up to deliver a couple of sharp kicks to the bag. The dog yelped, the priest cried out even louder than before, and the gyrations within the flopping canvas were astonishing to behold.

Vaspurakaners came up to enjoy the spectacle of their enemy thus entrapped and to add a kick or two of their own. "What was it you said, priest?" Bagratouni shouted. "'Whoever works evil on the wicked pleases Phos'? Phos tonight is mightily pleased."

From the noises inside the sack, it sounded as if Zemarkhos was being torn to pieces. Scaurus had no love for the fanatic priest, but did not think he deserved so bitter a death. "Let him go," he urged Bagratouni. "Alive, he could not hate you and yours more than he already does, but slain he would be a martyr and a symbol for vengeance for years to come."

The *nakharar* looked uncomprehendingly at the Roman, almost like a man interrupted in the act of love. His eyes filled with reluctant understanding. "In that young head an old mind you have," he said slowly. "Very well. It shall be as you ask."

His men moved with the same unwillingness their overlord displayed, but move they did, cutting the bag apart so its occupants could free themselves. The moment the hole they made was wide enough to let out the dog Vaspur, it darted through. The Vaspurakaners jumped back in alarm, but there was no fight left in the terrified beast. It streaked away into the night, its chain clattering behind it.

When Zemarkhos at last got loose from the swaddling canvas, he was a sight to glut even an appetite starved for revenge. There were deep bites on his arms and legs, and half of one ear was chewed away. Only luck had saved his face and belly from his animal's fangs.

Gorgidas leaped to his side at the sight of those wounds, saying, "Fetch me strips of cloth and a full winejug. We may be satisfied the dog was not mad, but the bites must be cleaned, lest they fester." When no Vaspurakaner stirred, the physician speared one with his eyes and snapped, "You! Move!" The man hurried back toward Bagratouni's house.

But Zemarkhos, lurching to his feet, would not let Gorgidas treat his injuries. "No heathen will lay hands on me," he said, and limped out through the gate of Bagratouni's estate. His priestly robe, torn by his dog's teeth, hung in flapping tatters around him. The *nakharar*'s men hooted in delight as the darkness swallowed up their chastised foe.

Viridovix came loping up to the gate with the Vaspurakaner Gorgidas had sent back for bandages. "What's all the rumpus in aid of? This omadhaun is after understanding my Videssian, but not a word of his can I make out."

When the Gaul learned of the stir he'd missed, he kicked at the ground in frustration. If he enjoyed anything more than his venery, it was combat. "Isn't that just the way of it? Another good shindy wasted because I was off friking in the bushes! It scarce seems fair."

"It's your own fault, you know. You could have been here with us if you hadn't gone skirt-chasing," Gaius Philippus said unkindly.

And Gorgidas demanded, "Is that all this would have been to you? Entertainment? Only a cruel man could take pleasure in watching the outcome of others' hatreds."

"Oh, get on with you," the Celt retorted. "You're only angry the now because that rascally priest ran off without letting you do the patching of him." There was just enough truth in that slander to reduce Gorgidas to sputtering fury.

Quintus Glabrio said quietly, "You needn't feel you lost out on a chance to take a risk, Viridovix. Or can you truly tell me you think loving any less dangerous than fighting?"

The Celt stared blankly, but Gorgidas' eyes narrowed in thought, as if he were seeing the young centurion for the first time. And when Gagik Bagratouni had the exchange translated—for most of it had been in Latin—he put his arm round Glabrio's shoulder, saying, "Clever I knew you were. Many men are clever, but now I see as well you are wise. This is a rarer and more precious thing. Scaurus, of this one you must take good care."

"Up to now he's been pretty well able to take care of himself, which is as it should be," Marcus answered. Thinking back, he realized just how true that was. Glabrio was so silently competent that days would sometimes go by with the tribune hardly noticing him, but the maniple he led was always perfectly drilled and, now that Scaurus was putting his mind to it, it seemed his men had fewer disciplinary problems than the other Romans. A good man to have around, Marcus thought, a very good man indeed.

XII

In a way, the tribune was disappointed when neither Helvis nor Amorion flared up as he had expected. His lady was so caught up by his account of Gagik Bagratouni's revenge on Zemarkhos that she forgot to be angry at not having been there. That the priest was of the orthodox Videssian faith only made his fall sweeter to her.

"More of them should be treated thus," she declared. "It would take their conceit down a peg."

"Is it not as wrong for you to rejoice in their downfall as it is for them to oppress your fellow believers?" Marcus asked, but her only reply was a look as blank as the one Viridovix had given Quintus Glabrio. He gave up—she was too convinced of her beliefs' truth to make argument worthwhile.

Amorion would have risen against its Vaspurakaners with the slightest word of encouragement from the Emperor, but that was not forthcoming. When Zemarkhos appeared at Mavrikios Gavras' tent to lay charges against Bagratouni, Gavras already had the accounts of the *nakharar* and the Romans. He sent the cleric away unhappy, saying, "Priest or no, you were unwelcome on the man's land and incited him by gross insult. He is not blameworthy for taking action against you, nor should he and his be liable to any private venture of vengeance."

More direct, his brother Thorisin added, "As far as I can see, you got what you deserved for meddling where you didn't belong." That was the feeling of most of the army, which appreciated the rough wit of Gagik's device. A chorus of barks and howls accompanied Zemarkhos as he limped out of the camp. His every glance was filled with hate, but the Emperor's threat restrained him while the army resupplied at Amorion.

Scaurus had the distinct feeling Mavrikios begrudged every minute he spent in the plateau town. The conflict between Zemarkhos and Gagik

Bagratouni, serious under most circumstances, was now but an unwelcome distraction to him. He had been like a horse with the bit between its teeth since the first skirmish with the Yezda and seemed on fire to join the great battle he had planned.

Yet it was as well that his host paused to refit before pushing northwest toward Soli. The journey, shorter than either of the first two stages, was worse than both of them rolled together. Whatever caches of food the local Videssian authorities managed to store up for the army had fallen instead to the invaders. The Yezda did their best to turn the land to desert, torching fields and destroying the canals that shared out what little water there was.

The nomads Yezd was funneling into the Empire were perfectly at home in such a desert. Trained to the harsh school of the steppe, they lived with ease where the Videssian army would have starved without the supplies it carried. More and more of them shadowed the imperial forces. When they thought the odds were in their favor they would nip in to raid, then vanish once more like smoke in a breeze.

Their forays grew bolder as time passed. About midway between Amorion and Soli, one band of about fifty broke through the army's screen of Khamorth outriders and dashed across the front of the marching column, spraying arrows into it as they rode.

Marcus saw the cloud of dust come rolling out of the west, but did not think much of it. Maybe, he thought, the scouts had spotted a good-sized Yezda party and were sending messengers back for aid.

Gaius Philippus disagreed. "There's too many there for that." His face went suddenly grim. "I don't think those are our men at all."

"What? Don't be absurd. They'd have to have—" Whatever argument the tribune was about to make died unspoken when one of the legionaries cried in pain and alarm as an arrow pierced his arm. The range was ungodly long, but quickly closed as the nomads, riding their light horses for all they were worth, zipped past the column's head, emptying their quivers as fast as they could. At their heels was a troop of Khamorth in imperial service.

"All maniples halt!" Gaius Philippus' battlefield roar rang out. "Shields up!" The Romans unslung their *scuta* and raised them to cover their faces.

There was nothing else they could do; the Yezda were racing by, far out of *pilum*-range. Adiatun and his slingers let fly with a few hasty bullets, but they fell short. What the Khamorth had thought all along, then, was true—the nomads' bows easily outranged any weapons the Romans had. Scaurus filed the fact for future worry.

The raiders broke up into groups of four and five and scattered in all directions. They had done nothing that could be called damage, but had managed to throw an army a thousand times their number into confusion.

Videssos' mercenary cavalry were still after the Yezda. More and more raced up to join the chase. Marcus was hard-pressed to tell friend from foe. In the swirling dust ahead, the nomads who fought under Yezd's banner looked little different from the Empire's hirelings. Perhaps the Khamorth themselves had the same problem, for not a handful of Yezda were brought down before the rest made good their escape.

The officers' meeting the Emperor called that night was not happy. The raiders' bravado stung Mavrikios, who was further infuriated by its going all but unpunished. "Phos' suns!" the Emperor burst out. "Half a day's march wasted on account of a few scraggly, unwashed barbarians! You, sirrah!" he barked at Ortaias Sphrantzes.

"Your Majesty?"

"What was that twaddle you were spouting? Something about the only people to catch nomads are other nomads?" The Emperor waited ominously, but Sphrantzes, with better sense than Scaurus had thought he owned—or was it simply terror?—kept silent.

Prudent though it was, his silence did not save him. "Those were your bloody nomads the Yezda rode through, boy. If they do it again, you can forget your precious left wing—you'll be back at the rear, in charge of horsedung pickup." When angry, Mavrikios was plainly Thorisin's brother. The Sevastokrator himself was saying no more than Ortaias Sphrantzes, but from his grin he was enjoying every bit of Mavrikios' tirade.

When the Emperor was through, Ortaias rose, bowed jerkily, and, muttering, "I'll certainly try to do better," made an undignified exit from the imperial tent.

266

His departure only partly pacified Mavrikios. He rounded on Sphrantzes' nominal subordinate Nephon Khoumnos: "You'll be right there with him, you know. I put the two of you together so your way of doing things would rub off on him, not the other way around."

"Anything can go wrong once," Khoumnos said stolidly. As was his style, he shouldered the blame without complaint. "They burst out of a wash and caught us napping. If it happens again, I deserve to be shoveling horseballs, by Phos."

"We'll leave it at that, then," the Emperor nodded, somewhat mollified.

Khoumnos was as good as his word, too; his cavalry pickets foiled ambush after ambush the rest of the way to Soli. The march slowed nonetheless. Skirmishes with the invaders were constant now, skirmishes that in a lesser campaign would have been reckoned full-scale battles. Time after time the army had to push the Yezda aside before it could press on.

The country through which it passed grew ever more barren, devastated. Save for the Videssian host and its foes, the land was nearly uninhabited, its farmers and hersdmen either dead or fled. The only substantial remaining population was in walled towns. There were not many of these after the long years of peace, nor were all of them unscathed. Where field and farm could not be worked, towns withered on the vine.

The army passed more than one empty shell of what had been a city but now housed only carrion birds—or, worse, Yezda who based themselves in abandoned buildings and fought like cornered rats when attacked.

Here as elsewhere, the invaders reserved their worst savagery for Phos' temples. Their other barbarities paled next to the fiendish ingenuity they devoted to such desecrations. Not all altars were so lucky as to be hacked to kindling; the bloody rites and sacrifices celebrated on others made mere desecration seem nothing more than a childish prank. As seasoned a veteran as Nephon Khoumnos puked up his supper after emerging from one ravaged shrine. Where before the Emperor had encouraged his troops to view their enemies' handiwork, now he began ordering the polluted fanes sealed so as not to dishearten them further.

"Such foulness points to Avshar, sure as a lodestone draws nails," Gorgidas said. "We must be getting near him."

"Good!" Gaius Philippus said emphatically. He had commanded the Roman party ordered to guard a sealed temple and used the privilege of his rank to break the seals and go inside. He came bursting out through the door an instant later, face pale beneath his deep tan and sweat beading on his forehead. "The sooner such filth is cleaned from the world, the better for all in it—aye, including the poor damned whoresons who follow him."

Marcus did not think he had heard his senior centurion ever speak thus of a foe. War was Gaius Philippus' trade, as carpentry might be another man's, and he accorded his opponents the respect their skills merited. Curious, the tribune wondered aloud, "What was it you saw in that temple?"

Gaius Philippus' face froze, as if suddenly turned to stone. Through clenched teeth he said, "If it please you, sir, never ask me that again. The gods willing, I may forget before I die."

The imperial army reached Soli a joyless force. What they found there did nothing to raise their spirits. The new town, wall-less in the fashion of so many Videssian cities, had snuggled against the Rhamnos River's turbid yellow waters, the better to lure trade. Old Soli on the hills above, a garrison against Makuran for hundreds of years, was all but deserted . . . until the Yezda came.

Then the new city fell in fire and death—sacked repeatedly, in fact, over the years, until nothing was left to loot. And Old Soli, far down the road to extinction, had a modest rebirth as survivors from the riverbank town patched its dilapidated walls and began to repair the tumbledown buildings from which their six-times-great-grandsires had sprung.

Heedless of the omens his men might draw, Mavrikios made camp amidst the ruins of the dead city by the Rhamnos. An army the size of his needed more water than Old Soli's wells and cisterns could provide, and the river was the logical place to get it. It made perfect military sense, but also made the soldiers edgy.

"Sure and there's bound to be angry ghosts about," Viridovix said, "all crying out for revenge on them that slew 'em. There!" he exclaimed. "Do you hear the keening of them?" Sure enough, a series of mournful cries came from the darkness outside the Roman camp.

"That's an owl, you great booby," Gaius Philippus said.

"Och, aye, it *sounds* like an owl." But the Gaul was anything but convinced.

Marcus shifted uneasily in his seat by the fire. He told himself he did not believe in ghosts and was able to convince the front part of his mind that he spoke the truth. Deeper down, he was not so sure. And if there were ghosts, they would surely live in such a place as this.

Most of the buildings of murdered Soli had perished either at the hands of the Yezda or through time's decay, but here and there a tower or a jagged section of some well-made building still stood, deeper blacknesses against the night sky. It was from these the owls' plaintive notes and the whirring call of the nightjar emanated—if that was what the noises were. No one seemed anxious to investigate, nor was the tribune inclined to ask for volunteers.

As if the place was not eerie enough, a thin mist crept up from the Rhamnos as the night wore on, half shrouding the imperial camp. Now it was Gaius Philippus' turn to fret. "I don't like this a bit," he declared as the fog swallowed one watchfire after another. "Belike it's some sending of Avshar's, to veil his attack till it's on us." He peered out into the rolling mist, trying to penetrate it by will alone. Inevitably he failed, which only increased his unease.

But Marcus had grown up in Mediolanum, hard by the Padus River's tributary the Olonna. He had to shake his head. "Mist often rises from a river at night—it's nothing to worry over."

"Quite so," Gorgidas agreed. "Nature has provided that particles go up into the air from oceans and streams. This fog is but the forerunner of a cloud. When the vapor rises to meet opposite emanations coming down from the ether which holds the stars, it will condense into a true cloud."

The Epicurean account of cloud formation did nothing to reassure the centurion. Viridovix tried to tease him back to good humor. "You didna trouble yoursel' when you saw the very land steam or ever we came to Garsavra. Of course," he added cunningly, "a good deal further from the Yezda we were then."

Not even the imputation of cowardice could get much response from Gaius Philippus. He shook his head, muttering, "It's this bloody place, that's all; even without fogs it's like camping in a tomb. We couldn't leave too soon to suit me."

But for all the senior centurion's wholehearted desire to be gone, the imperial army did not set forth at once. Scouts spying out the ways through Vaspurakan reported that the land west of Soli was a desolation stripped bare of almost every living thing.

Senpat Sviodo and his wife were among the riders who went into Vaspurakan. "There will be a reckoning for this, if it takes a thousand years," he said. What he had seen in his birthland had burned some of his youth away forever. The cold fury in his voice and on his face seemed better suited to a man of twice his years.

"Our poor people survive only in the mountain forests and in a few fastnesses," Nevrat said. She sounded weary beyond belief; her eyes were full of sorrow too bitter for tears. "The meadows, the farmlands—nothing moves there but Yezda and other beasts."

"I had hoped to bring a band of princes back with me, to fight under the Emperor's banner against the invaders," Senpat continued, "but no one was left to bring." His hands shook in impotent fury.

Marcus studied the harsh lines newly etched on either side of Senpat's mouth. The jolly youngster he'd met a few short days before would be a long time reappearing, and the tribune was not sure he cared for this grim almost-stranger who had taken his place. Nevrat clasped her husband's hands in her own, trying to draw the pain from him, but he sat staring straight ahead, only the vision of his ravaged homeland before him.

In such territory the army could not hope to live off the land; it would have to carry its own provisions through the wasteland. Mavrikios gave orders for grain to be brought up the Rhamnos from the coastal plain to the north, and then had to wait with his men until the boats arrived.

The onerous delay in such dismal surroundings strained the Emperor's disposition to the breaking point. He had been short-tempered since the handful of Yezda raiders disrupted the army's march. Now, stymied again, frustration ate at him when each day failed to see the coming of the needed supplies. Men walked warily around him, fearful lest his pent-up rage lash out against them.

The abcess burst on the fifth day at Soli. Scaurus happened to be close by. He wanted to borrow a map of Vaspurakan from the collection Mavrikios kept in his tent, the better to follow Senpat Sviodo's description of the land through which they would be passing if the supply ships ever came.

Two Halogai of the Imperial Guard pushed through the tentflaps, dragging a scrawny Videssian soldier between them. Three more Videssians nervously followed the northerners.

"What's this?" the Emperor demanded.

One of the guardemen answered, "This worthless piece of offal has been filching coppers from his mates." He shook his prisoner hard enough to make the teeth snap in his head.

"Has he now?" The Emperor looked up at the Videssian soldiers behind the Halogai. "You three are witnesses, I suppose?"

"Your Majesty, sir?" said one of them. All three had been gaping at the luxurious interior of the tent, its soft bed and cleverly designed light furnishings—Mavrikios was of less spartan taste than Thorisin.

"Witnesses, are you?" the Emperor repeated. By his tone, his patience was very short.

Between them, they got the story out. The prisoner, whose name was Doukitzes, had been caught emptying a coin pouch when his three fellows unexpectedly returned to the tent the four of them shared. "We thought a few stripes would make him keep his fingers off what don't belong to him," one of the soldiers said, "and these fellows," he pointed to the Halogai, "happened to be coming by, so—"

"Stripes?" Gavras interrupted. He gestured contemptuously. "A thief forgets stripes before they're done healing. We'll give him something he'll remember the rest of his days." He turned back to the Halogai and snapped, "Take his hand off at the wrist."

"No! Phos have mercy, no!" Doukitzes shrieked, twisting free of his captors to fall at Mavrikios' feet. He seized the Emperor's knees and kissed the hem of his robe, babbling, "I'll never do it again! By Phos I swear it! Never, never! Mercy, my lord, I beg, mercy!"

The luckless thief's tentmates looked at the Emperor in horror— they'd wanted their light-fingered comrade chastised, yes, but not mutilated.

Marcus was equally appalled at Gavras' Draconian judgment. In theory, thievery in the Roman army could be punished by death, but hardly over the trifling sum at issue here. He stood up from the mapcase through which he'd been searching. "Your Majesty, is this justice?" he asked through Doukitzes' wails.

Save only the prisoner, everyone in the imperial tent—Mavrikios, the Haloga guards, the Videssian soldiers, and the Emperor's ubiquitous servants—turned to stare at the Roman, amazed anyone would dare call the sovereign to account.

The Emperor was chilly as the eternal snow topping the peaks of Vaspurakan. "Captain of mercenaries, you forgot yourself. You have our leave to go." Never before had Mavrikios used the imperial "we" to the tribune; it was a manifest note of warning.

But Scaurus' ways were those of a land that knew no king, nor was he trained from birth to accept any one man as the embodiment of authority and law. Still, he was glad to hear the steadiness in his voice as he replied, "No, sir. I recall myself better than you. In your worry over great affairs, you are letting rancor get the better of you in small ones. To take a man's hand for a few coppers is not justice."

The tent grew very still. The imperial servitors flinched away from Scaurus, as if not wanting to be contaminated by his blasphemous practice of speaking the truth as he saw it. The Halogai might have been carved from wood; the Videssian common soldiers, even Doukitzes, faded from the tribune's perception as he waited to see if Mavrikios would doom him too.

The Emperor slowly said, "Do you know what I could do to you for your insolence?"

"No worse than Avshar could, I'm sure."

A chamberlain gasped, somewhere to Scaurus' left. He did not turn his head, keeping his attention only on the Emperor. Gavras was studying him as intently. Without removing his eyes from the tribune, Mavrikios said to the Halogai, "Take this grizzling fool"—He stirred Doukitzes with his foot—"outside and give him five lashes, well laid on, then let his mates take him back."

Doukitzes scuttled across the floor to Marcus. "Thank you, great lord, oh thank you!" He offered no resistance as the Halogai led him away.

"Does that satisfy you, then?" Mavrikios asked.

"Yes, your Majesty, completely."

"First man I've ever seen go happy to a whipping," the Emperor remarked, raising an ironic eyebrow. He was still watching Scaurus closely. "It wasn't just pride, then, was it, that made you refuse me the proskynesis back in Videssos all those months ago?"

"Pride?" That had never occurred to the Roman. "No, sir."

"I didn't think so, even then," Mavrikios said with something like respect. "If I had, you'd've regretted it soon enough." He laughed mirthlessly.

"Now get out of here," he went on, "before I decide I should have you killed after all." Scaurus left quickly, only half-sure he was joking.

"You were very brave, and even more foolish," Helvis said that night. Lazy after love, they lay side by side in her tent, his hand still curled over her breast. Her heartbeat filled his palm.

"Was I? I didn't really think about being either at the time. It didn't seem right, though, to have all Mavrikios' wrath come down on that poor wretch. His worst fault wasn't stealing a few pennies, it was being in the Emperor's way at the wrong time."

"His anger could have condemned you as easily as that worthless Videssian." Helvis sounded thoroughly afraid. She might come from a folk freer than the Empire's, Marcus thought, but she took the Avtokrator's absolute power as much for granted as any of Videssos' citizens.

Her fear, though, did not spring from any such abstract reason, but a far more basic concern. Her hand took his, guided it down the smooth softness of her belly. "You were a featherbrain," she said. "Would you want your child to grow up fatherless?"

"My . . . ?" The tribune sat up on the soft sleeping-mat, looked down at Helvis, who still held his hand against her. She smiled up at him. "You're sure?" he asked foolishly.

Her warm rich laughter filled the small tent. "Of course I am, simpleton. There is a way of knowing such things, you know." She sat up, too, and kissed him.

He returned the embrace eagerly, not from the lust but sheer gladness. Then something struck him funny. "How could I know this morning that I might be making my child an orphan, when I didn't know there was a child?"

Helvis poked him in the ribs. "Don't you go chopping logic with me, like some priest. I knew, and that's enough."

And so perhaps it was. Good omens had been scarce lately, but what could be better before a battle than the creation of new life?

The next morning, the patrols Mavrikios sent riding north finally met the supply barges toiling their way upstream. The squat, ugly vessels reached Soli late that afternoon. Their journey had not been easy; marauding Yezda along both banks of the Rhamnos had made it impossible to use horses to tow the boats, and their arrows made life hellish for the barges' rowers.

One had lost so many men it could no longer make headway against the stream and drifted aground in the shallows by the riverbank. The rest of the fleet picked up its surviving crew, but the Yezda gleefully burnt the stricken craft to the waterline.

That night there was no time for worry over haunted surroundings. Men labored till dawn, hurling sacks of grain into hundreds of wagons. When the sun rose, the army rumbled over the great stone bridge spanning the Rhamnos and pushed its way into Vaspurakan.

Marcus soon saw what had moved Senpat Sviodo to such bitter hatred. The Yezda had done their worst in Videssos, but the destruction they wrought there was but the work of a few seasons. Vaspurakan had felt the invaders' hand far longer and far more heavily; in some frequently ravaged passes, fair-sized second growth was already springing up to shroud the ruins of what, in happier times, were farm and villages.

The raiders had come so often to the princes' land, they were beginning to think of it as their proper home. Just as he had outside Imbros, the tribune watched herdsmen drive their flocks up into the mountains at the first sight of the army. But these were not Videssians afoot with their herd dogs; they were nomad archers mounted on shaggy steppe ponies, looking uncomfortably like the Khamorth with the imperial forces.

In Vaspurakan even walled cities were under Yezda control, either stormed or, more often, simply starved into submission. Mavrikios' host came to the first of these two days out of Soli—a town called Khliat, whose shadow in the afternoon sun ran long down the valley through which the army was traveling.

The Yezda commander refused surrender with a brusque message eerily close to Scaurus' retort to the Emperor: "If you conquer, you could do me no worse harm than my lords would, should I yield."

Gavras did not waste time in further negotiations. Using what light remained, he surrounded Khliat, quickly driving the Yezda skirmishers back inside the city's walls. Once the encirclement was complete, he rode round the town just out of bowshot, deciding where it was most vulnerable to siege engines.

Again the night was furiously busy, this time with soldiers unloading the precut timbers and other specialized gear of the siege train. At the officers' council that night, the Emperor declared, "Our assault party tomorrow will be made up of Romans and Namdaleni. As the most heavily armed troops we have, they are best suited to forcing their way through breached walls."

Marcus gulped. Mavrikios' reasoning was probably sound, but the attacking force's casualties could well be hideous. The Namdaleni would fill their ranks with new recruits from the Duchy, but where was he to find new Romans?

"May your Majesty it please," Gagik Bagratouni spoke up, "but I the privilege of leading this assault would beg for my men. It is their homes they are freeing. Their armors may be lighter, but their hearts shall be so too."

Mavrikios rubbed his chin. "Be it so, then," he decided. "Spirit has raised more than one victory where it had no right to grow."

"Well, well, the gods do look out for us after all," Gaius Philippus whispered behind his hand to Scaurus.

"You've been in this wizards' land so long you've taken up mind-reading," Marcus whispered back. The centurion bared his teeth in a silent chuckle.

After the meeting broke up, Soteric fell into step beside the tribune. "How interesting," he said sardonically, "and how lucky for you, to be chosen to share the butcher's bill with us. The Emperor is glad of our help, aye, and glad to bleed us white, too."

"Weren't you listening? The Vaspurakaners are going in our stead."

Soteric gestured in disgust. "Only because Bagratouni has more honor than sense. True, we're spared, but not forgotten, I promise you. Everyone knows what Mavrikios thinks of the men of the Duchy, and you did yourself no good when you stood up to him yesterday. You'll pay—wait and see."

"You've been talking to your sister again," Marcus said.

"Helvis? No, I haven't seen her today." Soteric eyed the tribune curiously. "By the Wager, man, don't you know? Every blasted Videssian is buzzing over how you saved twelve men from having their heads chopped off."

Scaurus exchanged a consternation-filled glance with Gaius Philippus. No matter how much he tried to evade the role, it seemed he was being cast as the Emperor's opponent. That notwithstanding, though, he thought Soteric was wrong. Mavrikios Gavras might be devious in his dealings with his foes, but there was never any doubt who those foes were.

When he said as much to the Namdalener, Soteric laughed at his naiveté. "Wait and see," he repeated and, still shaking his head over what he saw as the Roman's gullibility, went off about his business.

Gaius Philippus gave thoughtful study to the islander's retreating back. He waited until Soteric was too far away to hear him before delivering his verdict. "That one will always see the worst in things, whether or not it's there." Coming from the centurion, a pessimist born, the statement was startling.

Gaius Philippus glanced warily at Scaurus; after all, the man he was dispraising was the brother of the tribune's woman. Even so, Marcus had to nod. The characterization was too apt to gainsay.

276

Matching their commander's defiance, the Yezda inside Khliat roared their war cries at the Videssian army from the city's walls. The rising sun glinted bloodily off their sabers. It was a brave show, but not one to frighten the professionals in the audience. "This will be easy," Gaius Philippus said. "There aren't enough of them by half to give us trouble."

Events quickly proved him right. The imperial army's bolt-throwing engines and the strong bows of the Khamorth sent such floods of darts against Khliat's defenders that the latter could not stop Videssian rams from reaching the wall in three separate places. The ground shook as each stroke did its pulverizing work.

One ram was put out of action for a time when the Yezda managed to tear some skins from its covering shed and dropped red-hot sand on the men who worked it, but new troops rushed forward to take the place of those who fell. The sheds' green hides were proof against the burning oil and firebrands the nomads flung down on them, and many defenders bold enough to expose themselves in such efforts paid for their courage with their lives.

The wall crumbled before one ram, then, only minutes later, before a second. Yezda on the battlements shrieked in terror and anguish as they slid through crashing stones to the ground below. Others, cleverly stationed behind the masonry the rams were battering, sent withering volleys into the siege engines' crews.

Then the Vaspurakaners were rushing toward the riven wall, Gagik Bagratouni at their head. Their battlecries held a savage joy, a fierce satisfaction in striking back at the invaders who had worked such ruin on their homeland.

A Yezda wizard, an angular figure in flapping blood-colored robes, clambered onto shattered masonry in one of the breaches to hurl a thunderbolt at the onstorming foe. But Marcus learned what Nepos had meant when he spoke of battle magic's unreliability. Though lightning glowed from the mage's fingertips, it flickered and died less than an arm's length from his body. At his failure, one of his own soldiers sabered him down in disgust.

The fight at the breaches was sharp but short. The Yezda were not natural foot soldiers, nor was there any place for their usual darting cavalry tactics in the defense of a fortified town. More heavily armored than their opponents, the Vaspurakaners hammered their way through the nomads' resistance and into Khliat.

When he saw the enemy forces heavily committed against the "princes," Mavrikios gave the order for a general assault. Like a sudden bare-branched forest, ladders leaped upward at Khliat's walls. Here and there still-resolute defenders sent them toppling over with a crash, but soon the imperial forces gained a lodgement on the wall and began dropping down into the city itself.

The Romans were involved in little that deserved the name of fighting. The very heaviness of their panoplies, an advantage in close combat, made them slow and awkward on scaling ladders. The Emperor wisely did not use them thus until most danger was past. Khliat was largely in imperial hands by the time they entered it, a fact which brought advantages and disadvantages both. Their only casualty was a broken foot suffered when a legionary tripped and fell down a flight of stairs, but they found little loot, and some grumbled.

"Men are fools to complain over such things," Gorgidas remarked, bandaging the injured soldier's foot. "Think how much more booty there would be if the Yezda had killed everyone who got into the city before us, and how sorry we should be to have it."

Gaius Philippus said, "For a man who's followed the army a while, you're trusting as a child. Most of these lads'd cheerfully sell their mothers if they thought the old gals would fetch more than two coppers apiece."

"You may be right," Gorgidas sighed, "though I still like to think otherwise." Turning back to the Roman with the fracture, he said, "If you can, stay off that foot for three weeks. If you put your weight on it before it's healed, it may pain you for years. I'll change the dressings day after tomorrow."

"I thank you kindly," the legionary said. "I feel like a twit, falling over my own feet like that."

Gorgidas checked to make sure the bandage was not tight enough to risk necrosis in the Roman's foot. "Enjoy your rest while you can get it—you'll be back at your trade too soon to suit you, I promise you that."

The bravado of the Yezda cracked when it became plain they could not hold Khliat. They began surrendering, first one by one and then in groups, and were herded together like cattle in the city's marketplace. Some of the Videssians crowding round wanted to massacre the lot of them, but Mavrikios would hear none of it. In the glow of victory he was prepared to be merciful.

He threw a cordon of Halogai and Romans around the prisoners, then ordered the defeated enemy's common soldiers disarmed and sent back to Soli under guard. There they could await disposition until he had finished beating their countrymen. Most of them fought for Yezd instead of Videssos only because their wanderings first brought them to that land.

The chieftains were another matter. They knew full well the master they served and did so with open eyes. Yet their choice of overlord did not make the Yezda officers any less dauntless. Mavrikios came up to their commander, who was sitting dejectedly on the ground not far from where Marcus stood.

That captain and a handful of men had holed up in a house and would not yield until the Videssians threatened to burn it over their heads. Looking at him now, Scaurus did not think him wholly of the steppe blood, as were most of the warriors he led. He was more slimly built and finer of feature than they, with large liquid eyes; perhaps there were native Makuraners in his ancestry.

Thorisin Gavras was at his brother's side. "Rise for the Emperor, you!" he barked.

The Yezda did not move. "Were our positions reversed, I do not think he would rise for me," he said. His Videssian was fluent and almost without accent.

"Why, you impudent—" The Sevastokrator was furious, but Mavrikios checked him with a gesture. Not for the first time, Marcus saw the respect the Emperor gave forthrightness.

Mavrikios looked down at his captive. "Were our places reversed, what would you do with me?"

The Yezda stared back unflinchingly. He thought for a moment, then said, "I believe I would have you whipped to death."

"Keep a civil tongue in your head, filth!" said Zeprin the Red, hefting his axe. The Haloga officer tolerated the Romans treating Mavrikios with less than due ceremony; they were, after all, allies. This insolence from a prisoner he would not stomach.

The Emperor was unperturbed. He told the Yezda commander, "I will not be as harsh as you. You are a brave man—will you not renounce the evil you followed and join us in rooting it out?"

Something flickered in the Yezda's expressive eyes. Perhaps it was temptation. Whatever it was, it was gone before Marcus was sure he'd seen it. "I can no more foreswear myself than you could, were you sitting in this dust," the officer said, and won grudging nods of approval from both Thorisin Gavras and Zeprin the Red.

"As you wish," Mavrikios said. The quality of the man he faced made the Emperor eager to win him to his side. "I will not cast you in prison, though I will ship you to an island for safekeeping until I've beaten your khagan and his sorcerous minister. Then, maybe, your mind will change."

Scaurus thought the Yezda was, if anything, being treated too leniently, but the man only shrugged. "What you do to me does not matter. Avshar will dispose of me as he pleases."

The Emperor grew irritated for the first time. "You are under my control now, not your wizard-prince's." The Yezda shrugged again. Mavrikios spun angrily on his heel and strode away.

The next morning he sent men to take charge of the officer and ship him east. They found him dead, his lips burned from the poison he had swallowed. His stiff fist still clutched a tiny glass vial.

The news raised an unpleasant question in Marcus' mind. Had the Yezda killed himself for fear of the vengeance he thought Avshar would take on him, or was his suicide itself that vengeance? The implications were distasteful in either case.

Despite the questionable omen, the next two weeks went well for the imperial forces. Using Khliat as a base of operations, Mavrikios captured several other Yezda-held towns: Ganolzak and Shamkanor to the north, Baberd in the southeast, and Phanaskert due south of Khliat.

None of them put up a prolonged or difficult resistance. The Yezda were far more formidable on horseback than confined inside city walls, and the Videssian siege train proved its worth time and again. Moreover, the Vaspurakaners inside the towns hated their nomadic oppressors and betrayed them to the imperial forces at every opportunity. Large numbers of prisoners went trudging unhappily into the east; Videssian garrisons took their place.

Marcus noticed that Mavrikios Gavras was using troops of doubtful worth or loyalty to hold the newly captured cities, and appointing as garrison commanders officers whose allegiance he suspected. Gaius Philippus saw the same thing. He said, "He's stripping us down for the real action, right enough. Better to put the fainthearts where they might be useful than have them turn tail and run when he really needs them."

"I suppose so," Marcus agreed. Still, he could not help recalling the grief he'd come to by dividing his Romans on riot duty in Videssos.

Phanaskert was a good-sized city, though badly depopulated by the raids of the Yezda and their occupation. When Mavrikios took the rest of his forces back to Khliat, he left more than half his Namdaleni behind to hold the town's long circuit of walls against possible counterattack from the west.

Soteric was one of the islanders ordered to garrison duty. He invited his sister and Scaurus to share an evening meal with him before the bulk of the Videssian army returned to its base. Over captured Vaspurakaner wine—even thicker and sweeter than Videssian vintages—the Namdalener said to Marcus, "You see now what I meant outside the Emperor's tent. By one trick or another, Mavrikios finds ways to be rid of us."

Pretending not to take his meaning, the tribune answered, "Are you unhappy with your assignment? Holding a town from the inside strikes me as softer duty than fighting your way into one."

Soteric exhaled in exasperation at the Roman's dullness, but Helvis was coming to know him well enough to realize when he was dissembling. She said, "Must you always speak the Emperor fair? You have to see that the only reason he has for using the men of the Duchy so is his fear for our faithfulness."

Marcus usually dismissed Soteric's complaints over the Emperor's policies as the products of a slightly obsessed mind, but the more he thought about this one, the more likely it seemed. He knew Mavrikios thought along the lines Soteric was sketching; the Emperor had said as much himself, when talking of Ortaias Sphrantzes.

The tribune suddenly laughed out loud. Even people who always thought themselves persecuted could be right sometimes.

The joke fell flat when he made the mistake of trying to explain it.

Scaurus was drilling his men outside the walls of Khliat when he spied a horseman approaching the town from out of the west. "A nomad he is, from the look of him," Viridovix said, shading his eyes against the afternoon sun. "Now, will he be one of ours, or a puir lone Yezda struck from his wits by the heat and out to kill the lot of us at once?"

The rider was not hostile. He had ridden long and hard; his horse was lathered and blowing, and caked sweat and dust begrimed his clothes. Even so, he was so urgent to deliver his news that he reined in as he came up to the exercising Romans. He gave Marcus a tired wave that was evidently meant as a salute.

"Artapan son of Pradtak I am, a scout of Baan Onomag's army," he said, clipping the general's name in plainsman fashion. "I am not of the west—our watchword is 'Phos' light.'"

Onomagoulos had pushed west ten days before with a quarter of Mavrikios' remaining troops to seize the city of Maragha, which sat athwart the army's way into Yezd. "What word do you bring?" the tribune asked.

"Water first, I beg. This past half-day I rode with dry canteen," Artapan said, showing Marcus the empty waterskin at his belt. He swallowed the warm stale water from Scaurus' canteen as if it were chilled wine of ancient vintage, then wiped his mouth. "May the spirits be kind to you for that. Now you must take me into the city—Onomag is attacked, is pinned down less than a day's march from Maragha. We cannot go forward; no more can we go back. Without more men, we perish."

"Awfully bloody eager, isn't he?" Gaius Philippus said suspiciously.

"If I were setting a trap, he's sprouting the very story I'd use to send an army running pell-mell into it."

Marcus considered. The Yezda might well have had the chance to pick off an outrider and torture the password from him. Still—"There must be men inside Khliat who know this fellow, if he is in imperial service. He'd be a fool to think he wouldn't have his story checked. And if it's true—if it's true," the tribune said slowly, "then Mavrikios has done just what he hoped he would, and made the Yezda stand and fight."

In some excitement, he turned back to Artapan, but the nomad was no longer there. Impatient with the colloquy in a language he did not understand—for both the centurion and Scaurus had spoken Latin—he had booted his horse into a worn-out trot for the city.

"Out of our hands now," Gaius Philippus said, not altogether displeased at being relieved of the responsibility of choice. "Still, it's as you say—Mavrikios is too canny by half to sit down without looking first to see whether he's plunking his tail onto an anthill."

That the Emperor took Artapan's message seriously soon became clear. Marcus had been back from drills less than an hour when an orderly summoned him to an urgent officer's council.

"The Khamorth *is* genuine, then, sir," Quintus Glabrio guessed. The same enthusiasm that had gripped the tribune before was now beginning to run through his men.

Doing his best to present the calm front befitting a senior officer, Scaurus shrugged, saying merely, "We'll know soon enough, either way."

For all his efforts at impassiveness, he could not help feeling a tingle of excitement when he saw Artapan Pradtak's son seated close by the Emperor in what had been the main hall of Khliat's *hypasteos* or city governor. Another nomad, this one with a bandaged shoulder, was next to Artapan.

Scaurus and Gaius Philippus slid into chairs. Their curiosity, fired by the earlier meeting with the Khamorth scout, made them among the firstcomers. Their seats were the light folding type of canvas and wood, obviously from the imperial camp, not part of the hall's original furnishing.

The table at which they sat was something else again, being massively built from some heavy dark wood and looking as if it had held its place for centuries. It had the stamp of a Vaspurakaner product, calling to mind Gagik Bagratouni's fortress of a dwelling back in Amorion. The "princes" had become so used to life at bay that their very arts reflected their constant search for protection and strength.

The Yezda must have used the *hypasteos'* office as their headquarters before the Videssians drove them from Khliat, for the table was scarred with swordcuts and crude carvings. One symbol recurred constantly: twin three-pronged lightning bolts. Marcus thought nothing of them until Nephon Khoumnos sat down beside him and cursed when he saw them. "Filthy swine," he said, "putting Skotos' brand everywhere they go." The tribune remembered the dark icon in Avshar's suite at the capital and nodded in understanding.

Mavrikios brusquely called the meeting to order by slamming his palm down on the table. The low-voiced buzz of conversation disappeared. Without further preamble, the Emperor declared, "Baanes Onomagoulos has run into a nestful of Yezda a bit this side of Maragha. Without help, he says, he doesn't think he'll be able to hold out for long."

Heads jerked up in surprise—the Emperor had not announced the purpose of the meeting he was calling. Marcus felt smug at not being caught unawares.

"How did you learn that?" someone asked.

Gavras pointed to the nomad scouts. "You can thank these two— they slipped through the invaders to bring word. Spatakar"—That was the bandaged Khamorth—"came in just now with a written report of situation from Onomagoulos. The seals it bears have been checked— they're genuine. Not only that, both Spatakar and his fellow Artapan here are well known to their clansmen here in Khliat. This has also been checked. In short, gentlemen, this is what we've waited for."

Gaius Philippus touched Marcus' arm and whispered, "You were right." He need not have been so discreet. The whole room was in an uproar, with everyone talking at once, some exclaiming to their neighbors, others shouting questions at the Emperor.

The voice of Thorisin Gavras cut through the uproar. "Or, at any rate, it may be what we've waited for. As for me, I'm inclined to wait a trifle longer."

284

"Oh, Phos, here we go again," Nephon Khoumnos groaned.

Scaurus scratched his head at the sudden reversal of roles the two Gavrai were displaying. Thorisin was ever the impetuous one, with Mavrikios more inclined to wait on events. Yet now the Emperor was all for pushing ahead, while the Sevastokrator spoke out for caution. The tribune could make no sense of it.

Thorisin, having gained the council's attention, went on, "I would think three times before I set our whole army thundering to Baanes Onomagoulos' rescue because of his first reports of trouble. He may be a very able officer, but he is regrettably inclined to caution."

Baanes is a coward, Marcus translated. The Roman did not know Onomagoulos well, but did not think the Sevastokrator's thinly veiled charge was true. He grew surer he was right when he remembered Thorisin's longstanding jealousy of his older brother's comrade. Yes, things were clearer now. Nephon Khoumnos, who knew the Gavrai, must have seen all this from the moment Thorisin opened his mouth.

So, of course, did Mavrikios. He snapped, "Were it Khoumnos or Bagratouni out there, Thorisin, instead of Baanes, would you be counseling prudence?"

"No," his brother said at once. "And were it our good friend Ortaias here"—He did not bother hiding his contempt for young Sphrantzes—"would you go pounding after him?"

Mavrikios ground his teeth in frustration. "That is a low blow, Thorisin, and well you know it."

"Do I? We'll see." The Sevastokrator shot questions at Onomagoulos' Khamorth, and, indeed, their answers seemed to show his forces were not in such grim straits as it first appeared. His interrogation, though, reminded Marcus of nothing so much as a skilled lawyer at work, eliciting from witnesses only the facts he was after. But whether that was so or not, Thorisin succeeded in raising enough doubts in the council that it retired without taking any action at all.

"Grudges," Gaius Philippus said as he and Scaurus made their way to the Roman encampment. He put such a wealth of feeling in the word that it came out fouler than any swearing.

"You talk as if Rome were immune to them," the tribune answered. "Remember when Sulla and Gaius Flavius Fimbria each fought Mithridates without taking the other into account? When they joined forces, so many of Fimbria's men went over to Sulla that Fimbria killed himself from the sheer disgrace of it."

"And good riddance to him, too," Gaius Philippus said promptly. "He incited a mutiny against his commander to take charge of that army in the first place, the swine. He—" The centurion broke off abruptly, made a gesture full of disgust. "All right, I see your point. I still don't like it."

"I never said I did."

The next morning passed in anticipation, with the imperial forces in Khliat wondering whether Baanes Onomagoulos had managed to wriggle free of the Yezda trap . . . and if the trap was there at all. Around noon Scaurus got the summons to another council of war.

This time Onomagoulos' messenger was no Khamorth, but a Videssian officer of middle rank. His face was pinched with exhaustion and, but for the area his helm's nasal had covered, badly sun-blistered. Mavrikios introduced him to the assembled commanders as Sisinnios Mousele, then let him speak for himself.

"I thought all our riders must have been caught before they reached you," he said between swallows of wine; as was true of Artapan Pradtak's son, his journey had left him dry as the baking land round Khliat. "But when I made my way here, I learned two Khamorth were a day ahead of me.

"Why are you not on the move," he demanded, "when my news preceded me? Aye, we're holding our little valley against the Yezda, but for how long? The stream that carved it is only a muddy trickle in summer—we have almost no water and not much food. And the barbarians are thick as locusts in a wheatfield—I'd not thought there were so many Yezda in all the world. We could break out, perhaps, but they'd tear us to pieces before we got far. In Phos' holy name, brothers, without aid all of us will die, and die for nothing."

While Mousele was speaking, Mavrikios looked stonily at his brother. He made no public recrimination, though, over the day the army had lost to Thorisin's envious suspicion of Onomagoulos. In a way,

Marcus thought, that was encouraging—in the face of real crisis, the pretended feud between the Gavrai fell away.

Thorisin bore that out, asking the council, "Is there anyone now who feels we should not march? I own I was wrong yesterday; with your help and your men's, perhaps we can make good my mistake."

After Sisinnios Mousele's plea, there was almost no debate among the officers. The only question was how soon the army could start moving. "Don't worry, Sisinnios, we'll get your boys out!" a Videssian captain called.

Only when Mousele made no reply did all eyes turn toward him. He was asleep where he sat; his message delivered, nothing would have kept him awake another minute.

XIII

Khliat that afternoon was like a beehive poked with a stick. To speed the army's departure, Mavrikios promised a goldpiece to each soldier of the contingent first ready to leave. Men frantically dashed here and there, dragging their comrades from taverns and whorehouses.

There were also hurried farewells by the score, for the Emperor had no intention of delaying his advance with sutlers, women, children, and other noncombatants. Not a man complained; if they lost, better to have their loved ones safe behind Khliat's walls than in a battlefield camp at the mercy of an onstorming foe.

Helvis was a warrior's sister and a warrior's widow. She had sent men into battle before and knew better than to burden Scaurus with her fears. All she said was, "Phos keep you safe till I see you again."

"Bring me back a Yezda's head, Papa?" Malric asked.

"Bloodthirsty, aren't you?" Marcus said, hugging Helvis' son. "What would you do with it if you had it?"

"I'd burn it all up," the boy declared. "They're worse than Videssian heretics, Mama says. Burn it all up!"

The tribune looked quizzically at Helvis. "I won't say she's wrong. If I bring my own head back, though, that will be about enough for me."

The Romans won the Emperor's prize, as Marcus had been sure they would—fighting the Yezda was a less fearful prospect than facing Gaius Philippus after losing. But the rest of the army was close behind them, galvanized by the thought of rescuing their fellows from the Yezda. To the tribune's amazement, Khliat's gates swung wide an hour before sunset, and the last soldier was out of it before twilight left the sky.

In his urgency, Mavrikios kept the army moving through the early hours of the night. The endless drumbeat of marching feet, the clatter of iron-shod hooves, and the squeaks and rattles of hundreds of wagons filled with supplies and munitions were so pervasive the ear soon refused to hear them. Only the curses and thumps that followed missteps in the darkness really registered, in the same way that a skipped heartbeat demands attention while a steady pulse can be ignored.

Marcus was impressed by the amount of ground the imperial forces were able to make in that first, partial, day's march, despite the unfamiliar ground and the darkness. "You've forgotten what it's like, being with an army that's ready to fight," Gaius Philippus said. "I only hope Mavrikios doesn't wear us down by going too fast too soon."

"Och, the gods forfend!" said Viridovix. "I'm near as worn the now as ever I was when first we set out from Videssos all that while ago."

"You'd be in better shape if you hadn't said good-bye so thoroughly," the centurion pointed out. "You could hardly walk when you saw fit to come back to us."

"And can you think of a better way to pass a summer's afternoon?"

"No, damn you," Gaius Philippus said, and the patent envy in his voice drew laughter from around the Roman campfire.

The hot fire of enthusiasm kept the army surging westward the next day, and the next. Resistance was light. Onomagoulos' force had largely cleared the Yezda from the imperial line of march, and the small bands re-entering the territory between Khliat and Maragha were no match for Mavrikios' grand expedition. Most chose flight over combat.

In those first two heady days of travel, the host covered more than half the distance to Onomagoulos' embattled troops. But then, as Gaius Philippus had feared, the drive began to slow. The soldiers, pushed past their limits by nonstop marching, had to slow down. Their officers urged them to greater efforts, but they were as exhausted as their men.

Marcus lived in a hot gray world, his thoughts reaching no further than his next footsore stride, his cuirass chafing his shoulders, his sword bumping the outside of his thigh with every step he took. He found brief moments to be thankful the Romans marched at the imperial column's head; they kicked up dust for others to breathe instead of breathing it themselves.

When the army paused at night, he fell instantly into a slumber as deep as Sisinnios Mousele's. He woke dull and slow, as if he had been drugged.

In midmorning of the fourth day out from Khliat, Khamorth scouts rode in from the west to report a dustcloud, as of many marching men, approaching the Videssian force. Mavrikios took no chances, ordering his men to deploy from marching column into line of battle. Marcus felt a weary exultation when the command reached the Romans. One way or another, he thought, his ordeal would be over before long. He was so tired he hardly cared what the outcome would be.

Soon the Videssian army's main body could see the tan smudges of dust on the western horizon. Men looked to their weapons. Here and there a soldier spoke earnestly to his linemate, giving last instructions should he not survive the fight.

The dustclouds hid whoever stirred them up. The Emperor dispatched a couple of hundred Khamorth to learn what was ahead. Scaurus watched them shrink to black dots and vanish into the dust. The few minutes that passed before they came racing back seemed far longer.

As they galloped toward the imperial army, it was easy to see their excitement. They were wheeling and rearing their horses, and waving their fur caps—never abandoned, no matter what the weather—above their heads. They were shouting something, too, over and over. At last they were close enough for Marcus to understand it: "Onomag! Onomag!"

The tribune was worn out, but still felt a thrill course through him. Xenophon, he thought, must have known that same thrill when, from the rear of his battered Greek army, he heard men ahead crying, *"Thalassa! Thalassa! The sea! The sea!"*

Not only Onomagoulos' warriors were out ahead; Yezda were there too, harrying their retreat. Mavrikios flung cavalry against them— Videssians, Khamorth, Khatrishers, and finally Namdaleni. The islanders' powerful charge sent the lighter-armed enemy scattering in dismay and let the survivors of Baanes' division rejoin their comrades.

The army's joy at the meeting was short-lived; the first glimpse of the men staggering back through their lines dispelled it. The groans and cries of the wounded, and the sight of their distress, brought home all too vividly the dangers Mavrikios' force had yet to taste.

Onomagoulos himself was brought to safety in a litter, a great gash in his thigh bound up in the rags of his cloak.

"You will excuse me," Gorgidas said to Scaurus. "These poor devils need help." Without waiting for the tribune's leave, he hurried off to give the injured what aid he could.

Marcus' eyes, though, were on the warriors whose bodies had taken no blows. He liked none of what he saw. If ever any were, these were beaten troops. It showed in their eyes, in the haggard, numb bewilderment on their faces, in their slumped shoulders and dragging weapons. They had the look of men who tried in vain to stand against an avalanche.

Two words were on their lips. One was "Water!" Whenever a canteen was offered, it was tilted, drained, and, with gasped thanks, given back empty.

The other word was spoken softly. The defeated did not make it a warning to spread alarm through their rescuers. Marcus thought they would sooner have left it unsaid. But as often as little bands of them stumbled past his legionaries, he heard their voices drop and grow fearful. Because it was whispered, it took him a few minutes to catch the name of Avshar. After that, he understood.

Marcus saw his men's marching order thrown into disarray by Onomagoulos' fugitives. The sun was nearing the western horizon; rather than push forward under such unpromising circumstances, the Emperor ordered camp made so he could safely advance come morning.

His main body of troops fell to with a will. Marcus had to admit they did better work under the threat of imminent attack. Palisades and rough earthen barricades were built with a speed even the Romans could not fault, while the cavalry who had earlier driven the Yezda from Onomagoulos' men now screened them from the campsite.

They did not have an easy time of it. The iron charge of the Namdaleni had knocked the Yezda back on their heels, but not out of the fight. Constantly joined by more horsemen from the west, they made a battle of it, with all the confusion usual in big cavalry engagements. Squads of horsemen dashed back and forth, arrows flew in clouds, and sabers gleamed as they rose and fell.

"It's a good thing our works are going up fast," Gaius Philippus said, peering through the dusty haze to the west. "I don't think our horse is doing any too well out there. Those bloody bastards can ride—and how many of them are there, anyway?"

To that Scaurus could offer no reply. The dust and distance made numbers impossible to judge. Moreover, both the Yezda and their Khamorth cousins who fought under the Emperor's banner had strings of horses for each man, assuring them of a fresh mount each day and also making them seem far more numerous than they really were.

Numbers aside, the centurion was grimly correct. The Namdaleni might be the masters of the Yezda at close quarters, and the Khamorth their equals in speed. But the Videssians who formed the bulk of the imperial cavalry could neither crush them in close nor stay with them in a running fight. Slowly at first, Mavrikios' cavalry began drawing back toward and then into the field fortifications their comrades were still completing.

Marcus could hear horse shouts of triumph as the Yezda gave chase. Too many for all to enter at once, the Videssians and their mercenaries jammed together at the six gates of the imperial camp. Their foes, whooping with glee, sent flight after flight of arrows into those tempting targets. Men toppled in slow motion from their saddles; horses screamed as they were hit. The wounded beasts bolted in all directions, adding to the chaos round the gates.

Worse yet, in the turmoil and the fading light there was no way for the army to tell Khamorth friends from Yezda foes. More than a few invaders got into the camp in the guise of allies, then went on killing rampages until shot from their horses. Scaurus watched in horrified admiration as a Yezda sabered down three Videssian footsoldiers in quick succession, then leaped his horse over the breast-high palisade and into dusk's safety.

Khamorth were killed too, mistaken for enemies by panicky Videssians. Once or twice their clan-brothers, seeing comrades die before their eyes, took summary revenge. War within the Emperor's army was suddenly as real a threat as the enemy outside.

Much later, Marcus would hear Phostis Apokavkos retell the story of that dreadful night and say, "I'd sooner be dead than live through another time like that." From the proud, confident host that had set out from Videssos, the army was reduced in the early hours of that evening to little more than a terror-stricken mob, huddling behind the flimsy barricades that were all that kept it from the clutches of its foes.

If the Yezda had mounted an assault then and there, Marcus thought the Videssian force would have broken before them like so many dry sticks. But the nomads were leery of attacking a fortified camp, and perhaps the constant motion inside—in reality as meaningless as the scurrying of ants when their hill is disturbed—looked from outside like the preparations of battle-ready troops. The onslaught did not come, and little by little the Emperor began to get his men in hand once more.

He seemed everywhere at once, not in robes of state now but gilded armor above the crimson imperial boots. He dragged skulkers to the palisade from the false security of their tents. His army's position was hardly enviable, but he was far too much a soldier to quit without a fight.

When he came to the Roman section of the camp, weary approval lit his face. "Very neat," he complimented Scaurus. "Ditch, rampart, stakes—aye, and water too, I see—just like a drill. Are your men's spirits holding up?"

"Well enough, your Majesty," the tribune replied.

"There's no need to fret over that," Viridovix put in. "The lot of these Romans are too thick-skinned to be afraid."

Gaius Philippus bristled instinctively, but the Emperor waved him to silence. "Easy, there. On a night like this, you'd be better off if that were so. Phos knows, I wish I could say it." Not even the ruddy campfires could bring much color to his face; in their flickering light he looked wan and old. Shoulders bent as if under a heavy load, he turned and went his way.

His brother the Sevastokrator was rallying the staggered army too, in his own more direct fashion. "Phos' left hairy nut!" Marcus heard him shouting not far away. "Give me that bow, you worthless crock of dung!" A bowstring thrummed; Thorisin cursed heartily at a miss. He shot again. Somewhere in the gloom a horse gave a contralto shriek of agony. "There!" the Sevastokrator said. "That's how it's done!"

Strangely enough, Ortaias Sphrantzes also helped pull the Videssian army back together. He went wandering through the camp declaiming such pedantries as, "Wisdom-loving men—for I name you philosophers rather than soldiers—should show the barbarians that their eagerness is deathless," and, "The souls of the Yezda are not double, nor are their bodies made of adamant. They, too, are initiated into the mysteries of death."

The performance should have been ludicrous, and indeed it was. Men smiled to hear the young noble mouthing his platitudes, but in that place smiles were hard to come by. Moreover, however long-winded Sphrantzes was, he also spoke the truth, and those who took the time to listen were not worse for it.

Priests circulated, praying with the soldiers and re-swearing them to loyalty to the Empire. No one seemed to care this night if a Namdalener added a clause to the creed Videssos followed, or if a man of Vaspurakan styled himself a son of Phos' firstborn. In the face of peril, everyone was for once united.

When asked, the pagan Khamorth, too, took fresh oaths of allegiance. No priests would hear them, but before some of Mavrikios' scribes they swore by their swords to hold faith with the Emperor. Their very reluctance after the mishaps at the gates convinced Scaurus their word was good. Had they intended betrayal, he thought, they would have made their vows more readily, the better to deceive.

"Hello, hello." That was Nepos, who had been standing at the tribune's elbow for a couple of minutes without managing to be noticed. The little priest looked as somber as his plump, merry features would allow. He said diffidently, "Might I ask you and yours to join the rest of this army in pledging your loyalty to Videssos? I hold no suspicions and mean no offense, but this seems a time for renewing faith."

"Of course," Scaurus nodded. Had the Romans been singled out for such treatment he would have taken it ill, but, as the priest said, every man in the camp was reaffirming his loyalty. "What oath would satisfy you, though? Most of us do not follow your ways."

"Hmm." Nepos scratched his shaven head. "A poser—have you any suggestions?"

Marcus thought for a moment, then said, "It is our custom, when taking service in a legion, for one man to take the oath, and everyone swear to follow his example. If I swear that oath again, this time by my gods and your own, would it suffice?"

"I fail to see how I could ask for anything more."

"All right." At the tribune's command, the buccinators sounded their horns to gain the legionaries' attention. The clear trumpet notes cut through the tumult; Romans snapped their heads around to see what the matter was.

When Marcus saw they were all watching him, he asked if there was any man unwilling to give the promise Nepos asked. No one spoke. "Very well, then," he told them. "By the gods we brought from Rome and by the god we met here, I pledge myself to obey the Emperor and do his bidding as best I can. Do you now swear to do the same as I?"

"*Iuramus!*" they cried in the same Latin they had used when first joining their legions. "We swear it!" Nepos might not understand the word, but its meaning was unmistakable. He bowed his thanks to Marcus and hurried away to confirm some other unit's allegiance.

The din outside the camp was unbelievable. Not quite bold enough to storm its ramparts, the Yezda did everything they could to bring terror to the men within. Some rode up close to scream threats in broken Videssian, while others contented themselves with wordless shrieks of hate.

Worse still, Marcus thought, were the great drums that boomed around every Yezda campfire like the irregular heartbeats of a dying, demented god. The vibration came through the ground as much as through the air and seemed to echo and re-echo inside a man's bones.

To sleep in such circumstances was a forlorn hope, even for the phlegmatic Scaurus. He welcomed the messenger announcing Mavrikios' nightly council with enough eagerness to send the man off shaking his head in confusion. There was no need for directions to the Emperor's tent. Not only was it bigger than any other, it also stood on the highest ground in the campsite, to let Mavrikios have as good a view as he could of the surrounding terrain.

Reaching it, though, was like fighting through the crowds that always filled the forum of Palamas in the imperial capital. Men were on the move all through the camp, some with purposeful strides, others wandering aimlessly, using the simple fact of their motion as an anodyne against thought. Despite having a definite goal, the tribune also paid less attention to his surroundings than he might have. Gaius Philippus' warning was too slow to keep him from bumping into a Haloga from behind.

The blond giant swung round in annoyance; he wore a leather patch over his right eye. "Watch your feet, you oafish—" He stopped short.

"Skapti!" Marcus exclaimed. "I did not think you were with the Emperor's army. You should have visited us long ago."

"When I saw you last, I said we'd meet again." The commander of the Imbros garrison shrugged. To himself more than the Romans, he went on, "A man's weird is a strange thing—if he will not come to it, it comes to him instead."

He took Scaurus' hand in both his own in the Haloga fashion, then shook his head, rueful amusement on his face. Giving the Romans no time to puzzle out his riddle, he turned and went on his way, tall, lonely, and proud.

Staring at his back, Gaius Philippus said, "I've seen men with that look to them before. Fey, Viridovix would call him."

"Aye, and he seems to think somehow I'm part of his fate—may the gods prove him wrong." Something else struck Scaurus. "When did you, of all people, take to borrowing words from the Celt?"

The centurion wore the same expression Skapti Modolf's son had shown a moment before. "It does fit, though, doesn't it?"

"That I can't argue. Come on—let's see if Mavrikios' wizards have come up with a way to give us all wings and get us out of this pickle."

No wizards were at the battle conference, with or without word of wings. Mavrikios had brought them with his force, to be sure, but more to foil enemy sorcery than to use his own as a weapon of offense—he was a man of arms by birth and training. The fight he faced now might not be on the terms he wanted, but he did not intend to dodge it.

Indeed, he was surprisingly cheerful, saying to Ortaias Sphrantzes, "I don't think this is the way Kalokyres would have recommended luring the enemy into battle, but it shouldn't work out too badly. Unless I miss my guess, the nomads will be so pumped up from today's fighting that they'll stand against us for once. And when they do, we'll break them. In hand-to-hand they don't have a prayer against us."

Marcus thought the Emperor had every chance of being right. From what he had seen of the Yezda, victory would make them reckless. They would probably be so eager to finish off the Videssians as to be easy to snare.

296

The Emperor's thoughts were running along the same lines. He gave his orders to his brother and Sphrantzes accordingly, "You two on the wings will be crucial in making this work, since you have most of the light cavalry. Spread wide—funnel the Yezda down to the center. The heavy troopers there will stop them; once they're well engaged, close the wings like this." He brought his outstretched arms together in front of his body. "We'll surround them on three sides or, Phos willing, all four, and that should do it."

Thorisin quietly listened to Mavrikios' outline, now and then nodding as the Emperor made a point. "He's cool enough, isn't he?" Gaius Philippus murmured to Scaurus.

"Why not? This scheme can't be news to him. He and Mavrikios likely have been working it through since sundown."

Ortaias Sphrantzes was hearing it all for the first time, and his eyes glowed with excitement. "A classic ploy, your Majesty," he breathed, "and surely a trap to catch the undisciplined barbarian rabble." Scaurus was inclined to agree with the first part of what he said, but rather resented the rest. Mavrikios' plan reminded him of Hannibal's at Cannae, and that trap had closed around Romans.

The Emperor was pleased by the praise. "Thank you, Ortaias," he said graciously. "I look to you to hearten your men tomorrow with a fine rousing speech." Mavrikios was in a confident mood indeed, thought Marcus, if he was willing to be so courteous to his rival's nephew.

"I shall! I've prepared one against the day of need, nicely calculated to raise martial ferocity."

"Excellent."

Next to Scaurus, Gaius Philippus rolled his eyes and groaned, but so low in his throat only the tribune could hear. The senior centurion had listened to part of that speech, Marcus recalled, and was anything but impressed. It did not really matter. Scaurus had watched Nephon Khoumnos, well down in the formal order of precedence, listening to Mavrikios' scheme, and could fairly see the old warhorse plan its execution. Everyone—save possibly Ortaias Sphrantzes—knew the left wing was really his.

Out in the darkness beyond the encircled camp, the drums paused in their discordant pounding, were silent for a moment, then began anew, this time all together: *thump-thump, thump-thump, thump-thump.* The two-beat phrase, repeated endlessly, maddeningly, made teeth rattle in their sockets, brought dull pain to the head. The harsh voices of the Yezda joined the drums: "Avshar! Avshar! Avshar! Avshar!"

Marcus felt his hands curl into fists when he understood the invaders' chant. He glanced over to see Mavrikios' reaction. The Emperor met his eye, quirked an eyebrow upward. "All the pieces are on the board," he said. "Now we can play."

The day dawned clear and hot, the brassy sun fairly leaping into a sky of flawless blue. The tribune's eyes were gritty as he spooned up his breakfast porridge. The drums had not stopped throbbing all night, and what sleep he'd had was shallow and shot through with evil dreams. All through the Videssian camp, men yawned while they ate.

Quintus Glabrio scoured his empty bowl with sand, put it back in his pack. He was yawning too, but not worried about it. "Unless all the men out of Yezd are deaf, they had as much trouble sleeping as I did," he said. Marcus nodded, appreciating his sense of proportion.

Yezda tents lay scattered over the plain like multicolored toadstools. There were more of them to the west of the Videssian camp; many were grouped around a great pavilion of jet-black felt. Without need for conscious thought, Scaurus was sure it was Avshar's. Yezda streamed toward it. The tribune watched their battle line begin taking shape.

As he had feared, the nomads tried to keep the imperial army besieged in its camp, but Mavrikios was equal to that. Archers from behind the palisade made them keep their distance, and, when three or four dart-throwing catapults added their fire, the Yezda drew back toward their own lines. The Emperor then used his light horse as he had before, to form a curtain behind which his main force could deploy.

Sweat already beginning to make his shoulders raw under his cuirass, Scaurus led his Romans to their place in the Videssian line. They anchored the left flank of Mavrikios' strong center; to their own left was the cavalry contingent from Khatrish, which linked the center to Ortaias Sphrantzes' left wing.

The Khatrisher commander, a slim, pockmarked man named Laon

Pakhymer, waved when he saw the tribune. Marcus waved back. Ever since his first encounter with Taso Vones, he had liked the Khatrishers. He also preferred them on his flank to their Khamorth cousins. Some of the men from the plains of Pardraya were in a sullen mood, and Scaurus could scarcely blame them after their allies had shot at them by mistake.

Viridovix looked out over the barren plain toward the gathering enemy. He scratched his nose. His fair skin suffered under the fierce Videssian sun, burning and peeling without ever really tanning. "Not much like the last shindy the two of us were in, is it now?" he said to Marcus.

"It isn't, is it? Morning instead of night, hot instead of mild, this naked rockpile instead of your Gallic forest . . . why, we're even on the same side now."

"So we are." Viridovix chuckled. "I hadna thought of that. It should be a fine brawl all the same." Scaurus snorted.

Pipes whistled and drums thumped, ordering the imperial forces forward. The Romans did without such fripperies, except for their rallying horncalls, but the tribune was rather glad of the martial music surrounding his men. It made him feel less alone, less as if all the Yezda ahead were marking him as their target.

The invaders were advancing too, not in the neat articulated units of the Videssian army, but now here, now there, like a wave up an uneven beach. It was easy to recognize Avshar, even at the distance between the two forces. He chose to lead his host from the right rather than from the center like Mavrikios. His white robes flashed brightly against the sooty coat of the huge stallion he rode. Yezd's banner flapped lazily above his head.

"That is an evil color for a standard," Quintus Glabrio said. "It reminds me of a bandage soaked with clotted blood." The image was fitting, but surprising when it came from the Roman officer. It sounded more like something Gorgidas would say.

Gaius Philippus said, "It suits them, for they've caused enough to be soaked."

The two forces were about half a mile apart when Mavrikios rode his own roan charger out ahead of his men to address them. Turning his head left and right, Marcus saw Ortaias Sphrantzes and Thorisin doing the same in their divisions of the army. The Yezda, too, came to a halt while Avshar and their other chieftains harangued them.

The Emperor's speech was short and to the point. He reminded his men of the harm Yezd had inflicted on Videssos, told them their god was fighting on their side—the tribune was willing to bet Avshar was making the same claim to his warriors—and briefly outlined the tactics he had planned.

The tribune did not pay much attention to Mavrikios' words—their draft was plain after five or six sentences. More interesting were the snatches of Ortaias Sphrantzes' address that a fitful southerly breeze brought him.

In his thin tenor, the noble was doing his best to encourage his men with the same kind of sententious rhetoric he had used inside the Videssian camp the night before. "Fight with every limb; let no limb have no share of danger! The campaign of Yezd has justice opposed to it, for peace is a loathsome thing to them, and their love of battle is such that it honors a god of blood. Injustice is often strong, but it is also changed to ruin. I will direct the battle, and in my eagerness for combat engage the aid of all—I am ashamed to suffer not suffering . . ."

On and on he went. Marcus lost the thread of Sphrantzes' speech when Mavrikios finished his own and the men of the center cheered, but when their shouts subsided Ortaias was still holding forth. The soldiers on the left listened glumly, shifting from foot to foot and muttering among themselves. What they expected and needed was a heartening fierce speech, not this grandiloquent monologue.

The Sevastos' nephew built to his rousing conclusion. "Let no one who loves luxury's pleasures share in the rites of war and let no one join in the battle for the sake of loot. It is the lover of danger who should seek the space between the two armies. Come now, let us at last add deeds to words and let us shift our theory into the line of battle!"

He paused expectantly, waiting for the applause the two Gavrai had already received. There were a few spatters of clapping and one or two shouts, but nothing more. "He does have the brain of a pea," Gaius Philippus grumbled. "Imagine telling a mercenary army not to loot! I'm surprised he didn't tell them not to drink and fornicate, while he was at it."

Dejectedly, Sphrantzes rode back into line. Nephon Khoumnos was there to slap his armored back and try to console him—and also, Marcus knew, to protect the army from his flights of fancy.

It would not be long now. All speeches done at last, both armies were advancing again, and the forwardmost riders were already exchanging arrows. Scaurus felt a familiar tightening in his guts, suppressed it automatically. These moments just before fighting began were the worst. Once in the middle of it, there was no time to be afraid.

The Yezda came on at a trot. Marcus saw the sun flash off helmets, drawn swords, and lanceheads, saw their banners and horse-tail standards lifted high. Then he blinked and rubbed his eyes; around him, Romans cried out in amazement and alarm. The oncoming line was flickering like a candle flame in a breeze, now plain, now half-seen as if through fog, now vanished altogether. The tribune clutched his sword until knuckles whitened, but the grip brought no security. How was he to strike foes he could not see?

Though it seemed an eternity, the Yezda could not have remained out of sight more than a few heartbeats. Through the outcry of his own men, Scaurus heard counterspells shouted by the sorcerers who accompanied the imperial army. The enemy reappeared, sharp and solid as if they had never blurred away.

"Battle magic," the tribune said shakily.

"So it was," Gaius Philippus agreed. "It didn't work, though, the gods be thanked." He spoke absently, without turning to look at Scaurus. His attention was all on the Yezda, who, their ploy failed, were riding harder now, bearing down on the Videssians. "Shields up!" the centurion shouted, as arrows arced their way toward the Romans.

Marcus had never stood up under arrow fire like this. An arrow buzzed angrily past his ear; another struck his *scutum* hard enough to drive him back a pace. The noise the shafts made as they hissed in and struck shields and corselets was like rain beating on a metal roof. Rain, though, never left men shrieking and writhing when it touched their soft, vulnerable flesh.

The Yezda thundered forward, close enough for the tribune to see their intent faces as they guided their horses toward the gaps their arrows had made. *"Pila!"* he shouted, and, a moment later, "Loose!"

Men pitched from saddles, to spin briefly through the air or be dragged to red death behind their mounts. So stirrups had drawbacks after all, Scaurus thought. Horses fell too, or ran wild when bereft of riders. They fouled those next to them and sent them crashing to the ground. Warriors behind the first wave, unable to stop their animals in time, tripped over the fallen or desperately pulled back on their reins to leap the sudden barrier ahead—and presented themselves as targets for their foes.

The Roman volley shook the terrifying momentum of the Yezda charge, but did not, could not, stop it altogether. Yelling like men possessed, the nomads collided with the soldiers who would bar their way. A bushy-bearded warrior slashed down at the tribune from horseback. He took the blow on his shield while he cut at the nomad's leg, laying open his thigh and wounding his horse as well.

Rider and beast cried out in pain together. The luckless animal reared, blood dripping down its barrel. An arrow thudded into its belly. It slewed sideways and fell, pinning its rider beneath it. The saber bounced from his loosening grip as he struck.

A few hundred yards to his right, Marcus heard deep-voiced cries as the Namdaleni hurled themselves forward at the Yezda before them. They worked a fearful slaughter for a short time, striking with swords and lances and bowling the enemy over with the sheer weight of their charge. Like snapping wolves against a bear, the nomads gave way before them, but even in retreat their deadly archery took its toll.

Again the Yezda tried to rush the Romans, and again the legionaries' well-disciplined volley of throwing spears broke the charge before it could smash them. "I wish we had more heavy spearmen," Gaius Philippus panted. "There'd be nothing like a line of *hastati* to keep these buggers off of us." The *hasta*, though, was becoming obsolete in Rome's armies, and few were the legionaries trained in its use.

"Wish for the moon, while you're at it," Marcus said, putting to flight a nomad who, fallen from horse, chose to fight on foot. The Yezda scuttled away before the tribune could finish him.

Viridovix, as always an army in himself, leaped out from the Roman line and, sidestepping an invader's hacking sword-stroke, cut off the head of the nomad's horse with a single slash of his great blade. The Romans cried out in triumph, the Yezda in dismay, at the mighty blow.

The rider threw himself clear as his beast foundered, but the tall Celt was on him like a cat after a lizard. Against Viridovix's reach and strength he could do nothing, and his own head spun from his shoulders an instant later. Snatching up the gory trophy, the Gaul returned to the Roman ranks.

"I know it's not your custom to be taking heads," he told Scaurus, "but a fine reminder he'll be of the fight."

"You can have him for breakfast, for all I care," the tribune shouted back. His usual equanimity frayed badly in the stress of battle.

The legionaries' unyielding defense and the exploit of the Celt, as savage as any of their own, dissuaded the Yezda from further direct assaults. Instead, they drew back out of spear-range and plied the Romans with arrows. Marcus would have liked nothing better than to let his men charge the nomads, but he had already seen what happened when a Vaspurakaner company, similarly assailed, ran pell-mell at the Yezda. They were cut off and cut to pieces in the twinkling of an eye.

Still, there was no reason for the Romans to endure such punishment without striking back. Scaurus sent a runner over to Laon Pakhymer. The Khatrisher acknowledged his request with a flourish of his helmet over his head. He sent a couple of squadrons of his countrymen forward, just enough to drive the Yezda out of bowshot. As the nomads retreated, Marcus moved his own line up to help cover the allies who had protected him.

He wondered how the fight was going. His own little piece of it was doing fairly well, but this was too big a battle to see all at once. The numbers on both sides, the length of the battle line, and the ever-present smothering dust made that hopeless.

But by the way the front was bending, Mavrikios' plan seemed to be working. The Yezda, squeezed on both flanks, were being forced to hurl themselves at the Videssian line's center. Deprived of the mobility that gave them their advantage, they were easy meat for the heavy troops the Emperor had concentrated there. The great axes of his Haloga guardsmen rose and fell, rose and fell, shearing through the nomads' light small shields and boiled-leather cuirasses. The northerners sang as they fought, their slow, deep battle chant sounding steadily through the clamor around them.

———

Avshar growled, deep in his throat, a sound of thwarted fury. The Vides-sian center was even stronger than he had expected, though he had known it held his foes' best troops. And among them, he suddenly re-called, was the outlander who had bested him at swords. He seldom lost at anything; revenge would be sweet.

Three times he fired his deadly bow at Scaurus. Twice he missed; despite terrified rumor, the weapon was not infallible. His third shot was true, but a luckless nomad rode into the arrow's path. He fell, never knowing his own chieftain had slain him.

The wizard cursed to see that perfect shot ruined. "A different way, then," he rumbled to himself. He had intended to use the spell against another, but it would serve here as well.

He handed his bow to an officer by his side, calmed his horse with his knees till it stood still—the spell required passes with both hands at once. As he began to chant, even the Yezda holding the bow flinched from him, so frigid and terrible were his words.

Marcus' sword flared dazzlingly bright for an instant. It chilled him, but many magics were loose on the field today. He waved to the buccinators to call a lagging maniple into position.

Avshar cursed again, feeling his sorcery deflected. His fists clenched, but even he had to bow to necessity—back to the first plan, then. Yezda scouts had watched the imperial host drill a score of times and brought him word of what they had seen. Of all the men in that host, one was the key—and Avshar's spell would not go awry twice.

"There you go! There you go! Drive the whoresons back!" Nephon Khoumnos shouted. He was hoarse and tired, but increasingly happy over the battle's course. Ortaias, Phos be praised, was not getting in his way too badly, and the troops were performing better than he'd dared hope. He wondered if Thorisin was having as much success on the right. If he was, soon the Yezda would be surrounded by a ring of steel.

The general sneezed, blinked in annoyance, sneezed again. Despite the sweltering heat, he was suddenly cold; the sweat turned clammy on his body. He shivered inside his armor—there were knives of ice stabbing at his bones. Agony shot through his joints at every move. His eyes bulged. He opened his mouth to cry out, but no words emerged. His last conscious thought was that freezing was not the numb, painless death it was supposed to be.

"They appear to be stepping up the pressure," Ortaias Sphrantzes said. "What do you think, Khoumnos? Should we commit another brigade to throw them back?" Getting no reply, he turned to glance at the older man. Khoumnos was staring fixedly ahead and did not seem to be giving any heed to his surroundings.

"Are you all right?" Sphrantzes asked. He laid a hand on the general's bare arm, then jerked it back in horror, leaving skin behind. Touching Khoumnos was like brushing against an ice-glazed wall in dead of winter, but worse, for this was a cold that burned like fire.

Startled at the sudden motion, the general's horse shied. Its rider swayed, then toppled stiffly; it was as if a frozen statue bestrode the beast. A hundred throats echoed Sphrantzes' cry of terror, for Khoumnos' body, like a statue carved from brittle ice, shattered into a thousand frozen shards when it struck the ground.

"A pox!" Gaius Philippus exclaimed. "Something's gone wrong on the left!" Sensitive to battle's changing tides as a deer to the shifting breeze, the centurion felt the Yezda swing to the offensive almost before they delivered their attack.

Pakhymer caught the scent of trouble, too, and sent one of his riders galloping south behind the line to find out what it was. He listened as his man reported back, then shouted to the Romans, "Khoumnos is down!"

"Oh, bloody hell," Marcus muttered. Gaius Philippus clapped his hand to his forehead and swore. Here was a chance the Emperor had left unreckoned—responsibility for a third of the Videssian army had just landed squarely on Ortaias Sphrantzes' skinny shoulders.

The Khatrisher who brought the news was still talking. Laon Pakhymer heard him out, then spoke so sharply the Romans could hear part of what he said: "—mouth shut, do you under—" The horseman nodded, gave him an untidy salute, and rode back into line.

"Sure and I wonder what all that was about," Viridovix said.

Gaius Philippus said, "Nothing good, I'll warrant."

"You're a rare gloomy soul, Roman dear, but I'm afraid you have the right of it this time."

When his left wing faltered, Mavrikios guessed why. He sent Zeprin the Red south as fast as he could to rescue the situation, but the Haloga marshal found himself caught up in confused and bitter fighting that broke out when a band of Yezda cracked the imperial line and rampaged through the Videssian rear. The northerner's two-handed axe sent more than one of them to his death, but meanwhile Ortaias Sphrantzes kept command.

Like a ship slowly going down on an even keel, the left's plight grew worse. The various contingents' officers led them as best they could, but with Nephon Khoumnos gone their overall guiding force disappeared. Ortaias, in his inexperience, frantically rushed men here and there to counter feints, while failing to answer real assaults.

The left was also a liability in another way. Despite Pakhymer's silencing his messenger, rumors of how Khoumnos died soon ran through the whole Videssian army. They were confused and sometimes wildly wrong, but Avshar's name was writ large in all of them. Men in every section of the line looked south in apprehension, awaiting they knew not what.

The Emperor, seeing the failure of his scheme and the way the Yezda were everywhere pressing his disheartened soldiers back, ordered a withdrawal back to the camp he had left so full of hope. Using their superior mobility and the confusion on the left, the Yezda were beginning to slip small parties round the imperial army's flank. If enough got round to cut the Videssians off from their base, what was now nearly a draw could quickly become disaster.

Mavrikios did not intend to give up the fight. The Videssians could regroup behind their field fortifications and return to the struggle the next morning.

For a moment Marcus did not recognize the new call the drummers and pipers were playing. "Retreat," for obvious reasons, was not an often-practiced exercise. When he did realize what the command was, he read Mavrikios' intentions accurately. "We'll have another go at them tomorrow," he predicted to Gaius Philippus.

"No doubt, no doubt," the centurion agreed. "Hurry up, you fools!" he shouted to the legionaries. "Defensive front—get out there, you spearmen! Hold the losels off us." His fury came more from habit than need; the Romans were smoothly moving into their covering formation.

"Is it running away we are?" Viridovix demanded. "There's no sense of it. Aye, we've not beaten the spalpeens, but there's no one would say they've beaten us either. Let's stay at it and have this thing out." He brandished his sword at the Yezda.

Gaius Philippus sighed, wiped sweat from his face, rubbed absently at a cut on his left cheek. He was as combative as the Celt, but had a firmer grip on the sometimes painful realities of the field. "We're not beaten, no," he said. "But there's wavering all up and down the line, and the gods know what's going on over there." He waved his left arm. "Better we move back under our own control than fall apart trying to hold."

"It's a cold-blooded style of fighting, sure and it is. Still and all, there's a bright side to everything—now I'll have a chance to salt this lovely down properly." He gave a fond pat to the Yezda head tied to his belt. That was too much even for the hard-bitten centurion, who spat in disgust.

A deliberate fighting retreat is probably the most difficult maneuver to bring off on a battlefield. Soldiers equate withdrawal with defeat, and only the strongest discipline holds panic at bay. The Videssians and their mercenary allies performed better than Marcus would have expected from such a heterogeneous force. Warded by a bristling fence of spears, they began to disengage, dropping back a step here, two more there, gathering up the wounded as they went, always keeping a solid fighting front toward their foes.

"Steady, there!" Marcus grabbed the bridle of Senpat Sviodo's horse. The young Vaspurakaner was about to charge a Yezda insolently sitting his horse not thirty yards away.

"Turn me loose, damn you!"

"We'll get this one tomorrow—you've done your share for today." That was nothing less than the truth; Sviodo's fine wickerwork helm was broken and hanging loosely over one ear, while his right calf bore a rude bandage that showed the fighting had not all gone his way.

He was still eager for more, touching spurs to his mount to make it rear free of the tribune's grip.

Scaurus held firm. "If he hasn't the stomach to close with us, let him go now. All we have to do is keep them off us, and we'll be fine."

He glared up at the mutinous Vaspurakaner. To his legionaries he could simply give orders, but Senpat Sviodo was a long way from their obedience—and, to give him his due, he had better reason to hate that grinning Yezda than did the Romans. "I know how happy it would make you to spill his guts out on the dirt, but what if you get in trouble? To say nothing of your grieving your wife, we'd have to rescue you and risk getting cut off while the rest of the army pulled back."

"Leave Nevrat out of this!" Senpat said hotly. "Were she here, we'd fight that swine together. And as for the rest of it, I don't need your help and I don't want it. I don't care about the lot of you!"

"But want it or not, you'd have it, because we care about you, lad." Marcus released his hold on the bridle. "Do what you bloody well please—but even Viridovix is with us, you'll notice."

There was a pause. "Is he, now?" Senpat Sviodo's chuckle was not the blithe one he'd had before the army entered ruined Vaspurakan, but Marcus knew he'd won his point. Sviodo wheeled his horse and trotted it back to the Roman line, which had moved on another score of paces while he and Scaurus argued.

The tribune followed more slowly, studying as best he could how well the army was holding together. It really was going better than he'd dared hope; even the left seemed pretty firm. "You know," he said, catching up to the Vaspurakaner, "I do believe this is going to work."

Avshar watched Ortaias Sphrantzes canter down the Videssian left wing toward the center. Behind the robes that masked him, he might have smiled.

"Dress your lines! Keep good order!" Sphrantzes called, waving energetically to his men. This business of war was as exciting as he'd thought it would be, if more difficult. Decisions had to come at once, and situations did not easily fit into the neat categories Mindes Kalokyres outlined. When they did, they changed so quickly that orders were often worthless as soon as they were given.

The noble knew he had been outmaneuvered several times and lost troops as a result. It pained him; these were not symbols drawn on parchment or pieces to be taken cleanly from a board, but men who fought and bled and died so he could learn his trade.

Still, on the whole he did not think he had done badly. There had been breakthroughs, yes, but never a serious one—he did not know he still held command because of one of those breakthroughs. His mere presence, he thought, went a long way toward heartening his men. He knew what a fine warlike picture he made with his gilded helmet and armor, his burnished rapier with its jeweled hilt, and his military cape floating behind him in the breeze.

True, there had been that terrible moment when Avshar's sorcery reached out to slay Nephon Khoumnos. But even the white-shrouded villain was according him the respect he deserved, always shadowing him as he rode up and down the line.

He had done everything, in short, that a general could reasonably be expected to do . . . except fight.

Horns blared in the enemy ranks. Sphrantzes' lip curled at the discords they raised. Then the disdain vanished from his face, to be replaced by dread. A thousand Yezda were spurring straight at him, and at their head was Avshar.

"Ortaias!" the wizard-prince cried, voice spectrally clear through the thunder of hoofbeats. "I have a gift for thee, Ortaias!" He lifted a mailed fist. The blade therein was no bejeweled toy, but a great murdering broadsword, red-black with the dried blood of victims beyond number.

First among all the Videssians, Ortaias Sphrantzes in his mind's eye penetrated Avshar's swaddling veils to see his face, and the name of that face was fear. His bowels turned to water, his heart to ice.

"Phos have mercy on us! We are undone!" he squealed. He wheeled his horse, jabbed his heels into its flanks. Hunched low to ride the faster, he spurred his way back through his startled soldiers—just as Avshar, taking his measure, had foreseen. "All's lost! All's lost!" he wailed. Then he was past the last of his men, galloping east as fast as his high-bred mount would run.

A moment later the Videssian line behind him, stunned by its general's defection, smashed into ruin under the wizard's hammer-stroke.

Take a pitcher of water outside on a cold winter's day. If the water is very pure and you do not disturb it; it may stay liquid long after you would expect it to freeze. But let a snowflake settle on the surface of this super-cooled water, and it will be ice clear through in less time than it takes to tell.

So it was with the Videssian army, for Ortaias Sphrantzes' flight was the snowflake that congealed retreat into panic. And with a gaping hole torn in its ranks, and Yezda gushing through to take the army in flank and rear, terror was far from unwarranted.

"Well, that's done it!" Gaius Philippus said, angry beyond profanity. "Form square!" he shouted, then explained to Marcus, "The better order we show, the less likely the sods are to come down on us. The gods know they'll have easier pickings elsewhere."

The tribune nodded in bitter agreement. The amputated left wing of the army was already breaking up in flight. Here and there knots of brave or stubborn men still struggled against the nomads who were enveloping them on all sides, but more and more rode east as fast as they could go, throwing away shields, helms, even swords to flee more quickly. Whooping gleefully, the Yezda pursued them like boys after rabbits.

But Avshar kept enough control over the unruly host he led to swing most of it back for the killing stroke against the Videssian center. Assailed simultaneously from front and rear, many units simply ceased to be. They lacked the Romans' long-drilled flexibility and tore their ranks to pieces trying to redeploy. Even proud squadrons of Halogai splintered beyond repair. The Yezda surged into the gaps confusion created and spread slaughter with bow and saber. Survivors scattered all over the field.

Under the ferocious onslaught, the motley nature of the Videssian army became the curse Marcus had feared. Each contingent strove to save itself, with little thought for the army as a whole. "Rally to me!" Mavrikios' pipers signaled desperately, but it was too late for that. In the chaos, many regiments never understood the order, and those that did could not obey because of the ever-present, ever-pressing hordes of Yezda.

Some units held firm. The Namdaleni beat back charge after charge, until the Yezda gave them up as a bad job. Fighting with a fury born of despair, Gagik Bagratouni's Vaspurakaners also stopped the invaders cold. But neither group could counterattack.

As Gaius Philippus had predicted, the good order the Romans still kept let them push on relatively unscathed. Indeed, they attracted stragglers—sometimes by squads and platoons—to themselves, men seeking a safe island in a sea of disaster. Marcus welcomed them if they still showed fight. Every sword, every spear was an asset.

The additions came none too soon. One of the Yezda captains was wise enough to see that any organized force remained a potential danger. He shouted a word of command, wheeled his men toward the Romans.

Drumming hooves, felt through the soles as much as heard . . . "They come, aye, they come!" Viridovix yelled. Ruin all around him, he still reveled in fighting. He leaped out against the onrushing Yezda, ignoring arrows, evading swordstrokes that flashed by like striking snakes. The nomad captain cut at him. He jerked his head away, replied with a two-handed stroke of his own that sheared through boiled-leather cuirass and ribs alike, hurling his foe from his saddle to the dust below.

The Romans cheered his prowess, those not busy fighting for their own lives. *Pila* were few now, and the Yezda charge struck home almost unblunted. For all their discipline, the legionaries staggered under the blow. The front edge of the square sagged, began to crumple.

Marcus, at the fore, killed two Yezda in quick succession, only to have two more ride past on either side of him and hurl themselves against the battered line.

A mounted nomad struck him on the side of the head with a spear-shaft swung club-fashion. It was a glancing blow, but his vision misted, and he slipped to one knee. Another Yezda, this one on foot, darted forward, saber upraised. The tribune lifted his shield to parry, sickly aware he would be too slow.

From the corner of his eye he saw a tall shape loom up beside him. an axe bit with a meaty *chunnk*; the Yezda was dead before his dying cry passed his lips. Skapti Modolf's son put a booted foot on the corpse, braced, and pulled the weapon free.

"Where are your men?" Scaurus shouted.

The Haloga shrugged. "Dead or scattered. They gave the ravens more bones to pick than their own." Skapti seemed more a wolf than ever, an old wolf, last survivor of his pack.

He opened his mouth to speak again, then suddenly stiffened. Marcus saw the nomad arrow sprout from his chest. His one good eye held the Roman. "This place is less pleasant than Imbros," he said distinctly. His fierce blue stare dimmed as he slumped to the ground.

Scaurus recalled the fate the Haloga had half foretold when the Romans left his town. He had little time to marvel. Legionaries were falling faster than replacements could fill the holes in their ranks. Soon they would be an effective fighting force no more, but a broken mob of fugitives for the invaders' sport.

The tribune saw Gaius Philippus' head whipping from side to side, searching vainly for new men to throw into the fight. The centurion looked more harassed than beaten, annoyed over failing at something he should do with ease.

Then the Yezda shouted in surprise and alarm as they in turn were hit from behind. The killing pressure eased. The nomads streamed away in all directions, like a glob of quicksilver mashed by a falling fist.

Laon Pakhymer rode up to Marcus, a tired grin peeking through his tangled beard. "Horse and foot together do better than either by itself, don't you think?" he said.

Scaurus reached up to clasp his hand. "Pakhymer, you could tell me I was a little blue lizard and I'd say you aye right now. Never was any face so welcome as yours."

"There's flattery indeed," the Khatrisher said dryly, scratching a pockmarked cheek. He was quickly serious again. "Shall we stay together now? My riders can screen your troops, and you give us a base to fall back on at need."

"Agreed," Scaurus said at once. Even in the world he'd known, cavalry was the Romans' weakest arm, always eked out with allies or mercenaries. Here the stirrup and the incredible horsemanship it allowed made such auxiliaries all the more important.

While the Romans struggled for survival on the left center, a larger drama was building on the Videssian right wing. Of all the army, the right had suffered least. Now Thorisin Gavras, shouting encouragement to his men and fighting in the first rank, tried to lead it back to rescue his brother and the beaten center. "We're coming! We're coming!" the Sevastokrator's men cried. Those contingents still intact in the center yelled back with desperate intensity and tried to fight their way north.

It was not to be. The charge Thorisin led was doomed before it truly began. With Yezda on either side of them, the Sevastokrator's warriors had to run the cruelest kind of gauntlet to return to their stricken comrades. Arrows tore at them like blinding sleet. Their foes struck again and again, ruthless blows from the flank that had to be parried at any cost—and the cost was the thrust of the attack.

Thorisin and Thorisin alone kept his men moving forward against all odds. Then his mount staggered and fell, shot from under him by one of the black shafts Avshar's bow could send so far. The Sevastokrator was a fine horseman; he rolled free from the foundering beast and sprang to his feet, shouting for a new horse.

But once slowed, even for the moment he needed to remount, his men could advance no further. Against his will, one of his lieutenants literally dragging his mount's bridle, the younger Gavras was compelled to fall back.

A great groan of despair rose from the Videssians as they realized the relieving attack had failed. All around them, the Yezda shouted in hoarse triumph. Mavrikios, seeing before him the ruin of all his hopes, saw also that the last service he could give his state would be to take the author of his defeat down with him.

He shouted orders to the surviving Halogai of the Imperial Guard. Over all the din of battle Marcus clearly heard their answering, "Aye!" Their axes gleamed crimson in the sunset as they lifted them high in a final salute. Spearheaded by the Emperor, they hurled themselves against the Yezda.

"Avshar!" Mavrikios cried. "Face-to-face now, proud filthy knave!" The wizard-prince spurred toward him, followed by a swarm of nomads. They closed round the Halogai and swallowed them up. All over the field men paused, panting, to watch the last duel.

The Imperial Guard, steady in the face of the doom they saw ahead, fought with the recklessness of men who knew they had nothing left to lose. One by one they fell; the Yezda were no cowards and they, too, fought under their overlord's eyes. At last only a small knot of Halogai still stood, to the end protecting the Emperor with their bodies. The wizard-prince and his followers rode over them, swords chopping like cleavers, and there were only Yezda in that part of the field.

Whatever faint hopes the Videssian army had for survival died with Mavrikios. Men thought no further than saving themselves at any price and abandoned their fellows if it meant making good their own escape. Fragments of the right were still intact under Thorisin Gavras, but so mauled they could do nothing but withdraw to the north in some semblance of order. Over most of the battleground, terror—and the Yezda—ruled supreme.

More than anyone else, Gaius Philippus saved the Romans during that grinding retreat. The veteran had seen victory and defeat both in his long career and held the battered band together. "Come on!" he said. "Show your pride, damn you! Keep your ranks steady and your swords out! Look like you want some more of these bastards!"

"All I want is to get away from here alive!" a panicky soldier yelled. "I don't care how fast I have to run!" Other voices took up the cry; the Roman ranks wavered, though the Yezda were not pressing them.

"Fools!" The centurion waved his arm to encompass the whole field, the sprawled corpses, the Yezda ranging far and wide to cut down fugitives. "Look around you—those poor devils thought they could run away too, and see what it got *them*. We've lost, aye, but we're still men. Let the Yezda know we're ready to fight and they'll have to earn it to take us, and odds are they won't. But if we throw away our shields and flap around like headless chickens, every man for himself, not a one of us will ever see home again."

"You couldn't be more right," Gorgidas said. The Greek physician's face was haggard with exhaustion and hurt. Too often he had watched men die from wounds beyond his skill to cure. He was in physical pain as well. His left arm was bandaged, and the bloodstains on his torn mantle showed where a Yezda saber had slid along a rib. Yet he still tried to give credit where it was due, to keep the heart in others when almost without it himself.

"Thanks," Gaius Philippus muttered. He was studying his troops closely, wondering if he had steadied them or if stronger measures would be needed.

Gorgidas persisted, "This is the way men come off safe in a retreat, by showing the enemy how ready they are to defend themselves. Whether you know it or not, you're following Socrates' example at the battle of Delium, when he made his way back to Athens and brought his comrades out with him."

Gaius Philippus threw his hands in the air. "Just what I need now, being told I'm like some smockfaced philosopher. Tend to your wounded, doctor, and let me mind the lads on their feet." Ignoring Gorgidas' injured look, he surveyed the Romans once more, shook his head in dissatisfaction.

"Pakhymer!" he shouted. The Khatrisher waved to show he'd heard. "Have your riders shoot the first man who bolts." The officer's eyes widened in surprise. Gaius Philippus said, "Better by far to lose a few at our hands than see a stampede that risks us all."

Pakhymer considered, nodded, and threw the centurion the sharpest salute Marcus had seen from the easygoing Khatrishers. He gave his men the order. Talk of flight abruptly ceased.

"Pay Gaius Philippus no mind," Quintus Glabrio told Gorgidas. "He means less than he says."

"I wasn't going to lose any sleep over it, my friend," the physician answered shortly, but there was gratitude in his voice.

"The soft-spoken lad has the right of it," Viridovix said. "When he talks, that one"—He stabbed a thumb toward Gaius Philippus—"is like a fellow who can't keep his woman happy—things spurt out before he's ready."

The senior centurion snorted, saying, "I will be damned. This is the first time you've been on the same side of an argument as the Greek, I'll wager."

Viridovix tugged at his mustache as he thought. "Belike it is, at that," he admitted.

"And so he should be," Marcus said to Gaius Philippus. "You had no reason to turn on Gorgidas, especially since he was giving you the highest praise he could."

"Enough, the lot of you!" Gaius Philippus exclaimed in exasperation. "Gorgidas, if you want my apology, you have it. The gods know you're one of the few doctors I've seen worth the food you gobble. You jogged my elbow when I was in harness, and I kicked out at you without thinking."

"It's all right. You just paid me a finer compliment than the one I gave you," Gorgidas said. Not far away, a legionary cursed as an arrow pierced his hand. The physician sighed and hurried off to clean and bandage the wound.

He had fewer injuries to treat now. With their battle won, the Yezda slipped beyond even Avshar's control. Some still hunted Videssian stragglers, but more were looting the bodies of the dead or beginning to make camp among them; sunset was already past and darkness coming on. Sated, glutted with combat, the nomads were no longer eager to assail those few companies of their foes who still put up a bold front.

Somewhere in the twilight, a man screamed as the Yezda caught up with him at last. Scaurus shivered, thinking how close the Romans had come to suffering the same fate. He said to Gaius Philippus, "Gorgidas had the right of it. Without you we'd be running for cover one by one, like so many spooked cattle. You held us together when we needed it most."

The veteran shrugged, more nervous over praise than he had been when the fighting was hottest. "I know how to run a retreat, that's all. I bloody well ought to—I've been in enough of them over the years. You signed on with Caesar for the Gallic campaign, didn't you?"

Marcus nodded, remembering how he'd planned a short stay in the army to further his political hopes. Those days seemed as dim as if they had happened to someone else.

"Thought as much," Gaius Philippus said. "You've done pretty well yourself, you know, in Gaul and here as well. Most of the time I forget you didn't intend to make a life of this—you handle yourself like a soldier."

"I thank you," Scaurus replied sincerely, knowing that was as fulsome a compliment from the centurion as talk of Socrates was from Gorgidas. "You've helped me more than I can say; if I am any kind of soldier, it's because of what you've shown me."

"Hmp. All I ever did was do my job," Gaius Philippus said, more uncomfortable than ever. "Enough of this useless chitchat." He peered out into the dusk. "I think we've put enough distance between us and the worst of it to camp for the night."

"Good enough. The Khatrishers can hold off whatever raiders we draw while we're digging in." Scaurus spoke to the buccinators, who trumpeted out the order to halt.

"Of course," Pakhymer said when the tribune asked him for a covering force. "You'll need protection to throw up your fieldworks, and they will shelter all of us tonight." He cocked his head at the Roman in a gesture that reminded Scaurus of Taso Vones, though the two Khatrishers looked nothing like each other. "One of the reasons I joined my men to yours was to take advantage of your camp, if we saw today end with breath still in us. We have no skill at fortcraft."

"Maybe not, but you ride like devils loosed. Put me on a horse and I'd break my backside, or more likely my neck." The feeble jest aside, Marcus looked approvingly at the Khatrisher. It had taken a cool head to see ahead till nightfall in the chaos of the afternoon.

It was as well the Yezda did not press an attack while the camp was building. The Romans, dazed with fatigue, moved like sleepwalkers. They dug and lifted with slow, dogged persistence, knowing sleep would claim them if they halted for an instant. The stragglers who had joined them helped as best they could, hampered not only by exhaustion but also by inexperience at this sort of work.

Most of the non-Romans were merely faces to Scaurus as he walked through the camp, but some he knew. He was surprised to see Doukitzes busily fixing stakes atop the earthen breastwork the legionaries had thrown up. He would not have thought the skinny little Videssian whose hand he'd saved likely to last twenty minutes on the battlefield. Yet here he was, hale and whole, with countless tall strapping men no more than stiffening corpses . . . Tzimiskes, Adiatun, Mouzalon, how many more? Spying Marcus, Doukitzes waved shyly before returning to his task.

Zeprin the Red was here too. The burly Haloga was not working; he sat in the dust with his head in his hands, a picture of misery. Scaurus stooped beside him. Zeprin caught the motion out of the corner of his eye and looked up to see who had come to disturb his wretchedness. "Ah, it's you, Roman," he said, his voice a dull parody of his usual bull roar. A great bruise purpled his left temple and cheekbone.

"Are you in much pain?" the tribune asked. "I'll send our physician to see to you."

The northerner shook his head. "I need no leech, unless he know the trick of cutting out a wounded recall. Mavrikios lies dead, and me not there to ward him." He covered his face once more.

"Surely you cannot blame yourself for that, when it had to be the Emperor himself who sent you from him?"

"Sent me from him, aye," Zeprin echoed bitterly. "Sent me to stiffen the left after Khoumnos fell, the gods save a spot by their hearthfire for him. But the fighting was good along the way, and I was ever fonder of handstrokes than the bloodless business of orders. Mavrikios used to twit me for it. And so I was slower than I should have been, and Ortaias the bold"—He made the name a curse—"kept charge."

Anger roughened his voice, an anger cold and black as the storm-clouds of his wintry home. "I knew he was a dolt, but took him not for coward. When the horseturd fled, I wasn't yet nearby to stem the rout before it passed all checking. Had I paid more heed to my duty and less to the feel of my axe in my hands, it might be the Yezda who were skulking fugitives this night."

Marcus could only nod and listen; there was enough truth in Zeprin's self-blame to make consolation hard. With bleak quickness, the Haloga finished his tale: "I was fighting my way back to the Emperor when I got this." He touched his swollen face. "Next I knew, I was staggering along with one arm draped over your little doctor's shoulder." The tribune did not recall noticing Gorgidas supporting the massive northerner, but then the Greek would not have been easy to see under Zeprin's bulk.

"Not even a warrior's death could I give Mavrikios," the Haloga mourned.

At that, Scaurus' patience ran out. "Too many died today," he snapped. "The gods—yours, mine, the Empire's, I don't much care which—be thanked some of us are left alive to save what we can."

"Aye, there will be a reckoning," Zeprin said grimly, "and I know where it must start." The chill promise in his eyes would have set Ortaias Sphrantzes running again, were he there to see it.

The Roman camp was not so far from the battlefield as to leave behind the moans of the wounded. So many lay hurt that the sound of their suffering traveled far. No single voice stood out, nor single nation; at any moment, the listeners could not tell if the anguish they heard came from the throat of a Videssian grandee slowly bleeding to death or a Yezda writhing around an arrow in his belly.

"There's a lesson for us all, not that we have the wit to heed it," Gorgidas remarked as he snatched a moment's rest before moving on to the next wounded man.

"And what might that be?" Viridovix asked with a mock-patient sigh.

"In pain, all men are brothers. Would there were an easier way to make them so." He glared at the Celt, daring him to argue. Viridovix was the first to look away; he stretched, scratched his leg, and changed the subject.

Scaurus found sleep at last, a restless sleep full of nasty dreams. No sooner had he closed his eyes, it seemed, than a legionary was shaking him awake. "Begging your pardon, sir," the soldier said, "but you're needed at the palisade."

"What? Why?" the tribune mumbled, rubbing at sticky eyes and wishing the Roman would go away and let him rest.

The answer he got banished sleep as rudely as a bucket of cold water. "Avshar would have speech with you, sir."

"What?" Without his willing it, Marcus' hand was tight round his swordhilt. "All right. I'll come." He threw on full armor as quickly as he could—no telling what trickery Yezd's wizard-prince might intend. Then, blade naked in his hand, he followed the legionary through the fitfully slumbering camp.

Two Khatrisher sentries peered out into the darkness beyond the watchfires' reach. Each carried a nocked arrow in his bow. "He rode in like a guest invited to a garden party, your honor, he did, and asked for you by name," one of them told Scaurus. With the usual bantam courage of his folk, he was more indignant over Avshar's unwelcome arrival than awed by the sorcerer's power.

Not so his comrade, who said, "We fired, sir, the both of us, several times. He was so close we could not have missed, but none of our shafts would bite." His eyes were wide with fear.

"We drove the whoreson back out of range, though," the first Khatrisher said stoutly.

The druids' marks graven into Marcus' Gallic blade glowed yellow, not fiercely as they had when Avshar tried spells against him, but still warning of sorcery. Fearless as a tiger toying with mice, the wizard-prince emerged from the darkness that was his own, sitting statue-still atop his great sable horse. "Worms! You could not drive a maggot across a turd!"

The bolder-tongued Khatrisher barked an oath and drew back his bow to shoot. Scaurus checked him, saying, "You'd waste your dart again, I think—he has a protecting glamour wrapped round himself."

"Astutely reasoned, prince of insects," Avshar said, granting the tribune a scornful dip of his head. "But this is a poor welcome you grant me, when I have but come to give back something of yours I found on the field today."

Even if Marcus had not already known the quality of the enemy he faced, the sly, evil humor lurking in that cruel voice would have told him the wizard's gift was one to delight the giver, not him who received it. Yet he had no choice but to play Avshar's game out to the end. "What price do you put on it?" he asked.

"Price. None at all. As I said, it is yours. Take it, and welcome." The wizard-prince reached down to something hanging by his right boot,

320

tossed it underhanded toward the tribune. It was still in the air when he wheeled his stallion and rode away.

Marcus and his companions skipped aside, afraid of some last treachery. But the wizard's gift landed harmlessly inside the palisade, rolling until it came to rest at the tribune's feet. Then Avshar's jest was clear in all its horror, for staring sightlessly up at Scaurus, its features stiffened into a grimace of agony, was Mavrikios Gavras' head.

The sentries did shoot after the wizard-prince then, blindly, hopelessly. His fell laugh floated back to tell them how little their arrows were worth.

With his gift for scenting trouble, Gaius Philippus hurried up to the rampart. He wore only military kilt and helmet, and carried his *gladius* naked in his hand. He almost stumbled over Avshar's gift; his face hardened as he recognized it for what it was. "How did it come here?" was all he said.

Marcus told him, or tried to. The thread of the story kept breaking whenever he looked down into the dead Emperor's eyes.

The senior centurion heard him out, then growled, "Let the damned wizard have his boast. It'll cost him in the end, you wait and see. This"— He gave Mavrikios a last Roman salute—"doesn't show us anything we didn't already know. Instead of wasting time with it, Avshar could have been finishing Thorisin. But he let him get away—and with a decent part of army, too, once they start pulling themselves together."

Scaurus nodded, heartened. Gaius Philippus had the right of it. As long as Thorisin Gavras survived, Videssos had a leader—and after this disaster, the Empire would need all the troops it could find.

The tribune's mind went to the morning, to getting free of the field of Maragha. The legionaries' discipline would surely pay again, as it had this afternoon; overwhelming triumph left the Yezda almost as disordered as defeat did their foes. Now he had the Khatrisher horse, too, so he could hope to meet the nomads on their own terms. One way or another, he told himself, he would manage.

He stared a challenge in the direction Avshar had gone, said quietly, "No, the game's not over yet. Far from it."

AN EMPEROR FOR THE LEGION

WHAT HAS GONE BEFORE:

A SCOUTING COLUMN OF THREE COHORTS OF ROMAN LEGIONARIES, led by military tribune Marcus Aemilius Scaurus and senior centurion Gaius Philippus, was returning to Julius Caesar's main army when they were ambushed by Gauls. To prevent mass slaughter, the Gallic commander Viridovix offered single combat, and Marcus accepted. Both men bore druids' swords, that of Marcus being battle spoil. When the blades crossed, a dome of light sprang up around them. Suddenly the Romans and Viridovix were in an unfamiliar world with strange stars.

They soon discovered they were in the war-torn Empire of Videssos, a land where priests of the god Phos could work real magic. They were hired as a mercenary unit by the Empire and spent the winter in the provincial town of Imbros, learning the language and customs.

When spring came, they marched to Videssos the city, capital of the Empire. There Marcus met the soldier-Emperor Mavrikios Gavras, his brother Thorisin, and the prime minister, Vardanes Sphrantzes, a bureaucrat whose enmity Marcus incurred. At a banquet in the Romans' honor, Marcus met Mavrikios' daughter Alypia and accidentally spilled wine on the wizard Avshar, envoy of Yezd, Videssos' western enemy. Avshar demanded a duel. When the wizard tried to cheat with sorcery, Marcus' druid sword neutralized the spell, and Marcus won.

Avshar tried for revenge with an enchanted dagger in the hands of a nomad under his spell. The Videssian priest Nepos was horrified at the use of evil magic. Avshar forfeited the protection granted envoys.

Marcus was sent to arrest Avshar, accompanied by Hemond and a squad of Namdaleni, mercenaries from the island nation of Namdalen. But Avshar had fled, leaving a sorcerous trap that killed Hemond. Marcus was given Hemond's sword to take to his widow, Helvis.

Avshar's offenses served as justification for Videssos to declare war on Yezd, which had been raiding deep into the western part of the Empire. Troops—native and mercenary—flooded into the capital as Videssos prepared for war. Tension rose between Videssians and the growing number of Namdaleni because of differences in their worship of Phos. To the religiously liberal Romans, the differences were minor, but each side considered the other heretics. The Videssian patriarch Balsamon preached a sermon of toleration, which eased the tension for the moment.

But fanatic Videssian monks stirred up trouble again. Rioting broke out, and Marcus was sent with a force of Romans to help quell it. Going into a dark courtyard to break up a rape, he discovered that the intended victim was Helvis. Caught up in the moment, they made love. And after the riots subsided, she and her son joined him in the Romans' barracks. Other Romans had already found partners.

At last the unwieldy army moved west against Yezd, accompanied by women and dependents. Marcus was pleased to learn Helvis was pregnant, but shocked to discover Ortaias Sphrantzes commanded the army's left wing; he was only slightly mollified on finding the young man was a figurehead, hostage for Vardanes Sphrantzes' good behavior.

More troops joined the army in the westlands, including those of Baanes Onomagoulos and Gagik Bagratouni, a noble driven from his home in mountainous Vaspurakan by Yezda. Two other Vaspurakaners, Senpat Sviodo and his wife Nevrat, were acting as guides for the Romans. All Vaspurakaners were hated as heretics by a local priest, Zemarkhos, Zemarkhos cursed Bagratouni, who threw him and his dog into a sack, then beat the sack. Fearing a pogrom, Marcus interceded for him.

The Yezda began hit-and-run raids against the imperial army as it moved closer to Yezd. Then an advance force of Onomagoulos' troops was pinned down near the town of Maragha. Leaving the army's dependents behind at Khliat, the Emperor moved forward to rescue them.

In a great battle, Avshar commanded the Yezda. By sorcery, he slew the officer who truly commanded the imperial army's left wing. Ortaias Sphrantzes, suddenly thrust into real command, panicked and fled.

The whole wing collapsed. The battle, till then nearly a draw, turned to disaster. Mavrikios fell fighting, and Thorisin's desperate counterattack from the right failed, though he did manage to escape with a fair part of the army.

Roman discipline let the legionaries hold their ranks. They withdrew in good order and encamped for the night. Toward midnight, Avshar taunted them by throwing Mavrikios' head into their camp. As Gaius Philippus commented, the wizard should have pursued the forces of Thorisin instead.

The game was not over yet.

I

THE ROMANS' TREK EAST FROM THE DISASTROUS BATTLEFIELD WHERE the Emperor of Videssos lost his life was a journey full of torment. The season was late summer, the land through which they marched sere and burning hot. Mirages shimmered ahead, treacherously promising lakes where a mud puddle would have been a prodigy. Bands of Yezda invaders dogged the fugitives' tracks, skirmishing occasionally and always alert to pick off stragglers.

Scaurus still carried Mavrikios Gavras' severed head, the only sure proof the Emperor was dead. Foreseeing chaos in Videssos after Mavrikios' fall, he thought it wise to forestall pretenders who might claim the imperial name to aid their climbs to power. It would not be the first time Videssos had known such things.

"Sorry I am I wasna there when that black spalpeen Avshar flung you himself's noddle," Viridovix said to the tribune, his Latin musically flavored by his native Celtic speech. "I had a fine Yezda one to throw back at him." True to the fierce custom of his folk, the Gaul had taken a slain enemy's head for a trophy.

At any other time Marcus would have found that revolting. In defeat's bitter aftermath, he nodded and said, "I wish you'd been there, too."

"Aye, it would have given the whoreson something to think on," Gaius Philippus chimed in. The senior centurion usually enjoyed quarreling with Viridovix, but their hatred for the wizard-prince of Yezd brought them together now.

Marcus rubbed his chin, felt rough whiskers scratch under his fingers. Like most of the Romans, he had stayed clean-faced in a bearded land, but lately there had been little time for shaving. He plucked a whisker; it shone golden in the sunlight. Coming as he did from Mediolanum in northern Italy, he had a large proportion of northern blood in his veins. In Caesar's army in Gaul, he had been teased about looking like a Celt himself. The Videssians often took him for a Haloga; many of those warriors forsook their chilly home for mercenary service in the Empire.

Gorgidas worked ceaselessly with the wounded, changing dressings, splinting broken bones, and dispensing the few ointments and medicines left in his depleted store. Although hurt himself, the slim, dark Greek doctor disregarded his pain to bring others relief.

Covered by a screening force of light cavalry from Videssos' eastern neighbor Khatrish, the legionaries tramped east toward the town of Khliat as fast as their many injuries would allow. Had he led a force in the lands Rome ruled, Scaurus would have moved northwest instead, to join Thorisin Gavras and the right wing of the shattered imperial army. Hard military sense lay there, for the Emperor's brother—no, the Emperor now, Marcus supposed—had brought his troops away in good order. The fight against the Yezda would center on him.

But here Marcus was not simply a legionary officer, with a legionary officer's worries. He was also a mercenary captain. He had to deal with the fact that the legionaries' women, the families they had made or joined since coming to Videssos, were left behind in the Vaspurakaner city that had been the base for Mavrikios' ill-fated campaign. The Romans would disobey any order to turn away from Khliat. So, even more, would the hundreds of stragglers who had attached themselves to his troop like drowning men clinging to a spar.

For that matter, he never thought of giving such an order. His own partner Helvis, carrying his child, had stayed in Khliat, along with her young son from an earlier attachment.

That was to say, he hoped she had stayed in Khliat. Uncertainty tormented the legionaries as badly as the Yezda did. For all Scaurus knew, the invaders might have stormed Khliat and slain or carried into slavery everyone there. Even if they had not, fugitives would already be arriving with word of the catastrophe that had overtaken the Videssian army.

In the wake of such news; noncombatants might be fleeing eastward now. That was more dangerous than staying behind Khliat's walls. Marcus ran through the gloomy possibilities time after time: Helvis dead,

Helvis captured by the Yezda, Helvis struggling east with a three-year-old through hostile country . . . and she was pregnant, too.

At last, with a distinct effort of will, he banished the qualms to the back of his mind. Not for the first time, he was grateful for his training in the Stoic school, which taught him to cast aside useless imaginings. He would know soon enough, and that would be the time to act.

About a day and a half out of Khliat, a scout came riding back to the Roman tribune. "A horseman coming out of the east, sir," he reported. His staccato Khatrisher accent made him hard for Scaurus to understand—the tribune's own Videssian was far from perfect.

Interest flared in him when he realized what the scout was saying. "From the east? A lone rider?"

The Khatrisher spread his hands. "As far as we could tell. He was nervous and took cover as soon as he spotted us. From what little we saw, he had the seeming of a Vaspurakaner."

"No wonder he was leery of you, then. You look too much like Yezda." The invading nomads had ravaged Vaspurakan over the course of years, until the natives hated the sight of them. The Khatrishers were descended from nomads as well and, despite taking many Videssian ways, still had the look of the plains about them.

"Bring him in, and unhurt," Marcus decided. "Anyone fool enough to travel west in the face of everything rolling the other way must have a strong reason. Maybe he bears word from Khliat," the tribune added, suddenly hopeful in spite of himself.

The scout gave a cheery wave—the Khatrishers were most of them free spirits—and kicked his pony into motion. Scaurus did not expect him back for some time; for someone in the furs and leather of a plains-man, convincing a Vaspurakaner of his harmlessness would not be easy. The tribune was surprised when the Khatrisher quickly reappeared, along with another rider plainly not of his people.

The scout's companion looked familiar, even at a distance. Before the tribune was able to say more than that, Senpat Sviodo cried out in joy, and spurred his horse forward to meet the newcomer. "Nevrat!" the Vaspurakaner yelled. "Are you out of your mind, to journey alone through this wolves' land?"

His wife parted company from her escort to embrace him. The Khatrisher stared, slack-jawed. In her loose traveling clothes, her curly black hair bound up under a three-peaked Vaspurakaner hat of leather, and with the grime of travel on her, only her beardless cheeks hinted at her sex. She was surely armed like a man. A horseman's saber hung at her belt, and she carried a bow with an arrow nocked and ready.

She and Senpat were chattering in their throaty native tongue as they slowly rode back to the marching legionaries. The Khatrisher followed, still shaking his head.

"Your outrider has a head on his shoulders," she said, switching to Videssian as she neared Scaurus. "I took him and his comrades for Yezda, for all their shouts of 'Friends! Countrymen!' But when he said, 'Romans!' I knew he was no western jackal."

"I'm glad you chose to trust him," Marcus answered. He was fond of the intense, swarthy girl. So were many other Romans; scattered cheers rang out as the men realized who she was. She smiled her pleasure, teeth flashing white. Senpat Sviodo, proud of her exploit and glad beyond measure she had joined him safely, was grinning, too.

The question Senpat had shouted moments before was still burning in the tribune's mind. "In the name of your god Phos, Nevrat, why did you leave Khliat?" A horrid thought forced its way forward. "Has it fallen?"

"It still stood yesterday morning, when I set out," she answered. The Romans close enough to hear her cheered again, this time with the same relief Scaurus felt. She tempered their delight by continuing, "There's worse madness inside those walls, though, than any I've seen out here."

Gaius Philippus nodded, as if hearing what he expected. "They panicked, did they, when news came we'd been beaten?" The veteran sounded resigned; he had seen enough victories and defeats that the aftermaths of both were second nature to him.

The Romans crowded round Nevrat, calling out the names of their women and asking if they were all right. She told them. "As I said, I left early yesterday. When last I saw them, they were well. Most of you have sensible girls, too; I think they'll have wit enough to keep from joining the flight."

"There's flight, then?" Scaurus asked with a sinking feeling.

Nevrat understood his fears and was quick to lay them to rest. "Helvis knows war, Marcus. She told me to tell you she'd stay in Khliat till the first Yezda came over the wall." The tribune nodded his thanks, not trusting himself to speak. He felt suddenly taller, as if a burden had been lifted from his shoulders. Helvis, he knew, had no such reassurance that he lived.

There were messages from Khliat for some of the other Romans as well. "Is Quintus Glabrio here?" The junior centurion was almost at Nevrat's side, but as usual quiet nearly to the point of invisibility. He took a step forward; Nevrat laughed in surprise. "I'm sorry. Your lady Damaris also told me she would wait for you in the city."

"And much else besides, I'm sure," he said with a smile. The Romans who knew Damaris laughed at that; the hot-tempered Videssian girl was able to talk for herself and Glabrio both.

"Minucius," Nevrat continued in her businesslike way, "Erene says you should know she's stopped throwing up. She's beginning to bulge a bit, too."

"Ah, that's fine to hear," the burly legionary replied. After less than a week without a razor, his beard was coming in thick and black.

Nevrat turned back to Marcus for a moment, amusement in her brown eyes. "Helvis has no such message for you, my friend. I'm afraid she's green as a leek much of the time."

"Is she well?" he asked anxiously.

"Yes, she's fine. There's nothing at all to worry about. You men are such babies about these things."

She was so full of comforting, reassuring words from Khliat that someone finally called out, "If all's so well back there, why are they fleeing the city?"

"All's *not* well," she said flatly. "Remember, the messages I bring are from the folk with the wit to stay and the heart to think I'd find you and they'd see you again. All too many are of the other sort—they've been scurrying like rabbits ever since Ortaias Sphrantzes came galloping into the city with word all was lost."

Curses and angry shouts greeted the young noble's name. Command of the Videssian army's left wing had been his, and his terror-stricken flight turned an orderly retreat into rout. Nevrat nodded at the Romans' outburst. She might not have seen Ortaias flee the battlefield, but she had been in Khliat.

She said contemptuously, "He stayed just long enough to change horses—the one he'd ridden died next day of misuse, poor thing—and then he was flying east again. Good riddance, if anyone cares what I think."

"And right you are, lass." Gaius Philippus nodded. A professional soldier to the roots of his iron-gray hair, he asked, "On your way hither, what did you see of the Yezda—aye, and of our fellows, in the bargain?"

"Too many Yezda. They're thicker further east, but there's no order to them at all—they're like frogs after flies, striking at anything that moves. The only thing that brought them together was the imperial army. Now they've crushed it and they're breaking up again, looking for new land to push into . . . and all Videssos this side of the Cattle-Crossing lies open to them."

Marcus thought of Videssos' western lands laid waste by the nomads, the rich, peaceful fields put to the torch, cities so long at peace they had no walls now the playthings of invading barbarians, smoking altars heaped high with butchered victims for Yezd's dark god Skotos. Searching for any straw to contradict that horrid picture, he repeated the second half of Gaius Philippus' question: "What of the Empire's troops?"

"Most are as badly beaten as Ortaias. I watched three Yezda chasing a whole squad of horsemen, laughing themselves sick as they rode. One broke off to follow me, but I lost him in rocky ground." Nevrat dismissed two hours of terror in a sentence.

She went on, "I did see what's left of the Namdalener regiment still in good order, most of a day's ride ahead of you. The nomads were giving them a wide berth."

"That would be the way of it," Viridovix agreed. "Tough as nails, they are." The Romans concurred in that judgment. The warriors from the island Duchy of Namdalen were heretics in Videssos' eyes and as ambitious for themselves as any other mercenary soldiers, but they fought so well the Empire was glad to hire them.

336

"Did you see anything of Thorisin Gavras?" Scaurus asked. Again he thought of linking with Thorisin's forces.

"The Sevastokrator? No, nor heard anything, either. Is it true the Emperor's dead? Ortaias claimed he was."

"It's true." Marcus did not elaborate and did not mention his grisly proof of Mavrikios' passing.

Gorgidas caught something the tribune missed. The physician said, "How could Sphrantzes know? He was long fled when the Emperor fell." The Romans growled as they took in the implications of that.

"Perhaps he wished it true so badly, he never thought to doubt it," Quintus Glabrio suggested. "Men often believe what they most want."

It was like Glabrio to put as charitable a light as possible on the young noble's action. Marcus, who had been active in politics in his native Mediolanum, found another, more ominous interpretation. Ortaias Sphrantzes was of a house which had held the imperium itself; his uncle, the Sevastos—or prime minister—Vardanes Sphrantzes, was Mavrikios' chief rival.

Gaius Philippus broke into Scaurus' chain of thought. He demanded, "Have we chattered long enough? The sooner we're to Khliat, the sooner we can do something more than beating our gums over all this."

"Give a body a bit of a blow, will you now?" Viridovix said, wiping his sweaty, sunburned forehead with the back of his hand. "You're after forgetting not everyone's like that sleepless bronze giant I once heard a Greek tell of . . ."

He looked questioningly at Gorgidas, who gave him the name: "Talos."

"That's it," the Celt agreed happily. He was excitable, energetic, in short bursts of strength well-nigh unmatchable, but the senior centurion—indeed, many Romans—surpassed him in endurance.

Despite Viridovix' groans, Marcus decided Gaius Philippus was right. Progress was too slow to suit him anyway; there were many walking wounded, and others who had to be carried in litters. If Khliat still stood, the Romans had to get there as fast as they could, before the Yezda mounted an assault to overwhelm its feeble and no doubt demoralized garrison.

That thought led to another. "One last question before we march," he said to Nevrat: "Is there any word of Avshar?" For he was sure the wizard-prince was trying to organize the unruly nomads he led to deliver just that attack.

But she shook her head. "None at all, no more than of Thorisin. Curious, is it not?" She herself had seen war and skirmished against the Yezda when they first conquered Vaspurakan; she had no trouble following the tribune's logic.

By nightfall the Romans and their various comrades were less than a day from Khliat. Granted a respite by the Yezda, the legionaries erected their usual fortified camp. The protection had served them well more times than Marcus could recall. Men bustled about the campsite, intent on creating ditch, breastwork, and palisade. Eight-man leather tents went up in neat rows inside.

The Romans showed the Videssians and others who had joined them what needed to be done and stood over them to make sure they did it. At Gaius Philippus' profane urging, order was beginning to emerge again in the legionary ranks. Now the newcomers, instead of marching where they would, filled the holes fallen Romans had left in the maniples.

Scaurus approved. "The first step in making legionaries of them."

"Just what I thought." Gaius Philippus nodded. "Some will run away, but give us time to work on the rest, and they'll amount to something. Being with good troops rubs off."

Senpat Sviodo came up to Marcus, an ironic glint in his eye. "I trust you will not object if my wife spends the evening inside our works." He bowed low, as if in supplication.

Scaurus flushed. When the Videssian army was intact, he had followed Roman practice in excluding women from his soldiers' quarters. As a result, Senpat and Nevrat, preferring each other's company to legionary discipline, always pitched their tent just outside the Roman camp. Now, though—"Of course," the tribune said. "After we reach Khliat, she'll have plenty of company." He refused to say, or even to think, If we reach Khliat. . . .

"Good," Senpat said. He studied the tribune. "You can loosen up a bit after all, then? I'd wondered."

"I suppose I can," Marcus sighed, and the regret in his voice was so plain he and Sviodo both had to laugh. So it's to be our women with us wherever we go, is it? the tribune thought. One more step along the way from legionary officer to head of a mercenary company. He laughed at himself again, this time silently. In the Empire of Videssos, captain of mercenaries was all he'd ever be, and high time he got used to the notion.

The Yezda were thick as fleas round Khliat; the last day's march to the city was a running fight. But Khliat itself, to Scaurus' surprise, was not under siege, nor was any real effort made to keep the Romans from entering it. As Nevrat had remarked, in victory the nomads forgot the leaders who had won it for them.

That was fortunate, for Khliat could not have repelled a serious attack. Marcus had expected its walls to be bristling with spears, but only a handful of men were on them. To his shock, the gates were open. "Why not?" Gaius Philippus said scornfully. "There's so many running, the Yezda would be trampled if they tried to get in." A gray-brown dust cloud lay over everything eastward, the telltale banner of an army of fugitives.

Inside, panic still boiled. Plump sutlers, calculating men who could smell a copper through a wall of dung, threw their goods at anyone who would take them, so they could flee unencumbered. Singly and in small groups, soldiers wandered through the city's twisting streets and alleyways, calling the names of friends and lovers and hoping against hope they would be answered.

More pitiful yet were the women who crowded close by Khliat's western gate. Some kept a vigil doomed to heartbreak, awaiting warriors who would come to them no more. Others had already despaired of that and stood, bejeweled and gowned, offering themselves to any man who might get them safely away.

The Khatrishers were first into Khliat. Most of them were without women here, as they had taken service with Videssos for the one campaign alone and thus left wives and sweethearts behind in their forested homeland.

The tribune passed through the squat gray arch of stone and under the iron-spiked portcullis which warded the city's western gate. He looked up through the murder-holes and shook his head. Where were the archers to spit death at any invader who tried to force an entrance,

339

where the tubs of bubbling oil and molten lead to warm the foe's reception? Likely, he thought bitterly, the officer in charge of such things fled, and no one has thought of them since.

Then any concern over matters military was swept from him, for Helvis was holding him tightly, heedless of the pinch of his armor, laughing and crying at the same time. "Marcus! Oh, Marcus!" she said, covering his bristly face with kisses. For her, too, the agony of suspense was over.

Other women were crying out with joy and rushing forward to embrace their men. Three, comely lasses all, made for Viridovix, then halted in dismay and dawning hostility as they realized their common goal.

"I'd sooner face the Yezda than a mess like that," Gaius Philippus declared, but Viridovix met the challenge without flinching. With fine impartiality, the big Gaul had kisses, hugs, and fair words for all; the blithe charm that had won each girl separately now rewon them all together.

"It's bloody uncanny," the senior centurion muttered enviously. His own luck with women was poor, for the most part because he took no interest in them beyond serving his lusts.

"The Romans! The Romans!" Starting at the western gate, the cry spread through Khliat almost before the last legionary was in the city. Their dependents flocked to them, and many were the joyful meetings. But many, too, were the women who learned, some gently from comrades, others by the simple brutal fact of a loved one's absence, that for them there would be no reunions. There were Romans as well, who looked in vain for loved faces in the excited crowd and hung their heads, sorrow sharpened by their companions' delight.

"Where's Malric?" Marcus asked Helvis. He had to shout to make himself understood.

"With Erene. I watched her two girls yesterday while she kept vigil here at the gates. I should go to her, to let her know you've come."

He would not let her out of their embrace. "The whole city must know that by now," he said. "Bide a moment with me." He was startled to realize how much for granted he had come to take her beauty in the short time they had been together. Seeing her afresh after separation and danger was almost like looking at her for the first time.

Hers were not the sculptured, aquiline good looks to which Videssian women aspired. Helvis was a daughter of Namdalen, snub-nosed
and rather wide-featured. But her eyes were deepest blue, her smiling
mouth ample and generous, her figure a shout of gladness. It was too
soon for pregnancy to mark her body, but the promise of new life glowed
from her face.

The tribune kissed her slowly and thoroughly. Then he turned to
Gaius Philippus with orders: "Keep the single men here while those of us
with partners find them—the gods willing—and bring them back. Give
us, hmm—" He gauged the westering sun. "—two hours, then tell off a
hundred or so good, reliable men and rout out anyone fool enough to
think he'd sooner go it alone."

"Aye, sir." The grim promise on the centurion's face was enough to
make any would-be deserter think twice. Gaius Philippus suggested,
"We could do worse than using some Khatrishers in our patrols, too."

"There's a thought," Marcus nodded. "Pakhymer!" he called, and
the commander of the horsemen from Khatrish guided his small, shaggy
horse into earshot. Scaurus explained with he wanted. He phrased it as
request; the Khatrishers were equals, voluntary companions in misfortune, not troops formally subject to his will.

Laon Pakhymer absently scratched his cheek as he considered. Like
all his countrymen, he was bearded; he wore his own whiskers full and
bushy, the better to cover pockmarks. At last he said, "I'll do it, if all patrols are joint ones. If one of your troopers gets rowdy and we have to
crack him over the head, I want some of your men around to see it was
needful. It's easier never to have a feud than to stop one once started."

Not for the first time, Scaurus admired Pakhymer's cool good sense.
In shabby leather trousers and sweat-stained fox-skin cap, he looked the
simple nomad, a role many Khatrishers affected. But the folk of that land
had learned considerable subtlety since their Khamorth ancestors swept
down off the plains of Pardraya to wrest the province from Videssos
eight hundred years ago. They were like fine wine in cheap jugs, with
quality easy to overlook at a hasty drinking.

The tribune ordered the buccinators to trumpet "Attention!" The
legionaries stiffened into immobility. Marcus gave them his commands,
adding at the end, "Some of you may think you can steal away and never

be caught. Well, belike you're right. But remember what's outside and reckon up how long you're likely to enjoy your escape."

A thoughtful silence ensued. Gaius Philippus broke it with a bellowed, "Dis-*missed!*" Partnered men scattered through the city; their bachelor comrades stood at ease to await their return. Some moved toward the women clustered at the gates, intent on changing their status, permanently or for a little while. Gaius Philippus cocked an interrogative eyebrow at Scaurus. The tribune shrugged. Let his troops find what solace they could.

"Minucius," he said, "come on with Helvis and me? Erene is looking after Malric, it seems."

The legionary grinned. "I'll do that, sir. With three little ones running around, I'm sure of my welcome—seeing me's bound to be a relief."

Marcus chuckled, then translated for Helvis. Among themselves, he and his men mostly spoke Latin, and she had only a few words of it. She rolled her eyes. "You don't know how right you are," she said to Minucius.

"Oh, but I do, my lady," he answered, switching to Videssian for her. "The little farm I grew up on, I was the oldest of eight, not counting two who died young, and I still don't know when my mother slept."

Even in the most troubled times, some things in Khliat did not change. As Helvis, Marcus, and Minucius walked through the town's marketplace, they had to kick their way through the pigeons, blackbirds, and sparrows that congregated in cheeping, chirping hordes round the grain merchants' stalls. The birds were confident of their handouts and just as sure no one meant them any harm.

"They'll learn soon enough," Minucius said, sidestepping to avoid a pigeon which refused to make way for him. "Come a siege, there'll be a lot of bird pies the first day or two. After that they'll know their welcome's gone, and you won't get within fifty feet of one on the ground."

Beggars still lined the edge of the market place, though it seemed most of the able-bodied vagabonds had vanished for safer climes. In an expansive mood, Minucius dug into his pouch for some money to toss to a thin, white-bearded old man with only one leg who lounged in front of an open tavern door.

"You'd give him gold?" Marcus asked in surprise, seeing the trooper produce a small coin instead of one of the broad bronze pieces Videssos minted.

"That's what they'd like you to think, anyway. It's that pen-pusher Strobilos' money, and it's not worth a bloody thing." Ortaias Sphrantzes' great-uncle Strobilos had been Avtokrator until Mavrikios Gavras ousted him four years before. His coinage was cheapened even beyond the lows set by previous bureaucratic Emperors; the "goldpiece" on which his pudgy features were stamped was more than half copper.

Minucius flipped the coin to the beggar, who plucked it out of the air. Debased or no, it was a finer gift than he usually got; he dipped his head and thanked the Roman in halting, Vaspurakaner-flavored Videssian. That completed, he popped the coin into his mouth and dragged himself into the grogshop.

"I hope the old boy has himself one fine spree," Minucius said. "He doesn't look like there's many left in him."

Scaurus gave the legionary an odd look. Minucius had always struck him as sharing Gaius Philippus' single-minded devotion to the army, without the senior centurion's years of experience to give a sense of proportion. Such a thoughtful remark was not like him.

"If you're as eager to see Erene as she is to see you," Helvis said to Minucius with a smile, "it will be a happy meeting indeed. She hardly talks about anything but you."

Minucius' thick-bearded Italian peasant's face lit up in a grin that lightened his hard features. "Really?" he said, sounding shy and amazed as a fifteen-year-old. "These past few months I've thought myself the luckiest man alive. . . ." And he was off, praising Erene the rest of the way to the small house she and Helvis shared.

Listening to him as they walked along, Marcus had no trouble deciding where his unexpected streak of compassion came from. Here was a man unabashedly in love. In a way, the tribune was a trifle jealous. Helvis was a splendid bedmate, a fine companion, and no one's fool, but he could not find the flood of emotion in him that Minucius was releasing. He was happy, aye, but not heart-full.

Well, he told himself, you'll never see thirty again, and it's not likely Minucius has twenty-two winters in him. But am I older, he asked himself, or merely colder? He was honest enough to admit he did not know.

Helvis wore the key to her lodging on a string round her neck. She drew it up from between her breasts, inserted it into its socket, and drew out the bolt-pin. The door opened inward; Malric shot out, crying, "Mama! Mama!" and reaching up to seize his mother round the waist. "Hello, Papa!" he added as she lifted him and tossed him up in the air.

"Hello, lad," Marcus said, taking him from Helvis.

"Did you bring me a Yezda's head, Papa?" Malric said, remembering what he'd asked of Scaurus before the imperial army left Khliat.

"You'll have to ask Viridovix about that," the tribune told him.

Minucius barked laughter. "There's a warrior in the making," he said.

His voice brought a delighted cry of recognition from inside the house. Erene, a stocky little Videssian girl who barely reached his shoulder, came running through the door and almost bowled him over with her welcoming embrace.

"Easy, darling, easy!" he said, holding her out at arm's length. "If I squeeze you as tight as I want, I'd pop the baby out right now." He stroked her cheek with a sword-callused hand.

"Are you all right?" Erene asked anxiously. "You weren't hurt?"

"No, hardly even a scratch. You see, what happened was—"

Marcus gave a dry cough. "I'm afraid all this will have to wait. Erene, round up your girls and pack whatever you can carry without being slowed. I want to be out of this town before sunset."

Minucius looked at him reproachfully, but was too much a soldier to argue. He expected a protest from Erene, but all she said was, "I've been ready to leave for two days. This one"—She squeezed Minucius' arm— "knows how to travel light, and I've done my best to learn from him."

"And I," Helvis said when Scaurus turned his head toward her. "I've been with you long enough to know your craze for lugging everything around on your men's backs. What you have against supply wagons and packhorses I'll never understand." Her own folk's warriors fought mounted and were far more at home with horses than the unchivalric Romans.

"The more independent an army is of anything outside itself, the better it does. The Yezda show that only too well. Now, though, we really could use extra beasts and cars, what with all the noncombatants we'll have along. Will Khliat supply any, do you think?"

Erene shook her head. Helvis explained further: "Yesterday it would have, but last night Utprand brought his regiment through and emptied the horse-pens of what animals were left. He headed south at dawn this morning."

Likely, Marcus thought, the Namdalener captain was leading his troops to Phanaskert, to join his fellow easterners who were serving as a garrison in that city. From his own point of view that was a logical move: best to link all the men of the Duchy together. Utprand probably did not care—or even notice—that his march out of the path of the oncoming Yezda helped open Videssos to invasion. Mercenaries tended to think of themselves before their paymasters. As do I, the tribune realized, as do I.

His musing made him miss Helvis' next sentence. "I'm sorry?"

"I said that I suppose we'll be going in the same direction."

"What? No, of course not." The words were out of his mouth before he remembered her brother Soteric was part of the garrison at Phanaskert.

Helvis' full lips thinned; her eyes narrowed dangerously. "Why? From all I've heard, Utprand's men and yours fought the Yezda to a standstill, even after others fled." The normal contempt mercenary kin felt for the folk they were hired to defend was only made worse because Videssians and Namdaleni saw each other as heretics. Helvis went on, "Phanaskert is a stout city, stronger than Khliat. Surely behind its walls you could laugh at the scrawny nomads capering by."

The tribune swallowed a sigh of relief. He wanted no part of going to Phanaskert, and Helvis unwittingly provided him with a perfect military justification for not doing so. He also did not want to quarrel with her. She was strong-willed; her temper, once aroused, was fierce; and in any case he had no time to argue.

He said, "City walls are less protection against nomads than you think. They burn the fields outside, kill the peasants who work them, and starve the town into yielding. Think," he urged her. "You've seen it's true, in the Empire and here in Vaspurakan. May they rot for it, the Yezda are no better bargain in a siege than in the open field."

She bit her lip, wanting to disagree further but seeing Scaurus' mind was made up. "Very well," she said at last. Her smile was wry. "I won't argue with you over soldierly matters. Whether I'm right or not, it would do me no good."

Marcus was content to let it go at that. While what he had said was true, he knew it was far from the whole truth. Great events would be brewing in Videssos in the aftermath of Mavrikios' defeat and death. He did not intend to be stranded in a provincial town on the edge of nowhere while they took place without him. In his own way, he was as ambitious as all the other mercenary captains reckoning their chances of riding chaos' wind to glory. But with only his few precious legionaries behind him, his hopes, unlike theirs, had to center on the imperial government.

None of that calculation showed on his face. He mused how much easier it would have been to remain one of Caesar's junior officers, with clearly defined duties and with someone else to do his thinking for him. He shrugged inside his mail shirt. The Stoic doctrine he'd studied in Italy taught a man to make the best of what he had and not wish for the impossible—a good creed for a quiet man.

"If you're ready," he said to Helvis and Erene, "we'd best head back."

"Sure and I'm baked to a wee black cinder," Viridovix said as he tramped along. In fact he was not black, but red as any half-cooked meat. His fair Celtic skin burned under the ferocious Vaspurakaner sun, but refused to tan. Gorgidas smeared various smelly ointments on him. They sloughed away with each new layer of peeling hide.

The Gaul swore as a drop of sweat drew a stinging track down his face. "I have a riddle for the lot of you," he called. "Why is even the silly seagull wiser than I?"

"I could think of a dozen reasons without trying," Gaius Philippus said, not about to let such an opening slip by. "Tell us yours."

Viridovix glared, but gave the answer he had prepared. "Because it has the sense never to visit Vaspurakan."

The Romans, draggled and sun-baked themselves, chuckled in agreement. Senpat Sviodo, though, took offense to hear his native land maligned. He said loftily, "I'll have you know this is the first land Phos shaped when he made the world, and the home of our ancestor Vaspur, the first man."

Some of the Videssians who had joined the Romans hooted. The Vaspurakaners might call themselves Phos' princes, but no people outside the "princes'" land took their theology seriously.

Viridovix cared nothing for theology of any sort. His objections were more immediate. Tilting his head back so he could look down his long nose at the mounted Senpat, he said, "About your being kin to the first man I'll not speak one way or t'other. Of that sort of thing I ken nought. But I do believe this land your Phos' first creation, for one look about would tell anybody the puir fool needed more practice."

The legionaries whooped to see Sviodo speechless; the imperials— and Khatrishers, too—laughed louder yet at Viridovix' delicious blasphemy. "You've only yourself to blame for the egg on your face," Gaius Philippus told the young Vaspurakaner, not unkindly. "Anyone with a tongue fast enough to keep three lovelies—and keep them all happy with him—is more than a match for a puppy like you."

"I suppose so," Senpat murmured. "But who would have thought he could talk with it, too?" Sunburned as he was, Viridovix could go no redder, but his strangled snort said the Vaspurakaner had a measure of revenge.

The Romans and their comrades pushed east from Khliat in an order reminiscent of any threatened herd. As always, the Khatrishers served as scouts and outriders, screening the main body and warning of trouble ahead or to either side. At their center marched a hollow square of legionaries, old bulls protecting the women, children, and wounded within.

The force's good order and obvious readiness to stand and fight kept it from danger. A company of about three hundred Yezda paralleled the Romans' course for more than a day, like so many wolves waiting to pick off the stragglers from a herd of wisent. At last they concluded there was no hope of catching their quarry unaware and rode away in search of easier prey.

At nightfall now, Marcus could hardly protest women inside his camp. Helvis shared his tent, and he was glad of it. Nonetheless, the principle of the thing still galled him. When Senpat Sviodo began teasing him once more, the only answer he got was a stare cold enough to end any further raillery before it could start. Acquiescent Scaurus might be, but not enthusiastic.

Late in the fourth morning out from Khliat, a Khatrisher scout came riding up from the south. Flipping Marcus the usual offhand salute, he reported, "There's something funny going on up in the hills—sounds pretty much like fighting, but not quite. I didn't take a close look. It's better country for foot than horse—the grade is steep, and there's all kinds of loose rocks."

"Show me," the tribune said. He followed the Khatrisher's pointing finger. Sure enough, he saw a small dust cloud and, below it, occasional sparks of light as the sun flashed off a blade. Even allowing that the action was a couple of miles away, it did not seem very big.

Still, if it was Videssian stragglers or Vaspurakaners meeting the vanguard of a major Yezda force, that was something the Romans had to know. Scaurus turned to Gaius Philippus. "Detail me eight men with a good, sensible underofficer to find out what the skirmish means."

"Eight men it is, sir," the centurion nodded, quickly choosing a tentful of legionaries. "And for the party's leader," he said, "I'd suggest—"

On impulse, Marcus cut him off. "Never mind. I'll take them myself."

Gaius Philippus' face froze, except for one unruly eyebrow that climbed toward his hairline in mute expression of the scandalized feelings he was too well drilled to speak out loud. But Scaurus' ears were sharper than most. As he turned to take the reconnaissance squad away, he heard the senior centurion grumbling to himself, "Fool amateurs, always think they have to lead from the front."

Leadership, as it happened, had played almost no role in the tribune's sudden decision. Curiosity was a much bigger part of it, a curiosity piqued by the Khatrisher's odd description of what he had heard: "Pretty much like fighting, but not quite." That deserved a closer look.

"Double march," he told his men and hurried south, his long legs chewing up the distance. Though the legionaries were shorter and stockier, they kept pace. At double march—almost a trot, really—there was scant breath for chatter. The two miles vanished in a silence broken only by hard breathing, the slap of sandals on dirt, and the occasional clank of scabbards slapping off iron-studded military kilts.

The land began sloping up from the valley floor; loose rocks and gravel made the going hard. Marcus stumbled and had to put his hands out to save a fall. To the rear, one of his men cursed as the same thing happened to him. He realized the Khatrisher had been right in his reluctance to take his mount up the slope. Four legs might be quicker than two, but in this terrain two were far more agile.

He was close enough now to hear the noise the scout had reported, though a jumble of boulders ahead still hid its source. The Khatrisher had been right: at first it sounded like any bit of sharp fighting heard from outside, but as the Romans drew nearer they began cocking their heads and looking at one another in puzzlement. Steel on steel did not sound quite like this, nor did the shouts the combatants raised. Where was the noise of booted feet stamping and leaping, and what was the source of the high, almost inaudible keening that took its place?

Marcus drew his Gallic longsword; its weight was comforting in his palm. Behind him, he heard his men's stubby *gladii* rasp free of their brass scabbards. The Romans pushed past the last obstructions and up onto a stretch of ground flatter than that through which they had been struggling.

On the little plain, a dozen and a half Yezda, urged on by a hard-faced man in robes the color of dried blood, hewed and chopped at a double handful of Videssians clustered protectively around a plump, shave-pated fellow whose dusty garment might once have been sky blue. "Nepos!" Scaurus shouted, recognizing the rotund little priest of Phos.

Nepos' head whipped round at the cry; the struggle, going no better than most at odds of nearly two to one, promptly grew more desperate yet, the circle round the priest tighter. Neither the Videssian soldiers nor their foes appeared to notice the Romans' arrival.

"At them!" Marcus shouted. If the Yezda chose to be fools, it was none of his concern.

The red-robe who led them smiled thinly as the legionaries charged.

His men did not divert a minim of their attention from the enemy at hand, not even when the Romans were upon them. And the legionaries shouted in amazement and dread, for their swords drove through the

Yezda as if through smoke, and their bodies met no resistance from the solid-seeming foe.

The Videssian soldiers, for all their bellowed war cries, for all the ringing of their blades against those of the Yezda, were as insubstantial as the wraiths they fought. Marcus' brain stopped its brief terrorized yammering—Nepos was mage as well as priest, and the tribune knew Yezda sorcerers wore red-brown by choice. His men had stumbled across a wizards' duel—and Nepos' opponent was no weakling, not if he could force the fat priest to the defensive.

Then Scaurus' sword lashed across one of the phantom Yezda warriors. The marks set into the blade flared golden as it sheared through the sorcery. Like a doused candle flame, the soldier's seeming ceased to be. Another vanished to a second stroke, then another and another. The Yezda wizard's smile disappeared with them.

As their foes blew out, Nepos' projections swung to the attack, and it was his enemy's turn to draw his powers around himself for defense. But Marcus' blade, enchanted by vanished Gaul's druids, had shown itself proof against the spells of Avshar himself; an underling's magic was no match for it. The tribune pushed forward remorselessly, striking the Yezda's wraithly warriors out of existence.

Even when the last of them was gone, the red-robe proved neither coward nor weakling. His spells were still potent enough to hold off Nepos' assault; no phantom Videssian sword reached him, though they missed now by hairbreadths. Growling an oath in his own harsh tongue, he snatched out a dagger and leaped forward to grapple with Scaurus.

That was a contest with but one possible ending, despite the Yezda's courage. The Roman turned the wizard's stab with his shield, thrust out and up with the killing stroke of the legionaries. His blade bit flesh, not the filmy figments that had so far stood against him. Blood ran from the Yezda's mouth, to drown his dying curse half-uttered.

Nepos' seemings vanished when their creator's foe fell. The little Videssian priest staggered himself, a man in the last throes of exhaustion. Sweat was pouring from his shaven crown; drops sparkled in his beard. He came up to clasp the tribune's arm. "Praise Phos, who sends the light, for sending you to me in my desperate need." The priest's voice was a ragged, croaking caricature of his usual firm tenor.

He looked down at the crumpled form of the dead Yezda wizard, murmuring, "He would have killed me, I think, had you not come when you did."

"How did you get into a sorcerers' duel?" Marcus asked.

"We were dodging each other through these rocks. I saw he had a knife and wanted to frighten him off with phantoms. But he fought back—and he was strong." Nepos shook his head. "And yet he seemed but a shaman like a thousand others, while I, I am a mage of the Videssian Academy. Can it be true, then—is his dark Skotos a mightier god than mine? Is my life's work one long futility?"

Scaurus thumped his shoulder; Nepos was normally a jolly soul, but liable to fits of gloom when things went bad. The tribune said, "Buck up. He and all his kind are riding the hem of Avshar's robe—one win and they think they bestride the world." He studied the draggled priest. "And you, my friend, are not at your best."

"That's so," Nepos admitted. He scrubbed at the sweat-streaked dirt on his face with a grimy sleeve and shook his head in dismay. It was as if he was looking at himself for the first time in days. He managed a feeble smile. "I'm not in fine fettle, am I?"

"Hardly," Marcus said. "I can't promise you any elegant accommodations with my men, but they do beat straggling home alone."

Nepos' smile grew broader. "I should certainly hope so." He sighed, then turned to the legionaries. "I suppose that means I'll have to tramp back with you long-shanked gentlemen." The Romans grinned at him; they were all taller—and leaner—than the tubby little priest.

He did his valiant best to keep pace with them, his short legs churning over the ground. "Not bad," one of the soldiers commended him as they approached the Roman column. The trooper's smile turned sly. "There's plenty of Videssians with us already. Maybe we'll find you a coat of mail and a pack and make a real legionary out of you."

"Phos forfend!" Nepos panted, rolling his eyes.

"Or we could just lay you down and roll you along," another Roman suggested. The look the priest sent Marcus was so full of indignant appeal that the tribune coughed and put an end to his troopers' fun.

Gaius Philippus had been pulling out a full maniple of soldiers to come to Scaurus' rescue. He waved when he saw the squad coming back down into the valley. As soon as they were in earshot, he bellowed, "Everything all right?"

Marcus answered with the upraised thumb of the gladiatorial arena. The senior centurion gave back the signal and returned the maniple to the ranks. Despite Gaius Philippus' mutterings over amateurs and personal leadership, Scaurus saw no signs that anyone but the centurion was going to take that maniple forward.

A spare figure in chlamys and sandals loped out from the Roman column toward the returning squad. Gorgidas ignored Marcus; as for the legionaries, they might as well not have been there. The Greek doctor's attention was solely on Nepos. "Do you know your people's healing art?" he demanded. He leaned forward, as if willing an aye out of the priest.

"Why, yes, a bit, but—"

Gorgidas allowed no protest. He and Nepos had had many soul-searching talks, but the intense Greek would not spare time for them now. He clutched the priest's shoulder and dragged him toward the litters of the seriously wounded, saying, "The gods know I've been praying for days to run across a blue-robe with his wits about him. I've had to watch men die, beyond the power of my medicine to cure. But you lads, now—" He stopped short and shook his head, a rational man compelled to acknowledge the power of forces past reason.

Curious Romans, Marcus among them, followed the oddly matched pair. He had seen a healer-priest save Sextus Minucius and another legionary just after the Romans came to Videssos. But miracles, he thought, did not go stale with repetition.

Nepos was still protesting his unworthiness as Gorgidas tugged him onward. His expostulations faded when he came face-to-face with the horrid facts of injury. The worst-hurt soldiers were already dead, either of their wounds or from the sketchy care and jolting they had received during the Romans' grinding retreat.

Many who still clung to life would not for long. Shock, infection, and fever, coupled with scant water and constant baking sun, made death almost an hourly visitor. The stench of septic wounds turned the stomach even through the aromatic ointments Gorgidas had applied. Men witless from fever shivered in the noonday heat or babbled anguished gibberish. Here was war's aftermath at its grimmest.

In the face of such misery, Nepos underwent a transformation nearly as great as the one Gorgidas hoped he would work on the wounded. The rotund priest's fatigue fell from him. When he drew himself upright, he seemed inches taller. "Show me the worst of them," he said to Gorgidas, and suddenly it was his voice, not the Greek doctor's, that was filled with authority.

If Gorgidas noticed the reversal, it did not faze him. He was content to play a secondary role, should that be required to save his patients. "The worst?" he said, rubbing his chin with a slim-fingered hand. "That would be Publius Flaccus, I think. Over this way, if you will."

Publius Flaccus was beyond thrashing and delirium; only the low, rapid rise and fall of his chest showed he was still alive. He lay unmoving on his litter, the coarse stubble of his beard stark and black against tight-drawn, waxen skin. A Yezda saber had laid his left thigh open from groin to knee. Somehow Gorgidas managed to stanch the flow of blood, but the wound grew inflamed almost at once, and from mere inflammation quickly passed to mortification's horror.

Greenish-yellow pus crusted the bandages wrapping the gashed limb. Drawn by the smell of corruption, flies made a darting cloud around Flaccus. They scattered, buzzing, as Nepos stooped to examine the wounded Roman.

The priest's face was grave as he said to Gorgidas, "I will do what I can. Unbandage him for me, please; there must be contact between his flesh and mine." Gorgidas knelt beside Nepos, deftly undoing the dressings he had applied the day before.

Battle-hardened soldiers gagged and drew back as the huge gash was bared. Its stench was more than most men could stand, but neither priest nor physician flinched from it.

"Now I understand the *Philoktetes*," Gorgidas said to himself. Nepos looked at him without comprehension, for the doctor had fallen back into Greek. Unaware that he had spoken at all, Gorgidas did not explain.

Marcus also realized the truth in Sophokles' play. No matter how vital a man was, with this foul a wound his presence could become intolerable enough to force his comrades to abandon him. The thought flickered and blew out, for Nepos was leaning forward to take Publius Flaccus' thigh in his hands.

The priest's eyes were closed. He gripped the mangled leg so tightly his knuckles whitened. Had Flaccus been conscious, he would have shrieked in agony. As it was, he did not stir. Fresh pus welled up over the swollen lips of the wound to foul Nepos' hands. The priest ignored it, his spirit and will focused on the injury alone.

Back at Imbros, a year before, Gorgidas had spoken of a flow of healing from priest to patient. The words were vague, but Scaurus had found none better then, nor did he now. The short hairs on the nape of his neck tried to rise, for he could feel the current passing between Nepos and Flaccus, though not with any sense he could name.

To aid his concentration, Nepos whispered an endless series of prayers. The Videssian dialect he used was so archaic Scaurus only caught a word now and again. Even the name of the priest's god shifted. The divine patron of good was Phos in the modern tongue, but sounded more like "Phaos" in Nepos' elder idiom.

At first Marcus wondered if it was his hopeful imagination, but soon he had no doubt: the evil-smelling pus was disappearing from the filthy gash, its swollen, inflamed lips visibly shrinking. "Will you look there?" a Roman muttered, awe in his voice. Other legionaries called on gods they had known longer than Phos.

Nepos paid no attention. Everything around him might have vanished in a clap of thunder, and he would have crouched, oblivious, before the still form of Publius Flaccus.

The wounded legionary moaned and stirred, his eyes fluttering open for the first time in two days. They were sunk deep in their sockets, but had reason in them. Gorgidas slipped a steadying arm behind Flaccus' shoulder and offered him a canteen. The Roman drank thirstily. "Thank you," he whispered.

When nothing else had, his words penetrated Nepos' shell of concentration. The priest relaxed his clenched grip on Flaccus' thigh; like the legionary, he, too, seemed to become aware of his surroundings once more. He reached out to take one of Flaccus' hands in his own. "Phos be praised," he said, "for allowing me to act as his instrument in saving this man."

Marcus and the rest of the Romans looked with marvel at the wonder Nepos had wrought. The rotting, stinking wound which had been about to kill Publius Flaccus was suddenly clean, free of corruption, and showing every sign of being able to heal normally. And Flaccus himself, the killing fever banished from his system, was trying to sit and trading gibes with the soldiers crowding near him. Only the fly-swarming pile of pus-soaked bandages gave any evidence of what had just happened.

His face alight, Gorgidas came around Flaccus to help Nepos up. "You must teach me your art," he said. "Anything I have is yours."

The priest was wobbly on his feet; fatigue was flooding back into him. Nonetheless he smiled wanly, saying, "Speak not of payment. I will show you if I can. If the talent lies within you, Phos' servants ask nothing but that it be wisely used."

"Thank you," Gorgidas said softly, as grateful for the boon Nepos offered as Flaccus had been for the simpler gift of water. Then the physician grew brisk once more. "But for now there is only the one of you, and many more men who need your help. Cotilius Rufus, I think, is next worst off—his litter is over here." He tugged Nepos through the crowd round Flaccus.

The priest took three or four steps before his eyes rolled up in his head and he slid gently to the ground. Gorgidas stared in consternation, then bent over his prostrate form. He peeled back an eyelid, felt for Nepos' pulse. "He's asleep," the physician said indignantly.

Marcus laid a hand on his shoulder. "We've seen that this healing of theirs takes as much from the healer as it puts into the sufferer. And Nepos had been drawing heavily on his powers before you grabbed him. Let the poor fellow rest."

"Oh, very well," Gorgidas conceded with poor grace. "He is a man, after all, not a scalpel or a stick of collyrium to grind up for eyewash. I suppose it wouldn't do to kill off my chief healing tool from overwork. But he'd better wake up soon." And the physician settled himself beside the softly snoring Nepos to wait.

Soli, when the Romans and their companions reached it a few days later, had already had a visit from the Yezda. The ruins of the wall-less new town by the bank of the Rhamnos River had been sacked yet again, probably for the dozenth time in the two-score or so years since Yezd's nomads began pushing into Videssos. Little gray eddies of smoke still spiraled into the air, though Scaurus was hard-pressed to understand what the invaders had found to burn.

On the bluff overlooking the river, the partially rebuilt Old Soli had survived behind its walls. Cries of alarm and trumpet blasts came echoing from those walls when lookouts spied the approaching force. Marcus had trouble convincing the watchmen his troops were friendly, the more so as the Yezda had driven Videssian prisoners ahead of them to masquerade as an imperial army.

When the town's stout gates swung open at last, its *hypasteos* or city governor came out through them to greet the Romans. He was a tall, thin man of about forty, with stooped shoulders and a permanently dyspeptic expression. The tribune had not seen him on the army's westward march, but remembered he was called Evghenios Kananos.

Kananos studied the newcomers with wary curiosity, as if still unsure they were not Yezda in disguise. "You're the first decent-sized bunch of our troops I've seen. Was starting to think there weren't none left," he said to Marcus. He had an up-country twang that matched his dour mien.

"Some regiments did get free," the tribune answered. "We—"

Kananos kept right on, as if Scaurus had not spoken. "Ayuh," he said, "I don't believe I've seen hardly a one, but for the miserable little band that rode in with the Emperor yesterday. On his way to Pityos, he was, and then by sea to the capital, I suppose."

Marcus stared at the *hypasteos,* his mouth falling open. Everyone close enough to hear stood similarly frozen in his tracks. "The Emperor?" It was Zeprin the Red who asked the question, elbowing his way up through the Roman ranks. The burly Haloga had been one of the commanders of Mavrikios' Imperial Guard, and his failure to save his overlord had plunged the once-ebullient northerner so deep into depression that he marched along day after day with hardly a word. Suddenly his face and voice were alive again. "The Emperor?" he repeated eagerly.

"That's what I said," Kananos agreed. He used his words sparingly; it seemed to pain him to have to go back over ground once covered.

To the point as always, Gaius Philippus demanded, "How could Thorisin Gavras have come through here without us getting word he was close? And I'd hardly call the troops he had with him a 'miserable little band'—he got clear in pretty fair order."

"Thorisin Gavras?" Evghenios Kananos stared at the centurion in surprise and a little suspicion. "Didn't say a word about Thorisin Gavras. I was talking about the Emperor—the Emperor Ortaias. Far as I know, there ain't no other."

II

"YOUR HONOR, YOU'RE A RARE STUBBORN MAN," VIRIDOVIX TOLD SCAU-
rus the day after Kananos' shattering news, "but you can march the legs
off the lot of us, and we'll still never catch up to that omadhaun of a
Sphrantzes."

Weary and frustrated, the tribune halted. His outrage over Ortaias'
gall in assuming the imperial title had made him fling his small army
north to drag the usurper to earth. But Viridovix was right. When looked
at rationally and not through the red haze of anger, the Romans had no
chance to overtake him. Sphrantzes was mounted, had no women and
wounded to encumber him, and had a day's lead. Moreover, the further
north Scaurus led his men, the more Yezda they met, and the more hostile the nomads were.

The legionaries clearly saw the futility of pursuit. Roman discipline
kept them pushing toward Pityos, but their hearts were not in it. They
were harder to get moving after every halt, and slower on the march. And
only the fear that leaving would be worse kept the men they had added
since Maragha with them. Everyone despised Ortaias Sphrantzes, but
they all knew they could not catch him.

Laon Pakhymer sensed this stop was different from the ones before.
He rode back to Marcus, asking, "Finally had enough?" His voice held
sympathy—he had no more use than the Romans for Sphrantzes—but
also a certain hardness, warning that he, too, was running out of patience with this useless hunt.

Marcus looked from him to the Gaul, then, as a last hope, to Gaius
Philippus, whose contempt for the would-be Emperor knew no bounds.
"Are you asking what I think?" the senior centurion said.

Marcus nodded.

"All right, then. There's not a prayer of catching up with the worthless son of a sow. In your heart you must know that as well as I do."

"I suppose so," the tribune sighed. "But if that's what you think, why didn't you say so when we set out?" Roman discipline or no, Scaurus rarely had doubts about Gaius Philippus' opinion.

"Simple enough—whether or not we nailed Sphrantzes, I thought Pityos a good place to head for. If Ortaias could sail back to Videssos the city, so could we, and save ourselves having to fight across the westlands. But from the look of things, there are too bloody many Yezda between us and the port to let us get there unmangled."

"I fear you're right. I wish we knew how Thorisin stands."

"So do I—or *if* he stands. Too many Yezda westward, though, to swing back and find out."

"I know." Marcus clenched his fist. Now more than ever, he wished for any word of the slain emperor's brother, but the choice he was forced to only made getting that word more unlikely. "We have to turn east, away from them."

They had spoken Latin; when the tribune saw Pakhymer's blank look, he quickly translated his decision into Videssian. "Sensible," the Khatrisher said. He cocked his head at the Romans in a gesture his people often used. "Do any of you know where you're headed? 'East' covers a lot of ground, and you're not from these parts, you know." In spite of his gloom, Marcus had to smile at the understatement.

Gaius Philippus said, "The Yezda can't have run everyone off the land. There's bound to be a soul or two willing to show us the way—if for no better reason than to keep us out of his own valley."

Laon Pakhymer chuckled and spread his hands in defeat. "There you have me. *I* wouldn't want this ragtag mob of ruffians camped near me any longer than I could help it."

The senior centurion grunted. He might have been pleased at gaining the Khatrisher's agreement, but hardly by his unflattering description of the legionaries.

The shrill sound of a squabble woke Marcus before dawn the next morning. He cursed wearily as he sat up in his bedroll, still worn from the previous day's march through broken country. Beside him Helvis sighed and turned over, fighting to stay asleep. Malric, who never seemed to sleep when the tribune and Helvis wanted him to, did not stir now.

Scaurus stuck his head through his tent flap. He was just in time to see Quintus Glabrio's companion Damaris stamp from the junior centurion's tent. She was still shouting abuse as she angrily stode away: "—the most useless man I can imagine! What I saw in you I'll never know!" She disappeared out of the tribune's line of vision.

In fact, Scaurus was more inclined to wonder what had attracted the Roman to her. True, she was striking enough in the strong-featured Videssian way, with snapping brown eyes. But she was skinny as a boy and had all the temper those eyes foretold. She was, the tribune realized, as hotheaded as Thorisin's lady Komitta Rhangavve—and that was saying a great deal. Nor did Glabrio have Thorisin's quick answering contentiousness. It was a puzzler.

Glabrio, rather in the way of a man who pokes his head out the door to see if a thunderstorm is past, looked out to see which way Damaris had gone. He caught sight of Marcus, shrugged ruefully, and withdrew into his tent once more. Embarrassed at witnessing his discomfiture, the tribune did the same.

Damaris' last outburst had succeeded in rousing Helvis, though Malric slept on. Brushing sleep-snarled brown hair back from her face, she yawned, sat up, and said, "I'm glad we don't fight like that, Hemond—" She stopped in confusion.

Marcus grunted, his lip quirking in a lopsided smile. He knew he should not be bothered when Helvis absently called him by her dead husband's name, but he could not help the twinge that ran through him every time she slipped.

"You might as well wake the boy," he said. "The whole camp will be stirring now." The effort to keep annoyance from his voice took all emotion with it, leaving his words flat and hard as a marble slab.

The unsuccessful try at hiding anger was worse than none at all. Helvis did as he asked her, but her face was a mask that did as little to hide her hurt as had his coldly dispassionate tone. Looks like a fine morning already, just a fine one, the tribune thought as he laced on his armor.

He threw himself into his duties to take his mind off the almost-quarrel. His supervision of breaking camp was so minute one might have supposed his troops were doing it for the first time rather then the three-hundredth or, for some, the three-thousandth. He heard Quintus Glabrio swearing at the men in his maniple—something rare from that quiet officer—and knew he was not the only one with nerves still jangling.

The matter of guides went as Gaius Philippus had guessed. The Romans were passing through a hardscrabble country, with scores of rocky little valleys running higgledy-piggledy one into the next. The coming of any strangers into such a backwater would have produced a reaction; the coming of an army, even a small, defeated army, came close to raising panic.

Farmers and herders so isolated they rarely saw a tax collector—isolation indeed, in Videssos—wanted nothing more than to get the Romans away from their own home villages before pillage and rape broke loose. Every hamlet had a young man or two willing, nay, eager, to send them on their way . . . often, Marcus noted, toward rivals who lived one valley further east.

Sometimes the tribune's men got a friendlier reception. Bands of Yezda, with their nomadic hardiness and mobility, had penetrated even this inhospitable territory. When a timely arrival let the Romans appear as rescuers, nothing their rustic hosts owned was too fine to lavish on them.

"Now this is the life for me, and no mistake," Viridovix said after one such small victory. The Celt sprawled in front of a campfire. A mug of beer was in his right hand, a little mountain of well-gnawed pork ribs at his feet. He took a long pull at the mug, belched, and went on, "You know, we could do a sight worse than kinging it here for the rest of our days. Who'd be caring enough to say us nay?"

"I, for one," Gaius Philippus answered promptly. "This place is yo-keldom's motherland. Even the whores are clumsy."

"There's more to life than your prick, you know," the Celt said. His righteous tone drew howls from everyone who heard him; Gaius Philippus mutely held out a hand with three upraised fingers. With the ruddy

361

firelight and his permanently sunburned skin, it was impossible to tell if Viridovix blushed, but he did tug at his sweeping mustaches in chagrin.

"But still," he persisted, "doesn't all this"—He reached out a foot and toppled the pile of bones—"make munching marching rations a thought worth puking on? Dusty porridge, stale bread, smoked meat with the taste of a herd of butchered shoes—a day of that would gag a buzzard, and we eat it week after week."

Gorgidas said, "You know, my Gallic friend, there are times you're naïve as a child. How often do you think this miserable valley can supply feasts like this?" He waved out into the dark, reminding his listeners of the poor, small, rocky fields they'd come through, fields that sometimes seemed to go straight up a mountainside.

"I grew up in country like this," the doctor went on. "The folk here will eat poorer this winter for feasting us tonight. If they did it two weeks running, some would starve before spring—and so would some of us, should we stay."

Viridovix stared at him without comprehension. He was used to the lush fertility of his northern Gallic homeland, with its cool summers, mild winters, and long, gentle rains. Cut firewood sprouted green shoots there; here in the Videssian uplands, rooted trees withered in the ground.

"There are more reasons than Gorgidas' for going on," Marcus said, disturbed that the idea Viridovix put forward half jokingly was getting serious attention. "However much we'd like to forget the world, I fear it won't forget us. Either the Yezda will flatten the Empire—which looks all too likely right now—or Videssos will somehow drive them back. Whoever wins will stretch their rule all through this land. Do you think we could stand against them?"

"They'd have to find us first." Senpat Sviodo gave Viridovix unexpected support. "To judge from the run of guides we've had, even the locals don't know the land three valleys over."

There were rumbles of agreement to that from around the campfire. Gaius Philippus muttered, "To judge from the run of guides we've had, the locals don't know enough to squat when they crap."

No one could dispute that, either. Glad to see the argument diverted, Scaurus said, "This last one is better," and the centurion had to nod. The

Romans' latest guide was a solidly built middle-aged man with a soldier's scars; his name was Lexos Blemmydes. He carried himself like a veteran, too, and his Videssian had lost some of its original hill-country accent. Marcus had a nagging feeling he'd seen Blemmydes before, but the guide's face did not seem familiar to any of his men.

The tribune wondered if Blemmydes was one of the refugees from Videssos' shattered army. The man had attached himself to the Romans a few days before, coming up to their camp one evening and asking if they needed a guide. Whoever he was, he certainly knew his way through this rocky maze. His descriptions of upcoming terrain, villages, and even village leaders ahead were unfailingly accurate.

He was, in fact, so much superior to earlier escorts that Scaurus looked from one campfire to the next until he spotted Blemmydes shooting dice with a couple of Khatrishers. "Lexos!" he called, and then repeated more loudly when the Videssian did not look up. The guide's head whipped around; Marcus waved him over.

He picked himself up from the game, though he still had his stiff gambler's face on when he came to the tribune's side. "What can I do for you, sir?" he asked. His voice had the resigned patience of any common soldier's before an officer, but the dice muttered restlessly to themselves in his closed right fist.

"Not much, really," Marcus said. "It's only that you know so much more of this country than other guides we've had, and we're wondering how you learned it so well."

Blemmydes could not have been said to change expression, but his eyes grew wary. He answered slowly, "I've made it my business to know the best ways through the land I travel. I wouldn't want to be caught napping."

Suddenly intent, Scaurus leaned forward. Almost he remembered where this frozen-faced soldier had crossed his path before. But Gaius Philippus was chuckling at Blemmydes' reply. "Your business and no one else's, hey? Well, fair enough. Go on, get back to your game." Blemmydes nodded, still unsmiling, and strode off. Marcus' half memory stayed stubbornly dark.

The senior centurion was still amused. "He's probably some sort of smuggler, or a plain horse thief. More power to him, says I; anyone with the imagination to get himself a fifteen-hundred-man armed guard to cover his tracks deserves to do well."

"I suppose so," Scaurus sighed, and shelved the matter.

That night the weather finally broke, a reminder summer would not, after all, last forever. The wind shifted; instead of the seemingly endless westerly from the baking plains of Yezd, it blew clean and cool off the Videssian Sea to the north. There was fog in the early morning, and the low gray clouds did not burn away until almost noon.

"Well, hurrah!" Viridovix exclaimed when he emerged from his tent and saw the murky daylight. "My puir roasted hide won't fry today. No more slathering myself with Gorgidas' stinking goo, either. Hurrah!" he said again.

"Aye, hurrah," Gaius Philippus echoed, with a morose look at the sky. "Another week of this and it'll start raining; and it won't let up till it snows. I don't know about you, but I'm not much for slogging my way through mud. We'll be stuck in the boondocks till spring."

Marcus heard that with disquiet, still loath to be isolated while uncertainty—and Ortaias Sphrantzes—reigned in Videssos. But Quintus Glabrio remarked, "If we can't move, odds-on no one else can either." The manifest truth there cheered the tribune, who had been thinking of his men as an entity unto themselves and forgetting that nature laid its hand on all alike—Roman, Videssian, Namdalener, or Yezda.

As requested, Lexos Blemmydes led Scaurus' band southeast toward Amorion. The tribune wanted to reach the town on the Ithome River before the fall rains made travel hopeless. Amorion controlled much of the west central plateau and would give him a base for the trouble he expected come spring—if Thorisin Gavras still lived to brew it.

Gorgidas all but held Nepos prisoner. The priest used his healing art on the legionaries and did his best to teach it to the Greek. But his efforts there were fruitless, which drove Gorgidas to distraction. "In my heart I don't believe I can do it," he moaned, "and so I can't."

Scaurus came to rely on Blemmydes more and more. The guide had an uncanny knowledge of which ways were open. Not only was he intimately familiar with the ground himself, but he also questioned everyone whose path he crossed—the few traders still abroad, village headmen, farmers, and herders. Sometimes the route he chose was roundabout, but it was always safe.

At evening a couple of days later, the Romans reached a place where what had been a single valley split into two. The rivers that carved them were dry now, but Marcus knew the fall downpour would soon make torrents of them.

Blemmydes cocked his head down each gap, as if listening. He paused a long time, longer than any similar decision had taken him before. Scaurus gave him a curious glance, waiting for his choice. "The northern one," he said at last.

Gaius Philippus also noticed the delay and looked a question at the tribune. "He's been right so far," Marcus said. The senior centurion shrugged and sent the Romans down the path Blemmydes had chosen.

Scaurus thought at first the guide had betrayed them. The valley was full of lowing cattle and their herdsmen—Yezda, or so they seemed. Dogs followed their masters' shouted commands, nipping at the cows' heels and driving them up the rocky mountainsides as the herdsmen saw the column of armed men coming toward them.

But the Romans' alarm proved unfounded. The herdsmen were Videssians who had taken Marcus' soldiers for invaders. Once they learned their mistake, they fraternized with the newcomers, though warily. Imperial armies could plunder as ruthlessly as any nomads. But when Scaurus actually paid for some of their beasts, the herders came close to geniality.

"This isn't the sort of thing you want to do too often," Senpat Sviodo remarked, watching money change hands.

"Hmm? Why not?" The tribune was puzzled. "The less we take by force, the better we should get along with the locals."

"True, but some may die from the shock of not being robbed."

Marcus laughed, but Nepos did not approve. The priest had finally managed to get away from Gorgidas for a few minutes and was wandering about watching the Romans run up their camp. He said to Senpat, "It's never good to mock a generous heart. Our outland friend shows here the same kindness he used in giving a disgraced man a chance to redeem himself."

The Vaspurakaner, not usually as cynical as his words suggested, looked contrite. But the last part of what Nepos had said made no sense to Scaurus. "What are you talking about?" he demanded of the priest.

Nepos scratched his head in confusion. He had not had any more chance than the Roman to shave, and the top of his skull was starting to get bristly. He said, "No need for modesty. Surely only a great-souled man would restore to trust and self-respect the soldier he himself ousted from the Imperial Guards."

"What in the world do you—" Marcus began, and then stopped cold, remembering the pair of guardsmen he had had cashiered for sleeping at their posts in front of Mavrikios' private chambers. Sure as sure, this was the elder of the two; Scaurus even recalled hearing his name, now that Nepos had made the association for him.

He also remembered the sullen insolence Blemmydes had shown when called to account and the way the snoozing guardsmen were ignominiously banished from the capital when their effort to shift the blame to him fell through. It was hard to imagine Blemmydes having any good will toward the Romans after that.

Which meant . . . The tribune shouted for a sentry. "Find the guide and bring him to me. He needs to answer some questions." The legionary gave the closed-fist Roman salute and hurried away.

Nepos and Senpat Sviodo were both staring at Scaurus. The priest said, "You weren't taking Lexos on faith, then?"

Pretending not to hear his disappointment, Marcus answered, "On faith? Hardly. The truth is, with everything that's happened in the months since I saw him that once, I forgot the whoreson existed. Why didn't you speak up a week ago?"

Nepos spread his hands regretfully. "I assumed you knew who he was, and thought the better of you for it."

"Splendid," muttered the tribune. He wondered if his lapse would cost the Romans, a worry that abruptly became a certainty when he saw the sentry returning alone. "Well?" he barked, unable to keep from lashing out to hold his own alarm at bay.

"I'm sorry, sir, he doesn't seem to be anywhere about," the legionary reported cautiously—unlike Gaius Philippus, the tribune usually did not take out his feelings on his men.

"That tears it," Marcus said, smacking fist into palm in disgust.

366

"Only a great-souled idiot would take in a man like that." And if Blemmydes was gone, he must have thought he had his vengeance.

Marcus' failure to follow up on his half recognition of the guide filled him with self-contempt. He could look at others' mistakes with the easy tolerance his Stoic background gave him—they were, after all, only men, and perfection could not be expected from them. His own shortcomings, on the other hand, brought a black anger fiercer in some ways than the one he turned against battlefield foes.

With difficulty, he pulled himself free from that useless rage and began thinking what he had to do to set things right. First, plainly, he had to find out what the situation was. "Pakhymer!" he called.

The Khatrisher appeared at his elbow. "I've gotten to know that tone of voice," he said with a lopsided smile. "What's gone wrong now?"

The tribune's answering grin was equally strained. "Maybe nothing at all," he said, not believing it for a minute. "Maybe quite a lot." He quickly sketched what had happened.

Pakhymer heard him out without comment, whistling tunelessly between his teeth. "You think he's buggered us, then?" he said at last.

"I'm afraid so, anyway."

Pakhymer nodded. "Which is why you called me. I really should charge for this, you know." But there was no malice in his words, only the amused mockery with which the Khatrishers so often faced life.

He went on, "All right, I'll send some of the lads out to see what's ahead—aye, and another bunch to track down your dear friend Blemmydes, if they can." Seeing Scaurus wince, he added, "No one can think of everything, not even Phos—if he did, Skotos wouldn't be here."

That thought consoled the tribune but dismayed Nepos; the Khatrishers had a theology as free and easy as themselves. Pakhymer left before Nepos could put his protest into words. The priest was a good man, more tolerant than many of his colleagues, but there were limits his tolerance could not overstep.

Marcus wondered how Balsamon would have reacted to the Khatrisher's remark. Likely, he thought, the patriarch of Videssos would have laughed his head off.

There was nothing to do but wait for the scouts' return. The party sent out in pursuit of Blemmydes came back first, empty-handed. Marcus was not surprised. The terrain was broken enough to give the disgruntled Videssian a hundred hiding places in plain sight of the camp.

The unusual comings and goings set tongues wagging, as Scaurus had known they would. For once, rumor might be an ally: if the men suspected trouble, they would be quicker to meet it. And if what the tribune was beginning to fear came true, speed would count soon.

He saw the Khatrishers come riding back out of the east, slide off their horses, and jog over to Pakhymer with their news, whatever it was. They said not a word to the soldiers who hurled questions at them. The horsemen might not have the Romans' stiff discipline, but they were all right, the tribune decided for the hundredth time.

Their commander's scarred face had no trace of his usual mirth as he came up to the tribune. "As bad as that?" Marcus asked, reading the trouble in his eyes.

"As bad as that," Pakhymer agreed somberly. "The next valley east is crawling with Yezda; from what my boys say, they must have two or three times as many men as we do, the damned cuillions."

"It figures," Scaurus nodded bitterly. "Blemmydes has his revenge, all right—he must have been looking for Yezda all along, and run off when he found a band big enough to sink us."

Pakhymer tried to keep him from falling into despair. "The count's not very fine, you understand—just a short peek over that ridge ahead to reckon up their tents and fires."

"Fires, aye," Marcus said—fires to eat the Romans up. But something else about fire teased at the back of his mind. The sensation was maddening and horribly familiar; he had felt it when he tried without success to remember where he'd seen Lexos Blemmydes. Now he stood stock-still, not forcing whatever it was, but letting it come if it would.

Pakhymer started to say something; seeing Scaurus abstracted, he was sensitive enough to keep silent a little longer.

The tribune drove his fist into his palm for the second time in less than an hour, but now in decision. "The gods be praised I learned to read Greek!" he exclaimed. It had no meaning for Laon Pakhymer, but he saw the Roman was himself again.

He started to leave, but Scaurus stopped him, saying, "I'll need your

368

men again, and soon. They're better herders and drovers than the legionaries ever will be."

"And if they are?" The Khatrisher was mystified.

Marcus started to explain, but Gaius Philippus strode up, demanding, "By Mars' left hairy nut, what's going on? The whole camp is seething like a boiled-over pot, but nobody knows why."

The tribune spelled it out in a few sentences; his second-in-command swore foully. "Never mind all that," Scaurus said. Now that his wits were working again, haste drove him hard. "Get a couple of maniples out there with Pakhymer's men. I want every cow in the valley down here at this end inside an hour's time."

Khatrisher and centurion stared at him, sure he'd lost his mind after all. Then Gaius Philippus doubled over with laughter. "What a wonderful scheme," he got out between wheezes. "And we won't be on the receiving end this time, either."

"You've read Polybius too?" Scaurus said, indignant and amazed at the same time; the senior centurion found written Latin slow going, and Marcus had not thought he could read Greek at all.

"Who? Oh, one of your pet historians, is he? No, not a chance." For once Gaius Philippus' smile had none of the wolf in it. "There's more ways to remember things than books, sir. Every veteran's known that trick since Hannibal used it, and known his head would answer if he fell for it."

"Will the two of you talk sense?" Pakhymer asked irritably, but the Romans, enjoying their common joke, would not enlighten him.

They did explain the scheme to Viridovix; Marcus had thought of a special role he could play, if he would. The Celt whooped when he'd heard them out. "Sure and I'd kill the man you tried to put in my place," he said.

The herdsmen who had praised Scaurus to the skies while the sun still shone cursed his name in the darkness as, without mercy or explanation, their cattle were taken away. They carried spears and knives to protect themselves against tax-collectors and other predators, but were helpless in the face of the legionaries' swords and mail shirts, and the Khatrishers' horses and bows.

Lowing resentfully at the change in their routine, the cattle shambled down the valley, prodded along by their confiscators. Some of the herd dogs, unreasoningly gallant, leaped to their defense, but reversed spearshafts drove them yelping back.

At the camp, Marcus found Gaius Philippus had been right. When he ordered the legionaries still there to chop the stakes of the palisade into arm-long lengths, they grinned knowingly and fell to like so many small boys involved in a mammoth practical joke. Their women and new non-Roman comrades watched with the same caution one gave any group of men suddenly struck mad.

The tribune did not need to give them the next set of orders. As fast as cattle arrived from the west, the Romans tied the newly made sticks to their horns.

"Marcus, if this is meddling I crave your pardon, but what on earth is going on?" Helvis asked.

"Once your brother Soteric said my men had an advantage fighting in this world because we had a bundle of tricks no one here knows," Scaurus answered elliptically. "It's time to see if he was right."

He probably would have given her the full explanation in another minute or two, but a Khatrisher scout brought him bad news: "Whatever you're playing at, it had better work soon. A couple of Yezda just stuck their heads into the valley to see what all the ruckus is about here. I took a shot at them, but in the dark I missed."

Scaurus gave his preparations a last look. Not so many cattle as he would have liked were festooned with sticks, but a good two thousand head were ready. "This is all fascinating," Pakhymer said ironically. "Do you suppose the Yezda will run from a stampeding forest?"

"I doubt it. But they just might, from a forest fire." The tribune took a burning piece of wood from a campfire's edge and walked toward the cattle.

Pakhymer's eyes got round.

"Strike them now, I say!"

"Rest easy, Vahush. They'll be there in the morning." The speaker, a stocky, middle-aged Yezda, pulled a spit from the campfire, and offered the sizzling meat on it to his nephew.

Vahush rejected it with an angry gesture. Hawk-nosed as any Videssian, he had a zealot's narrow face and moved with the barely controlled grace of a beast of prey. "When you find your foe, Prypet, smite him!" he snapped. "So says Avshar, and he speaks truly."

"And so we will," Prypet said placatingly. "It will be easy; if the scouts tell no lies, the imperials are running about like so many madmen. In any case, we outnumber them two to one at least." He waved out into the darkness, where felt tents dotted the valley like toadstools.

The flocks would grow fat in this wide new land, Prypet thought. He pulled at a wine jug, another of the spoils of war. True, he mused, Avshar had won the battle that gave the nomads room to grow, but who had seen him since? In any case, he, Prypet, led the clan, not this wizard whose face no one knew . . . and not his own wife's sister's son, either.

Still, the lad showed promise and should not be squelched. "We've had hard riding, these past weeks. We'll fight better for the night's rest. Sit yourself down and relax. Have some bread." He lifted the chewy, unleavened sheet from the light griddle that served the nomads in place of an oven.

"You listen too much to your belly, uncle," Vahush said, his confidence in his own lightness driving soft words from him—and wrecking any hope of making the older man listen.

Prypet got deliberately to his feet, the mildness gone from his face. Nephew or not, Vahush could go too far. "If you like, boy, you can find a fight closer than the next valley," he said quietly.

Vahush leaned forward. "Any time you—" He blinked. "Avshar's black bow! What's that?"

Beginning in the valley to the west, the low rumble could be felt through the soles of the feet as well as heard. Bass bellows of pain and terror accompanied it. Prypet snorted his contempt. "Get dry behind your ears, whelp. Don't you know cows when you hear them?"

Vahush flushed. "Of course. Skotos, I'm edgy tonight."

His uncle relaxed, seeing the fighting moment was past. "Don't worry about it. Farmers never could handle kine—look at them letting a batch run loose like that. It might not be a bad idea for a few men to saddle up at that, you know, and round up the stragglers as they come through."

"I'll do that," the younger man said. "It'll let me work off my nerves."
He turned toward his horse, then stopped dead, horror on his face.

Prypet looked west, too, and felt ice leap up his back. The thunder
was louder now, pounding its way into the valley where the Yezda took
their ease. Cattle? It was not, it could not be cattle, but the great rever-
beration of a rolling, chopping sea of flame washing toward them at the
speed of a fast man's run. And at the edge of the wave ramped a devil, his
banshee wail loud through the roar. The shifting fire struck scarlet sparks
from the sword he waved above the tide.

The clan leader was a warrior seasoned in countless fights, but this
was magic beyond his courage to face. "Flee for your lives!" he screamed.

Yezda tumbled from their tents, glanced west, and leaped for their
mounts in panic. "Demons! Demons!" they shrieked, and set spur to
their horses without another backward glance. Like an upset mug, the
valley emptied of nomads. The fiery sea rolled over their tents as if they
had never been.

Vahush would have fled with his uncle and his clanmates, but for
long minutes his terror, far worse than Prypet's, held him motionless.
You wanted to attack them, fool, his mind gibbered, when they've found
a wizard who could blow Avshar out like a candle.

Nearer and nearer came the roaring ocean of flame. The young
nomad stared into the shattered darkness, waiting numbly for it to sweep
him away. And then at last it was close enough for him to see the grinning riders driving the cattle on, see the bare burning branches lashed
hastily to horns, smell their smoke and the reek of singed hair and flesh.

Rage exploded in him, freeing spirit and body from panic's grip. He
sprang onto his tethered horse. With a single slash of his saber, he cut the
rope that held it. Now his spurs bit; he darted not away from the tortured
herd but toward it, blade bright in his hands. "Back! Come back! You've
been tricked!" he cried to his escaping comrades, but in the din and distance they did not hear.

Closer by, though, someone did. "Aren't you the noisy one, now?" an
oddly accented voice said. Too late, Vahush remembered the devil-cries
from the head of the stampede. There was a man on a pony in front of
those frenzied cattle. A long straight blade leaped at the nomad's neck.

His last thought as he slid from his horse in death was that the imperials did not fight fair.

Had the Yezda stopped their panic-struck flight and returned to investigate, they likely would have routed the Romans from the valley they had vacated. In the relief their deliverance brought them, Marcus' troops and Pakhymer's danced with their women in whooping circles round the campfires, clapping, stamping, snapping their fingers, and shouting with glee for all the world to hear.

Pakhymer took no part in the celebration, wandering through the camp like a man in a daze. When he found Scaurus reveling with the rest of his men, he pulled the tribune out of his circle, earning him a glare from Helvis as the dance whirled her away. The tribune was ready to be angry, too, until he saw the lost look in the Khatrisher's eyes.

"Cattle," Pakhymer said blankly. "Plainsmen who spend their lives with cattle, heathens who kill for the sport of it, running like frightened children from a harmless herd of cows." He thumped his forehead with the heel of his hand, as if trying to drive belief into it.

Marcus, who had taken on a good deal of wine, had no better answer for him than a shrug and a wide, foolish grin. But Gorgidas was close enough to hear Pakhymer's comment and sober enough to try to deal with it. He had kept the Greek habit of watering his wine and, moreover, found the pursuit of understanding a sweeter fruit than any that grew on a vine.

"We may have driven cattle against the Yezda," he said to the Khatrisher, "but do you think it was cattle the nomads saw, charging out of the night aflame? Would you, in this magic-steeped land? If you expect to find sorcery, you will—whether it's there or not."

His mouth quirked upward in something that was not a smile.

"Belief is all, you know. When I studied medicine I was trained to hate magic and everything it stood for. Now I've found a magic that truly heals, and it will not serve me."

"Perhaps you should serve it, instead," Pakhymer said slowly.

"Does everyone here talk like a priest?" Gorgidas snarled, but his eyes were thoughtful.

"Sure and they don't." Viridovix caught only what was said, not its overtones. He looked most unpriestly, with each arm encircling a girl's waist.

Marcus could not for the life of him remember which two of his three they were. For one thing, the tall Celt mostly called them "dear" or "darling," a part of his speech pattern that served him well, lessening the chance of an embarrassing slip. For another, while all three were of dainty, flowerlike beauty, none had enough character to leave much other impression on the mind.

Viridovix suddenly noticed Scaurus standing with the Greek doctor and Laon Pakhymer. He loosed his hold on the girls to fold the tribune into a bear hug; Marcus smelled the wine fumes clinging to him even through his own drunkenness.

The Gaul held him at arm's length for a moment, studying him with owlish intensity. Then he turned to Gorgidas, declaring, "Will you look at him now, standing there so quiet and all after the greatest joke any of us ever saw, the which saved all our necks besides. And here I am a hero for sitting on some smelly horse's back and scaring those poor omad-hauns all to bits, and where's the glory for the fellow who thought to put me there in the first place?"

"You deserve it," Marcus protested. "What if the Yezda had decided to ride toward you instead of away? One did, you know."

"Och, that puir fool?" Viridovix gave a snort of scorn. "A week and a half it seemed he gawped at me. It's probably only when he pissed himself that he woke up. Who would have thought I'd make a horseman?"

"Cowman might be better, thinking of the herd," Laon Pakhymer said with a sidelong glance.

"Hmm. That's hardly a name for a man." But the Gaul's eyes were twinkling. "If you'd called me bullman, now, you might be closer to the truth. Isn't that right, loves?" he said, leading the girls back toward the tent they shared. Their bodies swayed toward his in mute agreement with the boast.

Pakhymer gave Viridovix' back a frankly jealous look. "What does he *do* with them all?" he wondered aloud.

"Ask him," Gorgidas suggested. "He'll tell you. Whatever else he may be, our Celtic friend is not shy."

Pakhymer watched three bodies briefly silhouetted by lanternlight as Viridovix pulled back his tent flap. "No," he sighed, "I don't suppose he is."

Next morning, Marcus thought for a bleary moment the noise of raindrops muttering on the sides of his tent was his pulse hammering in his ears. Pain throbbed dully through his head; the taste of sewers was in his mouth. When he sat up too quickly, his stomach yelped, and his surroundings gave a queasy lurch.

His motion woke Helvis, who yawned, stretched lithely, and smiled up at him from the sleeping mat. "Good morning, love," she said, reaching out to touch his arm. "How are you?"

Even her smooth contralto grated. "Bloody awful," the tribune croaked, holding his head in his hands. "Does Nepos know how to heal a hangover, do you think?" He belched uncomfortably.

"If there were a cure for nausea, I promise you pregnant women would know it. We can be sick together," she said, mischief in her voice. But then, seeing Scaurus' real misery, she added, "I'll do my best to keep Malric quiet." The boy was stirring under his blanket.

"Thanks," Marcus said, and meant it. A rambunctious three-year-old, he decided, could be the death of him at the moment.

The downpour meant no cooking fires; the Romans breakfasted on cold porridge, cold beef, and soggy bread. The tribune ignored his soldiers' grumbles. The thought of food, any food, did not appeal.

He heard Gaius Philippus squelching his way from one group of men to the next, instructing them, "Don't forget, grease your armor, leather and metal both. Easier that than grinding out the rust and patching over the rotted hide just because you were too lazy to do what needed doing. And oil your weapons, too, though the gods help you if you need me to tell you that."

With Lexos Blemmydes vanished, there were no guides to show Scaurus' force the way to Amorion. Save for the Romans, the valley the invaders had held was empty of humanity. The angry herders whose cattle had served to rout the Yezda hid in the hills, unwilling to help the men who, from their viewpoint, first befriended and then betrayed them.

Much later than was pleasing to Marcus' senior centurion, the army finally began slogging southeast. The sky remained a sullen, leaden gray; hour after hour the rain kept falling, now in little spatters of drizzle, now in nearly opaque sheets driven by a wind with the early bite of winter in it.

There was no way to steer a steady course in those dreadful conditions. Drenched and miserable, the legionaries and their companions struggled through a series of crisscrossing little canyons more bewildering than Minos' labyrinth. They trudged glumly on, trusting in dead reckoning.

The storm blew itself out toward evening; through tattered clouds, the sun gave an apologetic peep at the world. And when it did, some soldiers fearfully exclaimed it was setting in the east, for it shone straight into their faces.

Listening to the men, Quintus Glabrio shook his head in resignation. "Isn't that the way of the world? They'd sooner turn the heavens topsy-turvy than face up to our own blundering."

"You spend too cursed much time hanging round Gorgidas," Gaius Philippus said. "You're starting to sound like him." Scaurus had the same impression, though, thinking back on it, he did not remember seeing the junior centurion and the physician together very often.

"Worse things have happened," Glabrio chuckled. Gaius Philippus was content to let it rest. If there were things he did not understand in the younger officer, he approved of enough to tolerate the rest.

Marcus was glad the chaffing went no further than it did. His hangover was gone at last, but he had not eaten all day and felt lightheaded. A real quarrel would have been more than he was up to dealing with.

Only bits of scudding gray showed the storm's passage when dawn came again—those, and the red-brown clinging mud that tried to suck sandals from feet. It was, Marcus thought with disquiet, almost the color of Yezd's banners. He was strangely pleased to see tiny green shoots thrusting up through it, fooled into thinking it was spring.

Gaius Philippus barked harsh laughter when he said that aloud. "They'll find out soon enough how wrong they are." He sniffed at the brisk northern breeze, weather-wise from a lifetime lived in the open. "Snow's coming before long."

376

Quite by accident, for they were still guideless, they came upon a town early that afternoon. Aptos, it was called, and held perhaps five thousand souls. Peaceful, unwalled, unknown to the Yezda, it nearly brought tears to the tribune. To him, towns like this were Videssos' greatest achievement, places where generation on generation lived in peace, never fearing that the next day might bring invaders to rape away in hours the fruit of years of labor. Such bypassed tranquil islands were already rare in the westlands; soon, too soon, none would be left.

Monks pulling weeds from the rain-softened soil of their vegetable gardens looked up in amazement as the battered mercenary company tramped past. True to the disciplined kindness of their vocation, they hurried into the monastery storehouses, returning with fresh-baked bread and pitchers of wine. They stood by the side of the road, offering the refreshments to any who cared to stop for a moment.

Scaurus had mixed feelings about the Videssian clergy. When humane, as these monks seemed to be, they were among the best of men: he thought of Nepos and the patriarch Balsamon. But their zeal could make them frighteningly, violently xenophobic; the tribune remembered the anti-Namdalener riots in Videssos the city and the pogrom the priest Zemarkhos had wanted to incite against the Vaspurakaners of Amorion. His mouth tightened at that—Zemarkhos was still there.

The gilded sun-globes atop the monastery's spires disappeared behind the Romans. As they marched through Aptos itself, a shouting horde of small boys surrounded them, dancing with excitement and firing questions like arrows: Was it true the Yezda were nine feet tall? Were the streets in Videssos paved with pearls? Wasn't a soldier's life the most glorious one in the world?

The boy who asked that last question was a beautiful child of about twelve; flushed with the first dreams of manhood, he looked ready, nay, eager to run off with the army. "Don't you believe it for a minute, son," Gaius Philippus said, speaking with an earnestness Marcus had rarely heard him use. "Soldiering's a trade like any other, a bit dirtier than most, maybe. Go at it for the glory and you'll die too damned young."

The boy stared in disbelief, as if hearing one of the monks curse Phos. His face crumpled. Tears come hard at twelve, and scald when they fall.

"Why are you after doing that to the lad?" Viridovix demanded. "Sure and there's no harm in feeding his dreams a mite."

"Isn't there?" The centurion's voice was like a slamming door. "My younger brother thought that way. He's thirty years dead now." He looked stonily at the Celt, daring him to take it further. Viridovix reddened and kept still.

Despite the peregrinations of the day before, Scaurus learned Amorion was only about four days' march southeast. Aptos' adults pointed the way, though no one seemed eager to lead the Romans there. Still, as one plump fellow declared with the optimism of rustics everywhere, "You can't miss it."

"Maybe not, but watch us try," Gaius Philippus muttered to himself. Marcus was inclined to agree with him. All too often a landmark was a landmark because a local saw it every day of his life. To a stranger, it was just another tree or hill or barn.

Worse, the rain returned at dawn the next day, not with the vicious onslaught it had shown before, but a steady downpour riding the seawind south. The road to Amorion, in bad shape already, soon became next to impossible. Wagons and traveling cars bogged down, axle-deep in greasy mud. Straining to push forward nonetheless, two horses in quick succession snapped legbones and had to be destroyed. The soldiers worked with their beasts to move the wains on, but progress was minute. The four days' journey promised in Aptos seemed a cruel mockery.

"I feel like a drowned cat," Gorgidas complained. Dapper by choice, the Greek was sadly disheveled now. His hair, its curl killed by hours of rain, splashed down onto his forehead and kept wandering into his eyes; his soaked mantle clung to him, more like a parasite than a garment. He was spattered with muck.

In short, he looked no different from any of his companions in wretchedness. Viridovix said so, loudly and profanely, perhaps hoping to jar him out of his misery and into a good soul-stirring fight. There was more subtlety to the Gaul than met the eye; Scaurus recalled his using that ploy before and succeeding.

But today the doctor would not rise to the bait. He squelched away in glum silence, a person from a sunny land hard-pressed to deal with foul

378

weather. Viridovix, to whom rain was an everyday likelihood, was better prepared to cope with it.

The storm closed down visibility and pattered insistently off every horizontal surface. Thus the Romans, intent on their own concerns, were not aware of the newcomers until they loomed out of the watery curtain ahead.

Marcus' sword was in his hand before he consciously wished it there. His men bristled like angry dogs, leaping back from their labors and likewise reaching for weapons. Gaius Philippus' chest swelled as he gulped the air he'd need to shout them into battle formation.

Before the centurion could give the order, Senpat Sviodo cried out in his own language and splashed forward to clasp the hand of the leading horseman ahead. "Bagratouni!" he exclaimed.

With the naming of that name, the fear fell from Scaurus' eyes, and he saw the newly come riders as they were: not a Yezda horde bursting out of the mist, but a battered squadron of Vaspurakaners, as much refugees as the Romans.

Gagik Bagratouni almost jerked his hand from Sviodo's in startlement. Like Marcus, the *nakharar* had seen what he thought he would see and was about to cry his men forward in a last doomed, desperate charge. Eyes wide, he, too, reconsidered. "It is the Romans, our friends!" he shouted to his forlorn command. Weary, beaten faces answered with uncertain smiles, as if remembering a word long unused.

As the tribune moved up to greet Bagratouni, he was shocked to see how the *nakharar* had shrunken in on himself since the battle before Maragha. His skin was looser over the strong bones of his face; dark circles puffed below his eyes. His nose seemed an old man's beak, not the symbol of strength it had been.

Worst of all, the almost tangible power and presence once his had slipped from his shoulders, leaving him more naked than a mere loss of clothes ever could have.

He dismounted stiffly; his second-in-command, Mesrop Anhoghin, was there to steady him. From the look of mute misery the lanky, thick-bearded aide wore, Scaurus grew sure his imagination was not tricking him. "Greetings," Anhoghin said—thereby, Marcus knew, exhausting most of his Videssian.

379

"Greetings," the Roman nodded. Senpat came to his side, ready to interpret for him. But Scaurus spoke directly to Gagik Bagratouni, who used the imperial tongue fluently, albeit with heavy accent. He asked, "Are the Yezda between here and Amorion too thick to stop us pushing on?"

"Amorion?" the *nakharar* repeated dully. "How do you know we to Amorion have been?"

"For one thing, by the direction you came from. For another, well—" Scaurus waved at the ragged group before him. Most of Gagik Bagratouni's men were Vaspurakaners driven from their native land by the Yezda who settled in or near Amorion with their women. They had left those women behind when they took the Emperor's service, but some were here now, looking as worn and beaten as the men they rode with.

Some were here now . . . but where was Bagratouni's wife, the fat, easygoing lady Marcus had met in the *nakharar*'s fortresslike home? "Gagik," he asked, alarm leaping in him, "is Zabel—?" He stopped, not knowing how he should continue.

"Zabel?" It might have been a stranger's name, the way Bagratouni said it. "Zabel is dead," he said slowly, and then began to weep, his shoulders shaking helplessly, his tears washed away by the uncaring rain.

The sight of the stalwart noble broken and despairing was somehow more terrible than most of the concrete setbacks the Romans had encountered. "Take care of him, can't you?" Scaurus whispered to Gorgidas.

The compassion in the doctor's eyes was replaced by a spark of exasperation. "You always want me to work miracles, not medicine." But he was already moving toward Bagratouni, murmuring, "Come with me, sir. I'll give you something that will let you sleep." In Greek he told Scaurus, "I'll give him something to knock him out for two days straight. That may help a little."

The *nakharar* let himself be led away, indifferent to what fate held for him. Marcus, who could not afford indifference, began questioning the rest of the Vaspurakaners through Senpat Sviodo to learn what had happened to them to bring their leader to such a state.

The answer was the one he'd feared. He knew Bagratouni's men had got free of the fatal field before Maragha; their furious despair at Videssos' failure to free their homeland helped them beat back the Yezda time and again. The younger men and bachelors scattered to Vaspurakan's mountains to carry on the fight; the rest bypassed Khliat and marched straight for their families in Amorion.

After the rigors of the battlefield and a forced march through western Videssos' ravaged countryside, what they found there was the cruelest irony of all. Videssians had fought at their side against the nomads, but in Amorion other Videssians, using the Vaspurakaners' heterodoxy as their pretext, turned on them more viciously than ever the Yezda had.

With sickening certainty, the tribune knew what was coming next: Zemarkhos had headed the pogrom. Marcus remembered the lean cleric's burning, fanatical gaze, his automatic hatred of anyone who did not conform precisely to his conception of how his god should be revered. And he remembered how he himself had stopped Gagik Bagratouni just short of doing away with Zemarkhos when the priest taunted the Vaspurakaners by naming his dog for Vaspur, the prince they claimed as their first ancestor. And the result of his magnanimity? A cry of "Death to the heretics!" and revenge exacted from the absent warriors' defenseless kin.

The mob's fury blazed so high it even dared stand against Bagratouni's men on their return. In street fighting, ferocity carried almost as much weight as discipline, and the Vaspurakaners were already worn down to shadows of themselves. It was all they could do to rescue their surviving loved ones; for most, that rescue came far too late.

Mesrop Anhoghin, his face expressionless, gave the story out flatly, pausing every few seconds to let Senpat translate. Finally that impassivity was more than Scaurus could bear. He was drowning in shame and guilt. "How can you stand to look at me, much less speak this way?" he said, covering his face with his hands. "Were it not for me, none of this might have happened!"

His cry was in Videssian, but Anhoghin could understand the anguish in his voice without an interpreter. He stumped forward to look the tribune in the face; tall for a Vaspurakaner, his eyes were almost level with Scaurus'. "We are Phos' firstborn," he said through Senpat Sviodo. "It is only just that he tests us more harshly than ordinary men."

"That is no answer!" the tribune moaned. Without strong religious beliefs of his own, he could not comprehend the strength they lent others.

Anhoghin seemed to sense that. He said, "Perhaps it is not, for you. Think of this, then: when you asked my lord to spare Zemarkhos, it was not from love, but to keep him from being a martyr and a rallying cry for zealots. You did not—you could not—force him to spare the swine. That he did himself, for reasons he found good, no matter where they came from. And who knows? Things might have been worse the other way."

It was not forgiveness Anhoghin offered; it was better, for he said none was needed. Scaurus stood silent for a long, grateful moment, ankle-deep in doughy mud, suddenly not minding the raindrops splashing against his face. "Thank you," he whispered at last.

Fury blazed in him that the Vaspurakaners, sober, decent folk who asked no more from the world than that it leave them at peace, could find it neither in their conquered homeland nor in the refuge-place round Amorion. About the first he could do nothing; that had proved beyond all the Empire's power.

As for the other . . . The wolfish eagerness in his own voice surprised him as he asked Anhoghin, "Shall we avenge you?" The heat of the moment swept away weeks of careful calculation.

Senpat Sviodo instantly shouted, "Aye!" The headstrong young Vaspurakaner could be counted on to press for any plan that called for action.

But when he translated for Mesrop Anhoghin, Bagratouni's aide shook his head. "What purpose would it serve? Those of us who could escape have, and the dead care not for vengeance. This land has war enough without stirring up more; the Yezda would laugh to see us fight among ourselves."

Scaurus opened his mouth to protest, slowly closed it again. Were the occasion different, he might have laughed to hear arguments he had so long upheld come back at him from another. But Anhoghin, standing there in the muck with rain dripping through his matted beard and only exhaustion and defeat in his eyes, was not an object of mirth.

The tribune's shoulders slumped inside his mail shirt. "Damn you for being right," he said tiredly, and saw disappointment flower on Sviodo's mobile features. "If the way forward is closed, we'd best go back to Aptos." Turning to give the necessary orders, he felt old for the first time in his life.

III

The hill town northwest of Amorion was not a bad choice for winter quarters; Scaurus soon saw the truth of that. Where the Romans would have had to storm Amorion, Aptos welcomed them. Not a Yezda had been seen in its secluded valley, but the cold wind of rumor said they were about—a friendly garrison was suddenly desirable.

More than rumor told the townsfolk of the disaster the Empire had met. The local noble, a minor magnate named Skyros Phorkos, had levied a platoon of farmers to fight the Yezda with Mavrikios. None had yet returned; only now were friends and kin beginning to realize none ever would.

Phorkos' son and heir was a boy of eleven; the noble's widow Nerse had picked up the authority he left behind. A woman of stern beauty, she viewed the world with coldly realistic eyes. When the Romans and their comrades struggled back into Aptos, she received them like a ruling princess, to the edification of the few townsmen who braved the rain to watch.

The dinner to which she invited Scaurus and his officers was equally formal. If the Romans noticed the large number of guards protecting Phorkos' estate, they made no mention of it—no more than did Nerse, at the double squad of legionaries escorting the tribune's party thither.

Perhaps as a result of those shared silences, the dinner—a roast goat cooked with onions and cloves, boiled beans and cabbage, fresh-baked bread with wild honey, and candied fruits—went smoothly enough. Wine flowed freely, though Marcus, noticing his hostess' moderation—and recalling too well the morning after his last carouse—did not drink deep.

When her servants had taken the last scrap-laden platter from the dining hall, Nerse grew businesslike. "We are glad you are here," she said abruptly. "We will be gladder yet when we see you intend to treat us as a flock to be protected, not as victims to be despoiled."

"Keep us supplied with bread and with fodder for our beasts, and we'll pay for whatever else we take," Marcus returned. "My troops are no plunderers."

Nerse considered. "Less than I hoped for; more than I expected—fair enough. Can you live up to it?"

"What would my promises mean? The only test will be how we behave; you'll have to judge that." Marcus liked the way she put Aptos' case without pleading. He liked, too, the straightforward way she dealt with him. She did not try to use her femininity as a tool, but treated the Roman as an equal and plainly expected the same from him.

He waited for the tiny threat that was the sole pressure she could bring to bear: that Aptos' inhabitants would only cooperate with his men to the extent they were well treated. Instead, she turned the conversation to less important things. Before long she rose, nodded graciously, and escorted her guests to the door.

Gaius Philippus had been almost silent during the dinner. His presence, like that of Scaurus' other companions, was more ceremonial than it was necessary. Once outside, though, he paused only to draw his cloak round himself against the rain before declaring, "There is a woman!"

He spoke so enthusiastically Marcus raised a quizzical eyebrow. He had trouble imagining the senior centurion as anything but a misogynist.

"Cold as a netted carp she'd be between the sheets, from the look of her," Viridovix guessed, automatically ready to disagree with the veteran.

"Not if properly thawed," Laon Pakhymer demurred. As soldiers will, they argued it all the way back to the soggy Roman camp.

The tribune was inside it before he realized that Nerse's threat had in fact been made. It was merely that she had not crudely put it into words, but let him make it himself in his own mind. He wondered if she knew the Videssian board game that, unlike its Roman counterparts, depended only on a player's skill. If so, he decided, he did not want to play against her.

Wintering at Aptos, Marcus thought, was like crawling into a hole and then pulling it in after himself. He and his men had been at the center of events since spring; he had hobnobbed with Videssos' imperial family, sparred with the chief minister of the Empire, made a personal foe of the wizard-prince who led its foes, fought in a great battle that would change Videssos' course for years to come . . . and here he was in a country town, wondering if its store of barley meal would hold out until spring. It was deflating, but gave him back a sense of proportion he had been in danger of losing.

Aptos was lonely enough at the best of times. News of the disaster before Maragha had reached it, aye; the distant kingdoms of Thatagush and Agder would know of that by now. But the Romans brought word of Ortaias Sphrantzes' assumption of the throne, and Aptos had been equally ignorant of the persecution of the Vaspurakaners not five days' march away.

The tribune was unwilling to leave some news to chance. He talked with Laon Pakhymer outside his tent one morning not long after rain turned to snow. "I'd like to send a couple of your riders west," he said.

"West, eh?" The Khatrisher raised an eyebrow. "Want to find out what's become of the younger Gavras, do you?"

"Yes. If all we have is a choice between Yezd and Ortaias, well, suddenly the life of a robber chief looks better than it had."

"I know what you mean. I'll get the lads for you." Pakhymer clicked his tongue between his teeth. "Hate to send them out with so little hope of making it back, but what can you do?"

"Making it back from where?" Senpat Sviodo's breath puffed out in a steaming cloud as he asked the question—he was just done with practice at swords and still breathing hard.

When Marcus explained, the handsome young Vaspurakaner threw his hands in the air. "This is foolishness! Would you throw birds in a river when you have fish handy? Who better to go to Vaspurakan than a pair of 'princes'? Nevrat and I will leave within the hour."

"The Khatrishers will be able to get in and out faster than you could.

They have the nomad way of traveling light," Marcus said. Beside him, Pakhymer nodded reluctantly.

But Senpat laughed. "They'll be able to get killed faster, you mean, likely mistaken for Yezda. Nevrat and I are of the country and will be welcome wherever our people live. We've gone in before and come back whole. We can again."

He sounded so certain that Scaurus looked a question at Pakhymer. The Khatrisher said, "Let him go, if he wants to so badly. But he should leave Nevrat behind—the woman is too well favored to waste so."

"You're right," Senpat said, which surprised the tribune until he went on, "I tell her so myself. But she will not have us separated, and who am I to complain of that?" He turned serious. "She can care for herself, you know."

After her long journey west from Khliat, Marcus could not argue that. "Go, then," he said, giving up. "Make the best time you can."

"That we will," Senpat promised. "Of course, we may do a little hunting along the way." Hunting Yezda, Marcus knew he meant. He wanted to forbid it, but knew better than to give an order he could not enforce. The Vaspurakaners owed Yezd even more than Videssos did.

The tribune had his own troubles settling into semi-permanent quarters. Campaign and crisis had let him pay Helvis and Malric only as much attention as he wanted, something suddenly no longer true.

And, under settled conditions, Helvis did not always prove easy to live with. Marcus, a lifelong bachelor before this attachment, was used to keeping his thoughts to himself until the time came to act on them. Helvis' past, on the other hand, made her expect confidences from him, and she was hurt whenever he did something that affected them both without consulting her first. He realized her complaints held justice and did his best to reform, but his habits were no easier to break than hers.

The irritations did not run in one direction alone. As her pregnancy progressed, Helvis grew even more prayerful. Every day, it seemed, a new icon of Phos or some saint appeared on the walls of the cabin she and Scaurus shared. By itself, that would have been only a minor nuisance to the tribune. Not religious himself, he was willing to tolerate—that is, to ignore as much as possible—others' practices.

In this theology-mad land, that was not enough. Like the rest of the Namdaleni, Helvis added a phrase to the creed Videssos followed; for the sake of half a dozen words, the two lands' folk reckoned each other heretics. As the lone supporter of her version of the true faith for many miles, she naturally sought Marcus' support. But to give it took more hypocrisy than was in him.

"I have no quarrel with what you believe," he said, "but I would be lying if I said I shared it. Does Phos need worshippers so badly he would not resent a false one?"

She had to answer, "No." There the matter rested. Scaurus hoped it was settled, not merely dormant.

If he and Helvis had difficulties, they managed to keep them below the level of conflagration. Others were not so lucky. One grayish-yellow morning when the fall rain had turned to sleet but not yet to snow, the tribune was rudely awakened by the crash of a pot against a wall, followed at once by a shrill volley of curses.

He pulled the thick wool blankets over his ears to muffle the fighting, but when a second pot followed the first to smithereens, he knew it was in vain. He rolled over onto one side and saw without surprise that Helvis was awake, too.

"They're at it again," he said unnecessarily, and added, "This is the first time I've ever resented having my officers' quarters close to mine."

"Shh," Helvis said. "I want to listen."

Asking him for quiet was hardly needful either; when provoked, Damaris' voice had a carry to it that any professional herald would have envied. " 'Turn on your stomach'!" she was shouting. " 'Turn on your stomach'! I've rolled over for the last time for you, I can tell you that! Find yourself a boy, or a cow, or whatever suits your fancy, but you'll not use me that way again!"

The door to Quintus Glabrio's cabin slammed with tooth-rattling fury. Scaurus heard Damaris splash away, still screaming imprecations. "Even when I got you to put me on my back, you were no damned good!" she cried from some distance. Then, mercifully, the wind's voice at last covered hers.

"Oh, dear," the tribune said, his ears feeling red-hot.

Unexpectedly, Helvis broke into giggles. "What's funny?" Marcus demanded, wondering how Glabrio was going to be able to hold his head up in front of his men again.

The harshness in his voice reached her. "I'm sorry," she said. "It's just one of those silly things you think of. You don't understand women's gossip, Marcus; we've done nothing but wonder why Damaris never got pregnant. Now I guess we know."

That had never occurred to Scaurus. He felt a chuckle of his own rising unbidden, sternly suppressed it. But even as he did, he wondered again how many Romans were sniggering at the junior centurion.

At breakfast Glabrio moved in the center of a circle of silence. No one was quite able to pretend he had not heard Damaris, but no one had the nerve to mention her to him.

He drilled his maniple with grim intensity. Usually he was patient with the Videssians struggling to learn Roman ways of fighting, but not today. And he pushed himself even harder than his legionaries, not wanting to give them any opening to mock him.

But every group of men has its wit, a fellow who takes pleasure in amusing many at the expense of one. Marcus was not far away when one of Glabrio's soldiers, in response to an order the tribune did not hear, stuck out his backside with deliberate impertinence.

Already tight-lipped, the junior centurion went dead pale. Scaurus hurried forward to deal with the insolent Roman, but there was no need. Quintus Glabrio, his face empty of all expression, broke his vine-stave—a centurion's staff of office—over the soldier's head. The man dropped without a sound into the mud.

Glabrio waited until he moaned and shakily tried to sit. The young officer tossed the two pieces of his staff into the legionary's lap. "Fetch me a whole one, Lucilius," he snapped, and waited over him until he staggered to his feet and did as ordered.

Seeing Marcus approach, the junior centurion stiffened to attention. "I'm more than capable of handling these things myself, sir. No need to involve yourself."

"So I see," Scaurus nodded. He dropped his voice until Glabrio alone could hear. "It does no harm for me to remind the men you're an officer, not a figure of fun. What happened to you could as easily have befallen one of them."

"Could it? I wonder," Glabrio murmured, as much to himself as to the tribune. His manner grew brisk once more. "Well, in any case I don't think I'll have any more trouble from the ranks. Now if you'll forgive me—" He turned back to his troops. "I hope you enjoyed the rest you got, for you'll need it. And—one—!"

There was no further trouble from the maniple. Nonetheless, Scaurus was not happy. Quietly but unmistakably, Glabrio had made any further conversation unwelcome. Ah, well, the tribune thought, that one usually has more on his mind than he shows. He stood watching for another couple of minutes, but the junior centurion had everything well in hand. The tribune shrugged, shivered in the cold wind, and found something else to do.

That afternoon Gorgidas sought him out. The Greek was diffident, something so far out of character that Marcus suspected he was about to announce a major calamity. But what he had to say was simple enough: the cabin Glabrio and Damaris had been sharing was, in the junior centurion's opinion, too big for one man by himself, and he had invited Gorgidas to share it with him.

Scaurus understood the doctor's hesitation. Everyone with more sensitivity than crude Lucilius had trouble speaking straight out about Glabrio's misfortune. Still—"No reason to come at me as if you thought I was going to bite," he said. "I think that's all to the good. Better for him to have someone to talk to than sit by himself and brood. From the way you went about it, I thought you were going to tell me the plague had broken out."

"I only wanted to make sure there would be no problems."

"None I can think of. Why should there be?" The tribune decided Gorgidas' continuing failure with Nepos' healing magic was making him imagine difficulties everywhere. "It might do you both good," he said.

"I," Nepos announced, "need a stoup of wine." He and Marcus were walking down Aptos' main street. Snow crunched under their boots.

"Good idea. Hot mulled wine, by choice," the tribune said. He rubbed the tip of his nose, which was starting to freeze. Like his men, he wore Videssian-style baggy woolen trousers and was glad to have them. Winter in the westlands was not weather for the toga.

Of Aptos' half a dozen taverns, the Dancing Wolf was the best. Its proprietor, Tatikios Tornikes, enjoyed his work immensely; he was stout enough to make Nepos seem underfed beside him. "Good day to you, gentlemen," he called with a smile when priest and Roman entered.

"And to you, Tatikios," Marcus replied, wiping his feet on the rushes strewn inside the doorway. Tornikes beamed at him—the taverner was a stickler for cleanliness.

Scaurus liked the Dancing Wolf and its owner. So did most of his men. The only complaint he'd heard came from Viridovix: "May his upper lip go bald."

The Celt had reason for envy. Going against usual Videssian fashion, Tatikios shaved his chin, but his mustachios more than made up for it. Coal-black as his hair, they swept out and up; the taverner waxed them into spiked perfection every day.

The tribune and Nepos, glad of the roaring fire Tatikios had going, sat down at a table next to it. A serving girl moved out from behind the bar to ask what they cared for.

Staring into the flames, Marcus hardly noticed her come up. His head jerked around as he recognized her voice. Someone had told him Damaris was working at the Dancing Wolf, he realized, but this was the first time he'd seen her here.

He frowned a little; for his money, Quintus Glabrio was well rid of the hellcat. Today, though, he felt too good to be petty. "Mulled wine, nice and hot," he said. Nepos echoed him.

His nose twitched at the spicy scent. The handleless yellow cup stung his hands as he picked it up. The Dancing Wolf did things right. "Ahhh," he said, savoring the hot cinnamon bite on his tongue. The wine slid down his throat, smooth as honey.

"That calls for another," he said when the cup was empty, and Nepos nodded. Now that they were warmed inside and out, they could savor the second round at leisure. He waved for Damaris.

While she heated the wine, Tatikios wandered over to their table.

"What's the news?" he asked. Like every taverner, he liked to be on top of things. Unlike some, he did not try to hide it.

"Precious little, and I wish I had more," the tribune answered.

Tornikes laughed. "I wish I did, too. Things get slow, once winter sets in." He went back behind the bar, ran a rag over its already gleaming surface.

"I wasn't joking, you know," Marcus said to Nepos. "I wish Senpat and Nevrat would get back with word of Thorisin Gavras, whether good or ill. Not knowing where we stand is hard to bear."

"Oh, indeed, indeed. But friend Tatikios was perhaps lighter than he knew—everything moves slowly in the snow, the Vaspurakaners no less than other men."

"Less than the nomads," Scaurus retorted. He shook his head, smiled wryly. "I worry too much, I know. Likely the two of them are holed up in some distant cousin's keep, making love in front of a fire just like this one."

"A pleasant enough way to pass the time," Nepos chuckled. Like all Videssian priests, he was celibate, but he did not begrudge others the pleasures of the flesh.

"It's not what I sent them out for," Marcus said, a little stiffly.

Carrying an enameled tray in one hand, Damaris took two steaming cups from it and set them down. "Why should you fuss over a man lying with a woman?" she said to Scaurus. "You're used to worse than that."

The tribune paused with the hot cup halfway to his mouth. His right eyebrow arched toward his hairline. "What might that mean?"

"Surely you don't need me to draw you pretty pictures," she said. The undertone in her voice sent a chill through him, crackling flames and warm wine notwithstanding.

Malice leaped into her eyes as she saw his confusion. "A man who uses a woman as he would a boy would sooner have a boy . . . or be one." Wine slopped in Marcus' cup as he grasped her meaning. She drove the knife home: "I hear my sweet Quintus has taken no new lover these past weeks—or has he?" Her laugh was vicious.

The tribune looked Damaris in the eye. The vindictive smile froze on her face. "How long have you been putting this filth about?" he asked. His voice might have been one of the winter winds gusting outside.

"Filth? This is true, it is—" As it had so often in arguments with Quintus Glabrio, her voice began to rise. Heads all round the tavern turned toward her.

But Scaurus was not Glabrio. He cut in: "If the slime you wallow in spreads widely, it will be the worse for you. Do you understand?" The quiet, evenly spaced words reached her when a shouted threat might have been ignored. She nodded, a quick, frightened movement.

"Good enough," the tribune said. He finished his wine at leisure and held up his end of the conversation with Nepos. When they were both done, he pulled coppers from his belt-pouch, tossed them on the table, and strode out, Nepos at his side.

"That was well done," the priest said as they walked back toward the Roman camp. "No rancor matches a former lover's."

"Too true," Marcus agreed. A sudden, biting breeze blew snow into his face. "Damn, it's cold," he said, and pulled his cape up over his mouth and nose. He was not sorry for the excuse to keep still.

Once inside the ramparts of the camp, he separated from Nepos to attend to some business or other. He did not remember what it was five minutes later; he had other things on his mind.

He feared Damaris was not simply letting her spite run free, but had truth behind her slurs. Frightening her into silence was easier than quieting his own mind afterward. The charge she hissed out fit only too well with too much else he had noticed without thinking about.

The whole camp knew—thanks to Damaris and that shrill screech of hers—more about Glabrio's choice of pleasures than was anyone's business. In itself that might mean anything or nothing. But the junior centurion was sharing quarters with Gorgidas now, and the physician, as far as Scaurus knew, had no use for women. Recalling how nervous Gorgidas had seemed when he said he and Glabrio were joining forces, Marcus suddenly saw a new reason for the doctor's hesitancy.

The tribune's hands curled into fists. Of all his men, why these two, two of the ablest and sharpest, and two of his closest friends as well? He thought of the *fustuarium*, the Roman army's punishment for those who, in their full manhood, bedded other men.

He had seen a *fustuarium* once in Gaul, on that occasion for an inveterate thief. The culprit was dragged into the center of camp and tapped with an officer's staff. After that he was fair game; his comrades fell on him with clubs, stones, and fists. If lucky, condemned men died at once.

Marcus visualized Gorgidas and Quintus Glabrio suffering such a fate and flinched away in horror from his vision. Easiest, of course, would be to forget what he had heard from Damaris and trust her fear of him to keep her quiet. Or so he thought, until he tried to dismiss her words. The more he tried to shove them away, the louder they echoed, distracting him, putting a raw edge to everything around him. He barked at Gaius Philippus for nothing, swatted Malric when he would not stop singing the same song over and over. The tears which followed did nothing to sweeten Scaurus' disposition.

While Helvis comforted her son and looked angrily at the tribune, he snatched up a heavy cloak and went out into the night, muttering, "There are some things I have to deal with." He closed the door on her beginning protest.

Stars snapped in the blue-black winter sky. Marcus still found their patterns alien and still attached to the groupings the names his legionaries had given them more than a year ago. There was the Locust, there the Ballista, and there, low in the west now, the Pederasts. Scaurus shook his head and walked on, sandals soundless on snow and soft ground.

Like most cabins, the one Glabrio and Gorgidas shared was shut tight against the night's chill. Wooden shutters covered its windows, the spaces between their slats chinked tight with cloth to ward off the freezing wind. Only firefly gleams of lamplight peeped through to hint that the thatch-roofed hut was occupied.

The tribune stood in front of the door, his hand upraised to knock. He bethought himself of the Sacred Band of Thebes, of the hundred fifty pairs of lovers who had fought to their deaths at Chaeronea against Macedón's Philip and Alexander. His hand did not fall. These were not Thebans he led.

But he hesitated still, unable to bring his fist forward. Through the thin walls of the cabin, he heard the junior centurion and the physician talking. Though their words were muffled, they sounded altogether at ease with each other. Gorgidas said something short and sharp, and Glabrio laughed at him.

As Marcus stood in indecision, the image of Gaius Philippus rose unbidden to his mind. The senior centurion was talking to him just after he brought Helvis back to the barracks: "No one will care if you bed a woman, a boy, or a purple sheep, so long as you think with your head and not with your crotch."

Where dead Greek heroes had not stayed his hand, a Roman's homely advice did. If ever two men lived up to Gaius Philippus' standard, they were the two inside. Scaurus slowly walked back to his own hut, at peace with himself at last.

He heard a door open behind him, heard Quintus Glabrio call softly, "Is someone there?" By then the tribune was around the corner. The door closed again.

On his return, Scaurus took the scolding he got as one who deserves it, which only seemed to irk Helvis more; sometimes acceptance of blame is the last thing anger wants. But if absentminded, the tribune's apologies were genuine, and after a while Helvis subsided.

Malric took his undeserved punishment in stride, Marcus was thankful to see; he played with his adopted son until the boy grew drowsy.

The tribune was almost asleep himself when he happened to recall something he was sure he had forgotten: the name of the founder of Thebes' Sacred Band. It was Gorgidas.

During the winter, Aptos' sheltered valley learned but slowly what passed in the world outside. News of Amorion came, of all things, from a fugitive band of Yezda. The nomads, after a quick reconnaissance, had decided the town was a tempting target. It had no wall, was empty of imperial troops, and should make easy meat.

The Yezda suffered a rude awakening. Zemarkhos' irregulars, blooded in the Vaspurakaner pogrom, sent the invaders reeling off in defeat—and what they did to the men they caught made it hard to choose between their savagery and the Yezda's.

After listening to the tale spun by the handful of half-frozen nomads, Gagik Bagratouni rumbled low in his throat, "Here is something in my life new: to tenderness feel toward Yezda. I would much give, to see

Amorion burn, and Zemarkhos in it." His great, scarred hands gripped empty air; the brooding glow in his eyes gave him the aspect of a lion denied its prey.

Scaurus understood his vengefulness and took it as a good sign; time was beginning to heal the Vaspurakaner lord. Yet the tribune did not altogether agree with Bagratouni. In this winter of imperial weakness, any obstacle against the Yezda was worth something. Zemarkhos and his fanatics were a nasty boil on the body of Videssos, but the invaders were the plague.

Near midwinter day, an armed party of merchants made its way northwest from Amorion to Aptos, braving weather and the risk of attack in hope of reaping higher profits in a town where their kind seldom came. So it proved. Their stocks of spices, perfumes, fine brocades, and elaborately chased brass-work vessels from the capital sold at prices better than they could have realized in a city on a more traveled route.

Their leader, a muscular, craggy-faced fellow who looked more soldier than trader, contented himself with remarking, "Aye, we've done worse." Even with his double handful of guardsmen close by, he would not say more. Too many mercenary companies made a sport of robbing merchants.

He and his comrades were more forthcoming on other matters, sharing with anyone who cared to listen the news they had picked up on their travels. To his surprise, Marcus learned Baanes Onomagoulos still lived. The Videssian general had been badly wounded just before Maragha. Till now, Scaurus had assumed he'd perished, either of his wounds or in the pursuit after the battle.

But if rumor was to be trusted, Onomagoulos had escaped. Some sort of army under his command beat back a Yezda raid on the southern town of Kybistra, near the headwaters of the Arandos River.

"Good for him, if it's true," was Gaius Philippus' comment, "but the yarn came a long way before it ever got to us. Likely as not, he's ravens' meat himself, or else was a hundred miles away bedded down with something lively to keep the cold away. Good for him if that's true, too." He sounded wistful, as odd from him as diffidence from Gorgidas.

Like towns all through the Empire, Aptos celebrated the days after the winter solstice, when the sun at last turned north again. Bonfires burned in front of homes and shops; people jumped over them for luck. Men danced in the streets in women's clothing, and women dressed as men. The local abbot brought his monks down through the marketplace, wooden swords in hand, to burlesque soldiers. Tatikios Tornikes turned the tables by leading a dozen shopkeepers in a wicked parody of fat, drunken monks.

Aptos' celebration was rowdier than the one the Romans had seen the year before in Imbros. The latter was a real city and tried to ape the sophisticated ways of Videssos the capital. Aptos simply celebrated, and cared not a fig for the figure it cut.

The town had no theater or professional mime troupe. The locals put on skits in the streets, making up with exuberance what they lacked in polish. Like the ones at Imbros, their sketches were topical and irreverent. Tatikios did a quick change with one of the monks and came out dressed as a soldier. The rusty old mail shirt he had squeezed into was so tight it threatened to burst every time he moved. Marcus took a while to recognize his headgear. It might have been intended for a Roman helmet, but the crest ran from ear to ear instead of front to back—

Beside him, Viridovix chortled. Gaius Philippus' jaw was tightly clenched. "Oh, oh," Marcus muttered. The senior centurion wore a transversely crested helm to show his rank.

Tatikios had eyes only for a tall, fuzzy-bearded man who wore a fancy gown much like one Nerse Phorkaina was fond of. Every time the mock-noblewoman looked his way, though, he pulled his cloak over his eyes, shivering with fright.

"I'll kill that whoreson," Gaius Philippus ground out. His hand was on the hilt of his *gladius;* he did not sound as though he was joking.

"Nay, fool, 'tis all in fun," Viridovix said. "Last year at Imbros they were after scoffing at me for a tavern fight. The bards in Gaul do the same to a man. There's twice the disgrace in showing the taunting hurts."

"Is there?" Gaius Philippus said. After a while, to Marcus' relief, he let go of the sword, He stood watching till the playlet was done, but the tribune had seen his face less grim in battle.

The next skit, luckily, brought back his good humor. It showed what Aptos thought of Videssos' self-proclaimed Emperor. Posturing foolishly, a gorgeously dressed young man, plainly meant to be Ortaias, led a squad of monk-soldiers down Aptos' main street. Suddenly a six-year-old in nomad's furs leaped out from between two houses. The mock-Emperor shrieked and clutched at the seat of his robes. Throwing scepter one way and crown the other, he turned and fled, trampling half his men in the process.

"That's the way of it! Faster, faster, you spalpeen!" Viridovix shouted after him, doubled over with laughter.

"Aye, and give 'em a goldpiece each as you go," Gaius Philippus echoed. "No, don't, or they'll be after you themselves instead of leaving you for the Yezda!"

That crack drew cries of agreement from the townsfolk around him. As soon as he reached Videssos the city, Ortaias had set the mints churning out a flood of new coins to announce and, he hoped, popularize his reign. But his copper and silver pieces were thin and ill-shaped, his gold even more adulterated than his great-uncle Strobilos' had been. None of his tax collectors had yet been seen so far west, but rumor said even they would not accept his money, demanding instead older, purer coins.

Marcus found that the differing real values of coins nominally at par made gambling devilishly difficult. After more than a year in Videssos, though, he was used to the problem, and evening saw him in front of a table in the Dancing Bear, watching the little bone cubes roll.

"Ha! The suns!" exclaimed the leader of the merchant company, and scooped up the stake. The tribune gave the twin ones a sour look. Not only had they cost him three goldpieces—one of them a fine, pure coin minted by the Emperor Rhasios Akindynos a hundred twenty years ago—to his mind they were by rights a losing throw. When the Romans played at dice they used three, and reckoned the best roll a triple six. But to the Videssians, sixes lost. They called a double six "the demons"; it cost a gambler his bet and the dice both.

One of the other merchants was sitting at Scaurus' right. "He's hot tonight!" the trader crowed. "Three crowns says he makes it again!" He shoved the bright coins forward. They were not Videssian issue, but minted by some of the petty lords of mine-rich Vaspurakan. In the Empire's westlands they circulated widely, the more so because they were of purer gold than recent imperial money.

Marcus covered him with two more from his dwindling store of old

Videssian coins; he would have needed six or seven of Ortaias' wretched issue to match the stake. The merchant captain threw the dice. Three and five—that meant nothing. Nor did double fours. One and—Marcus had an anxious second until the other die stopped spinning. It was a two. "Whew!" he said.

More meaningless rolls followed, and still more. Side bets multiplied. At last the trader threw twelve and had to surrender the dice to the man at his left. Scaurus gathered in the other merchant's Vaspurakaner gold, along with the other bets he'd put down. As was true of the "princes'" other arts, the portraits on their money were executed in a strong, blocky style. Some coins bore square Vaspurakaner letters, others the more sinuous Videssian script.

Behind the tribune, a copper basin set on the tavern floor rang like a bell from a well-tossed dollop of wine. He heard cries of admiration, and the clink of money changing hands. Without looking, he was sure Gorgidas was winning the applause. When the Greek had found the Videssians played kottabos, his joy was undiluted. No one in the capital could match him, and surely no one in this country town. If the locals did not know it yet, they soon would.

The dice traveled slowly round the table. When they got to Marcus, he held them to his mouth to breathe life into them. The rational part of his mind insisted such superstitious foolishness would do no good. But it could not hurt, so he did it anyway.

His first several throws were meaningless; the Videssian game could be slow. Someone pulled the door of the Dancing Wolf open. "Shut that, will you?" Scaurus grunted without turning around as frigid air knifed into the tavern's warmth.

"So we will, and wine for everyone to make amends!" The tribune was on his feet even before a cheer rang through the Dancing Wolf. Snow melting on his jacket and in his beard, Senpat Sviodo grinned at him. Nevrat was right behind her husband.

Marcus rushed over to them, hugged them both, and pounded their backs. "What news?" he demanded.

"You might say hello first," Nevrat said, her dark eyes sparkling with mischief.

"Your pardon, hello. Now, what news?" They all laughed. But the

398

tribune was not really joking. He had been waiting for the Vaspurakaners' return—and worrying over the word they would bring—too long for that.

"Are you going to throw or not?" an annoyed gambler called from the table where he had been sitting. "Give us the dice back if you aren't." Marcus flushed, realizing he was still holding them.

Nevrat pressed a coin into his hand; her fingers were still cold. "Here," she said. "Bet this."

He looked at the goldpiece. It was good money, not pale with silver or darkened by copper's blush—likely from a Vaspurakaner mint, he thought. But the inscription on the reverse was in Videssian letters: "By this right." Above the words stood a soldier brandishing a sword. Scaurus had not seen a coin like it before. He turned it over, curious to learn what lord had issued it.

The diemaker was skillful. The face on the obverse was no stylized portrait, but the picture of a living, breathing man. He was shaggy of hair and beard, with a proud nose, and a mouth bracketed by forceful lines. The tribune almost felt he knew him.

Scaurus stiffened. He did know this man, had seen his mouth wide with laughter and straight as a sword blade in wrath. The Roman looked up at the ceiling and whistled, soft and low.

He noticed the inscription under the portrait bust for the first time. "Avtokrator," it said, and then a name, but he needed no inscription to name Thorisin Gavras for him.

When the tribune got back to camp with his news, Helvis took it like any mercenary's woman. "This has to mean another round of civil war," she said. He nodded. She went on, "Both sides will be wild for troops—you can sell our swords at a good price."

"Civil war be damned," said Marcus, who remembered Rome's latest one from his childhood. "The only fight that counts is the one against Avshar and Yezd. Any others are distractions; the worse they get, the weaker the Empire becomes for the real test. With Thorisin as Emperor, Videssos may even have a prayer of winning; with Ortaias, I wouldn't give us six months."

"Us?" Helvis looked at him strangely. "Are you a Videssian? Do you think either Emperor would call you one? They hire swords—you have them. That's all you can hope to be to them: a tool, to be used and put aside when no longer needed. If Ortaias pays you more, you're a fool not to take his money."

The tribune had the uneasy feeling there was a good deal of truth in what she said. He thought of his men and goals as different from those of other troops Videssos hired, but did its overlords? Probably not. But the idea of serving a poltroon like young Sphrantzes was too much to stomach.

"If Ortaias melted down the golden globe atop the High Temple in Videssos and gave it all to me, I would not fight for him," he declared. "For that matter, I don't think my men would take his side either. They know him for the coward he is."

"Aye, courage speaks," Helvis admitted, but she added, "So does gold. And do you think Ortaias runs affairs in the city today? My guess is he has to ask his uncle's leave before he goes to the privy."

"That's worse, somehow," Scaurus muttered. Ortaias Sphrantzes was a fool and a craven; his uncle Vardanes, Marcus was sure, was neither. But try as he might to hide it, the elder Sphrantzes had a coldly ruthless streak his nephew lacked. The Roman would have trusted him further if he did not make such an effort to hide his true nature with an affable front. It was like perfume on a corpse, and made Marcus' hackles rise.

He made a clumsy botch of explaining, and knew it. But the feeling was still in his belly, and he did not think any weight of gold could make it leave.

He also knew he was far from convincing Helvis. The only principle the Namdaleni who fought for Videssos knew was expedience; the higher the pay and fewer the risks, the better.

She walked over to the small altar she'd lately installed on the cabin's eastern wall, lit a pinch of incense. "However you decide," she said, "Phos deserves to be thanked." The sweet fumes quickly filled the small stuffy space.

When the tribune remained silent, she swung round to face him, really angry now. "You should be doing this, not me. Phos alone knows why he gives you such chances, when you repay him nothing. Here," she said, holding out the little alabaster jar of incense to him.

That peremptory, outthrust hand drove away the mild answer that might have kept peace between them. The tribune growled, "Probably because he's asleep, or more likely not there at all." Her horrified stare made him wish he'd held his tongue, but he had said too much to back away.

"If your precious Phos lets his people be smashed to bloody bits by a pack of devil-loving savages, what good is he? If you must have a god, pick one who earns his keep."

A skilled theologian could have come up with a number of answers to his blunt gibe: that Phos' evil counterpart Skotos was the power behind the success of the Yezda, or that from a Namdalener point of view the Videssians were misbelievers and therefore not entitled to their god's protection. But Helvis was challenged on a far more fundamental level. "Sacrilege!" she whispered, and slapped him in the face. An instant later she burst into tears.

Malric woke up and started to cry himself. "Go back to sleep," Scaurus snapped, but the tone that would have chilled a legionary's heart only frightened the three-year-old. He cried louder. Looking daggers at the tribune, Helvis stooped to comfort her son.

Marcus paced up and down, too upset to hold still. But his anger slowly cooled as Malric's wails shrank to whimpers and then to the raspy breathing of sleep. Helvis looked up at him, her eyes wary. "I'm sorry I hit you," she said tonelessly.

He rubbed his cheek. "Forget it. I was out of turn myself." They looked at each other like strangers; in too many ways they were, despite the child Helvis carried. What was I thinking, Scaurus asked himself, when I wanted her to share my life?

From the half-wondering, half-measuring way she studied him, he knew the same thought was in her mind.

He helped her to her feet; the warm contact of the flesh of her hand against his reminded him of one reason, at least, why the two of them were together. Though her pregnancy was nearly halfway through, it had yet to make much of a mark on her large-boned frame. There was a beginning bulge high on her belly, and her breasts were growing heavier,

but someone who did not know her might have failed to notice her big-
ness.

But when Marcus tried to embrace her, she twisted free of his arms.
"What good will that do?" she asked, her back to him. "It doesn't settle
things, it doesn't change things, it just puts them off. And when we're
angry, it's no good anyway."

The tribune bit down an angry retort. More times than one, troubles
had dissolved in love's lazy aftermath. But her desire had grown fitful
since pregnancy began; understanding that such things happened, Scaurus accepted it as best he could.

Tonight, though, he wanted her, and hoped it would help heal the
rift between them. He moved forward, put the palms of his hands on her
shoulders.

She wheeled, but not in desire. "You don't care about me or what I
feel at all," she blazed. "All you can think of is your own pleasure."

"Ha!" It was anything but a laugh. "Were that so, I'd have looked
elsewhere long before this."

Having swallowed his anger once, Marcus hit too hard when he finally loosed it. Helvis began to cry again, not with the noisy sobs she had
used before but quietly, hopelessly, making no effort to wipe the tears
from her face. They were running down her cheeks when she blew out
the lamp and, as the wick's orange glow died, slid beneath the covers of
the sleeping mat.

Scaurus stood in darkness some endless while, listening to the careful sobs that let out grief without disturbing the sleeping boy. At last he
bent down to stroke her through the thick wool, not in want but to give
what belated comfort he might.

She flinched away, as if from a blow. Careful not to touch her further,
the tribune got under the blankets himself. The scent of incense was still
in his nostrils, sweet as death.

He stared up at the low ceiling, though there was nothing to see in
the darkness. Eventually he slept.

When he woke, the Roman felt wrung out and used up as after a day in
battle. Helvis' face was puffed and blotchy from crying. They spoke to

each other, moved around each other, with cautious courtesy, neither wanting to reopen last night's wound. But Scaurus knew it would be a long time healing, if it ever did.

He was glad of the excuse of seeing to his men to leave quickly, and Helvis seemed relieved to see him go. The soldiers, of course, were oblivious to their commander's private woes. They buzzed with excitement over the goldpiece he had come across. The tribune managed a wry smile at that; he had almost forgotten the coin and its meaning.

He soon found he had accurately gauged their mood. To a man, they felt contempt for Ortaias Sphrantzes. "The mimes had the right of it," Minucius said. "With Thorisin Gavras alive, there'll hardly be a fight. The other'll run till he falls off the edge of the world."

"Aye, the Gavras is much better suited for kinging it," Viridovix agreed. "A fine talker he is, a rare good-looking wight to boot, and the stomach of him can hold a powerful lot of wine."

Gorgidas gave the Celt an exasperated look. "What does any of that have to do with kingship?" he demanded. "By your reckoning, Thorisin Gavras would make an excellent sophist, a pretty girl"—Marcus blinked at his choice of that figure, but had to admit its aptness—"or a splendid sponge. But a king? Scarcely. What the state needs from a king is justice."

"Well be damned to you, you and your sponges," the Gaul said. "Forbye, be your would-be king never so just, if he talk like a sausage seller and look like a mouse turd, not a soul will pay him any mind at all. If you're a leader, ye maun fit the part." He preened ever so slightly, reminding his listeners he had been a noble with a large following himself.

"There's something to that," Gaius Philippus said. Reluctant as he was to go along with Viridovix on anything, he had led enough men to know how much of the art of leadership was style.

Gorgidas dipped his head in reluctant agreement. "I know there is. But it's too easy to look the part without having what's really needed to play it. Take Alkibiades, for instance." The name flew past centurion and Celt alike. Gorgidas sighed and tried another tack, asking Viridovix, "What good does it do a king to be able to outdrink his subjects?"

"Och, man, the veriest fool should be able to see that. After standing the yapping of nitpickers all the day"—Viridovix stared at Gorgidas until the doctor, reddening, urged him on with a rude gesture—"what better way to ease the sorrows than with sweet wine?" He smacked his lips.

"I must be going senile," Gorgidas muttered in Greek. "To be out-argued by a red-mustached Celt . . ." He let the sentence trail off as he walked away.

Marcus left the discussion, too, walking out to the frozen fields to watch his soldiers exercise. Laon Pakhymer's Khatrishers darted here and there on horseback, wheeling, twisting, suddenly stopping short. Others practiced mounted archery, sending shafts slamming through heaped-up mounds of straw. For all their camaraderie with the Romans, they were still very much a separate command.

The foot soldiers, now, were something else again. The hundreds of stragglers who had joined the Romans after Maragha, as well as Gagik Bagratouni's refugees, were beginning to blend into the legionaries' ranks. Their beards and the sleeves on their mail shirts still gave Vides-sians and Vaspurakaners an exotic look, but constant practice was mak-ing them as adept with *pilum* and stabbing *gladius* as any son of Italy.

Phostis Apokavkos gave the tribune a wave and a leathery grin. Scau-rus smiled back. He still felt good about taking the farmer-soldier out of the capital's slums and making a legionary of him. But then, Apokavkos had adopted the Romans as much as they him, shaving his face and pick-ing up Latin to become as much like his new comrades as he could.

His tall, lean frame almost hid Doukitzes beside him. They were fast friends; Scaurus sometimes wondered why. Doukitzes was the sort of man Phostis had refused to become during his hungry time in Videssos the city: a small-time thief. The tribune had saved Doukitzes from losing his hand to Mavrikios' angry judgment not long before Maragha. Per-haps in gratitude, he had not plied his trade—or at least had not been caught—since joining the Romans after the battle. He waved, too, a little more hesitantly than Apokavkos.

Marcus watched their maniple let fly with a volley of practice-*pila*. He had a good little army, he thought with somber pride. That was as well; it would need to be good, soon enough.

Out of the corner of his eye he caught a motion decidedly not mili-tary. Arms round one another's waists, intent only on each other, Senpat Sviodo and Nevrat were making their slow, happy way to their cabin.

The sudden stab of envy was like a knife twisting in Scaurus' guts. The feeling's intensity was frightening, the more so because only weeks before he had been half of such a pair.

The world of the legions was simpler, he decided. Private life would not run by the brute simplicity of orders. He sighed, shook his head, and turned back to make what peace he could with Helvis.

IV

THE SWARTHY KHAMORTH SCOUT, WEARING GRAY-BROWN FOXSKINS and mounted on a dun-colored shaggy pony, was like a lump of winter mud against the bright green of spring. Studying the plainsman closely, Marcus asked him, "How do I know you're from Thorisin Gavras? We've seen snares before."

The nomad gave back a contemptuous stare. He had no more use than his distant Yezda cousins for towns, plowed fields, or the folk who cherished them. But he had sworn loyalty to Gavras on his sword, and his clan-chief and the imperial contestant had drunk wine mixed with their two bloods.

Therefore he answered in his bad Videssian, "He bid me ask you what he say about excitable women, that morning in his tent."

"That they're great fun, but they wear," the tribune answered, instantly satisfied. He remembered the morning in question only too well, having been afraid Thorisin was about to arrest him for treason. He was surprised Gavras also recalled it. The then-Sevastokrator had been very drunk.

"You right," the Khamorth nodded. He grinned, a male grin that cut across all differences in way of life. "He right, too."

"There's something to it," Marcus agreed, and smiled back. By Thorisin's standards, though, Helvis hardly counted as excitable. The truce between her and Scaurus, brittle at first, had firmed as winter passed. If there were things they no longer spoke of, the tribune thought, surely that was a small enough price to pay for peace.

Any peace with a price on it, part of his mind said for the hundredth time, is too dearly bought. For the hundredth time, the rest of him shouted that part down.

The plainsman had said something while he was in his reverie. "I'm sorry?"

The disdain was back on the nomad's face; what good was this fellow, if he would not even listen? Scaurus felt himself flush. Speaking as if to an idiot child, the Khamorth repeated, "You be ready to break camp, three days' time? Thorisin, his men, so far behind me. I ride west meet them, bring here to you to join. You be ready?"

Excitement boiled in the tribune. Three days' time, and he would be cut off from the world no longer. Three days' time to break a camp that had housed his men for a season? If the Romans could not do it, they did not deserve their name.

"We'll be ready," he said.

The plainsman swept a skeptical eye over ditch, palisade, and the townlet that had grown up inside them. To him and his, getting ready to leave a place was a matter of minutes, not hours or days. "Three days' time," he said once more. He made it sound like a warning.

Without waiting for an answer, he wheeled his little horse and trotted away. From his attitude, he had already wasted enough of this fine riding day on farmer folk.

A Khatrisher posted at the eastern end of Aptos' valley waved his fur cap over his head. Close by Marcus, Laon Pakhymer waved back to show the signal was understood. Thorisin Gavras' outriders were in sight. The picket came galloping back.

"Form up!" the tribune yelled. The buccinators' trumpets and cornets echoed his command. His foot soldiers, Romans and newcomers together, quick-marched to their positions behind the nine manipular standards, the *signa*. Even after a year and a half without it, Scaurus still missed the legionary eagle his detachment had not rated.

Beside the infantry assembled the Khatrisher horsemen. Pakhymer did not try to form them into neat ranks. They looked like what they were: irregulars, longer on toughness than order.

Most of Aptos' population lined the road into town. Fathers carried small boys and girls pickaback so they could see over the crowd—Phos alone knew when next an Emperor, even one with so uncertain a right to that title, would come this way.

From the talk he'd heard since the Khamorth scout appeared, Marcus knew half the rustics were wondering whether the hooves of Thorisin's horse would touch the ground. Those who knew better, like Phorkos' widow Nerse, were there, too.

"Ahhh!" said the townsmen. Still small in the distance, the first pair of Thorisin Gavras' cavalry came into view. They carried parasols, and Scaurus knew them for the Videssian equivalent of Rome's lictors with axes and bundles of fasces, the symbols that power resided here. Another pair followed, and another, until a dozen bright silk flowers bloomed ahead of Gavras' men—the full imperial number, right enough.

Straining his eyes, the tribune saw Thorisin himself close behind them, mounted on a fine bay horse. Only his scarlet boots made any personal claim to rank; the rest of his gear was good, but no more than that. Not even assuming the imperium could make him fond of its trappings.

His army rumbled down the road behind him, almost all cavalry, as was the Videssian way. Of all the nations the Empire knew, only the Halogai preferred to fight afoot; Roman infantry tactics had been an eye-opener here. Gavras' troops were about evenly divided between Videssians and Vaspurakaners—no wonder he had coined money to the "princes'" standard of weight.

"Good-looking men," Gaius Philippus remarked, and Scaurus nodded. The unconscious arrogance with which they rode said volumes about the confidence Thorisin had drilled into them. After the disaster in front of Maragha, that was no mean feat. Marcus' spirits rose.

He tried to gauge how many warriors accompanied Gavras as they came toward him. Maybe a thousand in the valley so far . . . now two . . . three thousand—no, probably not that many, for they had a good-sized baggage train in their midst. Say twenty-five hundred.

A good, solid first division, the tribune thought. In a moment the rest of the army would show itself, and then he would have a better idea of its real capabilities. Thorisin spotted him in front of his assembled troops and gave him quite an unimperial wave. Warmed inside, he waved back.

It was certainly taking enough time for the next unit's van to appear.

Marcus reached up to scratch his head, felt foolish as fingers rasped on the iron of his helmet.

"Hercules!" Gaius Philippus muttered under his breath. "I think that's all of them."

Marcus wanted to laugh or cry, or, better, both at once. This was Thorisin Gavras' all-conquering horde, with which he would reclaim Videssos from the usurper and drive the Yezda out of the Empire? Counting Pakhymer's few hundred, he had almost this many men himself.

Yet as Gavras' parasol bearers rode past the assembled inhabitants of Aptos, they bowed low to give honor to the Emperor. And as Thorisin brought his forces up to the troops Marcus had drawn up in review, Laon Pakhymer went to his knees and then to his belly in a full proskynesis, giving him formal reverence as sovereign. So did Gagik Bagratouni and Zeprin the Red, who stood near Scaurus.

The Roman, true to his homeland's republican ways, had never prostrated himself for Mavrikios. He did not do so now, contenting himself with a deep bow. He remembered how furious the younger Gavras had been the first time he failed to bend the knee to the Emperor. Now Thorisin reined in his horse in front of the tribune and said with a dry chuckle, "Still stubborn as ever, aren't you?"

Directly addressed, Marcus lifted his head to study the Emperor at close range. Thorisin still sat his stallion with the same jauntiness that had endeared him to Videssos' citizenry when he was but Mavrikios' brother, still kept the ironic gleam in his eye that made one ever uncertain how seriously to take him. But there was a harder, somehow more finished look to him than the Roman remembered; it was very much like Mavrikios come again.

"Your Majesty, would you recognize me any other way?" Scaurus asked.

Thorisin smiled for a moment. His gaze traveled up and down the silent Roman ranks, estimating their numbers just as the tribune had reckoned his. "You give yourself too little credit," he said. "I'd know you by the wizardry that let you bring your troop out so near intact. You were there at the worst of it, weren't you?"

Scaurus shrugged. The worst of it had been where Mavrikios' Haloga bodyguard had fought for the Emperor to the last man and perished with him at the end. He said nothing of that, but Thorisin read it in his eyes. His smile slipped. "There will be a reckoning," he said quietly. "More than one, in fact."

The matter-of-fact promise in his voice almost made it possible to forget that Mavrikios had failed against the Yezda with an army of over fifty thousand men. His brother was undertaking that task, along with simultaneous civil war, and his forces, even adding in the Romans and their comrades, were less than a tenth as great.

"If you've a mind to," Thorisin said to Marcus, "you can dismiss your troopers. A little ceremonial takes me a long way. Gather your officers together, round up some wine, and we'll talk."

"So the pipsqueak really did start the rout?" Thorisin mused. "I'd heard it before, but it galled me to believe it, even of Ortaias." He shook his head. "One more reason for dealing with him—as if I needed another."

Bareheaded, a mug in his hand, his red-booted feet propped on a table, he looked like any long-time soldier taking his ease after travel. His commanders, Videssians and Vaspurakaners both, were as nonchalant. Mavrikios had used the elaborate imperial ceremonies to enhance his own dignity, though he thought them foolish. Thorisin simply could not be bothered.

He listened closely as Scaurus told of the Romans' wanderings, slapped his thigh with his left hand when the Roman explained how he had used Hannibal's trick to free himself from the Yezda. "Turning flocks back on the nomads, eh? A fine ploy and only just," he said.

The tribune did not mention Avshar's parting gift to him. As soon as the Khamorth scout let him know Thorisin was nearby, he had buried Mavrikios' head. With a real Gavras very much present, the risk of a false one seemed smaller.

"Enough of this chatter about us," Viridovix said to the Roman. He turned to Thorisin, asking him, "Where was it you disappeared to, man? For months not a one of us knew if you were alive or dead or off in fairyland to come back a hundred years from now, the which would be no use at all to anybody."

410

Thorisin took no offense, which was as well; Viridovix curbed his tongue for no one. His tale was about what the tribune had expected. His mauled right wing of the great Videssian army had been pushed back into Vaspurakan's mountain fastnesses, terrain even more rugged than that which the Romans had crossed. There, much of the army had melted away, beaten soldiers slipping off singly or in small groups to try to make their way eastward.

Gaius Philippus nodded, commenting, "It's what I would have guessed, looking at the men you have with you. The peasant levies and fainthearts are long gone, dead or fled."

"That's the way of it," Thorisin agreed.

In one important respect, the younger Gavras' troops had had a harder time of it than the Romans. The Yezda made a real pursuit after them, and it took two or three bitter rearguard actions to shake free. "It was that cursed white-robed devil," one of the Videssian officers said. "He stuck tighter than a leech—aye, and sucked more blood, too."

Marcus and his entire party leaned forward, suddenly alert. "So Avshar was trailing you, then," the tribune said. "No wonder there was no sign of him in these parts—we had no idea what was keeping him out of Videssos."

"I still don't," Gavras admitted. "He disappeared a couple of weeks after the battle, and I have no idea where he is. As much as anything, his going saved us—without him the Yezda are fierce enough, but a rabble. With him—" Thorisin fell silent; from his expression, the words stuck in his mouth were not to his taste.

The officer who had mentioned Avshar—Indakos Skylitzes, his name was—asked Marcus, "Has Amorion gone mad? We sent a man there to proclaim Thorisin, and they horsewhipped him out of town— for a day, we thought he might not live. Phos' little suns, even in civil war, heralds have some rights." As a Videssian baron, Skylitzes knew whereof he spoke.

"It's Zemarkhos' city now, and his word is law there," Marcus said. He paused as a new thought struck him. "Was your envoy a Vaspurakaner, by any chance?"

Skylitzes looked uncertain, but Thorisin nodded. "Haik Amazasp? I should say so. What has that to do with—? Oh." His scowl deepened as he remembered how Amorion's fanatic priest had wanted to start his persecution of the "heretics" with imperial backing. "Ortaias is welcome to his support—not that he'll get much use from him."

"You'll avenge us?" Senpat Sviodo exclaimed eagerly. "You won't regret it—Amorion is a perfect place to push east. You know that as well as I." The young Vaspurakaner came halfway out of his seat in enthusiasm. Gagik Bagratouni began to rise, too, more slowly, but with a frightening sense of purpose.

Thorisin, though, waved them down once more. "No, we're after Videssos the city, nothing else. With it, the whole Empire falls to us; without it, none of the rest is truly ours."

Seeing their outraged disappointment, he went on, "If you don't mind your revenge at second hand, I think you'll get it. The Namdaleni are moving east out of Phanaskert, and I expect Amorion will be in their line of march. They'll bring the town down around Zemarkhos' ears if he squawks of heresy at them—and he will. He's bigot enough." Gavras contemplated the meeting with equanimity, even grim amusement. So, after a moment, did the Vaspurakaners.

Scaurus was ready to agree. Any trap that closed on the Namdaleni would be kicked open from the inside by six or seven thousand heavy-armed cavalry. So the men of the Duchy were on the move, too, were they? he thought. Armies were flowing like driblets from melting icicles after the winter freeze.

Something else occurred to him: the Namdaleni had a good many more soldiers hereabouts than Thorisin did. He asked, "What sort of understanding do you have with the easterners?"

"Mutual mistrust, as always," Gavras answered. "If they see their way clear, they'll go for our throats. I don't intend to give them the chance."

"Maybe Onomagoulos' men can come up from the south to help keep an eye on them," Marcus suggested.

It was the Emperor's turn to be startled. "What? Baanes is alive?"

"If traders' tales can be trusted," Gaius Philippus said, still doubting the merchants' rumor. He set it forth for Thorisin, who did not seem to find anything improbable in it.

"Well, well, good for the old fox. There's tricks left in him after all," Gavras murmured, but he did not sound overjoyed to Scaurus.

When Aptos disappeared behind a bend in the road, Gaius Philippus heaved a long sigh. "First time in full many a year I'm sorry to be on the move once more," he said.

"By the gods, why?" Marcus asked, surprised. Marching under a spring sky was one of the pleasures of a soldier's life. The last rains had given the foothills a carpet of new grass and were recent enough to keep Videssos' dirt roads from turning into choking ribbons of dust. The air was fine and mild, almost tasty, and sweetly clamorous with the calls of returning birds. Even the butterflies looked fresh, their bright wings not yet tattered and tarnished by time.

"Canna you tell?" Viridovix said to Scaurus. "The puir lad's heart is all broken in flinders—or would be, if he remembered where he mislaid it."

"Oh, be damned to you," Gaius Philippus said, the measure of his upset shown by his falling into the Celt's idiom.

For a moment Marcus honestly had no idea of what Viridovix was talking about, or why the senior centurion took the gibe seriously. When he stopped to think, though, an answer did occur to him. "Nerse?" he asked. "Phorkos' widow?"

"What if it is?" Gaius Philippus muttered, plainly sorry he'd said anything at all.

"Well, why didn't you court her, then?" the tribune burst out, but Gaius Philippus was doing no more talking. The veteran set his jaw and stared straight ahead as he marched, enduring Viridovix' teasing without snapping back. After a while the Celt grew bored of his unrewarding fun and went off to talk about swordplay with Minucius.

Studying Gaius Philippus' grim expression, Marcus came to his own conclusions. Strange that a man who was utterly fearless in battle, and who took fornication and rape as part of the warrior's trade, should be scared witless of paying suit to a woman for whom he felt something more than lust.

Thorisin Gavras' army hurried northeast toward the shore of the Videssian Sea. Gavras hoped to commandeer shipping and swoop down on Ortaias in the capital before the usurper could make ready to meet him. But at each port his troops approached, shipmasters hurried their vessels out to sea and sent them fleeing to bring young Sphrantzes word of his coming.

The third time that happened, at a fishing village called Tavas, Thorisin's short temper neared the snapping point. "For two coppers I'd sack the place," he snarled, pacing up and down like a caged tiger, watching a bulky merchantman's brightly dyed sails recede into sea mist as it drove north out of the Bay of Rhyax before turning east for the long run to Videssos.

He spat in disgust. "Bah! What's left here? Half a dozen fishing boats. Phos willing, I could put a good dozen men in each."

"You ought to pillage these faithless traders and peasants. Teach them to fear you," Komitta Rhangavve said, walking beside him. The fierce expression on her lean, aristocratic features made her resemble a hunting hawk, beautiful but deadly.

Alarmed at the bloodthirsty advice Gavras' lady gave, Scaurus said hastily, "Perhaps it's as well the merchant got away; Ortaias must be forewarned by now in any case. If the fleet in the city stands with him, he'd smash anything you could scrape together here."

Komitta Rhangavve glared at even this indirect disagreement, but Thorisin sighed, a heavy, frustrated sound. "You're probably right. If I could have brought it off at Prakana, though, four days ago—" He sighed again. "What was that thing poor Khoumnos used to say? 'If ifs and buts were candied nuts, then everyone would be fat.'" Nephon Khoumnos, though, was half a year dead, struck down by Avshar's sorcery at the battle before Maragha.

Neither Gavras nor Marcus found that a pleasant thought to dwell on. Returning rather more directly to rebutting Komitta, the tribune said, "At least the people hereabouts are for you, whatever the shipmasters do."

The Emperor's smile was still sour. "Of course they are—we've come far enough east that folk have had a good taste of Ortaias' taxmen; aye,

414

and of his money, too, though they'd break teeth if they tried to bite it." Sphrantzes' wretched coinage was a standing joke in his opponent's army. As for his revenue agents, Scaurus had yet to see one. They ran from Thorisin even faster than the navarchs did.

Five days later came an envoy of Ortaias' who did not flee. Accompanied by a guard force of ten horsemen, he rode deliberately up to Thorisin's camp at evening. One of the troopers bore a white-painted shield on a spearstaff: a sign of truce.

"What can the henhearted wretch have to say to me?" Thorisin snapped, but let the emissary's party approach.

The soldiers with Sphrantzes' agents were nonentities—the hard shell of a nut, good only for protecting the kernel within. The envoy himself was something else again. Marcus recognized him as one of Vardanes Sphrantzes' henchmen, but could not recall his name.

Thorisin had no such difficulty. "Ah, Pikridios, how good to see you," he said, but there was venom in his voice.

Pikridios Goudeles affected not to notice. The bureaucrat dismounted with a sigh of relief. He'd sat his horse badly; from the look of his hands, the reins would have hurt them. They were soft and white, their only callus on the right middle finger. A pen-pusher right enough, Scaurus thought, feeling the aptness of the Videssian soldiery's contemptuous term for the Empire's civil servants.

Yet for all his unwarlike look, the small, dapper Goudeles was a man to be reckoned with. His dark eyes gleamed with ironic intelligence, and the quality of his nerve was adequately attested by his very presence in the rival Emperor's camp.

"Your Majesty," he said to Thorisin, and went to one knee, his head bowed—not a proskynesis, but the next thing to it.

Some of Gavras' soldiers cheered to see their lord so acclaimed by his foe's ambassador. Others growled because the acclamation was incomplete. Thorisin himself seemed taken aback. "Get up, get up," he said impatiently. Goudeles rose, brushing dust from the knee of his elegant riding breeches.

He made no move to speak further. The silence stretched. At last, conceding the point to him, Thorisin broke it: "Well, what now? Are you here to turn your worthless coat? What price do you want for it?"

Beneath the thin fringe of mustache, so like Vardanes', Scaurus noticed—perhaps irrelevantly, perhaps not—Goudeles' lip gave a delicate curl, as if to say he had noticed the insult but did not quite care to acknowledge it. "My lord Sevastokrator, I am merely here to help resolve the unfortunate misunderstanding between yourself and his Imperial Majesty the Avtokrator Ortaias Sphrantzes."

Every trooper who heard that shouted in outrage; hands tightened on sword hilts, reached for spears and bows. "String the little bastard up!" someone yelled. "Maybe after he's hung a while he'll know who the real Emperor is!" Three or four men sprang forward. Goudeles' self-control wavered; he shot an appealing glance at Thorisin Gavras.

Thorisin waved his soldiers back. They withdrew slowly, stiffly, like dogs whistled off a kill they think theirs by right. "What's going on?" Gaius Philippus whispered to Marcus. "If this rogue won't own Gavras as Emperor, by rights he's fair game."

"Your guess is as good as mine," the tribune answered. With Gavras' hot temper, Scaurus had expected him to deal roughly with Goudeles, ambassador or no—in civil war such niceties of usage were easy enough to cast aside. It was lucky Komitta was not in earshot of all this, he thought; she would already be heating pincers.

Yet Thorisin's manner remained mild. Though a warrior by choice, he had known his share of intrigue as well, and his years at his brother's right hand in the capital made him alert to subtleties less experienced men could miss. Voice still calm, he asked Goudeles, "So you do not reckon me rightful Avtokrator, eh?"

"Regrettably, I do not, my lord," Goudeles said, half-bowing, "nor does my principal." His glance at Thorisin was wary; they were fencing as surely as if they had sabers to hand.

"Just a damned rebel, am I?"

Goudeles spread his soft hands, gave a fastidious shrug.

"Then by Skotos' dung-splattered beard," Thorisin pounced, "why does your bloody principal"—He made the word an oath—"still style me Sevastokrator? Is that his bribe to me, keeping a title he'll make sure is empty? Tell your precious Sphrantzes I am not so cheaply bought."

The envoy from the capital looked artfully pained at Gavras' crudity. "You fail to understand, my lord. Why should you not remain Sevastokrator? The title was yours during your deeply mourned brother's reign, and you are still close kin to the imperial house."

Thorisin stared at him as if he had started speaking some obscure foreign tongue. "Are you witstruck, man? The Sphrantzai are no kin of mine—I share no blood with jackals."

Once again, the insult failed to make an impression on Goudeles. He said, "Then your Majesty has not yet heard the joyous news? How slowly it travels in these outlying districts!"

"What are you yapping of?" Gavras demanded, but his voice was suddenly tense.

His quarry vulnerable at last, Goudeles thrust home with suave precision. "Surely the Avtokrator will pay you all respect due a father-in-law, putting you in the late Emperor's place. Why, it must be more than a month now since his daughter Alypia and my lord Ortaias were united in wedlock."

Thorisin went white. Voice thick with rage, he choked out, "Flee now, while you still have breath in you!" And Goudeles and his guardsmen, with no ceremony whatever, leaped on their horses and rode for their lives.

Gaius Philippus took a characteristically pungent view of the marriage. "It'll do Ortaias less good than he thinks," he said. "If he's the same kind of lover as he is a general, he'll have to take a book to bed to know what to do with her."

Remembering the military tome constantly under Sphrantzes' arm, Scaurus had to smile. But alone in his tent with Helvis and the sleeping Malric later that evening, he burst out, "It was a filthy thing to do. As good as rape, joining Alypia to the house her father hated."

"Why so offended?" Helvis asked. She was very bulky now, uncomfortable, and often irritable. With a woman's bitter realism, she went on, "Are we ever anything but pawns in the game of power? Beyond the politics of it, why should you care?"

"The politics are bad enough." The marriage, forced or not, could only rob Thorisin Gavras of support and gain it for Ortaias and his uncle. Helvis was right, though: Marcus' anger was more personal than for his cause. "From the little I knew of her, I rather liked her," he confessed.

"What has that to do with the price of fish?" Helvis demanded. "Since the day you came to Videssos, you've known the contest you were in; aye, and played it well, I'll not deny. But it's not one with much room for things as small as likes."

Scaurus winced at that harsh picture of his career in his adopted homeland. In Videssos, scheming was natural as drawing breath. No one who hoped to advance could escape it altogether.

But Alypia Gavra, he thought, should not fall victim to it merely by accident of birth. Behind the schooled reserve with which she met the world, the tribune had felt a gentleness this unconsented marriage would mar forever. The image of her brought miserable and defenseless to Ortaias' bed made cold fury flash behind his eyes.

And how, he asked himself, am I going to say that to Helvis without lighting a suspicion in her better left unkindled? Not seeing any way, he kept his mouth shut.

Sentries' shouts woke Scaurus at earliest dawn. Stumbling to his feet, he threw on a heavy wool mantle and hurried out to see what the trouble was. Gaius Philippus was at the rampart before him, sword in hand, wearing only helmet and sandals.

Marcus followed the veteran's pointing finger. There was motion at the edge of sight in the east, visible at all only because silhouetted against the paling sky. "I give you two guesses," the senior centurion said.

"You can have the first one back—I know an army when I see it. Shows how sincere Goudeles' talk of Thorisin being an honored father-in-law was, doesn't it?"

"As if we needed showing. Well, let's be at it." The veteran's bellow made up for the cornets and trumpets of the still-sleeping buccinators. "Up, you weedy, worthless good-for-nothings, up! There's work to do today!"

Romans tumbled from their tents, pulling on corselets and tightening straps as they rushed to their places. Campfires banked during the night were fed to new life to light the running soldiers' paths.

Marcus and Gaius Philippus looked at each other and, in looking, realized they were hardly clad for battle. Gaius Philippus cursed. They dashed for their tents.

When the tribune emerged a couple of minutes later, he led his troops out to deploy in front of their fortified camp. Pakhymer's light cavalry screened their lines. The Khatrishers' winter-long association with the Romans made them as quick to be ready as the legionaries. The rest of Thorisin Gavras' forces were slower in emerging.

There was no time to plan elaborate strategies. Thorisin rode up on his highbred bay, grunted approval at the Romans' quiet steadiness. "You'll be on the right," he said. "Stay firm, and we'll smash them against you."

"Good enough," Marcus nodded. Less mobile than the mounted contingents of standard Videssian warfare, his infantry usually got a holding role. As Gavras' cavalry came into line, the tribune swung Pakhymer over to his own right to guard against outflanking moves from the foe.

"A rare lovely day it is for a shindy, isn't it now?" Viridovix said. His mail shirt was painted in squares of black and gold, imitating the checkered pattern of a Gallic tunic. A seven-spoked wheel crested his bronze helm. His sword, a twin to Scaurus', was still in its scabbard; his hand held nothing more menacing than a chunk of hard, dry bread. He took a healthy bite.

The tribune envied him his calm. The thought of food repelled him before combat, though afterwards he was always ravenous. It *was* a beautiful morning, still a bit crisp with night's chill. Squinting into the bright sunrise, Scaurus said, "Their general knows his business, whoever he is. An early morning fight puts the sun in our faces."

"Aye, so it does, doesn't it? What a rare sneaky thing to think of," the Celt said admiringly.

Ortaias' army was less than half a mile away now, coming on at a purposeful trot. It looked no larger than the one backing Thorisin, Marcus saw with relief. He wondered what part of the total force of the Sphrantzai it contained.

419

It was cavalry, as the tribune had known it would be. He felt the hoofbeats like approaching thunder.

Quintus Glabrio gave his maniple some last instructions: "When you use your *pila,* throw at their horses, not the men. They're bigger targets, less well armored, and if a horse goes down, he takes his rider with him." As always, the junior centurion's tone was measured and under firm control.

There was no time for more speechmaking than that; the enemy was very close. In the daybreak glare, it was still hard to see just what manner of men they were. Some had the scrubby look of nomads—Khamorth or even Yezda—while others . . . lanceheads gleamed briefly crimson as they swung down in a disciplined flurry. Namdaleni, Marcus thought grimly. The Sphrantzai hired the best.

"Drax! Drax! The great count Drax!" shouted the men of the Duchy, using their commander's name as war cry.

"At them!" Thorisin Gavras yelled, and his own horsemen galloped forward to meet the charge. Bowstrings snapped. A Namdalener tumbled from his saddle, unluckily hit below the eye at long range.

The enemy's light horse darted in front of the Namdaleni to volley back at Thorisin's men. But the field was now too tight for their hit-and-run tactics to be used to full effect. More sturdily mounted and more heavily armed, the Videssians and Vaspurakaners who followed Gavras hewed their way through the nomads toward the men of the Duchy who were the opposing army's core.

The count Drax was new-come from the Duchy. The only foot worth its pay he'd seen was that of the Halogai. Of Romans he knew nothing. He took them for peasant levies Thorisin had scraped up from Phos knew where. Crush them quickly, he decided, and then deal with Gavras' outnumbered cavalry at leisure. With a wave of his shield to give his men direction, he spurred his mount at the legionaries.

Dry-mouthed, Scaurus waited to receive the charge. The pounding hooves, the rhythmic shouting of the big men rushing toward him like

420

armored boulders, the long lances that all seemed aimed at his chest . . .
he could feel his calves tensing with the involuntary urge to flee. Longsword in hand, his right arm swung up.

Drax frowned in sudden doubt. If these were drafted farmers, why were
they not running for their paltry lives?

"Loose!" the tribune shouted. A volley of *pila* flew forward, and another,
and another. Horses screamed, swerved, and fell as they were hit, pitching riders headlong to the ground. Other beasts stumbled over the first
ones down. Namdaleni who caught Roman javelins on their shields
cursed and threw them away; the soft iron shanks of the *pila* bent with
ease, fouling the shields beyond use.

Still, the legionaries sagged before the slowed charge's momentum.
Trumpets blared, calling squads from the flank to hold the embattled
center. The mounted surge staggered, stalled, turned to melee.

The knight who came at Scaurus was about forty, with a cast in his
right eye and a twisted little finger. Near immobile in the press, he jabbed
at the tribune with his lance. Marcus parried, ducking under the thrust.
His strong blade bit through the wood below the lancehead, which flew
spinning. Eyes wide with fear, the Namdalener swung the ruined lance
as he might a club. Scaurus ducked again, stepped up and thrust, felt his
point pierce chain and flesh. Sphrantzes' mercenary gave a shriek that
ended in a bubbling moan. Scarlet foam on his lips, he slid to the ground.

Close by, Zeprin the Red raised his long-hafted Haloga war axe high
above his helmet, to bring it crashing down on a horse's head. Brains
flew, pink-gray. The horse foundered like a ship striking a jagged rock.
Pinned under it, its Namdalener rider screamed with a broken ankle, but
not for long. A second stroke of the great axe silenced him for good.

An unhorsed mercenary slashed at Scaurus, who took the blow on
his shield. His *scutum* was bigger and heavier than the horseman's lighter
shield. Marcus shoved out with it. The man of the Duchy stumbled backwards, tripped on a corpse's upthrust foot. A legionary drove a stabbing-
sword into his throat.

Though the Namdalener charge was checked, they still fought with the skill and fierceness Marcus had come to know. Foul-mouthed Lucilius stood staring at his broken sword, the hard steel snapped across by a cunning lance stroke. "Well, fetch me a whole one!" he shouted, but before anybody could, a man of the Duchy rode him down.

"By all the gods, why aren't these bastards on our side? They're too bloody much work to fight," Gaius Philippus panted. There was a great dent in the right side of his helmet, and blood flowed down his face from a cut over one eye. The tide of battle swept them apart before Scaurus could answer.

A Namdalener stabbed down at someone writhing on the ground before him. He missed, swore, and brought his blade back for another stroke. So intent was he on his kill that he never noticed Marcus until the tribune's Gallic longsword drank his life.

Marcus pulled the would-be victim up, then stared in disbelief. "Grace," said Nevrat Sviodo, and kissed him full on the mouth. The shock was as great as if he'd taken a wound. Slim saber in hand, she slipped back into battle, leaving him gaping after her.

"Watch your left, sir!" someone cried. The tribune jerked up his shield in reflex response. A lancehead glanced off it; the Namdalener swept by without time for another blow. Marcus shook himself—surprise had almost cost him his neck.

With a banshee whoop, Viridovix leaped up behind a mounted mercenary and dragged him from his horse. He jerked up the luckless man's chin, drew sword across his throat like a bow over a viol's strings. Blood fountained. The Gaul shouted in triumph, sawed through windpipe and backbone. He lifted the dripping head and hurled it into the close-packed ranks of the Namdaleni, who cried out in horror as they recoiled from the grisly trophy.

The count Drax was not altogether sorry to see retreat begin. These foot soldiers of Thorisin's, whoever they were, fought like no foot he had met. They bent but would not break, rushing men from quiet spots along the line to meet threats so cleverly that no new points of weakness appeared. Quite professional, he thought with reluctant admiration.

From his left wing, the Khatrishers were spraying his bogged-down men with arrows and then darting away, just as he had hoped his hireling nomads would to Thorisin Gavras' heavy horse. But his clans of plainsmen were squeezed between his own men and the oncoming enemy. Soon they would break and run—to stand against this kind of punishment was not in them.

With a wry smile, Drax of Namdalen realized it was not in him, either. When Gavras' cavalry broke through the nomads and stormed into his stalled knights, the result would be unpleasant. And in the end, a mercenary captain's loyalty was to himself, not to his paymaster. Without men, he would have nothing to sell.

He reined in, tried to wheel his horse among his tight-packed countrymen. "Break off," he shouted, "and back to our camp! Keep your order, by the Wager!"

Marcus heard the count's shout to his men but was not sure he understood it; among themselves, the Namdaleni used a broad patois quite different from the Videssian spoken in the Empire. Yet he soon realized what Drax must have ordered, for pressure eased all along the line as the men of the Duchy broke off combat. It was skillfully done; the Namdaleni knew their business and left the legionaries few openings for mischief.

The tribune did not pursue them far. In part he was ruled by the same concern that governed Drax: not to spend his men unwisely. Moreover, the notion of infantry chasing horsemen did not appeal. If the Namdaleni spun round and counterattacked, they could cut off and destroy big chunks of his small force. In loose order the Romans would be horribly vulnerable to the tough mounted lancers.

Gavras' cavalry and the Khatrishers followed Sphrantzes' men for a mile or two, harassing their retreat, trying to turn it to rout. But when the Romans were not added in, the Namdaleni and their nomad outriders probably outnumbered the forces opposed to them. They withdrew in good order.

Scaurus looked up in the sky, amazed. The sun, which had but moments before—or so it seemed—blazed straight into his face as it rose, was well west of south. Marcus realized he was tired, hungry, dry as the Videssian plateau in summer, and in desperate need of easing himself. A slash on his sword hand he did not remember getting began to throb, the more so when sweat ran down his arm into it. He flexed his fingers. They all moved—no tendon was cut.

Legionaries were plundering the corpses of their fallen opponents. Others cut the throats of wounded horses, and of those Namdaleni so badly hurt as to be beyond hope of recovery. Foes with lesser injuries got the same rough medical treatment the Romans did—they could be ransomed later and hence were more valuable alive than dead.

Seriously wounded Romans were carried back into camp on litters for such healing as Gorgidas and Nepos could give. Marcus found the fat priest directing a double handful of women as they cleaned and bandaged wounds. Of Gorgidas there was no sign.

Surprised at that, Scaurus asked where the Greek doctor was. "Don't you know?" one of Nepos' helpers exclaimed, and began to giggle.

The tribune, worn out as he was, could make no sense of that. He stared foolishly. Nepos said gently, "You'll find him at your own tent, Scaurus."

"What? Why is he—? Oh!" Marcus said. He began to run, though a moment before simply standing on his feet had been almost beyond him.

In fact Gorgidas was not in the tribune's tent, but coming back the way Scaurus was going. Dodging the tribune, he said, "Greetings. How went your stupid battle?"

"We won," Marcus answered automatically. "But—but—" he sputtered, and ran out of words. For once there were more urgent things than warfare.

"Rest easy, my friend. You have a son." His spare features alight, Gorgidas took the tribune's arm.

"Is Helvis all right?" Marcus demanded, though the smile on the physician's face told him nothing could be seriously amiss.

"As well as could be expected—better, I'd say. One of the easier births I've seen, less than half a day. She's a big-hipped girl, and it was not her first. Yes, she's fine."

"Thank you," Scaurus said, and would have hurried on, but Gorgidas kept the grip on his arm. The tribune turned round once more. Gorgidas was still smiling, but his eyes were pensive and far away. "I envy you," he said slowly. "It must be a marvelous feeling."

"It is," Marcus said, startled at the depth of sadness in the doctor's voice. He wondered if Gorgidas had meant to lay himself so bare, yet at the same time was touched by the physician's trust. "Thank you," he said again. Their eyes met in a moment of complete understanding.

It passed, and Gorgidas was his astringent self once more. "Go on with you," he said, lightly pushing the tribune forward. "I have enough to do, trying to patch the fools who'd sooner take life than give it." Shaking his head, he made his way down to the injured men not far away.

Minucius' companion Erene was with Helvis, her own daughter, scarcely two months old, asleep in the crook of her arm. The inside of the tribune's tent smelled of blood, the hot, rusty scent as thick as Scaurus had ever known it on the field. Truly, he thought, women fought battles of their own.

Perhaps expecting to see Gorgidas again, Erene started when Marcus, still sweating in his armor, pulled open the tentflap. She knew at once why he had come, but had her own concerns as well. "Is Minucius safe?" she asked anxiously.

"Yes, he's fine," Marcus answered, unconsciously echoing Gorgidas a few minutes before. "Hardly a scratch—he's a clever fighter."

His voice woke Helvis, who had been dozing. Scaurus stooped beside her, kissed her gently. Erene, her fears at rest, slipped unnoticed from the tent.

The smile Helvis gave the tribune was a tired one. Her soft brown hair was all awry and still matted with sweat; purple circles were smudged under her eyes. But there was a triumph in them as she lifted the small blanket of soft lambswool and offered it to Scaurus.

"Yes, let me see him," Marcus said, carefully taking the light burden from her.

"'Him'? You've already seen Gorgidas," Helvis accused, but Marcus was not listening. He looked down at the face of his newborn son. "He looks like you," Helvis said softly.

"What? Nonsense." The baby was red, wrinkled, flat-nosed, and almost bald; he looked scarcely human, let alone like anyone in particular. His wide gray-blue eyes passed across the tribune's face, then returned and seemed to settle for a moment.

The baby wiggled. Scaurus, unaccustomed to such things, nearly dropped him. An arm came free of the swaddling blanket; a tiny fist waved in the air. Marcus cautiously extended a finger. The groping hand touched it, closed in a grasp of surprising strength. The tribune marveled at its miniature perfection—palm and wrist, pink-nailed fingers and thumb, all compressed into a space no longer than the first two joints of his middle finger.

Helvis misunderstood his examination. "He's complete," she said; "ten fingers, ten toes, all where they should be." They laughed together. The noise startled the baby, who began to cry. "Give him to me," Helvis said, and snuggled him against her. In her more knowing hold, the baby soon quieted.

"Do we name him as we planned?" she asked.

"I suppose so," the tribune sighed, not altogether happy with a bargain they'd made months before. He would have preferred a purely Roman name, with some good Latin praenomen ahead of the Aemilii Scauri's long-established nomen and cognomen. Helvis had argued, though, and with justice, that such a name slighted her side of their son's ancestry. Thus they decided the child's use-name would be Dosti, after her father; when heavier style was needed, he had a sonorous patronymic.

"Dosti the son of Aemilius Scaurus," Marcus said, rolling it off his tongue. He suddenly chuckled, looking at his tiny son. Helvis glanced up curiously. "For now," he explained, "the little fellow's name is longer than he is."

"You're out of your mind," she said, but she was smiling still.

V

THE EARLY SUMMER SUN STOOD TALL IN THE SKY. THE CITY VIDESSOS, capital and heart of the Empire that bore its name, gleamed under the bright gaze. White stucco and marble, tawny sandstone, brick the color of blood, the myriad golden globes on Phos' temples—all seemed close enough to reach out and touch, even when seen from the western shore of the strait the Videssians called the Cattle-Crossing.

But between the army on that western shore and the object of its desire swung an endlessly patrolling line of bronze-beaked warships. Ortaias Sphrantzes might have lost the transmarine suburbs of the capital, but when his forces pulled out they left behind few vessels larger than a fishing smack. Not even Thorisin Gavras' impetuosity made him eager to risk a crossing in the face of the enemy fleet.

Balked from advancing further, his frustration grew with his army. He summoned an officers' council to what had been the local governor's residence until that bureaucrat fled to Ortaias. An east-facing window of clear glass gave a splendid view of the Cattle-Crossing and Videssos the city beyond. Marcus suspected Gavras had chosen the meeting place as a goad to his generals.

Baanes Onomagoulos said, "Thorisin, without ships of our own, we'll stay here till we die of old age, and that's how it is. We could have ten times the men we do, and they wouldn't be worth a counterfeit copper to us. We have to get control of the sea."

He thumped his stick on the table; his wound had left his right leg shrunken and lame.

Thorisin glared at him, not so much for what he said but for the patronizing way he said it. Short, lean, and bald, Onomagoulos had a hard, big-nosed face; he had been Mavrikios Gavras' comrade since they were boys, but had never quite got the idea that the dead Emperor's little brother was now a man in his own right.

"I can't wish ships here," Thorisin snapped. "The Sphrantzai pay their captains well, if no one else. They know they're all that's keeping their heads from going up on the Milestone."

Privately, Marcus thought that an exaggeration. Along with Videssos' proud buildings and elegant gardens, its fortifications—the mightiest the Roman had ever seen—were visible from this seaside house. Even with the Cattle-Crossing somehow overleaped, an assault on that double line of frowning dun walls was enough to daunt any soldier. One problem at a time, he thought.

"Onomagoulos is right, I t'ink. Wit'out ships, you fail. Why not get dem from the Duchy?" Utprand Dagober's son entered the debate for the first time, his island accent almost thick enough to pass for that of the Namdaleni's Haloga cousins. His men were new-come to the seacoast, having marched and fought their way from Phanaskert clear across the Videssian westlands.

"Now there's a notion," Thorisin said dryly. Plainly he did not much like it, but Utprand's forces had swelled his own by a third. It behooved him to walk soft.

The Namdalener smiled a wintry smile; winter seemed at home in his eyes, the chill blue of the ice his northern ancestors left behind when they took Namdalen from the Empire two hundred years before. Matching Gavras irony for irony, he asked, "You cannot misdoubt our good fait'?"

"Surely not," Thorisin replied, and there were chuckles up and down the table. The Duchy of Namdalen had been a thorn in Videssos' flesh since its stormy birth. Its Haloga conquerors did not stay rude pirates long, but learned much from their more civilized subjects. That learning made their mixed-blooded descendants dangerous, subtle warriors. They fought for the Empire, aye, but they and their paymasters both knew they would seize it if they could.

"Well, what would you?" Soteric Dosti's son demanded of Gavras. Helvis' brother sat at Utprand's left hand; the young Namdalener had risen fast since the tribune last saw him. He went on, "Would you sooner win this war with our help, or lose without?"

428

Scaurus flinched; Soteric always presented choices so as to make yea unpalatable as nay. Save for a proud nose that bespoke partly Videssian ancestry, his features were much like his sister's, but his wide mouth habitually drew up in a thin, hard line.

Thorisin looked from him to the tribune and back again. Marcus' own lips compressed; he knew the Emperor still carried misgivings over the ties of friendship and blood between Romans and Namdaleni. But Gavras' answer was mild enough: "There still may be other alternatives than those."

His gaze swung back to Scaurus. "What say you?" he asked. "Not much, so far."

The tribune was glad of a question he could deal with dispassionately. "That ships are needed, no one can doubt. As to how to get them, others here know better than I. We Romans always took more naturally to fighting on land than on the sea. Put me on the other side of the Cattle-Crossing and you'll hear advice from me in plenty, never fear."

Thorisin smiled mirthlessly. "I believe that—the day you don't speak your mind is the day I begin to suspect you. And I grant you, silence is better than breaking wind by mouth when you've nothing useful to say."

But, having just disclaimed knowledge of naval warfare, Marcus thought back to his lost homeland's past. "My people fought wars with a country called Carthage, which at first had a strong fleet where we had none. We used a beached ship of theirs as a model for our own and soon we were challenging them on the sea. Could we not build our own here?"

The idea had not occurred to Gavras, whose thinking had dealt solely with ships already in existence. He rubbed his bearded chin as he thought; Marcus thought the white streaks on either side of his jaw were wider than they had been a year ago. Finally the Emperor asked, "How long did it take your folk to get their navy built?"

"Sixty days for the first ship, it's said."

"Too long, too long," Thorisin muttered, as much to himself as to his marshals. "I begrudge every day that passes. Phos alone knows what the Yezda are doing behind us."

"Not Phos alone," Soteric said, but so low Gavras could not hear. Few of the tales that the Namdaleni brought from their journey across Videssos were gladsome. Though they had no love for Thorisin Gavras, they agreed that the sooner he won his civil war—if he could—the better his hope of reclaiming the westlands for Videssos.

The Emperor refilled his wine cup from a shapely carafe of gilded silver—like the house in which the council sat, a possession of the recently departed governor. Gavras spat on the dark slate floor in rejection of Skotos and all his works, then raised his eyes and hands on high as he prayed to Phos—the same ritual over wine Scaurus had seen his first day in the Empire.

He realized with some surprise, though, that now he understood the prayer. What Gorgidas had said so long ago was true; little by little, Videssos was setting its mark on him.

Half an hour's ride south of the suburb the Videssians simply called "Across," citrus orchards came down to the sea, leaving only a thin strand of white beach to mark the coastline. Scaurus tethered his borrowed horse to the smooth gray branch of a lemon tree, then cursed softly when in the darkness he scraped his arm on one of the tree's protecting spines.

It was nearly midnight on a moonless night; the men dismounting near the Roman were but blacker shadows under Videssos' strange stars. The light from the great city on the eastern shore of the strait was of more use than their cold gleam, or would have been, had not a war galley's cruel silhouette blocked most of it from sight.

Gaius Philippus nearly tripped as he dismounted. "A pox on these stirrups," he muttered in Latin. "I knew I'd forget the bloody things."

"Quiet, there," Thorisin Gavras said, walking out onto the beach. The rest of his party followed. It was so dark the members were hard to recognize. What little light there was glistened off Nepos' smooth-shaved head and showed his short, tubby frame; Baanes Onomagoulos' painful rolling gait was also unmistakable. Most of the officers were simply tall shapes, one interchangeable with the next.

Gavras unhooded a tiny lantern, once, twice, three times. A cricket chirped in such perfect imitation of the signal that men jumped, laughing quick, nervous, almost silent laughs. But the insect call was not the response Thorisin awaited.

"There's too many of us here," Onomagoulos said nervously. A few seconds later he added, "Your precious fellow out there will get the wind up."

"Hush," Gavras said, making a gesture all but invisible in the dark. From the bow of the silent warship came one flash, then a second.

Thorisin gave a soft grunt of satisfaction, sent back a single answering flash. All was dark and silent for a few moments, then Marcus heard the soft slap of waves on wood as a boat was lowered from that lean, menacing shape ahead.

The tribune's right hand curled round his sword hilt. "Other alternatives"—he recalled Gavras' words of a week before only too well. This parley struck him as suicidally foolish; if the admiral aboard that bireme—drungarios of the fleet was his proper title, Marcus remembered—chose treachery and landed marines, the rebellion against the Sphrantzai would be short-lived indeed.

Thorisin had only laughed at him when he put his fears into words. "You never met Taron Leimmokheir, or you wouldn't speak such nonsense. If he promises a safe meeting, a safe meeting there will be. It's not in him to lie."

The boat was beyond its parent vessel's shadow now, and Scaurus saw Gavras had been right. There were but three men in it: a pair of rowers and a still figure at the stern who had to be the drungarios. The rowers feathered their oars so skillfully that they passed silently over the sea. Only the green-blue phosphorescence that foamed up at each stroke told of their passage.

The little rowboat beached, its keel scraping softly against sand. The rowers leaped out to pull it past waves' reach. When it was secured, Leimmokheir came striding toward the knot of men waiting for him by the trees. Either he was a lucky man or his night sight was very keen, for he unerringly picked out Thorisin Gavras from among his followers.

"Hello, Gavras," he said, clasping Thorisin's hand. "This skulking around by night is a dark business more ways than one, and I don't care for it a bit." His voice was deep and hoarse, roughened by years of shouting over wind and wave. Even at first hearing, Marcus understood why Thorisin Gavras trusted this man; it was not possible to imagine him deceitful.

"A dark business, aye," Gavras agreed, "but one which can lead toward the light. Help us pass the Cattle-Crossing and oust Ortaias the fool and his uncle the spider. Phos, man, you've had half a year now to see how the two of them run things—they aren't fit to clean the red boots, let alone to wear 'em."

Taron Leimmokheir drew in a slow, thoughtful breath. "I gave my oath to Ortaias Sphrantzes when it was not known if you were alive or dead. Would you forswear me? Skotos' ice is the final home for oath-breakers."

"Would you see the Empire dragged down to ruin by your scruples?" Thorisin shot back. There were times when he sounded all too much like Soteric, and Scaurus instinctively knew he was taking the wrong tack with this man.

"Why not work with them, not against?" Leimmokheir returned. "They freely offer you the title you bore under your brother, may good Phos shine upon his countenance, and declare their willingness to bind themselves by any oaths you name."

"Were it possible, I'd say I valued the oaths of the Sphrantzai less even than their coins."

That got home; Leimmokheir let out a bark of laughter before he could check himself. But he would not change his mind. "You've grown bitter and distrustful," he said. "If nothing else, the fact that you and they are now related by marriage will hold them to their pledges. Doubly damned are those who dare against kinsmen."

"You are an honest, pious man, Taron," Thorisin said regretfully. "Because you have no evil in you, you will not see it in others."

The drungarios half bowed. "That may be, but I, too, must try to do right as I see it. When next we meet, I will fight you."

"Seize him!" Soteric said urgently. At the edge of hearing, Leimmokheir's two sailors snapped to alertness.

But Gavras was shaking his head. "Would you make a Sphrantzes of me, Namdalener?" Close by, Utprand rumbled agreement. Thorisin ignored him, turning back to Taron Leimmokheir. "Go on, get out," he said. Marcus had never heard such bitter weariness in his voice.

The drungarios bowed once more, this time from the waist. He walked slowly down to his boat, turned as if to say something. Whatever it was, it did not pass his lips. He sat down at the boat's stern; his men pushed it out until they were waist-deep in the sea, then scrambled aboard themselves. Oars rose and fell; the rowboat turned in a tight circle, then moved steadily back to the galley.

Marcus heard a rope ladder creak as it took weight, the sound faint but clear across the water. Taron Leimmokheir's raspy bass rumbled a command. The bireme's quiet oars awoke, sending it gliding south like some monster centipede. It disappeared behind an outjutting point of land.

Thorisin watched it go, disappointment plain in every line of his body. He said softly to himself, "Honest and pious, yes, but too trusting by half. One day it will cost him."

"If it doesn't cost us first," Indakos Skylitzes exclaimed. "Look there!" From the north, a longboat was darting toward the lonely stretch of beach; no little ship's gig this, but a twenty-footer packed to the gunwales with armed men.

"Sold!" Gavras said, disbelief in his voice. He stood frozen for a moment as the longboat came ashore. "Phos curse that baseborn treacher for all eternity. Belike he landed marines south of us, too, just as soon as he was out of sight, to make it a good, thorough trap."

His sword rang free of scabbard. It glittered coldly in uncaring starlight. "Well, as friend Baanes said, there's more of us here than he reckoned on. We can give this lot a fight. Videssos!" he yelled, and charged the longboat, where soldiers were still climbing out onto the beach.

Scaurus among them, his officers pounded after him, sand spraying up as they ran. Only Nepos and Onomagoulos hung back—the one was no warrior, while the other could scarcely walk.

It was four to three against Gavras' party, or something close to that; there must have been twenty men in the grounded boat. But instead of using their numbers to any advantage, they stood surprised, waiting to receive their foes' onset.

"Ha, villains!" Thorisin cried. "Not the easy assassination you were promised, is it?" He cut at one of the men from the boat, who parried and slashed back. Lithe as a serpent, Thorisin twisted, cut again. The man groaned, dropped his blade to clutch at the spurting gash below his left shoulder. A last stroke, this one two-handed, ripped into his belly. He slumped to the sand, unmoving.

Marcus never wanted to know another fight like this battle in the darkness. To tell friend from foe was all but impossible, and it was not easy even to strike a blow. The beach sand was as treacherous as the combat, sliding and shifting so a man could hardly keep his feet planted under him.

An attacker slashed at Scaurus; his saber hissed past the tribune's ear. He stumbled back, wishing for a cuirass or shield. To hold the man off, he lunged out in a stop-thrust, and his opponent, intent on finishing an enemy he thought at his mercy, rushed forward to skewer himself on the blade he never saw. He grunted, coughed wetly, and died.

If none of Gavras' companions wore armor, the same seemed true of their assailants; few men who traveled by sea would risk its perilous weight. And Thorisin's followers were masters of war, soldiers who had come to their high ranks through years of honing their fighting skills. When coupled with their fury at this betrayal-caused battle, that balanced the advantage their enemies' numbers gave them.

Soon the would-be assassins sought escape, but they found no more than they would have granted. Three tried to launch the longboat once more, but they were cut down from behind.

Long legs churning through the sand, Soteric raced down the beach after the last of the fleeing bravoes. Finding flight useless, the warrior whirled to defend himself. Steel rang on steel. It was too black for Marcus to see much of that fight, but the Namdalener beat down his foe's guard with hammer-strokes of his sword and stretched him bleeding and lifeless on the soft white strand.

Scaurus' eyes jumped everywhere looking for more enemies, but there were none. A worse task began—seeing who among Thorisin's men had fallen. Indakos Skylitzes was down, as were two Vaspurakaner officers the tribune did not know well and a Namdalener who had accompanied Utprand and Soteric. The tribune wondered who would receive the dead man's sword, and what lives would suddenly be wrenched askew.

Gavras was jubilant. "Well fought, well fought!" he yelled, his glee filling the beach. "Thus always to murderers! They—here, stop that! What in Phos' holy name are you doing?"

Baanes Onomagoulos had been stumping up and down, methodically slitting the throats of those attackers who still moved. His hands gleamed, wet, black, and slick in the stars' pale light.

"What do you think?" Onomagoulos retorted. "That accursed Leimmokheir's marines will be here any time. Should I leave these whoresons to tell 'em where we've gone?"

"No," Thorisin admitted. "But you should have saved one for questioning."

"Too late now." Onomagoulos spread his bloody hands. "Nepos," he called, "make a light. I'd wager we'll have the answer to any questions soon enough."

The priest came up to Onomagoulos' side. His breathing grew deep and steady. Gavras' officers muttered in awe as a pale, golden radiance sprang into being round his hands. Marcus was less wonder-struck than some; this was a miracle he had seen before, from Apsimar the prelate of Imbros.

For all the amazement Baanes Onomagoulos showed, Nepos might have lit a torch. The half-crippled noble painfully bent by one of the fallen attackers. His knife snicked out to slit a belt-pouch. Goldpieces—a surprising number of goldpieces—spilled onto the sand. Onomagoulos scooped them up, held them close to Nepos' glowing palms. Thorisin's marshals crowded close to look.

"'Ort. the 1st Sphr., Avt. of Vid.,'" Onomagoulos read from a coin, not bothering to stretch the abbreviation full length. "Here's Ort. the first again—again." He turned a goldpiece over. "And again. Nothing but Phos-curse Ort. the first, in fact."

"Aye, ahnd ahll fresh-minted, too." That flat-voweled accent had to belong to Utprand Dagober's son.

"What else would Leimmokheir use to pay his hired killers?" Onomagoulos asked rhetorically.

"How could the Sphrantzai have infected him with their treachery?" Thorisin wondered. "Vardanes must be leagued with Skotos, to have suborned Taron Leimmokheir."

No one answered him; the crackle of brush pushed aside, loud in the midnight stillness, came from the south. Swords flew up instinctively. Nepos' light vanished as he took his concentration from it. "The son of a manurebag did land marines!" Onomagoulos growled.

"I don't think so," Gaius Philippus said. Woods-wise, he went on, "I think the noise was closer to us, made by something smaller than a man—a fox, maybe, or a badger."

"You are right, I think," Utprand said.

Not even the centurion of the Namdalener, though, seemed eager to wait and test their guess. With their comrades, they hurried back to their mounts. Soteric, Scaurus, and Nepos quickly lashed the bodies of Gavras' slain commanders to their horses. Moments later, they were trotting north through the orchard. Branches slapped at the tribune before he knew they were there.

If Leimmokheir's marines were behind the officers, they never caught them up. When Thorisin and his followers emerged from the fragrant rows of trees, the Emperor galloped his horse a quarter of a mile in sheer exuberance at being alive. He waited impatiently for his men to join him.

When they reached him at last, he had the air of a man who had come to a decision. "Very well, then," he declared. "If we cannot cross with Leimmokheir's let, we shall in his despite."

" 'In his despite,' " Gorgidas echoed the next morning. "A ringing phrase, no doubt." The Roman camp was full of excitement as word of the night's adventure raced through Gavras' army. Viridovix, as was his way when left out of a fight, was wildly jealous and sulked for hours until Scaurus managed to jolly him from his sour mood.

The tribune's men bombarded him and Gaius Philippus with questions. Most were satisfied after one or two, but Gorgidas kept on, trying to pull from the Romans every detail of what had gone on. His cross-questioning was sharp as a jurist's, and he soon succeeded in annoying Gaius Philippus.

A more typical Roman than the thoughtful Scaurus, the senior centurion had little patience for anything without obvious practical use. "You don't want us," he complained to the doctor. "You want one of the buggers Onomagoulos let the air out of, to go at him with pincers and hot iron."

The Greek took no notice of his griping, but said, "Onomagoulos, eh? Thank you, that reminds me of something else I wanted to ask: how did he know he'd find Ortaias' monies in the dead men's pouches?"

"Great gods, that should be plain enough even to you." Gaius Philippus threw his hands in the air. "If their drungarios hired murderers, he'd have to pay in his master's coins." The centurion gave a short, hard laugh. "It's not likely he'd have any of Thorisin's. And don't think you can ignore me and have me go away," he went on. "You still haven't said the first thing about why you're flinging all these questions at us."

The usually voluble Greek stood mute. He arched one eyebrow and tried to stare Gaius Philippus down, but Marcus came in on the senior centurion's side. "Anyone would think you were writing a history," he told the physician.

A slow flush climbed Gorgidas' face. Scaurus saw that what he had meant for a joke was in grim earnest to the Greek. "Your pardon," he said, and meant it. "I did not know. How long have you been working on it?"

"Eh? Since I learned enough Videssian to ask for pen and parchment—you know as well as I there's no papyrus here."

"What language is it in?" the tribune asked.

"*Hellenisti, ma Dia!* In Greek, by Zeus! What other tongue is there for serious thought?" Gorgidas slipped back into his native speech to answer.

Gaius Philippus stared at him in amazement. His own Greek consisted of a couple of dozen words, most of them foul, but he knew the name of the language when he heard it. "In Greek, you say? Of all the bootless things I've heard, that throws the triple six! Greek, in Videssos that's never heard the word, let alone the tongue? Why, man, you could be Homer or what's-his-name—the first history writer, I heard it once but I'm damned if I recall it—" He looked to Scaurus for help.

"Herodotus," the tribune supplied.

"Thanks; that's the name. As I say, Gorgidas, you could be either of those old bastards, or even both of 'em together, and who'd ever know it, here? Greek!" he repeated, half-contemptuous wonder in his voice.

The doctor's color deepened. "Yes, Greek, and why not?" he said tightly. "One day, maybe, I'll be easy enough in Videssian to write it, or I might have one of their scholars help translate what I write. Manetho the Egyptian and Berosos of Babylon wrote in Greek to teach us Hellenes of their nations' past glories; it wouldn't be the worst deed to make sure we are remembered in Videssos after the last of us has died."

He spoke with the same determination he might have shown when facing a difficult case, but Marcus saw he had not impressed Gaius Philippus. What happened after his own end was of no concern to the senior centurion. He sensed, however, that he had chaffed Gorgidas about as much as he could. In his rough way he was fond of the doctor, so he shrugged and gave up the argument, saying, "All this gabbing is a waste of time. I'd best go drill the men; they're fat and lazy enough as is." He strode off, still shaking his head.

"The Videssians will be interested in your work, I think," Marcus said to Gorgidas. "They have historians of their own; I remember Alypia Gavra saying she read them, and I think—though I'm not sure—she might have been taking notes for a book of her own. Why else would she have been at Mavrikios' council of war?" Something else occurred to the tribune. "She might be able to help you get yours translated."

He saw gratitude flicker in the doctor's eyes, but Gorgidas was prickly as always. "Aye, so she might—were she not on the far side of the Cattle-Crossing, married to the wrong Emperor. But who are we to boggle at such trivia?"

"All right, all right, your point's made. I tell you this, though—if Alypia were on the far side of the moon, I'd still want to see that history of yours."

"That's right, you read some Greek, don't you? I'd forgotten that." Gorgidas sighed, said ruefully, "Truly, Scaurus, one reason I started the thing in the first place was to keep myself from losing my letters. The gods know I'm no, ah, what's-his-name?" The physician's chuckle had a hollow ring. "But I find I can put together understandable sentences."

"I'd like to see what you've done," Scaurus said, and meant it. He had always found history, with its dispassionate approach, a more reliable guide to the conduct of affairs than the orators' high-flown rhetoric. Thucydides or Polybios was worth twenty of Demosthenes, who sold his tongue like a woman her virtue and sometimes composed speeches for prosecution and defense in the same case.

Gorgidas broke into his musing. "Speaking of Alypia and the Cattle-Crossing," he said, "did Gavras say anything of how he planned to pass it by? I'm not asking as a historian now, you understand, merely as someone with certain objections to being killed out of hand."

"I have a few of those myself," Marcus admitted. "No, I don't know what's in his mind." Still thinking in classical terms, he went on, "Whatever it is, it may well work. Thorisin is like Odysseus—he's *sophron*."

"*Sophron*, eh?" Gorgidas said. "Well, let's hope you're right." The Greek word meant not so much having superior wits but getting the most distance from those one had. Gorgidas was not so sure it fit Gavras, but he thought it a fine description for Scaurus himself.

Black-capped terns wheeled and dipped, screeching their disapproval at the armed men scrambling down a splintery ladder into the waist of a fishing boat that had seen better days. "A pox on you, louse-bitten sea crows!" Viridovix shouted up at them, shaking his fist. "I like the notion no better than yourselves."

All along the docks and beaches of Videssos' western suburbs, troops were boarding by squads and platoons as motley a fleet as Marcus had ever imagined. Three or four grain carriers, able to embark a whole company, formed the backbone of Thorisin Gavras' makeshift armada. There were fishing craft aplenty; those the eye could not pick out at once were immediately obvious to the nose. There were smugglers' boats, with great spreads of canvas and lines greyhound-lean. There were little sponge-divers' vessels, some hardly more than rowboats, with masts no thicker than a spearshaft. There were keel-less barges taken from the river trade; how they would act on the open sea was anyone's bet. And there were a great many ships whose functions the tribune, no more nautical than most Romans, could not hope to guess.

He helped Nepos down onto the fishing boat's deck. "I thank you," the priest said. Nepos sagged against the boat's raised cabin. Timbers creaked under his weight, but he made no move to stand free. "Merciful Phos, but I'm tired," he said. His eyes were still merry, but there were dark circles under them and his words came slowly, as if getting each one out took effort.

"Well you might be," Scaurus answered. Aided by three other sorcerers, the priest had spent the past two and a half weeks weaving spells round the odd assortment of boats Thorisin had gathered from up and down the western coastlands. Most of the work had fallen on Nepos' shoulders, for he held a chair in sorcery at the Videssian Academy in the capital while his colleagues were local wizards without outstanding talent. At its easiest, sorcery was as exhausting as hard labor; what the priest had accomplished was hardly sorcery at its easiest.

Gorgidas descended, graceful as a cat; a moment later Gaius Philippus came down beside him, planting himself on the gently rocking deck as if daring it to shake him.

"Viridovix!" It was a soft hail from the next boat down the dock, a lateen-rigged fishing craft even smaller and grubbier than the one the Celt was sharing with the Roman officers.

"Aye, Bagratouni?" Viridovix called. "Is your honor glad to be on the ocean, now?" Coming from landlocked Vaspurakan, Gagik Bagratouni had professed regret that he knew nothing of the sea.

The *nakharar*'s leonine features were distinctly green. "Does always it move about so?" he asked.

"Bad cess to you for reminding me," Viridovix said, gulping.

"Use the rail, not my deck," warned the fishing boat's captain, a thin, dark, middle-aged man with hair and beard sun-and-sea-bleached to the grayish-yellow color of his boat's planking. The Gaul's misery mystified him. How could a man be sick on an all but motionless boat?

"If my stomach decides to come up, now, I'll use whatever's underneath me, and that without a by-your-leave," Viridovix said, but in Latin, not Videssian.

"What now?" Marcus asked Nepos, waving out to the patrolling galleys, their broad sails like sharks' fins. "Shall we be invisible to them, like the Yezda for a few moments during the great battle?" He still sweat cold every time he thought of that, though Videssian sorcerers had quickly worked counterspells that brought the nomads back into sight.

440

"No, no." The priest managed to sound impatient and weary at the same time. "That spell is all very well against folk with no magic of their own, but if any opposing wizard is nearby one might just as well light a bonfire at the bow of the boat." The captain's head whipped round; he wanted no talk of bonfires aboard his ship.

Nepos continued, "Besides, the invisibility spell is easy to overcome, and if it were broken with us on the sea, the slaughter would be terrible. We are using a subtler measure, one crafted in the Academy last year. We will, in fact, be in full sight of the galleys all the way to the eastern shore of the Cattle-Crossing."

"Where's the magic in that?" Gaius Philippus demanded. "I could swim out there and accomplish as much, though I'd have little joy of it."

"Patience, I pray you," Nepos said. "Let me finish. Though we'll be in plain sight of the foe, he will not see us. That is the artistry; his eye will slide over us, look past us, but never light on us."

"I see," the senior centurion said approvingly. "It'll be like when I'm hunting partridges and walk past one without ever noticing it because its colors blend into the brush and woods where it's hiding."

"Something like that," Nepos nodded. "Though there's rather more to it. We don't blend into the ocean, you know. The eye, yes, and the ear as well, have to be tricked away from us by magic, not simple camouflage. But it's a gentler magic than the invisibility spell and nearly impossible to detect unless a wizard already knows it's there."

"There's the signal now," the fishing captain said. Thorisin Gavras' flagship, a rakish smugglers' vessel almost big enough to challenge one of Ortaias' warcraft, was flying the sky-blue Videssian imperial pennant. The steady northwesterly breeze whipped it out straight, showing Phos' sun bright in its center.

A sailor undid the mooring lines that held the fishing boat to the dock at stern and bow, tossed them aboard, and leaped nimbly down into the boat. At the captain's quick orders, his four-man crew unreefed the single square-rigged sail. The sailcloth was old, sagging, and much patched, but it held the wind. Pitching slightly in the light chop, the boat slid out into the Cattle-Crossing.

Scaurus led his companions to the bow, both to be out of the sailors' way and to see what lay ahead. The western part of the channel was as full of boats as an unwashed dog with fleas, but not one of the biremes ahead paid them the slightest heed. So far, at least, Nepos' magic held. "What will you do if your spell should fail in mid-crossing?" Marcus asked the priest.

"Pray," Nepos said shortly, "for we are undone." But seeing it was a question seriously meant and not asked only to vex him, he added, "There would be little else I could do; it's a complex magic, and not one easily laid on."

As always, Viridovix was lost in a private anguish from the moment the little fishing boat began to move. Knuckles white beneath freckles from the desperation of his grip, he clutched the boat's rail, leaning over it as far as he could. Gaius Philippus, who did not suffer from seasickness, said to Nepos, "Tell me, priest, is your conjuring proof against the sound of puking?"

On firm ground such sarcasm would have sparked a quarrel with the Celt, but he only moaned and held on tighter. Then he suddenly straightened, amazement ousting distress. "What was that, now?" he exclaimed, pointing down into the water. The others followed his finger, but there was nothing to see but the cyan-blue ocean with its tracing of lacy white foam.

"There's another!" Viridovix said. Not far from the boat, a smooth, silver-scaled shape flicked itself into the air, to glide for fifty yards before dropping back into the sea. "What manner of fairy might it be, and what's the meaning of it? Is the seeing of it a good omen, or foul?"

"You mean the flying fish?" Gorgidas asked in surprise. Children of the warm Mediterranean, he and the Romans took the little creatures for granted, but they were unknown in the cool waters of the northern ocean that was the only sea the Gaul knew.

And because they were so far removed from anything he had imagined, Viridovix would not believe his friends' insistence that these were but another kind of fish, not even when Nepos joined his assurances to theirs. "The lot of you are thinking to befool me," he said, "and rare cruel y'are, too, with me so sick and all." His bodily woes only served to make him ugly; his voice was petulant and full of hostility.

"Oh, for the—!" Gaius Philippus said in exasperation. "Bloody fool of a Celt!" Flying fish were skipping all around the boat now, perhaps fleeing some maruading albacore or tuna. One, more intrepid but less lucky than its fellows, landed on the deck almost at the centurion's feet. As it flopped on the planks, he took his dagger, still sheathed, from his belt and, reversing the weapon, struck the fish smartly behind the head with the pommel.

He picked up the foot-long, broken-backed fish and handed it to the Gaul. The broad gliding fins hung limply; already the golden eyes were dimming, the ocean-blue back and silver belly losing their living sheen and fading toward death's gray. "You killed it," Viridovix said in dismay, and threw it back into the sea.

"More foolishness," the centurion said. "They're fine eating, butter-flied and fried." But Viridovix, still distressed, shook his head; he had seen a dream die, not a fish, and to think of it as food was beyond him.

"You should be grateful," Gorgidas observed. "With your interest in the flying fish, you've forgotten your seasickness."

"Why, indeed and I have," the Celt said, surprised. His quick-rising spirits brought a grin to his face. Just then a wave a trifle bigger than most slapped against the fishing boat's bow. The light craft rolled gently and Viridovix, eyes bulging and cheeks pale with nausea, had to seek the rail once more. "Be damned to you for making me remember," he choked out between heaves.

Some of Thorisin's boats were by the patrolling galleys now, and still no sign they had been seen. As it sailed toward the agreed-upon landing point a couple of miles south of the capital, the vessel Marcus rode passed within a hundred yards of a warship of the Sphrantzai.

Spell-protected or not, it was a nervous moment. The tribune could clearly read the name painted in gold on the ship's bow: *Corsair Breaker*. Her sharp bronze beak, greened by the sea, came in and out, in and out of view. There were white patches of barnacles on it and on those timbers usually below the waterline. A dart-throwing engine was on her fore-deck, loaded and ready to shoot; the missile's steel head blurred in bright reflection.

Corsair Breaker's two banks of long oars rose and fell in smooth uni-son. Even a lubber like Scaurus could tell her rowers were a fine crew;

indifferent to the wind, they drove her steadily north. Over the creak of oars in their locks and the slap of them in the sea came the bass roar of song they used to keep their rhythm:

"Lit-tle bird with a yellow bill
Sat outside my windowsill—"

The Videssian army sang that song, too, and the Romans with them as soon as they'd learned the words. There were, it was said, fifty-two verses to it, some witty, some brutal, some obscene, and most a mix of all three.

The hoarse ballad faded as *Corsair Breaker*'s superior speed swept the bireme away on her patrolling path. Under-officers stood at the twin steering oars at her stern; a lookout was atop her mast to cry danger at anything untoward. Marcus swallowed a smile. If Nepos' magic suddenly disappeared, the poor fellow likely would have heart failure.

The tribune's smile returned—and not swallowed, either—as he watched his Emperor's mismatched excuse for a fleet sneak its way over the Cattle-Crossing under the nose of the imperial navy. Some of the faster boats were almost to the shore; even the slow, awkward barges were past the galleys loyal to Ortaias. With fortune, Videssos the city should be too much stunned at the sight of Gavras' army appeared from nowhere under its walls to put much thought to resistance.

"Aye, a splendid job," he said expansively to Nepos. "Puts the whole war in hailing distance of being won."

Like all of Phos' priests, Nepos was pledged to humility. He flushed under Scaurus' praise. "Thank you," he said shyly. He was academic as much as priest and so went on, "This success will take an important new charm out of the realm of theory and into the practical sphere. The research, of course, was the work of many; it's mere chance that makes me the one to execute it. It—"

The priest lurched and turned purple: no blush of modesty this, but a darkening as if strangler's hands were round his neck. Marcus and Gorgidas darted toward him, both afraid the fat little man's labor had brought on a fit of apoplexy.

But Nepos was suffering no fit, though tears rolled down his cheek to lose themselves in his thicket of beard. His hands moved in desperate passes; he whispered cantrips fast as his lips could shape them.

"What's toward?" Gaius Philippus barked. Doubly out of his reckoning on the sea and treating with magic, he nonetheless knew trouble when he saw it. His hand snaked to his sword hilt, but the familiar gesture brought him no comfort.

"Counterspell!" Nepos got out between his quickly repeated charms. He was shaking like a man with an ague. "A vicious one—aimed at me as much as my spell. And strong—Phos, who at the Academy can it be? I've never felt such strength—almost struck me down where I stood." He had been incanting between sentences, sometimes between words, and returned wholly to his sorcery once the gasped explanation was through.

The priest's skill was enough to save himself, but could not keep his spell intact. Still at his miserable perch over the rail, Viridovix cried out, "Och, we're for it now! The cat's after kenning there's mice in the cupboard!"

Including *Corsair Breaker,* there were seven galleys in Marcus' sight. He could hardly imagine how Sphrantzes' ship captains and sailors must have felt, with the ocean full of their enemy's ships. Their reaction, though, was nothing like the palpitations the tribune had jokingly wished on them a few minutes before. They went charging against the small craft all around them like so many bulls rampaging through a herd of sheep.

Scaurus' heart leaped into his mouth to see one of the cruel-beaked ships bearing down on the rearmost barge, a craft that was, to his horror, filled with legionaries. But the bireme's captain, at least, was unnerved enough by his foes' apparition to make a fatal error of judgment. Instead of trusting to his vessel's ram, his port oars swept up and out of the way as he came gracefully alongside and demanded the barge's surrender.

In his pride, though, he forgot there was more to the bargain than his sleek ship against the slow-moving, clumsy river scow: there were men as well. Ropes snaked up to catch on belaying pins and the steering oar, binding ship to ship tight as a lover's embrace. And up those ropes and over the galley's low gunwales swarmed the Romans, whooping with wolfish glee. They pitched the handful of marines on board over the side;

those splashes marked their end for, not true sailors, they wore cuirasses which now were fatal, not protecting.

Seeing his ship taken from under him, the captain fled to the high stern. He, too, wore armor: gilded, in token of his rank. It flashed brilliantly for a moment as he leaped into the sea to drown, too proud to outlive his folly.

That mattered little, as far as the outcome went. The Romans, no sailors themselves, laid hold of the bireme's pilot and put a sword against his throat. Thus encouraged, he bawled orders to the crew. Oars came raggedly to life; the sail spread and billowed. Like a race horse among carters' nags, the galley sprinted for the beach.

Elsewhere, things went not so well. Warned by their comrade's blunder, Ortaias' warships made no further unwise moves. A fishing boat kissed by their sharp bronze simply ceased to be, save as sodden canvas, splintered timbers, and men struggling in the warm blue waters of the strait. Worse still, alarm bells were ringing in the city, and through the boom of surf off sea walls Marcus could hear officers shouting their men aboard fresh galleys.

But all that needed time, and the Sphrantzai had little time to spend. Already Gavras' boats were beginning to beach, soldiers jumping from them as fast as they could scramble. And each attack run stole precious minutes from the warships, for their targets jinked and dodged with all the desperate skill their crews could summon. Even after a ram bit home, there was more delay as the triumphant bireme backed oars to pull itself free of its prey. Unspining was a delicate task, lest the warships, like bees, were to leave stings behind in their wounds, and with results as damaging to themselves.

Marcus shouted himself hoarse to see what seemed a surely fatal stroke go wide. He was so intent on the sprawling seafight that he almost did not hear the helmsman's frightened cry: "Phos have mercy! One o' the buggers is on our tail!"

"Come a point north," the captain ordered instantly, gauging wind, coast, and pursuer in one comprehensive glance.

"'Twill lose us some of our wind," the helmsman protested.

"Aye, but it's a shorter run to the beach. Steer so, damn you!" Pale beneath his sun-swarthied skin, the helmsman obeyed.

Scaurus bit his lip, not so much from fright but frustration. His fate was being decided here, and not a thing he could do but impotently wait. If that sea-bleached fishing captain knew his business, the boat might come safe through it; if not, surely not. But either way, there was nothing the tribune could do to help or hurt. His skills were worthless here, his opinions of no value.

The shore seemed nailed in place before him, while from behind the galley came rushing up, shark-sure and swift. Too fast, too fast, he thought; Achilles would surely catch this tortoise.

Gaius Philippus was making the same grim calculation. "He'll be up our arse before we ground," he said. "If we shed our mail shirts now, we have hope to swim it."

Abandoning armor was an admission of defeat, but that was not what set Marcus against it. There were archers on that cursed bireme; already a couple of shafts had whistled past, more swift and slender than any flying fish. To be shot swimming defenselessly in the sea was not an end he relished.

If the bireme was in arrow range the end of the chase could not be far away. With sick fascination, the tribune watched the imperial pennant stiff in the breeze at the warship's bow. Below it was another, this one crimson with five bronze bars, the drungarios' emblem. So, Marcus thought, it was Taron Leimmokheir himself who'd sink him. He would willingly have forgone the honor.

But another ship was racing up alongside the imperial vessel, not so big, but packed to the gunwales with armed men . . . and also flying the imperial banner. "Go on, Leimmokheir, go on, you sneaking filthy knife in the night!" Thorisin Gavras roared across the narrowing space of water, his furious bellow like song in Scaurus' ears. "Ram, and then you face me! You haven't the stones in your bag for it!"

No taunt, no insult could have moved the Videssian admiral from his chosen course, but hard reality did. If he sank the fishing boat ahead, Gavras would surely come alongside and board—and with so many soldiers crammed into his ship, that fight could have but one outcome. "Hard to port," Leimmokheir cried, and his ship heeled on its side as it twisted free from danger.

Thorisin and his men yelled derision after him: "Coward! Traitor!"

"No traitor I!" That was Leimmokheir's rough bass. "I said I would fight you if I met you again."

"You thought that would be never, you and your hired murderers!"

Wind and quickly growing distance swept away the admiral's reply. Thorisin shook his fist at the retreating galley and sent after it a volley of curses that Leimmokheir never heard.

Marcus waved his thanks to the Emperor. "So it was you I rescued, was it?" Gavras shouted. "See, I must trust you after all—or maybe I didn't know who was in your boat!" The tribune wished Thorisin had not added that gibing postscript; all too likely it held a touch of truth.

"Shoaling, we are," one of the sailors warned, and grabbed the fishing boat's rail. Gorgidas and Nepos both had the wisdom to do the same. A moment later timbers groaned as the boat ran hard aground. Marcus and Gaius Philippus fell in a swearing heap; Viridovix, still leaning over the side, almost went overboard.

"This salt water'll play merry hell with my armor," Gaius Philippus said mournfully as he splashed ashore. Marcus followed, carrying his sword above his head to keep it safe from rust.

A wave knocked Viridovix off his feet. He emerged from the sea looking like a drowned cat, his mustaches and long red locks plastered wetly across his face. But a grin flashed behind that hair. "It's one man jolly well out of a boat I am!" he cried. As soon as he got above the tideline, he carefully dried his blade in the white sand. He was careless in some things, but never with his weapons.

The whole fringe of beach was full of small units from Thorisin Gavras' army, all trying to form up into larger ones. A full maniple of Romans came marching toward the tribune from the captured Videssian bireme a quarter of a mile down the beach; Quintus Glabrio was their head.

"I thought you were done for when that whoreson came up on you," Marcus said, returning the junior centurion's salute. " 'Well done' doesn't say enough."

As usual, Glabrio shrugged the praise aside. "If he hadn't made a mistake, it wouldn't have turned out so well."

Gavras' ship went aground next to the boat that had carried Scaurus and his companions. "Hurry, there!" the Emperor exhorted his men as they came up onto the land. "Form a perimeter! If the Sphrantzai have the wit to make a sally against us, we'll wish we were on the other shore again. Hurry!" he repeated.

He co-opted Glabrio's maniple as part of his guard force. Scaurus gave it to him without demur; he had been taking constant nervous glances at Videssos' frowning walls and great gates, wondering if the capital's masters would contest their rival's landing.

But rather than vomiting forth armed men, the city's gates were slamming shut to hold the newcomers out. The thunder of their closing was audible where Gavras' men stood. "Pen-pushers! Seal-stampers!" Thorisin said with contempt. "Ortaias and his snake of an uncle must think to win their war huddling behind the city's walls, hoping I'll grow bored and go away, or that their next assassination scheme won't miscarry, or suchlike foolishness. There can't be a real soldier among 'em, no one to tell them walls don't win sieges, not by themselves. That takes wit and gut both. The young Sphrantzes has neither, Phos knows; Vardanes I'll give credit for shrewdness, aye, but the only guts to him are the ones bulging over his belt."

Scaurus nodded at Gavras' assessment of his imperial foes, though he suspected there might be more to Vardanes Sphrantzes than Thorisin thought. But even after it was plain there would be no sally from Videssos, the tribune's eye kept drifting back to that double wall of dour brown stone. How much wit, he asked himself, would it take to keep men out, fighting from works like those?

He must have spoken his thoughts aloud, for Gaius Philippus commented soberly, "Close, but not quite on the mark. The real question is, how much wit will it take to get in?"

VI

Trumpets blared a fanfare, then skirled into a march beat. Twelve parasols, the imperial number, popped open as one, bright flowers of red, blue, gold, and green silk. Thorisin Gavras' army, formed in a great long column, lifted weapons in salute of their overlord. A herald, a barrel-chested stentor of a man, roared out, "Forward—ho!" and, with the usual Videssian love of ostentatious ceremony, the column stamped into motion. It slowly paraded from south to north just out of missile range from the imperial capital's walls, a fierce spectacle intended to give the city's defenders second thoughts on their choice of masters.

"Behold Thorisin Gavras, his Imperial Majesty, rightful Avtokrator of the Videssians!" the herald bellowed from his place between Thorisin and his parasol bearers. The Emperor's bay stallion, his accustomed mount, was still on the other side of the Cattle-Crossing. He rode a black, its coat curried to dark luster.

Gavras waved to the city, doffing his helmet to let Sphrantzes' troops on the wall see his face. For the occasion he wore a golden circlet around the businesslike conical helm; his boots were a splash of blood against the horse's jet-black hide. Otherwise he was garbed as a common soldier—it was to soldiers he would appeal, and in any case he had no patience with the jewel-encrusted, gold-stitched vestments that were an Avtokrator's proper garb.

There were warriors aplenty to watch his progress before the city. They lined the lower, outer wall; the greatest numbers, as was natural, defended the gates. Except for gate house forces, the massive inner wall, fifty feet tall or even a bit more, was not so heavily garrisoned.

"Why serve pen-pushers?" the herald cried to the troops inside Videssos. "They'd sooner see you serfs than soldiers." That, Marcus knew, was only the truth. Bureaucratic Emperors had held sway in Videssos for most of the past half-century and, to break the power of their rivals, the provincial nobles, the pen-pushers systematically dismantled the native Videssian army and replaced it with mercenaries.

But that process was far-gone now, and the force defending Ortaias Sphrantzes and his uncle was itself largely made up of hired troops. They hooted and jeered at Gavras, crying, "All your people are serfs! That's why they need real men to fight for 'em!" The regiment of Namdaleni started its shout of "Drax! Drax! The great count Drax!" to drown out Gavras' herald's words.

One mercenary, a man with strong lungs and a practical turn of mind, shouted, "Why should we choose you over the Sphrantzai? They'll pay us and keep us on, and you'd send us home poor!" Thorisin's lips skinned back from his teeth in a humorless smile; his distrust of mercenaries was too well known, even though his own army was more than half hired troops.

Forgetting his herald, he yelled back, "Why prop up a worthless turntail rascal? For fierce Ortaias cost us everything in front of Maragha by running away like a frightened mouse, him and his talk of being 'ashamed to suffer not suffering.' Bah!"

On the last few words Thorisin's voice climbed to a squeaky tenor mockery of his foe's; he wickedly quoted young Sphrantzes' speech to his men just before the disastrous battle. His own soldiers were mostly survivors of that fight; they added their shouts to Gavras' derision: "Aye, give him to us, the coward!" "Send him to the amphitheater—he'd ride rings round your jockeys!" "You'd best be brave, you on the walls, if you have to fight after one of his speeches!" And Gaius Philippus, loud in Marcus' ear: "Give him over—we'll show him more than's in his book, I promise!"

The torrent of scorn that poured from Gavras' army seemed to have an effect on Ortaias' soldiers. They were men like any others, and sensitive to their fellow professionals' taunts. When the army's abuse died away, there was thoughtful silence up on Videssos' walls.

But one of Sphrantzes' captains, a huge warrior who towered over his troops, roared out harsh, contemptuous laughter. "You ran, too, Gavras," he bellowed, "after your brother lost his head! How are you better than the lord we serve?"

Thorisin went red and then white. He dug spurs into his horse until it screamed and reared. "Attack!" he snouted. "Kill me that slime-tongued whore's get!" A few men took tentative steps toward the wall; most never moved from their places in column. Realistic with the stark good sense of men who risk their lives for pay, they knew such an impromptu assault on the city's works could only end in massacre.

While Gavras wrestled his stallion to stillness, Marcus hurried forward to try to calm the Emperor. Baanes Onomagoulos was already at his side, holding the horse's bridle and talking softly but urgently to the furious Gavras. Between them they brought his rage under control, but it did not abate for turning cold. He ground out, "The scum will pay for that, I vow." He shook his fist at the captain on the wall, who gave back a gesture herdsmen used when they talked of breeding stock.

The officer's cynical challenge gave spirit back to his comrades. They whooped at his obscene reply to Thorisin's fist and sent catcalls after Gavras as his military procession moved north.

As Scaurus returned to his place, he asked Baanes Onomagoulos, "Do you know that captain of Sphrantzes'? The bastard has his wits about him."

"So he does, worse luck for us. They were wavering up there until he opened his mouth." Onomagoulos shaded his eyes, peered at the wall. "Nay, I can't be sure, his helm is closed. But from the size of him, and that cursed wit, I'd guess he's the one calls himself Outis Rhavas. If it's him, he leads a real crew of cutthroats, they say. He's a new man, and I don't know much about him."

Marcus found that strange. By his name, Outis Rhavas was a Videssian, and the tribune thought Baanes, a fighting man of thirty years' experience, should be familiar with the Empire's leading soldiers. Still, he reminded himself, chaos was abroad in Videssos these days, and perhaps this Rhavas was a bandit chief doing his best to prosper in it.

Even as you are, he told himself, and shook his head, disliking the comparison.

Ortaias and his uncle seemed willing to stand siege, and Thorisin, after failing in his appeal at the city's walls, saw no choice but to undertake it.

His men went to work building an earthen rampart to seal off the neck of Videssos' peninsula.

Some troops were almost useless for the task. Laon Pakhymer's Khatrishers dug and carried merrily for a couple of days, then grew bored and tired of the entire process. "Can't say I blame them," Pakhymer pointedly told Thorisin when the Emperor tried to order them back to their labor. "We came to fight the Yezda, not in your civil war. We can always go home again, you know—truth is, I miss my wife."

Gavras fumed, but he could hardly coerce the Khatrishers without starting a brand new civil war in his own army. Not wanting to lose the horsemen, he sent them out foraging with his Khamorth irregulars—he had not even tried to acquaint the nomads with the use of shovel and mattock.

Rather to his surprise, Marcus found he, too, missed Helvis, their storms notwithstanding. He was growing used to the idea that those would come from time to time, the inevitable result of attraction between two strong people, neither much disposed to change to suit the other's ways. Between them, though, they had much that was good, Malric and Dosti not least. The tribune had come late to fatherhood and found it more satisfying than anything else he had set his hand to.

In the first days of the siege of Videssos, he had scant time for loneliness. Unlike Pakhymer's troops, his Romans were men highly skilled in siege warfare. Spades and picks were part of their regular marching gear, and they erected field fortifications every night when they made camp.

Thorisin Gavras and Baanes Onomagoulos rode up to inspect the work. The Emperor wore a dissatisfied look, having just come from the amateurish barricade some of Onomagoulos' men were slowly throwing up. As ever since his wounding, Onomagoulos' face was set and tight, though less so now than Scaurus had sometimes seen him. Sitting a horse pained him less than the rocking hobble that was the ruin of his once-quick step.

Gavras' expression cleared as he surveyed the broad ditch and stake-topped earthwork the legionaries already had nearly done. The Romans held the southernmost half-mile of Thorisin's siege line. "Now here's something more like it," the Emperor said, more to Onomagoulos than Marcus. "A good deal better than your lads have turned out, Baanes."

"It looks well, yes," the older noble said shortly, not caring for the criticism. "What of it? Outlanders have some few skills: the Khamorth with the bow, the lance to the Namdaleni, and these fellows with their moles' tricks. A useful talent now, I grant."

He spoke offhandedly, not caring if the tribune heard, his unconscious assumption of superiority proof against embarrassment. Nettled, Marcus opened his mouth to make some hot reply. Before the words passed his lips, he remembered himself in a Roman tent in Gaul, listening to one of Caesar's legates saying, "Now, gentlemen, we all know the Celts are headstrong and rash. If we hold the high ground, we can surely lure them into charging uphill. . . ."

His mouth twisted into a brief, wry grin—so this was how it felt, to be reckoned a barbarian. Helvis was right again, it seemed.

But no, not altogether; catching the sour flicker on his face, Thorisin said quickly, "One day Baanes will choke, shoving that boot of his down his throat."

Scaurus shrugged. Thorisin's apology felt genuine, but at the same time the Emperor was using him to score a point off the powerful lord at his side. Nothing in this land ever wore but one face, the tribune thought with a moment's touch of despair.

He brought himself back to the business at hand. "We're properly dug in," he said, "from here to the sea." He waved to the walls of Videssos the city, their shadow in the late afternoon sun reaching almost to where he stood. "Next to that, though, all we've done is no more than a five-year-old playing at sand castles along the beach."

"True enough," Gavras said. "It matters not so much, though. They may have their castles, but they can't eat 'em, by Phos."

"As long as they rule the sea, they don't have to," Marcus said, letting his chief fret loose. "They can laugh at us while they ship in supplies. Ships are the key to cracking the city, and we don't have them."

"The key, aye," Thorisin murmured, his eyes far away. Scaurus realized after a few seconds that the Emperor was not lost in contemplation. He was looking southeast into the Sailors' Sea, at the island lying on the misty edge of vision from Videssos. With abrupt quickening of interest, the Roman recalled the Videssian name for that island: it was called the Key.

454

But when he asked Gavras what was in his mind, the Emperor only said, "My plans are still foggy." He smiled, as if at some private joke. Onomagoulos, Marcus saw, had no more idea of what his overlord meant than did the tribune. Somehow, that reassured him.

By coincidence, that night was one of the misty ones common on the coast even in high summer, moon and stars swallowed up by the thick gray blanket rolling off the sea at sunset. Videssos' towers and crenelated walls disappeared as if they had never been. Torch-carrying sentries moved in hazy haloes of light; the taste of the ocean came with every indrawn breath.

Viridovix prowled along the earthwork, torch in his left hand and drawn sword in his right. "Sure and they can't be failing to take a whack at us in this porridge, can they?" he demanded when he ran into Scaurus and Gaius Philippus. "If that were me all shut up in there, I'd give the tails of the omadhauns outside a yank they'd remember awhile."

"So would I," Gaius Philippus said. His ideas of warfare rarely marched with the Gaul's, but this was such a time. He took the fog almost as a personal affront; it changed war from a game of skill, a professional's game, into one where any cabbagehead could make himself a genius with an hour's luck.

Marcus, though, saw what the centurion in his nervousness and the aggressive Celt missed: it was as foggy inside the city as out. "I'd bet Ortaias' marshals are pacing the walls themselves," he said, "waiting to hear scaling ladders shoved against them."

Viridovix blinked, then laughed. "Aye, belike that's the way of it," he said. "Two farmers, the each of 'em staying up of nights to watch his own henhouse for fear the other raid it. A sleepless, thankless job they both think it, too, and me along with 'em."

"It may be so," Gaius Philippus conceded. "The Sphrantzai haven't the imagination for anything risky. But what of Gavras? This should be a night to suit him—he's a gambler born."

"There you have me," Scaurus said. "When the fog came down, I expected something lively would happen, but it seems I was wrong." He recounted the afternoon's conversation to the Roman and the Celt.

"There's deviltry somewhere, right enough," Gaius Philippus said. He yawned. "Whatever it is, it'll have to get along without me until morning. I'm turning in." His torch held waist-high so he could see the ground ahead, he headed for his tent; the Roman camp itself was set near the sea on the flat stretch of land that had been the Videssian army's exercise ground.

Scaurus followed him to bed a few minutes later and, to his annoyance, had trouble falling asleep. The gods knew it was peaceful almost to a fault without Dosti waking up several times a night. But the tribune missed Helvis warm on the sleeping-mat beside him. It was hardly fair, he thought as he turned restlessly: not so long ago he'd found it hard to sleep with a woman in his bed, and now as hard without one.

At the officers' conference the next morning Thorisin Gavras seemed pleased with himself, though Marcus had no idea why; as far as the Roman knew, nothing had changed since yesterday.

"He probably found himself a bouncy girl who'd say yes and not much more," was Soteric's guess after the meeting broke up. "Compared to poison-tongued Komitta, that'd be pleasure enough."

"I hadn't thought of that," Marcus laughed. "You may well be right."

Businesslike but slow, the siege proper got under way. A few of the military engineers who had accompanied Mavrikios Gavras' army still survived to follow his brother. Under their direction, Thorisin's men felled trees and knocked down a few houses to get timber for the engines and ladders they would presently need. The legionaries proved skilled help for the artisans, as they were used to aiding their own engineer platoons.

Save for the countermarching men visible on the walls, Videssos did its best to ignore the siege. Ships moved freely in and out of her harbors, bringing in supplies and men. Scaurus wanted to grind his teeth every time he saw one.

"Next thing you know, the Sphrantzai will try to stir up a storm behind us and use it to hammer us on the city's anvil. That's the way Vardanes thinks, and it's far from a bad plan," the tribune said to Gaius Philippus.

The senior centurion, though, was for once an optimist. "Let them try. We're getting more troops coming over to us than they are."

That, Marcus had to admit, was probably true. The nobles of Videssos' eastern dominions were not such great magnates as their counterparts in the westlands, but all the grandees, great or small, hated the bureaucrats who had seized the capital. They flocked to Thorisin's banner, this one leading seventy retainers, that one forty, the next a hundred and fifty.

"Of course," Gaius Philippus went on, following Scaurus' unspoken thought, "how useful such bumpkins will prove in the fighting remains to be seen."

After four or five clear nights the fog came again, if anything thicker than it had before. Again the tribune wondered whether the besieged Sphrantzai would try to sally under its cover, and doubled the sentries facing the capital.

It must have been near midnight when he heard shouts of alarm coming from the north. "Buccinators!" he shouted. The horns' bright music ripped through the murk. Cursing as they scrambled from their bedrolls, legionaries poured out of the tents in camp and, still buckling on armor, began to form up.

Hoofbeats pounded toward the camp. "Are all our lads up there asleep? Sure and the spalpeens're behind himself's rampart, and it so much trouble to make and all," Viridovix said.

"How would you know that?" Gaius Philippus said. "You didn't do a lick of work on it."

"And why should I, like some hod-toting serf? If you want to work like a kern, 'tis your own affair entirely, but you'll not see me at it. Give me a real fight, any day."

"I don't think those are Ortaias' men at all," Quintus Glabrio said suddenly, a statement startling enough to quell the brewing quarrel at once. "There's no sound of fighting and no more challenges from our sentries, either."

The young officer was proved right a few minutes later, when a troop of about a hundred of Thorisin Gavras' best Videssian cavalry rode south past the Roman camp. "Sorry about the start we gave you," their captain called to Scaurus as he went by. "We almost trampled one of your men

457

up there in this Phos-cursed gloom." The tribune believed that; even with torches held high, the horsemen disappeared before they had gone another fifty yards.

"Blow 'stand down,'" Marcus ordered his trumpeters. The legionaries stood for a moment as if suspecting a trick, then, shaking their heads in annoyance, went back to their still-warm blankets.

"Wish he'd make up his bloody mind," grumbled one. And another: "A good night's sleep buggered right and proper." With a veteran's knack for making the best of things, a third said cheerily, "No matter. I had to get up to piss anyway."

The camp settled back into peace. Scaurus yawned. It was near high tide, and the boom of surf on the nearby beach was lulling as smooth wine, as soft deep drums in the distance.

The tribune paused, half-stooped, a hand on his tentflap. Why had he thought of drums, from the sound of sea meeting sand? He jerked upright as he recognized the noise for what it was: waves on wood. Ships offshore, and close!

The fear of treachery flooding through him, he shouted for the buccinators once more. This time his men came forth growling, as at any drill they disliked. He did not care; his alarm blazed brighter than the mist-shrouded torchlight.

"Peel me off two maniples, quick," he said to Gaius Philippus. "I think the Sphrantzai are landing on the beach. Set the rest of the men to defend here and send a runner to Gavras—I think we're betrayed. In fact, send Zeprin the Red—Thorisin's most likely to listen to him."

"I'll see to it he does," the burly Haloga promised, understanding Marcus' reasoning. Because of his former high rank in Mavrikios' Imperial Guards, he was well-known both to the younger Gavras and his men. Throwing a wolfskin cape over his mail shirt, he vanished into the mist.

The senior centurion was barking orders. As the legionaries rushed to the places they were assigned, he turned back to Scaurus. "Betrayed, is it? You think those dung-faced horse-boys are there for a welcoming party?"

"What better reason?"

"Not a one, worse luck. What's the plan—hold them until we get enough reinforcements to fling 'em back into the sea?"

458

"If we do. If we can." The tribune wished he knew more of what he would face; ignorance's fog could be more dangerous than the gray clammy stuff billowing around him.

Viridovix hurried up. He leaned his shield against his hip to give himself two free hands with which to fasten his helmet strap under his chin. "You'll not get away with another shindy without me," he said to Scaurus.

"Well, come along then. From the way you talk, anyone would think I did it on purpose."

"So they would," Viridovix agreed darkly. But when Marcus looked to see if he was as serious as he sounded, the Celt was grinning at him.

The legionaries quick-marched south, following the Videssian cavalry. Marcus felt something soft squash under his sandal; even in the fog and dark he did not have to ask what it was. He heard Viridovix swear in Gaulish, caught the name of the Celtic horse-goddess Epona.

The tribune slid and almost fell as his feet went from dirt to shifting sand. The Videssians were still invisible in the swirling mist ahead, but he heard their captain call, "Come ashore!"

"Are you daft, landlubber?" a sailor's answer came thinly back. "My leadsmen near wet their breeches getting this close. We'll send boats!"

"Battle line!" the tribune said softly. Smooth as if on parade, the legionaries deployed from their marching column. "Yell 'Gavras' when we charge," Scaurus ordered. "Let the traitors know we know what they're at."

He feared he was come just too late. Already he could hear oars splashing toward shore, hear the scrape of light boats beaching. Well, no help for it. "Forward!" he said.

"Gavras!" The shout roared from two hundred throats. Swords drawn, *pila* ready to fling, the Romans slogged forward through the sand.

Down at the waterline there was a sudden chaos. Most of the Videssians were dismounted, walking up and down the beach holding torches to guide the boats in. Faintly through the fog, Scaurus saw some of those torches drop when his men bellowed out their war cry. A horse screamed off to one side; some Roman had seen movement in the mist and let fly with his javelin.

Full of asperity and command, an unseen voice demanded of the Videssian cavalry leader, "What sort of welcome have you prepared for us, captain?"

"Hold up! Hold up! Hold up!" the tribune shouted frantically, and blessed the legionaries, good discipline for bringing them to a ragged halt.

"What now?" Gaius Philippus snarled. "So they've a bitch with them—what of it? Sometimes I think the imperials can't fight without their doxies alongside 'em."

The senior centurion's harsh voice ripped through the fog; Marcus thanked the gods whose existence he doubted that his comrade had spoken Latin. He answered in the same tongue; "Bitch she may well be, but that's Komitta Rhangavve out there, or I'm a Celt."

Gaius Philippus' teeth came together with an audible click. "Thorisin's woman? Oh, sweet Jupiter! Wait, though—she's on the other side of the Cattle-Crossing with all the other skirts and their brats . . . begging your pardon, sir," he added hastily.

Marcus waved the apology aside; in his confusion, he hardly heard the words that made it necessary. Those ships out there could not be Sphrantzes'—Komitta was a hellcat, but never a traitor. But they could not be Thorisin's, either. The boats in his makeshift flotilla had long since gone back to their usual tasks. That left nothing . . . except the reality just offshore.

Two torches bobbed toward the Romans. Marcus stepped out ahead of his men to meet them. The Videssian captain stumped along under one, a short, stocky, red-faced man with upsweeping eyebrows and an iron-gray beard. Carrying the other was indeed Komitta Rhangavve, her pale, narrow face beautiful and fierce as a falcon's.

The tribune gave them both his best courtier's bow, but then, to his mortification, he heard himself blurting, "Will one of you please tell me what in Skotos' name is going on?"

The captain frowned. He spat on the sand and looked through the fog toward heaven, his hands upraised. I've wounded his piety, Scaurus thought. Well, too bad for him.

Komitta looked down her elegant nose at the Roman. "The Emperor has decided it is time for his soldiers' companions and families to rejoin them," she said matter-of-factly. "Were you not informed of the move? A pity." She was the perfect aristocrat, asking a servant's pardon for some small oversight.

The tribune resisted an urge to take her by her sculpted shoulders and shake information out of her. It was the devout captain who came to his rescue: "The Key's ships have declared for Gavras, now that he's put the city under siege. They sailed up during the last fog; his Highness ordered them to stay hidden so they could take advantage of the next one to bring our kin across without interference from the Sphrantzai. Worked, too."

"The Key," Scaurus breathed. Now that someone had spelled it out for him in small simple words, he mentally kicked himself for his stupidity. The fleets of the island of the Key were second in importance in Videssos only to the capital's, something he had known for a year and more. But, land-oriented foreigner that he was, the fact had held no meaning for him, even after some broad hints from Thorisin Gavras.

Viridovix, subject to no discipline but his own, had been hanging back a couple of paces behind the Roman. Now he came forward to lay an indignant hand on Marcus' arm. "Is it that there's no fight here after all?" he said.

"So it would seem." The tribune nodded, still bemused.

"Isn't that the way of it?" the Gaul said loudly. "The first one his honor gives me a fair chance at, and it turns out there's not a fornicating thing for him to be giving, at all."

The Videssian captain, as much a professional at war as a Roman veteran, looked at the Celt as he would at any other dangerous madman. There was a smoldering interest in Komitta Rhangavve's eye, though, that Marcus hoped against hope Viridovix would not pick up.

Luck rode with him; the Gaul's noisy complaint had caught more ears than the ones close by. Guided by it, two of his lemans came running up the beach to smother him with hugs and squeals of, "Viridovix! Darling! We missed you so much!" Viridovix patted them as best he could with a torch in one hand and his shield in the other. To Scaurus' relief, Komitta's high-arched nostrils pinched as they might at a bad smell.

Turning back to his men, the tribune quickly explained what the real

461

situation was. The Romans raised a cheer, excited both by the new strength the Key's fleet gave Gavras and, probably more, by the prospect of seeing their loved ones again. There was, Scaurus admitted reluctantly, something to this Videssian custom of keeping a soldier's family close by him, however much it went against the Roman way. The men stayed in better spirits and seemed to fight harder knowing that their families' fate as well as their own depended on their valor.

"We came for the wrong reason," he said to the legionaries, "but now that we're here we can be useful. Take your torches down to the shore and help guide those boats in."

That was a task they set to with a will, some of them even splashing out into the sea so the lights they carried would reach further. As the small boats beached, the Romans kept calling the names of their loved ones. A glad cry would ring out every few minutes as couples reunited. Scaurus saw some of these walk into the mist in search of privacy, but pretended not to notice; after the tension of a few minutes before, that sort of release was inevitable.

Then he heard a familiar contralto calling, "Marcus!" and forgot about Roman discipline himself. He folded Helvis into an embrace so tight that she squeaked and said, "Careful of the baby—and of me, too, you and your ironworks." Dosti was sound asleep in the crook of her right arm.

"Sorry," he lied; even through armor the feel of her roused him. She laughed, understanding him perfectly. She leaned against his shoulder, tilted her head up for a kiss.

Malric ran his hands over the tribune's mail. The excitement of the trip had kept him wide awake. "Papa," he said, "I was on the ship with the sailors and then on the little boat going through the waves with mama, and—"

"Good," Marcus said, absently ruffling his stepson's hair. Malric's adventures could wait. Scaurus' other hand was sliding to tease Helvis' breast, and she smiling up from eyes suddenly heavy-lidded and sensuous.

Out of the fog came a volley of discordant trumpet blasts, the metallic clatter of men running in mail, and loud shouts: "Gavras! Thorisin! The Emperor!"

"Ordure," muttered the tribune, all thoughts of love-making ban-

462

ished. He cursed himself for a fool. Somehow he had managed to forget the warning Zeprin the Red had taken to Thorisin. The Haloga had done his job only too well, it seemed; from the sound of them, hundreds of men were rushing the beach to meet the nonexistent invaders.

"Gavras!" he yelled at the top of his lungs, and the legionaries took up the cry, feeling at first hand the predicament in which they'd put the Videssian cavalry an hour before. An unpleasant prospect, being attacked by one's own army.

The Emperor's horsemen on the beach shouted as loudly as the Romans.

"Are you handling the traitors out there, Scaurus?" Thorisin was quite invisible, but the tribune could hear amusement struggling with concern in his voice.

"Quite well, thank you. We might have done better if we'd known they were coming." Gavras had known that. "My plans are foggy," Marcus remembered him saying. Foggy, forsooth! But he had not seen fit to tell his commanders. The jolt he must have got when Zeprin the Red stormed his tent shouting treachery served him right, Scaurus decided; he must have wondered if his scheme had turned in his hand to bite him.

The tribune gave him credit for taking nothing for granted; he had come ready to fight at need, and quickly, too. Now that they saw there was no danger, the troopers he had brought with him came running down to the seaside to help the boats in. It grew crowded and confused on the beach, but happy.

Komitta Rhangavve shrieked when Thorisin, mounted on his borrowed black, scooped her up and set her in front of his saddle like a prize of war. Gaius Philippus clucked in disapproval. "There's times when I wonder if he takes this war seriously enough to win," he said.

"Remember Caesar," Marcus said.

The senior centurion's eyes grew sad and fond, as at the mention of an old lover. "That bald whoremonger? Him and his Gallic tarts," he said, pure affection in his voice. "Aye, but you're right, he was a lion in the field. Caesar, eh?" he echoed musingly. "If the Gavras does half so well, we'll get our names in more histories than Gorgidas', and no mistake. Along with a copper, that'll buy you some wine."

"Scoffer," the tribune snorted, but knew he'd made his point.

Afterglow upon him, Marcus took some of his weight on his elbows. Helvis sighed, an animal sound of content. He listened to the ocean rhythm of his pulse, more compelling than the surf muttering to itself in the distance.

"Why isn't it always like this?" he said, more to some observer who was not there than to Helvis or himself.

He did not think she heard him. His fingers curious now in a new way, he touched her face, trying to bridge the gap between them. It was no good, of course; she remained the stubborn mystery anyone outside the self must always be, however closely bodies join. He looked down at her in the darkness inside their tent and could not read her eyes.

So he was startled when she shrugged beneath him, her sweat-slick skin slipping against his. Her voice was serious as she answered, "Much good can come from love, I think, but also much evil. Each time we begin, we make Phos' Wager again and bet on the good; this time we won."

He blinked there in the gloom; a thoughtful reply to his question was the last thing he had expected. The Namdaleni used their wager to justify right conduct in a world where they saw good and evil balanced. Though they were not sure Phos would triumph in the end, they staked their souls on acting as if his victory was certain. The comparison, Marcus had to admit, was apt.

And yet it did not bring Helvis closer to him, but only served to make plain their differences. She reached for her god in explanation as automatically as for a towel to dry her hands.

Then his nagging thoughts fell silent, for they were moving together again, her arms tightening round his back. Her breath warm in his ear, she whispered, "Too many never know the good at all, darling; be thankful we have it when we do."

For once he could not disagree. His lips came down on hers.

Once he had used the cover of fog to bring his soldiers' households over the Cattle-Crossing, Thorisin Gavras unleashed his newfound navy against the city's fleet. He hoped the sailors in the capital would follow those from the Key into rebellion against the Sphrantzai. Several captains did abandon the seal-stampers' cause for Gavras, bringing ships and crews with them.

But Taron Leimmokheir, more by his example and known integrity than any overt persuasion, held the bulk of the city's fleet to Ortaias and his uncle. The sea fight quickly grew more bitter than the stagnant siege before Videssos. Raid and counterraid saw galleys sunk and burned; pallid, bloated corpses would drift ashore days later, reminders that the naval war had horrors to match any the land could show.

The leader of the Key's fleets was a surprisingly young man, handsome and very much aware of it. Like most of the Videssian nobles Scaurus had come to know, this Elissaios Bouraphos was a touchy customer. "I thought we sailed to help you," he growled to Thorisin Gavras at an early morning officers' conference, "not to do all your bloody fighting for you." He ran his hands through hair that was beginning to thin at the temples, a habitual gesture; Marcus wondered if he was checking the day's losses.

"Well, what would you have me do?" Thorisin snapped back. "Storm the walls in a grand assault? I could spend five times the men I have on that, and well you know it. But with your ships aprowl, the seal-stampers can't bring a pound of olives or a dram of wine into Videssos. They'll get hungry in there by and by."

"So they will," Elissaios agreed sardonically. "But the Yezda will be fat, for they'll have eaten up the westlands while you sit here on your arse."

Silence fell round the table; Bouraphos had said aloud what everyone there thought in somber moments. In the civil war the Sphrantzai and Gavras both mustered what men they could round the capital, leaving the provinces to fend for themselves. Time enough to pick up the pieces after the victory was won . . . if any pieces were left.

"By Phos, he's right," Baanes Onomagoulos said to Thorisin. As was true of a good many of Gavras' officers, he had wide holdings in the westlands. "If I hear the wolves are outside Garsavra, Skotos strike me dead if I don't take my lads home to protect it."

The Emperor slowly rose to his feet. His eyes blazed, but his temper was under the rein of his will; each word he spoke might have been cut from steel. "Baanes, pull one man out of line without my leave and you will be struck dead, but not by Skotos. I'll do it myself, I vow. You gave me your oath and your proskynesis—you cannot take them back at a whim. Do you hear me, Baanes?"

Onomagoulos locked eyes with him; Thorisin stared back inflexibly. It was the marshal's eyes that broke away, flicking down the table to measure his support. "Aye, I hear you, Thorisin. Whatever you say, of course."

"Good. We'll speak no more about it, then," Gavras answered evenly, and went on with the business of the council.

"He's going to let him get away with that?" Gaius Philippus whispered incredulously to Marcus.

"It's just Onomagoulos' way of talking," the tribune whispered back, but he, too, was troubled. Baanes still had the habit of treating Thorisin Gavras as a boy; Scaurus wondered what it would take to make him lose that image of the Emperor in his mind.

Such nebulous concerns were swept away when the Romans returned to camp. Quintus Glabrio met them outside the palisade. "What's gone wrong?" Marcus asked at once, reading the junior centurion's tight-set features.

"I—you—" Glabrio started twice without being able to go forward; he could not control his voice as he did his face. He made a violent gesture of frustration and disgust, then spun on his heel and walked off, leaving his superiors to follow if they would.

Scaurus and Gaius Philippus exchanged mystified glances. Glabrio was as cool as they came; neither of them had seen him anything but quietly capable—until now.

He led them south past the camp, down along the earthwork the legionaries had thrown up to besiege Videssos. A knot of men had gathered at one of the sentry posts. As he came closer, Scaurus saw they all bore the same expression of mixed horror and rage that welled up through Quintus Glabrio's impassive mask.

The knot unraveled at the tribune's approach; the legionaries seemed glad of any excuse to get away. That left two men shielding what lay there, Gorgidas and Phostis Apokavkos.

"Are you sure you want to see this, Scaurus?" Gorgidas asked, turning to the tribune. His face was pale, though as legionary physician he had seen more pain and death than a dozen troopers rolled together.

"Stand aside," Marcus said harshly. The Greek and Apokavkos moved back to show him Doukitzes' corpse. He moaned. He could not stop himself. Was it for this, he thought, that I rescued the little sneak thief from Mavrikios' wrath? For this? The body there before him mutely answered yes.

Splayed now in death, Doukitzes was even smaller than Scaurus remembered. He seemed more a doll cast aside by some vicious child than a man. But where would any child, no matter how vicious, have gained the horrendous skill for the deliberate, obscene mutilations that stole any semblance of dignity, of humanity, from the huddled corpse?

A pace behind him, he heard Gaius Philippus suck in a long, whistling breath of air. He did not notice his own hands clenching to fists until his nails bit into his palms.

"He must have died quickly," Gorgidas said, showing the tribune the neat slash that ran from under the little man's left ear to the center of his throat. A couple of purple-bellied flies buzzed indignantly away from his pointing finger. "He couldn't have been alive for the rest of—that. The whole camp—Asklepios, the whole city—would have heard him, and no one knew a thing until his relief came out and found him."

"A mercy for him, aye," Gaius Philippus grunted. "The only one he got, from the look of it."

"The Sphrantzai have Yezda fighting for them," Marcus said at last, groping for some sort of explanation. "This could be their work—they kill foully to terrify their enemies." But even as he spoke he doubted his own words. The Yezda were barbarians; they killed and tortured with savage gusto. The surgical precision of this butchery matched anything of theirs for brutality, but was far beyond it in cruel, cold malice.

Phostis Apokavkos said, "The Yezda had nothing to do with it, curse 'em. Almost wish they had—I'd come nearer understandin' then." The adopted Roman spoke Latin with the twang of Videssos' westlands; the accent only emphasized his grief. Though he shaved his face like his mates among the legionaries, he was still a Videssian in his heart of hearts. He and Doukitzes, two imperials making their way among the Romans, had been fast friends since the chaos after Maragha.

"You talk as if you know this wasn't sport for the nomads," Gaius Philippus said, "but at your folk's worst I can't imagine any of them doing it."

"For which I give you thanks," Apokavkos said, rubbing his long chin. More often than not he insisted on styling himself a Roman, but this once he accepted the Videssian label. "Don't have to imagine it, though—it's true. See here." He pointed to the dead man's forehead.

To Scaurus the wounds incised there had been just another sample of the hideous virtuosity Doukitzes' killer had displayed. He looked again; this time his mind's eye stripped away the black dried blood and grasped the pattern the knife had cut. It was a word, or rather a Videssian name: Rhavas.

"Sure and the son of a sow's a natural-born turnip-head to be after doing such a thing," Viridovix said that evening by the Roman campfire. "He must ken we'll not be forgetting soon." He was eating lightly, bread and a few grapes; his stomach, always sensitive save in the heat of battle, had heaved itself up at the sight of Doukitzes' pathetic corpse.

"Aye," Gaius Philippus agreed, his square, hairy hands closing as if round an invisible neck. "And a fool twice in the bargain, for he's cooped up there in the city where getting away won't be so easy."

"One more reason to take it," Marcus said. He held out his apricot-glazed wine cup for a refill. Still shaken by what he had seen, he drank deep to dull the memory.

"The worst of it, sir, is what you said this morning," Quintus Glabrio said to Gaius Philippus, "though not quite the way you meant it. Doukitzes wasn't nomad's sport. To mutilate him so after he was dead—there's purpose in it, right enough, but may the gods spare me from too fine an understanding of such purposes." He put the heels of his hands to his eyes, as though they had betrayed him by looking on Doukitzes.

Scaurus drank again, stuck out his cup for yet another dollop of the sweet, syrupy Videssian wine. His companions matched him draught for draught, but their drinking brought no cheer. One by one they sought their beds, hoping sleep would prove a better anodyne than wine.

The tribune thrust the tent flap open, came out through it still arranging his mantle about him. He let his feet take him where they would; one path was good as the next, so long as it led away from the tent. Phos' Wager, or any other, could be lost as well as won.

Sentries gave Scaurus the clenched-fist Roman salute as he walked out the camp's north gate and into the darkness. He returned it absently, wishing no one at all had to see him; save for a few men coming and going to the latrines, the camp was quiet, its fires no more than embers.

Every legionary sentry post was double-manned now, both in camp and along Thorisin's besieging earthwork. The tribune saw torches glowing all the way down to the sea. Tonight, he knew, no man would sleep at his station.

The night was clear and cool, almost chilly. The moon had long since set behind Videssos' walls, leaving the sky to the distant stars. Glancing up at their still-strange patterns, Scaurus wondered if the Videssians used them to reckon destinies. It seemed a notion that would fit their beliefs, but he could not recall hearing of it in the Empire. Nepos would know.

The thought was gone almost as soon as it appeared, drowned in a fresh wave of resentment. The tribune wandered on, still going north; before long he was past the Roman section of line and coming up on the Namdalener camp. He gave that a wide berth, too, not much wanting to see any of the islanders right now.

He heard shouting in the distance ahead, a woman's voice. After a moment he recognized it as Komitta Rhangavve's. About now Thorisin was probably wishing she was back on the western side of the Cattle-Crossing. Scaurus let out a sour chuckle. It was a feeling he fully understood.

His laugh had startled someone nearby. He heard a sharp intake of breath, then a half-question, half-challenge: "Who is it?"

Another woman's voice, lower than Komitta's and more familiar, too, with a guttural trace of accent. Marcus peered into the night. "Nevrat? Is that you?"

"Who—?" she said again, but then, "Scaurus, yes?"

"Aye." The tribune briefly warmed to hear her. She and her husband no longer camped with the legionaries, having joined several of Senpat Sviodo's cousins among the Vaspurakaners who marched with Gavras. Marcus missed them both, Senpat for his blithe brashness, his wife for her clear thinking and courage, and the two of them together as a model of what a happy couple could be.

She walked slowly toward him, minding each step in the dark. As usual, she dressed mannishly in tunic and trousers; a swordbelt girded her waist. Her shining hair, blacker than the night, fell curling past her shoulders.

"What are you doing out and about?" Scaurus asked.

"Why not?" she retorted. "I feel like a cat prowling through the darkness, looking for who knows what. And the night is very beautiful, don't you think?"

"Eh? I suppose it is," he answered; whatever beauties it held were lost on him.

"Are you all right?" she asked suddenly, lifting a hand to touch his shoulder.

He thought about it a moment. "No, not really," he said at last.

"Can I do anything?"

Crisp and direct as ever, he thought; Nevrat was not one to ask such a question unless she meant it to be taken seriously. Here, though, there could be only one answer. "Thank you, lady, no. This doesn't have that sort of cure, I fear."

He was afraid she would press him further, but she only nodded and said, "I hope you solve it soon, then." Her grip on his arm tightened for a second, then she was gone into the night.

Marcus kept walking, still without much goal. He was well among Gavras' Videssian contingents now. A couple of troopers passed within twenty feet of him, unaware of his presence. One was saying, "—and when his father asked him why he was crying, he said, 'This morning the baker came and ate the baby!'"

They both laughed loudly; they sounded a little drunk. Without the rest of the joke, the punchline was so much gibberish to Scaurus. Somehow that seemed to march very well with everything else that had happened that day.

A man on horseback trotted by, singing softly to himself. Caught up in his song, he, too, failed to notice the tribune.

An awkward footfall ahead, a muttered curse. As the woman approached, Marcus reflected there was scant need to ask her why she was walking through the night. Her slit skirt swung open with every step she took, giving glimpses of her white thighs.

Unlike the soldiers, she saw the tribune almost as soon as he knew she was there. She came boldly up to him. She was slim and dark and smelled of stale scent, wine, and sweat.

Her smile, half-seen in the darkness, was professionally inviting. "You're a tall one," she said, looking Marcus up and down. Her speech held the rhythm of the capital, quick and sharp, almost staccato. "Do you want to come with me? I'll make that scowl up and go, I promise." Scaurus had not known he was frowning. He smoothed his features as best he could.

The lacing of her blouse was undone; he could see her small breasts. He felt a tightness in his chest, as if he were trying to breathe deep in a too-tight cuirass. "Yes, I'll go with you," he said. "Is it far?"

"No, not very. Show me your money," she said, all business now.

That brought him up short. Save for the mantle he was naked, even his sandals left behind. But as he started to spread his hands regretfully, a glint of silver on his right index finger made him pause. He pulled the ring free, held it out to her. "Will this do?"

She hefted it, held it close to her face, then smiled again and reached for him with knowing fingers.

As she promised, her small tent was close by. Shrugging off his cloak, Scaurus wondered if she was what he sought. He doubted it, but lay down beside her nonetheless.

VII

"WHAT? RESAINA FALLEN TO THE YEZDA?" GAIUS PHILIPPUS WAS SAY-ing to Viridovix, astonishment in his voice. "Where did you hear that?"

"One o' the sailor lads it was told me, last night over knucklebones. Aye, it's certain sure, he says. What with their moving around so much and all, those sailors get the news or ever anyone else does."

"Yes, and it's always bad," Marcus said, spooning up a mouthful of his morning porridge. "Kybistra in the far south gone a couple of weeks ago, and now this." Resaina's loss was a heavier blow. The town was perhaps two days' march south of the Bay of Rhyax, well east of Amorion. If it had truly fallen, the Yezda were getting past the roadblock the latter city represented, in Zemarkhos' fanatic hands though it was.

And while the westlands were falling town by town to the invaders, the siege of Videssos dragged on. There were men beginning to slip over the wall at night now, and others escaping in small boats. They brought tales of tightened belts inside the city, of increasingly harsh and capricious rule.

Whatever the shortcomings of the regime of the Sphrantzai, though, the capital's double walls and tall towers were always manned, its defenders ready to fight.

"All Thorisin's choices are bad," the tribune brooded. "He can't go back over the Cattle-Crossing to fight the Yezda without turning Ortaias and Vardanes loose behind him, but if he doesn't, he won't have much of an empire left even if we win here."

Gaius Philippus said, "What we need is to win here, and quickly. But that means storming the walls, and I shake in my shoes every time I think of trying."

"Och, such a pair for the glooms I never have seen," Viridovix said.

"We canna go, we canna stay, and we canna be fighting either. Wellaway, we might as well the lot of us get drunk if nothing better's to be done."

"I've heard ideas I liked less," Gaius Philippus chuckled.

The Celt's casual dismissal of logic annoyed Marcus. Giving Viridovix an ironic dip of his head, he asked him, "What do you see left to us, now that you've disposed of all our choices?"

"I haven't done that at all, Roman dear," the Gaul retorted, his green eyes twinkling, "for you've left treachery out of the bargain, the which Gavras'll never do. Too honest by half, y'are."

"Hmp," Scaurus grunted—no denying Viridovix had a point. But he did not much care for the label the Celt gave him: "too credulous," it seemed to mean. Moreover, he did not feel he deserved it. He had not repeated that angry night with the whore, nor wanted to; even while she clawed his back, he knew she was not the answer to his troubles with Helvis. If anything, those had since grown worse. There were times when his guarded silence hung between them like a muffling cloak.

He was glad to have his unpleasant reverie broken by a tall Videssian he recognized as one of Gavras' messengers. He took a last pull of thin, sour beer; Videssian wine was too cloying for him to stomach in the early morning. To business, then. "What can I do for you?" he asked.

The soldier bowed as he would to any superior, but Scaurus caught his slightly raised eyebrow, his delicately curled lip—to aristocratic Videssians, beer was a peasant drink. "There will be an officers' conclave in his Majesty's quarters, to commence midway through the second hour."

Like the Romans, Videssos split day and night into twelve hours each, reckoned from sunrise and sunset. The tribune glanced at the sky; the sun was hardly yet well risen. "Plenty of time to make ready," he said. "I'll be there."

"Would your honor care for a wee drop of ale?" Viridovix asked the messenger, offering the little keg that held it. Marcus saw the beginnings of a grin lurking under his flame-red mustaches.

"Thank you, no," Thorisin's man replied, his face and voice now altogether expressionless. "I have others to inform." And with another bow he was gone, in almost unseemly haste.

As soon as he was out of sight, Gaius Philippus swatted Viridovix on the back. "'Thank you, no,'" mimicking the Videssian. Centurion and Celt broke up together, forgetting to snarl at each other.

"And would *your* honor care for a wee drop?" Viridovix asked him.

"Me? Gods, no! I hate the stuff."

"I'd best not waste it, then," Viridovix said, and swigged from the cask.

It was easy to divide the commanders in Thorisin's tent into two sets: those who knew of Resaina's fall, and the rest. A current of expectancy ran through the first group, though no one was sure what to look for. By contrast, the ignorant ones mostly wandered in late, as to any other meeting where nothing much was going to happen.

For a time it seemed they were going to be proved right. The first order of business was a fuzz-bearded Videssian lieutenant hauled in between a pair of burly guards. The youngster looked scared and a little sick.

"Well, what have we here?" Thorisin said impatiently, drumming his fingers on the table in front of him. He had more urgent things on his mind than whatever trouble this stripling had found for himself.

"Your Highness—" the lieutenant quavered, but Gavras silenced him with a look, turned his eyes questioningly to the senior guardsman.

"Sir, the prisoner, one Pastillas Monotes, last evening did most wickedly and profanely revile your Majesty in the hearing of his troops." The soldier's voice was an emotionless, memorized drone as he recited the charge against the luckless Monotes.

The Videssian officers at the table grew still, and Thorisin Gavras alert. To the Namdaleni, to the Khamorth, to the Romans, a free tongue was taken for granted, but this was the Empire, an ancient land steeped in ceremonial regard for the imperial person. Not even an Emperor so unconventional as Thorisin, perhaps, could take lèse-majesté lightly without forfeiting his respect among his own people. Marcus felt sympathy for the frightened young man before him, but knew he dared not interfere in this matter.

"In what way did this Monotes revile me?" the Emperor asked. His voice, too, took on the formal tone of a court.

"Sir," the guard repeated, still from memory, "the prisoner did state that, in failing to do more than blockade the city of Videssos, you were a spineless cur, a eunuch-hearted blockhead, and a man with a lion's roar but the hindquarters of a titmouse. Those were the prisoner's words, sir. In mitigation, sir," he went on, and humanity came into his voice at last, "the prisoner had consumed an excess of liquors."

Thorisin cocked his head quizzically at Monotes, who seemed to be doing his best to sink through the floor. "Like animals, don't you?" he remarked. Scaurus' hopes rose; the Emperor's comment was hardly one to precede a routine condemnation. Honest curiosity in his voice, Gavras asked, "Boy, did you really say all those things about me?"

"Yes, your Highness," the lieutenant whispered miserably, his face pale as undyed silk. He took a deep breath, then blurted, "I likely would've come up with worse, sir, if I'd had more wine."

"Disgraceful," Baanes Onomagoulos muttered, but Thorisin was grinning openly and coughing in his efforts not to snicker. After a moment he gave up and laughed out loud.

"Take him away," he said to the guards. "Run the wine-fumes out of him, and he'll do just fine. Titmouse, indeed!" he snorted, wiping his eyes. "Go on, get out," he said to Monotes, who was trying to splutter thanks, "or I'll make you wish I was one."

Monotes almost fell as the guards let him go; he scurried for the tent flap and was gone. Gavras' brief good humor disappeared with him. "Where is everyone?" he growled. Actually, only a few seats were still unfilled.

When the last Khamorth chieftain sauntered in, Thorisin glared him into his chair. The nomad was unperturbed—no farmer's anger could reach him, not even a king's.

"Good of you to join us," Gavras told him, but sarcasm was as wasted as wrath. The Emperor's next words, though, seized the attention of everyone up and down the long table. Still taken with Pastillas Monotes' phrase, he said, "I propose to move my feathered hindquarters against the city's works at sunrise, two days hence."

There was a moment's silence, then a babble louder than any Scaurus had heard from Thorisin's marshals. Above it rose Soteric's cry: "Then you are a blockhead and you've lost whatever wits you had!"

Utprand Dagober's son echoed him a second later: "Ya, what brings on t'is madness?" Where Soteric sounded furious, a cold curiosity rode the older Namdalener's words. He gave Thorisin the same careful attention he would a difficult text in Phos' scriptures.

"Trust the islanders not to know what's going on," Gaius Philippus said to Marcus, the uproar covering his voice. It had faint contempt in it; to a professional, knowledge was worth lives. The Namdaleni, mercenaries by trade, were taken by surprise too often to measure up to the senior centurion's high standards.

Scaurus understood his lieutenant's disapproval, but, more sophisticated in the ways of intrigue than the blunt centurion, also understood why the men of the Duchy were sometimes caught short. Not only were they heretics in Videssian eyes, but also subjects of a duke who would fall upon the Empire himself if he thought the time right. No wonder news reached them slowly.

Thorisin Gavras waited till the tumult subsided; Marcus knew he was at his most dangerous when his anger was tightly checked. "Lost my wits, have I?" the Emperor said coldly, measuring Soteric as an eagle might a wolf cub on the ground below.

Soteric's eyes eventually flinched away from that confrontation, but the tribune still had to admire his brother-in-law's spirit, if not his sense. "By the Wager, yes," the Namdalener replied. "How many weeks is it of sitting on our behinds to starve the blackguards out? Now, out of the blue, it's up sword and at 'em. Idiocy, I call it."

"Watch your tongue, islander," Baanes Onomagoulos growled, his dislike for Namdaleni counting for more than his mixed feelings toward Thorisin. Other Videssian officers rumbled agreement.

Had Soteric spoken to Mavrikios Gavras thus in Thorisin's hearing, the younger of the brothers would have exploded. When thorny speech came his own way, though, Thorisin met it straight on—just as his brother had, Marcus remembered.

"Not 'out of the blue,' Dosti's son," the Emperor said, and Soteric looked startled to hear his patronymic. Recalling the elder Gavras' use of his own full name, Scaurus knew Thorisin was borrowing another of Mavrikios' tricks.

"Listen," Thorisin went on, and in a few crisp sentences laid out his

476

plight. He stared into Soteric's face once more. "So, hero of the age," he said at last, "what would you have me do?" He sounded very tired and finally out of patience.

The young Namdalener, sensitive to the mockery that made up so much of Videssian wit, bit his lip in anger and embarrassment. The words dragged from him: "Storm the city—if we can." He did not say— he did not need to say—that no one, Videssian or foreign foe, had taken those walls by assault. Everyone at the table knew that.

Utprand said to Thorisin, "Aye, storm t'city. You say that, and it sounds so easy. But we from t'Duchy, we pay the bill to win your Empire for you, and pay in blood." Scaurus could not help nodding; a mercenary captain who wasted his troops soon had nothing left to sell.

"To Skotos' frozen hell with you, then," Gavras snapped, his temper lost now. "Take your Namdaleni and go home, if you won't earn your keep. You say you pay in blood? I pay double, outlander—every man jack who falls on either side of this war diminishes me, friend and foe alike, for I am Avtokrator of all Videssos, and all its people are my subjects. Go on, get out—the sight of you sickens me."

After that tirade Marcus looked to see Utprand stalk from the tent. Indeed, Soteric pushed back his chair and began to rise, but a glance from the older Namdalener stopped him. In Thorisin's hot words was a truth that had not occurred to him before, and he paused to give it the thought it deserved. "Be it so, then," he said at last. "Two days hence." He sketched a salute and was gone, sweeping Soteric along in his wake.

The council broke up swiftly, officers leaving a few at a time, gabbling over what they had heard like so many washerwomen. As Marcus turned sideways to ease through the open tent flap, his eyes happened to meet those of Thorisin, who was still plotting strategy with Bouraphos the admiral. Thorisin's glance held unmistakable triumph in it. Scaurus suddenly wondered how angry the Emperor had really been and how much he had made the Namdaleni talk themselves into doing just what he had planned for them in the first place.

Gavras' army readied itself for the attack. Stone- and arrow-throwers moved forward, ready to give covering fire for the assault on the walls.

Every archer's quiver was filled, to the same purpose. Inside sheds covered with green hides, rams swung on their chains.

"Very impressive," Gorgidas murmured, watching the bustle of military preparation. "And inside, I suppose, they're heating up their oil to give us the warm reception we deserve."

"*Absit omen*," Marcus said, but it was only too likely. Too much of the readying process was visible from the walls to leave Videssos' defenders in much doubt over what was about to happen, despite the army's best efforts at secrecy.

"If there was a commander in there with his wits about him and an ounce more guts than he needs to turn beans into wind, he'd sally now and set us back a week," Gaius Philippus said. He watched soldiers marching four abreast on the capital's battlements, insect-small in the distance.

Scaurus said, "I don't think it's likely. The pen-pushers inside must have their generals under their thumbs, or they'd've hit us long before this. Ortaias may play at being a warrior, but Vardanes' way of ruling is by taxes and tricks, not steel. He distrusts soldiers too much to turn them loose, I think."

"I hope you're right," the senior centurion said. Marcus noticed him doubling patrols and sentry postings all the same. He did not change the dispositions; watchfulness was seldom wasted.

The Romans, then, were not surprised when at twilight a raiding party came storming from a sally port all but hidden by one of the outer wall's towers. The marauders carried flaming brands, as well as swords and bows, and flung them at any pieces of matériel they saw. Flames clung and spread, unnaturally bright; the Videssians were skilled incendiary-makers.

Shouts of "Ortaias!" and "The Sphrantzai!" flew with the raiders' missiles. So did the sentries' cries of alarm, their answering yells of "Gavras!" and the first shrieks of the wounded. Another war cry was in the air, too, one that made Scaurus, who normally faced battle without delight, jam his helmet down over his ears and rush to the fight: "Rhavas!" the marauders cheered, "Rhavas!"

Many of the attackers stopped short at the earthen breastwork that sealed the city Videssos from Videssos the Empire. These skirmished with the Roman pickets there, threw their torches and shot fire arrows, then fell back when they saw the defense ready for them. They fought, indeed, much like the bandits Outis Rhavas was said to lead: a brave onset, but no staying power.

One determined band, though, came scrambling over the chest-high rampart to trade swordstrokes with the Romans beyond and hack at their siege engines with axes, crowbars, and mauls. At their head was a tall, strongly built man who had to be Rhavas himself. With a cry of, "Stand and fight, murderer!" Marcus rushed at him.

To the tribune's disappointment, his foe wore a bascinet with its visor down; he wanted to see this man's eyes as he killed him. Whatever else he was, Rhavas was no coward. He loped toward Scaurus, his long-sword held high. The two blades met with a ring of steel. Marcus felt the jolt clear to his shoulder. The druids' marks on his Gallic sword flared golden. They were hotter and brighter than he had seen them since his duel with Avshar the wizard-prince just after he came to the capital. His lips tightened—so Rhavas bore an enchanted blade, did he? It would do him no good.

But the fighting separated them after another inconclusive passage. Before the tribune could come to grips with Rhavas once more, Phostis Apokavkos attacked Ortaias' captain. In his fury to avenge Doukitzes, all the careful swordplay the legionaries had drilled into him was forgotten. He slashed and chopped with his *gladius,* a blade far too short for such work. Rhavas toyed with him like a cat with a baby squirrel, all the while laughing cruel and cold.

At length he tired of his sport and decided to make an end. His sword hurtled toward Apokavkos' helm. But the stroke was not quite true; Phostis reeled away, hand clapped to his head, but that head still rode his shoulders. With a bellow of fury, Rhavas leaped after him.

Gaius Philippus stepped deliberately into his path. "Stand aside, little man," Rhavas hissed, "or it will be the worse for you." Behind the senior centurion, Apokavkos was down on his knees, blood running from one ear. Gaius Philippus planted his feet to await the onslaught. He spat over the edge of his shield.

A storm of blows rained down on him, furious as the fall cloudbursts in the westland plateaus. The Roman, though, was wiser by years of hard fighting than Phostis Apokavkos and did not try to match Rhavas stroke for stroke. He stood on the defensive, his own sword flicking out in counterattack only when the thrusts brought no danger to himself.

Rhavas feinted, tried to spring around him. But the senior centurion side-stepped quickly and kept himself between the giant warrior and his prey. Then Marcus was hurrying forward to give him aid, a dozen legionaries close behind. Viridovix, as always an army in himself, stretched two of the skirmishers in the dirt and bore in on Rhavas from another direction.

Still snarling curses, Rhavas had to retreat. He led the rear-guard that held the Romans at bay while the rest of his raiders made their way back over the besieging rampart. He was the last to vault over it and, once on the other side, favored Scaurus with a mocking salute. "There will be other times," he called, and the grim certainty in his voice sent a thrill of danger down the tribune's back.

"Shall we give him a chase?" Gaius Philippus asked. The bandit chieftain was standing there in no man's land, fairly daring the Romans to pursue.

Marcus answered regretfully, "No, I think not. All he wants to do is lure us into range of the engines on the walls."

"Aye, more lives than the whoreson's worth," Gaius Philippus conceded. He flexed his left shoulder, winced and said, "He's strong as a bear, curse him. A couple of the ones he hit me, I thought he broke my arm. This *scutum* will never be the same again either." The bronze facing of the shield's upper rim was all but hacked away, while the thick boards of the frame beneath were chipped and split from the fierceness of Rhavas' attack.

Water would not douse the fires the raiders had managed to set; they had to be smothered with sand. Half a dozen dart-throwers and one big stone-throwing engine were destroyed, and several others had been wrecked by Rhavas' axemen and crowbar swingers. Scaurus was surprised the damage was not worse; luckily, the marauders had only had a few minutes to carry out their assault.

Casualties were similarly light. Viridovix had accounted for half the enemy dead in his one brief flurry, a feat Marcus was sure he would not hear the last of for weeks to come. Of the Romans, it seemed no one had been killed, which gladdened the tribune's heart. Every legionary lost was one less link to the world he would never know again, one more man who shared his memories gone forever.

The worst-hurt man was Apokavkos. Gorgidas bent over him, easing his helmet off and palpating the left side of his head with skilled, gentle fingers. Apokavkos tried to speak, but produced only a confused, stammering sound.

Scaurus was alarmed at that, but the Greek doctor grunted in satisfaction, recognizing the symptom. "The blow he took threw his brain into commotion, as well it might," he told the tribune, "and so he's lost his voice for a time, but I think he'll recover. His skull is not broken, and he has full use of his limbs—don't you, Phostis?"

The Videssian moved them all to prove it. He tried to talk again, failed once more, and shook his head in annoyance, a motion immediately followed by a wince. "Head hurts," he scrawled in the dust.

"So you can write, can you? How interesting," Gorgidas said, ignoring what was written. For a moment he looked at Apokavkos more as a specimen than a man, but caught himself with an embarrassed chuckle. "I'll give you a draft of wine mixed with poppy juice. You'll sleep the day around, and when you wake the worst of your headache should be gone. You ought to have your voice back by then, too."

"Thanks," Apokavkos wrote. As with his last message, he used Videssian; while he spoke Latin, he could not write it. He climbed painfully to his feet and followed Gorgidas to his tent for the promised medicine.

"It's a good thing Drax's Namdaleni and the regular Videssian troops in the city didn't follow Rhavas' cutthroats out on sally," Marcus said to Gaius Philippus later that night. "They could have set things back as badly as you said, and we can't afford it with things in the westlands as they are."

The centurion carefully gnawed the last meat from a roasted chicken thigh, then tossed the bone into the fire. "Why should they follow Rhavas?" he said. "You know the Namdaleni, aye, and the imperials, too. Think they have any more stomach for his gang of roughs than we do? Probably hoping we'd kill the lot of 'em. There wouldn't be many a tear shed in there if we had, I'd bet."

Marcus stopped to consider that and decided Gaius Philippus was probably right. The men on the other side were most of them soldiers like any others and no doubt despised bandits the same way all regular troops did. It was their leaders who chose such instruments, not the rank and file. "The Sphrantzai," he said, the word sliding slimily off his tongue. Gaius Philippus nodded, understanding him perfectly.

The morning Thorisin Gavras had chosen for his assault dawned gray and foggy—not the porridge-thick blinding fog that had masked the arrival of the ships from the Key, but still a mist that cut visibility to less than a hundred paces. "Well, not *all* my prayers were wasted," Gaius Philippus said, drawing faint smiles from the legionaries who heard him. For the most part they went about their business grim-faced, knowing what was ahead of them.

"A big part of what we can do out there will depend on your men and the covering fire they can give us," Marcus was saying to Laon Pakhymer. The Khatrisher had brought his archers back from their foraging duties to join in the effort against the capital.

"I know," Pakhymer said. "Our quivers are full, and we've been driving the fletchers crazy with all the shafts we've asked for." He looked around, eyeing the murky weather with distaste. "We can't hit what we can't see, though, you know."

"Of course," Scaurus said, suddenly less glad of the fog than he had been. "But if you keep the top of the wall well-swept, it won't matter that your bowmen aren't aiming at anyone in particular."

"Of course," Pakhymer echoed ironically, and the tribune felt himself flush—a fine thing, him lecturing the Khatrisher on the tricks of the archer's trade, when Pakhymer had undoubtedly had a bow in his hand since the age of three. He changed the subject in some haste.

The voice of a trumpet rang out, high and thin in the early morning stillness. Marcus recognized the imperial fanfare, the signal for the attack. Much of his apprehension disappeared. No more waiting now. The event, whatever it held, was here.

The trumpet's last note was still in the air when the buccinator's horns blasted into life. The Romans, shouting, "Gavras!" at the top of their lungs, rushed for the Silver Gate and the postern gate through which Rhavas' sally party had come. More legionaries flung hurdles, bundles of sticks, and spadesful of earth into the ditch that warded Videssos, trying to widen the front on which they could bring their arms to bear.

The first protection the capital's gates had was a chest-high work not much different from the one Gavras' men had thrown up, save that it was faced with stone. The few pickets manning it were quickly killed or captured; the Sphrantzai were not about to throw open the gates to rescue them, not with the enemy close behind.

High over the Silver Gate stood icons of Phos, reminders that Videssos was his holy city. They were being rudely treated now; buzzing over the Romans' heads like a swarm of angry gnats came the arrow barrage the Khatrishers were laying down, along with the more intermittent crack of dart-casting engines and the thump of the stone-throwers' hurling arms smacking into their rests.

"Reload there! Come on, wind 'em tight!" an artilleryman screamed to his crew—the perfect Videssian incarnation, Marcus thought, of Gaius Philippus. The senior centurion was crying the legionaries on, ordering the rams forward to pound at the Silver Gate's ironbound portals. The slope-sided sheds, covered with hides to foil fire, hot oil, and sand, ponderously advanced.

Looking up at the crenelated battlements over the gates, Scaurus felt a surge of hope. Much against his expectations, the missiles had briefly managed to drive the defenders from their posts. The rams took their positions unhindered. The passageway behind the gates echoed their first *booms* like a great drum.

Gaius Philippus wore a wolfish grin. "The timbers may last forever," he said, "but the hinges can only take so much." *Boom-boom, boom-boom* went the rams.

But the Khatrishers could only keep up their murderous fire so long; arms tired, bowstrings weakened, and arrows began to run short. Soldiers appeared on the walls again. One of Bagratouni's Vaspurakaners shrieked as bubbling oil found its way through the joints of his armor to roast the flesh beneath. Another defender was about to tip his cauldron of sizzling fat down on the Romans when a Khatrisher shaft caught him in the face. He staggered backward, spilling the blazing load among his comrades. The Romans below cheered to hear their cries of pain and fear.

Stones and missiles shot from the towers of the inner wall were now beginning to fall on the legionaries. There were not enough Khatrishers, nor could they shoot far enough, to silence the snipers and catapults atop those towers.

Loud even through the din of fighting, the cry of "Ladders! Ladders!" came from the north. Scaurus stole a glance that way, saw men climbing for their lives and knowing they would lose them if the enemy tipped those ladders into space before they reached the top. The legionaries carried no scaling ladders—too risky by half, was the tribune's cold-blooded appraisal.

The rams still pounded away. A chain with a hook on the end snaked down to catch at one of the heads as it drove forward, but the Romans, alert for such tricks, knocked it aside. The huge iron clasps joining gate to wall creaked and groaned at every stroke; the thick oak portals began to bend inwards.

"Sure and we have 'em now!" Viridovix cried. His eyes blazed with excitement. He waved his sword at the Videssians on the walls, hot to come to grips with them at last. This fighting at long range and the duel of ram and catapult were a poor substitute for the hand-to-hand combat he craved.

Marcus was less eager, but still felt his confidence rising. Ortaias' men were not putting up a strong defense. By rights, he thought, the Romans should never have been able to get their rams near the Silver Gate, let alone be on the point of battering it down. He wondered how many men Elissaios Bouraphos' ships were drawing off to ward the sea wall. There were times when navies had their uses.

The fight at the sally port was not going so well for the legionaries. A sharp dogleg in the wall protected it from engines and let the troops inside fire at the attackers' flanks. As casualties mounted, Scaurus pulled most of his soldiers back, leaving behind a couple of squads to keep the besieged Videssians from using the postern gate against them.

One last stroke of the rams, working in unison now, thudded into the battered timbers of the Silver Gate. They sagged back like tired old men. The Romans surged past the rams' protecting mantlets, shouting that the city was taken.

484

It was not. The passage between inner and outer portals was itself walled and roofed, and a stout portcullis barred the way. From behind it, archers poured death into the legionaries at point-blank range.

Brave as always, Laon Pakhymer's Khatrishers ran up to return their fire. In their light armor they suffered for it, Ortaias' bowmen on the walls taking a heavy toll. Watching his men fall, Pakhymer remained expressionless, but his pockmarks stood shadowy on a face gone pale. He sent his countrymen forward nonetheless.

More archers shot down at the Romans from the murder-holes above the passageway; unlike the ones at panicked Khliat the summer before, these were manned and deadly. *"Testudo!"* Gaius Philippus shouted, and *scuta* went up over the legionaries' heads to turn the hurtling darts. But worse than arrows rained down. Boiling water, sputtering oil, and red-hot sand poured through the death-holes, and the interlocked shields could not keep the soldiers beneath them altogether safe. Men cursed and screamed as they were burned.

Still more terrible were the flasks of vitriol the defenders cast down on the legionaries. The very facings of their shields bubbled and smoked, and whenever a drop touched flesh it seared it away to the bone.

Scaurus ground his teeth in an agony of frustration. Having forced the Silver Gate, his men were caught in a cruder trap than if they had failed at once. The rams, protected by their mantlets, were still inching forward and might yet batter down the portcullis, though, as he watched, a man inside the mantlet fell, pierced by an arrow that found its way over his shield.

But after the portcullis lay the second set of gates, stronger even than the ones already fallen. Could he ask his men to claw their way through that gauntlet and have any hope they could fight Ortaias' still-fresh troops afterward?

With unlimited manpower behind him, he might have tried it. His force, though, was anything but unlimited, and once gone, was gone for good. However much he wanted to aid Thorisin, the mercenary captain's creed came first: protect your men. Without them you can do nothing to help or hurt.

"Pull back," he ordered, and signaled the buccinators to blow retreat. It was a command the legionaries were not sorry to obey; they had charged to the attack in high excitement, but they recognized an impossibility when they saw one.

Again the Khatrishers did yeoman duty in covering the Romans, especially the withdrawal of the rams and their heavy shielding mantlets, of necessity a slow, painful business. Laon Pakhymer brushed thanks aside when Marcus tried to give them, saying only, "You did more for us, one day last year." He was silent for a moment, then said, "Could we beg use of your fractious doctor?"

"Of course," Scaurus said.

"Then I thank you. That arrow-pulling gadget of his is a clever whatsit, and his hands are soft, for all his sharp tongue."

"Gorgidas!" Marcus called, and the Greek physician came trotting up, a length of bandage flapping in his left hand.

"What do you want now, Scaurus? If you must put out a fire by throwing bodies on it, at least give me leave to cobble them back together. Don't waste my time with talk."

"Tend to the Khatrishers too, would you? The arrow-fire's hurt them worse than our men because they wear lighter panoplies, and Pakhymer here thinks well of your arrow-drawer."

"The spoon of Diokles? Aye, it's a useful tool." He pulled one from his belt; the smooth bronze was covered with blood. Gorgidas held the instrument up to the two officers. "Can either of you tell whose gore's been spilled on this—Roman, Khatrisher, or imperial for that matter?" He did not wait for an answer, but went on, "Well, neither can I; I haven't really stopped to look—nor will I. I'm a busy man, thanks to you two, so kindly let me ply my trade."

Pakhymer stared at his retreating back. "Did that mean yes?"

"It meant he has been tending them all along. I should have known."

"There are demons on that man's trail," Pakhymer said slowly. His eyes held a certain superstitious awe; he intended his words to be taken literally. "Demons everywhere today," he murmured, "pulling the Balance down against us." In Videssian eyes, the Khatrishers were sunk deeper in heresy than even the Namdaleni. Where the men of the Duchy spoke of Phos' Wager with at least the hope that Phos would at last overcome Skotos, Pakhymer's people held the struggle between good and evil to be an even one, its ultimate winner impossible to know.

486

Scaurus was too tired and too full of disappointment to exercise himself over the fine points of a theology he did not share. With some surprise, he realized the sky was bright and blue—where had the fog gone? His shadow was pointing away from Videssos' works; the sun was in his eyes as he looked toward them. The assault had lasted most of the day. For all it had accomplished, it might as well not have been made.

Jeers flew from the wall as the Romans retreated, loudest among them the booming, scorn-filled laugh of Outis Rhavas. "Go back to your mothers, little boys," the bandit chieftain roared, his voice loaded with hateful mirth. "You've played where you don't belong and got a spanking for your trouble. Go home and be good and you won't get hurt again!"

Marcus swallowed hard. He had thought he was beyond feeling worse, but found he was wrong. Defeat was five times more bitter at the hands of Rhavas. His head hung as he led the weary, painful trudge back to camp.

Inside Videssos the soldiers of the Sphrantzai celebrated their defense far into the night. They had reason to rejoice; none of Thorisin's other attacks had come as close to success as the Romans', and Scaurus knew how far from victory the legionaries had been.

The sound of the revels only made Gavras' defeated army more sullen as it licked its wounds back behind its rampart. The tribune heard angry talk round the Roman campfires and did not blame his soldiers for it. They had fought as well as men could fight; but stone, brick, and iron were stronger than flesh and blood.

When the Namdalener came up to the Roman camp, nervous sentries almost speared him before he could convince them he was friendly. He asked for Scaurus, saying he would speak to no one else. The tribune's sword was drawn as he walked to the north gate; apart from his own troops, he was not prepared to take anyone on trust.

But the islander proved to be a man he knew, a veteran mercenary named Fayard who had once been under the command of Helvis' dead husband Hemond. He stepped forward out of the darkness to take the tribune's hand between his two, the usual Namdalener clasp. "Soteric asks you to share a cup of wine with him at our camp," he said. Years in the Empire had left his Videssian almost accent-free.

"This is a message you were bidden to give to me alone?" Scaurus asked in surprise.

"I had my orders," Fayard shrugged. He had the resigned air of a soldier used to carrying them out whether or not he found sense in them.

"Of course I'll come. Give me a moment, though." Marcus quickly found Gaius Philippus, told him of Soteric's request. The senior centurion's eyes narrowed. He stroked his chin in thought.

"He wants something from us," was his first comment, echoing Scaurus' guess. Gaius Philippus followed it a moment later with, "He's not very good at these games, is he? By now the whole camp'll know you're off on some secret meeting, where if his man had just sung out what he wanted to the gate crew, nobody would have thought twice about it."

"Maybe I should take you off combat duty," Marcus said. "You're getting to be a fine intriguer yourself, you know."

Gaius Philippus snorted, knowing the tribune's threat was empty. "Ha! You don't need to be a cow to know where milk comes from."

Scaurus fought temptation and lost. "You're right—that would be udderly ridiculous." He walked off whistling, somehow feeling better than he had since the ill-fated attack began.

He and Fayard drew three challenges in the ten-minute trip to the Namdalener camp and another at its palisade. Guardsmen who would have ignored a platoon the night before now reached for spear or bow at the smallest movement. Defeat, Marcus thought, made men jump at shadows.

Yet another sentry stood, armed, in front of Soteric's tent. A trifle shortsighted, he peered closely into the tribune's face before standing aside to let him pass. Fayard ceremoniously held the tent flap open. "You aren't coming, too?" Marcus said.

"Me? By the Wager, no," the man of the Duchy answered. "Soteric pulled me out of a game of dice to fetch you, and just when I was starting to win. So by your leave—" He was gone before the sentence was complete.

"Come in, Scaurus, or at least let the flap drop," Soteric called. "The wind will put out the candles."

If Marcus had had any doubts that Soteric's invitation was not merely social, the company Helvis' brother kept would have erased them. A bandage on his forearm, Utprand Dagober's son sat on the sleeping mat by Soteric, his bearing and his cold eyes wolfish as always. Next to him were a pair of Namdaleni the tribune did not know, save by name: Clozart Leatherbreeches and Turgot of Sotevag, whose native town was on the eastern shore of the island Duchy. The four of them together spoke for most of the islanders who followed Gavras.

They shifted to give Scaurus room to sit. Turgot swore softly as he moved. "My arse is bandaged," he explained to the Roman. "Took an arrow right in the cheek, I did."

"He doesn't care a moldy grape for your arse," Clozart rumbled. Marcus thought he looked foolish in the tight leather trousers he affected—he was nearing fifty, and his belly bulged over their fastening—but his square face was hard and capable, the face of a man who acts and lets consequences sort themselves out afterward.

"Have some wine," Turgot said, pouring from a squat pitcher. "We wouldn't want Fayard forsworn, would we?" Marcus shook his head, sipped politely. For all their ostentatious contempt for Videssian ways, some Namdaleni played the game of indirection even more maddeningly than the imperials who had taught it to them.

Soteric, though, was not one of those. Tossing his own cup back at a gulp, he demanded bluntly, "Well, what did you think of today's fiasco?"

"About what I thought before," the tribune answered. "With those walls, a handful of lame old men could hold off an army, so long as they weren't too old to remember to keep dropping rocks on its head."

"Ha! Well said, t'at," Utprand said, baring his teeth in the grimace that served him for a chuckle. "But t'question has more behind it. Gavras sent us forward to be killed, against works he had no hope of taking. Why should we serve such a man as that?"

"So you're thinking of going over to the Sphrantzai?" Marcus asked carefully. If their answer was aye, he knew he would have to use all his guile to leave the islanders' camp, for that was a choice he could never make. And if guile failed . . . He shifted his weight, bringing his sword to a position where it would be easier to seize.

But Clozart spat in fine contempt. "I fart in Ortaias Sphrantzes' face," he said.

"A pox on the twit." Soteric nodded. "The seal-stamping fop's a worse bargain than Gavras ever would be, him and his pot-metal 'gold-pieces.'"

"What then?" Scaurus said, puzzled. "What other choice is there?"

"Home," Turgot said at once, and longing filled his eyes at the word. "The lads have had a bellyful, and so have I. Let the damned imperials bake in their own oven, and may both sides burn. Give me cool Sotevag again and the long waves rolling off the endless gray ocean, and if the Empire's recruiters come my way again I'll set the hounds to 'em like your Vaspurakaner friend did to the Videssian priest."

The tribune felt no longing, only a jealousy that by now itself was tired. In this world he and his had no home, nor were they likely to. "You make it sound simple," he said dryly. "But what do you propose to do, march through the Empire's eastlands until you come to your own country?"

His intended sarcasm fell on deaf ears. "Aye," Clozart said, "or rather the sea across from it. Why not? What do the imperials have between here and there to stop us?"

"It should be easy," Utprand agreed. "T'Empire stripped t'garrisons bare to fight the Yezda, and then again for t'is civil war. Once we get clear of Videssos, there would be no army dare come near us. And T'orisin has to let us go—if he tries to hold us, the Sphrantzai come out and eat him up."

The chilly logic was convincing, as was Utprand himself; if the bleak Namdalener said a thing could be done, it very likely could. The only question Marcus could find was, "Why tell me now?"

"We want you and yours to come with us," Soteric answered.

The tribune stared, surprised past speech. The Namdelener rushed on, "Duke Tomond, Phos love him, would be proud to have such fighters take service with him. There's room and to spare in the Duchy, enough to make your troops yeoman farmers, each with his own plot, and you, I'd guess, a count. How's the sound of that? 'Scaurus, Scaurus, the great count Scaurus!' if ever you chose to go on campaign again."

Soteric's tickling at his vanity left Marcus unmoved; he had more influence as a general in the Empire than he would with a fancy title of nobility in Namdalen. But for the first time since the Romans were swept to this world, he found himself tempted to cast aside his allegiance to Videssos. Here, freely offered, was the thing he had thought impossible: a home, a place of their own in which they could belong.

The offer of land alone would seem like a miracle to his troops. Civil wars had been fought in Rome to get discharged veterans the allotments their generals promised. "Room and to spare . . ."

"Aye, outlander, it's a lovely country we have," Turgot said, still sentimental over the motherland he missed. "Sotevag sits on the coast, between oak woods and croplands, and I spend much of my time there, I will say. But I have a steading up in the moors as well—the high hills, all covered with heather and gorse, and flocks of sheep on 'em. The sky's a different color from what it is here, a deeper blue, almost makes you think you can see *through* it. And the wind carries music on its breath, not the smell of horseshit and dust."

The Roman sat silent, all but overwhelmed by his own memories of Mediolanum lost forever, of the snow-mantled Alps seen from a safe, warm house, of tart, pungent Italian wine, of speaking his mind in Latin instead of picking through this painfully learned other tongue . . .

All four Namdaleni were watching him closely. Clozart saw his struggle for decision but, mistrusting everyone not of his island nation, mistook its meaning. Dropping into the thick patois the men of the Duchy used among themselves, he said to his comrades, "I told you we never should have started this. Look at him there, figuring whether to sell us out or no."

He did not think Scaurus could follow his speech; few Videssians would have been able to. But more than a year's time with Helvis had given the tribune a grasp of the island dialect. His quick-sprung optimism faded. He and his were as alien to the Namdaleni as to the imperials.

Soteric knew him better than the other three and saw he had understood. Giving Clozart a venomous glare, he apologized as handsomely as he could.

"We know your worth," Utprand agreed. "You would not be here else."

Marcus nodded his thanks; praise from a soldier like this one was praise to be cherished. "I'll put what you've said to my men," he said. Clozart's hard face reflected only disbelief, but the tribune meant it.

There was no point in keeping the Namdalener offer from the legionaries, and no way to do so short of shutting them all in camp and killing any islander who came within hailing distance. Better by far to lead events than be led by them.

When the tribune emerged from his brother-in-law's tent, Fayard was nowhere to be seen. The dice spoke loudly to Namdaleni, and he doubtless decided Scaurus knew the way back to his own quarters.

His mind was spinning as he walked back to the Roman camp. His first feeling at Soteric's proposal still held true: after a Roman upbringing and almost two years in the Empire of Videssos, being a count in the Duchy seemed rather like being a large wolf in a small pack. Nor was he eager to abandon the Empire. The Yezda were foes who needed fighting once the civil war was won—if it could be won.

On the other hand, when thinking only of the Romans' best interests, Namdalen looked attractive indeed. He still had a hard time believing there could be land to offer freely to soldiers. In Rome the Senate kept a jealous grip on it; in the Empire it was in the hands of the nobles, with small freeholders taxed to the wall. Land—it would draw his men, right enough.

And on another level altogether, Helvis would surely leave him if he said Soteric nay, and that he did not want. What was between them refused to die, batter it about as they would. And they had a son . . . Was nothing ever simple?

Gaius Philippus waited just inside the north gate, edgily pacing back and forth. His saturnine features lit as he saw Scaurus. "About time," he said. "Another hour and I'd have come after you, and brought friends with me."

"No need for that," Marcus said. "We have some talking to do, though. Fetch Glabrio and Gorgidas and meet me back here—we'll take a stroll outside the palisade. Bring the Celt, while you're at it; this affects him, too."

"Viridovix? Is it a talk you want, or a brawl?" Gaius Philippus chuckled, but he hurried away to do what the tribune asked. Marcus saw how the Romans followed him with their eyes; they knew something was afoot. Damn Soteric and his amateur theatrics, he thought.

It was only a couple of minutes before the men whose judgment he most trusted and respected were gathered round him, curiosity on their faces. He led them into the night, talking all the while of little things, doing his futile best to make the conference seem ordinary to his men.

Out of earshot of the camp, though, he dropped the façade and gave a bald recounting of what had passed. A thoughtful silence followed as his comrades began to work the thing through, much as he had on his way back from Soteric's tent.

Gaius Philippus was the first to break it. "Were it up to me, I'd tell 'em no. I haven't a thing against the islanders—they're brave men and fine friends to drink with, but I don't want to spend the rest of my days living among barbarians." The senior centurion had in full measure the sense of superiority the Romans felt for all other peoples save Greeks. In this world Videssos was the standard by which such things were gauged, and he identified himself with the imperial folk here, forgetting they reckoned him as barbarous as the Namdaleni.

Gorgidas understood that perfectly well, but his choice was the same. He said, "I left Elis for Rome years ago because I knew my home was a backwater. Am I to reverse that course now? I think not—here I stay. There's too much I have yet to learn, too much the men of the Duchy don't know themselves."

The other two were slower to answer. Viridovix said, "Sure and it's not an easy choice you set us, Scaurus dear, but I think I'm for the change, belike for all the reasons the last two were against it. I'm easier with the islanders than with these sly, haughty imperials, where you never know the thought in a man's head until one day there's a hired dagger between your ribs because he misliked the cut of your tunic. Aye, I'll go."

That left only Quintus Glabrio; to judge by the pain on his face, his was the hardest choice of all. "And I," he said finally. Gorgidas' sharp intake of breath only made him seem more miserable, but he went on, "It's the land, more than anything else. The hope of it was the only reason I took service in the legions; it was the chance to be my own man one day, not a slave to someone else's wages. Without land, no one really has anything."

"You're a worse slave to land than to any human master," Gaius

Philippus retorted. "I joined the eagles to keep from starving at the miserable little stone-bound plot where I was born. You *want* to walk behind an ox's arse from sunup to sundown, boy? You must be daft."

But Glabrio only shook his head; his dream was proof against the senior centurion's harsh memories, proof even against his bond with Gorgidas. The physician looked like a soldier doggedly not showing a wound pained him, but he made no complaint against his companion's decision, whatever his eyes might say. Marcus admired him the more, thinking of his own private fears and wondering how much they would sway his course.

The centurions were too well-disciplined and Gorgidas too polite to ask the obvious question, but Viridovix put it squarely: "And what does your honor intend to do?"

Scaurus had hoped some consensus might show itself in his comrades' answers, but they were as divided among themselves as he was in himself. He stood silent a long while, feeling his inner balance sway now one way, now the other.

At last he said, "With this attack gone for nothing, I don't think Gavras has any real chance to take the city, and without it he'll lose the civil war. I'll go to Namdalen, I think; under the Sphrantzai the Empire will fall, and in any case I would not serve them. The Yezda, almost, are better, for they wear no mask of virtue."

Even with the decision made, he was far from sure it was right. He said, "In this I will give no man orders. Let each one do as he will. Gaius, my friend, my teacher, I know you'll do gallantly with the men who feel as you do." They embraced; Scaurus was shocked to see tears on the veteran's cheeks.

"A man does what he thinks is right," Gaius Philippus said. "A long time ago, when I was hardly more than a boy, I fought on Marius' side in the civil war, while my closest friend chose Sulla. While the war lasted I would have killed him if I could, but years later I happened to meet him in a tavern, and we drank the place dry between us. May it be so with you and me one day."

"May it be so," Marcus whispered, and his own face was wet.

Viridovix was hugging Gaius Philippus now, saying, "The crows take me if I won't miss you, you hard-shell runt!"

"And I you, you great hulking savage!"

With their long habit of discretion, what Gorgidas and Quintus Glabrio thought they kept to themselves.

"There's no point in throwing the camp into an uproar tonight," Marcus said. "Morning muster will be the right time to let the men know their choice; keep it to yourselves until then."

There were nods all around. They walked slowly back to the palisade, not one picking up the pace, all thinking this might be the last time they were together. The raucous noises from behind the city's walls were an intrusion on their thoughts. Things sounded as much like a riot as a celebration, the tribune thought bitterly. He cursed the Sphrantzai yet again, for forcing him to a decision he did not want to make.

The sentries drooped like flowers in a drought when their officers passed them by without a hint of what they had discussed. All through the camp, men stared toward them.

"Be damned to you!" Viridovix shouted. "I've not grown a second head, nor a crest of purple feathers either, so dinna be dragging your eyes over me so!" The Celt's short temper was reassuringly normal; legionaries turned back to their food, their talk, or their endless games of chance.

Gorgidas said, "You'll forgive me, I hope, but I have wounded to attend to, crude as my methods are." Much to his own dismay, he still fought hurts with styptics and ointments, tourniquets and sutures. Nepos maintained he had the skill to learn Videssian healing arts, but his efforts bore no fruit. Scaurus suspected that was one reason, and not the least, he had decided to stay in Videssos.

Quintus Glabrio followed the physician, talking in a voice too low for Scaurus to hear; he saw Gorgidas dip his head in a Greek affirmative.

Someone hefted a skin of wine. Viridovix ambled toward it, drawn as surely as nails by a lodestone.

Helvis was sleeping when the tribune ducked into their tent. He touched her cheek, felt her stir. She sat up, careful not to wake Malric or Dosti. "It's late," she said, a sleepy complaint. "What do you want?"

Scaurus told her of her brother's plan, speaking as tersely as he had to his officers. She said nothing for a full minute when he was through, then asked, "What will you do?" It was a curiously uninflected question, all emotion waiting on the answer.

He said only, "I'll go." Reasons did not matter now; the essence of the thing was the choice itself.

Even in the darkness he saw her eyes go wide. She had been braced for a no and for the explosion that would follow it. "You will? We will?" she said foolishly. Then she laughed in absolute delight, forgetting her sleeping children. She flung her arms around the tribune's neck, planted a lopsided kiss on his mouth.

Her joy did not make him any easier over his decision; somehow it only brought into sharper focus the doubts he felt. Caught up in that joy, she did not notice his somber mood. "When will we leave?" she asked, eager and practical at the same time.

"In three or four days, I'd guess." Marcus answered with reluctance; putting a date to the departure made it painfully real.

Malric woke up, and crossly. "Stop talking so much," he said. "I want to go back to sleep."

Helvis scooped him up and hugged him. "We're talking so much because we're happy. We're going home soon."

Her words meant nothing to her son, who had been born in Videssos and known no life save that of the camp. "How can we go home?" he asked. "We *are* home."

The tribune had to smile. "How do you propose to explain that to him?"

"Hush," Helvis said, rocking the sleepy boy back and forth. "Phos be thanked, he'll learn what the word really means. And thank you, my very dear, for giving him the chance. I love you for it."

Scaurus nodded, a short, abrupt motion. He was still fighting his internal battle, and praise seemed suspect. But with his choice made, what need was there to load his qualms on her? Better, he thought, to hold them to himself.

He slid under the blanket; this day had drained him, and in another way the one upcoming would be worse. But it was a long time before he slept.

Turmoil outside woke him at first light of day. He knuckled his eyes, cursed groggily, and then sat bolt upright. The first cause for the uproar that crossed his mind was his men's somehow learning what was afoot. He scrambled into his cloak and dashed out of the tent. It would be all too easy for hubbub to turn to riot.

But there was no sign of riot, though the legionaries were not standing to muster in front of their eight-man tents. Instead they were packed in a shoving, shouting mass against the western wall of the camp, peering and pointing over the palisade in high excitement. More kept coming as the camp awakened.

The tribune pushed through the crowd; his men gave way with salutes as they recognized him. They were jammed so close together, though, that he took several minutes to work his way up to the palisade.

He did not have to be right by it—his inches let him see over the last couple of ranks of men. Someone next to him pounded him on the back: Minucius. The trooper's eyes were alight with triumph, his strong features stretched in a grin. "Will you look at that, sir?" he exclaimed. "Will you just look at that?"

For a moment Marcus still did not know what he meant. There ahead was Thorisin's earthwork and, beyond it, the capital's fortifications, silently indomitable as always.

That sentence had no sooner taken shape than it echoed like a gong inside him. No wonder the great double walls seemed silent in the dawn—not a defender was on them.

He felt giddy, as if he had gulped down a jug of neat wine. "Step aside! Make room!" he cried, ramming his way to the very front—he had to see as much as he could, be as close as he could. Normally he would have been ashamed to use his rank so, but in his excitement he did not give it a second thought.

There were the Silver Gates straight ahead, the works that had beaten back everything his men could throw at them. They were wide open now, and in them stood three men with torches, almost hopping in their eagerness to wave the besiegers into Videssos. Their shouts came thinly across the no-man's-land between the city and the siege-works: "Hurrah for Thorisin Gavras, Avtokrator of the Videssians!"

VIII

THE TORCH-WAVERS AND THEIR FRIENDS BEHIND THEM WERE AS UN-
savory a lot of ruffians as the tribune had ever seen. Gaudy in street
finery—baggy tunics with wide, flopping sleeves and tights dyed in an
eye-searing rainbow of colors—they swarmed around the orderly
Roman ranks, flourishing cudgels and shortswords and shouting at the
top of their lungs.

No matter who they were, though, their cries were what Scaurus
most wanted to hear: "Gavras the Emperor!" "Dig up Ortaias' bones!"
"To the Milestone with the Sphrantzai, the dung-munching Skotos-
lovers!"

As he looked north along the wall, the tribune saw Thorisin's army
loping by squads and companies through every wide-flung gate. The
Namdaleni were moving up from their stretch of siege line along with all
the rest. If Gavras was a winner after all, withdrawal suddenly looked
foolish.

"Reprieve," Gaius Philippus said, and Marcus nodded, feeling relief
like a cool wind in his mind. He blessed the mixed emotions that had
made him hesitate before announcing the pullout to his men. Never had
he come to a decision more reluctantly and never was he gladder to see
events overturn it.

Helvis would be disappointed, but victory paid all debts. She would
get over it, he told himself.

The news grew wilder with every step he took into the city, until he
had no idea what to believe. Ortaias had abdicated, taken refuge in the
High Temple, fled the city, been overthrown, been killed, been torn into
seven hundred pieces so even his ghost would never find rest. The rebellion had started because of food riots, treachery among Ortaias' backers,
and anger at the excesses of Outis Rhavas' men, of the great count Drax,

or of the Khamorth. Its leader was Rhavas, Mertikes Zigabenos—whom Scaurus vaguely remembered as Nephon Khoumnos' aide—the Princess Empress Alypia, Balsamon the patriarch, or no one.

"They don't know what's happening any more than we do," Gaius Philippus said in disgust as he listened to the umpteenth contradictory tale, all of them told with passionate conviction. "You might as well shut your ears."

That was not quite true. On one thing, at least, all rumors came together—though the rest of Videssos had slipped from their hands, the Sphrantzai still held the palace quarter. Unlike much of what he heard, that made sense to Scaurus. Many buildings in the palace complex were fortresses in their own right, perfect refuges for a faction beaten elsewhere.

It also decided Scaurus' course of action. The Silver Gate opened onto Middle Street, the capital's main thoroughfare, which ran directly to the palaces with but a single dogleg. The tribune told the buccinators, "Blow double-time!" Above the blare of horns he shouted, "Come on, boys! We've waited long enough for this!" The legionaries raised a cheer and quickstepped down the slate-paved street at a pace that soon left most of the rowdies gasping far behind them.

The tribune remembered the Romans' parade along Middle Street the day they first came to the capital. Then it had been slow march, with a herald in front of them crying, "Make way for the valiant Romans, brave defenders of the Empire!" The street had cleared like magic. Today pedestrians got no more warning than the clatter of iron-spiked sandals on the flagstones and, if Phos was with them, a shouted "Gangway!" After that it was their own lookout, and more than one was flung aside or simply run down and trampled.

Just as they had on that first day, the sidewalks filled to watch the troops go by; to Videssos' fickle, jaded populace, even civil war could become entertainment. Farmers and tradesmen, monks and students, whores and thieves, fat merchants and sore-covered beggars, all came rushing out to see what the new spectacle might be. Some cheered, some called down curses on the Sphrantzai, but most just stood and stared, delighted the morning had brought them this diversion.

Marcus saw an elderly woman point at the legionaries, heard her screech, "It's the Gamblers, come to sack Videssos!" She used city slang for the Namdaleni; even in the language of insult, theology came into play.

Curse the ignorant harridan, thought Scaurus. The crowds had just left off being a mob; they could become one again in an instant. But the leader of the street toughs, a thick-shouldered bear of a man named Arsaber, was still jogging along beside the legionaries and came to their rescue now. "Shut it, you scrawny old bitch!" he bellowed. "These here ain't Gamblers, they're our friends the Ronams, so don't you give 'em any trouble, hear?"

He turned back to the tribune, grinning a rotten-toothed grin. "You Ronams, you're all right. I remember during the riots last summer, you put things down without enjoying it too much." He spoke of riots and the quelling thereof with the expert knowledge someone else might show on wine.

Thanks to a bungling herald's slip at the imperial reception just after the Romans came to Videssos, much of the city still mispronounced their name. Marcus did not think the moment ripe for correcting Arsaber, though. "Well, thanks," he said.

The plaza of Stavrakios, the coppersmiths' district—already full of the sound of hammering—the plaza of the Ox, the red-granite imperial office building that doubled as archives and jail, and a double handful of Phos' temples, large and small, all flashed quickly by as the legionaries stormed toward the palaces.

Then Middle Street opened out into the plaza of Palamas, the greatest forum in the city. Scaurus flicked a glance at the Milestone, a column of the same red granite as the imperial offices. There must have been a score of heads mounted on pikes at its base, like so many gruesome fruit. Nearly all were fresh, but terror had not been enough to keep the Sphrantzai on the throne.

The plaza market stalls were open, but Thorisin Gavras' blockade had cut deeply into their trade. Bakers, oil sellers, butchers, and wine merchants had little to sell, and that rationed and supervised by government inspectors. Ironically, it was commerce in luxuries that flourished under the siege. Jewels and precious metals, rare drugs, amulets, silks and brocades found customers galore. These were the things that could always be exchanged for food, so long as there was food.

500

The eruption of more than a thousand armed men into the plaza of Palamas sent the rich merchants flying for their lives, stuffing their goods into pockets or pouches and kicking over their stalls in their panic to be gone. "Will you look at the loot getting away," Viridovix said wistfully.

"Shut up," Gaius Philippus growled. "Don't give the lads more ideas than they have already." His vine-stave staff of office thwacked down on the corseleted shoulder of a legionary who had started to stray. "Come on, Paterculus—the fight's this way! Besides, you bonehead, the pickings'll be better yet in the palaces." That prediction was plenty to keep the men in line—the troopers who heard him fairly purred in anticipation.

They thundered past the great oval of the Amphitheater, the southern flank of Palamas' plaza. Then they were into the quarter of the palaces, its elegant buildings set off from one another by artfully placed gardens and groves and wide stretches of close-trimmed emerald lawn.

A Roman swore and dropped his *scutum* to clutch at his right shoulder with his left hand. High overhead, an archer in a cypress tree whooped and nocked another shaft. His triumph was short-lived. Zeprin the Red's great two-handed axe was made for hewing heads, not timber, but the muscular Haloga proved no mean woodsman. The axe bit, jerked free, bit again. Chips flew at every stroke. The cypress swayed, tottered, fell; the sniper's scream of terror cut off abruptly as he was crushed beneath the trunk.

"The gardeners will be angry at me," Zeprin said. A longtime veteran of the Imperial Guard, he thought of the palace complex as his home and mourned the damage he had done it. For the dead enemy he showed no remorse.

"Dinna fash yoursel', Haloga dear," Viridovix told him dryly. "They'll be after having other things on their minds."

He waved ahead—a barricade of logs, broken benches, and levered-up paving flags scarred the smooth expanse of lawn. There were helmeted soldiers behind it and bodies in front—the high-water mark, it seemed, of the mob's attack on the palaces.

The makeshift works might have been strong enough to hold off rioters, but Scaurus' troops were another matter—and a second look told him the defenders were not many. "Battle line!" he ordered. His men shook themselves out into place, their hobnailed *caligae* ripping the smooth turf. His eyes caught Gaius Philippus'; they nodded together. "Charge!" the tribune shouted, and the Romans rolled down on the barricade.

A few arrows snapped toward them, but only a few. With cries of "Gavras!" and "Thorisin!" they hit the waist-high rampart and started scrambling over. Some of the warriors on the other side stayed to fight with saber and spear, but most, seeing themselves hopelessly outnumbered, turned to flee.

"Don't follow too close! Let 'em run!" Gaius Philippus roared out— in Latin, so the enemy could not understand. "They'll show us where their mates are lurking!"

The command tested Roman obedience to the utmost, for their foes used not only "The Sphrantzai!" and "Ortaias!" as war cries, but also "Rhavas!" It was all the senior centurion could do to hold his men in check. The battle-heat was on them, fanned hotter by lust for vengeance.

But Gaius Philippus' levelheaded order proved its worth. The enemy fell back, not on the barracks where Scaurus had expected them to make their stand, but through the ceremonial buildings of the palace complex and past the Hall of the Nineteen Couches to the Grand Courtroom itself, after Phos' High Temple the most splendid edifice in all Videssos.

The Hall of the Nineteen Couches had walls of green-shot marble and gilded bronze double doors that would have done credit to a keep. It was useless as a strongpoint, though, for a dozen low, wide windows made it impossible to hold against assault.

Marcus wished the same was true of the Grand Courtroom. It was a small compound in its own right, with outsweeping wings of offices making three sides of a square. Archers stood on the domed roof of the courtroom proper; others, looking for targets, peered through windows in the wings. Those windows were few, small, and high—the architect who designed the thickset building of golden sandstone had made sure it could double as a citadel.

"Zeprin!" Scaurus shouted, and the Haloga appeared before him, axe at port arms. The tribune said, "Since you've already turned logger, hack me down a couple of tall straight ones for rams."

"Rams against the Grand Gates?" Zeprin the Red sounded horrified.

"I know they're treasures," Marcus said with what patience he could. "But do you think those whoresons'll come out by themselves?"

After a moment the Haloga sighed and shrugged. "Aye, there are times when it's what must be done, not what should be." His thick muscles bunched under his mail shirt; he attacked the stately pines with a ferocity that told something of his dismay. The Romans were at the foot-and-a-half thick trunks as fast as they fell, chopping branches away and then tugging the trimmed logs up.

"All right, at 'em!" Gaius Philippus said. The men at the rams clumsily swung their heavy burdens toward the Grand Gates. Shieldmen leaped out on either side of them to cover them from arrow-fire. The makeshift batterers, of course, had no mantlets; Marcus hoped the enemy trapped inside the Grand Courtroom had not had time to bring anything more lethal than bowmen up to the roof.

The ram crews lumbered forward, warded by their comrades' upraised *scuta*. The Grand Gates groaned at the impact, as if in pain. The logs jolted from the Romans' hands. Men tumbled, writhing as they fell to keep from being crushed. They scrambled to their feet, lifted the rams once more, and drew back for another blow.

More legionaries fanned out to deal with the few dozen men who had fled to the Grand Courtroom too late to take shelter inside. Soon only Romans stood erect in the courtyard. Not one of Rhavas' men had asked for quarter—in that, at least, they perfectly understood the temper of their foes.

Out of the corner of his eye Marcus noticed the upper stories of the nearby Hall of Ambassadors. They were crowded with faces watching the fighting. The tribune had several friends among the foreign envoys. He hoped they were safe. This, he thought, was a closer view of Videssos' government in action than they were likely to want.

Rhavas' archers were hitting back. One sharpshooter high on the courtroom dome scored again and again. Then he crumpled, sliding down over the orange-red tiles to fall like so many limp rags to the greenery far below.

The range and upward angle had made him a nearly impossible mark. "Well shot!" Marcus cried, looking round to find out who had picked off the bowman. He saw Viridovix pounding a skinny, swarthy man on the back: Arigh Arghun's son, the envoy of the Arshaum to Videssos' court. His nomadic people dwelt on the steppe west of the Khamorth, and he carried a plainsman's short, horn-reinforced bow. Bitter experience against the Yezda had taught Scaurus how marvelously long and flat those bows shot; the dead sharpshooter was but another proof.

"Isn't he the finest little fellow now?" Viridovix crowed, gleefully thumping Arigh again. The big ruddy Celt and slight, flat-faced, black-haired nomad made a strange pair, but they had often roistered together when the Romans were stationed in the city. Each owned a fierce, un-complicated view of life that appealed to the other, the more so in the wordly-wise capital.

The tribune's brief musing was snapped by a scream within the Grand Courtroom, a woman's shriek of mortal anguish that sent the hairs on his arms and at the nape of his neck bristling upright. Hardened though they were, the Romans and their foes both stood frozen in horror for a moment before returning to their business of murdering one an-other.

Marcus' first thought after his wits began to work again was that Alypia Gavra might well be in the besieged courtroom. If that scream had been hers—"Harder, damn you!" he shouted to the men at the rams and shoved sword in scabbard so he could take hold of a log.

The ram crews needed no urging; the cry had put fresh spirit in them as well. They rushed forward. The Grand Gates tolled like a sub-bass bell. Scaurus fell, scraping elbows and knees and feeling the wind half knocked from him, almost as if he had run full-tilt into the gates him-self.

He leaped to his feet and ran back to the log, never noticing the fist-sized stone that smashed into the grass where he had sprawled. Then it was back and forward again, and yet again. The rough bark drew blood from even the most callused hands.

Twice as tall as a man, the burnished gates were leaning drunkenly back against the bar that held them upright. Quintus Glabrio's clear voice rang out, "Once more! This one pays for all." The rams crashed home. With the desperate sound a great plank makes on breaking, the bar gave way. The Grand Gates flew open, as if kicked. Cheering, the Romans surged forward.

A fierce volley met them, but Scaurus, expecting such, had put shieldmen in front of the ram crews to hold off the arrows. Then it was savage fighting at the breached gate. The small opening kept the Romans from bringing their full numbers into play, and Rhavas' bandits fought with the reckless fury of men who knew themselves trapped. Even so, the legionaries were better armed and better trained; step by bitter step they pushed their foes back from the entrance and into the courtroom.

As he fought his way past the Grand Gates, Marcus felt the dismay Zeprin the Red had known when the tribune ordered rams brought to bear against them. The high reliefs on them were exquisite, a wordless chronicle of the Emperor Stavrakios' conquest of Agder in the far northeast eleven hundred years before. Here the imperial troops led back prisoners, the bowed heads of the captive women agonizing portraits of despair. A little higher, engineers carved a road along the side of a cliff so the army could advance; a pack mule's hoof skittered on the edge of disaster. At the join of the gates Stavrakios led a counterattack against the Halogai. And over all stood the Miracle of Phos, when hot sun in midwinter melted a frozen river and trapped the barbarians without retreat. The Videssian god appeared in brooding majesty above his chosen folk.

But Agder was lost to the Empire these last eight long centuries, and now, the reliefs that showed its overthrow themselves met war. The rams had flattened mountains and crushed faces with impartial brutality. A tiny twisted bronze ear was trampled in the grass at the tribune's feet. Nothing can come into being without change, he told himself, but the maxim did little to console him.

He shouldered past one of Rhavas' bravoes, thrust home under the arm where his mail shirt was weak. The man groaned and twisted away, enlarging his own wound. As he fell, Scaurus tore his small round shield from him to replace the *scutum* left outside the courtroom.

Marcus' eyes took a few seconds to adjust to the relative gloom within. He had expected to face Outis Rhavas at the entrance—had Ortaias Sphrantzes' foul captain fled? No, there he was, by a seething iron cauldron in the very center of the porphyry floor; the rude log fire kindled on that perfect surface was a desecration in itself. A knot of men around him jostled one another, each trying to dip a surcoat sleeve into whatever mixture bubbled in the kettle.

By it sprawled a gutted corpse, naked, female. The druids' stamps on Marcus' blade flared into light, but he did not need them to warn him of magic.

The fight was not the well-planned, carefully orchestrated engagement in which Gaius Philippus could take pride. The Romans perforce broke ranks to battle through the Grand Gates; inside the courtroom it was a vicious sprawl of fighting, one on one, three against two, up and down the broad center aisle and around the tall columns of light-drinking basalt. A hanging of cloth of gold and scarlet silk came tumbling down to enfold a handful of warriors in its precious web.

Marcus fought his way toward Rhavas. He moved cautiously; his hobnailed *caligae* would not bite on the glass-smooth flooring, and he felt as if he were walking on ice.

When one of Rhavas' men stumbled against him, they both fell heavily. They grappled, so closely locked together Scaurus could smell his enemy's fear. He could not stab with his sword; it was too long. He smashed the pommel into the brigand's face until the clutching arms around him relaxed their grip.

The tribune staggered to his feet. There were shouts outside—more of Thorisin's men reaching the palace complex at last through Videssos' maze of streets. Scaurus had no time for them. Outis Rhavas loomed over him, a tower of enameled steel from closed helm to mailed boots.

Most Videssians fought by choice from horseback and thus preferred sabers. But as he had in the brush at the rampart, Rhavas swung a heavy longsword. His giant frame made it a wickedly effective weapon; even the tall Scaurus gave away inches of reach.

"A pity you scrape your face bare," Rhavas hissed, his voice full of venom. "It ruins the pleasure of shaving your corpse."

The tribune did not answer; he knew the taunt was only meant to enrage and distract him. Their blades rang together. As Marcus had already found, Outis Rhavas was as skilled as he was strong. Stroke by stroke, he drove the Roman back; it was all Scaurus could do to parry the storm of blows. After the protection of his lost *scutum,* the small shield he carried seemed no more useful than a lady's powder puff.

But for all their fell captain's might, Rhavas' band was falling back around him. They fought as bandits do, furiously but without order. Though the legionaries' maniples were in disarray, long training had drilled into them the notion that they were parts of a greater whole. Like a constricting snake's coils, they pressed constantly, never yielding an advantage once gained.

Thus when Rhavas threatened Marcus, he was alone, while Viridovix and half a dozen Romans leaped to the tribune's defense. Balked of his prey, Rhavas cursed horribly. But he gave ground, falling back until he was one of the last defenders of the cauldron that still boiled and steamed in the center of the courtroom.

Even through woodsmoke, Marcus caught its contents' sick-sweet carrion reek, but a score of Rhavas' soldiers had already wet their sleeves in the liquid. And not soldiers alone; the sleeve that went into the pot now was purple satin shot through with thread of silver and gold.

"Vardanes!" the tribune shouted, and at the cry the elder Sphrantzes jerked as if jabbed with a pin. Scaurus had rarely seen Ortaias' uncle other than perfectly composed or known that round, ruddy face with its fringe of neat black beard to reflect anything but what the Sevastos wanted seen. But now he wore the furtive, guilty look of a man surprised at a perversion.

The battle stiffened. Some of Rhavas' bandits, it seemed, would not fall, no matter what blows landed on them. Marcus heard Gaius Philippus snarl, "Go down, you bastard, go down!," heard the soft, meaty sound of a blade driven home.

But the senior centurion's foe only grinned like a snake. Scaurus saw the yellowish stain on his surcoat sleeve. He slashed back at the Roman, a clumsy stroke Gaius Philippus turned with his shield. But doubt clouded the veteran's eyes—how was he to beat a man he could not wound?

That same doubt appeared on more and more Roman faces. As Rhavas' anointed gained confidence in their invulnerability to steel, they began running risks no warrior would have thought sane, taking ten blows to land one. They taunted the legionaries, as boys will taunt a savage dog when safely behind a high fence. And, inevitably, they took their share of victims. The Roman advance stumbled.

Smiling wickedly, a tall, jackal-lean Videssian engaged Viridovix. The cutthroat swung his sword two-handed—what need had he of shield? The big Gaul slid to one side, light on his feet as a great hunting cat. His blade, twin to Scaurus' own, sang through the air, druids' marks flashing gold.

It bit through flesh and windpipe and bone. Before the expression of horrified surprise could form on the brigand's face, his head leaped from his shoulders, hitting the ground with a warm, splattery thud. The spouting corpse collapsed, its limbs thrashing, for a moment not realizing they were dead.

Viridovix's banshee howl of triumph filled the courtroom. He leaped forward. Another muck-sleeved ruffian fell, clutching at the guts the Celt's sword laid out into his hands, neat as an anatomical demonstration.

Marcus went hunting stained surcoats, too, realizing that, as had always been true in Videssos, his good Gallic blade was proof against sorcery. Like Viridovix, he killed his first man with ridiculous ease. Not knowing the weapon he faced, the bandit scarcely bothered to protect himself. He gasped as the tribune's sword found his heart, then tried to breathe, but coughed blood instead.

"Liar!" he whispered, slumping to the floor; his eyes were on Rhavas. The harsh captain's men wavered in their attack, newfound confidence faltering as they watched their comrades die so in surprise. Then Arsaber, the hulking street ruffian, felled yet another of their number, his heavy club making a shattered ruin of the left side of his opponent's face.

Gaius Philippus was no scholar, but in battle he missed nothing. "It's only iron won't hurt 'em!" he shouted to the legionaries. He snatched a *pilum* from one of the Romans, grabbing the shank to wield it clubwise. He shouted in fierce delight as the blow sent one of Rhavas' warriors spinning back, sword flying from nerveless fingers. Marcus did not think that man would rise again; the senior centurion had exorcised all his fear of magic in one prodigious swing.

"Stand, you ball-less rabbits!" Rhavas bellowed, and Vardanes Sphrantzes' well-trained baritone rose in exhortation: "Hold fast! Hold fast!" But they were shouting against a gale of fear roaring through their followers—sword and spear had not held the Romans, and now sorcery failed as well.

One desperate band cut its way clean through the legionaries; its handful of survivors dashed through the Grand Gates, intent only on escape. Marcus heard their cries of despair as they ran headlong into more of Thorisin Gavras' troops outside. With agility born of desperation, bandits clawed their way up wall hangings to insecure refuges in window niches ten feet above the floor. Others tried to surrender, but not many of Scaurus' men would let them yield. Quintus Glabrio kept more than one from being killed out of hand, but he could not be everywhere.

Outis Rhavas cut down a bolting man from behind, and then another, his own way of encouraging his bandits to stand and fight. But even with the hardiest of his irregulars at his side, the surging Romans at last drove him from his wizard's cauldron. He fell back toward the imperial throne.

Marcus traded swordstrokes with one of his lieutenants. The man was fast as a striking viper; he pinked Scaurus twice in quick succession, and a vicious slash just missed the tribune's eye. But the cutthroat's heel slipped in the great pool of blood that had gushed from the serving wench his master had killed. Before he could recover, Scaurus' blade tore out his throat. He fell across the girl's outraged corpse.

As the tribune pushed forward, he glanced down into the iron pot Rhavas had defended with such ferocity and found himself looking at horror. Floating in the boiling, scum-filled water was a dead baby, the soft flesh beginning to fall away from its bones. No, he corrected himself, not even a baby—the tiny body was no longer than the distance between the tips of his outstretched thumb and little finger.

His eyes slipped to the serving wench's opened belly, back in disbelief to the cauldron, and he was sick where he stood. He spat again and again to clear his mouth of the taste and wished he might somehow wipe his vision clear so easily.

Cold in him was the knowledge that there were, after all, worse evils than Doukitzes' tortured death. He was tempted to follow the creed of Videssos, for in Outis Rhavas surely Skotos walked on earth.

That thought led to another, and sudden dreadful certainty gripped him. "Rhavas!" he shouted; the name was putrid as the vomit on his tongue. Then he solved the other's anagram, his monstrous joke, and cried another name: "Avshar!"

It grew very still within the Grand Courtroom; blows hung in the air, unstruck. Outis Rhavas' name brought with it rage and hatred, but the wizard-prince of Yezd had struck cold terror into Videssos' heart for a generation. Inside the ranks of Rhavas' men, Marcus saw Vardanes Sphrantzes' red cheeks go pale as he understood his state's greatest foe had been a chief upholder of his rule.

Across the thirty feet that separated them, Rhavas—no, Avshar— dipped his head to the tribune in derisive acknowledgment of his astuteness. "Very good," he chuckled, and Scaurus wondered how he had not known that fell voice at first hearing. "You have more wit than these dogs, it seems—much good will it do you."

After that moment of stunned dismay, the legionaries hurled themselves with redoubled fury at the backers of him who had styled himself Outis Rhavas. The men they faced threw down their swords in scores. Rhavas the brigand chief was a captain they had followed in hope of blood and plunder, but few were the Videssians who would willingly serve Avshar.

A bandit leaped at his longtime master's back, saber upraised to cut him down. But Avshar whirled with the speed of a wolf; his heavy longsword smashed through helm and skull alike. "A dog indeed," he cried, "nipping at the heels he followed! Are there more?"

The men who had been his flinched away in fright, all save a black handful who still clove to him, who would have happily fought for him had they thought him Skotos enfleshed—the worst of his band, but far from the weakest. Almost all wore surcoats stained with his protective brew—no qualm of conscience had kept them from dipping their sleeves in that horrid pot.

Vardanes Sphrantzes stood in indecision, a spider caught in a greater spider's web. He did not think of himself as an evil man, merely a practical one, and he feared Avshar with the sincere fear a far from perfect man can have for one truly wicked. But the Sevastos was more afraid to yield himself to Scaurus and, through him, to Thorisin Gavras. He knew too well the common fate of losers in Videssos' civil wars and also knew his actions in raising his nephew to the throne—and since—were sure to doom him in the victor's eyes.

The wizard-prince saw Sphrantzes waver; he flayed him into motion with the whip of his voice: "Come, worm, do you think you can do without me now?" And Vardanes, who had felt only contempt for soldiers, looked once more at the Romans' crested helms and at their stabbing swords and long spears. It seemed they were all bearing down on him alone. His will failed him, and he fled with Avshar.

The way they chose—the only way they could have chosen—was a narrow spiral stair that opened out into the Grand Courtroom just to the right of the imperial throne's gold and sapphire brilliance. It had not been part of the throne room's original design, for it brutally abridged a delicate wall mosaic. Marcus wondered what ancient treason caused some cautious Emperor to put safety above beauty.

Once Avshar's few partisans had gained the stair, the legionaries' advance was easy no more. Those steps had been made so one man could hold back an army, and the wizard-prince himself was rear guard, a cork not to be lightly pulled from the bottle.

The tribune and Viridovix attacked by turns; not only were they nearest Avshar in size and strength, but theirs were blades to stand against his sorcery. At every stroke the druids' marks incised upon them flashed golden, turning aside the banes locked within his brand.

Legionaries, crowding close behind their champions, jabbed spears over them at Avshar. Warded as he was, the thrusts could not hurt him, but spoiled his swordstrokes and threatened to trip him up. His heavy blade hewed clear through more than one soft iron *pilum*-shank; nevertheless he was forced back, step by slow step.

"Let's the both of us fight him at the same time," Viridovix panted. Marcus shook his head. The stairway was so narrow two men abreast would only foul each other, but he would have refused had it been wider. The first time his sword had met the Gaul's, they were whirled here; were they to touch again, only the gods knew what might befall.

The spiral wound through three complete turns. Then Avshar's massive frame was silhouetted against a background lighter than the stairway's oppressive gloom. The wizard-prince drew back away from the topmost step, as if inviting his pursuers to come on.

That Marcus did, but warily, expecting deviltry. He remembered Avshar's escape from Videssos the year before—the sea-wall arsenal's sudden-slammed door, the corpse of the wizard's servant speaking with his master's voice, the swords and spears that flew to the attack with no man wielding them. Avshar was never more dangerous than when seeming to give way.

A blade slammed against his upraised shield, but there was a ruffian back of it, a red-faced man with a great mat of greasy black beard. Scaurus parried, countered. The thrust was clumsy, but his reach and long blade made his stocky foe give back a pace. He stepped up quickly, Viridovix only a single stair behind him, legionaries jamming the stairway behind.

The suite above the throne room had to be the Emperor's disrobing chamber, a private retreat from the ceremonial of the Grand Courtroom. There had been, Marcus saw, six or eight well-stuffed chairs and a couch set up in the outer room; Avshar's men had flung them against the seascape-painted walls to gain fighting room. The rough treatment had burst one, and gray feathers whirled in the air.

Even as he fenced with the black-bearded highbinder, Scaurus wondered why Avshar had yielded the stair so easily there at the end, why for the moment he was leaving the battle to his henchmen. Where was he? Hardly time to see, with this cutthroat hacking away like a berserker.

The tribune let his foe's slash hiss past, stepped forward inside the saber's arc, and ran him through the throat. Aye, there was Avshar, in front of a closed door with Vardanes Sphrantzes. He bent low to say something to the Sevastos, who shook his head. Avshar smashed him in the face with his gauntleted hand.

Vardanes, strong-willed in this ruin of all his hopes, still would not do the wizard's bidding. With cold deliberation, Avshar hit him again. Marcus saw something crumple inside the proud Sevastos. All his life the bureaucrat had upheld his faction by circumventing brute force, by bringing Videssos' proud soldiers to heel without violence. Now at last he had to confront it with no buffers, and found he could not. He pulled a brass key from his belt, worked the lock, and slipped into the room beyond.

Marcus forgot him almost as soon as he disappeared. Fighting back to back, the tribune and Viridovix cleared enough space to let the legionaries emerge, a couple at a time, from the stairwell. Even with reinforcements constantly added, the fight was savage. Save for Scaurus' sword and the Celt's, Roman blades would not wound Avshar's men. They had to be clubbed into submission with spearshafts and other makeshift bludgeons, or else disarmed by a clever sword-stroke and then wrestled to the floor and dispatched with bare hands. They made the Romans pay dearly for each life.

The price would have been higher yet, but Avshar, as if conceding all was lost, stood aloof from the struggle, watching his men die one by one. Only when a legionary drew too near the door he was guarding did his blade flash forth, wielded as always with skill and might to daunt a hero. There was no shame in seeking easier prey, and so in the end the wizard-prince stood all alone before that doorway.

Facing a lesser foe, the Romans would have rolled over him and after Vardanes Sphrantzes. But Avshar was like a lion brought to bay; the debased majesty in him carried awe mingled with the dread. Push forward, Scaurus thought—make an end. But Avshar's gaze came baleful through visor slits, and the tribune could not move. Even Viridovix, a stranger to intimidation, stood frozen.

A strange silence fell, broken only by the legionaries' panting and the moans of the injured. Without turning, Avshar rapped on the door behind him. His iron-knuckled hand made it jump on its hinges. Only silence answered him. He hit it again, saying, "Come out, fool, lest I stand aside and let them have you."

There was another pause, but as Avshar began to slide away from the door, Vardanes Sphrantzes drew it open. The Sevastos clutched a dagger in his right hand. His left cruelly prisoned the wrist of a young girl; she wore only a short shift of transparent golden silk that served but to accent her nakedness beneath.

For all its paint, her face was not a palace tart's; the knowledge on it was of a different kind. But not until her calm greeting, "Well met, Marcus Aemilius Scaurus," did the tribune know her for Alypia Gavra.

Caught by surprise, he took an involuntary step forward. Sphrantzes' dagger leaped for her throat. Light glinted off the mirror-bright sliver of steel. The stiletto was only a noble's jewel-encrusted toy, but it could let her life river out before any man could stop it. Alypia stood motionless under its cold caress.

Scaurus also froze, two paces away. "Let her go, Vardanes," he urged, watching Sphrantzes closely. Vardanes' plump face was unnaturally pale, save for two spots of red that marked the impact of Avshar's hand. A thin trickle of blood ran from his left nostril into his beard. His pearl-bedecked Sevastos' coronet sat awry on his head—for the dandy Sphrantzes was, a telling sign of disintegration. His eyes were wide and staring, trapped eyes.

"Let her go," Marcus repeated softly. "She won't buy your escape—you know that." The Sevastos shook his head, but the dagger fell—not much, but an inch or two.

Avshar chuckled, his mirth more terrible than a shriek of hate. "Aye, let her go, Vardanes," he said. "Let her go, just as you let Videssos go when it was in your hands. You took your pleasure from it as from her, and then watched with drool dribbling down your chin as it slipped through your fingers. Of course, let her go. What better way to end your bungling life? Even as a puppet you were worthless."

Marcus never knew whether Avshar's contempt was more than the Sevastos could endure or whether, in some last calculation of his own, Vardanes decided—and perhaps rightly—the wizard-prince's death might be the one coin to buy his safety from Thorisin Gavras. Whatever his reasons, he suddenly shoved Alypia forward, sending her stumbling into the tribune's arms, then whirled and drove his dagger into Avshar's armored breast.

The thin steel needle was the perfect weapon to pierce a cuirass, and Sphrantzes' desperate stab was backed by all the power his well-fed frame could give. Scaurus had always thought there was muscle under that fat. Now he knew it, for when Vardanes' hand came away, the stiletto was driven home hilt-deep.

But Avshar did not crumple. "Ah, Vardanes," he said, laughing a laugh jagged as broken glass. "Futile to the very end. My magics proofed you against cold iron's bite. Did you think they would do less for me, their maker? See now, it should be done this way."

Swift as a serpent's strike, he seized the Sevastos, lifted him off his feet, and flung him against the wall. Marcus heard his skull shatter—the exact sound, he thought, of a dropped crock of porridge. Blood sprayed over the painted waves; Vardanes was dead before he slid to the floor.

Avshar drew the dagger from his chest, tucked it into his belt. "A very good day to you all," he said with a last mocking bow, and darted into the farther chamber.

His flight freed the Romans from the paralysis with which they had watched the past minutes' drama. They rushed to the door; but though the locks were on the outside, they would not open. The Romans attacked the door with swords and their armored shoulders, but the apartment over the throne room was, among other things, a redoubt, and the portal did not yield.

Through the noise of their pounding came Avshar's voice, loudly chanting in some harsh tongue that was not Videssian. More magic, Marcus thought with a twist of fear in his guts. "Zeprin!" he shouted, and then cursed the confused pushing and shoving that followed as the Haloga bulled his way up the crowded spiral stair.

He burst puffing out of the stairwell; the climb had left his normally ruddy features almost purple. His head swiveled till he spied Scaurus' tall horsehair plume. The tribune stabbed his thumb at the door. "Avshar's on the other side. He—"

Marcus had been about to warn the Haloga that Avshar was brewing sorcery, but found himself ignored. Zeprin the Red had nursed his hatred and lust for vengeance since Mavrikios fell at Maragha; now they exploded. He hurled himself at the doorway, roaring, "Where will you run now, wizard?"

Legionaries scattered as his great axe came down. It was as well they did; in his berserk fury the Haloga paid them no heed. Timbers split under his hammerstrokes—no wood, no matter how thick or seasoned, could stand up to such an assault for long.

Scaurus realized his arms were still tight around Alypia Gavra; her skin was warm through the thin negligee. "Your pardon, my lady," he said. "Here." He wrapped her in his scarlet cape of rank.

"Thank you," she said, stepping free of him to draw it around her. Her green eyes carried gratitude, but only as a thin crust over pain. "I've known worse than the touch of a friend," she added quietly.

Before Marcus could find a suitable reply, Zeprin shouted in triumph as the door's boards and bolts gave up the unequal struggle. Axe held high, he shouldered his way past the riven timbers, followed close by

Scaurus and Viridovix, each with his strong blade at the ready. Gaius Philippus and more Romans pushed in after them.

The tribune had not got much of a glimpse beyond the shattered door when Vardanes opened it, nor again when Avshar took refuge behind it. He stared now in amazement. It was a chamber straight from an expensive brothel: the ceiling mirror of polished bronze, the obscene but beautifully executed wall frescoes, the scattered bright silks that were donned only to be taken off, the soft, wide bed with its coverlets pulled down in invitation.

And he stared for another reason, the same which brought Zeprin's rush to a stumbling, confused halt a couple of paces into the room—save for the invaders, it was empty. The Haloga's knuckles were white round the haft of his axe. Primed to kill, he found himself without a target. His breath came in sobbing gasps as he fought to bring his body back under the control of his will.

Marcus' eyes flicked to the windows, tall, narrow slits through which a cat could not have crawled, let alone a man. Viridovix rammed his sword into its scabbard, a gesture eloquent in its disgust. "The cullion's gone and magicked us again," he said, and swore in Gaulish.

For all the sinking feeling in his stomach, the tribune would not yet let himself believe that. He ordered the soldiers behind him, "Turn this place inside out. For all we know, Avshar's hiding under the bed or lurking in that closet there." They stepped past him; one suspicious legionary jabbed his *gladius* into the mattress again and again, thinking Avshar might somehow have got inside it.

"Nay, it's magic sure enough," Viridovix said dolorously as the search went on without success.

"Shut up," Marcus said, but he was not paying much attention to the Celt. He had just noticed the gilded manacles set into the bedposts and reflected that Vardanes Sphrantzes' death, perhaps, had been too easy.

"There's magic and magic," Gaius Philippus said. "Remember the whole Yezda battle line winked out for a second until the Videssian wizards matched their spell? Maybe that's the trick the whoreson's using here."

That had not occurred to the tribune. Though he had scant hope in it, he sent runners through the palace complex and others to Phos' High

Temple, all seeking Nepos the mage. He also posted legionaries shoulder to shoulder in the broken doorway, saying, "If Avshar can make himself impalpable as well as invisible, he deserves to get away."

"No he doesn't," Gaius Philippus growled.

The sound of more fighting pierced the slit windows. Scaurus went over for a look, but their field of view was too narrow to show him anything but a brief glimpse of running men. They were Videssians, but whether Thorisin's troops advancing or followers of the Sphrantzai counterattacking, he could not tell.

Worried, he decided to go downstairs to make sure the legionaries were in position to defend the Grand Courtroom at need. Their discipline should have been enough to make such precautions automatic, but better safe; what with Avshar's magic and the fight up the stairs, usual patterns could slip.

He left the doorway full of guards and put others in front of the stairwell. Their eyes told him they thought their posts absurd, but they did not question him; like Fayard the Namdalener, they carried out their orders without complaint.

Alypia Gavra accompanied the tribune down the spiral stair. "So now you have seen my shame," she said, still outwardly as self-possessed as ever. But Marcus saw how tightly she held his cape closed round her neck, how she tugged at its hem with her other hand, trying to make it cover more of her.

He knew she meant more than the wisp of yellow silk beneath that cape. He spoke slowly, choosing his words with care, "What does not corrupt a man's heart cannot corrupt his life, or do him any lasting harm."

In Rome it would have been a Stoic commonplace; but to the Videssians, deeds spoke louder than intentions, as suited a folk who saw the universe as a war between good and evil. Thus Alypia searched Marcus' face in the gloom of the stairwell, suspecting mockery. Finding none, she said at last, very low, "If I can ever come to believe that, you will have given me back myself. No thanks could be enough."

She stared straight ahead the rest of the way down the steps. Scaurus studied the stairwell's rough stonework, giving her what privacy he could.

Alypia gasped in dismay as they came down into the throne room. It no longer had the semblance of the Empire's solemn ceremonial heart, but only of any battlefield after the fighting is done. Bodies and debris littered the polished floor, which was further marred by drying pools of blood. Wounded men cursed, groaned, or lay silent, according to how badly they were hurt. Gorgidas went from one to the next, giving the aid he could.

A glance told Marcus there would be no trouble at the Grand Gates. Unobtrusively effective as always, Quintus Glabrio had a double squad of legionaries ready to hold off an attack. But they were standing at ease now, their *pila* grounded and swords sheathed. The junior centurion waved to his commander. "Everything under control," he said, and Scaurus nodded.

Avshar's accursed kettle still steamed in the center of the hall, though the fire under it had gone out. The tribune tried to lead Alypia by as quickly as he could, but she stopped dead at the sight of the pathetic mutilated corpse beside it.

"Oh, my poor, dear Kalline," she whispered, making Phos' circular sun-sign over her breast. "I feared it was so when I heard your cry. So this is your reward for loyalty to your mistress?"

She somehow kept her features impassive, but two tears slid down her cheeks. Then her eyes rolled up in her head, and she crumpled to the floor, her strong spirit at last overwhelmed by the day's series of shocks. The borrowed cape came open as she fell, leaving her almost bare.

"One of Vardanes' trollops, is she?" a Roman asked the tribune, leering down at her. "I've seen prettier faces, maybe, but by Venus' cleft there'd be a lively time with those long smooth legs wrapped around me."

"She's Alypia Gavra, Thorisin's niece, so shut your filth-filled mouth," Scaurus grated. The legionary fell back a pace in fright, then darted off to find something, anything, to do somewhere else. Marcus watched him go, surprised at his own fury. The trooper had jumped to a natural enough conclusion.

At the tribune's call, Gorgidas hurried over to see to Alypia. He put her in as comfortable a position as he could, then folded Scaurus' cape around her again. That finished, he stood and started to go to the next injured legionary. "Aren't you going to do anything more?" Marcus demanded.

"What do you recommend?" Gorgidas said. "I could probably rouse her, but it wouldn't be doing her any favor. As far as I can see, the poor lass has had enough jolts to last any six people a lifetime—can you blame her for fainting? I say let her, if that's what she needs. Rest is the best medicine the body knows, and I'm damned if I'll tamper with it."

"Well, all right," Scaurus said mildly, reminding himself for the hundredth time how touchy the Greek was when anyone interfered with his medical judgment.

Alypia was stirring and muttering to herself when Nepos came bustling in behind one of Marcus' runners. Despite a remorseful cluck at the damage the Grand Gates had taken, the fat priest was in high good spirits as he entered the throne room. He scattered blessings on everyone around him. Most Romans ignored him, but some of the legionaries had come to worship Phos; they and the Videssians who had taken service with them bowed as Nepos went past.

He saw Scaurus and bobbed his head in greeting, smiling broadly as he approached. But he was less than halfway to the tribune when he staggered, as at some physical blow. "Phos have mercy!" he whispered. "What has been done here?" He moved forward again, but slowly; Marcus thought of a man pushing his way into a heavy gale.

He looked into the cauldron with a cry of disgust, a deeper loathing even than Scaurus' own. The tribune saw the torture's wanton viciousness; but as priest and mage, Nepos understood the malignance of the sorcery it powered and recoiled in horror from his understanding.

"You did right to summon me," he said, visibly gathering himself. "That the Sphrantzai opposed us is one thing, but this—this—" At a loss for words, he paused. "I never imagined they could fall to these depths. Ortaias Sphrantzes, from all I know of him, is but a silly young man, while Vardanes—"

"Is lying dead upstairs," Scaurus finished for him. Nepos gaped at the tribune, who went on, "The wizardry we dealt with, but the wizard, now—" In a few quick sentences he set out what had passed. "We may have him besieged up there," he finished.

"Avshar trapped? Trapped?" Nepos burst out when he was through. "Why are you wasting my time with talk?"

"He may be," Marcus repeated, but Nepos was no longer listening. The priest turned and ran for the stairway, his blue robe flapping about his ankles. Marcus heard his sandals clatter on the stairs, heard him run into a descending Roman.

"Get out of my way, you rattlebrained, slouching gowk!" Nepos shouted, his voice squeaking up into high tenor in his agitation. There were brief shuffling sounds as he and the trooper jockeyed for position, then he was past and clashing upward again.

When the legionary emerged from the stairwell he was still shaking his head. "Who stuck a pin in *him*?" he asked plaintively, but got no answer.

Alypia Gavra's eyes came open. Nepos had hardly spared her a second glance; Avshar's foul sorcery and Scaurus' news that the wizard-prince might still be taken drove from his mind such trivia as the Emperor's niece.

She sat slowly and carefully. Marcus was ready to help support her, but she waved him away. Though she was still very pale, her mouth twisted in annoyance. "I thought better of myself than this," she said.

"It doesn't matter," the tribune answered. "The important thing is that you're safe and the city's in Thorisin's hands." Why, so it is, he thought rather dazedly. He had been too caught up in the fighting to realize this was victory at last. Excitement flooded through him.

"Oh, yes, I'm perfectly safe." Alypia's voice carried a weary, cynical undertone Marcus had not heard in it before. "My uncle will no doubt welcome me with open arms—me, the wife of his rival Avtokrator and plaything of—" She broke off, unwilling to bring even the thought to light.

"We all knew the marriage was forced," Scaurus said stoutly. Alypia managed a wan smile, but more at his vehemence than for what he said. Some of his elation trickled away. There could be an uncomfortable amount of truth in Alypia's worries.

He was distracted by the sound of Nepos coming down the spiral stairway. It was easy to recognize the priest by his footfalls; his sandals slapped the stone steps instead of clicking off them as did the Romans' hobnailed footgear. It was also easy to guess his mood, for his descending steps were slow and heavy, altogether unlike his excited dash upwards.

The first glimpse of him confirmed the tribune's fears; the light was gone from his eyes, while his shoulders slumped as if bearing the world's weight. "Gone?" Marcus asked rhetorically.

"Gone!" Nepos echoed. "The stink of magic will linger for days, but its author is escaped to torment us further. Skotos drag him straight to hell, is there no limit to his strength? A spell of apportation is known to us of the Academy, but it requires long preparation and will not let the caster carry chattels. Yet Avshar cast it in seconds and vanished, armor, sword, and all. Phos grant that in his haste he blundered and projected himself into a volcano's heart or out over the open sea, there to sink under the weight of his iron."

But the priest's forlorn tone told how likely he judged that, nor could Scaurus make himself imagine so simple an end for Avshar. The wizard-prince, he was sure, had gone where he wanted to go and nowhere else—whatever spot his malice chose as the one that would harm Videssos worst. And with that thought, what was left of the taste of triumph turned sour in the tribune's mouth.

IX

Viridovix said, "It only goes to show what I've said all along—there's no trust to be put in these Videssians. The city folk stand by the Sphrantzai all through the siege and then turn on 'em after they'd gone and won it."

"Things are hardly as simple as that," Marcus replied, leaning back in his chair. The Romans had returned to the barracks they occupied last year before Mavrikios set out on campaign against the Yezda. The sweet scent of orange blossoms drifted in through wide-flung shutters; fine mesh kept nocturnal pests outside.

Gaius Philippus bit into a hard roll, part of the iron rations every legionary carried, as supplies inside the city were very short. He chewed deliberately, reached out to the low table in front of him for a mug of wine to wash the bite down. "Aye, the bloody fools brought it on themselves," he agreed. "If Rhavas'—no, Avshar's, I should say—brigands hadn't been off plundering to celebrate beating us back, Zigabenos' coup wouldn't have had a prayer."

"His and Alypia Gavra's," Marcus corrected.

A pail dropped with a crash and made Gaius Philippus jump. "Have a care there, you thumb-fingered oafs!" he shouted. The barracks were not in the same tidy shape the Romans had left them. During the siege they had held Khamorth and, from the smell and mess, their horses as well. Legionaries swept, scrubbed, and hauled garbage away; others made up fresh straw pallets to replace the filthy ones that had satisfied the nomads.

Reluctantly, the senior centurion returned to the topic at hand. "Well, yes," he said grudgingly to Scaurus, slow as usual to give a woman credit for wit and pluck.

But here credit was due, Marcus thought. Rumors still flew through

Videssos; like cheese, they had ripened through the day and now at evening some were truly bizarre. But unlike most of the city, Scaurus had talked with some of the people involved in events and he had a fair notion of what had actually gone on.

"Lucky for us Alypia realized Thorisin would never take the city from outside," he insisted. "The timing was hers, and it could hardly have been better."

The princess and Mertikes Zigabenos—who had kept his post as an officer of the Imperial Guard—were plotting against the Sphrantzai before Thorisin's siege even began. Alypia's handmaiden Kalline made the perfect go-between; her pregnancy protected her from suspicion and, as it had resulted from a rape by one of Rhavas' roughs, bound her to the plotters' cause. But as long as it seemed Thorisin might capture Videssos, the conspiracy remained one of words alone.

After his assault failed, though, assault from inside the city suddenly became urgent. Alypia managed to get word to Zigabenos that Ortaias had closeted himself away in the isolation of the private imperial chambers to compose a victory address to his troops.

Gaius Philippus knew that part of the story, too. His comment was, "The lady could have sat tight one day more. If there wouldn't have been a mutiny after that speech, I don't know soldiers." The senior centurion had endured more than one of Ortais Sphrantzes' orations and exaggerated only slightly.

Most of the regiments of the Imperial Guard had been lost at Maragha. Though Mertikes Zigabenos kept his title, Outis Rhavas' troopers actually warded the Sphrantzai. But the Romans had given them a hard tussle at the walls, and afterward most of them went on a drinking spree which quickly led to fist-fights and looting. Their victims, naturally, fought back, which brought more of them out of the palace complex to reinforce their mates—and gave Zigabenos his chance.

He only commanded three squads of men, but at the head of one of them he descended on Ortaias' secluded retreat, seized the feckless Avtokrator at his desk, and spirited him away to the High Temple of Phos; Balsamon the patriarch had long been well inclined toward the Gavrai.

The other two squads attacked the Grand Courtroom to rescue Alypia and use her as a rallying point for rebellion. Their luck did not match their commander's. Kalline had been caught returning to her mistress. Rhavas himself questioned her; he soon tore through her protests of innocence.

"She started to scream an hour before midnight," Marcus remembered Alypia saying, "and when she stopped, I knew the secret was lost. I never thought Rhavas was Avshar, but I was sure he was not one to let her die under torture till it suited him." The princess' would-be rescuers walked into ambush. None walked out again.

But Zigabenos was either a student of past coups or had a gift for sedition. From the High Temple he sent criers to every quarter of the city with a single message: "Come hear the patriarch!"

Everyone who claimed to be quoting Balsamon's speech for Scaurus gave a different version. The tribune thought that a great pity. He could all but see Balsamon on the High Temple's steps, probably wearing the shabby monk's robe he preferred to his patriarchal regalia. The moment's drama would have brought out the best in the old prelate—torches held high against the night, a sea of expectant faces waiting for what he would say.

Whatever his exact words were, they swung the city toward Thorisin Gavras in a quarter of an hour's time. Marcus was sure the sight of Ortaias Sphrantzes trussed up and shivering at the patriarch's feet had a good deal to do with that swing, as did Rhavas' thieving band rampaging through the shops of Videssos' merchants. Once given focus by Balsamon, the city mob was plenty capable of taking matters into its own hands.

"Almost you could feel sorry for Vardanes," Viridovix said, wiping grease from his chin with the back of his hand; from somewhere or other in the hungry city he had managed to come up with a fat roast partridge. "The puppet master found he couldn't be doing without his puppet after all."

After what he had seen in the bedchamber over the throne room, there was no room in Marcus for pity over Vardanes Sphrantzes, but the Celt's observation was astute. Much like the Videssian army, the citizens of the capital found Ortaias' foppish, foolish pedantry more amusing than annoying, and so his uncle had no trouble ruling through him. But the elder Sphrantzes, though a far more able man than his nephew, was himself quite cordially despised throughout the city. Once Ortaias was overthrown, Vardanes found no one would obey him when he gave orders in his own name.

His messengers had hurried out of the palace with orders for the regiments on the walls to put down the rising. But some of those messengers deserted as soon as they were out of sight, others were waylaid by the mob, and those who carried out their missions found themselves ignored. The Sevastos' Videssian troops liked him no better than did their civilian cousins, and his mercenaries thought of their own safety before his—Gavras would likely pay them, too, if he sat on the throne.

In the end, only Rhavas' bandits and murderers stood by Sphrantzes. All hands were raised against them, just as they were against him; neither they nor he could afford fussiness.

"Vardanes got what he deserved," the tribune said. "There at the last he was more Avshar's puppet than even Ortaias had been his." Fish on a hook might be a better comparison yet, he thought.

Gorgidas said, "If Rhavas and Avshar are one and the same, we probably know why Doukitzes met the end he did."

"Eh? Why?" Marcus said foolishly, stifling a yawn. Two days of hard fighting left him too tired to follow the doctor's reasoning.

Gorgidas gave him a disdainful look; to the Greek, wits were for use. "As a threat, of course, or more likely a promise. You know the wizard has hated you since you bested him at swords that night in the Hall of the Nineteen Couches. He must have wished that were you under his knife, not just one of your men."

"Avshar hates everyone," Scaurus said, but Gorgidas' words carried an unpleasant ring of truth in them. The tribune had had the same thought himself and did not care for it; to be a viciously skilled mage's personal enemy was daunting. He was suddenly glad of his exhaustion; it left him numb to worry.

Despite the reassurances he had given himself that morning, Marcus was not eager to confront Helvis with the obvious fact that they were staying in Videssos. He put off the evil moment as long as he could, talking with his friends until his eyelids began gluing themselves shut.

The cool night air did little to rouse him as he walked to the barracks hall he had assigned to partnered legionaries. It was not the same one of the Romans' four they had used the year before. That hall, with its partitions for couples' privacy, had been primarily a stable to the Khamorth, and the tribune wished Hercules were here to run a river through it.

Though the hall he had chosen for partnered men was tidier than that, he found Helvis busily cleaning, not satisfied with the job the legionaries had done. "Hello," she said, pecking him on the cheek as she swept. "On campaign I don't mind dirt, but when we're settled, I can't abide it."

Under other circumstances that speech might have gladdened Scaurus, who was fairly fastidious himself when he had the time. But Helvis' voice was full of challenge. "We *are* going to be settled here, aren't we?" she pursued.

The tribune wished he had fallen asleep where he sat. Worn out as he was, he did not want a quarrel. He spread his hands placatingly. "Yes, for the time—"

"All right," Helvis said, so abruptly that he blinked. "I'm not blind; I can see it would be madness to leave Videssos now."

Marcus almost shouted in relief. He had hoped her years as a soldier's woman would make her understand how the land lay, but hadn't dared believe it.

She was not finished, though. The blue of her eyes reminded Scaurus of steel as she went on, "This time, well enough. But the next, we do what we must."

There was no doubt in the tribune's mind what she meant by that, but he was content to let it go. The issue was dead anyway, he thought; with the civil war done, defection would not come up again. He stripped off his armor and was asleep in seconds.

Thorisin Gavras was Avtokrator self-proclaimed for nearly a year; with Ortaias Sphrantzes beaten, no one disputed his claim. Yet he remained a pretender in the eyes of Videssian law until his formal coronation.

As with any other aspect of imperial life, formality implied ceremony. Gavras was hardly inside the city before the chamberlains took charge of him; the Empire's topsy-turvy politics had made them experts at preparing coronations on short notice. Thorisin, for once, did not squabble with them—his legitimacy as Emperor was too important to risk.

Thus Scaurus found himself routed from bed far earlier than would have suited him, given hasty instructions on his role in the upcoming ceremonial by a self-important eunuch, and placed at the head of a maniple of Romans close behind the sedan chair that would carry Thorisin from the palace compound to the High Temple of Phos, where Balsamon was to anoint and crown him Emperor of the Videssians.

Thorisin emerged, stiff-faced, from the Hall of the Nineteen Couches and walked slowly past his assembled troop contingents to the litter. By custom, the procession should have begun at the Grand Courtroom, but that building was already in the hands of a swarm of craftsmen repairing the damage it had suffered in the previous day's fighting.

In all other respects, though, the new Avtokrator followed traditional usage. On this day he put aside the soldier's garb he favored for Videssos' splendid imperial raiment. Above the red boots, his calves were covered by blue-dyed woolen leggings; his bejeweled belt was of links of gold, while the silken kilt hanging from it was again blue, with a border of white. His scabbard was similarly magnificent, but Marcus noticed that the sword in it was his usual saber, its leather grip dark with sweat stains. His tunic was scarlet, shot through with cloth of gold. Over it he wore a cape of pure white wool, closed at the throat with a golden fibula. His head was bare.

Namdaleni, Videssian soldiers, Videssian sailors, Khatrishers, more Videssians—as Thorisin Gavras strode by each company, the troops went to their knees and then to their bellies in the proskynesis, acknowledging him their master. That was still a custom Marcus, used to Rome's republican ways, could not bring himself to follow. He and his men bowed deeply from the waist, but did not abase themselves before the Emperor.

For a moment Thorisin the man peeped through the imperial façade. "Stiff-necked bastard," he murmured out of the side of his mouth, so low only the tribune heard. Then he was past, settling himself into the blue and gilt sedan chair that was used only for the coronation journey.

Mertikes Zigabenos and seven of his men were the imperial bearers, their pride of place earned by the coup that had toppled Ortaias. Zigabenos himself stood at the front right, a thin-faced, lantern-jawed young man who wore his beard in the bushy Vaspurakaner style. Slung over his back he bore a large, bronze-faced oval shield. It was nothing like any a present-day Videssian would carry into battle, but Marcus had been briefed on the role it would soon play.

"Are we ready?" Gavras asked. Zigabenos gave a curt nod. "Then let's be at it," the Emperor said.

A dozen bright silk parasols popped open ahead of the traveling chair, further tokens—as if those were needed—of the imperial dignity. Zigabenos' men bent to the handles at their commander's signal, then straightened, raising Thorisin to their shoulders. Their pace a slow march, they followed the parasol bearers and Thorisin's strong-lunged herald out through the gardens of the palace compound toward the plaza of Palamas.

"Behold Thorisin Gavras, Avtokrator of the Videssians!" the herald roared to the multitude assembled there. The citizens of the capital, like the court functionaries, knew their role in the coronation. "Thou conquerest, Thorisin!" they cried: the traditional acclamation for new Emperors, delivered in the archaic Videssian of Phos' liturgy.

"Thou conquerest! Thou conquerest!" they thundered as the imperial procession made its way through the square. Marcus was surprised at their enthusiasm. From what he knew of the city's populace, they would turn out for any sort of spectacle, but would almost rather face the rack than admit they were impressed.

He understood a few seconds later, when palace servants began throwing handfuls of gold and silver coins into the crowd. The Videssians knew the largess to which they were entitled on a change of Emperors, whether the tribune did or not.

"Hey, the money's real gold! Hurrah for Thorisin Gavras!" someone yelled, startled out of formal responses by the quality of Thorisin's coinage. The cheers redoubled. But Scaurus knew the Vaspurakaner mines from which Thorisin had taken that gold were now in Yezda hands, and wondered how long it would be before the currency was cheapened again.

Still, this was no time for such gloomy thoughts, not with the applause of thousands ringing in his ears. "Hurrah for the Ronams!" he heard, and caught a glimpse of Arsaber standing tall in the middle of a knot of prosperous-looking merchants. One or more of them, he suspected, would go home lighter by a purse.

More cheering crowds lined Middle Street; every window of the three-story government office building had two or three faces peering from it. "Look at all the damned pen-pushers, wondering if Gavras'll have 'em for lunch," Gaius Philippus said. "Me, I hope he does."

A few blocks past the offices, the imperial procession turned north toward Phos' High Temple. The golden globes atop its spires gleamed in the bright morning sun.

The High Temple's great enclosed courtyard was, if anything, even more packed than the plaza of Palamas had been. Priests and soldiers held a lane open in the crush and kept the throng from flowing onto the broad stairs leading up to the shrine.

At the top of the stairs, somehow not dwarfed by the looming magnificence of the temple behind him, stood Balsamon. The patriarch was a fat, balding old man with a mischievous wit, but it suddenly struck Scaurus how great his power was in Videssos. Ortaias Sphrantzes was not the first Emperor he had helped cast down, and Thorisin Gavras would be—what? the third? the fifth?—over whose accession he had presided.

But his time was not quite come. Mertikes Zigabenos and his guardsmen carried Gavras through the crowd, which grew quiet, knowing what to expect. Followed by the ceremonial contingents, the Emperor's litter climbed the stairs. It halted two steps below the patriarch. The bearers lowered the chair to the ground. Thorisin climbed out and waited while his troops arranged themselves on the lower stairs.

Zigabenos unslung his shield and laid it, face up, before the Emperor. Thorisin stepped up onto it; it took his weight without buckling. Marcus was already marching up toward him, as were the other commanders of the units he had chosen to honor: the admiral Elissaios Bouraphos, Baanes Onomagoulos, Laon Pakhymer, Utprand Dagober's son, and a Namdalener the tribune did not know, a tall, dour man with pale eyes that showed nothing of the thoughts behind them. Scaurus guessed he had to be the great count Drax, perhaps included here to show that his mercenaries were still wanted by the Empire, even under its new master.

Once again, though, Zigabenos had precedence. He took from his belt a circlet of gold, which he offered to Thorisin Gavras. Following custom, Thorisin refused. Zigabenos offered it a second time and was again refused. At the third offering, Gavras bowed in acceptance. Zigabenos placed it on his head, declaring in a loud voice, "Thorisin Gavras, I confer on you the title of Avtokrator!"

That was the cue Scaurus and Gavras' other officers had awaited. They stooped and lifted the ceremonial shield to shoulder height, exalting the Emperor atop it. The waiting, expectantly silent crowd below burst into cries of "Thou conquerest, Thorisin! Thou conquerest!"

Baanes Onomagoulos' lame leg almost gave way beneath him as the officers lowered Thorisin to the ground once more, but Drax and Marcus, who stood on either side of the Videssian, took up the weight so smoothly the shield barely wavered.

"Steady, old boy. It's all done now," Gavras said as he stepped off it. Onomagoulos whispered an apology. Scaurus was glad to see the two men, usually so edgy in each other's company, behave graciously now. It seemed a good omen.

No sooner had Gavras descended from the shield than Balsamon, clad in vestments little less splendid than the Emperor's, came down to meet him. The patriarch performed no proskynesis; in the precinct of the Temple, his authority was second only to the Avtokrator's. He bowed low before Thorisin, the wispy gray strands of his beard curling over the imperial crown which he held on a blue silk cushion.

As the patriarch straightened, his eyes, lively beneath bushy, still-black brows, flicked over Thorisin's companions. That half-amused, half-ironic gaze settled on Scaurus for a moment. The tribune blinked—had Balsamon winked at him? He'd wondered that once before, inside the Temple last year. Surely not, and yet—

Again, as before, he was never sure. Balsamon's glance was elsewhere before he could make up his mind. The patriarch fumbled, produced a small silver flask. "Not the least of Phos' inventions, pockets," he remarked. The top rank of soldiers might have heard him; the second one surely did not.

Then his reedy tenor expanded to fill the wide enclosure. A younger priest stood close by to relay what he said, but there was no need. "Bow your head," Balsamon said to Gavras, and the Avtokrator of the Videssians obeyed.

The patriarch unstoppered the little flask, poured its contents over Thorisin's head. The oil was golden in the morning sunlight; Scaurus caught myrrh's sweet, musky fragrance and the more bitter but still pleasing scent of aloes. "As Phos' light shines on us all," Balsamon declared, "so may his blessings pour down on you with this anointing."

"May it be so," Thorisin responded soberly.

Still holding the crown in his left hand, Balsamon used his right to rub the oil over Thorisin's head. As he did so, he spoke the Videssians' most basic prayer, the assembled multitude echoing his words: "We bless thee, Phos, Lord with the great and good mind, by thy grace our protector, watchful beforehand that the great test of life may be decided in our favor."

"Amen," the crown finished. Marcus heard the Namdaleni add their own closing to the Videssian creed: "On this we stake our very souls." Utprand spoke the addition firmly, but Drax, closer yet, was silent. Scaurus' head turned in surprise—had the great count adopted the Empire's usage? He saw Drax's lips soundlessly shaping the Namdalener clause and wondered whether courtesy or expedience caused his discretion.

The "Amens," fortunately, were loud enough to drown out most of the sound of heresy; it would have been a fine thing, Marcus thought, to have the coronation interrupted by a religious riot.

Balsamon took the crown, a low dome of gold inset with pearls, sapphires, and rubies, and placed it firmly on Thorisin Gavras' lowered head. The throng below let out a soft sigh. It was done; a new Avtokrator ruled Videssos. The murmuring died away quickly, for the crowd was waiting for the patriarch to speak.

He paused a moment in thought before beginning, "Well, my friends, we have been disabused of a mistake and abused by it as well. A throne is only a few sticks, plated with gold and covered by velvet, but it's said to enoble whatever fundament rests on it, by some magic subtler even than they work in the Academy. Having a throne of my own, I've always suspected that was nonsense, you know"—One bushy eyebrow raised just enough to show his listeners they were not to take this last too seriously—"but sometimes the choice is not between bad and good but rather bad and worse."

"Without an Avtokrator we would have perished, like a body without its head." Marcus thought of Mavrikios' end and shivered to himself. Coming from republican Rome, he had doubts about that statement as well, but Videssos, he reflected, had been an empire so long it was likely true for her.

Balsamon went on, "There is always hope when a new Emperor sits the throne, no matter how graceless he may seem, and a new sovereign's advisers may serve him as a man's brains do his face, that is, to give form to what would otherwise be blank."

Someone shouted, "Phos knows Ortaias has no brains of his own!" and drew a laugh. Marcus joined it, but at the same time he recognized the fine line Balsamon was treading, trying to justify his actions to the crowd and, more important, to Thorisin Gavras.

The patriarch returned to his analogy. "But there was a canker eating at those brains, one whose nature I learned late, but not too late. And so I made what amends I could, as you see here." He bowed low once more; Marcus heard him stage-whisper to Gavras, "Your turn now."

With a curt nod, the Emperor looked out over the throng. "For all his fancy talk, Ortaias Sphrantzes knows no more of war than how to run from it and no more of rule than stealing it when the rightful holder's away. Given five years, he'd have made old Strobilos look good to you—unless the damned Yezda took the city first, which is likely."

Thorisin was no polished rhetorician; like Mavrikios, he had a straightforward style, adapted from the battlefield. To the sophisticated listeners of the capital, it was novel but effective.

"There're not a lot of promises to make," he went on. "We're in a mess, and I'll do my best to get us out the other side in one piece. I will say this—Phos willing, you won't want to curse my face every time you see it on a goldpiece."

That pledge earned real applause; Ortaias' debased coinage had won him no love. Scaurus, though, still wondered how Thorisin planned to carry it out. If Videssos' pen-pushers, with all their bureaucratic sleights of hand, could not keep up the quality of the Empire's money, could a soldier like Gavras?

"One last thing," the Emperor said. "I know the city followed Ortaias at first for lack of anything better, and then perforce, because his troops held it. Well and good; I'll hear no slanders over who backed whom or who said what about me before yesterday morning, so rest easy there." A low mutter of approval and relief ran through the crowd. Marcus had heard of the informers who had flourished in Rome during the civil war between the Marians and Sulla, and of the purges and counter-purges. He gave Gavras credit for magnanimous good sense and waited for the Emperor's warning against future plots.

Thorisin, however, said only, "You'll not get more talk from me now. I said that was the last thing and I meant it. If all you wanted was empty words, you might as well have kept Ortaias."

Watching the crowd slowly disperse, a dissatisfied Gaius Philippus said, "He should have put the fear of their Phos in 'em."

But the tribune was coming to understand the Videssians better than his lieutenant, and realized the armored ranks of soldiers on the High Temple's steps were a stronger precaution against conspiracy than any words. An overt threat from the new Avtokrator would have roused contempt. Gavras was wise enough to see that. There was more subtlety to him than showed at first, Scaurus thought, and was rather glad of it.

"What should we do with him?" That was Komitta Rhangavve's voice, merciless and a little shrill with anger. She answered her own question: "We should make him such an example that no one would dare rebel for the next fifty years. Put out his eyes with hot irons, lop off his ears and then his hands and feet, and burn what's left in the plaza of the Ox."

Thorisin Gavras, still in full imperial regalia, whistled in half-horrified respect for his mistress' savagery. "Well, Ortaias, how does that program sound to you? You'd be the one most affected by it, after all." His chuckle could not have been pleasant in his defeated rival's ears.

Ortaias' arms were bound behind him; one of Zigabenos' troopers sat on either side of him on the couch in the patriarch's library. He looked as if he would sooner be hiding under it. In Scaurus' mind the young noble had never cut a prepossessing figure: he was tall, skinny, and awkward, with a patchy excuse for a beard. Clad only in a thin linen shift, his hair awry and his face filthy and frightened, at the moment he seemed to the tribune more a pitiful figure than a wicked one or one to inspire hatred.

There was a tremor in his high voice as he answered, "Had I won, I would not have treated you so."

"No, probably not," Gavras admitted. "You haven't the stomach for it. A safe, quiet poison in the night would suit you better."

A rumble of agreement ran around the heavy elm table that filled most of the floor space in the library—from Komitta, from Onomagoulos and Elissaios Bouraphos, from Drax and Utprand Dagober's son, from Mertikes Zigabenos. Nor could Marcus deny that Thorisin likely spoke the truth. He could not help noticing, though, the patriarch's silence and, perhaps more surprisingly, Alypia Gavra's.

In a somber tunic and skirt of dark green, the paint scrubbed from her face, the princess seemed once more to be as Scaurus had known her in the past: cool, competent, almost forbidding. He was pleased to see her at this council, a sign that, contrary to her fears, Thorisin still had confidence in her. But she kept her eyes downcast and would not look at Ortaias Sphrantzes. The silver wine cup in her hand shook ever so slightly.

Balsamon leaned back in his chair until it teetered on its hind legs, reached over his shoulder to pluck a volume from a half-empty shelf. Scaurus knew his audience chamber, on the other hand, was so full of books it was nearly useless for its intended function. But then, the patriarch enjoyed confounding expectations, in small things as well as great.

Thus the tribune was unsurprised to see him put the slim leather-bound text in his lap without opening it. Balsamon said to Komitta, "You know, my dear, imitating the Yezda is not the way to best them."

The reproof was mild, but she bristled. "What have they to do with this? An aristocrat deals with his foes so they can harm him no further." Her voice rose. "And a true aristocrat pays no heed to such milksop counsels as yours, priest, though as your father was a fuller I would not expect you to know such things."

"Komitta, will you—" Thorisin tried, too late, to cut off his hot-tempered mistress. Onomagoulos and Zigabenos stared at her in dismay; even Drax and Utprand, to whom Balsamon was no more than a heretic, were not used to hearing clerics reviled.

But the patriarch's wit was a sharper weapon than outrage. "Aye, it's true I grew up with the stench of piss, but then, at least, we got pure bleached cloth from it. Now—" He wrinkled up his nose and looked sidelong at Komitta.

She spluttered furiously, but Gavras overrode her: "Quiet, there. You had that coming." She sat in stiff, rebellious silence. Not for the first time, Marcus admired the Emperor for being able to bring her to heel—sometimes, at any rate. Thorisin went on, "I wasn't going to do as you said anyway. I tell you frankly I can't brook it, not for this sniveling wretch."

"Be so good as not to waste my time with such meetings henceforth, then, if you have no intention of listening to my advice." Komitta rose, graceful with anger, and stalked out of the room, a procession of one.

Gavras swung round on Marcus. "Well, sirrah, what say you? I sometimes think I have to pull your thoughts like teeth. Shall I send him to the Kynegion and have done?" A small hunting-park near the High Temple, the Kynegion was also Videssos' chief execution grounds.

In Rome capital punishment was an extraordinary sentence, but, thought Scaurus, it had been meted out to Catiline, who aimed at overthrowing the state. He answered slowly, "Yes, I think so, if it can be done without turning all the seal-stampers against you."

"Bugger the seal-stampers," Bouraphos ground out. "They're good for nothing but telling you why you can't have the gold for the refits you need."

"Aye, they're rabbity little men, the lot of 'em," Baanes Onomagoulos said. "Shorten him and put fear in all their livers."

But Thorisin, rubbing his chin as he considered, was watching the tribune in reluctant admiration. "You have a habit of pointing out unpleasant facts, don't you? I'm too much a soldier to like taking the bureaucrats seriously, but there's no denying they have power—too much, by Phos."

"Who says there's no denying it?" Onomagoulos growled. He jabbed

535

a scornful thumb at Ortaias Sphrantzes. "Look at this uprooted weed here. This is what the pen-pushers have for a leader."

"What about Vardanes?" That was Zigabenos, who had been in the city while Ortaias reigned and his uncle ruled.

Onomagoulos blinked, but said, "Well, what about him? Another coward, if ever there was one. Shove steel in a pen-pusher's face, and he's yours to do with as you will."

"Which is, of course, why there have been bureaucrats or men backed by bureaucrats on the imperial throne for forty-five of the last fifty-one years," Alypia Gavra said, her measured tones more effective than open mockery. "It's why the bureaucrats and their mercenaries broke—how many? two dozen? three?—rebellions by provincial nobles in that time, and why they converted almost all the peasant militia in Videssos to tax-bound serfs during that stretch of time. Clear proof they're walkovers, is it not?"

Onomagoulos flushed right up to the bald crown of his head. He opened his mouth, closed it without saying anything. Thorisin was taken by a sudden coughing fit. Ortaias Sphrantzes, with nothing at all to lose, burst into a sudden giggle to see his captors quarrel among themselves.

Still beaming at his niece, the Emperor asked her, "What do you want us to do with the scapegrace, then?"

For the first time since the meeting began, she turned her eyes toward the man whose Empress, at least in name, she had been. For all the emotion she betrayed, she might have been examining a carcass of beef. At last she said, "I don't think he could be put to death without stirring up enmities better left unraised. For my part, I have no burning need to see him dead. He in his way was as much his uncle's prisoner as was I, and no more in control of his fate or actions."

From his wretched seat on the couch, Ortaias said softly, "Thank you, Alypia," and, quite uncharacteristically, fell silent again. The princess gave no notice that she heard him.

Baanes Onomagoulos, still smarting from her sarcasm, saw a chance for revenge. He said, "Thorisin, of course she will speak for him. And why should she not? The two of them, after all, are man and wife, their concerns bound together by a shared couch."

"Now you wait one minute—" Scaurus began hotly, but Alypia

needed no one to defend her. Moving with the icy control she showed on most occasions, she rose from her seat and dashed her wine cup in Onomagoulos' face. Coughing and cursing, he rubbed at his stinging eyes. The thick red wine dripped from his pointed beard onto his embroidered silk tunic, plastering it to his chest.

His hand started to seek his sword hilt, but he thought better of that even before Elissaios Bouraphos grabbed his wrist. Through eyelids already swelling shut, he looked to Thorisin Gavras, but found nothing to satisfy him on the Emperor's face. Muttering, "No one uses me thus," he climbed from his chair and limped toward the door, his painful gait an unintentioned parody of Komitta Rhangavve's lithe exit a few minutes before.

"You may be interested in knowing," Balsamon's voice pursued him, "that last night I declared annulled the marriage, if such it may be called, between Sphrantzes and Alypia Gavra—at the princess' urgent request. You may also be interested in knowing that the priest who performed that marriage is at a monastery on the southern bank of the Astris River, a stone's throw from the steppe—and I ordered that the day I learned of the wedding, not last night."

But Onomagoulos only snarled, "Bah!" and slammed the heavy door behind him.

An ivory figurine wobbled and fell to the floor. Balsamon, more distressed than he had been at any time during the meeting, leaped to his feet with a cry of alarm and hurried over to it. He wheezed as he bent to retrieve it, peered anxiously at the palm-high statuette.

"No harm, Phos be praised," he said, setting it carefully back on its stand. Marcus remembered his passion for ivories from Makuran, the kingdom that had been Videssos' western neighbor and rival until the Yezda came down off the steppe and conquered it less than a lifetime ago. More to himself than anyone else, the patriarch complained, "Things haven't been where they ought to be since Gennadios left."

The dour priest had been as much Balsamon's watchdog as companion, Scaurus knew, and there were times when the patriarch took unecclesiastical glee in baiting him. Now that he was gone, it seemed Balsamon missed him. "What became of him?" the tribune asked, idly curious.

"Eh? I told you," Balsamon answered peevishly. "He's spending his time by the Astris, praying the Khamorth don't decide to swim over and raid the henhouse."

"Oh," Marcus said. The patriarch had not named the priest who married Alypia to Ortaias, but he was not surprised Gennadios was the man. He had been the creature of Mavrikios' predecessor Strobilos Sphrantzes and doubtless stayed loyal to the clan. It would have been commendable, Scaurus thought, in a better cause; he could not work up much regret at the priest's exile.

"Are we quite through shilly-shallying about?" Thorisin asked with ill-concealed impatience.

"Shilly-shallying?" Balsamon exclaimed, mock-indignant. "Nonsense! We've trimmed this council by a fifth in a half hour's time. May you do as well with the pen-pushers!"

"Hmp," the Emperor said. He plucked a hair from his beard, crossed his eyes to examine it closely. It was white. He threw it away. Turning back to Alypia, he asked, "You say you don't want his head?"

"No, not really," she replied. "He's a foolish puppy, not as brave as he should be, and a dreadful bore." Indignation struggled for a moment with the fright on Ortaias Sphrantzes' face. "But you'd soon run short of subjects, uncle, if you did to death everyone who fit those bills. Were Vardanes here, now—" Her voice did not rise, but a sort of grim eagerness made it frightening to hear.

"Aye." Thorisin's right hand curled into a fist. "Well," he resumed, "suppose we let the losel live." Ortaias leaned forward in sudden hope; his guards pushed him back onto the couch. The Emperor ignored him, growling, "Skotos can pull me down to hell before I just turn him loose. He'd be plotting again before the rope marks faded. He has to know— and the people have to know—what a complete and utter idiot he's been, and he'll pay the price for it."

"Of course," Alypia nodded; she was at least as good a practical politician as her uncle. "How does this sound . . . ?"

Almost all the units which accompanied Thorisin Gavras on his coronation march had been dismissed to their barracks while the Emperor and his councilors debated Ortaias Sphrantzes' fate. Only a couple of squads of Videssian bodyguards waited for the Emperor outside the patriarchal residence, along with the dozen parasol bearers who were an Avtokrator's inevitable public companions.

The streets were nearly empty of spectators, too. A few Videssians stood and gawped at the shrunken imperial party as it made its way back toward the palaces, but most of the city folk had already found other things to amuse them.

Thus Marcus saw the tall man pushing his way toward them at a good distance, but thought nothing much of him—just another Videssian with a bit of a seaman's roll in his walk. In the great port the capital was, that hardly rated notice.

Even when the fellow waved to Thorisin Gavras, Scaurus all but ignored him. So many people had done so much cheering and greeting that the tribune was numb to it. But when the man shouted, "Hail to your Imperial Majesty!" ice walked up Scaurus' spine. That raspy bass, better suited to cutting through wind and wave than to the city, could only belong to Taron Leimmokheir.

The tribune had met Ortaias' drungarios of the fleet but twice, once on a pitch-dark beach and the other time when being chased by his galley. Neither occasion had been ideal for marking Leimmokheir's features. Nor were those remarkable: perhaps forty-five, the admiral had a rawboned look to him, his face lined and tanned by the sun, his hair and beard too gray to show much of their own sun bleaching.

If Marcus, then, had an excuse for not recognizing Leimmokheir at sight, the same could not be said for Thorisin Gavras, who had dealt with the drungarios almost daily when his brother was Emperor. Yet Thorisin was more taken aback by Leimmokheir's appearance than was the tribune. He stopped in his tracks, gaping as at a ghost.

His halt let the admiral elbow his way through the remaining guardsmen. Exclaiming, "Congratulations to you, Gavras! Well done!" Leimmokheir went to his knees and then to his belly in the middle of the street.

He was still down in the proskynesis when Thorisin finally found his voice. "Of all the colossal effrontery, this takes the prize," he whispered. Then, with a sudden full-throated bellow of rage, "Guards! Seize me the treacherous rogue!"

"Here, what's this? Take your hands off me!" Leimmokheir struck out against his assailants, but they were many to his one—and there could hardly be a worse position for self defense than the proskynesis. In seconds he was hauled upright, his arms pinned painfully behind him—almost exactly, Marcus thought irrelevantly, as Vardanes Sphrantzes had held Alypia.

The drungarios glared at Thorisin Gavras. "What's all this in aid of?" he shouted, still trying to twist free. "Is this the thanks you give everyone who wouldn't fall at your knees and worship? If it is, what's that snake of a Namdalener doing beside you? He'd sell his mother for two coppers, if he thought she'd bring so much."

The count Drax snarled and took a step forward, but Thorisin stopped him with a gesture. "You're a fine one to talk of serpents, Leimmokheir, you and your treachery, you and your hired assassins after a pledge of safe-conduct."

Taron Leimmokheir's tufted eyebrows—almost a match for Balsamon's—crawled halfway up his forehead like a pair of gray caterpillars. Amazingly, he threw back his head and laughed. "I don't know what you drink these days, boy." Gavras reddened dangerously, but Leimmokheir did not notice. "But pass me the bottle if there's any left when you're done. Whatever's in it makes you see the strangest things." He spoke as he might to any equal, ignoring the guardsmen clinging to him.

Scaurus remembered what he'd thought the first time he heard the drungarios' voice—that there was no guile in him. That first impression returned now, as strong as before. His two years in the Empire, though, had taught him that deceit was everywhere, all too often artfully disguised as candor.

That was how the Emperor saw it. If anything, his anger was hotter at seeing himself betrayed by a man he had thought trustworthy. He said, "You can lie till you drop, Leimmokheir, but you're a tomfool to try. There's no testimony for you to argue away. I was there, you know, and saw your hired man-slayers with my own eyes—"

"That's more than I did," Leimmokheir shot back, but Gavras stormed on.

"Aye, and fleshed my blade in a couple as well." The Emperor turned to the guards. "Take this fine, upstanding gentleman to gaol. We'll give him a nice, quiet place to think until I decide what to do with him. Go on, get him out of my sight." Holding the drungarios as they were, the troopers could not salute, but they nodded and hauled him away.

Only then did Leimmokheir really seem to understand this was not some practical joke. "Gavras, you bloody nincompoop, I still don't know what in Skotos' frozen hell you think I did, but I didn't do it, whatever it was. Phos have mercy on you for tormenting an innocent man. Watch that, you clumsy oafs!" he shouted to his captors as they dragged him through a puddle. His protests faded in the distance.

Matters pertaining to Ortaias Sphrantzes had been scheduled for two days later, but it was pelting down rain, and they had to be postponed. It rained again the next day, and the next. Watching the dirty gray clouds rolling out of the north, Scaurus realized the storm was but the first harbinger of the long fall rains. Where had the year gone? he asked himself; that question never had an answer.

At last the weather relented. The north wind still blew moist and cool, but the sun was bright; it flashed dazzlingly off still-wet walls and made every lingering drop of water into a rainbow. And if it had not had enough time to dry every seat in Videssos' huge Amphitheater, the people whose bottoms were dampened did not complain. The spectacle they were anticipating made up for such minor inconveniences.

"Sure and there's enough people," Viridovix said, his eyes traveling from the legionaries' central spine up and up the sides of the great limestone bowl. "The poor omadhauns in the last row won't be after seeing what's happening today till next week, so far away they are."

"More Celtic nonsense," Gaius Philippus said with a snort. "I'll grant you, though, we won't be much bigger than bugs to them." His own practiced gaze slid over the crowd. "Worthless, most of 'em, like the fat ones back home"—He meant Rome, and Marcus winced to be reminded—"who come out on the feast days to watch the gladiators kill each other."

The tribune agreed with that assessment; the buzz of conversation floating out of the stands had a cruel undercurrent, and on the faces in the first few rows, the ones close enough to see clearly, the air of vulpine avidity was all too plain.

He caught a glimpse of Gorgidas in the contingent of foreign envoys some little distance down the spine. As an aspiring historian, the Greek had wanted a close-up view of this day's festivities, and preferred the ambassadors' company to disguising himself as a legionary. He was listening to some tale from Arigh Arghun's son and scribbling quick notes on a three-leafed wax tablet. Two more hung at his belt.

Taso Vones, the ambassador from Khatrish, waved cheerily to the tribune, who grinned back. He liked the little Khatrisher, whose sharp, jolly wits belied his mousy appearance.

Horns filled the Amphitheater with bronzen music. The crowd's noise rose expectantly. Preceded by his retinue of parasol bearers, Thorisin Gavras strode into the arena. The applause was loud as he mounted the dozen steps that led up to the spine, but it fell short of the deafening tumult Scaurus had heard before in the Amphitheater. The Emperor, for once, was not what the populace had turned out to see.

Each unit of troops Gavras passed presented arms as he went by; at Gaius Philippus' barked command the Romans held their *pila* out at arm's length ahead of them. Gavras nodded slightly. He and the senior centurion, both lifelong soldiers, understood each other very well.

Not so the bureaucrats Thorisin passed on his way to the throne. They looked nervous as they bowed to their new sovereign; Goudeles, for one, was pale against his robe of dark blue silk. But Gavras paid them no more attention than he did to the clutter of a millennium and a half of heroic art that he passed: statues bronze, statues marble—some painted, some not—statues chryselephantine, even an obelisk of gilded granite long ago taken as booty from Makuran.

The Emperor grew animated once more when he came to the foreign dignitaries. He paused for a moment to say something to Gawtruz of Thatagush, at which the squat, swarthy envoy nodded. Then Gavras included Taso Vones in the conversation, whatever it was. The Khatrisher laughed and gave a rueful tug at his beard, as unkempt as Gawtruz'.

Even without hearing the words, Marcus understood the byplay. He, too, thought the fuzzy beard looked foolish on Vones, who could have passed for a Videssian without it. But his ruler still enforced a few Khamorth ways, in memory of his ancestors who had carved the state from Videssos' eastern provinces centuries before, and so the little envoy was doomed to wear the shaggy whiskers he despised.

Thorisin seated himself on a high stool at the center of the Amphitheater's spine; the chair was backless so all the spectators could see him. His parasol bearers grouped themselves around him. He raised his right hand in a gesture of command; the crowd grew quiet and leaned forward in their seats, craning their necks for a better view.

They all knew where to look. The gate that came open was the one through which, on most days, racehorses entered the Amphitheater. Today the procession was much shorter: Thorisin Gavras' deep-chested herald, two Videssian guardsmen gorgeous in gilded cuirasses, and a groom leading a single donkey.

Ortaias Sphrantzes rode the beast, but it needed a guide nonetheless, for its saddle was reversed, and he sat facing its tail. Long familiar with their own idiom of humiliation, the watching Videssians burst into guffaws. An overripe fruit came sailing out of the stands, to squash at the donkey's feet. Others followed, but the barrage was mercifully short; Videssos had been under siege too recently for there to be much food to waste.

The herald, nimbly sidestepping a hurtling melon, cried out, "Behold Ortaias Sphrantzes, who thought to rebel against the rightful Avtokrator of the Videssians, his Imperial Majesty Thorisin Gavras!" The crowd shouted back, "Thou conquerest, Gavras! Thou conquerest!"—as heartily, Marcus thought, as if they had forgotten that a week before they called Ortaias their lord.

Accompanied by the crowd's jeers, Ortaias and his guardians made a slow circuit of the Amphitheater, the herald all the while booming out his condemnation. Marcus heard more fruit splattering around Sphrantzes; the breeze brought him a rotten egg's gagging stench.

Some of the hurled refuse found its target. By the time Ortaias Sphrantzes came back into the tribune's sight, his robe was dyed with bright splashes of pulp and juice. The donkey he rode, Scaurus decided, had to be drugged. It ambled on placidly, pausing only to dip its head to nibble at a fragment of apple in its path. Its leader jerked on the long guide rope, and it abandoned the tidbit to move ahead once more.

At last it completed the course and halted in front of the gate through which it had entered. The two guards came back and lifted Ortaias off his mount, then led him up before Thorisin Gavras.

When they released his arms, he went to the ground in a proskynesis. The Emperor rose from his stool. "We see your submission," he said, speaking for the first time, and such were the acoustics of the Amphitheater that his words, though spoken in the tone of ordinary conversation, could be heard in the arena's uppermost rows. "Do you then renounce, now and forever, all claim upon the sovereignty of our Empire, protected by Phos?"

"Indeed yes, I yield the throne to you. I—" The moment the answer Thorisin Gavras required was complete, he cut Ortaias off with the same imperious gesture he had used to summon him forth.

Gaius Philippus gave the ghost of a chuckle. "Some things never change. I'd bet the scrawny bastard just had a two-hour abdication speech nipped in the bud—and a good thing, too, says I."

Thorisin spoke again. "Receive now the reward for your treachery."

The guardsmen raised Ortaias to his feet. They quickly pulled the robe off over his head. The crowd whooped; Gaius Philippus muttered "Scrawny" again. One of the guards, the larger and more muscular of the pair, stepped behind the luckless Sphrantzes and delivered a tremendous kick to his bare backside. Ortaias yelped and fell to his knees.

Viridovix clucked in disappointment. "The Gavras is too soft by half," he said. "He should be packing a wickerwork all full of this spalpeen and howsoever many followed him, and then lighting it off. There'd been a spectacle for the people to remember, now."

"You and Komitta Rhangavve," Marcus said to himself, slightly aghast at the Gaul's straightforward savagery.

"'Tis what the holy druids would do," Viridovix said righteously. That, Scaurus knew, was only too true. The Celtic priests appeased their gods by sacrificing criminals to them . . . or innocent folk, if no criminals were handy.

As Ortaias Sphrantzes, rubbing the bruised part, rose to his feet, one of Phos' priests descended from the Amphitheater's spine and approached him, carrying scissors and a long, gleaming razor. The crowd fell silent; religion was always respected in Videssos. But Marcus knew no blood sacrifice was in the offing here. Another priest followed the first, this one bearing a plain blue robe and a copy of Phos' sacred scriptures, glorious in its binding of enameled bronze.

Ortaias bowed his head to the first priest. The scissors flashed in the autumn sun. A lock of stringy brown hair fell at the deposed Emperor's feet, then another and another, until only a short stubble remained. Then the razor came into play; Sphrantzes' scalp was soon shiny bare.

The second priest stepped forward. Folding the monk's robe over the crook of his arm, he held out the sacred writings to Ortaias and said, "Behold the law under which you shall live if you choose. If in your heart you feel you can observe it, enter the monastic life; if not, speak now."

But Ortaias, with everyone else, was aware of the penalty for balking. "I will observe it," he said. The great-voiced herald relayed his words to the crowd. There was a collective sigh. The creation of a monk was always a serious business, even when the reasons for it were blatantly political. Nor could faith and politics be neatly separated in the Empire; Scaurus thought of Zemarkhos in Amorion and felt his mouth compress in a thin, hard line.

The priest repeated the offer of admission twice more, received the same response each time. He handed the holy book to his colleague, then robed the new monk in his monastic garb, saying, "As the garment of Phos' blue covers your naked body, so may his righteousness enfold your heart and preserve it from all evil." Again the herald boomed out the petition.

"So may it be," Ortaias replied, but his voice was lost in the thousands echoing his prayer. Despite himself Marcus was moved, marveling at Videssos' force of faith. Almost there were times he wished he shared it, but, like Gorgidas, he was too well rooted in the perceptible world to feel comfortable in that of the spirit.

Ortaias Sphrantzes left the Amphitheater through the same gate he had entered, arm in arm with the two priests who had made him part of their fellowship. Well satisfied with the day's show, the crowd began to disperse. Vonders took up their calls: "Wine! Sweet wine!" "Spiced cakes!" "Holy images to protect your beloved!" "Raiii—sins!"

Unhappy to the end, Gaius Philippus grumbled, "And now he'll spend the rest of his stupid days living the high life here in the city, but with a bald head and a blue robe to make it all right."

"Not exactly," Marcus chuckled; Thorisin might be blunt, but he was hardly as naïve as that. The tribune thought it altogether fitting that Gennadios should gain some company in his monastery at Videssos' distant frontier. He and the new Brother Ortaias, no doubt, would have a great deal to talk about.

X

"WHAT DO YOU MEAN, NO FUNDS ARE AVAILABLE?" THORISIN GAVRAS asked, his voice dangerously calm. His gaze speared the logothete as if that financial official were an enemy to be ridden down.

The Hall of the Nineteen Couches grew still. Marcus could hear the torches crackling, hear the wind sighing outside. If he turned his head, he knew he would see snowflakes kissing the Hall's wide windows; winter in the capital was not as harsh as in the westland plateaus, but it was bad enough. He pulled his cloak tighter round himself.

The logothete gulped. He was about thirty, thin, pale, and precise. His name, Scaurus remembered, was Addaios Vourtzes; he was some sort of distant cousin to the city governor of the northeastern town of Imbros. He had to gather himself before going on in the face of the Emperor's hostility.

But go on he did, at first haltingly and then with more animation as his courage returned. "Your Majesty, you expect too much from the tax-gathering facilities available to us. That any revenues whatsoever have been collected should be praised as one of Phos' special miracles. The recent unpleasantness"—Now there, thought the tribune, was a fine, bureaucratic euphemism for civil war—"and, worse, the presence of large numbers of unauthorized interlopers"—By which he meant the Yezda, Marcus knew—"on imperial soil, have made any accrual of surplusage a manifest impossibility."

What was he talking about? the tribune wondered irritably. His Videssian was fluent by now, but this jargon left him floundering.

Baanes Onomagoulos' translation was rough but serviceable. "By which you're saying that your precious dues-takers pissed themselves whenever they thought they saw a nomad, and turned tail before they could find out if they were right." The noble gave a coarse laugh.

"That's the way of it," Drax the Namdalener agreed. He turned a calculating eye on Vourtzes. "From what I've seen of you pen-pushers, any excuse not to pay is a good one. By the Wager, you'd think the money came out of your purse, not the peasants'."

"Well said," Thorisin exclaimed, his usual distrust for the islanders quenched when Drax echoed a sentiment he heartily shared. The count nodded his thanks.

Vourtzes proffered a thick roll of parchment. "Here are the figures to support the position I have outlined—"

Numbers in a ledger, though, meant little to the soldiers he faced. Thorisin slapped the scroll aside, snarling, "To the crows with this gibberish! It's gold I need, not excuses."

Elissaios Bouraphos said, "These fornicating seal-stampers think paper will patch anything. That was why I put in with you, your Highness—I kept getting reports instead of repairs—and sick I got of them, too."

"If you will examine the returns I have presented to you," Vourtzes said with rather desperate determination, "you will reach the inescapable conclusion that—"

"—The bureaucrats are out to bugger honest men," Onomagoulos finished for him. "Everyone knows that, and has since my grandfather's day. All you ever wanted was to keep the power in your own slimy hands. And if a soldier reached the throne despite you, you starved him with tricks like this."

"There is no trickery!" Vourtzes wailed, his distress wringing a simple declarative sentence from him.

Marcus had no love for the harried logothete, but he recognized sincerity when he heard it. "I think there may be something in what this fellow claims," he said.

Thorisin and his marshals stared at the Roman as if disbelieving their ears. "Whose side are you on?" the Emperor demanded. Even Addaios Vourtzes' look of gratitude was wary. He seemed to suspect some trap that would only lead to deeper trouble for him.

But Alypia Gavra watched the tribune alertly; her expression was masked as usual, but Scaurus could read no disapproval in it. And unlike the Videssian military men, he had had civilian as well as warlike experience, and knew how much easier it was to spend money than to collect it.

Ignoring Thorisin's half-accusation, he persisted, "Gathering taxes could hardly have been easy this past year. For one thing, sir, your men and Ortaias' both must have gone into some parts of the westlands, with neither side getting all it should. And Baanes has to be partly right— with the Yezda loose, parts of the Empire aren't safe for tax collectors. But even where there are no Yezda at any given moment, the lands they've ravaged still yield no cash—you can't get wool from a bald sheep."

"A mercenary with comprehension of basic fiscal realities," Vourtzes said to himself. "How extraordinary." Almost as an afterthought, he added, "Thank you," to the tribune.

The Emperor looked thoughtful, but Baanes Onomagoulos' face grew stormy; Scaurus, watching the noble's bare scalp go red, suddenly regretted his chance-chosen metaphor.

Alypia took another jab at Baanes. "Not all arrears are the tax collectors' fault," she said. "If big landowners paid what they owed, the treasury would be better off."

"That is very definitely the case," Vourtzes said. "Legitimately credentialed agents of the fisc have been assaulted, on occasion even killed, in the attempt to assess payments due on prominent estates, some of them properties of clans represented in this very chamber." While he named no names, he, too, was looking at Onomagoulos.

The noble's glare was hot enough to roast the bureaucrat, Marcus, and Alypia Gavra all together. The tribune, seeing Alypia's eyebrows arch, nodded almost imperceptibly in recognition of a common danger.

As he had in Balsamon's library, Elissaios Bouraphos tried to ease Onomagoulos' wrath, putting a hand on his shoulder and talking to him in a low voice. But the admiral was himself a possessor of wide estates, and said to Thorisin, "You know why we held back payments to the pen-pushers—aye, you did the same on your lands before your brother threw Strobilos out. Why should we give them the rope to hang us by?"

"I won't say you're wrong there," the Emperor admitted with a chuckle. "Since I'm not a pen-pusher, though, Elissaios, surely you'll pay in everything you owe without a whimper?"

"Surely," Bouraphos said. Then he whimpered, so convincingly that everyone at the table burst into laughter. Even Addaios Vourtzes' mouth twitched. Marcus revised his estimate of the admiral, which had not in-cluded a sense of humor.

Utprand Dagober's son spoke up for the first time, and the somber warning in his voice snuffed out the mirth. "You can wrangle all you like over who pays w'at. W'at needs to be settled is who pays me."

"Rest easy," Thorisin said. "I don't see your lads on the streets beg-ging for pennies."

"No," Utprand said, "nor will you." That was not warning, but un-mistakable threat. The great count Drax looked pained at his country-man's plain speaking, but Utprand ignored him. They did not care much for each other; Scaurus suspected the Namdaleni were not immune to the disease of faction.

Gavras, for his part, was one to appreciate frankness. "You'll have your money, outlander," he said. Seeing Addaios Vourtzes purse his lips to protest, he turned to the logothete. "Let me guess," he said sourly. "You haven't got it."

"Essentially, that is correct. As I have attempted to indicate, the pre-cise situation is outlined—"

The Emperor cut him off as brusquely as he had Ortaias Sphrantzes in the Amphitheater. "Can you bring in enough to keep everyone happy till spring?"

Faced with a problem whose answer was not to his precious accounts scroll, Vourtzes grew cautious. His lips moved silently as he reckoned to himself. "That is dependent upon a variety of factors not subject to my ministry's control: the condition of roads, quality of harvest, ability of agents to penetrate areas subject to disturbances . . ." From the way the bureaucrat avoided it, Marcus began to think the word "Yezda" made him break out in hives.

"There's something he's leaving out," Baanes Onomagoulos said, "and that's the likelihood the damned seal-stampers are pocketing one goldpiece in three for their own schemes. Oh, yes, they show us this pile of turds." He pointed contemptuously at Vourtzes' assessment document, "But who can make heads or tails of it? That's how they've kept their power, because no one who hasn't grown up in their way of cheating knows he's swindled until it's too late for him to do anything about it."

Vourtzes sputtered denials, but Thorisin gave him a long, measuring stare. Even Alypia Gavra nodded, however reluctantly; she might despise Onomagoulos, but she did not make the mistake of thinking him a fool.

"What's needed then," Marcus said, "is someone to watch over these functionaries, to make sure they're doing what they say they are."

"Brilliant—you should join the Academy," Elissaios Bouraphos said sardonically. "Who's to do it, though? Who can, among the men to be trusted? We're the lot of us soldiers. What do we know about the clerks' tricks the pen-pushers use? I keep more records than most of us, I'd bet, having to keep track of ships' stores and such, but I'd founder in a week in the chancery, to say nothing of being bored out of my wits."

"You're right," the Emperor said. "None of us has the knowledge for the job, worse luck, for it's one that needs doing." His voice grew musing; his eyes, speculation in them, swung toward the tribune. "Or is that so indeed? When you came to Videssos from your other world, Scaurus, do I remember your saying you had held some sort of civil post as well as commanding your troops?"

"Yes, that's so; I was one of the praetors at Mediolanum." Marcus realized that meant nothing to Gavras, and explained, "I held one of the magistracies in my home town, responsible for hearing suits, publishing edicts, and collecting tribute to send on to Rome, our capital."

"So you know something of this sharpers' business, then?" Thorisin pressed.

"Something, yes."

The Emperor looked from one of his officers to the next. Their smirks said more plainly than words that they were thinking along with him. Few things are more pleasant than seeing someone else handed a task one would hate to do oneself. Thorisin turned to Scaurus again. "I'd say you just talked your way into a job." And to Vourtzes he added, "Ha, pen-pusher, what do you think of that? Try your number-juggling now and see what it gets you!"

"Whatever pleases your Imperial Majesty, of course," the logothete murmured, but he did not sound pleased.

Scaurus said quickly, "It's not something I'll put full time into; I have to pay heed to my men."

"Of course, of course," the Emperor agreed; Marcus saw Drax, Utprand, and Onomagoulos nodding with him. Thorisin continued, "That lieutenant of yours is a sound man, though, and more than up to handling a lot of the day-to-day things. Give it as much time as you can. I'll see if I can't come up with some fancy title for the job and a raise in pay to go with it. You'll earn the money, I think."

"Fair enough," the tribune said. Thorisin's marshals made sympathetic noises; Marcus accepted their condolences and countered their bad jokes with his own.

In fact, he was not nearly so displeased as one of them would have been. A moderately ambitious man, he had long since realized there were definite limits to how high an outlander infantry commander could rise in Videssos on the strength of his troops alone. And his plans at Rome had been ultimately political, not soldierly; the military tribunate was a step aspiring young men took, but not one to stand on forever.

So he had made his suggestion; if Thorisin Gavras did not act on it, nothing whatever was lost. But he had acted, and now the tribune would see what came of that. Anticipation flowered in him. Regardless of the contempt the soldier-nobles had for the palace bureaucracy, it maintained Videssos no less than they. Nor, as Alypia Gavra had pointed out, was it necessarily the weaker party.

He saw her watching him with an expression of ironic amusement and had the uneasy feeling that all his half-formed, murky plans were quite transparent to her.

"I am extremely sorry, sir," Pandhelis the secretary was saying to someone outside the office Marcus had taken as his own, "but I have specific instructions that the *epoptes* is to be disturbed on no account whatever." As promised, Thorisin had conferred an impressively vague title on the Roman, meaning approximately "inspector."

"Och, a pox take you and your instructions both." The door flew open. Viridovix stomped into the little room, Helvis just behind him. Seeing Scaurus, the Gaul clapped a dramatic hand to his forehead. "I've seen that face before, indeed and I have. Don't be telling me, now, the name'll come back to me in a minute, I'm sure it will." He wrinkled his brow in mock concentration.

Wringing his hands, Pandhelis said to the tribune, "I'm sorry, sir, they would not listen to me—"

"Never mind. I'm glad to see them." Marcus threw down his pen with a sigh of relief; a new callus was forming on his right index finger. Shoving tax rolls and reckoning beads to one side of the untidy desk, he looked up at his visitors. "What needs doing?"

"Nothing needs doing. We're here to collect you," Helvis said firmly. "It's Midwinter's Day, in case you've forgotten—time for rejoicing, not chaining yourself up like some slave."

"But—" Marcus started to protest. Then he rubbed his eyes, red-lined and scratchy from staring at an endless procession of numbers. Enough is enough, he thought, and stood up, stretching till his joints creaked. "All right, I'm your man."

"I should hope so," she said, a sudden smoky glow in her blue eyes. "I've started wondering if you remembered."

"Ho-ho!" Viridovix said with a wink. His brawny arm propelled Scaurus out from around the desk, out of the cubicle, and into the corridor, giving the tribune no chance to change his mind. "Come along with you, Roman dear. There's a party laid on to make even a stodgy spalpeen like you frolic."

As always, the first breath of frigid outside air made the tribune cough. His own breath sighed out in a great steaming cloud. Whatever one could say against them, the bureaucrats kept their wing of Grand Courtroom offices heated almost summery-warm. It made the winter outside twice as hard to endure. He shivered in his cloak.

Ice glittered on bare-branched trees; the smooth-rolled lawns that were the palace gardeners' emerald delight in summer now were patchy and brown. Somewhere high overhead a gull screeched. Most birds were long gone to the warm lands of the unknown south, but the gulls stayed. Scavengers and thieves, they were birds that fit the capital.

"And how's that bairn of yours?" Viridovix asked as they walked back toward the Roman barracks.

"Dosti? He couldn't be better," Marcus answered proudly. "He has four teeth now, two top and two bottom. He likes to use 'em, too—he bit my finger the other day."

"Your finger?" Helvis said. "Don't complain of fingers, my dear—high time the boy was weaned."

"Oww," Viridovix sympathized.

The big Gaul waved as soon as he was in sight of the barracks; Scaurus saw a Roman wave back from a window. "What sort of ambush are you leading me into?" he asked.

"You'll see soon enough," Viridovix said. The moment they walked into the barracks hall, he shouted, "Pay up the goldpiece you owe me, Soteric, for here's himself in the flesh of him!"

The Namdalener flipped him the coin. "It's not a bet I'm sorry to lose," he said. "I thought he was too in love with his inks and parchments to recall how the common folk celebrate."

"To the crows with you," Marcus said to the man he counted his brother-in-law, aiming a lazy punch that Soteric dodged.

Viridovix was biting the goldpiece he'd won. "It's not of the best, but then it's not of the worst either," he said philosophically and tucked it into his belt-pouch.

The tribune was not paying much attention to the Celt, looking instead from face to grinning face around him. "This is the crew you've gathered to carouse with?" he said to Viridovix. Grinning too, the Celt nodded.

"Then the gods look to Videssos tonight!" Marcus exclaimed, and drew a cheer from everyone.

There was Taso Vones, arm in arm with a buxom Videssian woman several inches taller than he was. Gawtruz of Thatagush stood beside him, working hard on a wineskin. "How about some for the rest of us?" Gaius Philippus said pointedly.

"What's a skin of wine, among one man?" Gawtruz retorted, and kept drinking. He lowered the skin again a moment later, but only to belch.

Soteric had brought Fayard and Turgot of Sotevag with him. Turgot needed no help from Gawtruz's wineskin; he was already unsteady on his feet. His companion was a very blond Namdalener girl named Mavia. Scaurus doubted she was out of her teens. In a dark-haired land, her bright tresses gleamed like a goldpiece among old coppers.

Fayard greeted Helvis in the island dialect; her dead husband had been his captain. She smiled and answered in the same speech.

Arigh Arghun's son was in the middle of telling a dirty story to all three of Viridovix' lemans. Marcus wondered again how the Celt kept them from catfights. Probably the happy-go-lucky Gaul's own lack of jealousy, he thought. Viridovix seemed altogether unconcerned when they exploded into laughter at the end of Arigh's tale.

Quintus Glabrio said something low-voiced to Gorgidas, who smiled and nodded. Next to them, Katakolon Kekaumenos of Agder stirred impatiently. "Are we then assembled?" he asked. "An it be so, let's to the revels." His accent was almost as archaic as the sacred liturgy; Agder, though once part of the Empire, had been severed from Videssos' more quickly changing currents of speech for many years. Kekaumenos himself was a solidly built, saturnine man whose jacket of creamy snow-leopard pelts was worth a small fortune in the capital.

Marcus also thought him something of a prig; as the party trooped out of the barracks hall, he asked Taso Vones, "Who invited the dog in the manger?"

Aesop meant nothing to the Khatrisher, as Scaurus should have known. He sighed. There were times, most often brought on by such trivial things, when he was sure he would never fit this world. He explained himself *sans* metaphor.

"As a matter of fact, *I* invited him," Vones said. The Roman's embarrassment seemed to amuse him; he shared with Balsamon a fondness for discomfiting people. "I have my reasons. Agder's a far northern land, you know, and the turn of the sun at midwinter means more to them than to the Videssians or me—they're always half afraid it won't come back. When they see it start north again they wassail hard, believe me."

Videssos might not have feared for the sun's return, but it celebrated all the same. The two midwinter fests Marcus had seen before were in provincial towns. The captial's holiday was perhaps less boisterous than their uninhibited rejoicing, but made up for it with more polish. And the city's sheer size let the tribune imagine himself in the middle of a world bent solely on pleasure.

Winter's early night was falling fast, but torches and candles everywhere gave plenty of light. Bonfires blazed on many street corners; it was reckoned lucky to jump through them.

Helvis slid free of Marcus' arm round her waist. She ran for one of the fires, jumped. Her hair flew out around her head like a dark halo; despite the hand she kept by her side, her skirt billowed away from her legs. Someone on the far side of the fire cheered. The tribune's pulse quickened, too. She came back to him flushed from the run and the cold, her eyes bright. When he put his arm around her again, she pressed his hand tight against the top of her hip.

Nothing escaped Taso Vones' birdlike gaze. With a smile up at his own lady—whose name, Scaurus learned, was Plakidia Teletze—he said, "Better than crawling through codices, isn't it?"

"You'd best believe it," the tribune answered, and tipped Helvis' chin up for a quick kiss. Her lips were warm and alive against his.

"It's a public disgrace you'll make of yourselves," Viridovix complained. To show how serious he was, he planted good, thorough kisses on all his lady friends. They seemed perfectly content with his gallant impartiality. From long practice, it had almost a polish to it, like a conjuror plucking his ten-thousandth gold ring out of the air.

Waves of laughter came rolling out of the Amphitheater, a sound like a god's mirth. Videssos' mime troupes, naturally, were the best the Empire could offer. Eyeing the failing day, Gorgidas said, "It's probably too dark for them to squeeze in another show. What say we find an eatery now, before the crowd coming out fills them all to overflowing?"

"Always is a good idea, food," Gawtruz said in the heavy Khamorth-flavored accent he affected most of the time. The envoy from Thatagush slapped his thick belly. His appetite was real, but Scaurus knew the boorishness was an act to lull the unwary. A clever diplomat hid beneath that piggish exterior.

Gorgidas' good sense got his comrades into an inn a few blocks off the plaza of Palamas while the establishment was still only half full. The proprietor and a serving girl shoved two tables together for them. Before they had finished their first round of wine—Soteric, Fayard, and Katakolon Kekaumenos chose ale—the room was packed. The owner hauled a couple of battered tables from the kitchens out into the street to serve a few more customers, planting fat candles on them to give his guests light. "I wish I'd bought that bigger place," Marcus heard him say to himself as he bustled back and forth.

Delicious odors wafted out of the kitchen. Scaurus and his friends nibbled on sweetmeats and drank, waiting for their dinner to cook. At last a servingmaid, staggering a little under its weight, fetched a fat, roast goose to the table. Steel flashed in the torchlight as she expertly carved the bird.

The tribune liked most Videssian cooking, and when the eatery's owner proclaimed goose "our specialty" he had gone along without a qualm. His first bite gave him second thoughts. The goose was smothered in a sauce of cinnamon and sharp cheese, a combination piquant enough to bring tears to his eyes. There were times when the Empire's sophisticated striving for pleasure through contrasting tastes went beyond what his palate could tolerate.

Gaius Philippus seemed similarly nonplused, but the rest ate with every sign of enjoyment. Stifling a sigh, the tribune took a handful of shelled almonds from a dish by the half-demolished goose. They were sprinkled with garlic powder. The sigh became a groan; why hadn't the garlic gone on the meat instead?

"You're not eating much," Helvis said.

"No." Perhaps it was just as well. Being chairbound day in and day out had made him gain weight. And, he thought, raising his cup to his lips, he had more room for wine.

"Here, pretty one, would you care to sit by me?" That was Gaius Philippus, greeting a courtesan in a clinging dress of thin yellow stuffs. He stole a chair from a nearby table; its owner had gotten up to go to the jakes. The fellow's companions glowered at the senior centurion. He stared them down; long years of command gave him a presence none of the city men could match.

The woman saw that, too. There was real interest on her face as she sat, not just a whore's counterfeit passion. She helped herself to food and drink. A pretty thing, Marcus thought, and was glad for Gaius Philippus, whose luck in such matters was usually poor.

The shade of yellow she wore reminded the tribune of the diaphanous silk gown Vardanes Sphrantzes had forced on Alypia Gavra, and of her slim body unconcealed beneath it. The thought warmed and annoyed him at the same time. There should have been no room for it with Helvis beside him, her fingers teasing the nape of his neck.

Turgot stretched across the table to reach for the dish of almonds. He popped a handful into his mouth, then tried to curse around them. "Stinking garlic!" he said, washing out the taste with a hefty swig of wine. "Back in the Duchy we wouldn't foul good food with the stuff." He drank again, his face losing its soldier's hardness as he thought of his home.

"Well, I like it," Mavia said with a flip of her head. Her hair flashed gold-red in the torchlight, almost the color of flame itself. To prove the truth of her words, she ate an almond, then another one. Marcus guessed she'd come to the Empire long ago as a mercenary's small daughter and learned Videssian tastes as well as the Duchy's. Turgot, sitting hunched over his wine cup, suddenly seemed sad and tired and old.

The Videssian whose chair Gaius Philippus had annexed returned. He stood in confusion for a moment, while his friends explained what had happened. He turned toward the Roman—an unsteady turn, for he had considerable wine on board. "Now you shee—*see*—here, sir—" he began.

"Go home and sober up," the senior centurion said, not unkindly. He had other things on his mind than fighting. His eyes kept slipping hungrily to the courtesan's dark nipples, plainly visible through the fabric of her dress.

Viridovix's admiring gaze followed his. Only when the drunken Videssian started a further protest did the Celt seem to notice him. He burst out laughing, saying to Gaius Philippus, "Sure and the poor sot's clean forgotten a prick's good for more things than pissing through."

He spoke in the Empire's language so everyone round the party's two tables could share the joke. They laughed with him, but the man he'd insulted understood him, too. With a grunt of sodden rage the fellow swung at him, a wild haymaking right that came nowhere near the Gaul.

Viridovix sprang to his feet, quick as a cat despite all he'd drunk himself. His green eyes glowed with amusement of a new sort. "Your honor shouldn't ought to have done that, now," he said. He grabbed the luckless Videssian, lifted him off his feet, and hurled him down *splash!* into the great tureen of sea-turtle stew that stood as the centerpiece of his comrades' table.

The sturdy table did not collapse, but greasy greenish stew and bits of white meat splattered in all directions. The drunk feebly kicked his legs as he tried to right himself; his friends, drenched by their dinners, swore and spluttered and wiped at their faces.

"What are you doing, you loose fish, you clapped-out poxy blackguard, you beggarly, lousy, beetle-headed knave!" Gaius Philippus' courtesan screeched as she daubed futilely at herself. A good-sized chunk of meat was stuck in her hair above the gold hoop she wore in her right ear, but she did not notice it.

Nor did the Celt pay her bravura curses any mind. The men he'd swashed were coming at him, with determination if no great skill. Viridovix flattened the first of them, but the next one dashed a cup of wine in his face. While he choked and gasped, the fellow jumped on him, followed a second later by a companion.

Gaius Philippus and Gawtruz of Thatagush hauled them off. "Two against one's not fair," the senior centurion said, still mildly, flinging his man in one direction. Gawtruz wasted no words on his, but tossed him in the other. If they had hoped to quell the fight, they could hardly have done a worse job of it. The hurled men went careening into tables, bowling over two men seated at one and a woman at the other. Food flew. What had been a private quarrel instantly became general.

Viridovix's banshee howl of fighting glee rose over the anguished cries of the inn's owner and the sound of smashing crockery. The two tables were a bastion under siege, and it seemed everyone else in the eatery was trying to storm them.

Marcus had heard reports of Viridovix' tavern brawling, but until now had never been caught up in it himself. A mug whizzed past his head, to shatter against the wall. A fat Videssian punched him in the belly. "Oof!" he said, and doubled over. He swung back, felt his fist sink into flab.

"You will excuse me, I pray," Taso Vones said, and dove under the table, pulling Plakidia Teletze with him. She let out an unladylike squawk of protest as she disappeared.

It was, Marcus thought, the most good-natured fight he had been in. Perhaps all the battlers were in holiday spirits, or was it simply that Viridovix, at heart a good-natured soul, had set the stamp of his character on the brawl he'd started? Whatever it was, none of the scrappers showed the slightest desire to reach for the knives that hung at most of their belts. They pounded each other with high gusto, but no serious blood was spilled.

"Yipe!" said Scaurus, thrashing frantically. Someone had pulled open his tunic and poured a bowlful of syrup-sweetened snow down his back. It felt like a million frozen, crawling ants.

The eatery's owner ran from one little knot of fighting to the next, shouting, "Stop this! Stop this at once, I tell you!" No one paid him any mind until the fat Videssian, annoyed at his noise, hit him in the side of the head. He stumbled out into the night. "The guard! The guard!" His cries faded as he ran down the street.

A city man, fists flailing, charged Arigh Arghun's son, who was not much more than half as big. There was a flurry of arms and legs—Marcus could not see all that went on, because he was trading punches with a man who reeked of wine—and the Videssian thudded to the ground. He lay still; whatever Arigh's handfighting technique was, it worked well.

A plate broke, almost in the tribune's ear. He whirled round to see a Videssian stagger away clutching his head. Helvis still had a piece of the plate in her hand. "Thank you, dear," he said. She smiled and nodded.

Nor was she the only Namdalener woman able to handle herself in a ruction. Mavia and Gaius Philippus' tart were going at it hammer and tongs, screeching and clawing and pulling hair, and it was easy to see the blonde was getting the better of the battle. But her foe was still game; when the senior centurion tried to drag her out of the fray she raked her nails down his cheek, missing his eye by no more than an inch. "Stay and fight, then, you mangy trollop!" he yelled, all vestiges of chivalry forgotten.

Katakolon Kekaumenos sat sipping his wine, a bubble of calm in the brabble around him. One of the brawlers was rash enough to mistake his quiet for cowardice and started to tip his chair over backward. Kekaumenos was on his feet and spinning toward the Videssian almost before it began to move. He punched him once in the face and once in the belly, then lifted his sagging body over his head and threw him through a window. That done, he straightened the chair and returned to his wine, quiet as a snow leopard just after it has fed.

"That'll teach you to be trifling with an honest man, won't it now?" Viridovix yelled after the Videssian. He got no answer.

The tribune took a punch over the ear. He saw brief stars, but his assailant howled and clutched his left fist round a broken knuckle. Scaurus, too experienced to throw that kind of punch, hit him in the pit of the stomach. He doubled over and fell, gasping for air. Turgot and Gawtruz both jumped on him.

"All right in there, enough now!" an accented tenor called from the doorway. "Break it up, or we'll use our spearshafts on you!" The mailshirted Vaspurakaners pushed into the shambles that had been the inn's common room. "Break it up, I said!" their officer repeated, and someone yelped as one of the troopers carried out the threat.

"Hullo, Senpat," Marcus said indistinctly. One of his hands was in his mouth, trying to find out if a back tooth was loose. It was. Spitting redly, he asked, "How's your lady?"

"Nevrat? She's fine—" The young Vaspurakaner noble broke off in mid-sentence, a comic expression of surprise on his handsome features. "You, Scaurus, of all people, tavern brawling? You, the sensible, sober fellow who keeps everyone else out of trouble? By Vaspur the Firstborn, I'd not have believed it without the seeing."

"Heresy," someone muttered, but softly; fifteen Vaspurakaners crowded the room, every one of them armed.

Embarrassed, the tribune so far forgot his Stoic principles as to cast the blame elsewhere. "It's Viridovix' fault. He started the thing."

"Don't listen to him for even a second, Sviodo dear," the Celt said to Senpat. "He was enjoying himself as much as the rest of us." And Marcus, wine and battle both still firing his blood, could not say him nay.

The taverner, staring in horrified dismay at overturned tables, broken chairs, assorted potshards, and half a dozen of his kitchen creations splashed everywhere, let out a baritone shriek of despair. Not only was his eatery wrecked, but this Phos-despised foreign guard captain turned out to be friends with the wreckers! "Who's going to pay for all this?" he moaned.

Abrupt silence fell. The men still standing looked at each other, at their comrades unconscious on the floor, at the door—which was full of Vaspurakaners. "Someone had better pay," the innkeeper went on, his tone moving from despondence to threat, "or the whole city'll know why, and then—"

561

"Shut up," Scaurus said; he'd seen enough anti-foreign riots in Videssos never to want to see another. He reached for his belt. The taverner's eyes widened in alarm, but he was seeking his purse, not his sword. "We share and share alike," he said, his gaze including his own party and everyone else in the inn.

"Why add me in?" Gorgidas demanded. "I didn't help break up the place." That was true enough; the Greek, not caring for fighting of any sort, had stayed on the sidelines.

"Then call it your fine for a liver full of milk," Viridovix hooted. "If you're after talking your way free, what's to stop the rest of these omadhauns from doing the same?"

Gorgidas glared at him and opened his mouth to argue further, but Quintus Glabrio touched his arm. The junior centurion was another who did not brawl for sport, but a swollen lip and a bruise on his cheek said he had not been idle. He murmured something. Gorgidas dipped his head in acquiescence, the Greek gesture giving his exasperation perfect expression.

There were no other arguments. Scaurus turned back to the innkeeper. "All right, what do you say this stuff is worth?" Seeing an ignorant outland mercenary in front of him, the man doubled the fair price. But the tribune laughed scornfully; it was folly to think of gulling someone with his nose fresh out of the tax rolls. At his counteroffer the taverner flinched and called on Phos, but grew much more reasonable. They settled quickly.

"Don't forget the fellow lying out there in the snow," Senpat Sviodo said helpfully. "The more shares, the less each one pays." Three of his Vaspurakaners dragged the fellow back and flipped water in his face until he revived. It took several minutes; Marcus was glad Kekaumenos was a friend.

"Is that everyone?" he asked, scanning the battered room.

"Should be," Gaius Philippus said, but Gawtruz broke in, "Vones, where is he?" His fat face was smug; he loved to score points off his fellow envoy.

Heads turned. No one saw the little Khatrisher. Then Viridovix remembered, "Dove clear out of the shindy, he did," the Celt said, and lifted a tablecloth. Plakidia Teletze screamed. Vones, quicker thinking, snatched the cloth out of Viridovix's hand and yanked it down.

"Begging your honor's pardon, I'm sure," Viridovix said, suave as any ambassador himself, "but when you're finished the rest of us would be glad for a word with ye." Then the effort of holding himself back was too much, and he doubled over with a guffaw.

Vones emerged a moment later, urbane as ever. "Wasn't what it seemed," he said blandly. "Merely a coincidence, you understand, the way we happened to fall."

Grinning, Arigh interrupted, "Your breeches are unbuttoned, Taso."

"Why, so they are." Not a bit nonplused, Vones did them up again. "Now then, gentlemen, what do I owe you for my share in the festivities?" Plakidia scrambled out while he was talking. She bolted away from him; at Senpat Sviodo's gesture his men stood aside to let her pass.

"It's not us you should be after paying at all, at all," Viridovix chuckled, and Vones got off free. Scaurus dug in his pouch, filled his free hand with silver. He counted out seventeen coins. It took twenty-four to equal a goldpiece of pure metal, but the tribune saw a couple of the city men spend two of Ortaias' debased coins to pay their shares, and even then the innkeeper looked unhappy.

Gaius Philippus saw that, too, and narrowed his eyes in disgust. "You could be getting steel, not gold," he pointed out, toying with the hilt of his shortsword. He had the look of a man who had scores of taproom fights behind him and had ended some of them just that way. The taverner wet his lips nervously as he counted the coins and pronounced himself satisfied. In fact he was hardly lying; too often threats were all he got after a brawl.

"Come by the barracks when you have the chance," Marcus urged Senpat Sviodo as they left the inn. "We haven't seen much of you lately."

"I'll do that," the young noble answered. "I know I should have long ago, but there's so much to see here in the city. It's like another world." Scaurus nodded his understanding; next to Videssos, Vaspurakan's towns were but backwoods villages.

The courtesan in yellow tried to make up to Gaius Philippus but, his cheek still smarting, he rounded on her with advice more pungent than he'd had for the innkeeper. She answered with a two-fingered gesture every Videssian knew, and cast sheep's eyes at the fat man who'd hit Marcus in the stomach. They strolled off arm in arm.

The senior centurion stared glumly after her. Viridovix clucked. "Foosh, it's a rare wasteful man y'are," he said. "That was a lass with fire in her; a rare ride she would have given you." Scaurus thought that an odd sentiment, coming from the Gaul—his own companions were all of them lovely, but none had any spirit to speak of.

"Women," Gaius Philippus said, as if the word was enough to explain everything.

"Only take the time to know 'em, Roman dear, and you'll find 'em not so strange," Viridovix retorted. "And they're great fun besides—isn't that right, my dears, my darlings?" He swept all three of them into his arms; the way they snuggled close spoke louder than any words of agreement.

Gaius Philippus did his best to stay impassive; Marcus was probably the only one who noticed his jaw jet, saw his eyes narrow and grow hard. The Celt's teasing, this time, had struck deep, though Viridovix himself did not realize it. When the Celt opened his mouth for another sally, the tribune stepped on his foot.

"Ow! Bad cess to you, you hulking looby!" Viridovix exclaimed, hopping. "What was the point o' that?"

Scaurus apologized and meant it; in his hurry, he'd trod harder than he intended.

"Well, all right then," the Gaul said. He stretched luxuriantly. "Indeed and the shindy was not a bad way to be starting the evening, if a bit tame. Let's be off to another tavern and do it ag—och, you black spalpeen, that was no accident!" The tribune had stepped on his other foot.

Viridovix bent down and flung a handful of snow in his face. Cheeks stinging and eyebrows frosted white, Marcus retaliated in kind—as did Helvis, who had taken some of the snow that missed the Roman. In an instant everyone was pelting everyone else, laughing and shouting and cheering each other on. Marcus was just as well pleased; a snowfight was safer than most things Viridovix reckoned entertainment.

Sitting secure in Videssos, it was easy to imagine the Empire still master of all its lands—or it would have been, had Scaurus not been wrestling with the imperial tax rolls. In his office he had a map of the westlands showing the districts from which revenues had been collected. Most towns and villages in the coastal lowlands had little bronze pins stabbed through them, indicating that imperial agents had taken what was due from them. The central plateau, though, the natural settling ground for nomads like the Yezda, showed virtually a blank expanse of parchment. Worse, a finger of that same ominous blankness pushed east down the Arandos River valley toward Garsavra. If the town fell, it opened the way for the invaders to burst forward all the way to the shore of the Sailors' Sea.

Baanes Onomagoulos was as well aware of the somber truth as the imperial finance ministry. The noble's estates were hard by Garsavra, and his patience with Thorisin, never long, grew shorter with every report of a new Yezda advance.

The Emperor knew the reason for Onomagoulos' constant reproaches and knew there was some justice to them. He bore them with more self-control than Marcus had thought he owned. He committed such aid as he could to the Arandos valley; more, in Scaurus' eyes, than Videssos, threatened all through the westlands, could readily afford to spend there. But at every session of the imperial council Onomagoulos' cry was always for more men.

Thorisin's patience finally wore thin. About six weeks after the midwinter fest, he told his captious marshal, "Baanes, I am not made of soldiers, and Garsavra is not Videssos' only weak point. The nomads are pushing out of Vaspurakan toward Pityos and they're raiding in the westlands' south as well. And the winter's cold enough to freeze the Astris, so the Khamorth'll likely poke south across it to see if we poke back. The company I sent west ten days ago will have to be the last."

Onomagoulos ran his fingers up over the crown of his head, a gesture, Marcus guessed, born when hair still covered it. "Two hundred seventy-five men! Huzzah!" he said sourly. "How many Namdaleni, aye, and these other damned outlanders, too," he added with a glance at Scaurus, "are sitting here in the city, eating like so many hogs?"

Drax answered with the cool mercenary's logic Marcus had come to expect from the great count: "Why should his Majesty throw my men away in a fight they're not suited for? We're heavier-armed than you Videssians care to be. Most times we find it useful, but in deep snow we're slow and floundering, easy meat for the nomads' light horse."

"The same is true of my men, but more so, for we aren't mounted," Marcus echoed.

The quarrel might have been smoothed over there, for Onomagoulos was a soldier and recognized the point the others made. But Soteric happened to be at the council instead of Utprand, who was ill with a coughing fever. Scaurus' headstrong brother-in-law took offense at Baanes' gibe at the Namdaleni and gave it back in kind. "Hogs, is it? You bloody cocksure snake, if you knew anything about nomads you wouldn't have let yourself get trapped in front of Maragha. Then you wouldn't be sitting here carping about the upshot of your own stupidity!"

"Barbarian bastard!" Onomagoulos shouted. His chair crashed over backward as he tried to leap to his feet; his hand darted for his sword hilt. But his crippled leg buckled, and he had to grab for the council table to keep from falling. He had taken the laming wound in the fight Soteric named, and the Namdalener laughed at him for it.

"Will you watch that polluted tongue of yours?" Scaurus hissed at him. Drax, too, put a warning hand on his arm, but Soteric shook it off. He and Utprand bore the count no love.

Onomagoulos regained his feet. His saber rasped free. "Come on, baseborn!" he yelled, almost beside himself with rage. "One leg's plenty to deal with scum like you!"

Soteric surged up. Marcus and Drax, sitting on either side of him, started to grab his shoulders to haul him down again, but it was Thorisin's battlefield roar of "Enough!" that froze everyone in place, Roman and great count no less than the combatants.

"Enough!" the Emperor yelled again, barely softer. "Phos' light, the two of you are worse than a couple of brats fratching over who lost the candy. Mertikes, get Baanes' chair—he seems to have mislaid it." Zigabenos jumped to obey. "Now, the both of you sit down and keep still unless you've something useful to say." Under his glower they did, Soteric a bit shamefaced but Onomagoulos still furious and making only the barest effort to hide it.

Speaking to Gavras as if to a small boy, the Videssian noble persisted, "Garsavra must have more troops, Thorisin. It is a very important city, both of itself and for its location."

The Emperor bridled at that tone, which he had heard from Onomagoulos for too many years. But he still tried for patience as he answered, "Baanes, I have given Garsavra twenty-five hundred men, at least. Along with the retainers you muster on your estates, surely enough warriors are there to hold back the Yezda till spring. They don't fly over the snow themselves, you know; they slog through it like anyone else. When spring comes I intend to hit them hard, and I won't piddle away my striking force a squad here and a company there until I have nothing left."

Onomagoulos stuck out his chin; his pointed beard jutted toward Gavras. "The men are needed, I tell you. Will you not listen to plain sense?"

No one at the table wanted to meet Thorisin's eye while he was being hectored so, but all gazes slid his way regardless. He said only, "You may not have them," but there was iron in his voice.

Everyone heard the warning except Onomagoulos, whose angry frustration made him exclaim, "Your brother would have given them to me."

Marcus wanted to disappear; had Baanes searched for a year, he could not have found a worse thing to say. Thorisin's jealousy of the friendship between Mavrikios and Onomagoulos was painfully obvious. Imperial dignity forgotten, Gavras leaned forward, bellowing, "He'd have given you the back of his hand for your insolence, you toplofty runt!"

"Unweaned pup, your eyes aren't open to see the world in front of your face!" Baanes was not yelling at the Avtokrator of the Videssians, but at his comrade's tagalong little brother.

"Clod from a dungheap! You think your precious estates are worth more than the whole Empire!"

"I changed your diapers, puling moppet!" They shouted insults and curses at each other for a good minute, oblivious to anyone else's presence. Finally Onomagoulos rose once more, crying, "There's one more man Garsavra will have, by Phos! I won't stay in the same city with you—the stench of you curdles my nose!"

"It's big enough," Thorisin retorted. "Good riddance; Videssos is well shut of you."

By now, Scaurus thought, I should be used to the sight of people stalking out of Thorisin's councils. Baanes Onomagoulos' stalk was in

567

fact a limp, but the effect remained the same. As he reached the polished bronze doors of the Hall of the Nineteen Couches, he turned round for a final scowl at the Emperor, who replied with an obscene gesture. Onomagoulos spat on the floor, as Videssians did before wine and food to show their rejection of Skotos. He hobbled out into the snow.

"Where were we?" the Emperor said.

Marcus expected Baanes to be restored to Thorisin's good graces; the Emperor's temper ran high at flood but quickly ebbed. Onomagoulos' anger, though, was of a more lasting sort. Two days after the stormy council he kept the promise he'd made there, sailing over the Cattle-Crossing and setting out for Garsavra.

"I mislike this," the tribune said when he heard the news. "He's flying in the face of the Emperor's authority." Though he was in the Roman barracks, he looked round before he spoke and then was low-voiced—the price of living in the Empire, he thought discontentedly.

"You're right, I fear," Gaius Philippus said. "If I were Gavras, I'd haul him back in chains."

"The two of you make no sense," Viridovix complained. "It was the Gavras who gave him leave to go—or ordered him, more like."

"Ordered him to drop dead, perhaps," Gorgidas said, "but not to go off and fight his own private war." He lifted an ironic eyebrow at the Gaul. "When will you learn words can say one thing and mean another?"

"Och, you think you're such a tricksy Greek. This I'll tell you, though—if it was my home in danger, I'd go see to it, and be damned to any who tried to stop me, himself included." The Gaul folded his arms across his chest, as if daring the doctor to disagree.

It was Gaius Philippus, though, who snorted at him. "Likely you would, and maybe lose your home and all your neighbors' in the bargain. Think of yourself first and your mates last and that's what happens. Why else do you think Caesar's been able to fight one clan of Celts at a time?"

Viridovix gnawed at his drooping mustache; the senior centurion's gibe was to the point. But he replied, "'Twon't matter a bit in the end. Divided or no, we'll be whipping the lot of you back home with your tails tucked into their grooves."

568

"Not a chance," Gaius Philippus said, and the old dispute began again. Ever since the Romans came to Videssos, he and Viridovix had been arguing over who would win the fighting in Gaul. They both took the question seriously, although—or perhaps because—they could never answer it.

Not much caring to listen, Marcus left for his desk in the pen-pushers' wing of the Grand Courtroom. The problems there were new ones, but they did not seem to have solutions more definite than his friends' debating topic.

Pandhelis fetched him ledgers and reports in an unending stream. They further confused issues about as often as they settled them. Videssian bureaucrats, with their rhetorical training, took pride in making their meaning as obscure as possible. Trying to thread his way through a thicket of allusions he barely understood, Scaurus wondered why he had ever wanted a political career.

He slept at his desk that night, stupefied by a pile of assessment documents written in a hand so tiny as to defy the eye. The legionaries were already at the practice field when he got back to the barracks. He walked down Middle Street to join them, breakfasting on a hard, square rye-flour roll dipped in honey, that he bought in the plaza of Palamas.

It was another chilly day, with little flurries of snow blowing through the streets. When the tribune came up to a bathhouse with an imposing façade of golden sandstone and white marble, his enthusiasm for practice abruptly disappeared. He wrestled his conscience to the mat and went in. Falling asleep to the press of work, he told himself, was enough to make anyone feel grimy.

The bathhouse's owner took his copper at the door with a broad smile, waving him forward into the undressing chamber. He gave another copper to the boy there to make sure his clothes would not be stolen while he was bathing, then shed his sheepskin coat, tunic, and trousers with a sigh of relief.

The sounds of the bath drew him on. As was true at Rome, Videssian baths were as much social places as ones devoted to cleanliness. Hawkers of sausages, wine, and pastries were crying their wares; so was the hair-remover, for those men who affected such fastidiousness. He fell silent for a moment, then Scaurus heard his client yelp as he began to pluck an armpit.

Usually the tribune, with Stoic abstemiousness, limited himself to a cold bath, but after coming in out of the snow that was intolerable. He sweated for a while in the steam bath, baking the winter out. Then the cold plunge seemed attractive rather than self-tormenting. He climbed out of the pool when the icy water began to bite, stretching himself on the tiles to relax for a few minutes before going on to soak in the pleasantly warm pool beyond.

"Scrape you off, sir?" asked a youth with a curved strigil in his hand.

"Thank you, yes," the tribune said; he'd brought along a little money for small luxuries like this, as it was next to impossible for a bather to scrape all of himself. He sighed at the pleasant roughness of the strigil sliding back and forth over his flesh.

Around him plump middle-aged men puffed as they exercised with weights. Masseurs pummeled grunting victims, now clapping hands down on their shoulders, now cupping them to produce an almost drumlike beat. Three young men played the Videssian game called *trigon*, throwing a ball unexpectedly from one to the next. They feinted and shouted; whenever one dropped the ball the other two would cry out as he lost a point. Off in a corner, a handful of more sedentary types diced the morning away.

There was a tremendous splash as someone leaped into the warm pool in the hall beyond, followed closely by cries of annoyance from the nearby people whom he'd drenched. The splasher came up not a whit dismayed. After blowing the water out of his mouth and nose, he started to sing in a resonant baritone.

"Everyone thinks he sounds wonderful in the baths," the youth with the strigil said, cocking his head critically. He fancied himself a connoisseur of bathhouse music. "He's not bad, I must say, for all his funny accent."

"No, he isn't," Marcus agreed, though his ear was so poor he could hardly tell good singing from bad. But only one man in Videssos owned that brogue. Tipping the youth a final copper, he got up and went in to say hello to Viridovix.

The Celt was facing the entranceway and broke off his tune in midnote when he saw the tribune. "If it's not himself, come to wash the ink off him!" he cried. "And a good deal of himself there is to wash, too!"

Scaurus looked down. He'd felt his middle thickening from days in a chair without exercise, but hadn't realized the result was so plain to see. Annoyed, he ran three steps forward and dove into the warm water a good deal more neatly than Viridovix had. It was a shallow dive; the pool was no more than chest-deep.

He swam over to the Celt. The two of them were strange fish among the olive-skinned, dark-haired Videssians: Marcus dark blond, his face, arms, and lower legs permanently tanned from his time in the field but the rest of him paler; and Viridovix, fair with the pink-white Gallic fairness that refused to take the sun, his burnished copper hair sodden against his head and curling in bright ringlets on his chest and belly and at his groin.

"Shirking again," they both said at the same time, and laughed together. Neither was in any hurry to get out. The pool was heated to that perfect temperature where the water does not register against the skin. Marcus thought of the sharp wind outside, then chose not to.

A small boy, drawn perhaps by the Celt's strangeness, splashed him from behind. Viridovix spun round, saw his laughing foe. "Do that to me, will you now?" he roared, mock-ferocious, and splashed back. They pelted each other with water until the youngster's father had to go and take his son, unwilling, from the pool. Viridovix waved to them both as they left. "A fine lad, and a fine time, too," he said to Scaurus.

"From the look of you, you had your fine time last night," the tribune retorted. He had been staring at Viridovix's back and shoulders when the Gaul turned them during the water fight. They were covered with scratches that surely came from a woman's nails. One or two of them, Scaurus thought, must have drawn blood; they were still red and angry.

Viridovix smoothed down his mustaches, fairly dripping smugness. He said a couple of sentences in his own Celtic tongue before dropping back into Latin, which he still preferred to Videssian. "A wildcat she was, all right," he said, smiling at the memory. "You canna see it under my hair, but she fair bit the ear off me, too, there at the end."

He was in so expansive a mood that Marcus asked, "Which one was it?" He was hard pressed to imagine any of the Celt's three women showing such ferocity. They seemed too docile for it.

"Och, none o' them," Viridovix answered, understanding the question and not put out by it: plainly he felt like boasting. "They're well enough, I'll not deny; still, the time comes when so much sweetness starts to pall. The new one, now! She's slim, so she is, but wild and shameless as a wolf bitch in heat."

"Good for you, then," Scaurus said. Viridovix, he thought, would likely jolly this new wench into joining the rest. He had a gift in such matters.

"Aye, she's all I hoped she would be," the Gaul said happily. "Ever since she gave me her eye, bold as you please down there on the foggy beach, I've known she'd not be hard for me to lure under the sheets."

"Good for—" the tribune started to repeat, and then stopped in horrified amazement as the full meaning of Viridovix' words sank in. His head whipped round to see who might be listening before he remembered they had been speaking Latin. One small thing to be grateful for, he thought—probably the only one. "Do you mean to tell me it's Komitta Rhangavve's skirt you're lifting?"

"Aren't you the clever one, now? But it's herself lifts it, I assure you— as greedy a cleft as any I've known."

"Are you witstruck all of a sudden, man? It's the Emperor's mistress you're diddling, not some tavern drab."

"And what o' that? A Celtic noble is entitled to better than such trollops," Viridovix said proudly. "Forbye, if Thorisin doesn't want me diddling his lady, then let him diddle her his own self and not stay up till dead of night kinging it. He'll get himself no sons that way."

"Will you give him a red-headed one, then? If no other way, he'll know the cuckoo by its feathers."

Viridovix chuckled at that, but nothing the Roman said would make him change his mind. He was enjoying himself, and was not a man to think of tomorrow till it came. He started singing again, a bouncy love song. Half a dozen Videssians joined in, filling the chamber with music. Marcus tried to decide whether drowning him now would make things better or worse.

XI

"Pandhelis, where have you hidden last year's tax register for Kybistra?" Scaurus asked. The clerk shuffled through rolls of parchment, spread his hands regretfully. Muttering a curse, Scaurus stood up from his desk and walked down the hall to see if Pikridios Goudeles had the document he needed.

The dapper bureaucrat looked up from his work as the tribune came in. He and Scaurus had learned wary respect for each other since the latter began overseeing the bureaucrats for Thorisin Gavras. "What peculations have you unearthed now?" Goudeles asked. As always, a current of mockery flowed just below the surface of his words.

When Marcus told him what he wanted, Goudeles grew brisk. "It should be around here someplace," he said. He went from pigeonhole to pigeonhole, unrolling the first few inches of the scrolls in them to see what they contained. When the search failed to turn up anything, his mobile eyebrows came down in irritation. He shouted for a couple of clerks to look in nearby rooms, but they returned equally unsuccessful. His frown deepened. "Ask the silverfish and the mice," he suggested.

"No, you probably trained them to lie for you," Marcus said. When the Roman first started the job the Emperor had set him, Goudeles tested him with doctored records. The tribune returned them without comment and got what looked to be real cooperation thereafter. He wondered if this was another, subtler snare.

But Goudeles was rubbing his neatly bearded chin in thought. "That cadaster might not be here at all," he said slowly. "It might already be stored in the archives building down on Middle Street. It shouldn't be— it's too new—but you never can tell. I don't have it, at any rate."

"All right, I'll try there. If nothing else, I'll get to stretch my legs. Thanks, Pikridios." Goudeles gave a languid wave of acknowledgment. A strange character, Scaurus thought, looking and acting the effete seal-stamper almost to the point of self-parody, but with the grit to confront Thorisin Gavras in his own camp for the Sphrantzai. Well, he told himself, only in the comedies is a man all of a piece.

The brown slate flags of the path from the Grand Courtroom to the forum of Palamas were wet and slippery; most of the snow that had blanketed the palace complex' lawns was gone. The sun was almost hot in a bright blue sky. The tribune eyed it suspiciously. There had been another of these spells a couple of weeks before, followed close by the worst blizzard of the winter. This one, though, might be spring after all.

The tribune had a good idea of the reception he would get at the imperial offices that housed the archives—nor was he disappointed. Functionaries herded him from file to musty file until he began to hate the smell of old parchment. There was no sign of the document he sought, or of any less than three years old. Some were much older than that; he turned up one that seemed to speak of Namdalen as still part of the Empire, though fading ink and strange, archaic script made it impossible to be sure.

When he showed the ancient scroll to the secretary in charge of those files, that worthy said, "You needn't look as if you're blaming me. What would you expect to find in the archives but old papers?" He seemed scandalized that anyone could expect him to produce a recent document.

"I have been through all three floors of this building," Scaurus said, fighting to hold his patience. "Is there any other place the scurvy thing might be lurking?"

"I suppose it might be in the sub-basement," the secretary answered, his tone saying he was sure it wasn't. "That's where the real antiques get stowed, below the prisons."

"I may as well try, as long as I'm here."

"Take a lamp with you," the secretary advised, "and keep your sword drawn. The rats down there aren't often bothered and they can be fierce."

"Splendid," the tribune muttered. It was useful information all the same; though he had known the imperial offices held a jail, he had not been aware there was anything beneath it. He made sure the lamp he chose was full of oil.

He was glad of the lamp as soon as he started down the stairway to the prison, for even that was below the level of the street and had no light save what came from the torches flickering in their iron brackets every few feet along the walls. The rough-hewn blocks of stone above them were thick with soot that had not been cleaned away for years.

It was time for the prisoners' daily meal. A pair of bored guards pushed a squeaking handcart down the central aisle-way. Two more, almost equally bored, covered them with drawn bows as they passed out loaves of coarse, husk-filled bread, small bowls of fish stew that smelled none too fresh, and squat earthen jugs of water. The fare was miserable, but the inmates crowded to the front of their cells to get it. One made a face as he tasted the stew. "You washed your feet in it again, Podopagouros," he said.

"Aye, well, they needed it," the guard answered, unperturbed.

The tribune had to ask his way down to the sub-basement. He walked past the rows of cells to a small door whose hinges creaked rustily as he opened it. As with many doorways in the imperial offices, an image of the Emperor was set above this one. But Scaurus blinked at the portrait: a roundfaced old man with a short white beard. Who—? He held up his lamp to read the accompanying text: "Phos preserve the Avtokrator Strobilos Sphrantzes." It had been more than five years now since Strobilos was Emperor.

Long before he reached the bottom of the stairway, Marcus knew he would never find the tax roll, even if it was here. The little clay lamp in his hand was not very bright, but it shed enough light for him to see boxes of records haphazardly piled on one another. Some were overturned, their contents half-buried in the dust and mold on the floor. The air tasted dead.

The lamp flickered. Scaurus felt his heart jump with it. There could be no worse fate than to be lost down here, alone in the blackness. No, not altogether alone; as the flame blazed up again, its glow came back greenly from scores of gleaming eyes. Some of them, the tribune thought nervously, were higher off the ground than a rat's eyes had any right to be.

He retreated, making very sure that little door was bolted. Strobilos stared incuriously down at him; even the imperial artist had had trouble portraying him as anything but a dullard.

Its torches bright and cheerful, the prison level seemed almost attractive compared to what was below it. The guards with their handcart had not moved ahead more than six or seven cells. Their rhythm was slow, nearly hypnotic—a loaf to the left, a bowl of stew to the right; a bowl of stew to the left, a loaf to the right; a water jar to either side; creak forward and repeat.

"You, there!" someone called from one of the cells. "Yes, you, outlander!" Marcus had been about to go on, sure no one down here could be talking to him, but that second call stopped him. He looked round curiously.

He had not recognized Taron Leimmokheir in his shabby linen prison robe. The ex-admiral had lost weight, and his hair and beard were long and shaggy; months in this sunless place had robbed him of his sailor's tan. But as Scaurus walked over to his cell, he saw Leimmokheir still bore himself with military erectness. The cell itself was neat and clean as it could be, cleaner, in fact, than the passageway outside.

"What is it, Leimmokheir?" the tribune asked, not very kindly. The man on the other side of those rust-flaked bars had come too close to killing him and was condemned to be here for planning the murder of the Emperor the Roman supported.

"I'd have you take a message to Gavras, if you would." The words were a request, but Leimmokheir's deep hoarse voice somehow kept its tone of command, prisoner though he was. Marcus waited.

Leimmokheir read his face. "Oh, I'm not such a fool as to ask to be set free. I know the odds of that. But by Phos, outlander, tell him he holds an innocent man. By Phos and his light, by the hope of heaven and the fear of Skotos' ice below, I swear it." He drew the sun-sign over his breast, repeating harshly, "He holds an innocent man!"

The convict in the next cell, a sallow man with a weasel's narrow wicked face, leered at Scaurus. "Aye, we're all innocent here," he said. "That's why they keep us here, you know, to save us from the guilty ones outside. Innocent!" His laugh made the word a filthy joke.

The Roman, though, paused in some uncertainty. Barefoot and unkempt Leimmokheir might be, but his speech still had the oddly compelling quality Marcus had noted when he first heard it on that midnight beach, still carried the conviction that here was a man who would not, or could not, lie. His eyes bored into the tribune's, and Scaurus lowered his first.

The food cart came groaning up. The tribune made his decision. "I'll do what I can," he said. Leimmokheir acknowledged him not with a nod, but with lowered head and right hand on heart—the imperial soldier's salute to a superior. If this was acting, Scaurus thought, it deserved a prize.

He began to regret his promise before he got back to the palace compound. As if he didn't have troubles enough, without trying to convince Gavras he might have made a mistake. Thorisin was much more mistrustful of his aides than Mavrikios had been—with reason, Marcus had to admit. If he ever learned the tribune had planned to defect . . . ! It did not bear thinking about.

If, on the other hand, he approached the Emperor through Alypia Gavra, that might blunt Thorisin's suspicions, the more so if she took his side. At least he could learn what she thought of Leimmokheir, which would give better perspective on how far to credit the ex-admiral. He smacked fist into open palm, pleased with his own cleverness.

She might even know where that fornicating tax roll was, he thought.

The eunuch steward Mizizios rapped lightly at the handsome door. Like most of those in the small secluded building that was the imperial family's private household, it was ornamented with inlays of ebony and red cedar. "Yes, bring him in, of course," Scaurus heard the princess say. Mizizios bowed as he worked the silver latch.

He followed the tribune into the chamber, but Alypia waved him away. "Let us talk in peace." Seeing the eunuch hesitate, she added, "Go on; my virtue's safe with him." It was, Marcus thought, as much the bitterness in her voice as the order itself that made Mizizios flee.

But she was gracious again as she offered the Roman a chair, urged him to take wine and cakes. "Thank you, your Majesty," he said. "It's kind of you to see me on such short notice." He bit into one of the little cakes with enjoyment. They were stuffed with raisins and nuts and dusted lightly with cinnamon; better here than over goose, he thought. That midwinter meal still rankled.

"My uncle has made it plain to both of us that the pen-pushers' iniquities are of the highest importance, has he not?" she said, raising her eyebrows slightly. Was that surprise at his thanks, Scaurus wondered, or lurking sarcasm? He could not read Alypia at all and did not think the reverse was true; he felt at a disadvantage.

"If I'm interrupting anything . . ." he said, and let the sentence drop.

"Nothing that won't keep," she said, waving to a desk as overloaded with scrolls and books as his own. He could read the title picked out in gold leaf on a leather-bound volume's spine: the *Chronicle of Seven Reigns.* She followed his eye, nodded. "History is a business that takes its own time."

The desk itself was plain pine, no finer than the one Marcus used. The rest of the furnishings, including the chairs on which he and Alypia sat, were as austere. The only ornament was an icon of Phos above the desk, an image stern in judgment.

At first glance, the princess seemed almost equally severe. She wore blouse and skirt of plain dark brown, unrelieved by jewelry; her hair was pulled back into a small, tight bun at the nape of her neck. But her green eyes—rare for a Videssian—held just enough ironic amusement to temper the harshness she tried to project. "To what pen-pushers' iniquities are we referring?" she asked, and Scaurus heard it in her voice as well.

"None," he admitted, "unless you happen to know where they've spirited away Kybistra's tax records."

"I don't," she said at once, "but surely you could have a mage find them for you."

"Why, so I could," Scaurus said, amazed. The notion had never entered his mind. For all his time in Videssos, down deep he still did not accept magic, and it rarely occurred to him to use it. He wondered how much sorcery went on around him, unnoticed, every day among folk who took it as much for granted as a cloak against the cold.

Such musings vanished as he remembered his chief reason for seeing the princess. "I'm not here on account of the pen-pushers, actually," he began, and set out the story of how Taron Leimmokheir had recognized him and insisted on his own innocence.

Alypia grew serious as she listened, alert and intent. The expression suited her face perfectly; Marcus thought of the goddess Minerva as he watched her. She was silent for several moments after he finished, then asked at last, "What do you make of what he said?"

"I don't know what to believe. The evidence against him is strong, and yet I thought the first time I heard his voice that he was a man whose word was good. It troubles me."

"Well it might. I've known Leimmokheir five years now, since my father won the throne, and never seen him do anything dishonorable or base." Her mouth twitched in a mirthless smile. "He even treated me as if I were really Empress. He may have been artless enough to think I was."

Scaurus rested his chin on the back of his hand, looked down at the floor. "Then I'd best see your uncle, hadn't I?" He did not relish the prospect; Thorisin was anything but reasonable on the matter of Leimmokheir.

Alypia understood that, too. "I'll come with you, if you like."

"I'd be grateful," he said frankly. "It would make me less likely to be taken for a traitor."

She smiled. "Hardly that. Shall we find him now?"

The bare-branched trees' shadows were long outside. "Tomorrow will do well enough. I'd like to see to my men with what's left of today; as is, I don't get as much chance as I should."

"All right. My uncle likes to ride in the early morning, so I'll meet you at midday outside the Grand Courtroom." She stood, a sign the audience was at an end.

"Thanks," he said, rising too.

He took another little cake from the enamelwork tray, then smiled himself as the memory came back. He'd had these cakes before and knew who baked them. "They're as good as I remembered," he said.

For the first time he saw Alypia's reserve crack. Her eyes widened slightly, her hand fluttered as if to brush the compliment away. "Tomorrow, then," she said quietly.

"Tomorrow."

When the tribune got back to the barracks he found an argument in full swing. Gorgidas had made the mistake of trying to explain the Greek notion of democracy to Viridovix and succeeded only in horrifying the Celtic noble.

"It's fair unnatural," Viridovix said. "'Twas the gods themselves set some folk above the rest." Arigh Arghun's son, who was there visiting the Gaul and soaking up some wine, nodded vigorously.

"Nonsense," Scaurus said. The Roman patricians had tried to put that one over on the rest of the people, too. It had been centuries since it worked.

But Gorgidas turned on him, snapping, "What makes you think I need *your* help? Your precious Roman republic has its nobles, too, though they buy their way to the role instead of being born into it. Why is a Crassus a man worth hearing, if not for his moneybags?"

"What are you yattering about?" Arigh said impatiently; the allusion meant nothing to him and hardly more to Viridovix. The Arshaum was a chieftain's son, though, and knew what he thought of the Greek's idea. "A clan has nobles for the same reason an army has generals—so when trouble comes, people know whom to follow."

Gorgidas shot back, "Why follow anyone simply because of birth? Wisdom would be a better guide."

"Be a man never so wise, if he comes dung-footed from the fields and speaks like the clodhopper born, no one'll be after hearing his widsom regardless," Viridovix said.

Arigh's flat features showed his contempt for all farmers, noble and peasant alike, but he followed the principle the Celt was laying down. In his harsh, clipped speech he said to Gorgidas, "Here, outlander, let me tell you a story to show you what I mean."

"A story, is it? Wait a moment, will you?" The physician trotted off, to return with tablet and stylus. If anything could ease him out of an argumentative mood, it was the prospect of learning more about the world in which he found himself. He poised stylus over wax. "All right, carry on."

"This happened a few years back, you'll understand," Arigh began, "among the Arshaum who follow the standard of the Black Sheep—near neighbors to my father's clan. One of their war leaders was a baseborn man named Kuyuk, and he had a yen for power. He toppled the clan-chief neat as you please, but because he was a nobody's son, the nobles were touchy about doing what he told them. He was clever, though, was Kuyuk, and had himself a scheme.

"One of the things the clan-chief left behind when he ran was a golden foot-bath. The nobles washed their feet in it, aye, and pissed in it, too, sometimes. Now Kuyuk had a goldsmith melt it down and recast it in the shape of a wind spirit. He set it up among the tents, and all the clansmen of the Black Sheep made sacrifice to it."

"Sounds like something out of Herodotus," Gorgidas said, little translucent spirals of wax curling up from his darting stylus.

"Out of what? Anyway, Kuyuk let this go on for a while and then called in his factious nobles. He told them where the image came from, and said, 'You used to wash your feet in that basin, and piddle in it, and even puke. Now you sacrifice to it, because it's in a spirit's shape. The same holds true for me: when I was a commoner you could revile me all you liked, but as clan-chief I deserve the honor of my station.'"

"Och, what a tricksy man!" Viridovix exclaimed in admiration. "That should have taught them respect."

"Not likely! The chief noble, whose name was Mutugen, stuck a knife into Kuyuk. Then all the nobles gathered round and pissed on his corpse. As Mutugen said, 'Gold is gold no matter what the shape, and a baseborn man's still baseborn with a crown on his head.' Mutugen's son Turukan is chief of the Black Sheep to this day—they wouldn't follow a nobody."

"True, your nobles wouldn't," Marcus said, "but what of the rest of the clan? Were they sorry to see Kuyuk killed?"

"Who knows? What difference does it make?" Arigh answered, honestly confused. Viridovix slapped him on the back in agreement.

Gorgidas threw his hands in the air. Now, put in a more dispassionate frame of mind by his ethnographic jotting, he was willing to admit Scaurus to his side. He said, "Don't let them reach you, Roman. They haven't experienced it, and understand no more than a blind man does a painting."

"Honh!" said Viridovix. "Arigh, what say you the two of us find a nice aristocratic tavern and have a jar or two o' the noble grape?" Tall Celt and short wiry plainsman strode out of the barracks side by side.

Gorgidas' note-taking and his own visit to Alypia Gavra reminded Marcus of the Greek doctor's other interest. "How is that history of yours doing?" he asked.

"It comes, Scaurus, a bit at a time, but it comes."

"May I see it?" the Roman asked, suddenly curious. "My Greek was never of the finest, I know, and it's the worse for rust, but I'd like to try, if you'd let me."

Gorgidas hesitated. "I have only the one copy." But unless he wrote for himself alone, the tribune was his only possible audience for his work in the original, and no Videssian translation, even if somehow made, could be the same. "Mind you care for it, now—don't let your brat be gumming it."

"Of course not," Scaurus soothed him.

"Well all right, then, I'll fetch it, or such of it as is fit to see. No, no stay there, don't trouble yourself. I'll get it." The Greek went off to his billet in the next barracks hall. He returned with a pair of parchment scrolls, which he defiantly handed to Marcus.

"Thank you," the tribune said, but Gorgidas brushed the amenities aside with an impatient wave of his hand. Marcus knew better than to push him; the physician was a large-hearted man, but disliked admitting it even to himself.

Scaurus took the scrolls back to his own quarters, lit a lamp, and settled down on the bedroll to read. As twilight deepened, he realized how poor and flickering the light was. He thought of the priest Apsimar back at Imbros and the aura of pearly radiance the ascetic cleric could project at will. Sometimes magic was very handy, though Apsimar would cry blasphemy if asked to be a reading lamp . . .

Concentration on Gorgidas' history drove such trivia from his mind. The going was slow at first. Scaurus had not read Greek for several years— it was distressing to see how much of his painfully built vocabulary had fallen by the wayside. The farther he went, though, the more he realized the physician had created—what was that phrase of Thucydides'?— a *ktema es aei*, a possession for all time.

Gorgidas' style was pleasingly straightforward; he wrote a smooth *koine* Greek, with only a few unusual spellings to remind one he came from Elis, a city that used the Doric dialect. But the history had more to offer than an agreeable style. There was real thought behind it. Gorgidas constantly strove to reach beyond mere events to illuminate the principles they illustrated. Marcus wondered if his physician's training had a hand in that. A doctor had to recognize a disease's true nature rather than treating only its symptoms.

Thus when speaking of anti-Namdalener riots in Videssos, Gorgidas gave an account of what had happened in the particular case he had observed, but went on to remark, "A city mob is a thing that loves trouble and is rash by nature; the civil strife it causes may be more dangerous and harder to put down than warfare with foreign foes." It was a truth not limited to the Empire alone.

Helvis came in, breaking Marcus' train of thought. She had Dosti in the crook of her arm and led Malric by the hand. Her son by Hemond broke free from his mother and jumped on Scaurus' stomach. "We went walking on the sea wall," he said with a five-year-old's frightening enthusiasm, "and mama bought me a sausage, and we watched the ships sailing away—"

Marcus lifted a questioning eyebrow. "Bouraphos," Helvis said. The tribune nodded. It was about time Thorisin sent Pityos help against the Yezda, and the drungarios of the fleet could reach the port on the Videssian Sea long before any force got there by land.

Malric burbled on; Scaurus listened with half an ear. Helvis set Dosti down. He tried to stand, fell over, and crawled toward his father. "Da!" he announced. "Da-da-da!" He reached for the roll of parchment the tribune had set down. Remembering Gorgidas' half-serious warning, Marcus snatched it away. The baby's face clouded over. Marcus grabbed him and tossed him up and down, which seemed to please him well enough.

"Me, too," Malric said, tugging at his arm.

Scaurus tried hard not to favor Dosti over his stepson. "All right, hero, but you're a bit big for me to handle lying down." The tribune climbed to his feet. He gave Dosti back to Helvis, then swung Malric through the air until the boy shrieked with glee.

"Enough," Helvis warned practically, "or he won't keep that sausage down." To her son she added, "And enough for you, too, young man. Get ready to go to bed." After the usual protests, Malric slipped out of shirt and breeches and slid under the covers. He fell asleep at once.

"What did you rescue from this one?" Helvis asked, hefting Dosti. "Are you bringing your taxes to bed now?"

"I should hope not," Marcus exclaimed; there was a perversion not even Vardanes Sphrantzes could enjoy. The tribune showed Helvis Gorgidas' history. The strange script made her frown. Though she could read only a few words of Videssian, she knew what the signs were supposed to look like, and was taken aback that a different system could represent sounds.

Something almost like fear was in her eyes as she said to Scaurus, "There are times when I nearly forget from how far away you come, dear, and then something like this reminds me. This is your Latin, then?"

"Not quite," the tribune said, but he could see his explanation left her confused. Nor did she understand his interest in the past.

"It's gone, and gone forever. What could be more useless?" she said.

"How can you hope to understand what will come without knowing what's come before?"

"What comes will come, whether I understand it or not. Now is plenty for me."

Marcus shook his head. "There's more than a little barbarian in you, I fear," he said, but fondly.

"And what if there is?" Her stare challenged him. She put Dosti in his crib.

He took her in his arms. "I wasn't complaining," he said.

It always amused Scaurus how students and masters of the Videssian Academy turned to watch him as he made his way through the gray sandstone building's corridors. They could be priest or noble, graybeard scholar or ropemaker's gifted son, but the sight of a mercenary captain in the halls never failed to make heads swing.

He was glad Nepos kept early hours. With luck, the chubby little priest could find his missing tax roll for him before he was due to meet Alypia Gavra. At first it seemed he would have that luck, for Nepos' hours were even earlier than he'd thought; when he peered into the refectory a drowsy-looking student told him, "Aye, he was here, but he's already gone to lecture. Where, you say? I think in one of the chambers on the third floor, I'm not sure which." The young man went back to his honey-sweetened barley porridge.

584

Marcus trudged up the stairs, then walked past open doors until he found his man. He slid into an empty seat at the back of the room. Nepos beamed at him but kept on teaching. His dozen or so students scribbled notes as they tried to keep pace.

Now and then a student would ask a question; Nepos dealt with them effortlessly but patiently, always asking at the end of his explanation, "Now do you understand?" To that Scaurus would have had to answer no. As near as he could gather, the priest's subject matter was somewhere on the border between theology and sorcery, and decidedly too abstruse for the uninitiated. Still, the tribune judged him a fine speaker, witty, thoughtful, self-possessed.

"That will do for today," Nepos said as Marcus was beginning to fidget. Most of the students trooped out; a couple stayed behind to ask questions too complex to interrupt the flow of the lecture. They, too, looked curiously at Scaurus as they left.

So did Nepos. "Well, well," he chuckled, pumping the tribune's hand. "What brings you here? Surely not a profound interest in the relation between the ubiquity of Phos' grace and proper application of the law of contact."

"Uh, no," Scaurus said. But when he explained why he had come, Nepos laughed until his round cheeks reddened. The tribune did not see the joke, and said so.

"Your pardon, I pray. I have a twofold reason for mirth." He ticked them off his fingers. "First, for something so trivial you hardly need the services of a chairholder in theoretical thaumaturgy. Any street-corner wizard could find your lost register for a fee of a couple of silver bits."

"Oh." Marcus felt his face grow hot. "But I don't know any street-corner wizards, and I do know you."

"Quite right, quite right. Don't take me wrong; I'm happy to help. But a mage of my power is no more *needed* for so simple a spell than a sledgehammer to push a pin through gauze. It struck me funny."

"I never claimed to know anything of magic. What else amuses you?" Feeling foolish, the tribune tried to hide it with gruffness.

"Only that today's lecture topic turns out to be relevant to you after all. Thanks to Phos' all-pervading goodness, things once conjoined are ever after so related that contact between them can be restored. Would you have, perhaps, a tax roll from a city close by Kybistra?"

Scaurus thought. "Yes, back at my offices I was working on the receipts from Doxon. I don't know that part of the Empire well, but from my maps the two towns are only a day's journey apart."

"Excellent! Using one roll to seek another will strengthen the spell, for, of course, it's also true that like acts most powerfully on like. Lead on, my friend—no, don't be foolish, I have no plans till the afternoon, and this shan't take long, I promise."

As they walked through the palace compound, the priest kept up a stream of chatter on his students, on the weather, on bits of Academy gossip that meant little to Scaurus, and on whatever else popped into his mind. He loved to talk. The Roman gave him a better audience than most of his countrymen, who were also fond of listening to themselves.

Marcus thought the two of them made a pair as strange as Viridovix and Arigh: a fat little shave-pate priest with a fuzzy black beard and a tall blond mercenary-turned-bureaucrat.

"Do you prefer this to the field?" Nepos asked as the tribune ushered him into his office. Pandhelis the secretary looked up in surprise as he saw the priest's blue robe out of the corner of his eye. He jumped to his feet, making the sun-sign over his breast. Nepos returned it.

Scaurus considered. "I thought I would when I started. These days I often wonder—answers are so much less clear-cut here." He didn't want to say much more than that, not with Pandhelis listening. He returned to the business at hand. Doxon's cadaster was where he'd left it, shoved to one corner of his desk. "Will you need any special gear for your spell?" he asked Nepos.

"No, not a thing. Merely a few pinches of dust, to serve as a symbolic link between that which is lost and that which seeks it. Dust, I think, will not be hard to come by in these surroundings." The priest chuckled. Marcus did, too; Pandhelis, a bureaucrat born, sniffed audibly.

Nepos got his dust from the windowsill, carefully put it down in the center of a clean square of parchment. "The manifestations of the spell vary," he explained to Scaurus. "If the missing object is close by, the dust may shape itself into an arrow pointing it out, or may leave its resting point and guide the seeker directly. If the distance is greater, though, it will form a word or image to show him the location of what he's looking for."

In Rome the tribune would have thought that so much hog-wash, but he knew better here. Nepos began a chant in the archaic Videssian dialect. He held Doxon's tax roll in his right hand, while the stubby fingers of his left moved in quick passes, amazingly sure and precise. The priest wore a smile of simple pleasure; Marcus thought of a master musician amusing himself with a children's tune.

Nepos called out a last word in a commanding tone of voice, then stabbed his left forefinger down at the dust. But though it roiled briefly, as if breathed upon, it showed no pattern.

Nepos frowned, as Scaurus' imaginary musician might have at a lute string suddenly out of tune. He scratched his chin, looked at the Roman in some embarrassment. "My apologies. I must have done something wrong, though I don't know what. Let me try again." His second effort was no more successful than the first. The dust stirred, then settled meaninglessly.

The priest studied his hands, seemingly wondering if they had betrayed him for some reason of their own. "How curious," he murmured. "Your book is not destroyed, of that I'm sure, else the dust would not have moved at all. But are you certain it's in the city?"

"Where else would it be?" Scaurus retorted, unable to imagine anyone wanting to spirit off such a stupefying document.

"Shall we try to find out?" The question was rhetorical; Nepos was already examining the contents of his belt-pouch to see if he had what he needed. He grunted in satisfaction as he produced a small stoppered glass vial in the shape of a flower's seed-capsule. He put a couple of drops of the liquid within on his tongue, making a face at the taste. "Now this not every wizard will know, so you did well coming to me after all. It clears the mind of doubts and lets it see further, thus increasing the power of the spell."

"What is it?" Scaurus asked.

Nepos hesitated; he did not like to reveal his craft's secrets. But the drug was already having its way with him. "Poppy juice and henbane," he said drowsily. The pupils of his eyes shrank down almost to nothing. But his voice and hands, drilled by years of the wizard's art, went through the incantation without faltering.

Again the finger darted at the dust. Marcus' eyes widened as he watched the pinches of dead stuff writhe like a tiny snake and shape themselves into a word. Successful magic never failed to raise his hackles.

"How interesting," Nepos said, though his decoction dulled the interest in his voice. "Even aided, I did not think the cantrip could reach to Garsavra."

"Fair enough," Scaurus answered, "because I didn't think the tax roll could be there either." He scratched his head, wondering why it was. No matter, he decided; Onomagoulos could always send it back.

The tribune dispatched Pandhelis to take Nepos to the Roman barracks and put him to bed. The priest went without demur. The potion he had swallowed left his legs rubbery and his usually lively spirit as muffled as a drum beaten through several thicknesses of cloth. "No, don't worry for me. It will wear off soon," he reassured Scaurus, fighting back an enormous yawn. He lurched off on Pandhelis' arm.

Marcus looked out the window, then quickly followed the secretary and priest downstairs. By the shortness of the shadows it was nearly noon, and it would not do to keep Alypia Gavra waiting.

To his dismay, he found her already standing by the Grand Gates. She did not seem angry, though. In fact, she was deep in conversation with the four Romans on sentry duty for her uncle.

"Aye, your god's well enough, my lady," Minucius was saying, "but I miss the legion's eagle. That old bird watched over us a lot of times." The legionary's companions nodded soberly. So did Alypia. She frowned, as if trying to fix Minucius' remark in her memory. Marcus could not help smiling. He'd seen that expression on Gorgidas too often not to recognize it now—the mark of a historian at work.

Spotting his commander, Minucius came to attention, grounding his spear with a sharp thud. He and his comrades gave Scaurus the clenched-fist Roman salute. "As you were. I'm outranked here," the tribune said easily. He bowed to Alypia.

"Don't let me interfere between your men and you," she said.

"You weren't." Back in his days with Caesar in Gaul, the least breach of order would have disturbed him mightily. Two and a half years as a mercenary captain had taught him the difference between spit and polish for their own sake and the real discipline that was needed to survive.

The chamberlain inside the Grand Gates clicked his tongue between his teeth. "Your Highness, where are your attendants?" he asked.

"Doing whatever they do, I imagine. I have no use for them," she answered curtly, and ignored the functionary's indignant look. Scaurus noted the edge in her voice; her natural leaning toward privacy could only have been exaggerated by the time she spent as Vardanes Sphrantzes' captive.

The court attendant gave an eloquent shrug, but bowed and conducted them forward. As the tribune walked up the colonnaded central hall toward the imperial throne, he saw the damage of the previous summer's fight had been repaired. Tapestries hung untorn, while tiny bits of matching stone were cemented into chipped columns.

Then Scaurus realized not all the injuries had been healed. He strode over a patch of slightly discolored porphyry flooring, a patch whose polish did not quite match the mirrorlike perfection of the rest. It would have been about here, he thought, that Avshar's fire blazed. He wondered again where the wizard-prince's sorcery had snatched him; through all the winter there had been no report of him.

Alypia's eyes were fathomless, but the closer she drew to the throne— and to the passageway beside it—the tighter her mouth became, until Marcus saw her bite her lip.

Another chamberlain led Katakolon Kekaumenos back from his audience with the Emperor. The legate from Agder gave Scaurus his wintry smile, inclined his head to Alypia Gavra. Once he was out of earshot, she murmured, "You'd think he paid for every word he spoke."

Their guide fell in the proskynesis before the throne. From his belly he called up to Thorisin, "Her Highness the Princess Alypia Gavra! The *epoptes* and commander Scaurus the Ronam!" Marcus stifled the urge to kick him in his upraised backside.

"Phos' light, fool, I know who they are," the Emperor growled, still with no use for court ceremonial. The attendant rose. He gaped to see the tribune still on his feet. Alypia was of royal blood, but why was this outlander so privileged? "Never mind, Kabasilas," Thorisin said. "My brother made allowances for him, and I do, too. He earns them, mostly." Kabasilas bowed and withdrew, but his curled lip spoke volumes.

Gavras cocked an eyebrow at the tribune. "So, *epoptes* and commander Scaurus, what now? Are the seal-stampers siphoning off gold-pieces to buy themselves counting-boards with beads of ruby and silver?"

"As for that," Marcus said, "I'm having some trouble finding out." He told the Emperor of the missing tax register, thinking to slide from an easy matter to the harder one that was his main purpose here.

"I thought you know better than to come to me with such twaddle," Thorisin said impatiently. "Send to Baanes if you will, but you have no need to bother me about it."

Scaurus accepted the rebuke; like Mavrikios, the younger Gavras appreciated directness. But when the Roman began his plea for Taron Leimmokheir, the Emperor did not let him get past the ex-admiral's name before he roared, "No, by Skotos' filth-filled beard! Are you turned treacher, too?"

His bellow filled the Grand Courtroom. Courtiers froze in mid-step; a chamberlain almost dropped the fat red candle he was carrying. It went out. His curse, a eunuch's contralto, echoed Gavras'. Minucius poked his head into the throne room to see what had happened.

"You were the one who told me it wasn't in the man to lie," Marcus said, persisting where a man born in the Empire might well quail.

"Aye, so I did, and came near paying my life for my stupidity," Thorisin retorted. "Now you tell me to put the wasp back in my tunic for another sting. Let him stay mured up till he rots, and gabble out his prayers lest worse befall him."

"Uncle, I think you're wrong," Alypia said. "What little decency came my way while the Sphrantzai reigned came from Leimmokheir. Away from his precious ships he's a child, with no more skill at politics than Marcus' foster son."

The tribune blinked, first at her mentioning Malric and then at her calling him by his own praenomen. When used alone, it was normally a mark of close personal ties. He wondered whether she knew the Roman custom.

She was going on, "You know I'm telling you the truth, uncle. How many years, now, have you known Leimmokheir? More than a handful, surely. You know the man he is. Do you really think that man could play you false?"

The Emperor's fist slammed down on the gold-sheathed arm of his throne. The ancient seat was not made for such treatment; it gave a painful creak of protest. Thorisin leaned forward to emphasize his words. "The man I knew would not break faith. But Leimmokheir did, and thus I knew him not at all. Who does worse evil, the man who shows his wickedness for the whole world to see or the one who stores it up to loose against those who trust him?"

"A good question for a priest," Alypia said, "but not one with much meaning if Leimmokheir is innocent."

"I was there, girl. I saw what was done, saw the new-minted gold-pieces of the Sphrantzai in the murderers' pouches. Let Leimmokheir explain them away—that might earn his freedom." The Emperor laughed, but it was a sound of hurt. Marcus knew it was futile to argue further; feeling betrayed by a man he had thought honest, Gavras would not, could not, yield to argument.

"Thank you for hearing me, at least," the tribune said. "I gave my word to put the case to you once more."

"Then you misgave it."

"No, I think not."

"There are times, outlander, when you try my patience," the Emperor said dangerously. Scaurus met his eye, hiding the twinge of fear he felt. Much of the position he had built for himself in Videssos was based on not letting the sheer weight of imperial authority coerce him. That, for a man of republican Rome, was easy. Facing an angry Thorisin Gavras was something else again.

Gavras made a dissatisfied sound deep in his throat. "Kabasilas!" he called, and the chamberlain was at his elbow as the last syllable of his name still echoed in the high-ceilinged throne room. Marcus expected some sonorous formula of dismissal, but that was not Thorisin's way. He jerked his head toward his niece and the tribune and left Kabasilas to put such formality in the gesture as he might.

The steward did his best, but his bows and flourishes seemed all the more artificial next to the Emperor's unvarnished rudeness. The other court functionaries craned their necks at Scaurus and Alypia as he led them away, wondering how much favor they had lost. That would be as it was, Marcus thought. He laughed at himself—a piece of fatalism worthy of the Halogai.

When they came out to the Grand Gates once more, Alypia stopped to talk a few minutes longer with the Roman sentries there, then departed for the imperial residence. Scaurus went up to his offices to dictate a letter to Baanes Onomagoulos; Pandhelis' script was far more legible than his own. That accomplished, he basked in a pleasant glow of self-satisfaction as he started back to the barracks.

It did not last long. Viridovix was coming toward him, a jar of wine in his hand and an anticipatory grin on his face. The Gaul threw him a cheery wave and ducked into a small doorway in the other wing of the Grand Courtroom.

Maybe I should have drowned him, Marcus thought angrily. Had Viridovix no idea what he was playing at? There was no more caution in him than guile in Taron Leimmokheir. What would he do next, ask Thorisin for the loan of a bedroom? The tribune warned himself not to suggest that—Viridovix might take him up on it.

With the Celt gone, Scaurus was surprised to see Arigh at the barracks. The Arshaum was talking to Gorgidas again while the Greek took notes. Gorgidas was asking, "Who sees to your sick, then?"

The question seemed to bore Arigh, who scratched beneath his tunic of sueded leather. At last he said indifferently, "The shamans drive out evil spirits, of course, and for smaller ills the old women know of herbs, I suppose. Ask me of war, where I can talk of what I know." He slapped the curved sword that hung at his side.

Quintus Glabrio came in; he smiled and waved to Gorgidas without interrupting the physician's jottings. Instead he said to Marcus, "I'm glad to see you here, sir. A couple of my men have a running quarrel I can't seem to get to the bottom of. Maybe they'll heed you."

"I doubt that, if you can't solve it," the tribune said, but he went with Glabrio anyhow. The legionaries stood stiff-faced as he warned them not to let their dislike for each other affect their soldiering. They nodded at the correct times. Scaurus was not deceived; anything the able junior centurion could not cure over the course of time would not yield to his brief intercession. The men were on formal notice now, so perhaps something was accomplished.

Arigh had gone when he returned. Gorgidas was working up his notes, rubbing out a word here, a phrase there with the blunt end of his stylus, then reversing it to put his changes on the wax. "Viridovix will think you're trying to steal his friend away," the tribune said.

"What do I care what that long-shanked Gaul thinks?" Gorgidas asked, but could not quite keep amusement from his voice. Sometimes Viridovix made his friends want to wring his neck, but they remained his friends in spite of it. Less pleased, the doctor went on, "At least I can learn what the plainsman has to teach me."

There was no mistaking his bitterness. Marcus knew he was still seeing Nepos and other healer-priests, still trying to master their arts, and still falling short. No wonder he was putting more energy into his history these days. Medicine could not be satisfying to him right now.

Scaurus yawned, cozily warm under the thick wool blanket. Helvis' steady breathing beside him said she had already dropped off; so did her arm flung carelessly across his chest. Malric was asleep on her other side, while Dosti's breath came raspy from his crib. The baby was getting over a minor fever; Marcus drowsily hoped he would not catch it.

But an itchy something in the back of his mind kept him from following them into slumber. He rehashed the day's events, trying to track it down. Was it his failure to gain Taron Leimmokheir's release? Close, he thought, but not on the mark. He had not expected to win that one.

Why close, then? He heard Alypia Gavra's voice once more as she talked with the legionaries outside the Grand Courtroom. Whatever else she knew about their ways, he realized, she was perfectly familiar with the proper use of Roman names.

He was a long time sleeping.

XII

THE TRIBUNE SNEEZED. GAIUS PHILIPPUS LOOKED AT HIM IN DISGUST. "Aren't you through with that bloody thing yet?"

"It hangs on and on," Marcus said dolefully, wiping his nose. His eyes were watery, too, and his head seemed three times its proper size. "What is it, two weeks now?"

"At least. That's what you get for having your brat." Revoltingly healthy himself, Gaius Philippus spooned up his breakfast porridge, took a great gulp of wine. "That's good!" He patted his belly. Scaurus had scant appetite, which was as well, for his sense of taste had disappeared.

Viridovix strode into the barracks, splendid in his cape of crimson skins. He helped himself to peppery lamb sausage, porridge, and wine, then sank into a chair by the tribune and senior centurion. "The top o' the day t'ye!" he said, lifting his mug in salute.

"And to you," Marcus returned. He looked the Celt up and down. "Why such finery so early in the morning?"

"Early in the morning it may be for some, Scaurus dear, but I'm thinking of it as night's end. And a rare fine night it was, too." He winked at the two Romans.

"Mmph," Marcus said, as noncommittal a noise as he could muster. Normally he enjoyed Viridovix in a bragging mood, but since the Gaul had taken up with Komitta Rhangavve the less he heard the better. Nor did Gaius Philippus' incurious expression offer Viridovix any encouragement; the senior centurion, Marcus was sure, was jealous of the Celt, but would sooner have been racked than admit it.

Irrepressible as always, Viridovix needed scant prompting. After a long, noisy pull at his wine, he remarked, "Would your honor believe it, the wench had the brass to tell me to put all my other lassies to one side and have her only. Not ask, mind you, but tell! And me sharing her with

594

himself without so much as a peep. The cheek of it all!" He bit into the sausage, made a face at its spiciness, and drank again.

"Sharing who with whom?" Gaius Philippus asked, confused by pronouns.

"Never mind," Marcus said quickly. The fewer people who knew of Viridovix' trysting, the longer word of it would take to get back to Thorisin Gavras. Even Viridovix saw that, for he suddenly looked sly. But his report of what Komitta had said worried the tribune enough to make him ask, "What did you tell the lady?"

"What any Celtic noble and gentleman would, of course: to go futter the moon. No colleen bespeaks me so."

"Oh, no." Scaurus wanted to hold his aching head in his hands. With Komitta's savage temper and great sense of her own rank, it was a wonder Viridovix was here to tell the tale. In fact—"What did she say to that?"

"Och, she carried on somewhat, sure and she did, but I horned it out of her." Viridovix stretched complacently. The tribune looked at him in awe. If that was true, the Gaul was a mighty lanceman indeed.

Viridovix routed a piece of gristle out from between his teeth with a fingernail, then belched. "Still and all," he said, "if ye maun play the tomcat of evenings, then the day's the time for lying up. A bit o' sleep'd be welcome now, so by your leaves—" He rose, finished his wine, and walked out, whistling cheerily.

"Enough of your 'never minds,' " Gaius Philippus said as soon as the Celt was gone. "You don't go fish-belly color over trifles. What's toward?"

So Marcus, his hand forced, told him and had the remote pleasure of watching his jaw drop to his chest. "Almighty Jove," the senior centurion said at last. "The lad doesn't think small, does he now?"

He thought another minute, then added, "He's welcome to her, too, for my silver. I'd sooner strop my tool on a sword blade than go near that one. All in all, it's safer." The tribune winced at the image, but slowly nodded; down deep inside he felt the same way.

As spring drew on, Scaurus spent less time at tax records. Most of the receipts had come in after the fall harvest, and he was through most of the backlog by the time the days began to grow longer once more. He knew he had done an imperfect job of overseeing the Videssian bureaucracy. It was too large, too complex, and too well entrenched for any one man, let alone an outsider, to control it fully. But he did think he had done some good and kept more revenue flowing into the imperial treasury than it would have got without him.

He was only too aware of some of his failures. One afternoon Pikridios Goudeles had mortified him by coming into the offices with a massy golden ring set with an enormous emerald. The minister wore it with great ostentation and flashed it at the tribune so openly that Marcus was sure its price came from diverted funds. Indeed, Goudeles hardly bothered to deny it, only smiling a superior smile. Yet try as Scaurus would, he could find no errors in the books.

Goudeles let him stew for several days, then, still with that condescending air, showed the Roman the sly bit of jugglery he'd used. "For," he said, "having used it myself, I see no point in letting just anyone slide it past you. That would reflect on my own skill."

More or less sincerely, Marcus thanked him and said nothing further about the ring; he had fairly lost this contest of wit with the bureaucrat, just as he had won the one before. They remained not-quite-friends, each with a healthy regard for the other's competence. As Scaurus came less often to his desk in the Grand Courtroom wing, he sometimes missed the seal-stamper's dry, delicate wit, his exquisite sense of where to place a dart.

Before long, only one major item was outstanding on the tribune's list: the tax roll for Kybistra. Onomagoulos ignored his first request for it; he sent out another, more strongly worded. "That echo will be a long time returning, I think," Goudeles told him.

"Eh? Why?" Marcus asked irritably.

The bureaucrat's eyebrow could not have lifted by the thickness of a hair, but he contrived to make the Roman feel like a small, stupid child. "Ah, well," Goudeles murmured, "it was a disorderly time for everyone."

Scaurus thumped his forehead with the heel of his hand, annoyed with himself for missing what was obvious, once pointed out. Onomagoulos had taken refuge at Kybistra after Maragha; the tribune wondered what part of his accounts would not bear close inspection. Thorisin, he thought, would be interested in that question, too.

So it proved. The imperial rescript that went out to Garsavra all but crackled off its parchment. By that time Marcus cared less than he had. He was working hard with his troops as they readied themselves for the coming summer campaign. As he sweated on the practice field, he was gratified to see the beginning potbelly he had grown during the winter's inactivity start to fade away.

Roman training techniques were enough to melt the fat off anyone. The Videssians, Vaspurakaners, and other locals who had taken service with the legionaries grumbled constantly, as soldiers will over any exercises. Gaius Philippus, naturally, worked them all the harder for their complaints. As for Scaurus, he threw himself into the drills with an enthusiasm he had not felt when he first joined the legions.

The troops exercised with double-weight weapons of wood, and fought at pells until their arms ached, thrusting now at the dummy posts' faces, now at their flanks, and again at thigh level. They used heavy wicker shields, too, and practiced advancing and retreating from their imaginary foes.

"Hard work, this," Gagik Bagratouni said. The Vaspurakaner *nakharar* still led his countrymen and had learned to swear in broken Latin as foully as in his hardly more fluent Videssian. "By the time comes real battle, a relief it will be."

"That's the idea," Gaius Philippus said. Bagratouni groaned and shook his head, sending sweat flying everywhere. He was well into his forties, and the drill came hard for him. He worked at it with the fierce concentration of a man trying to forget past shadows, and his countrymen showed a spirit and discipline that won the Romans' admiration.

The only thing that horrified the mountaineers was having to learn to swim. The streams in their homeland were trickles most of the year, floods the rest. Learn they did, but they never came to enjoy the water legionary-style, as a pleasant way to end a day's exercises.

The Videssians among the legionaries were not quite at their high pitch. A dozen times a day Marcus would hear some Roman yelling, "The point, damn it, the point! A pox on the bloody edge! It isn't good for anything anyway!" The imperials always promised to mend their swordplay and always slipped back. Most were ex-cavalrymen, used to the saber's sweet slash. Thrusting with the short *gladius* went against their instincts.

More patient than most of his fellows, Quintus Glabrio would explain, "No matter how hard you cut, armor and bones both shield your foe's vitals, but even a poorly delivered stab may kill. Besides, with the stabbing stroke you don't expose your own body and often you can kill your man before he knows you've delivered the stroke." Having nodded in solemn agreement, the Videssians would do as they were ordered—for a while.

Then there were those to whom Roman discipline meant nothing at all. Viridovix was as deadly a fighter as Scaurus had seen, but utterly out of place in the orderly lines of the legionaries' maniples. Even Gaius Philippus acknowledged the hopelessness of making him keep rank. "I'm just glad he's on our side," was the senior centurion's comment.

Zeprin the Red was another lone wolf. His great axe unsuited him for action among the legionaries' spears and swords, as did his temperament. Where Viridovix saw battle as high sport, the Haloga looked on it as his cold gods' testing place. "Their shield-maidens guide upwards the souls of those who fall bravely. With my enemy's blood I will buy my stairway to heaven," he rumbled, testing the edge of his double-bitted weapon with his thumb. No one seemed inclined to argue, though to Videssian ears that was pagan superstition of the rankest sort.

Drax of Namdalen and his captains came out to the practice field several times to watch the Romans work. Their smart drill impressed the great count, who told Scaurus, "By the Wager, I wish that son of a pimp Goudeles had warned me what sort of men you had. I thought my knights would ride right through you so we could roll up Thorisin's horse like a pair of leggings." He shook his head ruefully. "Didn't quite work that way."

"You gave us a bad time, too," the tribune returned the compliment. Drax remained a mystery to him—a skilled warrior, certainly, but a man who showed little of himself to the world outside. Though unfailingly courteous, he had a stiff face a horse trader would envy.

"He reminds me of Vardanes Sphrantzes with the back of his head shaved," Gaius Philippus said after the islander left, but that far Marcus would not go. Whatever Drax's mask concealed, he did not think it was the unmourned Sevastos' cruelty.

However much the Namdaleni admired the legionaries, the senior centurion remained dissatisfied. "They're soft," he mourned. "They need a couple of days of real marching to get the winter laziness out of 'em once and for all."

"Let's do it, then," Marcus said, though he felt a twinge of trepidation. If the troopers needed work, what of him?

"Full kits tomorrow," he heard Gaius Philippus order, and listened to the chorus of donkey brays that followed. The full Roman pack ran to more than a third of a man's weight; along with weapons and iron rations, it included a mess kit, cup, spare clothes in a small wicker hamper, a tent section, palisade stakes or firewood, and either a saw, pick, spade, or sickle for camping and foraging. Small wonder the legionaries called themselves mules.

Dawn was only a promise when they tramped out of the city, northward bound. The Videssian gate crew shook their heads in sympathy as they watched the soldiers march past. "Make way, there!" Gaius Philippus rasped, and waggoners hastily got their produce-filled wains out of the roadway. Like most of the Empire's civilians, they distrusted what little they knew about mercenaries and were not anxious to learn more.

Marcus pulled a round, ruddy apple from one of the wagons. He tossed the driver a small copper coin to pay for it and had to laugh at the disbelief on the man's face. "Belike their puir spalpeen was after thinking you'd breakfast on him instead of his fruit," Viridovix said.

There was less room for good cheer as the day wore along. The military step was something the Romans fell into with unthinking ease, each of them automatically holding his place in his maniple's formation. The men who had taken service since they came to Videssos did their best to imitate them but, here as in so many small ways, practice told. And because the newcomers were less orderly, they tired quicker.

Still, almost no one dropped from the line of march, no matter how footsore he became. Blistered toes were nothing to the blistering Gaius Philippus gave fallers-out, nor was any trooper eager to face his fellows' jeers.

Phostis Apokavkos, first of all the Videssians to become a legionary, strode along between two Romans, hunching forward a little under the weight of his pack. His long face crinkled into a smile as he flipped Scaurus a salute.

The tribune returned it. He hardly reckoned Apokavkos a Videssian any more. Like any son of Italy's, the ex-farmer's hands were branded with the mark of the legions. When he learned the mark's significance, Apokavkos had insisted on receiving it, but Scaurus had not asked it of any of the other recruits, nor had they volunteered.

By afternoon the tribune was feeling pleased with himself. There seemed to be a band of hot iron around his chest, and his legs ached at every forward step, but he kept up with his men without much trouble. He did not think they would make the twenty miles that was a good day's march, but they were not far from it.

Already they were past the band of suburbs that huddled under Videssos' walls and out into the countryside. Wheat-fields, forests, and vineyards were all glad with new leaf. There were newly returned birds overhead, too. A blackcap swooped low. "Churr! Tak-tak-tak!" it scolded the legionaries, then darted off on its endless pursuit of insects. A small flock of linnets, scarlet heads and breasts bright, twittered as they winged their way toward a gorse-covered hilltop.

Gaius Philippus began eyeing likely looking fields for a place to camp. At last he found one that suited him, with a fine view of the surrounding area and a swift clear stream running by. Woods at the edge of the field promised fuel for campfires. The senior centurion looked a question toward Scaurus, who nodded. "Perfect," he said. Even though this was but a drill, from skill and habit Gaius Philippus was incapable of picking a bad site.

The buccinators' horns blared out the order to halt. The legionaries pulled tools from their packs and fell to work on the square ditch and rampart that would shelter them for the night. Stakes sprouted atop the earthwork wall. Inside, eight-man tents went up in neat rows that left streets running at right angles and a good-sized open central forum. By the time the sun was down, Marcus would have trusted the camp to hold against three or four times his fifteen hundred men.

Some of the farmers hereabout must have reported the Romans' arrival to the local lord, for it had just grown dark when he rode up to investigate with a double handful of armed retainers. Marcus courteously showed him around the camp; he seemed a bit unnerved to be surrounded by so much orderly force.

"Be gone again tomorrow, you say?" he asked for the third time. "Well, good, good. Have a pleasant night of it, now." And he and his men rode away, looking back over their shoulders until the night swallowed them.

"What was all that in aid of?" Gaius Philippus demanded. "Why didn't you just tell him to bugger off?"

"You'd never make a politician," Marcus answered. "After he saw what we had, he didn't have the nerve to ask for the price of the firewood we cut, and I didn't have to embarrass him by telling him no right out loud. Face got saved all around."

"Hmm." It was plain Gaius Philippus did not give a counterfeit copper for the noble's feelings. The tribune, though, found it easier to avoid antagonizing anyone gratuitously. With the touchy Videssians, even that little was not always easy.

He settled down by a campfire to gnaw journeybread, smoked meat, and an onion, and emptied his canteen of the last of the wine it held. When he started to get up to rinse it out, he discovered he could barely stagger to the stream. The break—the first he'd had from marching all day—gave his legs a chance to stiffen, and they'd taken it with a vengeance.

Many legionaries were in the same plight. Gorgidas went from one to the next, kneading life into cramped calves and thighs. The spare Greek, loose-limbed himself after the hard march, spotted Marcus hobbling back to the fireside. *"Kai su, teknon?"* he said in his own tongue. "You too, son? Stretch out there, and I'll see what I can do for you."

Scaurus obediently lay back. He gasped as the doctor's fingers dug into his legs. "I think I'd rather have the aches," he said, but he and Gorgidas both knew he was lying. When the Greek was done, the tribune found he could walk again, more or less as he always had.

"Don't be too proud of yourself," Gorgidas advised, watching his efforts like a parent with a toddler. "You'll still feel it come morning."

The physician, as usual, was right. Marcus shambled down to the stream to splash water on his face, unable to assume any better pace or

601

gait. His sole consolation was that he was far from alone; about one legionary in three looked to have had his legs age thirty years overnight.

"Come on, you lazy sods! It's no further back than it was out!" Gaius Philippus shouted unsympathetically. One of the oldest men in the camp, he showed no visible sign of strain.

"Och, to the crows with you!" That was Viridovix; not being under Roman discipline, he could say what the legionaries felt. The march had been hard on the Gaul. Though larger and stronger than almost all the Romans, he lacked their stamina.

However much Gaius Philippus pressed as the legionaries started back, he did not get the speed he wanted. It took a good deal of marching for the men to work their muscles loose. To the senior centurion's eloquent disgust, they were still a couple of miles short of Videssos when night fell.

"We'll camp here," he growled, again choosing a prime defensive position in pastureland between two suburbs. "I won't have us sneaking in after dark like so many footpads, and you whoresons don't deserve the sweets of the city anyway. Loafing good-for-naughts! Caesar'd be ashamed of the lot of you." That meant little to the Videssians and Vaspurakaners, but it was enough to make the Romans hang their heads in shame. Mention of their old commander was almost too painful to bear.

When Marcus woke the next morning, he found to his surprise that he was much less sore than he had been the day before. "I feel the same way," Quintus Glabrio said with one of his rare smiles. "We're likely just numb from the waist down."

There were quite a few bright sails in the Cattle-Crossing; probably a grain convoy from the westlands' southern coast, thought Scaurus. A city the size of Videssos was far too big for the local countryside to feed.

Less than an hour brought the legionaries to the capital's mighty walls. "Have yourselves a good hike?" one of the gatecrew asked as he waved them through. He grinned at the abuse he got by way of reply.

It was hardly past dawn; Videssos' streets, soon to be swarming with life, as yet were nearly deserted. A few early risers were wandering into Phos' temples for the sunrise liturgy. Here and there people of the night—whores, thieves, gamblers—still strutted or skulked. A cat darted away from the legionaries, a fishtail hanging from the corner of its mouth.

The whole city was sweet with the smell of baking bread. The bakers were at their ovens before the sun was up and stayed till it was dark once more, sweating their lives away to keep Videssos fed. Marcus smiled as he felt his nostrils dilate, heard his stomach growl. Journeybread fought hunger, but the mere thought of a fresh, soft, steaming loaf teased the appetite to new life.

The legionaries entered the palace compound from the north, marching past the Videssian Academy. The sun gleamed off the golden dome on its high spire. Though the season was still early spring, the day already gave promise of being hot and muggy. Marcus was glad for a granite colonnade's long, cool shadow.

Hoofbeats rang round a bend in the path, loud in the morning still-ness. The tribune's eyebrows rose. Who was galloping a horse down the palace compound's twisting ways? A typical Roman, Scaurus did not know that much of horses, but it hardly took an equestrian to realize the rider was asking for a broken neck.

The great bay stallion thundered round the bend in the track. Mar-cus felt alarm stab into his guts—that was the Emperor's horse! But Thorisin was not in the saddle; instead Alypia Gavra bestrode the beast, barely in control. She fought it to a halt just in front of the Romans, whose first ranks were giving back from the seeming runaway.

Not liking the check, the stallion snorted and tossed its head, eager to be given free rein once more. Alypia ignored it. She stared down the long Roman column, despair on her face. "So you've come to betray us, too!" she cried.

Glabrio stepped forward and seized the horse's head. Scaurus said, "Betray you? With a training march?"

The princess and the Roman shared a long, confusion-filled look. Then Alypia exclaimed, "Oh, Phos be praised! Come at once, then—a band of assassins is attacking the private chambers!"

"What?" Marcus said foolishly, but even as he was filling his lungs to order the legionaries forward he heard Gaius Philippus below, "Battle stations! Forward at double-time!"

Scaurus envied the senior centurion's immunity to surprise. "Shout 'Gavras!' as you come," he added. "Let both sides know help's on the way!"

The legionaries reached back over their shoulders for *pila*, tugged swords free from brass scabbards. "Gavras!" they roared. The Emperor's horse whinnied in alarm and reared, pulling free of Quintus Glabrio's grasp. Alypia held her seat. She could ride, as befitted a onetime provincial noble's daughter. Though Thorisin's frightened charger would have been a handful for anyone, she wheeled it and cantered forward at the Romans' head.

"Get back, my lady!" Marcus called to her. When she would not, he told off half a dozen men to hold her horse and keep her out of the fighting. They ignored her protests and did as they were ordered.

Nestled in the copse of cherry trees just now beginning to come into fragrant bloom, the private imperial residence was a dwelling made for peace. But its outer doors gaped open, and before them a sentry lay unmoving in a pool of blood. "Surround the place!" Marcus snapped, maniples peeled off to right and left.

For all his hurry, he was horribly afraid he had come too late. But as he rushed toward the yawning doorway, he heard fighting within. "It's a rescue, not revenge!" he yelled. The legionaries cheered behind him: "Gavras! Gavras!"

An archer leaped out into the doorway and let fly. Close behind Scaurus, a Roman clutched at his face, then skidded down on his belly. No time to see who had fallen, nor could the Videssian get off a second shot. He threw his bow to one side and drew saber.

He must have known it was hopeless, with hundreds of men thundering toward him. He set his feet and waited nonetheless. The tribune had a moment to admire his courage before their swords met. Then it was all automatic response: thrust, parry, slash, riposte, parry—thrust! Marcus felt his blade bite, twisted his wrist to make sure it was a killing blow. His foe groaned and slowly crumpled.

The Romans spilled down the hallway, their hobnailed *caligae* clattering on the mosaic floor. The light streaming through the alabaster ceiling panels was pale and calm, not the right sort of light at all to shine on battle. And battle there had already been aplenty: the corpses of sentries and eunuch servants sprawled together with those of their assailants. The red tesserae of hunting mosaics were overlain by true blood's brighter crimson; it spattered precious icons and portrait busts of Avtokrators centuries forgotten.

Marcus saw Mizizios lying dead. The eunuch had a sword in his hand and wore an ancient helmet of strange design, loot from a Videssian triumph of long ago. He had been a quick thinker to clap it on his head, but it had not saved him. A great saber cut opened his belly and spilled his entrails out on the floor.

Shouts and the pounding of axes against a barricaded door led the legionaries on. They rounded a last corner, only to be halted by a savage counterattack from the squadron of assassins. In the narrow corridor numbers were of scant advantage. Men pushed and cursed and struck, gasping when they were hit.

The assassins' captain was a burly man of about forty in a much-battered chain-mail shirt. He carried a torch in his right hand, and shouted through the door to Thorisin, "Your bully-boys are here too late, Gavras! You'll be roast meat before they do you any good!"

"Not so!" cried Zeprin the Red, who was fighting in the first rank of legionaries. He still blamed himself for Mavrikios Gavras' death, and would not let a second Emperor weigh on his conscience. The thick-muscled Haloga flung his great war axe at the torch-carrier. The throw was not good; quarters were too close for that. Instead of one of the gleaming steel bits burying itself in the Videssian's chest, it was the end of the axe handle that caught him in the pit of the stomach. Mail shirt or no, he doubled over as if kicked by a steer. The smoking torch fell to the floor and went out.

Snarling an oath, one of the trapped attackers sprang at Zeprin, who stood for a second weaponless. The Haloga did not—could not—retreat. He ducked under a furious slash, came up to seize his foe and crush him against his armored chest. The tendons stood out on his massive arms; his opponent's hands scrabbled uselessly at his back. Scaurus heard bones crack even through the din of combat. Zeprin threw the lifeless corpse aside.

At the same moment Viridovix, with an enormous two-handed slash, sent another assassin's head springing from his shoulders. The tribune could feel the enemy's spirit drain away. A quiet bit of murder was one thing, but facing these berserkers was something else again. Nor were the Romans themselves idle. Their shortswords stabbed past the Videssians' defenses, while their large *scuta* turned blow after blow. "Gavras!" they shouted, and pushed their foes back and back.

Then the blocked door flew open, and Thorisin Gavras and his four or five surviving guards charged at the enemy's backs, crying, "The Romans! The Romans!" It was more gallant than sensible, but Thorisin had an un-Videssian fondness for battle.

Some of the attackers spun round against him, still trying to complete their mission. Gaius Philippus cut one down from behind. "You bloody stupid bastard," he said, jerking his *gladius* free.

Marcus swore as a saber gashed his forearm. He tightened his fingers on his sword hilt. They all answered—no tendon was cut—but blood made the sword slippery in his hand.

Thorisin killed the man he was facing. The Emperor, not one to relish having to flee even before overpowering numbers, fought now with savage ferocity to try to ease the discredit only he felt. When he had been Sevastokrator he probably would have let his fury run away with him, but the imperial office was tempering him as it had his brother. Seeing only a handful of his assailants on their feet, he cried, "Take them alive! I'll have answers for this!"

Most of the assassins, knowing what fate held for them, battled all the harder, trying to make the legionaries kill them outright. One ran himself through. But a couple were borne to the floor and trussed up like dressed carcasses. So was their leader, who still could hardly breathe, let alone fight back.

"Very timely," Thorisin said, looking Marcus up and down. He started to offer his hand to clasp, stopped when he saw the tribune's wound.

Scaurus did not really feel it yet. He answered, "Thank your niece, not me. She lathered your horse for you, but I don't think you'll complain."

The Emperor smiled thinly. "No, I suppose not. Took the beast, did she?" He listened as the Roman explained how he had encountered Alypia.

Thorisin's smile grew wider. He said, "I never have cared for her scribbling away behind closed doors, but I won't complain of that any more, either. She must have gone out the window when the barney started, and run for the stables. Fire-foot's usually saddled by dawn." Marcus remembered Gavras' fondness for a morning gallop.

Thorisin prodded a dead body with his foot. "Good thing these lice were too stupid to throw a cordon round the building." He slapped Scaurus on the back. "Enough talk—get that arm seen to. You're losing blood."

The tribune tore a strip of cloth from the corpse's surcoat; Gavras helped him tie the rude dressing. His arm, numb a few minutes before, began to throb fiercely. He went looking for Gorgidas.

The doctor, Marcus thought with annoyance, did not seem to be anywhere within the rambling imperial residence. However much the legionaries outnumbered the twoscore or so assassins, they had not beaten them down without harm to themselves. Five men were dead— two of them irreplaceable Romans—and a good many more were wounded, more or less severely. Grumbling and clenching his fist against the hurt, the tribune went outside.

He saw Gorgidas kneeling over a man in the pathway—a Roman, from his armor—but had no chance to approach the physician. Alypia Gavra came rushing up to him. "Is my uncle—" she began, and then stopped, unwilling even to complete the question.

"Unscratched, thanks to you," Scaurus told her.

"Phos be thanked," she whispered, and then, to the tribune's glad confusion, threw her arms round his neck and kissed him. The legionaries who had kept her from the residence whooped. At the sound she jerked away in alarm, as if just realizing what she had done.

He reached out to her, but reluctantly held back when he saw her shy away. However brief, her show of warmth pleased him more, perhaps, than he was ready to admit. He told himself it was but pleasure at seeing her wounded spirit healing, and knew he was lying.

"You're hurt!" she exclaimed, spying the oozing bandage for the first time.

"It's not too bad." He opened and closed his hand to show her he could, though the proof cost him some pain. True to his Stoic training, he tried not to let it show on his face, but the princess saw sweat spring out on his forehead.

"Get it looked at," she said firmly, seeming relieved to be able to give advice that was sensible and impersonal at the same time. Scaurus hesitated, wishing this once for some of Viridovix' brass. He did not have it, and the moment passed. Anything he said would too likely be wrong.

He slowly walked over to Gorgidas. The doctor did not notice him. He was still bent low over the fallen legionary, his hands pressed against the soldier's face—the attitude, Marcus realized, of a Videssian healer-priest. The Greek's shoulders quivered with the effort he was making. "Live, damn you, live!" he said over and over in his native tongue.

But the legionary would never live again, not with that green-feathered arrow jutting up from between the doctor's fingers. Marcus could not tell whether Gorgidas had finally mastered the healing force, nor did it matter now; not even the Videssians could raise the dead.

At last the Greek felt Scaurus' presence. He raised his head, and the tribune gave back a pace from the grief and self-tormenting, impotent anger on his face. "It's no use," Gorgidas said, more to himself than to Scaurus, "Nothing is any use." He sagged in defeat, and his hands, red-black with blood beginning to dry, slid away from the dead man's face.

Marcus suddenly forgot his wound. "Jupiter Best and Greatest," he said softly, an oath he had not sworn since the days in his teens when he still believed in the gods. Quintus Glabrio lay tumbled in death. His features were already loosening into the vacant mask of the dead. The arrow stood just below his right eye and must have killed him instantly. A fly lit on the fletching, felt the perch give under its weight, and darted away.

"Let me see to that," Gorgidas said dully. Like an automaton, the tribune held out his arm. The doctor washed the cut with a sponge soaked in vinegar. Stunned or no, Scaurus had all he could do to keep from crying out. Gorgidas pinned the gash closed, snipping off the tip of each *fibula* as he pushed it through. With his arm shrieking from the wound and the vinegar wash, Marcus hardly felt the pins go in. Tears began streaming down the Greek's face as he dressed the cut; he had to try three times before he could close the catch on the complex *fibula* that secured the end of the bandage.

"Are there more hurt?" he asked Scaurus. "There must be."

"Yes, a few." The doctor turned to go; Marcus stopped him with his good arm. "I'm sorrier than I know how to tell you," he said awkwardly. "To me he was a fine officer, a good man, and a friend, but—" He broke off, unsure how to continue.

"I've known you know, for all your discretion, Scaurus," Gorgidas said tiredly. "That doesn't matter any longer either, does it? Now let me be about my business, will you?"

Marcus still hesitated. "Can I do anything to help?"

"The gods curse you, Roman; you're a decent blockhead, but a block-head all the same. There he lies, all I hold dear in this worthless world, and me with all my training and skill in healing the hurt, and what good is it? What can I do with it? Feel him grow cold under my hands."

He shook free of the tribune. "Let me go, and we'll see what miracles of medicine I work for these other poor sods." He walked through the open doorway of the imperial residence, a lean, lonely man wearing anguish like a cloak.

"What ails your healer?" Alypia Garva asked.

Scaurus jumped; lost in his own thoughts, he had not heard her come up. "This is his close friend," he said shortly, nodding at Glabrio, "and mine as well." Hearing the rebuff, the princess drew back. Marcus chose not to care; the taste of triumph was bitter in his mouth.

"Lovely, isn't it?" Thorisin said to Marcus late that afternoon. He was speaking ironically; the little reception room in the imperial chambers had seen its share of fighting. There was a sword cut in the upholstery of the couch on which the tribune sat; horsehair stuffing leaked through it. A bloodstain marred the marble floor.

The Emperor went on, "When I set you over the cadasters, outlander, I thought you would be watching the pen-pushers, but it seems you flushed a noble instead."

Scaurus grew alert. "So they were Onomagoulos' men, then?" The assassins had fought in grim silence; for all the tribune knew, Ortaias Sphrantzes might have hired them.

Gavras, though, seemed to think he was being stupid. "Of course they're Baanes'. I hardly needed to question them to find that out, did I?"

"I don't understand," Scaurus said.

"Why else would that fornicating, polluted, pox-ridden son of a two-copper whore Elissaios Bouraphos have brought his bloody collection of boats back from Pityos? For a pleasure cruise? Phos' light, man, he's not hiding out there. You must have seen the galleys' sails as you marched in this morning."

Marcus felt his face grow warm. "I thought it was a grain convoy."

"Landsmen!" Gavras muttered, rolling his eyes. "It bloody well isn't, as anyone with eyes in his head should know. The plan was simple enough—as soon as I'm dealt with, across comes Baanes to take over, smooth as you like." Thorisin spat in vast contempt. "As if he could—that bald pimple hasn't the wit to break wind and piddle at the same time. And while he tries to murder me and I settle him, who gains? The Yezda, of course. I wonder if he's not in their pay."

The Emperor, Scaurus thought, had a dangerous habit of underestimating his foes. He had done so with the Sphrantzai, and now again with Onomagoulos, who, loyal or not, was a capable, if arrogant, soldier. Marcus started to warn Gavras of that, but remembered how the conversation had opened and asked instead, "Why credit"—That seemed a safer word than *blame*—"me with Baanes' plot?"

"Because you kept hounding him for Kybistra's tax roll. There were things in it he'd have done better not to write down."

"Ah?" Marcus made an interested noise to draw the Emperor out.

"Oh, truly, truly. Your friend Nepos filled the assassins so full of some potion of his that they spewed up everything they knew. Their captain, Skotos take him, knew plenty, too. Did you ever wonder why friend Baanes did so careful a job of slitting throats when we were waylaid last year after the parley?"

"Ah?" Marcus said again. He jumped as several men in heavy-soled boots tramped down the hallway, but they were only workmen coming to set things to rights once more. Live long enough in Videssos, he thought, and you'll see murderers under every cushion—but the day you don't, they'll be there.

Caught up in his own rekindled wrath, Thorisin did not notice the tribune's start. He went on, "The dung-faced midwife's mistake hired the knives himself and paid a premium for Ortaias' coin so no fingers would point his way even if something went wrong. But he put everything down on parchment so he could square himself with the Sphrantzai if he did kill me—and put it down on Kybistra's register. Why not? He had the thing with him; after all, he'd collected those taxes, when he ran there after Maragha. After that he could hardly let you see it, but he couldn't send a fake either, now could he?" The Emperor chuckled, imagining his rival's discomfiture.

Scaurus laughed, too. Videssian cadasters were invalid if they bore erasures or crossed-over lines; only fair copies went to the capital. And once there, they were festooned with seals of wax and lead and stamped with arcane bureaucratic stamps—to which, of course, Onomagoulos had no access once he was out in the provinces.

"He must have filched it as soon as he found out I was going to look over the receipts," the tribune decided.

"Very good," Gavras said, making small clapping motions of sardonic applause. Marcus' flush deepened. There were times when the subtle Videssians found his Roman straightforwardness monstrously amusing. Even seemingly bluff, blunt types like Thorisin and Onomagoulos proved as steeped in double-dealing as candied fruit in honey.

He sighed and spelled things out, as much for himself as for the Emperor: "A clerk, even a logothete, wouldn't have made much of some money-changing—probably figured he was lining his own purse and not worried much about it. But he knew I was on that beach, and he must have thought I'd connect things. I recall the fuss he made about its being Ortaias' money, aye, but I'd be lying if I said I was sure a few lines in a dull tax roll would have jogged my memory. He'd have been smarter letting things ride."

This time humorlessly, Thorisin chuckled again. "'The ill-doer's conscience abandons the assurance of Phos' path,'" he said, quoting from the Videssian holy books like a Greek from Homer. "He knew his guilt, whether you did or not."

"And if he is guilty, then that means Taron Leimmokheir is innocent!" Marcus said. Certainty blazed in him. He could not keep all the triumph from his voice, but did not think it mattered. There was such perfect logical clarity behind the idea, surely no one could fail to see it.

But Thorisin was frowning. "Why are you obsessed by that gray-whiskered traitor? What boots is that he plotted with Onomagoulos instead of Ortaias?" he said curtly. Recognizing inflexibility when he heard it, Scaurus gave up again. It would take more than logic to change Gavras' mind; he was like a man with a writing tablet who pushed his stylus through the wax and permanently scarred the wood beneath.

"Buck up, Roman dear, it's a hero y'are tonight, not the spook of a dead corp, the which wouldn't be invited to dinner at all, at all," Viridovix said as they walked toward the Hall of the Nineteen Couches. He deliberately exaggerated his brogue to try to cheer up Marcus, but spoke Videssian so Helvis and his own three companions would understand.

"Crave pardon; I didn't realize it showed so plainly," the tribune murmured; he had been thinking of Glabrio. Helvis squeezed his left arm. His right, under its bandages, he wished he could forget. The smile he managed to produce felt ghastly from the inside, but seemed to look good enough.

The ceremonies master, a portly man—not a eunuch, for he wore a thick beard—bowed several times in quick succession, like a marionette on a string, as the Roman party came up to the Hall's polished bronze doors. "Videssos is in your debt," he said, seizing Marcus' hand in his own pale, moist palm and bowing again. Then he turned and cried to those already present, "Lords and ladies, the most valiant Romans!" Scaurus blinked and forgave him the limp handclasp.

"The captain and *epoptes* Scaurus and the lady Helvis of Namdalen!" That one was easy for the fellow; worse challenges lay ahead. "Viridovix son of Drappes and his, ah, ladies!" The Celt's name was almost unprounceable for Videssians; the protocol chief's brief pause conveyed his opinion of Viridovix' arrangement. Marcus suddenly groaned—silently, by luck. Komitta Rhangavve would be here tonight.

He had no time to say anything. The ceremonies master was plowing ahead. "The senior centurion Gaius Philippus! The junior centurion Junius Blaesus!" Blaesus was a longtime underofficer and a good soldier, but Scaurus knew he was hardly a replacement for Quintus Glabrio. "The underofficer Minucius, and his lady Erene!" Not "the lady," Scaurus noted; damned snob of a flunky. Minucius, proud of his promotion, had burnished his chain mail till it gleamed.

Two more names completed the legionary party: "The *nakharar* Gagik Bagratouni, detachment-leader among the Romans! Zeprin the Red, Haloga guardsman in Roman service!" Despite persuasion, Gorgidas had chosen to be alone with his grief.

Bagratouni, too, still mourned, but time had dulled the cutting edge of his hurt. The leonine Vaspurakaner noble swept through the slimmer Videssians as he made his way toward the wine. Scaurus saw his eyes moving this way and that; no doubt Bagratouni was very conscious of the figure he cut, and of the ladies among whom he cut it.

The tribune and Helvis drifted over to a table covered with trays of crushed ice, on which reposed delicacies of various sorts, mostly from the ocean. "A dainty you won't see every day," said an elderly civil servant, pointing at a strip of octopus meat. "The curled octopus, you know, with only one row of suckers on each arm. Splendid!" Scaurus didn't know, but took the meat. It was chewy and vaguely sea-flavored, like all the other octopus he'd ever eaten.

He wondered what the gastrophile beside him would have thought of such Roman exotica as dormice in poppy seeds and honey.

A small orchestra played softly in the background: flutes, stringed instruments whose names he still mixed up, and a tinkling clavichord. Helvis clapped her hands in delight. "That's the same rondo they were playing when we first met here," she said. "Do you remember?"

"The night? Naturally. The—what did you call it? You'd know I was lying if I said yes." A lot had happened that evening. Not only had he met Helvis—though Hemond had still been alive then, of course—but also Alypia Gavra. And Avshar, for that matter; as always, he worried whenever he thought of the sorcerer-prince.

They drifted through separate crowds of bureaucrats, soldiers, and ambassadors, exchanging small talk. Scaurus was unusual in having friends among all three groups. The two imperial factions despised each other. The Videssian officers preferred the company of mercenaries they distrusted to the pen-pushers they loathed, which merely confirmed their boorishness in the civil servants' eyes.

Taso Vones, an imposingly tall Videssian lady—*not* Plakidia Teletze—on his arm, bowed to the tribune. "Where are you come from?" he asked with a twinkle in his eye. "How to shoe a heavy cavalry horse, or the best way to compose a memorandum on a subject of no intrinsic worth?"

"The best way to do that is not to," Helvis said at once.

"Blasphemy, my dear; seal-stampers burn people who express such thoughts. But then, I find cavalry horses no more inspiring." With that attitude, thought Scaurus, it was easy to see why Vones held aloof from warriors and bureaucrats alike.

"His Sanctity, Phos' Patriarch Balsamon!" the ceremonies master called, and the feast paused for a respectful moment as the fat old man waddled into the chamber. For all his graceless step, he had a presence that filled it up.

He looked round, then said with a smile and a mock-rueful sigh, "Ah, if only you paid me such heed in the High Temple!" He plucked a crystal wine goblet from its bed of ice and drained it with obvious enjoyment.

"That man takes nothing seriously," Soteric said disapprovingly. Though he did not shave the back of his head in usual island fashion, Helvis' brother still looked very much the unassimilated Namdalener in high tight trousers and short fur jacket.

Marcus said, "It's not like you to waste your time worrying over his failings. After all, he's a heretic to you, is he not?" He grinned as his brother-in-law fumbled for an answer. The truth, he thought, was simple—the Videssian patriarch was too interesting a character for anyone to ignore.

Servants began carrying the tables of hors d'oeuvres back to the kitchens and replacing them with dining tables and gilded chairs. From previous banquets in the Hall of the Nineteen Couches, Marcus knew that was a signal the Emperor would be coming in soon. He realized he needed to speak to Balsamon before Thorisin arrived.

"What now, my storm-crow friend?" the patriarch said as Scaurus approached. "Whenever you come up to me with that look of grim determination in your eye, I know you've found your way into more trouble."

Like Alypia Gavra, Balsamon had the knack of making the tribune feel transparent. He tried to hide his annoyance, and was sure Balsamon saw that, too. More flustered than ever, he launched into his tale.

"Leimmokheir, eh?" Balsamon said when he was done. "Aye, Taron is a good man." As far as Scaurus could remember, that was the first time he'd heard the patriarch judge anyone so. But Balsamon went on, "What makes you think my intercession would be worth a moldy apple?"

"Why," Marcus floundered, "if Gavras won't listen to you—"

"—He won't listen to anyone, which will likely be the case. He's a stubborn youngster," the patriarch said, perfectly at ease speaking thus of his sovereign. His little black eyes, still sharp in their folds of flesh, measured the Roman. "And well you know it, too. Why keep flogging a dead mule?"

"I made a promise," Marcus said slowly, unable to find a better answer.

Before Balsamon could reply, the ceremonies master was crying out, "Her Majesty the Princess Alypia Gavra! The lady Komitta Rhangavve! His Imperial Majesty, the Avtokrator of the Videssians, Thorisin Gavras!"

Men bowed low to show their respect for the Emperor; as the occasion was social rather than ceremonial, no proskynesis was required. Women dropped curtsies. Thorisin bobbed his head amiably, then called, "Where are the guests of honor?" Servitors rounded up the Romans and their ladies and brought them to the Emperor, who presented them to the crowd for fresh applause.

Komitta Rhangavve's eyes narrowed dangerously as they flicked from one of Viridovix' lemans to the next. She looked very beautiful in a clinging skirt of flower-printed linen; Marcus would sooner have taken a poisonous snake to bed. Viridovix did not seem to notice her glare, but the Celt was not happy, either. "Is something wrong?" the tribune asked as they walked toward the dining tables.

"Aye, summat. Arigh tells me the Videssians will be sending an embassy to his clan. They're fain to hire mercenaries, and the lad himself will be going with them to help persuade his folk to take service with the Empire. A half-year's journey and more it is, and him the bonniest wight to drink with I've found in the city. I'll miss the little omadhaun, beshrew me if I won't."

Stewards seated the legionaries in accordance with their prominence of the evening. Marcus found himself at the right hand of the imperial party, next to the Princess Alypia. The Emperor sat between her and Komitta Rhangavve, who was on his left. Had she been his wife rather than mistress, her place and the princess' would have been reversed. As it was, she was next to Viridovix, an arrangement Scaurus thought ill-omened. Unaware of anything amiss, the Gaul's three longtime companions chattered among themselves, excited by their high-ranking company.

The first course was a soup of onions and pork, its broth delightfully delicate in flavor. Marcus spooned it down almost without tasting it, waiting for the explosion on his left. But Komitta seemed to be practicing tact, a virtue he had not associated with her. He relaxed and enjoyed the last few spoonfuls of soup and and was sorry when a servant took the empty bowl away. His goblet of wine, now, never disappeared. Whenever it was empty, a steward would be there to fill it again from a shining silver carafe. Even if it was sticky-sweet Videssian wine, it dulled the ache in his arm.

Little roasted partridge hens appeared, stuffed with sautéed mushrooms. Balsamon, who sat next to Helvis at the tribune's right, demolished his with an appetite that would have done credit to a man half his age. He patted his ample belly, saying to Scaurus, "You can see I've gained it honestly."

Alypia Garva leaned toward the patriarch, saying, "You would not be yourself without it, as you know full well." She spoke affectionately, as to a favorite old uncle or grandfather. Balsamon rolled his eyes and winced, pantomiming being cut to the quick.

"Respect is hard for a plump old fool like me to get, you'll note," he said to Helvis. "I should be mighty in my outrage like the patriarchs of old and be a prelate to terrify the heretic. You *are* terrified, I hope?" he added, winking at her.

"Not in the least," she answered promptly. "No more than you convince anyone when you play the buffoon."

Balsamon's eyes were still amused in a way, but no longer merry. "You have some of your brother's terrible honesty in you," he said, and Scaurus did not think it was altogether a compliment.

Courses came and went: lobster tails in drawn butter and capers; rich pastries baked to resemble peahens' eggs; raisins, figs, and sweet dates; mild and sharp cheeses; peppery ground lamb wrapped in grape leaves; roast goose—sniffing the familiar cheese and cinnamon sauce, Marcus declined—cabbage soup; stewed pigeons with sausage and onions . . . with, of course, appropriate wines for each. Scaurus' arm seemed far away. He felt the tip of his nose grow numb, a sure sign he was getting drunk.

Nor was he the only one. The great count Drax, who wore Videssian-style robes, unlike Soteric and Utprand, was singing one of the fifty-two scurrilous verses of the imperial army's marching song, loudly accompanied by Zeprin the Red and Mertikes Zigabenos. And Viridovix had just broken up the left side of the imperial table with a story about—Marcus dug a finger in his ear, trying not to believe he was hearing the Celt's effrontery—a man with four wives.

Thorisin roared out laughter with the rest, stopping only to wipe his eyes. "I thank your honor," Viridovix said. Komitta Rhangavve was not laughing. Her long, slim fingers, nails painted the color of blood, looked uncommonly like claws.

Dessert was fetched in, a light one after the great feast: crushed ice from the imperial cold cellars, flavored with sweet syrups. A favorite winter treat, it was hard to come by in the warmer seasons.

The Emperor rose, a signal for everyone else to do the same. Servants began clearing away the mountains of dirty dishes and bowls. But even if the food was gone, wine and talk still flowed freely—perhaps, indeed, more so than before dinner.

Balsamon took Thorisin Gavras to one side and began speaking urgently. Marcus could not hear what the patriarch was saying, but Thorisin's growled answer was loud enough to turn heads. "Not you, too? No, I've said a hundred times—now it's a hundred and one!" Rather muzzily, the tribune wished he could disappear. It did not look as though Taron Leimmokheir would see the outside of his dungeon any time soon.

As the guests decided no further trouble was coming on the heels of Gavras' outburst, the level of conversation picked up again. Soteric came over to tell Helvis some news of Namdalen he'd got from one of Drax' aides. "What? Bedard Wood-tooth, become count of Nustad on the mainland? I don't believe it," she said. "Excuse me, darling, I have to hear this with my own ears." And she was gone with her brother, exclaiming excitedly in the island dialect.

Left to his own devices, the tribune took another drink. After enough rounds, he decided, Videssian wine tasted fine. The interior of the Hall of the Nineteen Couches, though, wanted to spin whenever he moved his head.

"Piss-pot!" That was Komitta Rhangavve's wildcat screech, aimed at Viridovix. "The son of a pimp in your joke would be no good to any of his wives after he had his ballocks cut off him!" She threw what was left in her goblet in the Celt's face and smashed the cut crystal on the floor. Then she spun and stamped out of the hall, every step echoing in the startled silence.

"What was that in aid of?" the Emperor asked, staring at her retreating back. He had been talking with Drax and Zigabenos and, like Scaurus, missed the beginning of the scene.

Red wine was dripping from Viridovix's mustaches, but he had lost none of his aplomb. "Och, the lady decided she'd be after taking offense at the little yarn I told at table," he said easily. A servitor brought him a damp towel; he ran it over his face. "I wish she had done it sooner. As is, I'm left wearing no better than the dregs."

Thorisin snorted, reassured by the Celt's glib reply and by what he knew of Komitta's fiery temper—which was plenty. "All right, then, let's hope this is more to your taste." He beckoned a waiter to his side and gave the man his own goblet to take to Viridovix. People murmured at the favor shown the Gaul; the room relaxed once more.

Gaius Philippus caught Marcus' eye from across the hall and hiked his shoulders up and down in an exaggerated sigh of relief. The tribune nodded—for a moment, he'd been frightened nearly sober.

He wondered just how much he had drunk; too much, from the pounding ache that was beginning behind his eyes. Helvis was still deep in conversation with a couple of Namdalener officers. The dining hall suddenly seemed intolerably noisy, crowded, and hot. Marcus weaved toward the doors. Maybe the fresh air outside would clear his head.

The ceremonies master bowed as he made his way into the night. He nodded back, then regretted it—any motion was enough to give his headache new fuel. He sucked in the cool nighttime air gratefully; it felt sweeter than any wine.

He went down the stairs with a drunken man's caution. The music and the buzz of talk receded behind him, nor was he sorry to hear them fade. Even the tree frogs piping in the nearby citrus groves grated on his ears. He sighed, already wincing from tomorrow's hangover.

He peered up at the stars, hoping their calm changelessness might bring him some relief. The night was clear and moonless, but the heavens still were not at their best. Videssos' lights and the smoke rising from countless hearths and fireplaces veiled the dimmer stars away.

He wandered aimlessly for a couple of minutes, his hobnailed *caligae* clicking on the flagstone path and then silent as they bit into grass. An abrupt intake of breath made him realize he was not alone. "Who the—?" he said, groping for his sword hilt. Visions of assassins flashed through his head—a landing party from Bouraphos' ships out there, perhaps, stealing up on the Hall of the Nineteen Couches.

"I'm not a band of hired killers," Alypia Gavra said, and Scaurus heard the sardonic edge that colored so much of her speech.

His hand jerked away from the scabbard as if it had become red-hot. "Your pardon, my lady," he stammered. "You surprised me—I came out for a breath of air."

"As did I, some little while ago, and found I preferred the quiet to the brabble back there. You may share it with me, if you like."

Still feeling foolish, the tribune approached her. He could hear the noise from the dining hall, but at a distance it was bearable. The light that streamed through the Hall's wide windows was pale, too, the princess beside him little more than a silhouette. He took parade rest unconsciously, a relaxed stance from which to savor the night.

After they stood a while in silence, Alypia turned to him, her face musing. "You are a strange man, Marcus Aemilius Scaurus," she said finally, her Videssian accent making the sonorous sounds of his full name somehow musical. "I am never quite sure what you are thinking."

"No?" Scaurus said, surprised again. "It's always seemed to me you could read me like a signboard."

"If it sets your mind at ease, not so. You fall into no neat category; you're no arrogant noble from the provinces, all horsesweat and iron, nor yet one of the so-clever seal-stampers who would sooner die than call something by its right name. And you hardly make an ordinary mercenary captain—there's not enough wrecker in you. So, outlander, what are you?" She studied him, as if trying to pull the secret from his eyes.

The question, he knew, demanded an honest answer; he wished his wits were clearer, to give her one. "A survivor," he said at last.

"Ah," she said very low, more an exhalation than a word. "No wonder we seem to understand each other, then."

"Do we?" he wondered, but his arms folded round her as her face tilted up.

She felt slim, almost boyish, under his hands, the more so because he was used to Helvis' opulent curves. But her mouth and tongue were sweet against his—for a couple of heartbeats, until she gave a smothered gasp and wrenched herself away.

Alarmed, Marcus tried to flog his brain toward an apology, but her sad, weary gesture stopped him before he could begin. "The fault is not yours. Blame—times now gone," she said, casting about for a circumlocution. "No matter what I wish to feel, there are memories I cannot set aside so easily."

The tribune felt his hands bunch into fists. Not the least of Avshar's crimes, he thought once more, was the easy death he gave Vardanes Sphrantzes.

He reached out to touch her cheek. It was wet against his hand. She started to flinch again, but sensed the gesture was as much one of understanding as a caress. Her wounded strength, the mix of vulnerability and composure in her, drew him powerfully; it was all he could do to stand steady. Yet however much he wanted to take her in his arms, he was sure he would frighten her away forever if he did.

She said, "When I was a painted harlot you showed me a way to bear what I had been, but because of what I was then, I can have no gift for you now. Life is a tangled skein, is it not?" Her laugh was small and shaky.

"That you are here and healing is gift enough," Scaurus replied. He did not say he thought he might be too drunk to do a woman justice in any case.

But that was one thought Alypia missed. Her drawn features softened; she leaned forward to kiss him gently. "You'd best go back," she said. "After all, you are the guest of honor."

"I suppose so." The tribune had nearly forgotten the banquet.

Alypia stayed beside him no more than a second before drawing back. "Go on," she said again.

Reluctantly, Marcus started back toward the Hall of the Nineteen Couches. When he turned round for a last look at Alypia, she was already gone. A trace of motion among the trees might—or might not—have been her, slipping toward the imperial residence. The tribune trudged on, his head whirling with wine and thought.

He knew most mercenaries, if offered a chance at an imperial connection, would cut any ties that stood in the way. Drax would, instantly, he thought; the man who was too adaptable by half. What was the nickname that Athenian had earned during the Peloponnesian War? "The stage boot," that was it, because he fit on either foot.

But Scaurus could not find it in himself to imitate the great count. For all the attraction and fondness he felt for Alypia Gavra, he was not ready to cast Helvis aside. They both sometimes strained at the bond between them, but despite quarrels and differences it would not break, nor, most of the time, did he want it to. Then, too, there was Dosti. . . .

"We missed you, my lord," the ceremonies master said with another low bow as Marcus stumbled back into the hall. The Roman hardly heard. For a man who called himself a survivor, he thought, he had an uncommon gift for complicating his life.

XIII

"Phos blast that insolent Treacher Bouraphos into a thousand pieces and roast every one of them over a dung fire!" Thorisin Gavras burst out. The Emperor stood on Videssos' sea wall, watching one of his galleys sink. Two more fled back to the city, closely pursued by the rebel drungarios' ships. Heads bobbed in the water of the Cattle-Crossing as sailors from the stricken vessel snatched at spars or swam toward Videssos and safety. Not all would reach it; tiny in the distance, black fins angled toward them.

Gavras ran an irritable hand through his hair, ruffled by the sea breeze. "And why have I no admirals with the sense not to piss into the wind?" he grated. "A two-year-old in the bathhouse sails his toy boat with more finesse than those bullheads showed!"

Along with the other officers by the Emperor, Scaurus did his best to keep his face straight. He understood Thorisin's frustration. Onomagoulos, on the western shore of the Cattle-Crossing, led an army far weaker than the one Gavras had mustered against it. What did it matter, though, when the Emperor could not come to grips with his foe?

"Now if you had some ships from t'Duchy—" Utprand Dagober's son began, but Thorisin's glare stopped even the blunt-spoken Namdalener in mid-sentence. Drax looked at his countryman as if at a dullard. Everyone knew the Emperor suspected the islanders, his eye seemed to say and to ask what the point was of antagonizing him without need.

Cross as a baited bear, Gavras swung round on Marcus. "I suppose you'll be after me next, telling me to turn Leimmokheir loose."

"Why, no, your Majesty, not at all," the tribune said innocently. "If you were going to listen to me, you would have done that long since."

He scratched at his arm. It itched fiercely. Still, it was healing well enough that Gorgidas had pulled the pins from it the day before. The feel of the metal sliding through his flesh, though not painful, had been unpleasant enough to make him shudder at the memory.

"Bah!" Thorisin turned his gaze out to the Cattle-Crossing again. Only scattered timbers showed where his warship had sunk; Bouraphos' vessels were already resuming their patrol. As if continuing an argument, the Emperor said, "What would it gain me to let him go? He'd surely turn against me now, after being shut up all these months."

Unexpectedly, Mertikes Zigabenos spoke up for Leimmokheir. The guards officer had come to admire the older sailor, who showed repeatedly while the Sphrantzai held Videssos how a good man could keep his honor under a wicked regime. Zigabenos said, "If he grants you an oath of loyalty, he will keep it. No matter what you say, sir, Taron Leimmokheir would not forswear himself. He fears the ice too much for that."

"And besides," Marcus said, thrusting home with a pleasure for which he felt no guilt at all, "what's the difference if he does betray you? You'd still be outadmiraled and hardly worse off, whereas—" He fell silent, leaving Thorisin to work the contrary chain of logic for himself.

The Emperor, still in his foul mood, only grunted. But his hand tugged thoughtfully at his beard, and he did not fly into a rage at the very notion of releasing Leimmokheir. His will was granite, thought the tribune, but even granite crumbles in the end.

"So you think he'll let him go?" Helvis said that evening after Scaurus recounted the day's events. "One for you, then."

"I suppose so, unless he does turn his coat once he's free. That would drop the chamber pot into the stew for fair."

"I don't think it will happen. Leimmokheir is honest," Helvis said seriously. Marcus respected her opinion; she had been in Videssos years longer than he and knew a good deal about its leaders. Moreover, what she said confirmed everyone else's view of the jailed admiral—except the Emperor's.

But when he tried to draw her out further, she did not seem interested in matters political, which was unlike her. "Is anything wrong?" he asked at last. He wondered if she had somehow guessed the attraction growing between himself and Alypia Gavra and dreaded the scene that would cause.

Instead, she put down the skirt whose hem she had been mending and smiled at the tribune. He thought he should know that look; there was a mischievous something in her eyes he had seen before. He placed it just as she spoke, "I'm sorry, darling, my wits were somewhere else. I was trying to reckon when the baby will be due. As near as I can make it, it should be a little before the festival of sun-turning."

Marcus was silent so long her sparkle disappeared. "Aren't you pleased?" she asked sharply.

"Of course I am," he answered, and was telling the truth. Too many upper-class Romans were childless by choice, beloved only by inheritance seekers. "You took me by surprise, is all."

He walked over and kissed her, then poked her in the ribs. She yelped. "You like taking me by surprise that way," he accused. "You did when you were expecting Dosti, too."

As if the mention of his name was some kind of charm, the baby woke up and started to cry. Helvis made a wry face. She got up and unswaddled him. "Are you wet or do you just want to be cuddled?" she demanded. It proved to be the latter; in a few minutes Dosti was asleep again.

"That doesn't happen as often as it used to," Marcus said. He sighed. "I suppose I'll have to get used to waking up five times a night again. Why don't you arrange to have a three-year-old and save us the fuss?" That earned him a return poke.

He hugged her, careful both of her pregnancy and his own tender arm. She helped him draw the blouse off over her head. Yet even when they lay together naked on the sleeping-mat, the tribune saw Alypia Gavra's face in his mind, remembered the feel of her lips. Only then did he understand why he had paused before showing gladness at Helvis' news.

He realized something else, too, and chuckled under his breath. "What is it, dear?" she asked, touching his cheek.

"Nothing really. Just a foolish notion." She made an inquisitive noise, but he did not explain further. There was no way, he thought, to tell her that now he understood why she slipped every so often and called him by her former lover's name.

"Let's have a look at that," Gorgidas ordered the next morning. Marcus mimed a salute and extended his arm to the doctor. It was anything but pretty; the edges of the gash were still raised and red, and it was filled with crusty brown scab. But the Greek grunted in satisfaction at what he saw and again when he sniffed the wound. "There's no corruption in there," he told the tribune. "Your flesh knits well."

"That lotion of yours does good work, for all its bite." Gorgidas had dosed the cut with a murky brown fluid he called barbarum: a compound of powdered verdigris, litharge, alum, pitch, and resin mixed in equal parts of vinegar and oil. The Roman had winced every time it was applied, but it kept a wound from going bad.

Gorgidas merely grunted again, unmoved by the praise. Nothing had moved him much, not since Quintus Glabrio fell. Now he changed the subject, asking, "Do you know when the Emperor intends to send his embassy to the Arshaum?"

"No time soon, not with Bouraphos' ships out there to sink anything that sticks its nose out of the city's harbors. Why?"

The Greek studied him bleakly. Marcus saw how haggard he had become, his slimness now gaunt, his hair ragged where he had chopped a lock away in mourning for Glabrio. "Why?" Gorgidas echoed. "Nothing simpler; I intend to go with it." He set his jaw, meeting Scaurus' stare without flinching.

"You can't," was the tribune's first startled response.

"And why not? How do you propose to stop me?" The doctor's voice was dangerously calm.

"I can order you to stay."

"Can you, in law? That would be a pretty point for the barristers back in Rome. I am attached to the legions, aye, but am I of them? I think not, any more than a sutler or a town bootmaker who serves at contract. But that's neither here nor there. Unless you choose to chain me, I will not obey your order."

"But why?" Marcus said helplessly. He had no intention of putting Gorgidas in irons. That the Greek was his friend counted for less than his certainty that Gorgidas was stubborn enough not to serve if made to remain against his will.

"The why is simple enough; I plan to add an excursus on the tribes and customs of the Arshaum to my history and I need more information than Arigh can—or cares to—give me. Ethnography, I think, is something I can hope to do a proper job of."

His bitterness gave Scaurus the key he needed. "You think medicine is not? What of all of us you've healed, some a dozen times? What of this?" He held his wounded arm out to the physician.

"What of it? It's still a bloody mess, if you want to know." In his wretchedness and self-disgust, Gorgidas could not see the successes his skill had won. "A Videssian healer would have put it right in minutes, instead of this week and a half's worth of worry over seeing if it chooses to fester."

"If he could do anything at all," Marcus retorted. "Some hurts they can't cure, and the power drains from them if they use it long. But you always give your best."

"A poor, miserable best it is, too. With my best, Minucius would be dead now, and Publius Flaccus and Cotilius Rufus after Maragha, and how many more? You're a clodhopper to reckon me a doctor, when I can't so much as learn the art that gave them life." The Greek's eyes were haunted. "And I can't. We saw that, didn't we?"

"So you'll hie yourself off to the steppe, then, and forget even trying?"

Gorgidas winced, but he said, "You can't shame me into staying either, Scaurus." The tribune flushed, angry he was so obvious.

The Greek went on, "In Rome I wasn't a bad physician, but here I'm hardly more than a joke. If I have some small talent at history, perhaps I can leave something worthwhile with that. Truly, Marcus," he said, and Scaurus was touched, for the doctor had not used his praenomen before, "all of you would be better off with a healer-priest to mend you. You've suffered my fumblings long enough."

Clearly, nothing ordinary would change Gorgidas' mind. Casting about for any straw, Marcus exclaimed, "But if you leave us, who will Viridovix have to argue with?"

"Now that one strikes close to the clout," Gorgidas admitted, surprised into smiling. "For all his bluster, I'll miss the red-maned bandit. It's still no hit, though; as long as he has Gaius Philippus, he'll never go short a quarrel."

Defeated, Scaurus threw his hands in the air. "Be it so, then. But for the first time, I'm glad Bouraphos joined the rebels. Not only does that force you to stay with us longer, it also gives you more time to come to your senses."

"I don't think I've left them. I might well have gone even if—things were otherwise." The Greek paused, tossed his head. "Uselessness is not a pleasant feeling." He rose. "Now if you'll excuse me, Gawtruz has promised to tell me of his people's legends of how they overran Thatagush. A comparison with the accounts by Videssian historians should prove fascinating, don't you think?"

Whatever Marcus' answer was, he did not wait to hear it.

The tribune stood at stiff attention, below and to the right of the great imperial throne. For this ceremony he did not enjoy the place of honor; Balsamon the patriarch was a pace closer to the seated Emperor. Somehow Videssos' chief prelate contrived to look rumpled in vestments of blue silk and cloth-of-gold. His pepper-and-salt beard poured down in a disorderly stream over the seed pearls adorning the breast of his chasuble.

At the Emperor's left side stood Alypia Gavra, her costume as somber as protocol would permit. Scaurus had not seen her save at a distance since the feast two weeks before; twice he had requested an audience, and twice got no reply. He was almost afraid to meet her eye, but her nod as they assembled in the throne room had been reassuring.

With no official status, Komitta Rhangavve was relegated to the courtiers who filed in to flank the long central colonnade. In that sea of plump bland faces her lean, hard beauty was like a falcon's feral grace among so many pigeons. At the sight of the Roman, her eyes darted about to see if Viridovix was present; Marcus was glad he was not.

An expectant hush filled the chamber. The Grand Gates, closed after the functionaries' entrance, swung slowly open once more, to reveal a single man silhouetted against the brightness outside. His long, rolling strides seemed alien to that place of gliding eunuchs and soft-footed officials.

Taron Leimmokheir wore fresh robes, but they hung loosely about his prison-thinned frame. Nor had his release robbed him of the pallor given by long months hidden from sun and sky. His hair and beard, while clean, were still untrimmed. Scaurus heard he had refused a barber; his words were, "Let Gavras see me as he had me." The tribune wondered what else Leimmokheir might refuse. So far as he knew, no bargains had been struck.

The ex-admiral came up to the imperial throne, then paused, looking Thorisin full in the face. In Videssian court etiquette it was the height of rudeness; Marcus heard torches crackle in the silence enveloping the courtroom. Then, with deliberation and utmost dignity, Leimmokheir slowly prostrated himself before his soverign.

"Get up, get up," Thorisin said impatiently; not the words of formula, but the court ministers had already despaired of changing that.

Leimmokheir rose. Looking as if every word tasted bad to him, the Emperor continued, "Know you are pardoned of the charge of conspiracy against our person, and that all properties and rights previously deemed forfeit are restored to you." There was a sigh of outdrawn breath from the courtiers. Leimmokheir began a second proskynesis; Thorisin stopped him with a gesture.

"Now we come down to it," he said, sounding more like a merchant in a hard bargain than Avtokrator of the Videssians. Leimmokheir leaned forward, too. "Does it please you to serve me as my drungarios of the fleet against Bouraphos and Onomagoulos?" Marcus noted that the first person plural of the pardon had disappeared.

"Why you and not them?" Prison had not cost Leimmokheir his forthrightness, Scaurus saw. Courtiers blanched, appalled at the plain speech.

The Emperor, though, looked pleased. His answer was equally direct. "Because I am not a man who hires murderers."

"No, instead you throw people into jail." The fat ceremonies master, who stood among the high dignitaries, seemed ready to faint. Thorisin sat stony-faced, his arms folded, waiting for a real reply. At last Leimmokheir dipped his head; his unkempt gray locks flopped over his face.

"Excellent!" Thorisin breathed, now with the air of a gambler after throwing the suns. He nodded to Balsamon. "The patriarch will keep your oath of allegiance." He fairly purred; to a man of Taron Leimmokheir's religious scruples, that oath would be binding as iron shackles.

Balsamon stepped forward, producing a small copy of the Videssian scriptures from a fold of his robe. But the drungarios waved him away; his seaman's voice, used to overcoming storm winds, filled the throne room: "No, Gavras, I swear no oaths to you."

For a moment, everyone froze; the Emperor's eyes went hard and cold. "What then, Leimmokheir?" he asked, and danger rode his words. "Should your say-so be enough for me?"

He intended sarcasm, but the admiral took him at face value. "Yes, by Phos, or what's your pardon worth? I'll be your man, but not your hound. If you don't trust me without a spiked collar of words round my neck, send me back to the jug, and be damned to you." And he waited in turn, his pride proof against whatever the Emperor chose.

A slow flush climbed Thorisin's cheeks. His bodyguards' hands tightened on their spears. There had been Avtokrators—and not a few of them—who would have answered such defiance with blood. In his years Balsamon had seen more than one of that stripe. He said urgently, "Your Majesty, may I—"

"No." Thorisin cut him off with a single harsh word. Marcus realized again the overwhelming power behind the Videssian imperial office in its formal setting. In chambers, Balsamon would have rolled his eyes and kept on arguing; now, bowing, he fell silent. Only Leimmokheir remained uncowed, drawing strength from what he had already endured.

The Emperor still bore him no liking, but grudging respect slowly replaced the anger on his face. "All right, then." He wasted no time with threats or warnings; it was clear they meant nothing to the reinstated admiral.

Leimmokheir, as abrupt as Gavras, bowed and turned to go. "Where are you away so fast?" Thorisin demanded, suspicious afresh.

"The docks, of course. Where else would you have your drungarios go?" Leimmokheir neither looked back nor broke stride. If he could have slammed the Grand Gates behind him, Scaurus thought, he would have done that, too. Between them, the stubborn admiral and equally strong-willed Emperor had managed to turn Videssian ceremonial on its ear. The assembled courtiers shook their heads as they trooped from the throne room, remembering better-run spectacles.

"Don't you just wander off," Thorisin said to the tribune as he started to follow them out. "I have a job in mind for you."

"Sire?"

"And spare me that innocent blue-eyed gaze," the Emperor growled. "For all the wenches it charms, it goes for nothing with me." Marcus saw the corner of Alypia Gavra's mouth twitch, but she did not look at him. Her uncle went on, "You were the one who wanted that gray-bearded puritan loose, so you can keep an eye on him. If he so much as breathes hard, I expect to hear about it. D'you understand me?"

"Aye." The Roman had half expected that order.

"Just 'aye'?" Gavras glared at him, balked of the chance to vent his anger further. "Go on, take yourself off, then."

As Marcus walked back to the legionaries' barracks, Alypia Gavra caught him up. "I have to ask your pardon," she said. "It was wrong of me to pretend I never got your requests to see me."

"The situation was unusual," the tribune replied. He could not speak as freely as he would have liked. The path was busy; more than one head turned at the sight of a mercenary captain, even one of the prominence Scaurus had won, walking side by side with the Avtokrator of the Videssians' niece.

"To say the least." Alypia raised one eyebrow. She, too, used phrases with many meanings. Marcus wondered if she had deliberately chosen to meet him in public to keep things between them as impersonal as possible.

"I hope," he said carefully, "you don't feel I was, ah, taking undue advantage of the situation."

She gave him a steady look. "There are many benefits an officer with an eye for the main chance might gain; something, I might add, I am as capable of seeing as any officer of that stripe."

"That is the main reason I hesitated so long."

"I never believed here"—Alypia laid her hand on her left breast—"you were such a man. It is, though, something one considers." She cocked her head, still studying him. "'The main reason'? What of your young son? What of the family you've made since you came to Videssos? At the banquet you seemed well content with your lady."

Scaurus bit his lip. It was chastening to hear his own thoughts come back at him from the princess' mouth. "And you claimed to have trouble reading me!" he said, embarrassed out of indirection.

For the first time Alypia smiled. She made as if to put her hand on his arm, but stopped, remembering better than he where they were. She said quietly, "Were those thoughts not there to read, the, ah, situation"—Her mockery of the tribune's earlier pause was gentle—"Would never have arisen."

The path divided. "We go different ways now, I think," she said, and turned toward the flowering cherries that concealed the imperial residence.

"Aye, for a while," Marcus answered, but only to himself.

"Look what Gavras gives me to work with!" Taron Leimmokheir shouted. "Why didn't he tell me to go hang myself from a yardarm while I was about it?" He answered his own question, "He thought my weight'd break it, and he was right!" He looked disgustedly about the Neorhesian harbor.

The capital's great northern anchorage was not a part of the city Scaurus knew well. The Romans had patrolled near the harbor of Kontoskalion, on Videssos' south-facing coast, and had also embarked on campaign against the Yezda from there. But Kontoskalion was a toy port next to the Neorhesian harbor, named for the long-dead city prefect who had supervised its building.

There were ships aplenty at the docks jutting out into the Videssian Sea, a veritable forest of masts. But all too many of them belonged to fat, sluggish trading ships and tiny fishing craft like the one Marcus had sailed on when Thorisin's forces sneaked over the Cattle-Crossing. These, by now, rode high in the water. Their cargoes long since unloaded, they were trapped

631

in Videssos by Elissaios Bouraphos outside. As had been only proper—
then—Bouraphos had taken the heart of the Empire's war fleet when he
sailed for Pityos and kept it when he joined Onomagoulos in rebellion.

Leimmokheir had precious little left: ten or so triremes, and perhaps
a dozen smaller two-banked ships like the ones the tribune knew as Liburnians. He was outnumbered almost three to one, and Bouraphos also
had the better captains and crews.

"What's to do?" Marcus asked, worried the drungarios thought the
task beyond him. After his outburst, Leimmokheir was staring out to
sea, not at the choppy little waves dancing inside the breakwater, but
beyond, to the vast sweep of empty horizon.

The admiral did not seem to hear him for a moment; he slowly came
back to himself. "Hmm? Phos' light, I truly don't know, left here with the
lees to drink. Wait and watch for a bit, I expect, until I understand how
things have gone since I was taken off the board. I've come back facing a
new direction, and everything looks strange."

In the Videssian board game, captured pieces could be used against
their original owners and change sides several times in the course of a
game. It was, Scaurus thought, a game very much in its makers' image.

Seeing the Roman troubled by his answer, Leimmokheir slapped
him on the shoulder. "Never lose hope," he said seriously. "The Namdaleni are heretics who imperil their souls with their belief, but they have
the right of that. No matter how bad the storm looks, it has to end sometime. Skotos lays despair before men as a snare."

He was the living proof of his own philosophy, Scaurus thought; his
imprisonment had dropped from him as if it had never been. But the
tribune noted he had still not answered the question.

The last clear notes of the pandoura faded inside the Roman barracks.
Applause, a storm of it, followed swiftly. Senpat Sviodo laid aside his
stringed instrument, a smile of pleasure on his handsome, swarthy face.
He lifted a mug of wine in salute to his audience.

"That was marvelous," Helvis said. "You made me see the mountains of Vaspurakan plain as if they stood before me. Phos gave you a
great gift. Were you not a soldier, your music would soon make you rich."

"Curious you should say that," he answered sheepishly. "Back in my teens I thought about running off with a troupe of strummers who were playing at my father's holding."

"Why didn't you?"

"He found out and stropped his belt on my backside. He had the right of it, Phos rest him. I was needed there; even then, the Yezda were thick as tax collectors round a man who's dug up treasure. And had I gone, look what I would have missed." He slid his arm round Nevrat beside him. The bright ribbons streaming from his three-peaked Vaspurakaner cap tickled her neck; she brushed them away as she snuggled closer to her husband.

Marcus sipped from his own wine cup. He had nearly forgotten what good company the two young westerners made, not just for Senpat's music but for the gusto and good cheer with which he—indeed, both of them—faced life. And they were so obviously pleased with each other as to make every couple around them happier simply by their presence.

"Where is your friend with the mustaches like melted bronze?" Nevrat asked the tribune. "He has a fine voice. I was hoping to hear him sing with Senpat tonight, even if Videssian songs are the only ones they both understand."

"'Little bird with a yellow bill—'" Gaius Philippus began, his baritone raucous. Nevrat winced and threw a walnut at him. Ever alert, he caught it out of the air, then cracked it with the pommel of his dagger.

The distraction did not make her forget her question. She quirked an eyebrow at Scaurus. He said lamely. "There was some business or other he said he had to attend to; I don't know just what." But I can make a fair guess, he thought.

Nevrat's other eyebrow went up when she saw him hesitate. Unlike most Videssian women, she did not pluck them to make them finer, but they did nothing to mar her strong-featured beauty.

In this case, Marcus was immune to such blandishments. He wished he had no part of Viridovix' secret and would not spread it further.

Nevrat turned to Helvis. "You're a big girl, dear. You should do more than pick at your food."

Said in a different tone, the words could have rankled, but Nevrat was obviously concerned. Helvis' answering smile was a trifle wan. "There'd just be more for me to give back tomorrow morning."

Nevrat looked blank for a moment, then hugged her. "Congratulations," Senpat said, pumping Marcus' hand. "What is it, the thought of going west that makes you randy? This'll be twice now."

"Oh, more than that," Helvis said with a sidelong glance at the tribune.

When the laughter subsided, Senpat grew serious. "You Romans will be going west, not so?"

"I've heard nothing either way," Scaurus said. "For now, no one goes anywhere much, not with Bouraphos at the Cattle-Crossing. Why should it matter to you? You've been detached from us for months now."

Instead of answering directly, Senpat exchanged a few sentences in guttural Vaspurakaner with Gagik Bagratouni. The *nakharar*'s reply was almost a growl. Several of his countrymen nodded vehemently; one pounded his fist on his knee.

"I would rejoin, if you'll have me," the younger noble said, giving his attention back to Scaurus. "When you go west, you'll do more than fight rebels inside the Empire. The Yezda are there, too, and I owe them a debt." His merry eyes grew grim.

"And I," Nevrat added. Having seen her riding alone through them after Maragha and in the press when the legionaries fought Drax' men, Marcus knew she meant exactly what she said.

"You both know the answer is yes, whether or not we move," the tribune said. "How could I say otherwise to seasoned warriors and bold scouts who are also my friends?" Senpat Sviodo thanked him with unwonted seriousness.

Still caught up in his own thoughts, Bagratouni said hungrily, "And also Zemarkhos there is." His men nodded again; they had more cause to hate the fanatic priest than even the nomads. Likely their chance for revenge would come, too, if the legionaries went west. On the way to Maragha, Thorisin had mocked Zemarkhos, and so the zealot acknowledged Onomagoulos as his Avtokrator. His followers helped swell the provincial noble's forces.

The hall grew silent for a moment. The Romans were loyal to the state for which they fought, but it was a mercenary's loyalty, ultimately shallow. They did not share or fully understand the decades of war and pogrom which tempered the Vaspurakaners as repeated quenchings did steel. The men who styled themselves princes rarely showed that hardness; when they did, it was enough to chill their less-committed comrades.

"Out on the darkness!" Senpat Sviodo cried, feeling the mood of the evening start to slide. "It's Skotos' tool, nothing else!"

He turned to Gaius Philippus. "So you Romans know the little bird, do you?" His fingers danced over the pandoura's strings. The legionaries roared out the marching song, glad to be distracted from their own thoughts.

"Are you well, Taron?" Marcus asked. "You look as if you hadn't slept in a week."

"Near enough," Leimmokheir allowed, punctuating his words with an enormous yawn. His eyes were red-tracked, his gravelly voice hoarser than usual. The flesh he had begun gaining back after his release looked slack and unhealthy. "It's a wearing task, trying to do the impossible." Even his once-booming laugh seemed hollow.

"Not enough ships, not enough crews, not enough money, not enough time." He ticked them off on his fingers one by one. "Outlander, you have Gavras' ear. Make him understand I'm no mage, to conjure up victory with a wave of my hand. And do a good job, too, or we'll be in cells side by side."

Scaurus took that as mere downheartedness on the admiral's part, but Leimmokheir grew so insistent the tribune decided to try to meet with the Emperor. Exhaustion had made the drungarios of the fleet irritable and unable to see any viewpoint but his own.

As luck would have it, the tribune was admitted to the imperial presence after only a short wait. When he spoke of Leimmokheir's complaints, Thorisin snapped, "What does he want, anchovies to go with his wine? Any fool can handle the easy jobs; it's the hard ones that show what a man's made of."

A messenger came up to the throne, paused uncertainly. "Well?" Gavras said.

Recognized, the man went down in full proskynesis. When he rose, he handed the Avtokrator a folded leaf of parchment. "Your pardon, your Majesty. The runner who delivered this said it was of the utmost urgency that you read it at once."

"All right, all right, you've given it to me." The Emperor opened the sheet, softly read aloud to himself: " 'Come to the sea wall and learn what your trust has gained you. L., drungarios commanding.' "

His color deepened at every word. He tore the sheet in half, then turned on Scaurus, shouting, "Phos curse the day I heeded your poisoned tongue! Hear the braggart boasting as he turns his coat!

"Zigabenos!" Gavras bellowed, and when the guards officer appeared the Emperor profanely ordered him to send troops hotfoot to the docks to stop Leimmokheir if they could. He grated, "It'll be too bloody late, but we have to try."

The fury he radiated was so great Marcus stepped back when he rose from the throne, afraid Thorisin was about to attack him. Instead Gavras issued a curt command: "Come along, sirrah. If I must watch the fruit of your folly, you can be there, too."

The Emperor swept down the aisleway, an aghast Scaurus in his wake. Everything the Roman had believed of Leimmokheir looked to be a tissue of lies. It was worse than betrayal; it spoke of a blindness on his part humiliating to contemplate.

Courtiers scurried out of Gavras' path, none daring to remind him of business still unfinished. Swearing under his breath, he stalked through the grounds of the palace compound; he mounted the steps of the sea wall like an unjustly condemned man on his way to the executioner. He did not so much as look at Scaurus.

What he saw when he peered over the gray stone battlements ripped a fresh cry of outrage from him. "The pimp's spawn has stolen the whole fleet!" Sails furled, the triremes and lighter, two-banked warships were rowing west from the Neorhesian harbor. Sea foam clotted whitely round their oars at every stroke. Marcus' heart sank further. He had not known it could.

"And look!" the Emperor said, pointing to the suburban harbor on the far shore of the Cattle-Crossing. "Here comes that cow-futtering

Bouraphos, out to escort him home!" The rebel admiral's ships grew swiftly larger as they approached. Thorisin shook his fist at them.

Boots rang on the stairway. A swearing trooper trotted up to the Emperor. He panted, "We were too late, your Majesty. Leimmokheir sailed."

"Really?" Gavras snarled. The soldier's eyes went wide as they followed his outflung arm.

Leimmokheir's ships shook themselves out into a line facing the rebels, his heavier galleys in the center with the Liburnians on either wing. Even in an element not his own, Marcus knew a tactical maneuver when he saw one. "That's a battle formation!" he exclaimed.

"By Phos, it is!" Thorisin said, acknowledging his presence for the first time. "What boots it, though? Treacher or zany, your precious friend will wreck me either way. Bouraphos'll toy with him like a cat with a grasshopper. Look at the ships he has with him."

Whether or not Gavras thought Leimmokheir a turncoat, plainly Elissaios Bouraphos did not. His entire fleet was there to form a line of battle, its horns sweeping forward to flank the smaller force it faced. The curses Thorisin had called down on Leimmokheir's head he now switched to Bouraphos. Zigabenos' messenger listened admiringly.

Marcus scarcely heard the Emperor. Watching a fight in which he could take no part was worse than combat itself, he discovered. In the hand-to-hand there was no time to reflect; now he could do nothing else. His nails bit into his palms as he watched the rowers on both sides step up the stroke. Their ships leaped at one another. The tribune wondered if Leimmokheir had in fact gone mad, if the egotism that seemed to lurk in every Videssian's soul deluded him into thinking his powers godlike.

The fleets were less than a furlong apart when one of Bouraphos' two-banked craft swerved inward to ram the trireme next to it square amidships. The heavier galley, taken utterly by surprise, was ruined. Oars snapped; faint over the water, Marcus heard screams as rowers' arms were wrenched from their sockets. Water gushed into the great hole torn in the trireme's side. Almost with dignity, the stricken ship began to settle. The Liburnian backed oars and sought another victim.

As if the first treacherous attack had been a signal, a score and more of the rebel admiral's ships turned on their comrades, throwing Boura-phos' line into confusion. No longer sure who was friend and who foe, ships still loyal lost momentum as their captains looked nervously to either side. And into the chaos drove Taron Leimmokheir.

On the sea wall Thorisin Gavras did three steps of a jig. "See how it feels, you bastard!" he screamed to Bouraphos. "See how it feels!" Scaurus abruptly understood Leimmokheir's sleepless nights; the drungarios had been sowing this field for many days and come to harvest it now that it was ripe.

But for all the sowing, the sea fight was far from won. Even with his suddenly revealed recruits, Leimmokheir was still outnumbered, and Elissaios Bouraphos a resourceful commander. It was his ships, though, that were pressed back into a circle, with Leimmokheir's prowling round them. And when he tried to strike outward, a galley of his that had bided its time drew in its starboard oars and sheared away its neighbor's portside bank with its projecting bulkheads. The crippled ship wallowed helplessly; its conqueror joined the enemy; Bouraphos' attacking squadron, daunted, pulled back.

To add to the disorder, both sides flew the imperial pennant with its central sun. Tiny in the distance, Marcus saw another banner at a trireme's bow, this one scarlet barred with gold—the emblem of the drungarios of the fleet. Bouraphos must have decided the only way out of his predicament was to kill his rival admiral, for four of his own galleys surged toward Leimmokheir's, sinking a Liburnian as they came.

No ships were close by to help. The drungarios' trireme spun in the water, backing oars to port while pulling ahead on the starboard side. It turned almost in its own length and sped away from the attackers. Some of Leimmokheir's fleet might not be perfectly trained, but he tolerated no slackness on his flagship.

The wake foamed up under the galley's bow; it was driving almost straight back toward Scaurus, past the slowly settling hulk of the first trireme sunk when Bouraphos' ships began changing sides. One after the others, the rebels gave chase.

"Skotos and his demons take them, they're gaining," Thorisin said, his hands clutching the battlements until knuckles whitened. Where minutes before he had been ready to dip Leimmokheir an inch at a time into boiling oil, now he was in an agony of suspense lest the drungarios come to harm.

But Leimmokheir knew what he was about. Even at a range of more than a quarter of a mile, his mane of gray-white hair made him recognizable. His arm came down to emphasize an order. Twisting like a snake, the trireme darted round the sinking galley and rammed its leading pursuer before the startled rebels could maneuver. Bouraphos' other three ships stopped dead in the water, as if Leimmokheir had shown himself to be a dangerous wizard as well as a seaman.

His daring put new heart into his fleet and seemed to be the blow that broke his foes. In a desperate charge across the water, about twenty of them broke through his line, but all fight was out of them. They fled toward the suburbs of the opposite shore. Another group, seeing the way the wind was blowing, went over to the winners and fell on their erstwhile comrades.

Thorisin began to dance in earnest. Heedless of the imperial dignity, he pounded Marcus and the messenger on the back and grinned as he was pummeled in return.

One squadron of about fifteen ships kept up the fight; Scaurus was unsurprised to spot a second drungarios' pennant among them. Game to the end, Elissaios Bouraphos and his surviving loyal followers gave their fellows the chance to escape. They tried to be everywhere at once, whirling and dashing forward to the attack like so many dogs at bay.

Facing so many, the battle could have had only one result, but the end came quicker than the tribune had expected. All at once the coordinated defense dissolved into a series of single-ship actions. White shields came up on poles as the last of Bouraphos' captains began to yield.

"Sink 'em all!" Gavras shouted, and then a moment later, reluctantly, "No, we'll need them against Namdalen one day." He sighed and said to Marcus, "I'll turn forethoughtful yet, damn me if I won't. This wretched job will see to that." He sighed again, remembering the freedom of irresponsibility.

By the time the Emperor reached the Neorhesian harbor he was jovial again. The space by the docks was filled with a milling crowd of civilians and soldiers. To the people of the city, Leimmokheir's triumphal return was a spectacle to make the day pass more quickly. The soldiers knew how much more it meant. Now at last they could face Baanes Onomagoulos; the shield that had separated them was hacked to bits.

Thorisin nodded to every captain coming ashore. He carefully made no distinction between the men who had sailed out with the drungarios and former rebels. The latter, knowing his reputation for a swift temper, approached him warily, but found their role in the victory outweighing earlier allegiance. They left the imperial presence quite relieved.

Taron Leimmokheir's galley was among the last to put in. It had taken damage, Marcus saw. Some oars trailed limply in the water for lack of men to pull them, and a ten-foot stretch of the port rail was smashed to stove-wood.

Gavras' soldiers cheered the admiral, who ignored them until the trireme was tied up at the dock. Then a single short wave sufficed him. With the agility of a much younger man, he scrambled up onto the pier. He elbowed through the press until he stood before the Emperor.

He bowed low, saying, "I trust my message sufficed to lay your concern to rest." Holding the bow, he tipped a wink to Scaurus with his left eye, which Thorisin could not see.

The Emperor, coloring, inhaled ominously. But before he could blast Leimmokheir, he spied Marcus trying to swallow a grin. "Then you're too fornicating trusting by half," he growled, but without sincerity. "I've said so for years, you'll recall."

"So now my task is done, it's back to the cell, eh?" The drungarios returned Thorisin's banter, but Scaurus heard nothing light in his tone.

"After the scare you threw into me, you deserve a yes to that." Gavras' eyes swung to the flagship. "What have we here?"

Two corseleted marines brought their prisoner before the Emperor. They had to half support him; the left side of his handsome face and head was bloody from a slingstone's glancing blow. "You would have done better to stay at Pityos, Elissaios," Thorisin said.

Bouraphos glared at him, shaking his head to try to clear it. "We were nearly holding our own till that cursed rock flattened me, even with the bolters. I'd bolt 'em proper, I would." The wordplay was feeble, but Marcus had to respect the rebel's spirit for essaying it at all.

"You're not likely to have the chance," Thorisin said.

"I know." Bouraphos spat at Taron Leimmokheir's feet. "When will you fight for yourself, Gavras? You used me to counter this bag of turds, and then him against me. What sort of warrior does that make you?"

"The master of you both," the Emperor replied. He turned to the marines, who came to attention, expecting the order. "Take him to the Kynegion."

As they began to lead Bouraphos away, Gavras stopped them for a moment. "In memory of the service you once gave me, Elissaios, your lands will not stand forfeit to the fisc. You have a son, I think."

"Yes. That's good of you, Thorisin."

"He's never harmed me. We can keep your head off the Milestone, too."

Bouraphos shrugged. "Do as you like there. I'll have no further use for it." He eyed the marines. "Well, let's go. I trust I don't have to show you the road?" He walked off between them, his back straighter and stride firmer at every step.

Unable to hold the thought to himself, Marcus said, "He dies very well."

"Aye, so he does," the Emperor nodded. "He should have lived the same way." To that the tribune had no good reply.

The small crowd studied the ship moored at the pier. "What's that written on its stern?" Gaius Philippus asked.

The letters were faded, salt-stained. "*Conqueror*," Marcus read.

The senior centurion pursed his lips. "It'll never live up to that."

The *Conqueror* bobbed in the light chop. Beamier than the lean Vides-sian warships, it carried a wide, square-rigged sail, now furled, and a dozen oarports so the crew could maneuver in and out of harbors at need.

Gorgidas, who knew more of ships than the Romans, seemed satis-fied. "It wasn't built yesterday or the day before, either, but it'll get us across to Prista, and that's what counts." He stirred a large leather ruck-sack with his foot. Having helped him pack it, Marcus knew that rolls of parchment, pens, and packets of powdered ink make up a good part of its bulk.

The tribune remarked, "The Emperor wastes no time. Less than a week since he gained the sea, and already you're off to the Arshaum."

"High time, too," Arigh Arghun's son said. "I miss the feel of a horse's barrel between my legs."

Pikridios Goudeles gave a delicate shudder. "You will, I fear, have all too much chance to grow thoroughly used to the sensation, as, worse luck, will I." To Scaurus he said, "The upcoming campaigns, both against the usurper and against the Yezda, shall be difficult ones. Good Arigh's men will be too late for the first of them, it seems, but surely not for the second."

"Of course," Marcus said. That Thorisin had enough faith in Goudeles to send him as ambassador surprised the Roman—or was the Emperor clearing the stage of a potential danger to himself?

Whatever Gavras' reasons, his trust for the smoothtongued bureaucrat plainly was not absolute. Goudeles' fellow envoy was a dark, saturnine military man named Lankinos Skylitzes. Scaurus did not know him well and was unsure whether he was brother or cousin to the Skylitzes who had died in the night ambush the year before. In one way, at least, he was a good choice for the embassy—the Roman had heard him talking with Arigh in the nomad's tongue.

Perhaps knowledge of the steppe was his speciality, for he said, "There's another reason for haste. A new set of dispatches came from Prista last night. Avshar's on the plains. Belike he's after soldiers, too; we'd best forestall him."

Marcus exclaimed in dismay, and was echoed by everyone who heard Skylitzes' news. In his heart he had known the wizard-prince escaped Videssos when the Sphrantzai fell, but it was always possible to hope. "You're sure?" he asked Skylitzes.

The soldier nodded once. No garrulous imperial here, Scaurus thought with a smile.

"May the spirits let us meet him," Arigh said, pantomiming cut-and-thrust. Marcus admired his bravado, but not his sense. Too many had made that wish already and got no joy when it came true.

Gaius Philippus undid the shortsword at his belt and handed it to Gorgidas. "Take it," he said. "With that serpent's spawn running free, you'll need it one day."

The Greek was touched by the present, but tried to refuse it, saying, "I have no skill with such tools, nor any desire to learn."

"Take it anyway," Gaius Philippus said, implacable. "You can stow it in the bottom of your duffel for all of me, but take it."

He sounded as if he were taking a legionary to task, not giving a gift, but Gorgidas heard the concern behind his insistence. He accepted the *gladius* with a word of thanks and proceeded to do just what the senior centurion had advised, packing it away in his kit.

"Very moving," Goudeles said dryly. "Here's something with a sweeter edge to it." He produced an alabaster flask of wine, drank, and passed it to Scaurus. It went down smooth as cream—nothing but the best for Pikridios, the tribune thought.

A gangplank thudded into place. The *Conqueror*'s captain, a burly man of middle years, shouted, "You toffs can come aboard now." He wagged his head in invitation.

Arigh left Videssos without a backward glance, his right hand on the hilt of his saber, his left steadying the sueded leather bag slung over his shoulder. Skylitzes followed, equally nonchalant. Pikridios Goudeles gave a theatric groan as he picked up his duffel, but seemed perfectly able to carry it.

"Take care of yourself," Gaius Philippus ordered, thumping Gorgidas on the back. "You're too softhearted for your own good."

The physician snorted in exasperation. "And you're so full of feces it's no wonder your eyes are brown." He embraced the two Romans, then shouldered his own rucksack and followed the rest of the embassy.

"Remember," Marcus called after him, "I expect to read what you say about your travels, so it had best be good."

"Never fear, Scaurus, you'll read it if I have to tie you down and hold it in front of your face. It's fitting punishment for reminding me you're my audience."

"That's the lot of you?" the captain asked when the Greek came aboard. Getting no contradiction, he called to his crew, "Make ready to cast off!" Two half-naked sailors pulled in the gangplank; another pair jumped onto the dock to undo the fat brown mooring lines that held the *Conqueror* fore and aft.

"Hold on, avast, belay, whatever the plague-taken seaman's word is!"

The pier shook as Viridovix came thudding up, his helmet on his head and a knapsack under his arm. He was crimson-faced and puffing; sweat streamed down his cheeks. He looked to have come from the Roman barracks on the dead run.

"What's happened?" Marcus and Gaius Philippus asked together, exchanging apprehensive glances. Except in battle and wenching, such exertion was alien to the Gaul's nature.

He got no chance to answer them, for Arigh shouted his name and leaped out of the *Conqueror* to greet him. "Come to see me off after all, are you?"

"Not a bit of it," Viridovix replied, dropping his bag to the boards of the pier with a sigh of relief. "By your leave, I'm coming with you."

The nomad's grin flashed white in his swarthy face. "What could be better? You'll learn to love the taste of kavass, I promise you.".

"Are you daft, man?" Gaius Philippus asked. Pointing to the *Conqueror,* he went on, "If you've forgotten, that is a ship. Your stomach will remember, whether you do or not."

"Och, dinna remind me," the Celt said, wiping his face on a tunic sleeve. "Still and all, it's that or meet the headsman, I'm thinking. On the water I'll wish I'm dead, but to stay would get me the wish granted, the which I don't fancy, either."

"The headsman?" Scaurus said. Thinking quickly, he shifted to Latin. "The woman turned on you?" As long as no names were named, Arigh—and the listening sailors—could not follow.

"Didn't she just, the fickle slut," Viridovix answered bitterly in the same tongue. His happy-go-lucky air had deserted him; he was angry and self-reproachful. Catching the gleam in Marcus' eye, he said, "I've no need for your told-you-so's, either. You did that, and rightly. Would I were as cautious a wight as you, the once."

That admission was the true measure of his dismay, for he never tired of chiding the Romans for their stodginess. "What went awry?" the tribune asked.

"Can you no guess? That one's green as the sea with jealousy—like a canker it eats in her. And so she was havering after me to set aside my Gavrila and Lissena and Beline, and I said her nay as I've done before.

They'll miss me, puir girls, and you must be after promising not to let herself's wrath fall on 'em."

"Of course," Scaurus said impatiently. "On with it, man."

"Och, the blackhearted bitch started shrieking fit to wake a dead corp, she did, and swore she'd tell the Gavras I'd had her by force." A fragment of the Celt's grin appeared for a moment. "Belike she'd make himself believe it, too. She's after seeing enough of me to give sic charge the weight of detail, you might say."

"She'd do it," Gaius Philippus said without hesitation.

"The very thought I had, Roman dear. I couldna be cutting her throat, with it so white and all. I had not the heart for it, to say naught of the hurly-burly it'd touch off."

"What did you do, then?" Marcus demanded. "Let her go free? By the gods, Viridovix, the imperial guards'll be on your heels!"

"Nay, nay, you see me revealed a fool, but not a damnfool. She's swaddled and gagged and tied on a bed in the sleazy little inn where we went. She'll be a while working loose, but I'm thinking the exercise'll not improve her temper, and so it's away with me."

"First Gorgidas, and now you, and both for reasons an idiot would be ashamed to own," the tribune said, feeling the wrench as his tightly knit company began to unravel. Again he gave thanks that the Romans had not had to split themselves between Namdalen and Videssos; it would have torn the hearts from them all.

Impatient with the talk in a language he did not understand, Arigh broke in, "If you're coming, come."

"I will that, never fear." Viridovix clasped Scaurus' hand. "Take care o' the blade you bear, Roman. It's a bonny un."

"And you yours." Viridovix' longsword hung at his right hip; he would have seemed naked without it.

The Celt's jaw dropped as he noticed Gaius Philippus weaponless. "Wore it out, did you?"

"Don't be more foolish than you can help. I passed it on to Gorgidas."

"Did you now? That was a canny thing to do, or would be if the silly lown had the wit to realize what grand sport war is. As is, like as not he'll lose it, or else slice himself." Viridovix' lip curled. A second later he brightened. "Och, that's right, I'll have the Greek to quarrel with. Nothing like a good quarrel to keep a day from going stale."

Marcus remembered his own words to Gorgidas when the doctor told him he was leaving. At the time they had been a desperate joke, but here they were coming back at him in all seriousness from the Gaul's mouth. Viridovix lived to wrangle, whether with swords or with words.

The captain of the *Conqueror* made a trumpet of his hands. "You there! We're sailing, with you or without you!" The threat was empty— while Viridovix meant nothing to him, he could hardly set off without the Arshaum, who meant everything to the embassy.

The aggrieved shout underlined Arigh's unrest. "Let's do it," he said, taking the Celt's arm. Viridovix' rawhide boots clumped on the planking of the dock; the nomad, shod in soft calfskin, walked silent as a wildcat.

Looking like a live man going to his own funeral, the Gaul tossed his duffel to a sailor. Still he hesitated before following it down. He sketched a salute to Scaurus, waved his fist at Gaius Philippus. "Watch yourself, runt!" he called, and jumped.

"And you, you great bald-arsed lunk!"

To the captain's shouted directions, his crew backed water. For a few seconds it seemed the *Conqueror* was too bulky to respond to the oars, but then it moved, inching away from the pier. When well clear, it turned north, ponderous as a fat old man. Marcus heard ropes squeal in pullies as the broad sail unfurled. It flapped loosely, then filled with wind.

The tribune watched until the horizon swallowed it.

With regained mastery of the sea, Thorisin Gavras threw Drax and his Namdalener mercenaries at Baanes Onomagoulos. Leimmokheir's galleys protected the transports from rebel warships; the men of the Duchy landed in the westlands at Kypas, several days' march south of the suburbs opposite Videssos.

A great smoke rose in the west as Onomagoulos fired his camp to keep Thorisin from taking possession of it. Baanes retreated toward his stronghold round Garsavra. He moved in haste, lest the Namdaleni cut him off from his center of power. Thorisin, acting like a man who feels victory in his grasp, retook the western suburbs.

Marcus waited for a summons from the Emperor, expecting him to order the legionaries into action against Onomagoulos. He drilled his men furiously, wanting to be ready. He still had doubts about the great count, despite the successes Drax was winning for Gavras.

No orders came. Thorisin held military councils in plenty, but to plan the coming summer campaign against the Yezda. He seemed certain anyone fighting Onomagoulos had to be his friend.

Scaurus tried to put his suspicions into words after one officers' meeting, saying to the Emperor, "The nomads attack Baanes, too, you know, but not in your interest. Drax wars for no one but Drax; he travels under your banner now, but only because it suits him."

Thorisin frowned; the Roman's advice was clearly unwelcome. "You've given me good service, outlander, and that sometimes in my despite," he said. "There have been stories told of you, just as you tell them now against the Namdalener. A prudent man believes not all of what he sees and only a little of what he hears. But this I tell you: no rumor-seller has ever come to me with news that Drax purposed abandoning me at the hour of my peril."

Scaurus' belly went heavy as lead—how had that report reached the Emperor? Unsure how much Gavras knew, he did not dare deny it. Picking his words with care, he said, "If you believe such tales, why hold me and mine to your service?"

"Because I trust my eyes further than my ears." It was dismissal and warning both—without proof, Gavras would not hear charges against the great count. Glad the Emperor was taking the other question no further, Marcus left hastily.

He had expected a great hue and cry after Viridovix, but that, too, failed to materialize. Gaius Philippus' misogyny led him to a guess the tribune thought close to the mark. "I'd bet this isn't the first time Komitta's played bump-belly where she shouldn't," the veteran said. "Would you care to advertise it, were you Gavras?"

"Hmm." If that was so, much might be explained, from Thorisin's curious indifference to his mistress' tale of rape to her remaining mistress instead of queen. "You're getting a feel for the politics hereabouts," Marcus told the senior centurion.

"Oh, horseturds. When they're thick on the ground as olives at harvest time, you don't need to feel 'em. The smell gives them away."

In the westlands Drax kept making gains. When his dispatches arrived, Thorisin would read them out to his assembled officers. The great count wrote like an educated Videssian, a feat that roused only contempt in his fellow islander Utprand.

"Would you listen to that, now?" the mercenary captain said after one session. " 'Goals achieved, objectives being met.' Vere's Onomagoulos' army and w'y hasn't Drax smashed it up? T'at's what needs telling."

"Aye, you're right," Soteric echoed vehemently. "Drax greases his tongue when he talks and his pen when he sets ink to parchment."

Marcus put some of their complaint down to jealousy at Drax' holding a greater command than theirs. From cold experience, he also knew how much such complaints accomplished. He said, "Of course the two of you are but plain, blunt soldiers of fortune. That you were ready to set Videssos on its ear last summer has nothing to do with intrigue."

Utprand had the grace to look shamefaced, but Soteric retorted, "If the effete imperials can't hold us back, whose fault is that? Ours? By the Wager, they don't merit this Empire of theirs."

There were times when Scaurus found the islanders' insistence on their own virtues and the decadence of Videssos more than he could stomach. He said sharply, "If you're speaking of effeteness, then betrayal should stand with it, not so?"

"Certainly," Soteric answered; Utprand, more wary than his lieutenant, asked, "W'at do you mean, betrayal?"

"Just this," Marcus replied. "Gavras knows we met at the end of the siege, and what befell. By your Phos, gentlemen, no Roman told him. Leaving Helvis out of the bargain, only four ever learned what was planned, and it never went beyond them. Some one of your men should have his tongue trimmed, lest he trip on it as it flaps beneath his feet."

"Impossible!" Soteric exclaimed with the confidence of youth. "We are an honorable folk. Why would we stoop to such double-dealing?" He glared at his brother-in-law, ready to take it farther than words.

Utprand spoke to him in the island dialect. Marcus caught the drift:

648

secrets yielded accidentally could hurt as much as those given away on purpose. Soteric's mouth was still thin with anger, but he gave a grudging nod.

The tribune was grateful to the older Namdalener. Unlike Soteric, Utprand had seen enough to know how few things were certain. Backing what the officer had pointed out, Marcus said, "I didn't mean to suggest deliberate treachery, only that you islanders fall as short of perfection as any other men."

"You have a rude way with a suggestion." Soteric had a point, Scaurus realized, but he could not make himself regret pricking his brother-in-law's self-importance.

"A priest to see me?" the tribune asked the Roman sentry. "Is it Nepos from the Academy?"

"No, sir, just some blue-robe."

Curious, Marcus followed the legionary to the barracks-hall door. The priest, a nondescript man save for his shaved pate, bowed and handed him a small roll of parchment sealed with the patriarch's sky-blue wax. He said, "A special liturgy of rejoicing will be celebrated in the High Temple at the eighth hour this afternoon. You are bidden to attend. The parchment here is your token of entrance. I also have one for your chief lieutenant."

"Me?" Gaius Philippus' head jerked up. "I have better things to do with my time, thank you."

"You would decline the patriarchal summons?" the priest said, shocked.

"Your precious patriarch doesn't know my name," Gaius Philippus retorted. His eyes narrowed. "So why would he invite me? Hmm—did the Emperor put him up to it?"

The priest spread his hands helplessly. Marcus said, "Gavras thinks well of you."

"Soldiers know soldiers," Gaius Philippus shrugged. He tucked the parchment roll into his belt-pouch. "Maybe I'd better go."

Putting his own invitation away, Scaurus asked the priest, "A liturgy of rejoicing? In aid of what?"

"Of Phos' mercy on us all," the man replied, taking him literally. "Now forgive me, I pray; I have others yet to find." He was gone before Marcus could reframe his question.

The tribune muttered a mild curse, then glanced around to gauge the shadows. It could not be later than noon, he decided; at least two hours until the service began. That gave him time to bathe and then put on his dress cape and helmet, sweltering though they were. He ran a hand over his cheek, then sighed. A shave would not be amiss, either. Sighing as well, Gaius Philippus joined him at his ablutions.

Rubbing freshly scraped faces, the Romans handed their tokens of admission to a priest at the top of the High Temple's stairs and made their way into the building. The High Temple dominated Videssos' sky-line, but its heavy form and plain stuccoed exterior, as always, failed to impress Scaurus, whose tastes were formed in a different school. As he did not worship Phos, he seldom entered the Temple and sometimes forgot how glorious it was inside. Whenever he did go in, he felt transported to another, purer, world.

Like all of Phos' shrines, the High Temple was built round a circular worship area surmounted by a dome, with rows of benches north, south, east, and west. But here, genius and limitless resources had refined the simple, basic plan. All the separate richnesses—benches of highly polished hardwoods, moss-agate columns, endless gold and silver foil to reflect light into every corner, walls that imitated Phos' sky in facings of semiprecious stones—somehow failed to compete with one another, but were blended by the artisans' skill into a unified and magnificent whole.

And all that magnificence served to lead the eye upward to contemplate the Temple's great central dome, which itself seemed more a product of wizardry than architecture. Liberated by pendentives from the support of columns, it looked to be upheld only by the shafts of sunlight piercing its many-windowed base. Even to Marcus the stubborn non-believer, it seemed a bit of Phos' heaven suspended above the earth.

"Now here is a home fit for a god," Gaius Philippus muttered under his breath. He had never been in the High Temple before; hardened as he was, he could not keep awe from his voice.

Phos himself looked down on his worshippers from the interior of the dome; gold-backed glass tesserae sparkled now here, now there in an

650

ever-shifting play of light. Stern in judgment, the Videssian god's eyes seemed to see into the furthest recesses of the Temple—and into the soul of every man within. From that gaze, from the verdict inscribed in the book the god held, there could be no appeal. Nowhere had Scaurus seen such an uncompromising image of harsh, righteous purpose.

No Videssian, no matter how cynical, sat easy under that Phos' eyes. To an outlander seeing them for the first time, they could be overwhelming. Utprand Dagober's son stiffened to attention and began a salute, as to any great leader, before he stopped in confusion. "Don't blame him a bit," Gaius Philippus said. Marcus nodded. No one tittered at the Namdalener; here the proud imperials, too, were humble.

Fair face crimsoning, Utprand found a seat. His foxskin jacket and snug trousers set him apart from the Videssians around him. Their flowing robes of multicolored silks, their high-knotted brocaded fabrics, their velvets and snowy linens served to complement the High Temple's splendor. Jewels and gold and silver threadwork gleamed as they moved.

"Exaltation!" A choir of boys in robes of blue samite came down the aisles and grouped themselves round the central altar. "Exaltation!" Their pure, unbroken voices filled the space under the great dome with joyous music. "Exaltation! Exaltation!" Even Phos' awesome image seemed to take on a more benign aspect as his young votaries sang his praises. "Exaltation!"

Censer-swinging priests followed the chorus toward the worship area; the sweet fragrances of balsam, frankincense, cedar oil, myrrh, and storax filled the air. Behind the priests came Balsamon. The congregation rose to honor the patriarch. And behind Balsamon was Thorisin Gavras in full imperial regalia. Along with everyone else, Marcus and Gaius Philippus bowed to the Avtokrator. The tribune tried to keep the surprise from his face; on his previous visits to the High Temple, the Emperor had taken no part in its services, but watched from a small private room set high in the building's eastern wall.

Balsamon steadied himself, resting a hand on the back of the patriarchal throne. Its ivory panels, cut in delicate reliefs, must have delighted the connoisseur in him. After resting for a moment, he lifted his hands to the Phos in the dome, offering his god the Videssians' creed: "We bless thee, Phos, Lord with the right and good mind, by thy grace our protector, watchful beforehand that the great test of life may be decided in our favor."

The congregation followed him in the prayer, then chorused its "Amens." Marcus heard Utprand, Soteric, and a few other Namdalener officers append the extra clause they added to the creed: "On this we stake our very souls."

As always, some Videssians frowned at the addition, but Balsamon gave them no chance to ponder it. "We are met today in gladness and celebration!" he shouted. "Sing, and let the good god hear your rejoicing!" His quavery tenor launched into a hymn; the choir followed him an instant later. They swept the worshippers along with them. Taron Leimmokheir's tuneless bass rose loud above the rest; the devout admiral, his eyes closed, rocked from side to side in his seat as he sang.

The liturgy of rejoicing was not commonly held. The Videssian notables, civil and military alike, threw themselves into the ceremony with such gusto that the interior of the High Temple took on a festival air. Their enthusiasm was contagious; Scaurus stood and clapped with his neighbors and followed their songs as best he could. Most, though, were in the archaic dialect preserved only in ritual, which he still did not understand well.

He caught a quick stir of motion through the filigreed screening that shielded the imperial niche from mundane eyes and wondered whether it was Komitta Rhangavve or Alypia Gavra. Both of them, he thought, would be there. He hoped it was Alypia.

Her uncle the Emperor stood to the right of the patriarchal throne. Though he did no more than pray with the rest of the worshippers, his presence among them was enough to rivet their attention on him.

Balsamon used his hands to mute the congregation's singing. The voices of the choir rang out in all their perfect clarity, then they, too, died away, leaving a silence as speaking as words. The patriarch let it draw itself out to just the right length before he transformed its nature by taking the few steps from his ivory throne to the altar at the very center of the worship area. His audience leaned forward expectantly to listen to what he would say.

His eyes twinkled; he plainly enjoyed making them wait. He drummed his stubby fingers on the sheet silver of the altartop, looking this way and that. At last he said, "You really don't need to hear me at all today." He beckoned Gavras to his side. "This is the man who asked me to celebrate the liturgy of rejoicing; let him explain his reasons."

Thorisin ignored the irreverence toward his person; from Balsamon it was not disrespectful. The Emperor began almost before his introduction was through. "Word arrived this morning of battle just east of Gavras. Forces loyal to us"—Even Gavras' bluntness balked at calling mercenaries by their right name—"decisively defeated their opponents. The chief rebel and traitor, Baanes Onomagoulos, was killed in the fighting."

The three short sentences, bald as any military communique, touched off pandemonium in the High Temple. Bureaucrats' cheers mingled with those of Thorisin's officers; if the present Avtokrator was not the pen-pushers' choice, he was a paragon next to Onomagoulos. For once, Gavras had all his government's unruly factions behind him.

Master of his own house at last, he basked in the applause like a sunbather on a warm beach. "Now we will deal with the Yezda as they deserve!" he cried. The cheering got louder.

Marcus nodded in sober satisfaction; Gaius Philippus' fist rose and slowly came down on his knee. They looked at each other with complete understanding. "Our turn to go west next," the senior centurion predicted. "Still some work to do to get ready."

Marcus nodded again. "It's as Thorisin said, though—at least we'll be fighting the right foe this time."

HARRY TURTLEDOVE is the award-winning author of the alternate-history works *The Man with the Iron Heart; Guns of the South; How Few Remain* (winner of the Sidewise Award for Best Novel); the Worldwar saga: *In the Balance, Tilting the Balance, Upsetting the Balance,* and *Striking the Balance;* the Colonization books: *Second Contact, Down to Earth,* and *Aftershocks;* the Great War epics: *American Front, Walk in Hell,* and *Breakthroughs;* the American Empire novels: *Blood & Iron, The Center Cannot Hold,* and *Victorious Opposition;* and the Settling Accounts series: *Return Engagement, Drive to the East, The Grapple,* and *In at the Death.* Turtledove is married to fellow novelist Laura Frankos. They have three daughters: Alison, Rachel, and Rebecca.